Gainsbourg: The Biography
by Gilles Verlant

TRANSLATED FROM THE FRENCH BY
PAUL KNOBLOCH

BOOKS

Originally published in French *GAINSBOURG* by Albin Michel in 2000

GAINSBOURG © Editions Albin Michel
© Gilles Verlant 2012
Translation by Paul Knobloch ©2012
© TamTam Books, 2012
First published by TamTam Books in the U.S.A. In 2012
Printed in the United States of America

TamTam Books want to thank: Lun*na Menoh, Shirley Berman, Ichiro Shimizu, Kimley Maretzo, Bethany Handler, Nicki Wong, Paul Knobloch, Emi Kamei, Sam Freilich, Ron Mael, Russell Mael, Gilles Verlant, Josephine Tran, Sophie Schiavo, James Bae, Boris Vian, Jane Brown, Kyra Lunenfeld, Jason, Brady, Marlowe, Arrow & the beauty of Serge Gainsbourg's music

TamTam Books is edited and published by Tosh Berman

TamTam Books are art directed and designed by Tom Recchion
GAINSBOURG interior design & typography by Mark Holley

tosh.berman@gmail.com
www.tamtambooks.com
www.tamtambooks-tosh.blogspot.com

ISBN 9780966234671

Distributed by ARTBOOK | D.A.P.
155 6th Avenue, 2nd Floor
New York, NY 10013
www.artbook.com

contents

Prologue · · · · · · VIII

Yeah, I'm Ginsburg · · · · · · 14

My First Yellow Star · · · · · · 32

I Admit, I Suffered Dear · · · · · · 66

My Illusions Open Onto The Courtyard · · · · · · 92

There Is No Sunshine In My Life · · · · · · 122

An Anthracitic Mood · · · · · · 158

Be Pretty And Keep Quiet · · · · · · 180

Let's Take A Walk Inside Of Me · · · · · · 198

To The Beat Of The Yé-Yés · · · · · · 222

Don't Listen To Pop Stars · · · · · · 240

Who's "In" Who's "Out" · · · · · · 258

Lollipop Annie · · · · · · 278

Zip! Shebam! Pow! Blop! Wizz! · · · · · · 298

Jane B., English, Sex: Female · · · · · · 332

Erotic '69 · · · · · · 356

Ah! Melody 368

O Di Doo Di Doo Dah 388

There Are Days I'd Give God Knows What
To Be Able To Shit My Whole Being Away 412

I'm Cabbage-Head Man 428

Le Jour De Gloire Est Arrivé 446

Yeah, I'm Gainsbarre 466

Escape Happiness Before It Escapes You 492

A Whore Among Whores 510

Hey Man Amen 534

I'll Die On A Sunday, My Suffering True
And Tried 550

Epilogue 572

Bio Page 578

Index Of Names 580

Photographs & Images Credits 588

prologue

Constantinople, 1919. Vociferous cries of rage. The smell of Turkish tobacco and alcohol hangs in the air. A shady bar with French sailors on one side and English on the other. Every so often a brawl breaks out and the place explodes. A real free-for-all.

In the back of the room, oblivious to all the noise, a young man of twenty-three plays Chopin on an upright piano. His touch is at once light, nostalgic, and sensitive. As his fingers run over the keys he seems to be lost in his memories.

His name is Joseph Ginsburg, born in Kharkiv on March 27, 1896. Ashkenazi. A Russian Jew. Crazy for music. Also nuts about painting, but he decided to abandon that a few years earlier. His story is incredible, typically Slavic. He was on the Trans-Siberian railway, carrying in his humble student bag a portrait he had done of a young girl with whom he was madly in love. During the long trip he dozed off. When he awoke, the painting was gone. Clenching his fists in pain like some tortured Dostoyevskian hero, Joseph swore to himself that day that he would never again touch a paintbrush.

At the bar in Constantinople our little pianist is still playing. He's moved from Chopin onto a sad little number that the French sailors are singing along with... Russia is closer than ever, but the young man knows that his exile is for good.

His mind harkens back to the twelve months of happiness he shared with his wife in that pretty little port on the Black Sea, at Theodosia, in Crimea on the Ukrainian peninsula. Postcards of a vanished universe, the Russia of tsars and troikas.

Old memories flow back into his mind. He sees himself at five years of age in Mariupol, on the Azov Sea. He then remembers fleeing with his four brothers and his sister when his father, a schoolteacher who had no desire to enlist in the tsar's army, decided to leave the Ukraine for Belarus. It was 1904, the height of the Russo-Japanese war.

In 1916 – he's now twenty years old – Joseph finds himself in Ekaterinoslav, the future Dnepropetrovsk, where he assiduously frequents the conservatory.

> JOSEPH GINSBURG: *"All I desired at that time, after my tenure at the conservatory, was a professorship, for example in Petrograd or Moscow. Something that would permit me to hang a sign on my door reading - Joseph Ginsburg, Laureate of the Conservatory of... A grand piano in a big hall and a copper nameplate on the door... That's all I would have needed to attract a throng of students."*

The pogroms of 1905 left their traces in the Ukraine: in Odessa, the Christian population, manipulated by a power base that wanted to create a diversion in the face of all the discontentment, had massacred three hundred Jews and left thousands of others injured. There was also great lamentation over the numerous victims in Theodosia. It's there, however, where Joseph settles in 1917. He's offered a room at 21, Rue Sainte-Catherine, with the Besman family and their eight children. It's love at first sight for one of the girls, Brucha Goda, nicknamed Olia, born on January 15, 1894. Very beautiful, vivacious, buoyant. A beautiful voice. Mezzo-soprano with a uniquely expressive Russian timbre...

> JOSEPH GINSBURG: *"Her parents called her Olia, her friends Olga Yacovlevna, and those intimate with her called her Oletchka... And me, I later called her Olioucitchka... When I finally asked her to sing something*

*for me it didn't take much coaxing. She accompanied herself, starting with
a little love song that was in vogue at the moment, and had I grasped the
literal meaning of the words she was singing I would have run away and
never looked back:*

> *Go away, fly*
> *What's the use to beg and cry*
> *Words of love leave me cold as ice...*

But how could I have fled when the singer was so young, so charming, so attractive, and so full of passion and talent? [...] I stood there admiring her, and said to myself: The man who marries her will be a happy soul, indeed. [...] My time in Theodosia was the happiest of my life. Just imagine: I was twenty-one, with no real money problems (I had students), living in a bright and shining city, in a warm and welcoming house with a magnificent girl who never refused my kisses. Plus, I was able to completely devote myself to my passion: the piano."

But then comes the rumbling of that terrible revolution, of one Vladimir Ilyich Lenin and all blood that would flow. Olia has to leave for Saint Petersburg where she works as a nurse in the tsar's army hospital. It's civil war: Joseph traverses the whole of Russia in order to join her, three days and three nights, non-stop, except for the occasional interruption by Bolshevik troops or those of General Wrangel, who wants to force inscription on all the students and beat back the opposition. Joseph barely escapes, hiding under the enormous skirts of some peasant women who take pity on him.

> OLIA GINSBURG: *"One evening, we went to the Bolshoi to hear Fedor
> Chaliapin, and during the interlude we heard the bang-bang-bang of firearms. We weren't frightened. We were in love..."*

Joseph and Olia are married in the middle of this nightmare, on June 18, 1918. They immediately make the most important decision of their lives: to escape at any cost. In 1919 they find themselves in Batoum, Georgia, on the Black Sea, near the end of a very risky trip.

OLIA GINSBURG: *"A ship, reserved for liberated soldiers on their way to Caucasus, was leaving from our town. They weren't even selling tickets. I begged the officer to let us board. I was quite attractive when I was young, so I'm sure that had an effect on him. "O.K.," he said. "We'll put you hull, under the military tarps.""*

JOSEPH GINSBURG: *"The Crimean itinerary truly stands out in our memories with startling clarity. Having left Crimea, the beautiful homeland of my wife and a marvelous country, we had a stop over at Batoum, one which lasted... a year. [...] The mountains of Caucasus, violet and sundrenched and affectionate... the luxuriant flora, the Black Sea... green. A year of earthly paradise."*

But still, flee they must. They're able to board a Greek cargo ship: "We passed along the Turkish coast. And then a real layover – a year in Constantinople." The Turkish capital is flooded with expatriates hoping that the revolution fails so that they might return as soon as possible. But the situation is hopeless. The Ginsburgs get someone to forge phony documents for them and decide to make for Marseilles - a multitude of Russians are settling in the area of Côte d'Azur, where the climate reminds them of Crimea - but for the Ginsburgs, it will be but a brief stop before the trip north to Paris.

JACQUELINE GINSBURG: *"At that time, crossing the Black Sea was dangerous because of the pirates. When my mother's younger brother, Michel Besman, wanted to join my parents in Constantinople, he had quite an adventure. He was very young, hardly 15 years-old..."*

GAINSBOURG: *"... He was always the unlucky one in the family. Anyway, he takes off on a Turkish boat and gets nabbed by pirates who, instead of cutting his throat, strip off his clothing, shove him in a barrel and toss him into the sea, shouting at him: "Have fun getting yourself out of this mess."*

In 1921, the year the Ginsburgs settle in the capital, Joseph finds work at La Chope d'Anvers, Boulevard de Rochechouart, for 20 francs per day. There are already more than 31,000 Russian immigrants in France. In 1924, the League of Nations estimates that the number is over 100,000. Some have become naturalized French (those who applied); others maintain their status as refugees without a country and are granted an international identity certificate guaranteed by the League of Nations.

There are essentially three categories of Russian immigrants: soldiers in the Russian expeditionary corps from the French and Macedonian fronts who never made it back home after World War I; soldiers in the White Army under Denikine or Wrangel who had taken off from ports in the Black Sea and come to find refuge in France, the only nation that recognized the government of General Wrangel; finally, civilians like the Ginsburgs who feared suffering hardships as a result of the measures taken by the new Bolshevik government (in general, those who suffered the most: landlords, high-ranking officials, Ukrainian nationalists, members of non-Bolshevik parties, and Jews, of course, inasmuch as Ukraine's 1918 declaration of independence had incited numerous pogroms across the land and given birth to the slogan "Death to the bourgeois and death to the Jews").

In any case, the page has turned. Joseph, twenty-five, and Olia, twenty-seven, have but one desire: to raise a family far away from the tumult of revolution. In France, the Ginsburgs owe nothing to anyone: they manage on their own, tightening their purse strings, and they succeed rather well, despite the sadness they feel at having left behind parents, brothers, and sisters from whom they will never hear again. Their entire life will be built on this very model, which will be a source of both arrogance and pride, and their three children will never forget this lesson...

one

Yeah, I'm Ginsburg...

.

H e's named Lucien and he's crying in his cradle in the kitchen of a gloomy little apartment at 35, Rue de la Chine in the 20th arrondissement. He is born on April 2, 1928, at 4:55 in the morning, Hospital Hôtel Dieu on l'île de la Cité, just seconds after his twin sister Liliane. What he doesn't know yet is that he also has an elder sister – barely two years older – named Jacqueline.

When Oletchka had discovered she was pregnant shortly after the birth of Jacqueline, the couple hesitated for a considerable time. They had lost a first baby, which was born in 1922, a year after their arrival in Paris: a nasty case of bronchitis took little Marcel from them at the age of six months. In 1926, Joseph, who wanted a girl, had his wish fulfilled. But this new pregnancy just came too quickly. They made the decision to go and see an abortionist. One can imagine what a sordid affair it is at that time – Pigalle, some filthy quack of a doctor, a cracked enamel basin full of suspect colors. Beside herself, Mother Ginsburg simply fled. This was the first in a long series of reprieves that Gainsbourg, this survivor and son of survivors, would later take pleasure in describing.

Olia tells herself that perhaps she is expecting a boy, her dream... Or two, since she soon learns that she is pregnant with twins. At the moment of birth, catastrophe – it's Liliane who arrives first. Oletchka bursts out in tears, imaging herself with three girls in her arms.

Finally, little Lulu pops out.

Constantinople is already a distant memory. In Paris, Joseph has makes a name for himself as a nightclub pianist. Each time an engagement comes to an end he heads to the musicians' market at Place Pigalle. Léo Parus, also a pianist, remembers having met him.

> Léo Parus: *"I knew Serge's father when he worked as a pianist in cabarets, bars, and Russian restaurants. Joseph was an amiable sort, distinguished, always well dressed. He had an aristocratic side, a fine and delicate appearance which stood out in the milieu of musicians. His French was very good, even refined. Because the two of us were both Jews of Russian origin, we spoke Russian when we were together. He was serious. When it came to work you could always count on him. He was conscientious, the best sort of man. At that time, especially before the war, there were plenty of musicians because there was all sorts of work in restaurants, bars, and bistros. In Pigalle, there was a kind of "Musicians' Market." We'd get together with other musicians between five and eight o'clock on the terreplein across from Café Pigalle to look for work. The engagements lasted anywhere from one night to a week. We were well paid. We'd earn as much as 100 francs per day while a schoolteacher, for example, would only make 1,200 a month. The work varied: accompaniment for singers, or work as a musician in a little bistro combo performing popular songs or excerpts from opera, maybe Viennese waltzes, a little jazz or cabaret music. Sometimes you had to play requests from the clientele, which didn't inspire a lot of passion. The groups consisted of three to eight musicians. 95% of the time we played without sheet music, five to six hours at a stretch. It was an exhausting job. During the summer we played the holiday seasons in casinos or spas because there wasn't any work in Paris."*

After the birth of the twins, Joseph does, as a matter of fact, work a great deal in the provinces, most notably in Sète and Bordeaux, making 80 to 90 francs a night. Nothing glorious, but no life of misery either. While they aren't rich, the Ginsburgs do belong to the petite bourgeoisie of the artistic set. During the 30s, they even succeed in saving enough to buy a little apartment at 59, Rue Caulaincourt, which they rent out. The tiny monthly payment they receive enables them to survive during the war.

What else do we know about the Ginsburg parents? That they never reside – neither at Rue de la Chine, nor at Rue de Montreuil, nor later at Rue Chaptal – in the Jewish neighborhoods (for example, within the triangle formed by République/Bastille/Hôtel de Ville). That they aren't practicing Jews who go to synagogue. That they don't follow a kosher diet or observe Jewish holy days. In the Ukraine, where they had lived before, most Jews were not religious. Isn't there a Jewish proverb that states: "The fires of hell surround Odessa?"

"Religion wasn't practiced in our household," remembers Jacqueline: "My father was a self-declared free-thinker."

We know that they come from a country where anti-Semitism (chronic, traditional, deep-rooted in society) is much more pronounced than in France, where it arises in moments of crisis, as in the Dreyfus Affair between the years of 1894 and 1906; we know that they are fascinated with occidental culture but they don't completely deny their roots: prior to the birth of Jacqueline in 1925, Olia sings regularly at the Russian conservatory, Rue de Rochechouart in the 9th arrondissement, at the time when the Ginsburgs still live at 110, Rue de Montreuil. Finally, we know that Joseph – while he plays piano several hours a night – still practices his scales daily at home.

> GAINSBOURG: *"My first memories, as a boy of one or two years of age, were esthetic and musical. My father, for his own pleasure, played Scarlatti, Bach, Vivaldi, Chopin, or Cole Porter. He would interpret Manuel de Falla's La Danse du feu or South American tunes. He was a complete pianist. It was all a prelude to my musical education: I heard my father's piano every day of my life, from zero to twenty. This was very important..."*

> LILIANE ZAOUI: *"As for painting, my father had a very open mind. He particularly appreciated Matisse, Cézanne, Vlaminck, Derain, and the Impressionists. He regularly followed the sales of paintings at the Hôtel Drouot. The words "esthetic" and "eclectic" were a staple of his speech. "Avant-garde" was the ultimate praise, "pompous" or "philistine" an irrevocable condemnation."*

In 1970, a year before his death, Joseph Ginsburg, encouraged by his son, began to write his memoirs, *Voici déjà l'hiver*, in a little notebook. A random glance at the pages reveals this moving profession of faith:

For me, Art with a capital "A" is what counted most. A man who didn't make art was a poor fool, a philistine even! Epictatus, whom I'd read perhaps too young, inculcated in me a disdain for the professions of men: it was all small-minded, narrow. This Greek was perhaps the precursor of Russian nihilism. For me, the only Art that counted was high art. The rest was matter-of-fact, and therefore negligible.

A happy coincidence: the artistic life in Paris had never been as exciting as in the 1920s. First of all, in April 1921, at the Sans-Pareil, there is the opening of the "Grand Saison Dada," with André Breton and his friends, followed in May by the arrival of Marcel Duchamp and Max Ernst's Dadaist exposition. Furthermore, Erik Satie presents *Le piège de Méduse* at the Théâtre Michel. In June of the same year, at the "Salon Dada," text and poems by Tristan Tzara, Benjamin Péret, Louis Aragon, Paul Éluard, as well as photos by Man Ray, are exhibited at the Galerie Montaigne above the Théâtre des Champs–Elysées. In 1924, Breton publishes his first *Surrealist Manifesto*. In 1928, the year of Serge's birth, there's the famous "Surrealist Exposition" at the Galerie Goemans in Paris. Finally, in December, 1929, Breton publishes his *Second Surrealist Manifesto* in the twelfth issue of the periodical *La Révolution surréaliste*, a revue which he and Péret had been co-editing for the last five years. Meanwhile, the Parisian public, which had barely recovered from the scandal created by the Suprematism of Malevich's "Carré noir sur fond blanc," has the chance to discover the works of Piet Mondrian, the pictorial equivalent of the Dutch architects of the De Stijl school, while the German Bauhaus, until it is condemned by the Nazis in 1933, continues to be extremely influential with its professors such as Klee, Kandinsky, and Maholy-Nagy, who are creating a synthesis of the major arts (architecture) and the minor arts (the decorative arts and furniture). In 1921, Le Corbusier's essay "L'Ésprit Nouveau" links him to the Bauhaus esthetic.

As for music at the beginning of the 20s, Paris welcomes King Oliver and his Original Creole Band, the first real jazz group in the history the music. Prokofiev presents his magical opera *L'Amour des trois oranges* followed by his *Third Concerto for Piano and Orchestra*, and Maurice Ravel presents his adaptation of Mussorgsky's *Pictures from an Exhibition*. The 1920s also see the publication of both volumes of James Joyce's Ulysses, performances of Cocteau and Radiguet's *Mariés de la Tour Eiffel* at the Théâtre de l'Œuvre, Sacha Guitry's first plays, Chaplin's *The Kid* and *The Gold Rush*, Erich Von Stroheim's scandalous film *Foolish Wives*, Fritz Lang's *Dr. Mabuse*, F.W. Murnau's *Nosferatu*, Cecil B. DeMille's *The Ten Commandments*, Abel Gance's *La Roue*, G.W. Pabst's *Street of Sorrow* with the young Greta Garbo, and also Eisenstein's *Battleship Potemkin*, censored in France for its "revolutionary propaganda and demoralization of the army."

While Joseph never lacks for work, he still has trouble finding prestigious engagements. He doesn't have access to the network of musicians who work for recording studios or for big music hall stars of the epoch, such as Alibert ("Constantinople"), Mistinguett ("Gosse de Paris"), Josephine Baker ("J'ai deux amours"), Maurice Chevalier ("Valentine"). In September, 1932, Joseph meets a pioneer of French jazz, Fred Adison, who'd just arrived in Paris, and instead of using his famous big band he instead employs a small combo that performs in the afternoon at the restaurant Chez Maxim's.

> LÉO PARUS: *"Joseph Ginsburg wasn't a crack player, nor was he very highly regarded in his field. They used him to fill in when regulars couldn't make it, in nightclubs or Russian restaurants like Le Shéhérazade, Le Novi, or Le Drap d'Or, where a lot of musicians were Jewish and where above all you had to play gypsy music and eastern European tunes. But even though he had good classical training, he really didn't have the background necessary for this type of work. He wasn't on par with the more notable pianists, such as Berinsky, Niagu, or Coldolban. He was more of a pick-up musician than a regular. The violinist would always team up with the same pianist, but a big name violinist, for example a Volodarski or a Krikava, would never use Joseph as an accompanist."*

In 1934, during a five-month engagement at the Casino de la Corniche in Algiers, Joseph brings along the entire family. Upon his return to Paris, he finds a job as a pianist at Aux Enfants de la Chance, where he'll work for three straight seasons, until the end of 1937. Serge will never forget the name of this club, taken from a novel by Kessel – he will in fact use it as the title of a song in 1987.

The Ginsburgs had long since abandoned the idea of returning to Russia. Perfectly integrated and in love with French culture, they often attend concerts and never miss an art exposition, which helps to keep alive the passion for art and painting that they had developed in Russia. The next step is naturalization, a simple formality. On March 11, 1927, Joseph submits an application for French nationality for Jacqueline and it is automatically granted. In 1932, still in possession of the false documents that claim he was born in Constantinople, he sets in motion the steps necessary for the rest of the family, and thus the decrees of naturalization are published on June 9, 1932 in *Le Journal official* for Joseph, Liliane, Lucien, and ten days later for Olia, after the obligatory inquest into morality and the questioning of neighbors.

Moving time: The Ginsburg family settles in at 11 bis,[1] Rue Chaptal, third floor, four windows. Plus, it's just two steps away from SACEM (The Society of Authors, Composers, and Music Publishers) and from the Hot-Club de France, located across from the famous Renan-Scheffer Masion, which has since become Le Musée de la vie romantique. The choice of this street and this neighborhood is by no means haphazard. First of all, it's practical: from now on, Joseph will be living in the musicians' district, near all the Pigalle nightclubs in which he works (when you have to hoof it back at five in the morning, before the metro opens, it's good to live nearby). Also, the area is rich in history and haunted by the memory of great artists who lived there in the previous century. In fact, since the 1820s people have often spoke of this 9th arrondissement, which was in a state of constant transformation. They spoke of the neighborhoods of Saint-Georges and Nouvelle-Athens (just below Rue Chaptal, bordering Rue de la Rochefoucauld, Rue de la Tour-des-Dames, Rue Taitbout, Rue d'Aumale, Rue Notre-Dame-de-Lorette, etc.), recently created boroughs where the members of the "Société des artistes parisiens" would often find lodging. Among the celebrities one might run across included actors Talma and Mademoiselle Mars, but there were also painters like Horace Vernet, Eugène Delacroix, Théodore Géricault, Eugène Isabey, Gustave Moreau, etc. The area around the Square d'Orléans also played host in 1830 to Alexandre Dumas, George Sand, and Frédéric Chopin.

---

[1] The French often use the word "bis" with addresses. For example, if there is already an address 11 on a street, then bis would indicate another separate residence, an 11 B, as it were. (T.N.)

At the end of the century, Monet resided there, a detail that the much refined Joseph surely knew of and appreciated.

In November, 1976, when Serge was interviewed by Thomas Sertilange and Gilles Davidas for the program *L'Oreille en coin* on Inter-France, he strolled through the neighborhood of his youth, overcome with emotion. He could see himself back in 1932, his eyes filled with tears as he walked through the doors of the nursery school across the street from his home at 11 bis, Rue Chaptal.

GAINSBOURG: *"The barber was here, and I had problems with him because he desperately wanted to use a bunch of hair lotion on me. But all I had was the money for the cut. Plus my ears stuck out... I already had a bunch of hang-ups... Also close to 11 bis there was a hardware dealer. This really captured my fancy because there were marbles for sale. [...] Here, at Rue Henner, I'd fly down the streets on roller-skates and often end up taking a spill. [...] It was always a calm neighborhood, but even so, at that period you'd occasionally hear some gunfire from gangsters in Pigalle who'd strayed from their usual stomping grounds to come and settle a score. [...] Each Thursday, if we got good grades, we'd be treated to a cake, so all three of us, hand in hand, would walk down to the bakery, which I believe is still there..."*

Two years later, in September, 1934, Lucien starts attending the primary school at Rue Blanche, where he will spend the next five years. That takes us to 1939. Much like 98% of the Jews living in France, who are always worried about perfectly integrating into French society, the Ginsburgs send their children to a secular and republican public school: Catholic schools don't accept practicing Jews and a private school is above their means.

Joseph and Olia speak Russian to each other. When they shift into French, they really can't manage to hide rather pronounced accents. When they quarrel, they sometimes send insults flying through the air in Russian or Yiddish slang, believing the children incapable of understanding. But they're wrong. At the table, on this little plot of uprooted Russia, they eat borscht, pierogies, and other typical dishes.

At the age of four, Jacqueline starts on the piano. Both Liliane and Lulu will follow suit. Upon returning from school, each child has the right to a one-hour lesson. Knowing what's in store for them, the three children place handkerchiefs at the end of the keyboard: they are aware that every lesson ends in tears. If Lulu plays an F instead of an F sharp, his father scolds him in a loud and authoritarian voice: "Why did you do that?" Lucien murmurs: "My finger slipped," and then starts to cry, his sisters following suit.

When the lesson is finished and all the noses wiped, the kids do their homework. Jacqueline is a brilliant student and runs away with every award of excellence. Very early on, she devotes all her energy to achieving academic success, which delights her parents but troubles her little brother, already traumatized by a previous incident...

> GAINSBOURG: *"I remember throwing a furious tirade when I was two years old because I had seen my father take my little sister somewhere, completely pampering her, while I had to stay with a nanny in the country."*

Liliane doesn't work quite as hard and Lucien is a model young lad but has no real passion for school. It's important to note that one teacher, a certain Charlet, takes an instant dislike to Serge and even goes so far as to refer to him as "the little Jew." One day, Charlet passes by him and blurts out: "It smells like cat piss here," much to the shame of young Lulu.

Nevertheless, Mama and Papa Ginsburg have high hopes – their children will be doctors or lawyers. If need be, dentists or professors. Nothing else is imaginable. Unless, of course, their son decides to become a painter.

> GAINSBOURG: *"In grade school I started stealing and became a little kleptomaniac. I swiped pricey toy soldiers made of lead, miniature race cars, pistols, all of which I grabbed from display windows and shoved into my school bag. But bringing them home was out of the question: they would have been discovered and I wouldn't have been able to explain how I got them. Theft was just a thrill - the thrill of transgression. I just gave the stuff away to my friends, the sons of maintenance men who were every bit as poor as me. That is until the day I got nabbed. The store manager caught me red-handed and said: "Wait here. We're going to go get your father!"... But I'd given him a fake address. When he found out, the guy literally started kicking my ass. That was that. Afterwards, I was so humiliated that I never stole again... My father was harsh. He especially adored Jacqueline, or at least I thought so. When I was a kid and I did something stupid, he'd take off his belt and threaten to beat me bare-assed, Cossack-*

style. My mother would wait for a while outside the room and then come to my rescue. I could live with this disciplinarian side of his nature, but what I found intolerable is that in the evening, during the family supper, he would apologize for his brutality. Little birdbrain that I was, I would have preferred that he were harsh and unrelenting. But having a heart of gold, he needed to justify himself before me, and I found that perturbing."

JACQUELINE GINSBURG: *"Sometimes my dad would lock him in the cupboard, and my brother had a terrible fear of the dark. He was really a very fearful kid. Anyway, when the door was open he'd come out in tears, runny nose and all, and my sister and I would start laughing. All of a sudden, he'd start laughing too, and we'd make fun of him even more, calling him Jean-qui-rit, Jean qui pleure.[2] He wasn't supposed to have any light in the cupboard, but there was a switch and he'd turn it on all the same. His punishment really didn't do much good. He'd always say, I won't do it again, I won't do it again, but he always did."*

GAINSBOURG: *"Little brats sometimes have a masochistic side: after a thrashing, I'd lie on my back, on my little iron bed, and cry... But at the same time I'd tell myself: I'm the happiest and also the saddest little kid on earth... You know why? Because I treasured the moment when my tears would flow down the side of my head into the openings of my ears..."*

Certain people who've commented on Gainsbourg's life have dramatized the educational methods of Joseph Ginsburg to the point of sensationalism. A few licks of the belt have transformed our hero into a beaten child, the victim of a sadist. Well, first of all, this was a time when corporal punishment was common practice and had not yet been denounced by child psychologists. Furthermore, this wasn't simply gratuitous punishment: a muscular version of the traditional slap on the ass was reserved for when Lulu had really crossed the line. Joseph, of course, never laid a hand on the girls, which may have troubled young Lucien. But they were much better behaved and knew that they had nothing to fear as long as they brought home good report cards. On the other hand, since he often stressed the inconsistency of his parents' behavior (the apologies after getting the strap) one might search

---

[2] John who laughs, John who cries. There are all sorts of poems and rhymes and drawings of this famous French caricature. (T.N.)

here for the origin of the rejection of Joseph's authority, amplified by Serge's tenacious contempt for his father's modest career, which will be illustrated in the following chapters.

> LILIANE ZAOUI: *"Apart from my father's fits of anger, the atmosphere in the house was very festive. My mother would often hum Russian love songs and we were proud of the deep tenderness that united my parents. My father simply adored my mother. If she was troubled by something, she wouldn't sing, and he would immediately notice this. They were very much in love, but Mama could be a bit of a bitch and she wasn't very demonstrative, so I was especially moved by the attention my father showed her. He would kiss her, calling her "my joy" or "my sunshine." They always held hands when they walked."*

Little Lulu is not only shy, as are his two sisters, but also cowardly. When he goes to sleep - he has no room of his own and must make do with a folding iron bed in the kitchen - he calls for his older sister to make sure no one is hiding behind the curtains. His imagination is hard at work. As soon as his parents are in bed, his sister comes down quietly, and after verifying everything the two of them begin to whisper and giggle. Jacqueline always explodes in laughter and Mama Ginsburg cries: "Get to sleep, right now!"

Like all kids at that time, his favorite reading material is *Le Journal de Mickey* and Robinson.[3] Lucien is especially fond of Luc Bradefer, Guy l'Éclair, Mandrake, La Famille Illico, Bicot, and Burroughs' Tarzan.

> GAINSBOURG: *"Comic books immediately captured my imagination. A long time ago, I had first editions of Mickey and Robinson. That was 1936 or 1937. I remember Luc Bradefer in Robinson. In Mickey, there was the aunt, whose name was translated as Madame Bellecour, and the uncle, who was called Monsieur Dusabot. In the drab world of my childhood it was like a utopian universe in primary colors. Pim Pam Poum was extraordinary!"*

Lucien quickly starts to amuse himself by drawing his own little comics under the title "Les aventures du Professeur Flippus,"[4] as well as illustrations in color crayons that look like something pulled from the pages of a fairy-tale book. He in fact devours his first book, given to him by Jacqueline,

---

[3] Popular comic books.
[4] "The adventures of Professor Flippus" (T.N.)

a collection of tales by Jacob and Wilhelm Grimm. Lucien escapes into these imaginary and often terrifying worlds. Among his favorite tales is the story "The Seven Crows," in which a man's seven sons, the victims of his curse, are transformed into brilliant, black crows that fly away in a flurry. Another is the atrocious story of "The Problem Child":

Once upon a time there was a little problem child of rather stubborn disposition who never did what his mother asked of him. And so the Good Lord, who was not at all happy with the lad, visited upon him a sickness that not a single doctor was capable of curing. The boy soon found himself resting in his coffin. But after they had put him into his grave and covered it up with dirt, his little arm popped straight back up into the air. No matter how many times they placed him back in his coffin and covered him with dirt, the little arm would still pop out. It was finally necessary for his mother to go to his gravesite, take a rod, and beat the arm back down. Her punishment was eventually successful, and alas the child found abiding peace underground.

GAINSBOURG: *"Being a kid, I projected my own being onto my Mecanno toy – I could destroy and then reconstruct myself at will. I had the instructions – in English, a premonition – and all the bolts in my hand."*

Most of the time Lucien plays by himself. He doesn't have any pals. His sisters have friends, but Lucien is simply forgotten. Among his toys there is a gyroscope, a sort of tank that spits out sparks with a little air gun. One day he uses it to hurl a pebble that ends up cracking a tile in one of the classrooms of the elementary school across from his house at 11 bis. Sometimes, he wanders as far as the Square de la Trinité – a church ("Horrible, the ugliest thing I ever saw") which sends shivers up his spine, as does "the groundskeeper, no doubt a survivor of the trenches, who had but one arm." There, Lulu plays with a ball or uses the pond to launch his little sailboat: "It's all so sad... I see the shadow of a boy who is no longer himself, who is dead... best to forget about it, just forget it, forget it."

At the house on Rue Chaptal, they listen to the radio plays, police stories that are broadcast on Friday evenings. But they never listen to popular music. Papa Ginsburg disapproves. "Stop singing that crap!" he orders his son, who is fond of humming the popular tunes. For Joseph, these songs belong to a populist genre, and are in no way on a par with Stravinsky, Milhaud,

Shostakovich, Chopin, or Debussy... "During that time," remembers Liliane, "we were accustomed to hearing the tunes that were popular at the moment because at home my father would practice the repertory that he had to perform in nightclubs." Among the popular tunes of 1936-37 include "Vas-y Léon," sung by Monthéhus, "Les mômes de la cloche," by Edith Piaf, "Quand on se promène au bord de l'eau" by Jean Gabin, and "Ça vaut mieux que d'attraper la scarlatine," by Ray Ventura et ses Collégians.

In 1936, the year of Serge's eighth birthday, we see that two other songs will become imbedded in his memory and reemerge many years later. The first is "Sombre Dimanche," by Damia, one of the defining tunes of this period and also the object of parody ("Triste Lundi" by Georgius) because of its ill-fated reputation: legend has it that the song creates such melancholy that those who listen to it assiduously are often driven to suicide. Gainsbourg will reprise it on the 1987 album *You're Under Arrest*, under the title, "Gloomy Sunday." On the same album we find his remake of "Mon legionnaire," which is a rather startling coincidence. It was also an enormous success from 1936-1937, written by Marguerite Monnot and Raymond Asso and recorded by Marie Dubas in Marseille in April of 1936. A year later it was covered by the young "Môme,"[5] Piaf, who at that time had just recently bounced back from the famous scandal involving Louis Leplée, her impresario. For a while, Piaf was a suspect.[6] So half a century later, in his role as "Gainsbarre" - his monstrous alter ego - he will breathe new life into these two old songs. A walk down memory lane, a moving flashback.

> GAINSBOURG: *"When I was at elementary school, I was so cute that they called me Ginette – Hey, Ginette... Where are you going, Ginette? One day, I went to the vegetable store with my mom and because it was raining, I'd put my hood over my head. And so the keeper of the stall bent over and said to me: "And what do you want mademoiselle?" Ooohh... did that hurt! Anyway, I started out cute... but that quickly deteriorated."*

---

[5] "Kid" or "Brat" in French. (T.N.)

[6] Gainsbourg preferred the original recording, by Marie Dubas, whose songs were later banned during the war because she was Jewish. According to legend, it was based on a crush that a seventeen-year-old Piaf had developed on a soldier she met during a tour of the barracks. The soldier later met his fate in the colonies. It was written for Marie Dubas because Edith at that time didn't yet believe in herself enough to tackle the piece.

JACQUELINE GINSBURG: *"My brother would always make us break out in laughter, my sister and me. He'd literally put us into a trance when he played the clown and he always had a colossal sense of humor and a spirit of mockery that he would direct at himself and others. Why, you might ask? It's just the type of idiotic fooling around that makes children laugh. For example, my brother would hide behind the window and watch people passing down the street. He would imitate them and sing a fanfare, and these little tunes were so ridiculous that we'd laugh until our eyes were full of tears. He had a very critical eye, the eye of a caricaturist. He would fill up his notebooks with pages of designs, influenced most notably by American cartoons and Walt Disney."*

From time to time, Joseph and Olia cave under the pressure of their three children and take them to the movies. Lucien, as lily-livered as ever, leaves the theatre terrorized by an episode of Paul Fejos' *Fantomas*. He wets his bed again that same night.

At ten years of age, the rather well behaved young lad receives the cross of honor from his school. He's wearing a black shirt with red trim upon which he proudly pins his prize. On the way home, he runs into Fréhel, the great realist *chanteuse*. Fréhel - her real name is Marguerite Boulc'h – is forty-eight years of age at the time of this meeting although she looks twenty years older. A notorious dope fiend, legend has it that she was never without her powder compact, which was larger than a container of Camembert and filled with cocaine (they also say that when she would make her dog sniff at her handkerchief, the mutt would run around the room in circles like a lunatic). Her career was launched by La Belle Otéro,[7] her former lover. Maurice Chevalier was also in love with Fréhel, but later abandoned her for her rival, Mistinguett, when he found that his relationship with Fréhel was turning him into cocaine addict. After a suicide attempt, we find her in 1914 singing in the honky-tonks of Bucharest. In 1922, while touring through Europe and the fringes of the Orient, she was deported from Constantinople by the French Embassy due to the severity of her addiction. In the thirties, even though she was physically speaking a wreck, Fréhel won back her audience with such songs as "Où est-il donc?" and "Tel qu'il est." A few months before

[7] Carolina Otero (1868-1965), Spanish-born actress, dancer, and high-class prostitute. (T.N.)

the war, she had even managed to record the biggest hit of the second half of her career, the famous "Java Bleue."

GAINSBOURG: *"Around 1937 or 38 - I was about nine or ten years old - I ran into Fréhel, who looked like death warmed over. She lived just a few steps away, at l'impasse Chaptal, home of the Grand Guignol. She was strolling down the street in a dressing gown with a Pekingese under each arm, followed by a gigolo at the prescribed distance: five meters, like in the army. I was on my way home from grade school and I had my cross of honor pinned to my smock. Fréhel stopped me, and running her hands through my hair, she said: "You're a good little boy..." She certainly didn't know me! "I can see from your cross of honor that you've been a proper young lad at school, so I'm going to buy you a drink..." I can recall the scene perfectly. We were on the terrace of a café at the corner of Rue Chaptal and Rue Henner. She had a huge glass of red wine and she treated me to a Shirley Temple and a cherry tart! So my first contact with the world of show business was considerable. This was a woman of some importance."*

Among her most legendary hits was "La Coco," which Gainsbourg liked to recite from memory:

> As the band played a tango, the couple did sway
> In his arms he held his treasure
> But there on the table, I found a blade
> And my vengeance was beyond all measure
> Yes I was soused, I behaved like a louse
> I killed my gigolo
> In front of my friends, I was at my wit's ends
> Through his heart my knife did go
> Give me coco to ease the woe

During this period, Joseph plays the piano in nightclubs. He spends most of 1938 and the first five months of 1939 at Mimi Parson's in addition to picking up a franc here and there on the side. The pay is not bad, but the job brings with it several demands. For example, he has to play requests, which means knowing how to segue from an interlude by Bach into "Les roses de Picardie." And what's more, he has to stay until the very last customer has left.

JANE BIRKIN: *"On each and every New Year's, Serge's father would work until six in the morning, and one of the children's most lively recollections was finding on the living room table - while their father was still asleep - all the hats, confetti, and little trumpets that he had gathered together for them after the celebration. For the kids, January first was like a second Christmas..."*

Summer is even better. Joseph plays the casinos, and at a time when there is no such thing as a paid holiday, the modest Ginsburgs spend their summers in Arcachon (1929-1932), Cabourg (1933), Trouville (1935), or Fouras, in Charente-Maritime (1936).

GAINSBOURG: *"That's where I saw a vast array of elegant automobiles, those superb cars, the Delages, the Bugattis... Proper etiquette demanded that the car stop and the man remain at the wheel while his lady stepped out, sublime and dressed to kill in haute couture with a purebred dog at her side. I was mingling with high society... I remember the carriages and horses all festooned with ribbons, all those rich bastards walking out of their luxury hotels..."*

This fascination with wealth and elegant women is something Serge would always carry with him, as we will see later on. But at this period, he has other concerns...

GAINSBOURG: *"When I was ten years old, my favorite singer was Charles Trenet. I was in love with him, fixated... I remember my vacations, one at the seaside. I was smitten with a lovely young girl about the same age as me. At that time, songs from the TSF[8] were broadcast over the loudspeakers and I fell in love with her while listening to "J'ai ta main dans ma main," by Trenet. It made a real impression on me, and that's why I believe very strongly in the connection between image and sound in one's memories... It was a dazzling love, one of absolute purity. She was so pretty: I had already developed a penchant for esthetics."*

In 1981, prefacing a collection of texts by Trenet which he admitted having "defiled" when he was a kid, Gainsbourg wrote this respectful homage:

[8] Generally speaking, TSF means the "wireless," just another way of saying "radio." (T.N.)

At the edge of memory and forgetfulness
Where young boys of barbed wire gold
Arabesque in the realm of my secret reverie
I spy a smuggler of dreams
Wearing a bright velvet halo
As dazzling as the sun in a time before war

He sings the song of a male mermaid
To which conical loudspeakers
Floating above the stirring sands
Of my first vacations[...]
Bestow the gift of ubiquity
And the power of sorcerers [...]

I listen and I want to let others hear
That my initial adolescent passion
Whose initials are those of that crazy songster
Was asexual, yet sensual
Purely homosexual and as somber as amethyst [...]

At the end of the summer of 1939, when war is declared, the Ginsburgs find themselves in Dinard. Father Ginsburg had signed a contract to play at the municipal casino, Le Balnéum, a colonial-style establishment. Joseph became a French citizen in 1932 but was exempted from military service the following year because he was over thirty years of age and had children to support. He is recalled, however, on September 2, as part of a general mobilization order. Several days later, the entire family accompanies him to the train station at Dinard, from where he departs, still without a uniform. Assigned to the 223rd RAT, which he joins on September 19, he is sent back home on October 23 after digging a few trenches and is officially dismissed from the army on November 17, 1939.

During this time, Olia returns to Paris with the children in order to plead a case on the behalf of Liliane. Her school had given her a failing score on

---

[9] Secondary school. Thus, a lycée de guerre is a school established during wartime. (T.N.)

the entry exam for grade 6 over a trifling matter: when asked: "What is your favorite season?" she replied as one would expect a child of a musician to reply, "The season at Trouville." Her instructors did not find this amusing. In fact, the decision is upheld and Olia's youngest daughter is refused entry to the sixth grade and the family immediately returns to Dinard, where mother Olia, ever resourceful, succeeds in enrolling her three children in a "lycée de guerre"[9] hastily thrown together at the Villa Nahan, a magnificent estate comprised of a mansion surrounded by an immense park on the banks of the Rance.

> JACQUELINE GINSBURG: *"Thanks to that, our life was a dream from 1939 to 1940. A year of vacation! Seeing as how young children are oblivious to what's happening, the big attraction was to go down to the market square to see the arrival of all the trucks and carts involved in the exodus..."*

> GAINSBOURG: *"Before abandoning Saint-Malo, the English set fire to the gasoline reserves and we watched as huge, thick black clouds spiraled towards the heavens, a fantastic spectacle. A few days later, we were playing around the levee at Dinard and we saw a little silhouette approaching, all alone on the beach. It was the first German soldier."*

two

My First Yellow Star...

At Dinard, in spite of the overcrowded class (44 students), Lucien does a pretty fair job finishing the school year, and afterwards, he is admitted into level five with no objections.

In May, 1940, at the end of the eight month "phony war," [1] the armies of the Reich go on the attack and enter France after first having conquered Belgium and the Netherlands. On June 14, the Germans parade through Paris while two million refugees hit the road, fleeing from the invaders and the bombardments. On June 18, de Gaulle makes his famous "appeal" over the waves of the BBC. Then on June 22, Pétain signs the shameful armistice at Rethondes. As July begins, Olia and the children return to Paris. Joseph had been there since his discharge and continually sends money to ensure that the family is able to meet its daily expenses.

The Ginsburgs had witnessed the powerful surge in anti-Semitism during the 1930s, but just like many other thousands of Jews at that time, it had done nothing to diminish their loyalty towards the French republic. They are, however, quite shaken when they see the first anti-Semitic posters appear in their neighborhood: it starts in August, 1940, in a café on Rue de

---

[1] The period of October, 1939 to April, 1940, before the Nazis invaded France.(T.N.)

Châteaudun, some 300 meters from Rue Chaptal, with a sign that states "No Israelites."

Among the first workers affected by the laws of exclusion in the summer of 1940 are the most obvious: Jewish musicians, opera house singers, and chansonniers are fired from the theatres and cabarets where they appear. Jewish journalists no longer have anywhere to publish and Jewish painters have no access to galleries where they can exhibit or sell their work. Practitioners of these various professions – and soon it would come to include every segment of the Jewish population, without exception – were among the first of the growing ranks of poor Jews who had no other means of nourishment other than the soup kitchen. A year later, in the summer of 1941, it is estimated that 50% of the Jewish population in France is deprived of any and all means of existence.

Beginning in autumn of 1940, anti-Semitism invades the streets and one can see reprehensible graffiti start to spread all over. Some examples: "When you're a Jew, best hightail it to Palestine and make yourself scarce," "The Jews will soon be reduced to rubble, so pack your bags, little girl," "One, two, three... Bang! Watch your store explode," or "What's the matter, kike? Don't you understand French?" On September 27, 1940, an ordinance from the chief of the German military administration in France defines the word Jew: "One who belongs to the Jewish religion or has more than two Jewish grandparents, which is to say belonging to the Jewish religion." On October 2, the Jews of Paris and the Département de la Seine[2] learn from the newspapers that they must undergo a new census: from October 3 to October 20, they are summoned, in alphabetical order, to present themselves to the various police headquarters. October 8 is the day for the letter G...

OLIA GINSBURG: *"I'll tell you, the Jews were downright stupid, unforgivably dense! They'd said: "The Jews won't be harmed. We just have to register so they know how many of us there are." So everyone has to go to the police and give their names, and all. I say to my husband: "You know, I do not want you to do this." He responds: "No! We have to!" So I say: "You'll see. There'll be problems." And he says: "No way, it'll never happen."*

---

[2] An administrative area including Paris and the surrounding cities that bordered the Seine. First established in 1790. (T.N.)

Those who stray from their duty to register are rare. Docilely, "out of a refusal to deny their origins and a habit for obeying the law," the Jews, whom no Jewish organization had advised to abstain from the obligation to declare, line up in front of their respective police headquarters to register. During this census, in order to streamline the process and ensure that they could easily round up those who resisted, "the police precincts are directed to take all necessary measures to ensure that Jewish identity cards are recognizable by certain marks. To this effect, the surface of every identity card must have a red stamp reading either *Jew* or *Jewess*." The Jews are thus once again summoned, individually this time, starting on October 22, for their ID cards or visas to be adorned with this infamous mark. Ever obedient, Joseph adheres to this new formality. And yet, troubling signs start to emerge: Jewish shopkeepers have until October 31 to place a special poster in their windows which states "Judiches Geschäft/Jewish business." At the beginning of December there are already 4,660 boutiques and artisanal shops that bear this mark of shame – more than 400 in the 9th arrondissement alone. The next stage consists, evidently, of confiscating these "Jewish enterprises" and finding owners who are 100% French. On July 22, 1941, it's a done deal – the law declares an "Aryanization of all enterprises, goods and monies belonging to Jews."

Meanwhile, there's something that profoundly shocks the Ginsburg children, even more so than the book *How do you recognize a Jew?*, by professor Georges Montando, which they see on display in the windows of bookstores, and more than the anti-Semitic propaganda posters that flourish in the metro: it is the poster that promotes the *Le Juif Süss*, a hateful propaganda film. Thirty-five years later, Serge is quite able of remembering it when he pens the lyrics of "Est-ce est-ce si bon" on the album *Rock Around the Bunker*.

On the March 29, 1941, the authorities of the Vichy government create the General Commission on Jewish Affairs in order to establish a policy of exclusion and methodically spread propaganda. Come autumn of 1941, the police are handling Jewish matters. During this interval, the first roundups start to take place in Paris: on the afternoon of May 13, 1941, roughly 6,700 summonses are presented by agents of the French police.

Later, more than 3,700 Jews (mostly Polish) present themselves at the gymnasium of Japy, la caserne Napoléon, la caserne des Minimes, or other centers of summoning. Those called are detained, while the family members who accompany them are sent back with their personal effects. From the Gare d'Austerlitz, they are transported to camps. That same day, the daily paper *Paris-Midi* states: "Five thousands Jews have left, and last night they spent their first evening in a concentration camp. Five thousand less parasites for our great city of Paris, which had been infected by their deadly presence."

Nevertheless, Lucien manages to pass level 5 during the 1940-41 school year. He's still at Condorcet, in spite of a professor who happens to be particularly disagreeable and who goes out of his way to call attention to Lucien's name: Gins-burg, Gins-burg, Gins-burg... At the age of thirteen, with his boxes of watercolors, his pastels, his charcoal, and his crayons – all purchased from a shop on Rue Chaptal – he has for a good time now displayed his penchant for drawing and painting.

> GAINSBOURG: *"My father, who had sworn to never again touch a paintbrush, brings me to painting school in Montmartre. There, I take classes with two old Post-Impressionists, Camoin and Jean Puy. My initiation into the erotic... one day a girl passes by – I was already quite gallant – a young, very pretty girl. She was a model. I hadn't yet done any nudes: I was working with plaster and drawing in charcoal. After that, there was another model, an African who called herself Josepha. One day I saw part of a feminine napkin between her legs. I was disgusted..."*

Also at the age of thirteen, Lucien, while in the process of masturbating, is caught by his father. Joseph orders him to put an immediate stop the behavior but offers no explanation. This is the beginning and the end of his only course in sexual education. Brief, to be sure, but at least it spares him all that "it makes you deaf" and "you'll go to hell if you do that" nonsense.

> GAINSBOURG: *"Things were super-strict in my household, Russki... Judeo-Russki strict. There was this one day when my father - because I'd pissed on the sides of the crapper - he said to me: "Take hold of your dick and control the stream." He didn't really say "dick," he said "pee-pee." That's it: "Take hold of your pee-pee and control it. Never piss on the sides." That in a nutshell is the miserable relationship we had when it came to sexual matters."*

In 1984, during an interview with Pablo Rouy and Marco Lemaire for the gay magazine *GPH*, Serge "the chameleon" gives us a more embellished version of the incident...

> GAINSBOURG: *"One day my father tells me: "You shouldn't jerk off." I had, without a doubt, made a few stains on my sheets. The next day I stuck my finger up my ass and said: "Ah, interesting." I didn't say it exactly like that, all cool. Anyway, it was a diversion that was at once sexual, physiological, and instinctual. I quite liked it. Since the old man had forbidden travel in one direction, I took a trip the other way. But it never did stop me from returning to women."*

At the beginning of the 1941 school year, which corresponds to level 4, Lucien, for health reasons, is no longer enrolled in Condorcet, and the Jewish situation in the capital is worsening day by day: starting in June, 1941, for example, Propangastaffel starts putting up huge anti-Semitic posters. On the night of October 2, seven explosive devices wreak havoc in as many synagogues (Rue de la Victoire, Rue des Tournelles, Rue Pavée, etc.). A few days later, the National Anti-Semitic League of France distributes pamphlets posing the question: "Do we want to live as French, or die as Jews?" In the beginning of January, 1942, Doriot and his Parti Populaire Français[3] chime in by publishing small, public notices which state that "the Jews of France have stolen 500 billion francs worth of French jobs." At the same time, at the Palais Berlitz, there is an exposition called "The Jew and France" which attracts more than 200,000 visitors welcomed by "a large allegorical composition representing a sort of vampire with a long beard, thick lips, and a hooked nose, whose bony fingers, like those of a bird of prey, have a chokehold on planet Earth."

After the very difficult season of 1940-1941, Joseph (officially, he had not worked but two months at l'Ange rouge) is still able to find a job at la Cabane Cubaine, where he will spend the good part of the season of 1941-1942. Yet out of caution, no doubt, he doesn't respond to the musicians union, which writes him in February, 1942 to ask why he has not taken care of his dues. But Joseph and Olia have other worries: Lucien is not able to enroll in level four because he falls ill. He'd never been a strong lad. Like his parents, he has no

---

[3] French Popular Party. A fascist, pro-Nazi group headed by Doriot.

interest in sports and goes through a stage during which he's rather scrawny. At first, the doctors can't make heads or tails of his ailment: weakened, unable to get up, he coughs and remains bed ridden for weeks, his stomach distended and painful. Could it be typhus? He refuses to eat. Olia makes him little sandwiches but he only pretends to pick at them and then hides them under his bed when his mother turns away.

In fact, he is suffering from tubercular peritonitis, which in those days was fatal 99% of the time. Explanation: first, the tuberculosis settles in. A farandole of Koch bacillus. Then the infection spreads, through the blood, to the peritoneum membranes that cover the intestines. Finally, the great French specialist and pediatrician, Professor Robert Debré, is called to the bedside of little Lucien. In extremis, he saves him with the correct diagnosis – the problem at that time is that there was no treatment for this type of infection. The only solution: send the boy off to take the cure, where he can breathe good mountain air. They head for the country and Lucien is whisked off to Courgenard, a small village of 500 inhabitants in La Sarthe. The sickness leaves him in a pitiful state. He looks like a frail old man and the children in the little farming town almost feel as if they should pray for him.

Why Courgenard? Because the Ginsburgs just spent their vacation there, during the summer of 1941, on the advice of their neighbor, Mrs. Choisy, who often spends her leisure time at La Bassetière, two steps from the Romanesque church, with the Dumurs, a family of farmers. For a miniscule sum, they rent out a small, separate two bedroom cottage on their farm and the little family settles in, "sleeping on straw beds," according to Jacqueline. The Dumurs had already welcomed several families to this little house, most notably in June, 1940, during the exodus.

Going to Courgenard is like a true expedition inasmuch as the trip carries with it a certain number of risks. Making sure to avoid the security at the stations, they take the train as far as la Ferté-Bernard. There, papa Dumur comes to fetch them in a carriage. And if he doesn't show for the rendezvous, that's some tough luck, because the walk is nine kilometers on foot, with luggage...Once at the farm, the Ginsburgs are welcomed by Jean, the eldest son, 18 years old as of August, 1941, and his three sisters. Many years later he would become the mayor of this little village.

JEAN DUMUR: *"At the beginning of the summer of 1941, the five of them arrived, and soon after, maybe a few weeks, the father returned to Paris leaving behind the mother and her children. During the day, I'd work in the fields and Lucien would accompany me, and while he was too young to work he would sometimes help me by picking apples up off the ground. He later came back alone and lived with my parents. But my little sister, Thérèse, remembers it best. She has the photos and drawings that he made of the family."*

THÉRÈSE GAUGAIN: *"With Lulu's health still fragile, his parents asked mine if he might stay with us during his convalescence so that he could eat a balanced diet, the products of the farm. He was calm and sedate, and he became a part of the family. During the day, he would make drawings. He would accompany us everywhere and he observed us while we worked on the farm, helping our parents. My parents were very attentive to him. But we came from different backgrounds, so we didn't really know how to talk to one another. As they say, people of La Sarthe aren't very communicative about either their joys or sorrows."*

This bubble of serenity and kindness would later summon a great nostalgia in the minds of the Ginsburg parents: they would come back to Courgenard in the middle of the 60's and spend several days at the village's café-hotel-restaurant. Serge himself made two or three pilgrimages along with Jane.

It is without a doubt that at this time, in the country, he had his first erotic experience. The following account comes from the 1990 novel *Les Animals* by Bayon, the writer drawing inspiration from Serge's own words: "I found myself a puppy, a little dog, and then just like that, I'd say 'instinctually,' I was in the fields with her. She was so cute, the little mutt, and I took – I don't know if it's the little finger or the ring finger – and I put it in her... How sweet a sheath it was! You know, I never again found that kind of feeling in a woman. And then the little dog looked back at me thoroughly pleased. I tried to slip my dick in but was unable to: I was just a kid [...] I couldn't get a hard-on."

Nursed back to health by the good country air and a little exercise ("At 13, after my illness, they had me lift weights," we read in *l'Equippe*, forty years later), Lucien returns to Paris. He's lost virtually an entire year of school. His parents, who don't want him to repeat the grade (for the Ginsburgs, nothing is as shameful as academic failure), pay for private courses at Cours du Guesclin before enrolling him for the school year of 1942-1943. Meanwhile, life for the Jews of Paris has become a living hell.

The first steps of the final solution were underway in France, with the obligatory wearing of the yellow star instituted in June, 1942 by order of the German military command. Besides the humiliation and fear, this measure serves as a test of the of the rapport between Jews and the rest of French society: wearing the "Yellow Star"[4] means announcing to one's neighbors, shopkeepers, and even the people one passes on the street, that you are Jew, a pariah. Mandatory for any Jew six years of age or older, the star must be of cloth, solid yellow, and must spell out in black inscription the word "Jew"; it must be the size of the palm of one's hand with a black outline. Finally, it must be worn, solidly stitched and clearly visible on the left side of one's chest, starting on the date of June 7, 1942.

> I have earned my 'Yellow Star'
> And upon this 'Yellow Star'
> Yellow words inscribed all bright
> Hieroglyphics rife with fright

Thus, Joseph goes out to pick up the stars: carefully ironed, the kids pin them on their coats, not bothering to have them sewn on. Moreover, had they gone outside without them, the landlord, a collaborator and former nurse during World War I, wouldn't have missed the opportunity to denounce them. Olia, who had advised against submitting to the Jewish census in October, 1940, sees her worst fears realized.

OLIA GINSBURG: *"Then they forbade us from going out after 8 o'clock at night, and we could no longer travel or take the trains. Well me, I went to the country each week to look for supplies. I didn't wear the insignia, I wasn't afraid! I brought big basketfuls of stuff for my kids – they had plenty to eat up till then! Eggs, pork, rabbit, knobs of butter big like so, and all while other families were dying of hunger. But I risked a lot. One day I was in a compartment with some French citizens. A German walks in and shouts: "All of you, out!" I was afraid then: had they asked for my*

---

[4] Yellow Star" became a song on Rock around the Bunker, 1975.

papers – I wasn't yet carrying fakes – they would have seen "Ginsburg"
and said : "Ah, ha! You're traveling! What right have you?" I would have
been sent directly to a camp. Everyone said to me: "You're risking much
too much." But I would just say "Too bad. I've made up my mind about
what I'm going to do.""

Not wearing the star is indeed risky. The General Union of Israelites in France even launches a campaign to incite Jews to "wear the sign with dignity, for all to see." It is these folks who rename the star their "decoration," often wearing it with pride in order to assure their children and also to "give a clear example of how the Germans were failing in their attempt to humiliate the Jews." During the early stages, the Jews in effect do have strong feelings about wearing the star. It is a supplementary humiliation, destined to isolate them even more from the rest of the population and stir up a movement of hostility against them. They are afraid of being hounded in the metro or in the lines in front of food stores where at anytime they might run across collaborators or informants, and they are apprehensive about sending their kids off for the first day of school, fearing that they might become whipping boys for their fellow classmates.

In reality, wearing the yellow star created, according to certain commentators, a wave of sympathy among the population. Many are indignant about this latest measure. In the streets, this is manifested in gestures of complicity, smiles, a discreet tipping of the hat, although the most widespread reaction consists of simply pretending not to notice, as if it were nothing. This unexpected indifference reassures those Jews who fear being the objects of a rather creepy curiosity.

JACQUELINE GINSBURG: *"Even when wearing the star, I never had any*
problems nor did I hear any remarks from the students at the Lycée Jules
Ferry. They were all very warm with me and the five other Jews in my
class. For us, life went on as usual. They let us attend, which was the most
important thing."

In order to reduce the risks, the movements of Jacqueline and Liliane are restricted to trips to and from Lycée Jules Ferry. The rest of the time they stay at home. But they start to get tired of being confined to the house.

It is now impossible for Joseph to find work. The parents reach the end of their meager savings and the small amount of rent money they receive from the apartment on Rue Caulaincourt is not enough to feed the tribe. A few days after having picked up the stars, Joseph makes a heartbreaking decision: in order to meet the needs of the family, they have to head for the unoccupied zone. He makes contact with a smuggler, but the expedition soon turns into an ordeal. Forced to make part of the journey on foot, he becomes terribly fatigued and loses 20 kilos. From Nice, he sends a photo of himself on the Promenade des Anglais. He's unrecognizable. As soon as he recuperates, he sets off zigzagging across the south of France. Some forty years later Serge talks about how Parisian musicians had threatened his father and provoked his departure.

> GAINSBOURG: *"They told him: "You have no right to play because you're a Jew. Beat it!" Harsh, very harsh... They wanted to steal his job. He had to [...] make for the unoccupied zone. That I will never forget. [...] He sent us money in his letters, discreetly. There's also a photo of him in which he's terrifyingly thin. You could see he was worried. Emaciated, pale..."*

Not wearing the star or simply pinning it on is enough to get someone arrested. Since the middle of June, 1942, more than 100,000 Jews had been sent to Drancy for this very reason. But the worst is yet to come: when in Paris on June 30, Adolf Eichmann, chief of the Jewish division of the German police, calls for the deportation of all the Jews in France, and to do so he reinforces the powers of the SS agents based in Paris while also taking new and more vexing measures.

After having been deprived of the radio (starting September 1, 1941, all Jews are supposed to hand in their wireless radios to the police), they are now forced to ride in only the last car on the metro. The 9th German ordinance (July, 1942) limits their access to stores: they may shop only from the hours of three to four o'clock. The PTT[5] receives instructions to cut telephone service to all Jewish subscribers, and finally, establishments open to the public are now off limits (restaurants, cafés, cinemas, concert halls, music halls, pools, museums, libraries, galleries, and even phone booths!).

---

[5] The organization that controlled phone and postal services during World War II. (T.N.)

The round-ups increase all over France during the month of July, 1942. Then on July 16, there's the Vel D'Hiv raid organized by René Bousquet. At four in the morning, 4,500 French police undertake the mission of arresting 27,361 Jews who have no citizenship, including all women from the ages of 2 to 55 and all men aged 2 through 60. The Compagnie du métropolitain[6] puts fifty busses at their disposal. The following day, at five o'clock in the afternoon, they arrest 3,031 men, 5,802 women, and 4,051 children. Many men had been warned in time and are able to flee. The final result of the roundup is a little less than half of what they aimed for: 13,152 Jews. The families are taken to the Vélodrome d'Hiver and the unmarried are sent directly to Drancy. 8,160 men, women, and children stand waiting, ready to be sent off to the camps. The chaos is nightmarish, a tragedy beyond all description.

The vice-grip is tightened. One of Liliane's classmates is rounded up, as is Michel Besman, the unlucky uncle who'd been thrown overboard in that trunk in the Black Sea... Born November 27, 1902 in Theodosia, he lives during this period at 3, Avenue Wilson in Saint Denis and works as a mechanic. Five days after his arrest in the raids of July 16 and 17, he is sent to Auschwitz from the Bourget-Drancy station along with 1,000 other Jews, 615 men (including 16 year-old adolescents) and 385 women, the majority of whom are Polish and another twenty-five per cent Russian, all of humble vocation (shoemakers, upholsterers, tailors, roofers, locksmiths, seamstresses, hatters, etc.). From this convoy, which arrives on July 24, there will be but five survivors.[7]

After the raids in Paris, the youth of the PPF (Parti Populaire Français, French Nazis) spread terror on the terraces of cafés while fear sends an uninterrupted flow of Jews who take for the road beyond the lines of demarcation. We see, for example, exhausted, penniless, and sick families arrive in Lyon. Their departures are disorganized: these are frantic flights rooted in fear and panic. The daily newspapers, ordered to keep quiet, publish nothing about the raids between July 16 and July 31, 1942. Several months later,

[6] The organization that controlled busses and the metro. (T.N.)

[7] Research done at the Centre du Documentation Juive Contemporaine (Contemporary Jewish Resource Center). Between March 27 and September 30, 1942, 38, 206 Jews are deported from France in 41 convoys – one convoy of a thousand Jews every three or four days from July 17 through September – all headed for Auschwitz. In 1945, only 779 survivors are accounted for. All in all, 75,721 French Jews were deported during the war – only 3% returned.

Hitler had coldly announced his intentions of multiple reprisals, notably on February 26, 1942 in *Paris-Soir*: "This war will not annihilate the Aryan population but rather the Jewish element. Preparations are being made that will settle the matter for good."

OLIA GINSBURG: *"One day, I saw it with my own eyes but didn't want to believe it. In front of a French police station they were telling them "Get on, climb aboard!," and then they took them away in trucks. They would leave and never come back. And my daughter Jacqueline almost got deported! My husband had left for the unoccupied zone with a musician friend. His friend wrote to his wife asking her to join him. She had found a smuggler and came to see me: "Give me Jacqueline. I'll take her to her father. She'll be safe with me!" I said: "Never in my life do I want to be separated from my children!" Her retort: "But your husband is out there with mine!" I told her: "When he writes and tells us to come, we'll all go together." So she left alone, but someone denounced her and she was caught..."*

In September, 1942, while Jacqueline and Liliane return to Lycée-Jules-Ferry, Serge, fourteen and a half, finds himself in level 3 at Du Guesclin, a private school on Rue de Turin, still in the 9th arrondissement but near the Place de l'Europe neighborhood. In class, he meets a boy of his age named Daniel Foucret, crazy about drawing, like him, but also about soccer, which Lucien was oblivious to. Lucien is the only one in class who wears the star, but neither the students nor the professors care at all.

DANIEL FOUCRET: *"The war was truly bothersome for all the little Parisian students; everything was difficult: the discipline, the food supply, the alerts, the metro, the men who hated us because we hadn't fought in World War I and wouldn't have to fight in this war either... We didn't have the right to anything while we were there together, so we thought about only one thing: laughing, playing around, finding some sort of diversion. Our life was nothing but a hassle, and worrying about other people's hassles just wasn't our problem. He talked to us about the yellow star, but we never brought up the rationing."*

This weariness, this frustration with interdictions of all kind is also expressed in song, as Jacques Vassal remembers in his *Encyclopédie de la chanson française des années 40 à nos jours*: While Lucienne Boyer sings "Je ne crois plus au Père Noël"[8] (A Santa with a white moustache and a military hat, no doubt), a youth party, squarely opposing the Service of Obligatory Work,[9] thumbs its nose at the occupiers and the Vichy collaborators. They call themselves the Zazous and flaunt their differences, first of all by way of clothing (long coats down to the knees, super-short pants) and also with their hairdos (long hair and powder puffs) in stark contrast to the to the strict dress and short cropped hair extolled by the keepers of mainstream morality... As for music, they pledge their allegiance to swing and swing alone (the rhythm is synonymous with freedom and livelihood, the dance of sensuality), which is considered from Berlin to Vichy as the degenerate expression of depravation itself. After Charles Trenet, Lucien's idol, and his "Poule Zazou," comes his ex-partner in crime, the Swiss Johnny Hess – not so neutral after all – who becomes the champion of the movement recording "J'suis swing" and "Ils sont Zazous" in 1943.

Between February and March of 1943, when Hitler's Minister of the Interior and mastermind of the concentration camps, Heinrich Himmler, announces his coming visit to Paris, new and violent anti-Semitic articles are published simultaneously in *Paris-Soir* (under the pen name of Jean Bosc we see "The crime of the Jews"), *Le Matin* (under the pen name of Jacques Ploncard, who calls for the "creation of a ministry of race"), and Appel, where Pierre Constantini demands a "Ferocious cleansing." The simple truth is that at a time when the crime of having certain characteristics buys you a one-way ticket to Auschwitz, Lucien has a terrible problem, as Foucret has noticed and as other witnesses will attest to later on.

> DANIEL FOUCRET: *"Some might say that he was the obvious Jewish type, that he stood out as a "little Jew," with his big ears, his nose, his big, black eyes...and what's more he was small, a very important detail, and he grew during the year. When he came back to school he must have been just under five feet and then he grew suddenly and at the end of the school year was half a head taller than me..."*

Among the Ginsburgs, Lucien is, in effect, the one who resembles most closely the characteristic representation made by anti-Semites of their favor-

[8] I don't believe in Santa any more. (T.N.)

[9] A program that took French goods and workers and sent them to Germany. (T.N.)

ite targets. Should we look here for one of the sources of the terrible complex with ugliness that he developed during adolescence?

In the meantime, while he might be a zero in math, Lucien is interested in other subjects. In Latin, he finds delectable delight in the story of the conquest of the Gauls by Julius Caesar and also the poetry of Catullus (he had taken precious care of this school book, from the Garnier collection, 1931 edition, which is in his library at Rue de Verneuil). His French professor introduces him to the art of the sonnet, one of the most perfect of poetic forms (he tries his hand at this style and succeeds with the typical prowess he's now known for on the album *Melody Nelson* in 1971) by way of the Trophées of the "decadent" poet (an expression dating from 1870) José Maria de Heredia, whose verses he would take pleasure in quoting forty years later.

His timidity, on the other hand, is something he can't come to terms with. It is perhaps this shyness that prevents Lucien from ever speaking with his classmates in his drawing classes at the academy in Montmartre. Or perhaps it's because some of them are particularly talented: a certain Lallemand, son of an illustrator, amuses himself by putting on his friends with a sketch of a horse head. Foucret himself manages quite well, and even ends up operating a gallery and working as an agent for painters.

> DANIEL FOUCRET: *"What Lulu really liked were the pornographic little comic strips I designed. A pair of breasts or some garters was enough to get him going… These comics were all the rage in our little group."*

After six months of treating his peritonitis in the country and after catching up on his schoolwork at home and at the Du Guesclin school, where he was apparently accepted for level 3 without having really made up the time he missed (at the Ginsburg house, one does not repeat a school year), Lucien becomes completely disinterested with the lycée while his passion for painting and sketching grows all the more. At the academy in Montmartre, he wears the yellow star, but the studio is a real no man's land, a protected universe. Right next to him, a German officer is at work at his easel. Walking through the doors and seeing Lucien, he could have had a completely different reaction…

During the school year, things become complicated for Jacqueline and Liliane. Constantly fearing a raid, of course, their mother decides to send the girls to a boarding house with nuns, in Senlis, in a convent willing to hide them. They stay there from April to June, 1943, but at the end of the trimester the mother superior warns Olia that she can no longer keep the two girls because it has become too risky. In spite of the danger, Jacqueline and her sister are enrolled once again in Lycée Jules-Ferry for the trimester of September, 1943, while Serge returns of course to Du Guesclin, just at the moment when the food shortages become even worse: in June, a number of bakeries close due to lack of flour; at the end of summer, meat becomes scarce. The month of September also marks the bombing of Paris by Allied troops, and the suburbs encounter 300 dead and 1,500 wounded. Since the capitulation of von Paulus at Stalingrad in January, 1943, it is clear that things are beginning to turn sour for the Nazis. They had already witnessed the Allies landing in Sicily in 1942 and Montgomery's defeat of the Afrika Korps in May, 1943 in Tunisia. In France, they see the development of the National Council of the Resistance, and then in July, there's the German debacle at Koursk, the fall of Mussolini, and the bombing of Hamburg. These are indelible images that will resurface later in the song "Rock Around The Bunker":

No calm
Just bombs
The blasts
Reblast
Sublime
The lead
That flies
A world
That dies
In slime

But it will take months of waiting before seeing the results of the Allied landings that everyone had hoped for - a wait that becomes all the more palpable as the days pass. Images of the destruction of Berlin by Allied bombers are saluted with applause in the cinema of Place-Italie during the first show on December 25, 1943 (After that, the newsreels are projected in lighted halls so that the shows ensue without incident).

In the meantime, Olia and her children are comforted upon learning that Joseph is safe near Limoges. Better yet, he makes arrangements in order to meet them: under the name of Guimbard, he moves into the old neighborhood of Viraclau, near Place de la République, which is quite a lively quarter, even in 1943-44, with no less than thirteen bars and four café-concerts. He finds a place to stay at 13, Rue de Combes (which has since become number 11), in a little two-bedroom, one of eight furnished rooms in a hotel belonging to Mr. Phillipe Nadaud, who sells soft drinks and brandy at this same location (his little café, called 'Le Café de la Mère Nadaud,' is on the first floor). The neighboring establishments along Rue des Combes include a bathhouse, other bistros, such as the L'Enchanson or Chez Cafassier, the headquarters of the daily paper *Le Populaire*, and also, next to number 13, the hair salon of Mr. Pierre Riou.

Centrally located, Rue de Combes nevertheless presents certain dangers: in the uppermost section of the neighborhood there's a sort of blockhouse run by the Germans, who often ask for papers. Two hundred meters away, on Rue Général Cerez, is the staff headquarters of the militia, one of whose chiefs, Dr. Chadoune, will be elected mayor of Limoges after the Liberation. At the end of Rue de Combes, a number of shows are presented at a circus-theatre.

Joseph, under the pseudonym of "Jo d'Onde," works most notably at La Coupole in Place de la République, at Cyrano, and also at Café Riche, where he happens to be engaged when his family comes to join him. Among his friends is bandleader and violinist Pierre Guyot, who helps him enormously during these somber times. It's thanks to him that he finds a place to live, and upon his advice Joseph succeeds in hiding his girls in a religious institution and his son in the high school Saint-Léonard-de-Noblat. In Limoges, Josephs also runs across an old acquaintance...

> LÉO PARUS: *"I ran into Joseph in Limoges, where my wife and I were refugees, along with many other Alsatian Jews. All the Jews had fake identity documents. Nobody wore the yellow star. In Limoges, I had found work in one of the five or six cafés in the city that had a band. During the first year, the Vichy government forbade music, and after that only classical music was permitted. We often played "La Marche Lorraine" for the Germans."*

In excerpts from Mrs. Léo Parus' intimate journals, we learn that Joseph is a regular visitor. He even comes to celebrate the New Year on December 31, 1943, just a few days after his family had arrives. Among his other friends and acquaintances is the violinist Monique d'Anglade, whose real name is Yvette Hervé.

YVETTE HERVÉ: *"Joseph, alias Jo d'Onde, played with me and my husband Jean Hervé in a group in Limoges around 1942-43. There were five of us: two violins (myself and Armand Bitsch), a cellist (my husband), a bassist (named Pendola) and the pianist (Léo Parus). After Léo was arrested, we needed a pianist and Jo d'Onde replaced him. He was a good player but not as good as Parus. We played two sets: one from 5 to 7 and one from 9 to 11. Our repertory was eclectic: classical, jazz, operetta, gypsy tunes, etc. The clientele was chic - it was the bourgeoisie that came to listen to the music. There were sometimes German officers. In the evening, the café was shut up. They pulled down iron grids over the windows. Towards 11 o'clock we could hear the bombing. Jo d'Onde was a man of great distinction. Delicate, charming, the type who would kiss a lady's hand. He was very cultivated. His accent was quite pronounced but his French was very refined. One day we had a long exchange about the letters of Madame de Sevigny. He was a Russian from the time of the tsars, in an era when speaking French was considered elegant. He dressed in a very austere manner, in very somber suits, and contrary to his son, he really had no typically Jewish traits."*

In December, 1943, Joseph finally signals to Olia that is time to leave. As Jacqueline is the eldest, 17, and her passage considered the most hazardous, she leaves alone, supplied with false documents still under the name of Guimbard. She has the fear of God put into her as she passes security at the Vierzon train station. Safe and sane, she is greeted upon arrival by Joseph. On January 9, Joseph presents her to Léo Parus and his wife. The family is finally reunited: Olia, Liliane, and Lucien arrive after an uneventful train trip. Before leaving, their mother, decidedly very clever, takes the trouble, along with the help of neighbors Mr. and Mrs. Fiancette, to stage a phony move out of their apartment. Knowing that Germans and collaborators systematically loot the apartments of Jews heading for unoccupied territory, she finds, thanks to the Fiancettes, a maid's room a bit down the road on Rue Chaptal, and there she crams in all their furniture, except for Joseph's piano, which is stored at a friend's home. Result: after the Liberation, the Ginsburgs are able to move back in without any problems as we will see later on...

Pierre Riou, the hairdresser on Rue des Combes in Limoges, who was twenty-two in 1944, recounts his memories in 1998, after the closing of his salon:

> PIERRE RIOU: *"The children stayed for six months, no longer. I often saw their father, who was distinguished and sported a fine moustache, but mother Gainsbourg did no go out very often. They were the only refugees in the building. One day, in March, 1944, there was a raid. The father was able to escape. My little clerk, Narcisse, died in the crossfire of the militia at the Caserne des Dragons, in Cité Blanqui."*

The religious institution of Sacré-Cœur is on Rue Portail-Imbert, near Rue des Combes, and there, Jacqueline and Liliane find boarding on the advice of Pierre Guyot. They see their parents only on Sundays, after mass at the cathedral in the company of all the other high school students in Limoges. It's a mass that they attend in pretense, of course.

Lucien is sent some 20 kilometers to the east of Limoges, to the school of Saint-Léonard-de-Noblat, a pretty little medieval town in a countryside of rolling hills. At the bottom of the hill overlooking Saint-Léonard flows the Vienne River. The Romanesque church is a place of pilgrimage: as legend has it, the women who kiss the iron door lock there will become fertile. The school where Lucien stays in January, 1944 opened its doors in 1887. It's an austere looking building shaped like a U, with light gray walls and a central building of two stories and two wings of three floors each. It is situated at the exit point of the village and frequented especially by the sons of farmers or craftsmen (the children of more well-off parents go to Limoges). To enter, you pass through an iron grill and cross the garden. The playground, small in size, opens on to the rolling hills of the countryside. At the end of the courtyard there are restrooms and a garden where the director, Louis Chazelas, grew a few vegetables, and a lower courtyard off to the right. Chazelas is an organized man: he heads expeditions for his students, on bicycle, in order to collect eggs from the farms... One eats better at Saint-Léonard than at Sacré-Cœur de Limoges. The children's menu includes soup in the afternoon and evening and a stew seven days a week, with large portions of potatoes and carrots (as for meat, that's only on Saturdays). The last detail, which as we will later learn is important, is that only a part of the left wing is used along with the dining hall. The other part burned down in 1941.

For the second time in his life, after six months of convalescence in Courgenard, Lucien is separated from his parents. A new experience traumatizes his life as a young adolescent, who is 15 years and nine months old at the time the following lines are written. He has, in fact, started keeping an intimate journal in a little notebook, only two pages of which – written in tiny script on both sides of the page – have been found (the sudden cut-off at the end of the second page indicates that there were even more). The sentences are short and Serge moves constantly from line to line, which is due not only to the size of the notebook: one might guess that he wanted to do it that way, clumsily, naively, to give a rhythm to his text and render it more dramatic:

—Well, good-bye sir!
The door closed and mother disappeared...

I stood there face to face with the director. His fat gut inspired in me a certain confidence.

—Grab your bags and follow me, he said.

I leaned down over my grimy bundles. How could I carry this stuff all by myself? My mother had to help me here, dragging it along and swearing as sweat dripped from her brows!

When I'd grabbed a little more than half of my bundles by their strings, my clenched fingers refused to open again. Through the space between my legs, I caught a glimpse of the director's two shoes as he waited in silence.
—Let me take that. I'll help you, he said suddenly.
He took what remained. He wasn't a proud man...He then left, leading the way.
I was staggering.
A bag full of cookies cracked open.
We went up the shiny, yellow staircase. Not bad for a high school!, I said.
But it was just an illusion.
On the second floor, the director opened a door and what I saw made me forget my embarrassment and shyness.

Iron beds, white walls...

A veritable hospital room!

That's what a dormitory is! I was worried.

Further on, in a little recess, a ceramic washbasin and lead pipes. A toilette, even!

Downstairs, in the courtyard, the black slate of the urinals left me feeling crushed.

I made a quick study of my surroundings.

A maddening wall of hair, berets, eyes...

With all those eyes are fixed on us that way, in large numbers, they acquire a certain power.

Hell! The children and even the young men didn't intimidate me, especially seeing as they were just a bunch of country kids.

They study hall was in a state of total disorder. Papers of all size and color littered the tiles of the floor.

Filthy walls, all scratched up.

A smoking stove.

By the time I sat down in the first row, the director had disappeared. I then noticed the supervisor, and examining his sullen face I had no illusions about becoming chummy with him.

In the evening I was back in the dormitory.

We had to sit at the foot of the bed, and upon a signal from the supervisor we undressed.

It was the first time for me sleeping among strangers.

Well, I have to admit that I hid myself away.

The lights went out.

And the hall was dark.

Through the windows, I saw the second dormitory and the one above it, whose lights went out one after the other.

I suddenly felt a presence behind me, near my nightstand.

I rolled my head over on my pillow.

—You're not cold?

It was the voice of the director. I lay there in my sheets and yawned "No...," which I don't think he heard. Then he walked away.

I heard the door squeak in the distance, and that was all.

I was finally able to calmly sink into self-pity, contemplating my unfortunate fate.

But I was able to fall asleep.

—Touch my shoes and I'll break your face!

It was Morelon who had said that, laughing like an idiot.

It's now eight days that I've been at school.

I have now become used to the place and the freakishness of these country hicks.

An Alsacian, Brumpt, who had become my friend, and the aforementioned Morelon, guided and "protected" me!

I already had a nickname: "The Philosopher."

Only the hicks know why!...

I got along fine with the supervisors, Lebras and "Pampelune." By Pampelune I mean Mr. Calien. His wards showed him no mercy...

We were studying.

As the bell for recess was about to ring, we didn't worry about too much about raising our voices, especially since it was Pampelune who was in charge.

Still, from time to time some bookworm would raise his voice, all bent out of shape:

—Hey! This isn't a bordello!

I was sitting behind Morelon, next to Brumpt.

His blond hair, arched nose, and prominent chin give him a special demeanor, which I like.

Unfortunately, there was something thickheaded and dull about him, which earned him the moniker of "boor."

He was in the middle of explaining something to me with [cuts off]

We've found many of his classmates, including the nephew and the son of the director of the school, Louis Chazelas, but we couldn't track down Morelon and Brumpt. Still, a number of witnesses confirm what we have already ascertained about the qualities and shortcomings of Lucien Ginsburg the student...

ROBERT FAUCHER: *"He was seated next to me in class and he didn't talk much. He never brought up his personal life, but we knew about it because he wasn't the only one in the class. There were always about a dozen Jews in permanent residence at the school. The teachers did their best so that they could lose themselves amongst the crowd. They arranged things so that they could pass by unnoticed. Gainsbourg didn't really fit in at all. English was all he was really good at, and he seemed to speak it fluently. During class, he'd spend his time drawing, sometimes nudes. He drew very quickly – just three strokes of the brush and you'd have something recognizable."*

GUY MOREAY: *"My father was a gendarme in Saint-Léonard. He knew about the children hidden at the school. Furthermore, there were a lot of Jews hiding in the village."*

It is obviously out of the question for Lucien Guimbard to write directly to his parents in Limoges, Rue des Combes. Too risky. Other more reliable means are organized. That's why on February 24, 1944, he sends his mail to "Miss Jacqueline Ginsburg 9 (sic!) at the home of Mrs. Sansonnet / Le Grand Vedeix (Saint-Cyr)":

Dear Mother and Father,
Jacqueline and Liliane

I have just received your package!!!
I put it in the corner and finished some things I had to do, then without hurrying too much I went up to the dormitory and opened it up...
–A sweater! Marvelous!
–A pair of shoes – Great!
My old ones are worn out.
–And this is nice : a sewing kit.
Now what's in here??? Ah, Yes! Nice!
–What is it that you would like to know?
The proper thing to do is to offer you my most sincere thanks.
Thus, I thank you, mother, from the bottom of my heart, and from the
bottom of my appetite...
Now that's a record!

I haven't yet tasted anything. I am conserving it jealously so that it might last me a long time!

I haven't yet been back home! Jacqueline and Liliane, I stick my tongue out at the both of you!

I know that you couldn't care less – I'm sure that for you, Limoges is better than a piece of cake, big as it is, right?

But as for me, I'd rather have cake, especially a big slice... respectfully, rather than anything else!

[several missing lines]

[...] who handles the service. And when it comes to distributing the grub, that's the best sort of friendship.

–You want some of that?

–What is it?

–Beans!

–Yes, a few!

–That's all?

–A little more...

–That? That's all? Shit! So that's that?

So when someone doesn't want something, someone else steps in and takes advantage. Me, I often take advantage. They don't like the boudin here. But it's good! When they serve it, everyone gets a piece as big as my finger (true, my finger isn't all that big...)

So certainly, I take advantage of that:

Who wants my boudin?

–Me!

–You want mine?

–Yeah!

–And mine?

–Yeah!

–Take mine, too!

–Bring it on!

And just like that, I've collected quite a respectful quantity!

But enough of this piggishness!

After the meal, it's time for the older students to horse around.

When you're nineteen, you've got to come up with something more than shoving breadcrumbs up your friend's nose. That's why certain amusing accidents take place. Not amusing for the recipient, of course. When somebody has a bottle of water poured all over his coat, it's wet, but not so funny. Me, I received a lesson when I found a mashed up potato in my pocket.

There are even jokes (in a manner of speaking) played in the dormitory. Finding an apple pie in your bed isn't so bad. Sometimes, when the weather permits, you get a snowball between your sheets.

In the evening, when the supervisor is absent, it's pillow fights (we have long, round pillows) Smack! And smack again! The feathers fly... You can hear the cries of the combatants mixed in with the dull thuds of the pillows landing forcefully on the head. A pretty harmony. I can tell you that I really like seeing a guy get walloped, but I have no desire to be woken up at night by a series of feathery blows. In the bigger dormitories, in the gallery, it's a real terror when they have at it. There's no supervisor capable of stopping it (especially the night before our "escape" [the last day of school]). When a friend is targeted, there's nothing to do but submit. Most of the time it's a surprise attack. Here's how it happens: the guy is sleeping. Two others move in on his bed, stick their hand under the mattress, and "wham!" – he falls out of his bed and finds himself under his mattress. And there you have it.

When there's a lot of snow, there are non-stop snowball fights. When somebody is targeted the whole crowd takes after him! That's how I was trapped when two guys came up on me from behind and a third crushed an ice-cold snowball into my face. It can really shake a guy up!

But telling you about all these pranks must make you think that life here is just a journey on a hell bound train. You mustn't believe that. Those things happen from time to time, but otherwise it's pretty calm. I know you're not very happy, but at least you guys have your Thursdays and Sundays!

All my love,
Lucien

JEAN CHAZELAS: *"During the war, among a total of 150 students, about 80 of them were boarders occupying three dormitories. There were two kinds of students who weren't from the surrounding area: those from dis-placed families that had to flee because of the circumstances of the war, especially people from the north of Alsace who weren't really hiding, and then there were children of Jews escaping persecution. The presence of the first group made it easier for the second to pass by incognito among the mass of students. My uncle had found some solutions for the older ones: for example, they become supervisors. On the second floor of the left wing, which had partially burned down in 1941, there was a room with three or four beds and the windows had curtains. There they would hide children who were on the run, those not attending class. We never saw a yellow star during the war, or even knew it existed. The war didn't penetrate our establishment."*

GEORGES CHAZELAS: *"Each year there were at least 20 students who hid out at the school. Interested parties knew they could send their children to the school, but my father was never part of the Resistance. He acted independently. In 1944, the militia descended upon the school after an in-fringement, but they found nothing."*

On the nights of February 26 and 27, 1944, a courageous officer from the Royal Navy smuggles in a messenger from the Resistance, on a secret mission from Dartmouth to Brittany. The officer is David Birkin, the future father of Jane, who will be born on December 14, 1946. As for the messenger, legend has it that he is named François Mitterrand (later, as the president of France, he awarded the Legion of Honor to David Birkin in official recognition of the event, at a time when his past activities during the occupation where causing him some problems).

Still, in Limoges, danger always lies in wait. The militias, more and more menacing, breed panic along Rue des Combes.

GAINSBOURG: *"In the sordid little two-bedroom that we occupied, my mother had hidden our fake papers under the wax tablecloth in the kitchen. One fine day, a search, not by the SS but rather the French militia, lands us in some hot water. My mom is seated on the corner of the table. There are about 10 men and she tells them to look wherever they please. They search everywhere, but forget to ask my mom to stand up and thus leave empty handed."*

After this initial warning, his parents are stopped and detained for 48 hours and it's only by way of an enormous web of lies that they are able to worm themselves out of it.

OLIA GINSBURG: *"I had two fake pieces of identity under the name of Guimbard and I had claimed, without budging an inch, that I was the Ginsburg's maid. But my husband cracked under more severe interrogation... My worst memory is that of being locked up with a bunch of prostitutes, vile women, who were smoking and insulting one another so much so that my ears were burning. The boss at the place where my husband worked was immediately alerted and had dinner sent over to us. It's thanks to him that we were able to get out..."*

MRS. PIERRE GUYOT: *"Joseph was arrested during band rehearsal. When the police came, they immediately took him into custody. It was my husband who brought them something to eat."*

The Ginsburgs are released, but forbidden to leave Limoges. Still, that doesn't stop them from fleeing for the countryside the very next day, to Grand Vedeix in Saint-Cyr, and the home of the Sansonnets. We caught up with the daughter, Gabrielle, just a few weeks before her death.

GABRIELLE SANSONNET: *"It's a story about everyday life, really... Gainsbourg's parents lived with mine in Grand Vedeix, in a little house next to ours in the hamlet. It was 1944. Serge's father showed up one day and I was all alone at the house. People had told them that we could provide them lodging. At the time, people were ready to stay anywhere. They didn't need any creature comforts. They wanted to hide, and here, while it's not a part of the country that's really off the maps, it's also not a place anyone will come looking for you. They were very nice people. They never understood that we knew they were Jews. I'd often go out with the girls, who were a little younger than me – I was twenty – and we'd take off on bicycles. I remember one time we passed a little village and I said, "Look, those people are Israelites." I was trying to get them to say it, but Jacqueline and Liliane never said "Us, too." I would go to mass with the two of them, but they remained secretive about the truth."*

After the death of her parents, Gabrielle Sansonnet found in a shoebox the pages of a diary as well as letters from Lucien. As of March, 1944, he still writes to his parents, using a coded language (weak = Jew, my health = the fact that I am a Jew, etc.) but also show signs of a feeling of superiority and snobbism that is rather outlandish. At the time of this writing, he is 15 days from his sixteenth birthday:

Dear Mother and Father,
Jacqueline and Liliane,

I have received your package, but seeing as that I had just sent you a voluminous letter of some fifteen pages, I was waiting to receive your response to it.
I received it at noon.
I now write you.
Although I could have survived without this package, it has warmed my heart, not to mention delighting my palate and tongue...
Upon opening it, I first noticed the back of the underpants, the one's with the color of an African's head on a background of café-crème... Another two or three holes and I would have had Scottish underwear... Ten more like that and I would have had chestnut-colored pants with little brown spots... witty...
Now onto the victuals.
Chocolate? – Ah! Marvelous!
(A little bit is already missing)
And what's in this little, slightly dented box? – hmm! I'm sniffing... I think it's... but the taste will tell me more than the smell... this knife I have is worthless... a piece of tongue... That's what I thought! Excellent paté! Great! Just great!
And here's a little knob of butter. I hope it's not rancid... Let's see... Not at all... no... very good butter. It's getting better and better...
And let's see what's in this packet... Wow! The mother lode! These little cookies are delicious!
(Two of them missing already)
I don't think I've overlooked anything... When I read your letter I was saddened to hear that you've been worrying about my health here.
From day one, we have known that [missing a few words]
The director has a nephew whom he tells everything to, and this nephew tells his friends everything, and then if they don't get it from him they get it

from someone else. Nothing one can do. The length of my nose, about which I say [? ? ?]...

And so, I'll say it again, there's nothing to do about it without risking repeating a level. But don't go thinking that just because they know I'm weak means that things aren't just fine here.

What's more, there are three real nice guys here and nobody pays attention to my weakness, so have no concerns over that matter. The boys that insult the weak sometimes get a good ass kicking from the others.

But I'll tell you again that nobody has ever said a word to me and nobody will. I am kind of on my own here, but not because of that. It's rather that this place is peopled with farmer's sons and modest administrators with mediocre minds.

So it is they who have put me at a distance because of my ideas about the future, the ideas in general expressed in my drawing (The Artist), and because of my books (The Poet, The Philosopher).

And I will not, simply in order to become more popular, pretend or feign interest in those who idealize the culture of carrots and cabbage, the profession of schoolteacher or postman, or that of telegraph or telephone operator...

From what I've just told you must not imagine that I am intentionally trying to play the part of the outsider!

A friend helped me to understand the situation I was in:

–"You're here," he said, when I told him about my ideas and my projects, "in a world of farmers and clerks. And if you use the word 'farmer' with such little respect (we were discussing the future), you'll soon find yourself an outsider."

I then understood that I had better put the brakes on, so to speak, and not say what I feel. And for that reason I never tell them what I'm thinking. So I'm never surprised when, behind my back or even to my face, I hear "the artist!" or "the philosopher!", "Watteau!", "Raphael!" and so on... Anyway, it doesn't bother me... Caesar said it's better to be first in a village than second at Rome. That's debatable...

But back to the matter at hand.

I can tell you again for the millionth time that I am at no risk here. All the boys in my same situation know one another here. There have never been any problems. In any case, please don't worry.

The director asked for information about my situation at the Ministry of Instruction, and in spite of my health and even the health of certain supervisors, we are constantly under the protection of the director here.

But outside of the college, it is well understood that no one speaks about the wickedness of my dear uncle...

I will now respond to this morning's letter. Thank you for the money. I will no longer ask for anything from the director.

[several missing words]

I'll ask the director what to do about my watch. Surely he can bring it to a watchmaker. If not, I'll give it to my "Latin teacher" because he's in charge of going to the post office to mail letters. So I'm bringing the cover and the note-book with the sonatas.

I will buy one-way only ticket, as you have instructed (just to show you that I'm writing this letter with yours beneath my very eyes and that I have understood what remains to be done...)

On Monday, I gave my dirty laundry to another laundress – all is fine on this end. I only deposited:

7 handkerchiefs

1 washcloth

1 shirt (yellow collar)

1 pair of underwear

[some missing words]

I've got a dirty shirt on, some cotton flannel, my sheets (which are lovely!) and two pairs of socks.

Should I ask the laundress to mend my sheets and socks? Because one of the little sheets has a small hole and each night my foot slips through and my socks are too worn out for me to mend them myself: the sheet has a hole big enough to disappear into and I could pass my head through the holes in my socks.

Well, almost.

I await your instructions.

And I send you my love and hope for the best.

Lucien

Let's try to interpret this. His parents have been arrested and have made this understood to Lucien. They are worried about him, but Chazelas, the director, thanks to his "Ministry of Instruction" (surely one or more informants who keep him up to date as to the current raids by the militia and the SS), watches over Lucien's "health" and that of the other Jews at the school, including the two supervisors mentioned in the letter. In the school, no one bring ups "the wickedness of my dear uncle" (Adolph Hitler, of course). Still, Joseph and Olia give him a set of instructions so that he will be able to leave at any moment in case a problem arises (with the help of the director, who must bring "my watch [...] to the watchmaker") and join them ("one-way only") in Grand Vedeix. Lucien appears quite boastful, but this is just a facade. With his fearful nature, one can easily imagine him being tortured with fright. And who wouldn't be in his situation? Expecting an eventual and sudden departure, his imagination is at work, nourished by the adventure books that he devours at that time, penned by Fenimore Cooper (*The Last of the Mohicans*, which had him crying at the end), Trelawney (*Memoirs of a Gentleman Pirate*), Daniel Defoe (*Robinson Crusoe*), and Rudyard Kipling (*The Jungle Book*). This is why we can legitimately doubt the following anecdote, although it is recounted numerous times by Serge during the 1980s...

> GAINSBOURG: *"One day, the director of the establishment calls me in and says, "My lad, the militia is going to drop in today and verify whether or not there are any Jews in the school. So here's what I want you to do: Take this axe and go hide out in the woods. If someone asks, you're just the son of a woodsman." So I head off like Tom Thumb and build myself a little hut. It was a real adventure. Unfortunately, when night fell a storm broke out; in less than an hour I'm soaked to the bones. The next day, some of the smaller boys came and brought me some food. When all was clear, I made my way back."*

Did this little adventure really take place? Did he, a few weeks after the previous letter, cook up a romantic account of his expedition so that he might rejoin his family? Did he later draw inspiration, in order to construct his legendary exploit, from elements given to him in a story by his friend Gert Alexander in the house of Champsfleur, in Mensil-le-Roy, as we will see later on?

June 6, 1944. The Allies land in Normandy. On June 10, a detachment of an SS division, "Das Reich," decide on taking a punitive expedition to Oradour-sur-Glane, barely 20 kilometers from Grand-Vedeix, in order to avenge the abduction and (supposed) assassination of one of their officers. One of the surviving witnesses tells us: "They asked all the men to assemble in four or five groups. Each group was then led into a barn and the Germans locked the doors behind them. It was about two o'clock in the afternoon. At that very moment, we heard machine gun fire coming from the neighboring villages and saw smoke rising from the village and the nearby farms. After having been searched from top to bottom, which took several hours, houses were burned down one after the other. At about five o'clock, the SS came back to the church. They placed a sort of case on top of the prie-dieu used for communion and brought out some burning fuses. The air quickly became unbreathable [...] And then the Germans started to shoot through the windows of the church. They went in and finished off the rest of the survivors with machine guns and then tossed something on the ground and the church went up in flames... Towards six o'clock, the Germans stopped a train right on the tracks as it was passing by. They made everyone who was heading for Oradour-sur-Glane get off and then proceeded to pump them full of bullets and deposit their cadavers in the fire...."

All tolled, the Oradour massacre takes the lives of 642 inhabitants. Of the village's total population, only seven are miraculously spared: "The German officer who ordered this butchering," said Serge, "could have easily pointed his finger just two centimeters to the side on his map at staff headquarters." After having escaped that abortionist's wash basin and the peritonitis when he was 16, he would later come to interpret this as yet another reprieve...

"During the year of 1944, in particular the months of May through August, the militias engaged in numerous crime sprees and abuses of power in the region of Limoges," reports the Chief of the Central Directorate of the Judicial Police on April 27, 1945. And he adds: "To our knowledge, 42 people were killed during this time in various circumstances by militia men, while 106 others were victims of arbitrary arrests, violence, theft, or the pillaging of apartments." Yet it is the very same police force in Limoges that less than a month earlier put out the following "wanted" notice:

POLICE FORCE OF LIMOGES

REGIONAL SECURITY SQUAD

Bureau of Identification and Diffusion

5, cours Vergniaud, Limoges

Telephone: 34-70

Notice Number 27/44 N, June 22, 1944

WANTED INDIVIDUALS:

1 – GINSBURG Joseph, born 3/27/1896 in Constantinople of parents Hérich and Bata Chava SMILOVICI, French citizen by naturalization – pianist – last known place of residence: Limoges, 3, Rue St-Paul.

Subject to arrest and internment by the Regional Police Chief of Limoges

2 – BESMAN Goda, wife of Ginsburg, born on 1/2/1894, French citizen by naturalization, same address.

Subject to arrest and internment by the Regional Police Chief of Limoges

Subject to house arrest in Limoges.

–If found, the above-named persons will be taken and held by the Limoges Police and the Intendancy of the Department of Law and Order will be informed. (Cabinet – Internment Services).

Joseph and Olia ignore both the fact that their escape has been discovered in Limoges and the new danger that hovers above their heads. At the Sansonnets, they are, of course, well hidden, but not at all under lock and key. They are waiting for the end of the school year so that the family can once again be reunited, which will be a done deal come the beginning of July.

Paris is liberated on August 25. The next day, there's immense jubilation as de Gaulle parades down the Champs-Elysées. From July 21 to 25, 250 children are still arrested in the houses of the UGIF (Union Générale des Israélites de France) in the region of Paris and sent to camps. On August 17, the last convoy leaves Drancy for Buchenwald. All told, nearly 76,000 French Jews disappear during the war, either executed or deported.

In their unhappiness, and in spite of the anguish and fear every hour of the day for four straight years, we can confirm that the Ginsburgs manage to escape unscathed. Other than for uncle Besman, who died in Auschwitz, the family is intact. They have escaped the raids, avoided deportation, confiscations, and execution. Upon returning to Paris, thanks to their kindly neighbors, they have their apartment and all of their furniture. Jacqueline has passed her bac, and despite an education that has been turned upside down (a year in Dinard, the Lycée Jules-Ferry, the convent at Senlis, Sacré-Cœur de Limoges), Liliane also graduates with honors. For Lucien, on the other hand, the results, as we will see in the next chapter, are clearly less positive.

Like hundreds of thousands of other Jews who survived the Nazi terror, the Ginsburgs will never again speak, among themselves, of the trials they went through. It's a total black-out, out of respect for the dead and modesty towards those who lost everything. No talking on the radio, either, with the notable exception of the astonishing interview with Olia, improvised by Andrew Birkin, Jane's brother. A passionate story that is told in the 1970s. Serge's position as a public figure would eventually change everything, but he would wait until the 1980s before really expressing himself on the subject, even though in 1975 – thirty years after the German surrender – he recorded Rock Around The Bunker, a record which was a sort of exorcism.

Never again will he have to wear a "Yellow Star." Or rather, yes. In 1969, Serge will sport a new Star of David, but this time it's platinum, and comes from Cartier...

three

I Admit, I Suffered Dear

Although Olia and the kids settle back into their Parisian residence, Joseph decides to work for a few more months in Limoges. While still at the Sanosonnet's in Grand-Vedeix, he gets a letter from a musician friend who tells him that "the bands here in Limoges started playing again last night." Joseph starts performing there on Sunday, October 1, in a new club on "Avenue de la Libération" (still with quotation marks because it's entirely new!). "There's a rehearsal Saturday morning and an audition for the boss that same afternoon." He's only making 300 francs a day, far from the 900 he was earning before the war. On October 8, Joseph visits Léo Parus and his wife. On November 15, he writes to Gabrielle Sansonnet, to whom he announces his departure on the morning of October 21. He finally heads back up to Paris where a host of troubles await him: Lucien, who returned to Condorcet, has received simply disastrous grades.

His penchant for dreaming has taken over. Rather than do his homework, he prefers the delights of reading: Flaubert's *Madame Bovary*, Daniel Defoe's *A Journal of the Plague Year* (according to Serge "the first journalistic record in the history of literature.") He then discovers *Down There* and *Against Nature* by Joris-Karl Huysman, whose "cold and almost inhuman esthetic," is something that he would encounter again later on, he states, in Nabokov's *Lolita*. The symbolic and decadent quest of the hero, des Esseintes,[1] the neurotic perfection of style, the absurd richness of the vocabulary, the constant search for an arcane word – all this serves to hurl adolescent Gainsbourg, who is approaching his sixteenth birthday, into a world of a morbid fascination. Among the Russians, Gorky is his favorite ("very hardcore"), As he will explain very clearly later on, in an interview published in 1985 in *L'Humanité*, he discovers Rimbaud, Baudelaire, and Edgar Allan Poe[2] shortly thereafter, at the time when he is also deeply into his education in painting.

But let's get back to *Adolphe*,[3] which he will continue to quote from during his entire career, beginning with the appearance of his first album in 1958 and continuing through the dialogues on *Charlotte For Ever* in 1986:

Tell me, she wrote. Is there any country that I would not follow you to? Is there any hiding place where I would not hole up with you in order to be near your, being sure not to be a burden that weighs you down? But no, that's not what you want. Every idea I suggest, all timid and trembling because you have left me frozen with fear, is impatiently brushed aside. The best I can hope for is your silence. Such cruelty is not in step with your character. You are good, your actions noble and dedicated, but why are these actions wiped out by your words? These acerbic words resound around me. I hear them at night. They follow and devour me and make all else you do wither away. So must I die? I think you would be happy. She died, that poor little creature that you looked after... but she's also the one you keep on hitting twice as hard. She will die, this troublesome Ellénore that you can't stand to have in your presence, that you consider an obstacle, and for whom you can nowhere on earth find a spot where she will not be a tiresome bother for you. She will die. You shall walk alone in the middle of the crowd that you have always been so eager to be a part of. You know them, those men whom, this very day, you thank for being indifferent. And perhaps one day, crushed by their bloodless hearts, you will regret the heart

---

[1] Protagonist, or antihero, of Huysman's Against Nature. (T.N.)

[2] His copy of A Journal of the Plague Year w as a first French edition (Denoël, 1928). As for Poe, two volumes of Tales of Horror and Mystery from l'Édition Gründ are given to him in 1947. They are all numbered and come complete with hallucinatory illustrations by Gus Bofa. In 1949, he buys - perhaps after having loaned out or lost a first copy? – The works of Arthur Rimbaud from Éditions Mercure de France, which he dedicates touchingly, "To myself."

[3] By Benjamin Constant.

you threw away, the one that lived for your affection, who braved thousands
of dangers in your defense, the one whom you will not even dignify with the
slightest regard... [4]

At a time when people are looking for heroes that they can identify with,
in a world that inspires nothing but horror and disgust, crushed by his complex over his ugliness, his nose, and his ears, which for so long had tortured
him at the time of the raids, ridiculed for his juvenile appearance (he has
no facial hair during these long years and he smokes in order to look older),
aware of his superiority (pride a major trait among the Ginsburgs), he is yet
profoundly romantic and idealistic (his fantasies revolve around art with a
capital "A" and take form in his painting), and there are numerous reasons
for this – reasons whose roots we may find in the authentic revelation which
seizes him during the reading of *Adolphe*, a portrait of a cold man, too demanding with himself, persuaded that all passion is doomed to end in failure
and deception, all written in a very dry and terribly concise style. [5]

The return to Condorcet. His second trimester is even worse. He scores
0.25 (18th in his class) in French, 0 in Latin translation, 0 in Greek translation, and the other scores are in keeping with those. "He was wasting his
time in class, simply trying to stay awake," the headmaster remarks, and his
teacher in French, Latin, and Greek even claims that his "compositions are
worthless," and that Serge "has no place in level 1." The others remarks, more
laconic, are along the line of "weak," "very weak," "a bit weak"... He isn't
a troublemaker, nor even rebellious. He has simply been failing in his academic pursuits since his "virtual" level 4, which he failed because of illness.
He just loses all interest in lycée, and often ditches class. One instructor, still
discreetly a Francist of the Pétain persuasion, clearly displays his scorn for
Ginsburg the student and for the "race" he represents. Anti-Semitism has
not quieted down after the Allied landing: while there may no longer be any
denunciations or raids, it still manifests itself in waves, such as during the
spring of 1945 when we see shopkeepers who had taken over confiscated

---

[4] See Movies (the complete edition of his screenplays), a publication established and annotated by Frank
Lhomeau, Éditions Joseph K., Nantes, 1944 (pp.208-209).

[5] One might also note that his primary reference books, from Adolphe to [Sartre's] Nausea, and including Against Nature, Lautréamont's Maldoror, and even Defoe's Robinson Crusoe, are novels with a single
main character... Just as in Evguénie Sokolov, Serge's parabolic tale published in 1980 (thanks to Xavier
Lefebvre).

Jewish stores refuse to hand them back. There are still even anti-Jewish protests in certain arrondissments throughout Paris.

Serge would never finish his last year or pass his bac. On March 2, 1945, a month before his seventeenth birthday, there's a revolution at the Ginsburg home: while his elder sister Jacqueline is doing brilliantly at the Sorbonne, Lucien decides to interrupt his studies. That or he's simply kicked out of Condorcet, according to the official version, which may not be true. For his parents, who had always stressed scholarly success and had struggled to give their three children a proper education even while facing the occupation and all the other whims of fate, the blow is terrible. The only consolation for Joseph, the frustrated painter, is that Lucien continues to pursue his passion in his drawing and painting classes in Montmartre. Still, as Serge confides some twenty years later in on France-Inter,[6] his father wanted him to be a painter (key phrase: his father wanted him to be a painter), but he found himself "so crushed when I didn't want to work any longer, to pursue my studies – I dropped everything at Lycée Condorcet – and I went to study architecture at the school of fine arts."

At the Académie Montmartre, soon to be rebaptized as the Académie Fernand Léger, Lucien meets the painter and (future) sculptor Jacob Pakciarz, seven years his elder. Born in Poland, he is a member of the communist party, not to mention a survivor. Imprisoned at Drancy on August 20, April 1941, he manages to escape and hides out in Switzerland until the Liberation. His entire family was deported and killed in Auschwitz. In Paris, he paints lampshades in order to make a living.

JACOB PAKCIARZ: *"He invited me to his parents' home for someone's birthday. It was in a little apartment on Rue Chaptal, a modest place with a piano. He was rather rebellious in front of his family. We were there, a group several young people, and he said: "You can always manage to do what you want to do. If you really want it." He had plenty of energy and ambition. At that time, he showed a great deal of hostility towards his father. He despised him for being a nightclub musician. He saw him as a failure. I think that his words, "You can always manage to do what you want," hinted at this contempt, as if he wanted to say, "My father wasted his life. He didn't show enough perseverance in order to become a great*

---

[6] French radio station. (T.N.)

*pianist, and I will never be like him." This, in my opinion, is the origin of
his melancholy. He was not proud of his father. He suffered from this and
at the same time he felt guilty."*

There were surely some sort of summit-like negotiations between
Lucien, Olia, and Joseph. At that time, you didn't need your bac to enroll as
an architecture student at the school of fine arts. You just had to pass a test
and take some prerequisite courses. One might imagine the following pact:
rather than make up a year and move to another lycée, he lets himself be
convinced to study architecture even though his passion is painting. It would
have made much more sense for him to enroll as a painting major, but mother
Ginsburg must have been very persuasive. She already has enough with one
artist to take care of, with Joseph coming home at all hours now that he is
back on the nightclub circuit in Montmartre.

Finally, everything becomes orderly - everyone reconciles and waits for
the return to school in September. Remember that in the Ginsburg home,
the family is close-knit, and that the war, which brought them only closer, is
still fresh in their minds. Joseph is crazy about his wife and Lucien adores
his mother. Still, the boy has no friends and does not appreciate the company of people his own age. He has but one companion, an old Catalan poet
and novelist, an ex-deputy in the parliament of Catalonia who fled Spain in
1936 to live at Place Clichy. Joan Puig i Ferreter (pronounced "Pooch") is 63
years old and has a white beard that makes him look like Victor Hugo. The
bastard child of a landowner and one of his female servants, towards the age
of 18, he almost shoots and kills the man who sired him upon discovering the
secret of his birth, but he loses his nerve at the crucial moment. Romantic
and sanguine, he is 20 years old at the beginning of the century, leading a
bohemian life in the south of France and resorting to theft when he gets too
hungry... In 1904, he publishes a collection of poems and his first theatre
piece, staged in Barcelona, where he takes up residence a few years later. He
becomes a journalist, and is very famous in the years following 1925, after
the publication of his novel *Les Facèies de l'amour*, which is followed by an
autobiographical account of his experiences as journalist who is a slave to the
commercial press (*Servitude*).

In 1929, although he receives a prize for a new work during a posh evening ceremony, he unloads with an aggressive rant about the scheming and

envious atmosphere that dominates the literary milieu of Barcelona. Arriving in Paris after an adventurous journey (with his family, he travels in the cargo hold which transports anti-Francists funds set aside for the purchase of arms), he starts to write again. We then see his name in the papers after he beats up his wife's lover with an iron.

"Pooch" and the kid engage in never-ending discussions that leave Lucien dazzled.... But also underway are his introductory lessons in the realm of music, with Joseph, whose contempt for popular song has not changed one iota.[7] When together, they prefer to listen to the family phonograph: 78's of Stravinsky's *Sacre du Printemps*, Béla Bartok's *Music for Strings, Percussion, and Celesta*, Claude Debussy's opera *Pelléas et Mélisande* and Alban Berg's *Lulu*. There are also Joseph's favorites, Shostakovitch and Prokofiev, and of course Chopin, especially the interpretations of Alfred Cortot, a brilliant pianist who had studied the world over but unwisely accepted the position of Minister of Culture, at a time when it was still called "High Commissioner of the Fine Arts," under the Vichy government.

After a short while, Joseph takes his son, as he used to before the war, to listen to rehearsals of the great concerts at the Théâtre des Champs-Elysées. They take place in the afternoon and are free, and one day, Cortot is the featured artist.

> GAINSBOURG: *"Alfred Cortot was not only the greatest interpreter of Chopin, but he was able to see right to the soul of the musical score. I can see him walking onto the stage, coming to the piano amidst the boos from the crowd, and then being thrown out... He was a notorious collaborator and even played for the SS, but being a kid, I said to myself: "How can this be?" We were there for the music, not to make a political statement. I felt sorry for him..."*

Joseph watched over every aspect of his son's awakening to the world of literature, music, and painting. As for sex, for which a fierce fire was starting to burn, he had to manage on his own. Having to sketch nude women at the Académie Montmartre left him thinking of sex and sex alone. The young Gainsbourg, "with his little dick, would jerk off looking at sepia-tinted copies

---

[7] The years of 1945-46 are nevertheless those of "La vie en rose" (Edith Piaf), "La Mer" (Charles Trenet), "Les trios cloches" (Edith Piaf et les Compagnons de la Chanson), "Dans les plaines du Far-West" (Yves Montand), etc.

of *Paris-Hollywood* in which the pubic hair was brushed out," had only one thing on his mind: losing his virginity. Not so easy when one is considered to be, like him, extremely ugly. Particularly when he comes home from the hairdresser, inspecting his crooked part in the mirror, as well as that face of his, with those huge ears – a face to which he starts swearing ferocious hatred.

> GAINSBOURG: *"Obviously, I was flat broke, but I decided to treat myself to a little whore. So I headed over towards Barbès where I came upon a group of five prostitutes, five poor young girls, and overcome with emotion, I chose the one who was least attractive, but also, without a doubt, the kindest. When she closed the door of her room, I was frightened to death. She showed me the way to her viscous and sorry-looking little love box and when it was over, she told me I wasn't at all clumsy. When I came back to my parents place, I had the impression that they could tell. I went into the crapper and had a good wank in order to bring back the memories of my virginity. And that's the whole story."*

After that experience, Lucien would pay for other escapades in Barbès. One hooker keeps insulting him and won't stop chewing her gum, even at the moment of climax. Another refuses to let herself be caressed, saying: "No way! Don't touch my perm!" The last one sends him packing, telling him: "You're very cute, but come back when you're older!" We will meet these ladies again in 1958, when Serge sings "L'alcool" on his first album:

> *Lots of tarts are strutting 'round if you've the need*
> *Those who like to chew their gum while doing the deed*
> *But what will you find in such a bloodless body?*
> *Nothing but indifference and melancholy*

In September, 1945, Lucien is actually enrolled as a student and audits classes at the École National Supérieure des Beaux-Arts,[8] in a preparatory architecture workshop - a new initiation, and a strict one this time, into the perfection of golden section, the beauty of pure lines. But the following year, in math, he is completely sunk, in spite of private lessons paid for by his father. It's a sordid hazing for his dad, who had already had so much trouble tolerating the promiscuity, and it leaves him disgusted. After two years,

---

[8] National School of Fine Arts. (T.N.)

maybe less,[9] Serge abandons architecture, and a new conflict takes place with his father.

Meanwhile, the Ginsburgs have moved. In 1946, their nice little plan of buying another apartment to rent out is a success. They find a place on Avenue Bugeaud in the 16th arrondissement, two steps from Avenue Foch and Place de la Dauphine, and they quickly settle negotiations with a renter who moves in right away.

> GAINSBOURG: *"That was when my father started making me think about how I was going to be able to support myself. As for my painting, my instructors all predicted a brilliant future and spoke of my forceful personality. But my father knew that trying to make a living as a painter often meant going hungry, so he made it a point to give me guitar lessons. It was a gypsy who taught me to play. He had extraordinarily dark hair, like that of a crow. At that time, we still used Sergeant-Major ink pens and he would draw out the fingering positions for me. When he got a drop of ink on his fingers he's just wipe it off by running his hand through his hair..."*

As a guitarist, Serge is heavily influenced by Django Reinhardt, who is at the peak of his glory. In order for Serge to make a few bucks, he finds a series of jobs that are mediocre, but not displeasing. He finds himself strumming his guitar at balls, dances, weddings, baptisms, and bar mitzvahs. One day, after an argument, Lulu decides to go it on his own, and, at right then and there, he finds a one-eyed singer who specializes in Italian ditties like "O Sole Mio." They play the bistro terraces for two days straight without making a penny. Lulu heads back home, a bit contrite.

> GAINSBOURG: *"In Place Pigalle, we played in the streets, trying to find work – I'd learned how to play the guitar and we would stand there waiting for someone to steer us towards a Saturday night dance. We'd often just be left there, hanging out... And my father would push me, do all he could for me because he was in a position to help - he played all the nightclubs in Pigalle. My guitar playing wasn't much at that time - I played rhythm guitar.... There were four categories of musicians, which I didn't know at that time. The rank amateurs stood around on the street; the second tier, who had more or less stable jobs, sat waiting at the café across the street; and the crack musicians, or at least those I considered crack*

---

[9] In spite of all our efforts, we have not been able to locate a single one of his classmates.

players, were downstairs at the café. There you could find saxophonists like André Ekyan, or the pianist Léo Chauliac... Then there are the super-crack players, the ones you never saw, those who worked the recording sessions. Me, I played everything: Paso-dobles, dance tunes, and I even sang in Spanish..."

At the time of his seventeenth birthday, Lucien is still essentially a dreamer, shy, inhabiting another world. He hasn't the slightest hint of any facial hair to put a razor to and he smokes like a chimney...

GAINSBOURG: *"I started at 13... following some low-life who had tossed away a cigarette that was still lit. I picked it up and took a drag. At that time I didn't have any money. I smoked Parisian cigarettes - the "P4" brand. You could buy them one at a time. I would smoke them down to here (he displays a stub about 5 millimeters long), until it burned my fingers. That's where you get all the tar and nicotine!"*

On Avenue Begeaud, his parents give him what he had always wished for: the maid's room. He appreciates the illumination that filters through the sole fanlight at the break of day. In his attic, Lucien paints like a mad-man. He's trying to find himself but never seems satisfied with his results. As time passes, he continues to scribble all over canvases yet never saves a one. Driven by fear and respect for the great masters, he wants to attain a level of perfection that is impossible. Genius or nothing. He will always carry inside him this complex, an eternal distinction between great art and minor art. As an esthetic challenge, he radically changes his style of writing, suppressing anything that might make his hand move backwards, even at the expense of proper spelling. No more accents marks – no accent grave, no accent aigu, no circonflexe. He doesn't even use apostrophes, cross his t's or dot his i's...

JACOB PAKCIARZ: *"I can recall Lucien and his disgusting fur-lined jacket that he used to wipe his paintbrush on. He would play his guitar in order to earn a paltry handful of coins at night in the bars. We got along because of our mutual love of Bonnard. He was our idol. We were haunted by the ex-plosion of light and color in Bonnard's work. A painting without tragedy, without drama. Also by the straight lines in Cézanne's vision of the world: structure and light before all else. Lucien did still life - gracious, likeable, and very subtle. A bit like Villon. Lucien was gifted but overcautious. He never took risks."*

Bonnard's influence is evident, especially in one of Serge's prettiest canvases, signed Ginsbourg (with an "o"), which is now owned by Juliette Greco. It's an image of two children at the beach ("My twin sister and I playing in the sand," dixit Serge). Bonnard, the Nabi[10] whom he will never mention, will later become one of his favorite painters. But at eighteen he is haunted by him. Will Serge find that his tastes are closer to those of his father - who loved the Impressionists and Post-Impressionists – even though he takes courses given by André Lhote and Fernand Léger, both from the Cubist school? Will he simply skip over abstract art, which was born in the 20th century and began to explode in the 20s and 30s?

What is clear is that he hates Léger ("Léger? A clod..."),[11] whose comments he completely ignores. André Lhote, on the other hand, although he is today considered a minor painter and one of the lesser Cubist masters, is above all a great theorist. He had a decisive influence upon Serge: "Magnificent professor and excellent technician [...] We called him 'The hair stylist', and I don't really know why. His treatise was for a long time my favorite bedside reading." Lhote's classes consist of theory, visits to museums, and exercises that he would comment on. At the Louvre, where Lucien spends entire days, he copies the work of Delacroix, Titian, Géricault, and Courbet, who fascinates him: "I stood for hours in front of *The Artist's Workshop*. At the Museum of Fine Arts, I said to myself: I will be Courbet or I will be nothing. He was the Flaubert of painting. With him, art toppled into scandal. His subjects were daring." 33 years later, when writing the parabolic tale *Evguénie Sokolov*, he would recall his professors:

> *I looked upon my instructors with secret disdain in spite of the fame that they had garnered from their personal work, appreciating neither the neoclassicism of one group nor the modernism of the others. Nor did I like having to call them "Master," like some 17th century African slave. Only much later did I become grateful for their having given me an initiation into such a noble art form.*

---

[10] An influential group of avant-garde, Post -Impressionist Parisian painters in the 1890s. (T.N.)

[11] In French: "Léger? Un lourd..." The pun is untranslatable, but Serge is playing with the words: "léger" means light and "lourd" means heavy, or dull-witted. (T.N.)

Among his other comrades at Léger's academy, the painters Simone Véliot, Claudine Sonjour, and Vacha Neubert were more than willing to share their memories:

VACHA NEUBERT: *"Serge was about 18 and I was 20. He called me Papa. For about two years he'd come and visit me at home. He painted mostly still life, oil on Ingres paper, and he did a lot of nudes. He liked bright colors, pastel-like. His painting was delicate and diaphanous, almost Chinese in style. For a New Year's Eve party at the academy he'd designed a poster in the style of Toulouse-Lautrec. At that time, Serge was a shy lad and already a big smoker. He had a very elegant way about him, but not at all gay. One could feel his disdain. He never tried to sell his paintings and never seemed to be concerned with success. One day he told me that he wanted to have his ears and his nose fixed. He was very timid about approaching women and he told me that he went to prostitutes. One day I asked him to make me a painting. He did a nude, spreading her legs and putting on a slipper: The red slipper. Later, one day when I was flat broke, I painted over it so I could re-use the canvas."*

SIMONE VÉLIOT: *"I was very good friends with Gainsbourg for a year, from 1946-47. The day I arrived at the academy I entered the huge workroom, where there was a platform. It was Lucien who welcomed me. He was alone. As he settled in I saw he was dressed to the nines: starched white collar, tie, impeccable suit, leather gloves. He was always dressed like that. Not at all bohemian. He told me: "I'll set up an easel for you." He was really sweet. The professor at that time was Yvan Cerf, who was later replaced by André Bouhéret. Lucien was quite assiduous. He came every morning but didn't take painting lessons. He would work all alone. He would do oils and gouaches. It reminded me of Bonnard. The first day, he painted a beggar who had come to pose. It was in blue tones, I found it very lovely. I felt that he had a certain sensibility."*

CLAUDINE SONJOUR: *"I came to know Lucien at the Académie Montmartre, around 1947. He was rather elusive. He didn't talk much, but it wasn't as if he had nothing to say. It was more like he was just someone who wasn't looking to make relationships. He seemed to have a high opinion of himself and I think he didn't give a damn about what the professors had to say. As for painting, he only liked curved lines. He said: "There aren't any straight lines in nature."*

Among the songs one would hear in 1947, we can easily imagine Serge ignoring the likes of "Ma Cabane au Canada" (by Line Renaud) to focus on songs such as "J'ai bu" by Georges Ulmer, "Revoir Paris" by Charles Trenet, or "Les feuilles mortes" by Prévert and Kosma, the song from the Marcel Carné film *Les Portes de la nuit*, sung by Cora Vaucaire and Yves Montand.[12]

> *Dead leaves, shoveled all together*
> *You see, I did not forget*
> *Dead leaves, shoveled all together*
> *My memories, and all my regrets*

Simone Véliot tells us that at this period Serge is very much in love with a girl named Olga Tolstoï, "who would stop by class from time to time, especially, I believe, to visit Lucien. She was a pretty girl. The Russian type – very tall and elegant and a bit eccentric."

VACHA NEUBERT: *"At that time, he knew a very pretty young girl, the Countess Olga Tolstoï. She was 18, and capricious. Serge was courting her. I was living in a hotel on Rue Blanche and told him he could use my room when he wanted to be alone with her. I bought him a bottle of wine to give him some courage and I let them into my room. I came back to find them sitting on the bed. They hadn't done a thing. He was quite timid."*

GAINSBOURG: *"She was the granddaughter or great granddaughter of Tolstoï. A virgin. I had taken her up to an attic room, but once I had her under me she became frightened and I respected her wishes. The next day, we were supposed to meet again, but she never came. I waited for her, telling myself, like a beast, that I was wrong not to have made love to her. She had hurt me, that cow... I was desperate, and that bitch was finished. I had my revenge 15 years later, in February, 1962. It was in Algiers, at the end of the Algerian war... I was supposed to appear on TV – I was already famous... There I received a calling card: "Olga Tolstoï – then there was another name – would like to see you." In other words, she wanted to be jumped. So I see this girl again, already worn out from housework and*

---

[12] These "Feuilles mortes" ("Autumn Leaves") were of course referenced in Gainsbourg's "La Chanson de Prévert" in 1961.

childbirth, but I can still recognize her from her teeth, her smile. That time it was me who didn't want any..."

Almost imperceptibly, he starts to feel the first rumblings of the birth of a tenacious misogyny, amplified by this initial unhappy love affair and by other misadventures...

SIMONE VÉLIOT: *"One day he stops by and says, "You have to do me a favor. There's a girl who wants to kill me. She's following me around with a revolver. She wants my head. I'd like you to talk to her, try to reason with her." I refused and he was upset with me. That was the end of our friendship."*

In the spring of 1947, still at the Académie Léger, Serge meets the woman who, in 1951, will become his first wife: Elisabeth Levitsky. Their liaison will become more serious in October of the same year. In the beginning, things didn't really click. She is beautiful and sophisticated. He is intimidated and sarcastic... Two years his elder (he is 19, she is 21), Elisabeth, the daughter of Russian immigrant aristocrats, works as a model. The first time she comes to class, she tells us, she's in a suit from Lucien Lelong's (a big couture house in the thirties and forties), with high-heels and a violet hat: "I felt that someone was making fun of me. I turned around and it was him. I was red-faced with shame."

Several months later, in October, 1947, things click when he accompanies her once again to her family's boarding house where she resides near Place Clichy...

ELISABETH LEVITSKY: *"After a week of playing this game, he ends up asking me – rather than just standing there in the street – if he can come up. It seemed to me that he was really shy and had a hard time making up his mind. He had his guitar. He gave me a little jazz concert and I made him a cup of tea. We were still addressing each other formally, and he explained to me all his most complicated chords. I was on my bed in my little room and I said to myself: "What's he waiting for?" It was too late for the last metro, so I got into bed and said, "Come on!" He sat down next to me, put his guitar to the side and shut off the lights. And since he was able to fuck me seven times in a row that night, he never forgot it. "Seven times in a row! Just like the little tailor!" he would always repeat later."* [13]

Elisabeth has a job as secretary to the surrealist poet Georges Hugnet. He had published *Une petite anthologie poétique du surrealisme* in 1934, some ten years after the first publication of André Breton's *Surrealist Manifesto.* He had brought together the texts of Breton, Salvador Dali, René Char, Paul Eluard, René Crevel, Paul Nougé, Benjamin Péret, as well as some of his own poems and instructions for several Surrealist games. In his *Manuel de Saint-Germain-des-Prés*,[14] Boris Vian shows his respect: "He's a poet, painter, avant-garde filmmaker, bookbinder, and creator of bizarre objects, all done in his workshop at 13, Rue de Bucci during the glory days of Surrealism." In 1947, we find Hugnet living in an apartment on Boulevard du Montparnasse, which is "overflowing with fascinating knick-knacks." The driving force behind the restaurant Le Catalan, on Rue des Grands Augustins, whose ground floor is decorated with his collection of turn-of-the-century objects, Hugnet is sort of a stalwart of the Left Bank. During the liberation he was part of a group that included Michel Leiris, Picasso, Jean-Paul Sartre, Simone de Beauvoir, Raymond Queneau, etc. In April of 1947, a date which also corresponds to the opening of the club Tabou in a cellar cave on Rue Dauphine, Hugnet organizes and introduces an exposition of "restaurant tablecloths" at the Paul Morihien bookstore - drawings improvised by all his friends, artists and writers, on paper tablecloths from Le Catalan. His wife, Myrtille, whom he meets in 1949, remembers the role played by Elisabeth.

MYRTILLE HUGNET: *"We called her Lise. She was George's secretary for two years. She was in charge of taking inventory at the library and also served as Hugnet's assistant. He was agoraphobic and also suffered form vertigo, so he needed to be accompanied when he went out. It was Lise who would accompany him, and she went everywhere with him. He let her go when we met each other. Lise never even mentioned the existence*

---

[13] An unimaginably obscure reference to a Mickey Mouse cartoon based on a Grimm Brothers fairy tale. In The Brave Tailor, the kingdom is looking for someone to kill a giant. Well, one day while at work, Mickey managed to kill seven flies in a row. In the give and take between the peasants who are discussing their problems, someone asks him if he had ever killed any [giants]. He says that indeed he had, seven at one time! Of course he meant flies, not giants. This is another reference to Serge's fascination with cartoons and also possibly a pun. (T.N.)

[14] The Manual of Saint-Germain-des-Prés. Translated by Paul Knobloch and published by Rizzoli International, 2005. Co-edited by Tosh Berman, publisher of Tam Tam Books.

of Gainsbourg to my husband. Rather, she frequented a group of people from Martinique, which included the poet Edouard Glissant and the lawyer Roland Souvelor-Danceny, and she informed my husband that she was Glissant's companion."

GAINSBOURG: *"She succeeded in getting her hands on the keys to Dali's apartment, and we went there. The place was dazzling, an apartment of sumptuous beauty. We spent a few nights there. I fucked her like a madman in a huge bed some three meters square, covered in fur. The salon was covered in astrakhan carpeting and I trampled over works by Miro, Ernst, Picasso, and even Dali – canvasses not yet framed. What class!... In Gala's bathroom there was a Roman tub and hundreds of bottles of perfume, lotions of every kind. There was an odor of regret that reigned there, a flashback-like sentiment, one of outrageous luxury... I was 19 and I was studying painting. It was hallucinating."*

MYRTILLE HUGNET: *"In 1940, Salvador Dali and Gala had for all intents and purposes left Paris, and they gave the keys to the enormous apartment they rented, at 147, Rue de l'Université, to Paul Eluard, asking that he find someone to occupy the place because unoccupied apartments were requisitioned. Knowing that Hugnet didn't have enough space at his apartment on Boulevard de Montparnasse, Eluard suggested that he use the apartment to store some of his things. The apartment also housed different people, among them an Irish poetess and even Lise herself. I don't know how she succeeded in obtaining the keys to rooms that contained Dali's paintings and personal belongings, especially the famous astrakhan room, for which only Eluard had a copy..."*

By September, 1947, Lucien has completely forgotten about architecture and enrolls in the École Normale de Musique de Paris, founded by Alfred Cortot and situated at 114 bis, Boulevard Malesherbes in the 17th arrondissement. Cortot is at the end of his career, and like a relic from the past century the concert pianist resembles in a rather troubling way his hero, Chopin: a visage from beyond the grave, menacing eyes, sunken-in cheeks, and pursed lips. But Lucien doesn't take the classes of the old professor. He takes courses on theory and harmony for the entire scholastic year. He wants to improve his technique and he has obviously decided to become a composer of songs (Serge the auteur would, as we will see, manifest himself later on). Also, his student status permits him to push back the date of his obligatory military service. In December, Elisabeth moves to the Left Bank and the home of the artists of the Schola Cantorum.[15] But a problem arises: she is able to earn a living, albeit modest, but Serge struggles. "I didn't want to sell my work. I was highly principled when it came to painting," he explains in retrospect, while speaking into the microphone at France-Inter in 1976. Yet more than likely he is embellishing the pathetic reality: the reason he doesn't dare offer his canvases to salesmen is "not out of pride but timidity." One can also presume that the arrogant Lucien is afraid of failure, afraid of being met with rejection, even though he could have probably, through the intervention of Georges Hugnet (whom he had yet to meet), approached important players in the art world.

> GAINSBOURG: *"So I was twenty years old and sponging off Elisabeth. One day, a terrible scene unfolded between my father and me. He told me: "I don't want any gigolo for a son. I'm about ready to give you a good slap in the face..." And then something horrible ensues. I raise my fists and say, "Bring it on! You'll soon see I'm not a kid any more!" It was atrocious. We both lowered our fists."*

According to his friend Jacob Pakciarz (who two years later would hire Lucien at the Champsfleur home, at Maison-Lafitte),[16] "although he was starving, he could have returned to his father's home, but he refused. Serge and his first wife didn't make a very happy couple. Things were morose." In 1948, we know that Lucien and Lise, in addition to their painting classes with André Lhote and Fernand Léger, are also enrolled in the Académie de la Grand Chaumière, just a stone's throw from the Carrefour Vavin in Montparnasse.[17] When summer arrives, Lucien, who had received his military papers and knows he will be called up on November 15, decides to go and recuperate at Camp Sokols in Sciez-sur-Léman, near Thonon-les-Bains. The whole outfit is run by charity groups. It's a sort of scout camp of Czech origin where people go through rigorous exercise and it's frequented espe-

---

[15] A French music school.

[16] Grand Chaumière had opened its doors in 1902 on the site of the most famous old ballroom of 19th century Paris. Since its inception, the academy had played a primordial role in the artistic life of Paris. It still had a fine reputation when Serge and Lise enrolled.

[17] A place which housed Jewish children and concentration camp survivors. Serge would teach drawing and direct the choir. It was here where he would also write some of his first songs. (T.N.)

cially by adolescents and young adults from Russian expatriate families. We met up with a young man who remembers very precisely these vacations in Haute-Savoie...

BORIS FIAKOLVSKY: *"We lived in American tents, with the boys and girls separated. Each morning upon waking we would sing old-fashioned hymns. Gainsbourg was about five years older than the rest of us. There were five or six of us. What set him apart was that he didn't speak Russian very well while the rest of us were quite fluent. Seeing as he was older and his parents more fortunate than ours, we envied his creature comforts. He didn't really show off his wealth but he received lots of packages and money... Lulu never participated much in the activities. He preferred watching the girls... He bragged about knowing a pretty, blue-eyed blonde girl in the camp who must have been about the same age as him. He told us that he had slept with her! The rest of us weren't that interested in girls, except for Jean-Conrad, with whom he had a sort of rivalry..."*

The camp supervisors organize athletic competitions but Lulu just keeps to himself. Being a loner, he spends his time reading and strumming his guitar. Knowing that his military service is nearing, he gets used to the discipline, the strict routine of each day, which includes waking up at eight o'clock, showering, saluting the flag, having breakfast, etc. During his one-month stay, Lucien pays for trips to Geneva in order to bring back American cigarettes, which are still pretty rare at that time. All the kids are envious, to the point where they even steal some from him.

BORIS FIAKOLVSKY: *"Me, my brother, and a friend of ours, well, we had to leave the camp before the end of the month because of this incident! We had sent my brother to go and swipe a pack or two of those first-rate cigarettes, taking advantage of the moment when we were all in the canteen. He noticed what was happening, complained to the authorities, and we were sent packing right then and there. It was no laughing matter in those days!"*

"I was simply a sad and stern young man. That's all," Serge tells us years later while speaking into the microphone of Michelle Lancelot and his "doctor" during a sequence of "Radio Psychose" on Europe 1...

GAINSBOURG: *When I was twenty, I was invited to parties and I was rather stern and puritanical. I didn't like young people disappearing into side rooms to fool around.*

THE DOCTOR: *But in all honesty, that's what you do when you're 20, what you call this "fooling around." Why didn't you participate? Why didn't you do what the others were doing, rather than being content to play the role of judge and spectator?*

GAINSBOURG: *Because I was a romantic and I was searching for love. And I wasn't yet at that stage of pure physical love. [...]*

THE DOCTOR: *It must have happened to you sometime in your life, when you were younger, hanging around with groups of other people. What happened?*

GAINSBOURG: *What happened? As soon as I arrived, the mood went dead. The ambiance was broken. Perhaps it was because of that rigid stare of mine, I don't know. People thought that I was judging them, which is true. Too much lucidity. Anyway, the only means to overcome it, the method which I employed in the army because it is necessarily rife with promiscuity, is alcohol.*

THE DOCTOR: *And it worked?*

GAINSBOURG: *With alcohol? Yeah... I was a bit of a joker like the others. And it's something I still do now. I drink because I'm a brute. It's difficult to get to know me... I'm too... too cold. I know that it's not really pleasant, especially for others.*

On November 15, 1948, Lucien Ginsburg is called to duty at the barracks of Charras à Courbevoie (Hauts-de-Seine) and placed in the 93rd infantry, 1st battalion regiment (whose escutcheon carries the inscription: "For such men, nothing is impossible.") He will serve for 12 months. At first, military service isn't that bad. He makes friends who are more or less humble lads, including the son of a pub owner and an apprentice pastry chef, etc. There are 50 to a room, in bunk beds. With his mates, he learns to drink. Whenever they have leave they get dead drunk on cheap red wine, and that's to say dead like cadavers. Lulu makes extremely suggestive little erotic sketches that make their eyes pop out of their heads. He is conscious of the effect this produces: most of them have never seen anything like this outside of the graffiti on public toilet stalls (at that time, only well-off individuals could afford pornographic drawings or erotically illustrated novels). On his guitar, he plays them such distinguished numbers as "That's that! I can see that I'm fucked!"[18]

> GAINSBOURG: *"At Dali's place, I had discovered a portion of his collection of precious erotic objects and photos. I stole two of the photos, very small but superb, in which one can see two young girls, barely seven years old, who are tickling each other, there... During my sleep those scoundrels swiped them from me."*

Among those called to duty with Serge, we find a number of Alsatians. Behind his back, some of them call him "dirty Jew." He's aware of this: "Because I belonged to the Jewish population of the 9th arrondissement, my punishment grew worse. You could always see discriminatory tendencies at work in the army. This particular racism is neither political nor religious: rather, it is based on the reputation of material wealth of the Israelites, which people envy and are jealous of."

We have tracked down several of his Alsatian comrades, most notably Jules Schneider (farmer), Jacques Apffel (carpenter), André Boehli (baker/pastry chef), as well as the nurse, Léonard Zurlinden.

> LÉONARD ZURLINDEN: *"He was in the infirmary with the flu for three or four days during the winter of 1948-49. He played his guitar a lot and kept to himself. The others, who were much sicker than he was, complained about the noise. I don't think he sang, but rather played around with chord progressions. He also did a lot of other annoying shit. First of all, it was forbidden to smoke in the infirmary, and he insisted on smoking all the time. Then, one Saturday evening, he jumped the wall with his guitar - probably to go make a little dough - and he didn't return until the next morning. It was very risky because if had been caught then we'd all have had to take the rap. After that episode, he was booted out of the infirmary by the head nurse."*

> JULES SCHNEIDER: *"I remember him from the infirmary. He told us that he played in a band. I was immediately struck by his eyes and his*

---

[18] There other possible translations, such as "you really made a fool of me." But given the sarcastic context created by the author, I think this translation gets to the point much more realistically. (T.N.)

ears. He had a cold, and when the doctor passed by he asked him, "Your name, please?" He murmured so low that the doctor said, "Louder!" But he responded very quietly, "I can't." Then, when the doctor left, he started speaking normally again. He was such a lazy bastard, the laughing stock of the entire ward. He never wanted to do anything. We went up to do firing exercises at Mont-Valérien, and on the current site of Place de la Défense, they were doing their marching drills around the monument. The 93rd were specialists in marching because we had good music. But I don't believe he did much of that because you had to march in a straight line, and he never learned how to march in step."

The one thing that Lucien just can't tolerate is waking at dawn, at five in the morning when the bugler plays. In winter, the butts of the rifles are ice cold. Some soldiers even lose consciousness and faint.

To the woman who would soon become his wife, Serge writes very passionate letters, rife with romantic sensitivity:

Yes, when hearing your voice I understood that reality would surpass in beauty anything said in our letters. I can recall even the slightest detail of your body and this waiting is driving me mad. My violent and passionate love for you knows no bounds.

GAINSBOURG: *"My fondest memory is that of the barracks at Charras, in the visitor's room. A wooden panel roughly shoulder-high separated us from the sergeant in charge of supervision. I was in my fatigues, waiting for my little doll. I had her kneel down, and completely unperturbed by the officer's presence, I let her bring me to climax..."*

After five months at Courbevoie, the first battalion is transferred to the camp at Frileuse in the Yveline, some 20 kilometers from Versailles. A model camp, set up by Marshall Lattre de Tassigny and run with an iron-fisted discipline, Serge would always describe it as a "prison camp" where, if we are to believe him, he becomes an elite marksman with his lightweight machine gun. "It was no piece of cake at Frileuse," Léonard Zurlindin reminds us. "The 'obstacle course' for those training to be parachutists was particularly tough."

On leave in Paris, Lucien runs across his friend Pakciarz and complains about the training imposed on him: Sliding down ropes, hurling oneself into a pile of sand in order to avoid crashing into a concrete wall. "I can't do it" he confides to his friend, "I'm going to desert..."

"Every day there you ran the risk of cracking your skull..." he tells Guy Vidal in *Pilote* in 1964. One day, on the assault course, he suffers a spell of vertigo; then he gets sick during a long-distance run. On July 14, 1948, he takes part in a military review for Marshall Lattre de Tassigny, who had come to inspect the troops. In Paris, Elisabeth patiently awaits his return.

> *You wanted to buy a bra so please don't deprive yourself of this. We'll be going out on the town now and then and we'll have to be a little thrifty, but since we are so in love the slightest little indulgence will be charming, right (...) Tell me that you love me like I love you, as my one and only, THE FIRST AND THE ONLY... how much I adore you.*
>
> *Lucien*

These letters, published after his death, show us another side of his personality: idealistic, still somewhat the adolescent, very much in love, incapable of thinking about tomorrow. Miles away from imagining that one day he would be Gainsbourg.

Serge would later admit to having lived through great moments of despair during his time in the service. His misanthropy grows as he is confronted by promiscuity: Lucien the dandy, the aficionado of art and literature, is suffering in this closed and feudal universe. All the more so after the occurrence of some rather ambiguous happenings... One evening with his friends, he goes and gets plastered outside the barracks. An officer passes by, reprimands him, and Lucien responds by indicating he doesn't give damn about him. The officer, enraged, slaps him. His friends come to his defense. The officer – who had already been demoted for a similar incident – evidently had no right to strike him. The next day, he calls Lucien to his office: "Listen, Ginsburg, if I had really wanted to break your face, here's how I'd do it." And then, Serge tells us, "He grabbed me by my khaki shirt and enacted for me the manner in which he would go about doing it." The officer then says, "I simply wanted to sober you up." So there on the spot, Serge figures that he can denounce the officer but would run the risk of getting a month in the clink for insubordination. He decides to keep his mouth shut.

GAINSBOURG

We have, on the other hand, great doubts concerning another anecdote which occurs at the camp in Frileuse towards May, 1949.

GAINSBOURG: *"The most atrocious memory is of the day when they asked for volunteers to go and shoot a collaborator who had been sentenced to death. The officer came out and told us: "We need volunteers to go and liquidate a female collaborator." I said to myself: What? Gun down a woman? This is no good... Even shooting a guy is out of the question. Point blank? Their hands tied behind a pole? No. Out of the question. I am not an executioner." A friend of mine said: "I'll go!" Can you visualize a dozen twenty-year old fiends gunning down a girl? I asked my friend: "Hey, are you going too?" He later told me: "They gave us each one bullet, one of which is a blank, and we're going to execute her." So the poor sod comes back, all white. Not white like linen but pure white - blemished, pale, and bloodless. "So, you've won! Why do you look so pale?" "Listen, Lucien [...] it's atrocious, it's atrocious what's happened to me. We all had a rifle (it was a MAS 48 at that time, refurbished), and we used our rifles to gun her down. And part of the ritual includes the lieutenant going over to blow out her brains, to give her the coup de grace right through the skull. Afterwards, the lieutenant says: Now go and get a sponge and clean up the execution pole. Get it clean and get all the brain matter off." My friend took the sponge - he was the one whose rag was full of the girl's brains. That guy was marked for life, but he had wanted to do it. I told him: "Well, old pal, you wanted it and you got it!" And he cried."*

Another time he concluded his story, now smoothly rehearsed, with these words: "He left in the cold of the morning as a hero. He retuned a broken man, a swine." Yet there is much that leads us to believe that Serge did not experience this event first hand: one can imagine that rather, it was related to him by a non-com during an evening of binge drinking. This is for the simple reason that chronologically, things just don't add up: in the spring of 1949, there are no more death sentences for female collaborators, including (the majority of them) termed "horizontal collaborators" or "Kraut kittens." During the "tonte" of the summer of 1944, even if they happened discreetly, summary executions did take place. Usually, women who slept with the occupiers were publicly judged, exhibited, and insulted in the face of an angry crowd. The Liberation committees then humiliated them by shaving their heads and forcing them to wear dunce caps. Beginning in mid-August and lasting through June, 1945, these trials were organized by the revolutionary tribunals of the Liberation, and they decided to execute "those found most guilty of being traitors to the country and furthermore to avenge the young men who were tortured." Others received various punishments, such as two to three years of forced labor. Still, and this is the source of the anecdote, some of these women were gunned down by firing squads made up of young men before their two or three year prison terms had expired. We know that this type of execution certainly took place in the "model" camp of Frileuse, but by 1949, the survivors had been released...

On November 14, 1949, Lucien is sent on "congé libérable," which in French means the end of his military service. "I almost ended up in the EOR (the school for reserve officers)" he recounts, "but I hated the idea of giving people orders, so I got out of that..." Before his time in the army, he only drank water. When he came out, if we are to believe him, he was an "alcoholic of the worst ilk." Rather, let's simply say that he learned to drink, that he discovered the virtues alcohol and how it helped him cope with his hangups. 35 years later, in the 80s, he admitted that his cop friends reminded him of his drinking buddies in the army.

So now Lucien returns to civilian life and painting, to the studios of La Grande Chaumière and the Académie Montmartre. As he must find a way to eat, Lucien also starts playing music again, with his guitar and his espagnolades. Just exactly what were they singing in 1949-50? Henri Salvador, just starting out (he becomes well known two years later with his "Clopin-clopant" and "Mathilde d'amour"), does his version of "Parce que ça me donne du courage" by Mireille and Jean Nohain. Piaf sings "L'hymne à l'amour" while André Claveau croons "Cerisier rose et pommier blanc." Also, Yves Montand gives us "Une demoiselle sur une balançoire."

Towards the end of 1949 and into 1950, if we follow the chronology established by Elisabeth Levitsky (the only source we have for certain years of his bohemian period, which she was part of), after having lived a while at the foyer d'artistes of the Schola Cantorum, the couple moves into the Hôtel Royer-Collard, in the room once shared by Verlaine and Rimbaud, where their neighbors are none other than Léo Ferré and Madeleine.

ELISABETH LEVITSKY: *"We had a room in the artists' quarters, the only place where pianos were permitted. It overlooked the interior courtyard of the Schola Cantorum. Next door there was an Anglican chapel, in a state of neglect. The acoustics there were great, and it was frequently rented out to orchestras and jazz singers for rehearsals. In the back of our room there was a closet for our clothing, and in the closet there was an old door, nailed shut, that led to the chapel. The musicians strictly forbade anyone from listening to them or interrupting them. Lulu spent hours in that closet, spying on them like a voyeur, through the little crack in the door, exquisitely terrified at the thought of being discovered. Hunched over on a stool in the dark, surrounded by all the dresses and pants hanging down, he was all ears, avidly trying to understand their styles and techniques. It's funny how much you can learn when things are forbidden!"*

They are still flat broke, but Lucien continues to nourish his brain. For example, he is quite impressed with discovering Jean-Paul Sartre, who in 1948 published *La Nausée* and *Les Mains sales* one after the other.[19] In the first work, a novel of quintessential solitude, he is fascinated by the character of Antoine Roquentin, an idealist somewhere in his thirties for whom artistic creation becomes the sole vehicle through which he can escape the emptiness and boredom that haunts his life. In *Les Mains sales*, he is attracted to Hugo, a young, bourgeois revolutionary seduced by communism and provocation, and directed by the party to assassinate Hoederer, whose ideas (that strategy is more important than theory) are too dangerous for the cause, but who becomes a visionary martyr once executed.[20]

Lucien reads the Surrealists, in particular Péret and Breton, as well as the Dadaists, Tzara for sure, but also Picabia. His celebrated *Jésus-Christ Rastaquouère*, a thousand copies of which were printed in 1920, is something

---

[19] Nausea and Dirty Hands. (T.N.)

[20] Although there is no textual link with Gainsbourg's work, these books (such as Adolphe and others cited above) surely contributed to the attitude and personality that he was forging at that time (and let's not forget that he's only twenty-one and fresh out of the army), a personality that he would polish and perfect throughout the course of his life: alternately cynical, savage, melancholic - a disenchanted man, affected less by his failures in love and friendship than by his inability to experience happiness.

Lucien would read again and again. As for poetry, it is Rimbaud, forever and again. He also gets his hands on a Dutch copy of Guillaume Apollinaire's *Onze Mille Verges*,[21] a banned book in France, and meanwhile Jean Genet publishes his autobiographical *The Thief's Journal*, Simone de Beauvoir gives us *The Second Sex*, and Aragon publishes his novel Les Communistes. Boris Vian's last novel, *L'Herbe rouge*, fails to have the impact of his two preceding works, *L'Écume des jours* (1946) *and L'Automne à Pékin* (1947).[22] All the same, he manages to titillate the consumers of gossip rags with his third pseudo-crime thriller, *Elles se rendent pas compte*, published under the pen name of Vernon Sullivan (the first of these was *J'irai cracher sur vos tombes*, 1946).[23] The prince of Saint-Germain-des-Prés, Vian is simply having a good laugh while in the meantime he plays his pocket trumpet at Le Tabou.[24] In fashion, everyone's talking about the "new look" launched by Christian Dior. In painting, the New York school is all the rage – especially the "Action Painting" of Jackson Pollock – and it is exhibited at the Venice Biennial. In Paris, André Lhote, Lucien's professor, publishes his *Traité de la figure*.

Humbled and amazed by all this, Lucien is nevertheless in love and continues to paint. He is obviously living through one of the happiest periods of his life, despite his financial difficulties. Two declarations, one made in 1974 on Canadian radio and the other in 1976 on France-Inter, seem to confirm this. A small sample...

> GAINSBOURG: *"I was truly influenced by painting. In found it to be a major art, and one which stabilized me intellectually. Singing and the fame that followed left me unstable. I was happy with painting... I adored it so, [and I regret so much] having abandoned it..."*

---

[21] The Eleven Thousand Rods. (T.N.)

[22] Both published by TamTam Books as Foam on the Daze (translation by Brian Harper) and Autumn in Peking (translation by Paul Knobloch) respectively. (T.N.)

[23] Elles se rendent pas compte has yet to be translated into English. The latter was published by TamTam in 1998 as I Spit on Your Graves and is translated by Vian and Milton Rosenthal. TamTam has since brought out two other Sullivan/Vian titles, Les morts on tous la même peau (The Dead all Have the Same Skin) and Et on tuera tous les affreux (To Hell with the Ugly), translated by Paul Knobloch. (T.N.)

[24] A famous cellar club in Saint-Germain-des-Prés. See The Manual of Saint-Germain-des-Prés, op. cit.

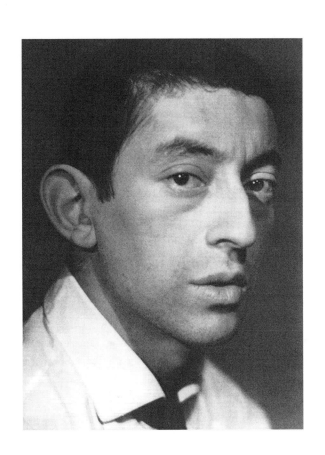

four

My Illusions Open Onto The Courtyard

It's 1950. We are at l'Hôtel Saint-André-des-Arts, and Lucien is think-ing about a few things: wouldn't it be advantageous, while waiting to make his mark as a painter, to earn a little money, simply in order to avoid having to pack up and leave once again in the middle of the night?

His friend, Jacob Pakciarz, who meanwhile manages to find a job teach-ing drawing at the Maisons-Laffite education center, an institution for Jewish children and young refugees from Nazi concentration camps, tells Serge that he should consider applying for a job as a counselor. The story of Champsfleur, officially the "Home of Israelite Refugees" at 6, Avenue de la République – today a Red Cross retirement home – and that of its direc-tor, Serge Pludermacher, are worthy of a detailed account, especially since Serge will spend two years of his life here, from the age of 22 to 24, and also because, as we will see, it isn't simply a means of putting food on the table but another stage in his personal development.

The education center at Champsfleur, located halfway between Maisons-Laffite and Le Mensil-le-Roi, had opened its doors in 1947. More than 200 deported Jewish children – some hoping to one day locate their lost rela-tives – are immediately welcomed after the war. Serge Pludermacher, born in 1918 in Vilna, Lithuania, is the son of Gerchon Pludermacher, one of the founders of the Bund (a Jewish socialist party, founded in Russia in 1897). Champsfleur, as many other establishments of its type – there were about forty in and around Paris -, is financed by various parties, including the Bund, l'Ose (Office de secours à l'enfance),[1] and Le Joint (a fund established by the Jewish-American community). During the war, Pludermacher had been imprisoned during a raid along with a group of Jewish children whom he had been looking after. They were threatened with deportation and placed in the Château de Chabannes. Miraculously, they managed to escape. Along with Rachel, who would become his wife in 1945, he then works as an educator in other homes where Jewish children are hidden, first in Moutiers and then in Izieu, before going into hiding near Guéret, in La Creuse, where their son Georges Pludermacher, today a pianist internationally renowned for his interpretations of Xenakis and Debussy, was born in July, 1944.

In 1991, Albert Hirsch, now a sculptor and former resident of the Champsfleur home, published a touching book on Pludermacher and the center that he directed. Born in 1940 to parents of Polish origin, little Albert spent the war hiding out on a farm. He then lost his father, and his mother, a seamstress, was no longer able to feed him. She heard about Maisons-Laffite and Albert was accepted in 1947.

> ALBERT HIRSCH: *"There were children there whose families had been decimated and they were awaiting adoption. Although the atmosphere was extraordinary, it couldn't make up for the absence of parents. The children of Champsfleur were all melancholy, in a state of despair. Some had escaped from the camps. The teachers were not all Jewish, including Jean Cizaletti, who was in charge of assessing the students' aptitudes. During the day, we went to a secular school at Maisons-Laffite, in Carrières-sous-Bois at Mensil-le-Roi, etc. Everyday we would run into children from the village. After school there were always fights. It was pure anti-Semitism. The fact that we were getting a privileged education at Champsfleur didn't go over well. It created a lot of jealousy."*

Before Champsfleur, Serge Pludermacher – ten years older than Lucien – had in April of 1945 opened La Maison de Buissons in Mans, for the same

---

[1] An organization that saved hundreds of Jewish refugee children in Vichy France during WWII. (T.N.)

reasons. All of the witnesses we have found draw a picture of an exceptional man, authoritarian but generous, whose ideas about education were in the end very similar to those professed in the Ginsburg home: the semiotician Claude Zylberberg, who was placed at Maisons-Laffite with his sister Huguette Attelan when they were children, recalls the visionary "who was thirty or forty years ahead of the rest of the world," and who wanted "above all to be a pioneer, like a Jewish Robinson Crusoe the day after the shipwreck, whose vast influence nobody would have the right to question." Pludermacher favored culture in all its forms, especially the type one acquires through initiation. With this goal in mind, he introduces courses in classical dance, mandolin, painting, etc., given by talented professors (a former star from the world of dance, a first chair violinist, a remarkable piano teacher named Olga Goldenstein, who was Georges Pludermacher's first professor). At Champsfleur, the children draw, sculpt in wood, do pyrography, embroidery, sewing, and study the history of music. On Thursdays, weekends, and during holiday breaks, in addition to sports (which Lucien participates in nominally) the children are taken to the theatre, the cinema, and to concerts. During their meals, which are eaten alongside the teachers and directors, they listen to records or important radio broadcasts. Current events are always a part of the discussions that take place between children and adults. Some learn Yiddish, taught by Rachel Pludermacher, and this includes traditional songs led by a refugee from both Treblinka and Auschwitz, Frida Welinsky, who also directs the choir and the mandolin ensemble.

> CLAUDE ZYLBERBERG: *"Lucien was one of many counselors. He was in no way a supervisor, but rather part of the managerial staff, an adult presence for the children. When he came to Champsfleur, there were 30 or 40 of us children, all being schooled. We left home in the morning to go to school and we didn't get back until the evening."*

> ALBERT HIRSCH: *"Gainsbourg came to Champsfleur strictly out of financial concern: he was fed and lodged, his clothes were washed, and he also received a modest salary. When he arrived, he didn't give a damn about education. He said to himself: "I'm going to take it easy and continue to paint." Pludermacher took him on a trail basis and he turned out to be a very popular teacher with the students. Step by step, he learned the game. He became interested and even passionate about it. I clearly remember*

the day he arrived, wearing a beige duffle coat in the style of the guys from Saint-Germain-des-Prés. His hair was cropped short and he was cleanly shaved. In one hand he was holding on to his girlfriend, Lili; in the other he carried a guitar. His girl was a real Saint-Germain type, with a haircut like Gréco's. She was a real beauty, with big eyes, and she always wore tight-fitting suits. Pludermacher put Lucien in charge of my group, and we could be rather troublesome. When we first met him, we started to make fun of his scrawny physique. We'd never seen anybody like him, most of all because he was decked out in the latest fashion. Nobody in Mensil-le-Roi struts around in a duffel coat! And he looked younger than he actually was. He was quite shy, but seeing as he didn't want to be eaten alive he asserted himself in order to gain our respect. When we didn't behave, he would tug on our ears. He was strict, but he never raised his voice. He would just say: "Don't give me any crap." He swayed us with his charm."

So he moves to Champsfleur, along with Lise (who doesn't work and spends her days in Paris). Lucien becomes friends with a guy named Gert Alexander, alias "Mäneken" (which means "little buddy," in reference to his stature), also known as Mickey. Born in Berlin, he arrives in France in July, 1939, twelve years old, without his parents but accompanied by 40 Jewish boys who were saved by a benefactor, Monsieur de Monbrison, a French Catholic who owned a chateau and who, in 1936, had already saved forty girls who were Spanish republicans.

At Champsfleur, Gert and Lucien mostly look after the older kids, a group of about 30. Their duties are relatively simple: they have to wake them up in the morning, make sure they bathed, have breakfast, and then take them to school. From 9 to 11:30 they are free. The kids come back for lunch, then return to school, and starting at 4:30 the two of them make sure that all homework is completed before the students engage in different cultural activities.

ALBERT HIRSCH: *"In the morning, Lucien would come and wake us up and then take us to school, about a kilometer and a half away. We went on foot but he had a racing bike. When he went to Paris he would leave his bike at the train station. Sometimes he'd lend me the bike so I could go get him some Gitanes or Troupes. Or sometimes he'd even ask me to go to the store and get a liter of wine, which had to be wrapped up in newspaper because wine was forbidden at Champsfleur. On Thursdays, Saturdays, and*

Sundays, he'd teach us drawing and painting. He was a good instructor but he never drew alongside us. He would give us themes and then describe what he wanted us to do. He noticed that I had a talent for drawing. There was a rather well known painter, Dobrynski, from the École de Paris, a colleague of Modigliani and a friend of Soutine who came on Sundays to paint the children. Lucien was quite impressed and could tell that he was a true artist. Then there was the choir, run by Frida, who also, as I recall, gave piano lessons to Lucien. There were two pianos at Champsfleur and some great players: Frida, Olga Goldenstein, Edmond Rosenfeld, and Georges Pludermacher, a child prodigy. I think Lucien had a bit of an inferiority complex because of them. But Frida, a woman of extraordinary enthusiasm, encouraged him."

GEORGES PLUDERMACHER: *"I was about six or seven when I met Gainsbourg. He was funny: a slender fellow who looked really tall in that all too short duffel court. And he had a strange sort of walk, as if he were skipping around like an elf. He had roving eyes and spoke in soft, steady tones. He always spoke very quietly, like he had a secret to tell you. In those days, musicians, such as Les Frères Englander, would come to Champsfleur maybe once or twice a month. One of them, a violinist, organized a mandolin ensemble with the kids. When he stopped coming, Lucien took his place. I played the piano, which I had started studying at the age of three and a half. My professor was Olga Goldenstein. She had little appreciation for Lucien, and said: "He always leaves the piano out of tune, playing all that jazz!" One day Lucien decided to sketch a portrait of me in pencil, very seriously. I met with him several times to pose. While I sat for him, he would talk to me just so things wouldn't get too boring."*

Lucien paints at Champsfleur, but not assiduously. It's as if he's already beginning to distance himself from his first passion. Huguette Attelan remembers having seen him two or three times, with his inks, painting in the students' assembly room, where the light is great. He gives two canvases to Mäneken, his friend with whom he spends every afternoon playing checkers and listening to classical music. One is a portrait and the other a view of the Seine in winter at Mensil-le-Roi. For "Jojo" Pludermacher, he does a sketch. When he's not playing checkers with his pal – the same age as him, more or less – he amuses himself by organizing a little competition around the record player, where they take turns guessing the musician's name or the title of the piece.

There is a photo of him playing his guitar along with the children's mandolin ensemble. After the departure of Frida Wilensky, Lucien takes charge of the choir and begins by changing the repertory. Gone are the Yiddish and revolutionary hymns of the Bund, now replaced by Chœrs des chasseurs from an opera by Weber or Beethoven's Ruines d'Athènes for which he prepares arrangements for children. "He liked directing the choir," recalls Albert Hirsch. "When we did stuff with him, he would always bring out something new. When we drew, we always made fabulous drawings."

Serge also serves as the night steward. When the lights go out, he makes his rounds through the boys' dormitory, which is always clean, and then the girls' quarters, where it always smells of pee.

GAINSBOURG: *"I have never understood why, but this olfactory memory has always stayed with me. But what's most important is that I got these drawings from these magnificent children. One, for example, was from a little girl who had drawn a locomotive on a rooftop, and it was sublime, surreal! In class, I put no restraints upon them. I told them that things would deteriorate as they got older: sooner or later, eggs would start looking oval, and cubes would look like cubes. All the poetry would vanish."*

Not only to amuse the children but also because it is likely that he is thinking about it more and more, Lucien starts to write and compose his very first songs at Champsfleur. All of our witnesses have confirmed this.

GERT ALEXANDER: *"He composed with his guitar, in his room, but especially on the rehearsal piano that was used in dance class. He worked there while the kids were in school. He wrote a song called "Lolita" for a very pretty Spanish girl who worked as a maid and did the laundry. Lolita was her first name. He was a bit in love with her, as was I. As bizarre as it might seem, I was also Lucien's first impresario. You see, in Mensil-le-Roi, in the forest of Saint-Germain-en-Laye, there's a clearing where they hold a carnival every July 14 and there's a platform and a band. It's like being in the country: you can dance and there are little stalls where you can have a drink, etc. And what's more, it was covered by local radio. We were there with Lucien and some of the older children from the home when I said: "Lucien, why don't you go up on stage, just to give it a try, seeing as how you want to be a singer?" So he says: "Oh, no way..." He was really shy and wouldn't dare try. So I slipped behind to see who was running the show and I said: "You know, I've got a semi-professional here who would love to come up and try out one of his songs." So he borrowed a guitar and got up on stage. The result was catastrophic. First of all, it was the first time he ever sang in public – there must have been about 300 to 400 people there. Plus, you could barely hear him, so nobody understood his song. The result? He was booed off the stage."*

ALBERT HIRSCH: *"These organized evening events were special moments that we all looked forward to. They took place once a month. Gainsbourg exploded onto the scene in extraordinary fashion. It was then when he started to sing his songs like "Robinson Crusoe" and "Lili." These were by no means children's songs. Lili went like this: "You were no beauty, this is true / But I risked my life for you..." He said the song was about him. He accompanied himself on guitar, with one leg up on a chair, like Brassens.[2] He also sang a song based on a poem by Ronsard: "L'amour de moi..." He even taught that one to the choir. His love for Trenet led him to cover "Il pleut dans ma chambre." Everyone came to these little concerts and everyone prepared something: sketches, excerpts from plays, etc. Like the others, Lucien would sometimes play emcee during these evenings. One time he dressed up as a wizard in a hounds-tooth jacket and a turban on his head, and did extraordinary card tricks for us. He was incredibly dexterous and it was all done with great seriousness."*

GEORGES PLUDERMACHER: *"I remember one of his tricks in which he would make a candelabra move over a table. Actually, he was using a magnet, but us kids, we were amazed! He already had a great flair for the theatrical."*

Because Lucien was hanging around with Serge Pludermacher for two years, whom everyone considered an exceptional fellow, we must ask the question: was he or wasn't he an influence on Lucien Ginsburg? Albert Hirsch seems convinced. He even wonders if Serge didn't choose his first name as an homage to Georges Pludermacher's father.

---

[2]Georges Brassens was one of the most famous and prototypical of the French poet-singer-songwriters, what they refer to today in France as a chansonnier. It was a genre that Gainsbourg would both pay homage to and transform into something uniquely his own. (T.N.)

ALBERT HISRCH: *"Serge was nice to Lucien and gave him the best advice in the world. He helped him find himself artistically, most notably in steering him towards music rather than painting. It was like a trigger. When he arrived in Champsfleur he was a bohemian, and there he understood that he'd have to work if he wanted to become a professional."*

GEORGES PLUDERMACHER: *"When he left Champsfleur, we never heard about him again. A few years later we discovered he was a singer when he released "Le poinçonneur de Lilas." My father, Serge, seemed a bit irritated. He said: "Why did he change his first name? Why doesn't he call himself Lucien?""*

His stay at Maisons-Lafitte was marked by two events only. The first was his absence, in July, 1951, for military maneuvers: the west was caught up in the cold war, and the army was embroiled in the squabble and called back its grunts. Lucien had noticed that after two years his ex-pals had become adults, most of them married with children. And then he got married. Upon the insistence of his partner, moderately enthusiastic but really out of conformist pressure, he presented himself on Saturday, November 3, 1951 at the city hall of Mensil-le-Roi.

GAINSBOURG: *"I married her because I had told myself it wasn't good for children to have unmarried parents. Then we ended up never having any kids..."*

During either the summer or the beginning of the 1952 school year, the couple returns to Paris and moves into a hotel on Rue de l'Échaudé. What happens in the capital during these two years? The world of painting is swept away by the Cobra movement, which gives us Jorn and Alechinsky. In official artistic circles, the pitiful Matieu publishes his first thesis, *Essay on poetics and the signifier.*[3] Alexander Calder headlines the Venice Biennial with his stabile sculptures in sheet metal. The first performance of concrete music is given at the École Normale in Paris. The world of literature and the theatre is particularly rich: Camus publishes *The Rebel*, Eugene Ionesco stages *The Bald Soprano*, and Henri de Montherlant his Maltesta. Sartre wins acclaim with *The Devil and the Good Lord* while Jean Vilar creates the TNP (Théâtre

---

[3] Note sur la poétique et le signifiant. (T.N.)

National Populaire) to stage Brecht's *Mother Courage* right before Samuel Beckett causes a scandal with *Waiting for Godot* in 1952. On the big screen (the television having only reached a few initiates), Hitchcock paralyzes with fear the viewers of *Strangers on a Train*. Visconti moves away from neo-realism with the melodrama *Belissima*, and Vittorio De Sica makes *Miracle in Milan*. In France, Robert Bresson reveals his austere style with *Diary of a Country Priest*. In 1952, René Clément receives first prize at the Venice Film Festival for *Forbidden Games*, while André Cayatte receives the Special Jury Prize at Cannes for *We Are All Murderers*. Jacques Becker makes *Casque d'or*, Max Olphus *Le Plaisir*, Christian-Jaque *Fanfan la tulipe*, René Clair *Les Belles de nuit*, and Jean Boyer introduces us to Brigitte Bardot in *Le trou normand*, with Bouvril.

Encouraged by his father, Lucien starts playing background music again in nightclubs and at dances as a guitarist-pianist, giving him a good reason to move further away from painting. It's impossible to do both: as a musician, he gets home at all hours of the night, but as a painter, he must wake at the break of day to take advantage of the beautiful light. The question is whether he is abandoning a passion, or it is leaving him...Serge thinks of it as abandon, driven by fear and laziness, but he will later admit a doing so out of "a fear of poverty."

> LILIANE ZAOUI: *"The only canvases that remain are the ones he had given my parents. When he asked to have them discarded, they were completely opposed to the idea."*

This is why Liliane is in possession of the largest collection of paintings signed *Lucien Ginsburg*: two oils and one pastel! Not to mention a self-portrait and a painted vase from the fifties... Then there's Gert Alexander and his two paintings. Now Liliane possesses but one, as does Juliette Greco, and an art dealer in Pau, Eric Lhoste, who in 1986, for 5,000 francs, purchased an oil painting from one Mrs. Paulette Franckhauser, the daughter of a café owner in Argelès-Gazost in the Hautes-Pyrénées, where Serge would have cocktails during the summers of 1951 and 1952 while he played for a band at the local casino.

From February to May, 1953, Mr. and Mrs. Ginsgurg take a room in a full-service pension in Home Saint-Jacques, on a street of the same name.

The place is usually reserved for students at the Schola Cantorum, situated right next door, but the management sometimes makes exceptions for artists and painters. The rent is 35,000 (old) francs per month for the two of them. Beginning in June, Elisabeth Ginsburg stays there alone and pays the rent herself, now 20,000 francs per month. Has Lucien returned to his parents' home? In any case, he's broke.

> GAINSBOURG: *"At that time I was making a lot of collages, and to earn a little dough I'd paint flowers on old furniture to reproduce fake Louis XIII pieces, among others. I would also colorize black and white photos for the outside of movie theatres, a little trick that I got very good at. I even painted some of the red lips on the Marilyn Monroe photos for Niagara. I worked in aniline, for one franc per photo – one franc at that time – I was barely getting by."*

In the meantime, Joseph sees all his hopes go up in flames. The fact that his son might be happy colorizing movie photos simply revolts him. Yet in September, 1953, the financial situation seems to improve. Mr. and Mrs. Ginsburg are living once again under the same roof, but in separate rooms, which costs them 46,500 francs per month. This only lasts for two months: in February and March of 1954, Lucien is living alone in the room at number 8. Around February 15, at the Blue Note, he listens fervently as Billie Holiday sings "Gloomy Sunday," and he is blown away. Then he leaves home: thanks to his father, who had also worked there, he is employed for the first time, during Easter vacation in 1954, playing background music on the piano at the Club de la Forêt, at Flavio's in Toquet. At the end of this trial run, they give him a contract for the coming summer.

Le Toquet, on the Côte d'Opal, is a very chic seaside resort. Rich, young Parisians headed there like they head to Deauville today, thus the name "The Toquet-Paris-Plage," The Parisians rub elbows with people from the neighboring Boulogne, and the English, who assiduously frequent the Casino (gambling is forbidden across the channel). All of these "beautiful people" gather together at the Hôtel Westminster, an elegant palace on the edge of the forest, where the club (of the same name) is opened in the summer of 1949. They come they for an aperitif, or maybe one last drink, or even to celebrate after an evening at the casino. It's not yet a real restaurant, but one can snack on a croque-monsieur, some foie-gras, caviar, or lobster. Flavio Cucco, the boss of the joint, is a well-known figure of the Toquet nightlife. Before the war he had already run the Chatham, a nightclub on the main drag. Born in England to an Italian father and a British mother, his flawless knowledge of the language is appreciated by the English clientele. An article published in La Voix du Nord in June, 1950 describes his establishment: "The Club de la Forêt has as a manager of great class, our friend Flavio. Someone who knows how to create an ambiance in a quality setting with a single pianist playing gently, quite gently, almost muted in order not to bother anyone and at the same time lighten everyone's spirits. That is unless some ardent youngsters ask him to abandon the melody in favor of swing."

> FLAVIO CUCCO: *"In 1954, Gainsbourg's father had come during the four days of Easter weekend and he immediately spoke of his son, telling me: "He's young, and that's what you need here. What's more, he's a much better player than me." The next weekend he came down and I immediately signed him on. He worked out well: in the afternoon, on the terrace at tea-time; at the start of the evening, aperitif time, playing in the bar; then later in the evening he'd continue playing until two in the morning..."*

In the meantime, Lucien's two sisters are married; in April of 1954, Liliane meets the love of her life in Italy and the couple soon settles in Casablanca, where Serge's twin finds work as an English professor in a French lycée.

Toquet is where Lucien spends his first summer season. But first let's talk about another episode which is chronologically situated at the same time and which we will always regret not having brought up with Serge, discovering as it were, a mother lode of information at SACEM just three months after his death. In the spring of 1954, Joseph manages for his son to take courses in composition and orchestration so that Serge might pass the entrance exam for SACEM – a difficult exam at that time (Brassens failed it the first time) - which would give him the right to collect copyright royalties as an arranger... or eventually as a composer. Elisabeth lent a hand to Lucien in transcribing musical scores. On July 1, 1954, Serge is accepted as a composer: given a theme ("Notre premier baiser"), he tosses out these lines, which are in no way a precursor of any greatness:

> *Time has now erased*
> *Inside my bitter heart*

The sadness of my past
Which now today does part
But I cannot forget
It lives within me still
The feeling when we met
And our lips knew such thrill

According to the stories that Serge would recount concerning the beginning of his career, stories carefully polished after the fact in order to wipe away the years of wandering and disappointment, everything happened quite quickly, between the moment when he saw Boris Vian on stage – the famous incitation that we'll come back to later – and the moment when he composed "Le poinçonneur de Lilas." Now we know that August 26, 1954, he puts down six of his first tunes, some two months after his entrance exam at SACEM. One of the titles is almost a premonition: "Ça vaut pas la peine d'en parler." He also gives us "Les amours perdues," which he also offers to Gréco before recording his own version on his third album in 1961:

Yes this heart it bleeds so
Yes it's hard to let go
Hold me hard in your arms
My love I need you so

A few weeks later, a new attempt at flirting with distress ("It's the last page, the last amend/ Our beautiful love has come to its end.") We understand from this why the future Gainsbourg still hides behind the clever pseudonym of Julien Grix (or Gris: Julien standing for Stendhal, Gris for the painter Juan Gris, and perhaps also a nod at Le Grix, the married name of his older sister Jacqueline), a name that he will abandon in 1956. It is in fact in 1954 that Lucien decides to launch his career in the world of song, at least as a composer and lyricist. He is perhaps trying to get his songs into the hands of publishers or even directly to singers. It is also not beyond the realm of belief that he wants to follow the example of a certain Francis Lemarque, whose works had been performed for years by Yves Montand ("A Paris," "Marjolaine," "Quand un soldat") or one Léo Ferré, who gave us "Le piano du pauvre" and "Paris Canaille," sung by Catherine Sauvage in 1953-54. Or still yet a certain Aznavour, who since 1951 had had multiple hits with both male and female singers alike. One must remember that at this time, the world of French song still operates on a global level – even if a new generation of singer-songwriters is making itself known with Brassens, Ferré, and others – according to an old and established model in which the professions are separated, with one group writing songs and the other group making them popular. So what are people listening to in 1953 and 1954? Rubbish like "L'amour est un bouquet de violettes" (Luis Mariano) and "Le chien dans le vitrine" (Line Renaud).[4]

It's probably upon his return from Touquet in 1954 that Lucien once again replaces his father, this time in Paris, in the 18th arrondissement at Cabaret Madame Arthur, where he becomes the pianist and band director (there were only two other musicians: a drummer and a saxophonist-violinist). It was a position that Joseph had occupied since 1947. This is also something he never spoke of and it is also research done at SACEM in the spring of 1991 that permits us to understand this episode at once as passionate and fulfilling as any of his years of apprenticeship. It's hard to understand why he was so tight lipped about it all, this man who reveled in recalling other more sordid anecdotes of his career, who never hesitated about dressing up as a transvestite for the cover of his album *Love On The Beat* in 1984, an album on which several songs revolve around the theme of homosexuality.

Today, as it was in 1954, Madame Arthur is a club renowned for its transvestite acts (at the time it was still called "transformiste"). The young Gainsbourg, steadfastly heterosexual, finds himself surrounded by queens and spends the night as an accompanist for transvestite routines, which oscillate between the tacky and the burlesque, and even the troubling, some forty years before the word "drag queen" even becomes a common term. There he meets Louis Laibe, the artistic director, with whom he will soon compose an entire series of bits, the heart of the spectacle at the center of the lovely evenings at Madame Arthur's during the seasons of 1954-55 and 1955-56.

> LOUIS LAIBE: *"Joseph Ginsburg, who we called Papa Jo, was very sweet, but when he walked he looked like an undertaker. Not at all the funny type. When Serge came to replace him, he didn't even know what blue jeans were, or what it was to wear your shirt unbuttoned. He was always*

---

[4] The last title is the insipid "How much is the doggy in the window."

*dressed like a kid from a respectable family, and I'll tell you straight out
we didn't give him any ribbing – he was as serious as his father. Serge was
taught by his father to be anti-homosexual. He was very discreet about it,
and I never saw Gainsbourg hang out with a transvestite or a fag at that
time. That's why I was flabbergasted some years later when I saw him sing
"Mon legionnaire": I asked myself where that had come from! He's a lad
who always surprised me."*

One of the most celebrated cabaret stars is Coccinelle, a super-glamor-
ous transvestite who two years later would become the most famous tran-
sexual in France after undergoing surgery in Morocco. But she doesn't sing
any of the songs penned by Lucien. Then between February and June of
1955, Lucien gives Louis Laibe a series of songs with exotic titles (she takes
credit for most of the lyrics), including "Zita la panthère," "Tragique cinq
à sept," "Arthur Circus," "Pourqoui," "Charlie," "Locura Negra (Frénésie
noire)," "Maximambo," "Jonglerie chinoise," "La trapéziste," "La danseuse
de corde," and "L'haltérophile."

LOUIS LAIBE: *"At Madame Arthur's, we were never shocking or smutty:
our objective was to make people forget the little bit of the viciousness
with the attractiveness of the performance. You had to be careful at that
time if you didn't want to get hauled off to La Tour Pointue[5] or have your
head busted open when leaving. I quickly got the idea to write songs with
Lucien for our new revue, which centered on a circus theme and was an
important show at the club. At that time, there were about 30 to 35 artists
on stage – the space was tiny but our shows were known the world over!
"Arthur Circus" was the opening number, and then there was "La trapéziste," written in remembrance of the old circus star Médrano, who suffered an accident. "Zita la panthère" was sung by my partner, Maslowa,
a hot-headed kid. It told the story of a tigress in love with her trainer...
For this number he was disguised as a panther and at the end of his long
tail there was a zipper from which he'd take a powder-puff and touch up
his snout. It was quite funny. "I am Zita the panther, and you can ask
me anything..." Among our other performers, there was Toinou Coste, a
250 pound kid who imitated Fréhel, and Lucky Carcell, a former houseboy*

[5] Quai des Orfèvres – Site of a famous police station in Paris and title of the 1947 film by
Henri-Georges Clouzot.

*for Mistinguett who was later fired from the Folies-Bergère after having
screwed up his entrance on stage because he was out doing coke on the
stairway. He was ugly, but had nice legs: I would introduce him as the only
singer who sings with his legs..."*

This Lucky Sarcell is in reality the first to perform one of Gainsbourg's
tunes when he's offered "Antoine le casseur" at the start of 1955. Gainsbourg
also wrote the lyrics to this one:

> *I whored myself out for this lad*
> *Selling my ass and my name*
> *And he was sex crazed and mad*
> *About me you could say the same*
> *The brothels I worked left me cold with fright*
> *It was only Antoine who had the right*
> *My feelings are so profound*
> *That only his love abounds*

Pretty spicy stuffy, hey? Musically speaking, this place was, just as his
experience as a nightclub pianist at Toquet, a prodigious place of learning...
With Laibe, he wrote songs in every style: blues, waltzes, java rave-ups,
African tinged airs, South American mambos, and pure dance hall stuff. It
was an experience he would remember years later when working for Zizi
Jeanmaire at the Casino de Paris and at Bobino.

LOUIS LAIBE: *"I had written a poem as a response to Aznavour's song
"Parce que," which was simply titled "Pourquoi." I thought the song was
quite pretty and I put it in my repertory. One morning at four o'clock,
when most of the clientele had left, we happened to do a number off the
cuff. At that hour, my customers were mainly whores from la Chapelle.
They had finished their work for the night and before waking up to start
all over again they would come by with their madams, all lined up like
at boarding school! They would always take the tables in the rear and
the madams would order champagne for them if they'd had a good night.
When the show was finished, they had to get back to work. The madam
would stand up and tap them on the hands, saying: "Come on girls, time to
hit the streets!" The girls really liked that song for which Serge had written the music. I remember the last time I saw Gainsbourg, towards 1975
on a winter night at Arthur's. He told me: "You know there were some
good things in those songs we wrote together. 'Pourquoi,' for example, was*

really good." I said: "You bastard! You never released it because you pre-
ferred to do the words and music yourself, so that you don't have to share
royalties!""

So how long did Serge actually work at Madame Arthur's? In spite of all
our research, it's difficult to confirm. From autumn 1954 to spring 1955? It's
probable if we use as reference points the copyright dates of certain songs.
It's also possible that he left the cabaret in mid-season to accept a new engagement, once again arranged by Joseph, at Milord l'Arsouille, which
several witnesses attest to. At every crossroad in his life - Serge has often
repeated this – we find his father. This time, Joseph learned through the network of musicians that they were looking for a pianist-guitarist for the Left
Bank cabaret. But it was situated on the "wrong" side of the Seine because it
was on Rue Beaujolais, some two steps from the Pails-Royal.

People speak a lot about what happened, in effect, starting at the end of
the 1940s. It's a true style, launched already before the war at Bœuf sur le
Toit or at Agnès Capri's and later developed after the liberation at l'Ecluse
(opened in 1947) or at l'Echelle de Jacob (1948). It's there where we hear
Cora Vaucaire, Marcel Mouloudji, and les Frères Jacques. The Left Bank
Style – inspired by the songs of Prévert and Cosma and by the Groupe
Octobre – was formed at the time of Juliette Gréco, and then a new generation of cabarets made a name for themselves during the second half of the
fifties: La Colombe, on the l'île de la Cité, Le Cheval d'Or on Rue Descartes,
Le Port du Salut or the Fontaine de Quatre Saisons run by Pierre Prévert (the
brother of Jacques) on Rue Grenelle. There you could hear Vian, Mouloudji,
or even Germaine Montero, Monique Morelli, and Philippe Clay. The Left
Bank stands for "poetic song" before becoming a synonym for political com-
mitment. The style is also exported across the Seine, to Patachou's and Aux
Trois Baudets in Montmartre, and also to the Milord l'Arsouille.

ROMAIN BOUTEILLE: *"When I made the scene in the left bank, things*
were really happening at La Contrescarpe, Le Cheval d'Or, and at l'Ecluse.
That's where tomorrow's talents were being molded – talents we would
later find earning more dough on the Right Bank. There was also Le
Bâteau Ivre, Chez Bernadette, l'Echelle de Jacob, and Le Port du Salut,
with Bobby Lapointe, who like me was another unmarketable talent. What
these places all had in common was their tiny size. People would sit any-

where and any way, on chairs with a little, red, ten-cent balloons. They
would listen to a dozen numbers that were short, but inspired. Very cere-
bral. It was the circuit of the penniless, a moody scene. On the Right Bank,
it isn't so much about invention, but rather recuperation. They really know
their jazz because it's dear to them."

André Halimi, who would make his name as a television director, was
at that time a beginning journalist who would make the rounds of cabarets
and music halls. In 1959, he will also publish his book, *On connaît la chanson*
(Histoire vivante et panier des crabes de la chanson contemporaine), which left
him out of favor with musicians for some time.

ANDRÉ HALIMI: *"Le Milord Arsouille was unique in that it was situ-*
ated on the Right Bank and quite bourgeois. But the artists – even Léo
Ferré sung there – came from the Left Bank. It was very expensive, much
more so than the cellar clubs of Saint-Germain. Francis Claude had a fol-
lowing from Neuilly, very 16th arrondissement, "Right Bank anarchist."
People would come to rub shoulders with the riffraff in the cabarets, where
there was an air of impertinence and insolence. Sort of a mixture of Sacha
Guitry and Léo Ferré. There was a certain vibe."

A vibe perhaps inherited from the time when Cora Vaucaire – the interpreter of "Feuilles mortes," henceforth nicknamed "the lady in white," in contrast to Gréco, who was always dressed in black – had held court at the spot,
beginning in 1950, when the cabaret was still called le Caveau Thermidor.
But the place was sold the following year and another prince of Parisian
nightlife named Francis Claude had rechristened it Milord l'Arsouille. Born
in Paris, Francis was of Basque origin and preparing to enter the Department
of the Treasury. Still, at a young age, he was passionate about the world of
theater. After a brief interlude in the colonies in 1939, followed by a stint in
the Foreign Legion, he made his debut on stage at the Perroquet in Nice.
After the Liberation he opened Le Quod Libet in Saint-Germain before taking over at Milord, where he was both artistic director and star, thanks especially to his sketches and monologues known for their wit and elegance.

FRANCIS CLAUDE: *"I liked the place. It's where the Marseillaise was*
first sung after the French Revolution and where Danton and Camille
Desmoulins edited the first issues of La Lanterne. During the Restoration
they called it le Caveau de Aveugles because the owner would only hire

blind musicians so that they couldn't see the orgies that the clientele was engaging in."[6]

The name Milord l'Arsouille is suggested to Serge by one of the eras most licentious characters, Lord Seymour, a half-English, bastard count who led a double life as a raging wild man in disguise. He would get into brawls and toss money out his window. The lesson to be learned from all of this: he was only himself when wearing a mask: "A scoundrel among lords and a lord among scoundrels." The story is rich, and one that seduced Marcel Carné, who had thought about turning it all into a film with Pierre Brassard in the lead role.

From its opening in 1950, the cabaret is met with enormous success. Léo Ferré and Jacques Douai are among the first artists booked. Francis Claude presents a little philosophical number in which he spits out a bunch of witty remarks. In a duet with Louis Lion, Claude narrates the screwball adventures of two peasants form the southwest named Darrigade and Fouziquet. At Milord, you might run into Orson Welles, Jacques Charron, Francis Carco, Jean Cocteau, Maurice Chevalier, Robert Hirsch, or Mireille. Among the regulars at the club, those who are practically a part of the décor until Francis Claude threw in the towel in 1962, include Jacques Dufilho, Maurice Biraud, and the singer Michèle Arnaud, a future interpreter of Gainsbourg whose "poetic presence and warm voice enchant the public."[7] But on the stage of Milord other stars would follow, such as Alain Barrière, Mouloudji, Hélène Martin, Georges Moustaki, Catherine Sauvage, Jacques Brel (Francis Claude hired him in 1954, just before he played l'Ecluse), Guy Béart, and later Jean Ferrat – all of the great stars of the time except one: Georges Brassens.

GAINSBOURG: *"One evening, at Milord, I spy Boris Vian, all pale under the spotlight, spewing forth a series of ultra-aggressive texts before a dumbfounded crowd. That night I really got an earful from him. Vian had a hallucinatory presence on the stage, but it was also a sickly and pathological presence. He was stressed, pernicious, caustic. It was while listening to him that I said to myself: "I can do something with this minor art..."*

---

[6] The Restoration of the Bourbons, the royal family, in 1830. (T.N.)

[7] All this information comes from Le Cabaret-Théâtre 1945-1965.

URSULA VIAN: *"It's true that he could be terrifying because he had this awful stage fright. His rigidity could turn off the public."*

ALAIN GORAGUER: *"On stage, Boris was absolutely stiff. He was decked out in Maoist gear, long before it was fashionable, with clean, straight lines and plenty of buttons. It was almost a uniform. What's more, Boris was a strapping fellow. Thus, when he sang "Monsieur le Président, je vous fait une letter," it was sung with pure aggression. He even delivered his comic songs with this intensity."*

Boris Vian. So the name has been dropped... As biographer Philippe Boggio reminds us, "One is immediately drawn to his intriguing physical presence: long, slender silhouette, icy gray-blue eyes, and that hatchet face with an immense forehead that is almost alien-like."[8] Boris Vian had recently been drawn to the world of song out of necessity, curiosity, and because he had not yet delved into this form of expression. He had already displayed his talent as novelist (*L'Écume des jours*), a journalist (his countless articles on jazz), a sort of literary con man (*J'irai cracher sur vos tombes*, which Vian claimed to have translated from an original American work), and a nightclub impresario (the famous nights at Le Tabou with Juliette Gréco, Anne-Marie Cazalis, and other cohorts, among whom Vian was a constant fixture).

And yet just like Gainsbourg, Vian really doesn't like popular song until he delves into it. In an article published in the magazine *Arts* in September, 1953, he speaks out about his admiration for Ferré, Trenet, Brassens, Mouloudji, and Leclerc. Beginning 1954, he starts to really give all his energy to music, as does his partner, Ursula, who also starts singing. Straightaway, he composes songs that are contentious and anarchistic. For example, on February 15, 1954, he registers the text and music of his veritable anti-militarist hymn called "Le déserteur." The song is his most famous, and Mouloudji even records his own watered down version the day the French forces are defeated at Diên Biên Phu. In springtime of the same year, Boris meets Jacques Canetti, who gives his songs to Philippe Clay, Juliette Gréco, Suzy Delair, and Renée Lebas (through whom Vian meets Jimmy Walter, a man who will

---

[8] Boris Vian, Éditions Flammarion, Paris, 1993. Most of the information that follows is from this reference source.

set several of Boris' texts to music, including "Je suis snob.") Finally, Vian has to face the facts: in order to get his songs heard, he'll have to sing them himself. Boggio would write about "the need to be popular and recognized, a need which hides beneath a pathological shyness. An intense psychological necessity which one has to confront." So Vian auditions in December, 1954 at the Théâtre des Trois Baudets. His own official debut takes place at the same spot on January 4, 1955, with his "coat as somber as that of a clergyman, like a preacher who had lost his faith... Boris was pale, mortified, and motionless, standing stiff and straight as if trying to avoid falling backwards." It was like a droning: "Like a spoken-word song, with no vibrato. He doesn't really sing, but simply struggles to make it through... The audience is infected by his obvious malaise and they snub him." After a couple of tries, "either out of indifference or embarrassment, he insults the audience..." Vian wants to quit, but Canetti keeps pushing him to continue. On July 28, he sings at Pierre Prévert's place, La Fontaine des Quatre Saisons.

> JULIETTE GRÉCO: *"I believe that in a certain way, Serge and Boris are like brothers. They share the same violence, the same reserved nature, the same mystery. They are one in their derision, their cruelty, and their tenderness"*

At the end of April, 1955, Vian records a dozen titles (which would be collected on two rare EPs, *Chansons impossibles* and *Chansons possibles*, released later that year) in the big studios at Philips. Along with Jimmy Walter, Claude Bolling, and some help from arranger-composer Alain Goraguer – Gainsbourg's future arranger – they put out a biting satire, "La Java des bombes atomiques," which would garner Vian the honor of the front page of *Le Canard enchaîné* on June 13, 1955. Among other songs – many now standards – we find "Je suis snob," "La complainte du progrès," and even "Je bois":

> *I drink*
> *Whenever there's time*
> *Just to get high*
> *To forget this mug of mine*
> *I drink*
> *But I find no relief*
> *I just put off the grief*
> *Of admitting it's the end*

Outraged by Vian's "Déserteur," former soldiers, in an attempt to get the song banned, organize several protests, first in Nantes and then in Lorient and Perros-Guirec, They consider Vian a communist and shout out, "Back to Russia! Back to Russia!" In Dinard, the concert evolves into a political scuffle as the mayor, Monsieur Verney, supported by a group of ex-soldiers and cheered on by the crowd, climbs up on the stage and pleads with Vian to leave. At the start of the new school year, the scandal is reported by *Le Canard enchaîné*. On September 20, 1955, Vian gives a show at L'Amiral which is a complete flop. Then in July, 1956, he has a serious bout with pulmonary edema, which demands several months of rest. His days of performing on stage are over, but he continues to write and compose. Thus, his period as a songster lasts from December, 1954 to March, 1956: a mere 20 months, 15 of which are spent on stage.

In the summary of similarities, we can't help but be amused by another coincidence: Boris records a song with Brigitte Bardot on November 16, 1956, which remains unreleased. It's called "La Parisienne" and is penned by Alain Goraguer:

> Morals and girdles
> Aren't really hurdles
> To making your score
> Sure as day dawns
> When both stacked and blond
> The world is all yours

But back to Lucien, who despite his stints at Madame Arthur's and Milord l'Arsouille, is perpetually broke. He stills works touching up the color on thousands of cinema stills that he delivers to MGM on the Champs-Elysées, but he can no longer stomach the work. In order to help out Lucien and his wife, who's starting to put on weight in an untimely and uncontrollable fashion, Joseph and Olia suggest that he move into the maid's quarters beneath the rooftops of Avenue Bégeaud. Joseph had resumed his position at Madame Arthur's and we also know that he was playing in a luxury hotel in Brittany, at Tréboul... Up in the attic, Lucien is already starting to show off his esthetic mania, which will grow into true paroxysm in the salon on Rue de Vernueil, where each photo and knick-knack has its own precise place. At the beginning, he has nothing but an ashtray, a lighter, and a pack of smokes.

Nevertheless, he looks for the most harmonious way to arrange them, placing everything atop a flat piece of wood on a stool, which serves as a table. Three floors down, at his parents place, Lucien plays records by Art Tatum and Dizzy Gillespie.

In July, 1955, Lucien registers two titles with SACEM: one with Paul Aly and another with Billy Nencioli, who wrote the lyrics to "Abomey." The latter is four years younger than Lucien, a former musician for dance bands who had just started singing at College Inn and at Milord. Invited by Francis Claude, who also does a well-known radio show dedicated to popular song, Nencioli is discovered by publisher Raoul Breton, who offers him songs such as "Tante Amélie," "On ne trouve ça qu'à Paris," "Porte de Lilas," etc. But he's called back to Algeria six months later and does not release his first 45 on Columbia until 1957, which is prefaced by Aznavour. In 1958, he wins le prix de l'Académie du disque for his song "Porte des Lilas."[9]

Serge suggests that Nencioli write the music for one of his texts, "Les mots inutiles." However, Nencioli never finishes the music. Serge does it himself and registers the song under the title "Vienne à Vienne," changing three words of the original text submitted in 1955. It's regretful that he never recorded it, inasmuch as the lyrics are for the first time authentically "Gainsbourgian" and also because they seem to express his feelings about the love song and even love in general:

Words are tattered and worn
They've revealed their apathy
And the shadow of years forlorn
Haunts my vocabulary
Take me far from the maddening crowd
Make me forget that what you say
That everything you speak aloud
Is but another cliché
Come to Vienna, you'll speak no more
Take my hand and walk out the door
And you'll see in this smile of mine
That speaking is not worth the time
I have no use for witty banter

---

[9] Porte de Lilas is also a 1957 film by René Clair with Georges Brassens, Pierre Brasseur, Danny Carrel and Henri Vidal. The aforementioned award is similar to the American Grammy. (T.N.) 1957 is also the year when Gainsbourg registered "Le poinçonneur de Lilas" with SACEM.

For the heart's but a savage youth
More powerful than language
It reveals a deeper truth

The marriage with Elisabeth is floundering, and Serge's dalliances are becoming more frequent, often long-distance affairs that happen when he's in Troquet. There were also some one-night stands after his night gigs at Milord l'Arsouille. Nencioli recalls a night when they picked up a couple of American girls at The Whisky à Gogo on Rue de Beaujolais.

BILLY NENCIOLI: *"Now this big character, ugly and as thin as a rail, thinks about nothing but women. Anyway, we meet a pretty little brunette and a big blonde bombshell. At that time I was earning 1,500 francs at Milord – old currency of course – and Serge must have been making about a thousand. Well, at the Whisky, a scotch went for 800 francs – really expensive, but we still offered to buy them a drink. Then I saw Serge take the blonde back to her hotel. It just took him a few words, while I had wasted all my time on a girl who was saving herself for marriage."*

Gainsbourg – still performing as Julien Grix – is hired on as a background pianist at Milord. Early in the evening, he provides ambiance and accompanies certain artists on the bill. A little later, towards midnight, Michèle Arnaud hits the stage. Jacques Lasry takes over on piano and Serge picks up a guitar. A third guy, an opera singer by trade, plays bass. One can get a very good example of the atmosphere at Milord by listening to the album *Une soirée chez Milord l'Arsouille*, released in 1956 by Ducretet. It features Michèle Arnaud, Jacques Dufilho, Francis Claude, and Maurice Mérane. Lasry, who along with Baschet was the future creator of *Structures sonores*, had been a major player at Milord for several years before Serge had burst onto the scene.

JACQUES LASRY: *"I came to Milord in 1951, thanks to Francis Claude. He had also hired me for a weekly radio broadcast called Isabelle, où es-tu?, which featured new singers. Francis was dedicated to helping launch young talent, but their songs had to have interesting lyrics. I was in charge of auditioning young singers at my place on Avenue des Ternes. I would do the arrangements and accompany them on the radio. At Milord, they didn't mess about with little pop ditties. It was much more than just popular song. I composed "Le pont Mirabeau" for Michèle Arnaud, which was based on a text by Apollonaire, and I also set to music a piece by Oscar Wilde which was adapted by Francis Claude."*

JACQUES DUFILHO: *"The crowd at Milord was very evolved and preferred true poetry to simple affectation. People would come after the theatre... I played there for five years. As soon as my little comic routine was finished at Milord, I would run straight to Galerie 55. I can certainly say that my encounters with Serge were furtive. Michèle Arnaud was the queen of the joint. She would discover writers and help launch them. She would also sing with great restraint and delicateness – there was nothing sloppy about her repertory."*

Soon after Lucien's arrival, Michèle Arnaud wants to fire him because of problems with his amp and rotten, old guitar; his money problems still haunt him. Lasry hears about it and tells Michèle that if she fires him, he'll quit too. Gainsbourg: "I'll never forget what you've done."

JACQUES LASRY: *"It was me who brought Lucien to Milord. One day Michèle had asked me to find another musician because we were starting to do more and more galas. We needed someone who could sit in on for me piano while I was on tour with Michèle, some one who could also play guitar with me at Milord. So I called over to Place Pigalle, where all the musicians hung out. A few days later I got a call from Gainsbourg, who told me in an almost inaudible voice, "I'm looking for work. I play guitar and piano. Would you like to hear me?" He came by my place and I was instantly charmed by his gentle nature and good manners; he was possessed of enormous discretion and exquisite politeness. He played "The Man I Love" on the piano, which I found quite nice, and we immediately hit it off."*

It's high time that we say a few more words about the beautiful and haughty Michèle Arnaud, a major player in Gainsbourg's career. She is born Micheline Caré in Toulon in 1919 (making her ten years older than Serge). Daughter of a naval officer, she studies law and political science, and then finally she gets her degree in philosophy. In her mid-forties, she discovers existentialism and starts to frequent Le Tabou, La Rose Rouge, and also Le Quod Libet, run by her future husband Francis Claude. After seeing Léo Ferré, she launches her own musical career by covering his songs: in fact, she even records "L'Ile de Saint-Louis," done by Léo three years earlier, and then she wins the Prix de Deauville the same year for "Tu voulais...," one of Florence Véran's tunes. Now the permanent headliner at Milord, her first 25 cm (ten-inch LP) contains all her hits from the stage: "L'Ile de Sain-Louis," "Tu voulais," "Sur deux notes" (by ex-Collégien Paul Misrali), and "La complainte de infidèles" by Mouloudji. "Her gift was in her mix of intelligence, humor, and style," stated monthly *Platine* in May, 1998, two years after her death at the age of sixty-nine. "Her diction was perfect, but her coldness would limit her success. She would always remain a club singer." And she always lives up to her nickname, "the intellectual of song" (in earlier times she would probably have held court in a literary salon), because of her first rate choice of material and excellent interpretations (after Ferré, she would sing Béart, and at just the right moment she had the good taste to be able to hear future greatness in Gainsbourg). Real success would, nevertheless, evade her. Her look is obviously a problem: other than the certain physical and vocal resemblance to Cora Vaucaire, most people simply take her for a snob. In the press, we learn that she has married again, with an industrialist this time, and there are photos of the two at her place in Chatou, surrounded by her collections of canvases by Bernard Buffet... She is close to the circles of power, and her admirers come from all over the political landscape: as Serge strums his guitar at her side, one might even see Minister of the Interior François Mitterrand in the front row, flanked by his faithful friend André Rousselet.

The Milord is a great success. The shows are from 10:00 p.m. to 1:00 a.m. nightly and it's always packed. Michèle is the joint's main attraction; she sings seven or eight songs at the end of the program.

JACQUES LASRY: *"We'd finish the show at one o'clock, and since we were no longer tired we'd go and have coffee with Francis Claude at Café Washington, where we would run into all the prostitutes from the neighborhood. Lucien and I addressed each other formally. He was exactly ten years younger than I. Seeing as how I lived on Avenue des Ternes and he with his parents near La Porte Dauphine, I would accompany him home each night. We often stayed talking in the car for thirty minutes or even an hour, discussing painting, literature - everything but music. One day his parents invited me over to dinner in order to say thanks for getting Serge the job at Milord. His father was wearing a tuxedo that evening. He got*

up in the middle of the meal and announced, "I've got to go to work now!"
He was playing somewhere in a cabaret..."

1955 comes to a close with no new titles registered at SACEM. Still Lucien must note with great interest the rise of a singer with a look heretofore considered difficult, Philippe Clay, the revelation of the year, who wins the Académie Charles-Cros prize for his first 45, a four-song disc which includes "Le noyé assassiné" and "La goualante du pauvre Jean." He quickly follows with his first 33 for Phillips, covering a poem by Boris Vian, another by Prévert, and Léo Ferré's "Le danseur de Charleston," "Si j'avais un piano," etc. The other big stars of the moment include Yves Montand, Sidney Bechet (3,000 of his fans literally sacked the Olympia in 1954, the year in which this legendary venue was turned into a music hall thanks to Bruno Coquatrix), Gilbert Bécaud, and Eddie Constantine. The list also includes Luis Mariano, Les Frères Jacques, Mick Micheyl, as well as Bouvril and Georges Guétary, who triumphs with the operetta *La Route fleurie*. There's also the steady rise of Aznavour, and a new kid named Jacques Brel. As for international stars, the overseas hype surrounding Elvis Presley is late to reach France: instead, people start to speak of the emotive style of Johnnie Ray who, in the U.S., has hits like "Please Mr. Sun" and "Here Am I – Broken Hearted." Three years later, Serge would cite him as being among his favorite artists even though the exaggerated, expressive style of Ray (deaf in one ear, half-Indian, Ray would weep onstage over the slightest thing) - a sort of missing link between Sinatra and Presley - seemed the complete antithesis of his. It is perhaps on Johnnie Ray's records that Serge hears electric guitars for the first time, unless he found it on the records of another of his favorites, Ray Conniff.

Other than the fact that his marriage is disintegrating, we know little about 1956, the final year of his apprenticeship before things really get serious. Still, the couple's financial situation improves a bit. They leave their attic on Rue Bugeaud for a maid's quarter on the sixth floor of a quaint, bourgeois dwelling at 6, Rue Eugène-Labiche, in the 16th arrondissement. As Lise recounts, at the moment they were to move in they were forced to bring their piano up the service stairs in disassembled pieces, a story that would later inspire "Le Charleston des déménageurs de piano," a song that Boris Vian might have penned:

If you want to make us cry
Better get an early start
You know that there are guys
Who use this ruthless engine's heart
To make us believe in a simpleton's ruse -
That life is but a piano's muse

If 1956 seems to be an unremarkable year for the Gainsbourg biographer it's because Lucien is immersed in his personal life. Simply put, he's having marital problems. Far from simple household squabbles, "the discussions [become] more and more strained," and as the months pass Serge becomes more distant. Had he stopped loving her because she had changed, physically or emotionally? Had she stopped because he had abandoned painting? The bohemian lifestyle, the poverty – were these the reasons behind all the passion in the letters? Gainsbourg has remained evasive and avoided questions about the "errors of his youth." The divorce, finalized on October 9, 1957, will be amicable.

Lucien is also surely irked about not having succeeded in getting his songs heard, other than at Madame Arthur's. And the royalties coming in from last year's songs are just peanuts. In fact, in the following months he registers but two songs with SACEM, for which he writes both music and lyrics, still under the pen name of Julien Grix. On June 25, 1956, one year before "Le poinçonneur de Lilas," we encounter "On me siffle dans la rue!," probably written for a female singer but certainly not for Michèle Arnaud. Could this be a belated commission from one of the drag queens at Madame Arthur's? The lyrics are cause for thought:

Some behold you with a cynic's gaze
And others with superior air
The timid are lost in romantic haze
But most fall for your blue-eyed stare
Are mad in love without a care

So why when I walk with my hair in the wind
Do the people chuckle and scratch their chins?

Serge would never speak about these songs. He is much more open about his summer gigs at Club de la Forêt. From June 1 to September 30, 1956, he returns to the neighborhood of his pal Flavio. He's once again among his friends, including Kostio, who is both a very elegant and very homosexual lady, as well as Madame A., a shopkeeper and specialist in wool garments at whose house he happens to spend the night. But when he invites Dani, the fifteen year-old daughter of Flavio, to the cinema, it is only with the purest of intentions.

> DANI DELMOTTE: *"Lucien didn't drink at all, and he was quite educated and cultivated. When the club was empty, he would spend the afternoons composing on our wreck of a piano. Whenever he didn't have a girl-friend or was feeling blue, he'd take me to the Cinéma du Casino, where they would often show original language versions, with no subtitles, for the English clientele. He would translate for me during the course of the movie."*

Lucien has a good time during the summers in Toquet: he works hard and discovers his talents as a crooner. Then along comes his future arranger, Alain Goraguer, Boris Vian's right-hand man.

> Alain Goraguer: *"I was in Toquet as a tourist. I was having an aperitif and there he was, sitting at his piano. A lot of times we don't notice piano players in bars, unless they are very good or very bad. But what I noticed in Serge was his song choice, nothing but beautiful American standards almost murmured rather than sung. And his face was striking – he had an air of great sadness."*

> JACQUELINE GINSBURG: *"My brother had invited me to Club de la Forêt, and I was immediately stunned by those English girls who were all falling at his feet. He was no heartthrob - I mean with that awful hair and those ears sticking out... Even where he wasn't known, he'd just attract women like a magnet. He always had such a great auditory memory and could recall any "mi corazón" style Spanish song in just a few seconds. He'd belt out the song in his penetrating way and the women would simply lose it."*

> GAINSBOURG: *"Being a pianist in a bar is the best education. My repertory ranged from Léo Ferré's "Monsieur William" to Aznavour's "Parce que," and included Cole Porter, Gershwin, Irving Berlin, and even Mouloudji's "Comme un petit coquelicot." I can still see myself singing "Les escaliers de la Butte sont durs aux miséreux," watching the rich break open their lobster, all decked out in tuxedos... I earned 2,000 old francs per night... Two bagfuls! But I was already a huge snob. I would never play non-stop: I was always due a break. So I'd head to the bar and say: "Now I'm a client! Serve me... What's the damage?... 2,000? Here you go..." I was content... must have also been stupid... Maybe not so stupid... I was proud... Another*

night, I was at the piano and a guy gave me a one franc piece. In all my arrogance, I got up and told him "Buddy, I'm not a juke box!"..."

FLAVIO CUCCO: *"One thing's for sure, he didn't live like any choirboy, and seeing as his job put him in the position of being able to easily woo the female heart, well, he by no means deprived himself. Towards 11:00 p.m. I would see the girls in the neighborhood start to arrive, the ones who worked at Toquet or those on vacation who couldn't afford Club de la Forêt. And take it from me, his charms of seduction never faltered."*

DANI DELMONTE: *"I remember a ravishing English woman... big, slender, blonde... Her first name was Faye, and she spent her vacations in Toquet, with her sister-in-law. She was married to an Englishman in the chewing gum business. During the week, their husbands would return to London on business, leaving behind their women, who took advantage of their husbands' absence to really live it up. I can still see Faye moving all alone on the little dance floor under Serge's watchful gaze. During the following days he would make trips back and forth from Westminster. He would come back with a rumpled tie and his shirt half-open."*

This adventure would quickly turn sour: caught red-handed with Faye, Serge is hauled before the London courts: adultery was no laughing matter back then...

Once back in Paris, Lucien returns to Milord, which is still hotter than ever, especially since the recent success of Michèle Arnaud. In spring of 1956, she plays Bobino, on the same bill as Pierre and Jean-Marc Thibault, where she has great success singing Ferré's "L'inconnu de Londres" and "La Truite" in the style of Schubert. On May 24, she plays Luxembourg during the first season of the "Grand Concours Eurovision" with her song "Ne crois pas." On September 13, still accompanied by Jacques Lasry, she makes her first appearance at Olympia, opening for Eddie Constantine. Finally, in 1956, she sings Aznavour's "Sa Jeunesse" and Doris Day's American hit "Que Sera, Sera." But once again, she is copied by another singer, Jacqueline François. For years now she has been singing but has never had true success. Whenever she chooses a song – and her fine taste is never in question – it's always a case of bad luck. Her dream, she tells herself, would be to find a talented songwriter just starting out who would write for her exclusively. This rare bird is right under her nose, even though she hasn't grasped this yet.

five

There's No Sunshine In My Life

With his hair cropped short and those ears that stuck out, eyes half-closed and consumed by shyness, Lucien is hopelessly in love with Michèle Arnaud. She calls him "That dear Serge," not doubting for an instant that he will soon offer her up a smorgasbord of finely crafted tunes that she so desperately needs. Serge? Oh, yeah... Lulu has two pseudonyms: Julien Grix for SACEM, and Serge when he plays the piano.

Gainsbourg: "So the name change came about because all this "Lucien" business was getting to my head. Everywhere I'd go I would see *Chez Lucien – Men's Hair Stylist*, or *Lucien – Salon for Ladies*. Psychologists say that the most important thing in life is your first name. Some names are lucky and others are curses. At the time, Serge, with its Russian sonority, seemed to suit me fine. As for the 'o' and the 'a' in the spelling, well that's a tribute to those high school professors who used to butcher my name."

Smoke from a Gitane illuminates his palm and predicts international voyages, a tortured love life, and a brush with death at forty years of age. Those who believe in fate will see that all these things will come to pass. In the meantime, even though he is supposed to be working on new tunes in Toquet, he has yet to register a single song. His first attempts as a lyricist are, to be frank, disastrous. Serge is perhaps dismayed at the level of stupidity surrounding this minor art, especially at the end of 1956... On one side are the big stars: Brassens, who sings "Je m'suis fait tout p'tit," often sees his songs banned on waves of the RTF;[1] Aznavour continues to spit out hits – or "tubes," if we adopt the slang term just created by Boris Vian – such as "Sur ma vie" and "Vivre avec toi"; Bécaud puts out his third LP, "Alors raconte," and winds up the year in lovely fashion with "La corrida"; Léo Ferré does "Pauvre Rutebeuf" and "Le temps du plastique." Brel, who is nicknamed "l'abbé Brel" by Tonton Georges, has yet to shave his moustache.[2] 1956 is the year when rock and roll is unveiled to the young French public though the medium of cinema: "Rock around the Clock," the title song from Blackboard Jungle, makes chubby Bill Haley into an international superstar. The Platters hit pay dirt with "Only You" while country singer Tennessee Ernie Ford finds luck with "16 Tons." It's a piece that Serge really likes: "I love '16 Tons,' it's super... the words ... *If you see me comin', better step aside, A lotta men didn't, a lotta men died.* Great stuff!..."

1956 will also usher in a new fad that will, for a time being, eat at the stomachs of the lovers of good French pop: the "exotic" hits by singers and songstresses with foreign accents. Before being blown away by Dalida (who made a thunderous breakthrough with "La plus bell chose au monde," the French version of "Love is a Many Splendored Thing"), we see that same year one Gloria Lasso fly from success to success (L'amour, castignettes et tango," "L'étranger au paradis," "Mandolino," "Lisboa Antigua," etc.). Lucienne Delyle sings "Arrivederci Roma," Caterina Valente gives us "Coco Polka," Tino Rossi does "Méditerranée," Georges Guétary records "Domani," and Dario Moreno stays on top of the charts for nine months with "J'irai revoir ma blonde"... A total nightmare, in other words, and we have haven't even started to talk about the debut of Marino Marini in Paris on French TV's *Musicorama*.

It's in this hellish context that Serge quietly begins, once again, to write music and lyrics. On January 3, we see for the first time, on a receipt of deposit, a piece signed "Serge Gainsbourg." It's called "Cha cha cha intellectual," and nothing but a few lines have survived on the back of the document:

[1] French Radio and Television Broadcasting. (T.N.)

[2] L'abbé means "abbot" or "priest." (T.N.)

I'm not an intellectual
No I think life is just much too dear
To waste my time inside of books
When all this pleasure is so near

The same day, he registers "La ballade de la vertu" with lyrics by Serge Barty. Serge, whose true name is Serge Barthélémy, has nothing to do with the music hall world. He actually occupies a position as an economist in the Ministry of Finance. A few years later we'll see him offer Gainsbourg another text, the lovely "Ronsard 58," whose misogyny fits perfectly with the disposition of our hero... But if one follows the chronology of songs registered at SACEM, we find one last rough draft from April of 1957, "La chanson du diable":

One day the devil was tortured
By the flesh of hell's desire
And left his bachelor's standing
Buried deep beneath the fire

Finally, in June, Lucien Ginsburg completes his metamorphosis into Serge Gainsbourg. On the 28, he actually puts out four songs that finally reveal a unique talent: "Mes petites odalisques," "La jambe de bois (Friedland)," "Le poinçonneur de Lilas," and "La cigale et la fourmi." The last of these, recorded for Editions Musicales Tutti (the first publisher to give him a contract, in February, 1958), will never be issued. It contains, nevertheless, funny little quips:

Having sung all summer in old Pigalle
Desiree found herself poor as dirt
Walking nude down Avenue Marceau
With not so much as a shirt
She woke up nude in a babbling brook
At the end of a bout of hunger
And being deprived of subsitent fare
She decided to sell her body bare
By next season, this I promise
I'll buy myself, she claims
A mink to warm my shoulders
It's must-have in this game

July 19, 1957, Serge starts his fourth and final summer season, a month-long gig at Club de la Forêt. Accompanied by guitarist Romain Tonazzi, also known as Tony Romain, he earns 62,000 old francs for 31 days of work, or 2,000 francs a day, a part of which he sends to Lise, who's living in Paris. As usual, Joseph played the role of go-between: his son balked at the idea of doing another season alone in Toquet. So an acquaintance of his, Antonio Tonazzi, alias Scylio, also a bandleader, recommends his son as a partner. Serge and the other lad, who are being put up at Flavio's, are both heavy into jazz and make a connection, often exchanging instruments at the end of the night. They play the Boston, a dance tune that the English are crazy for, and standards like "True Love" and "On the Sunny Side of the Street." During the afternoon, Serge works on arrangements for "Le poinçonneur de Lilas." Sometimes he sings at night.

Before playing, they dine together. Tonazzi (deceased in 1998) recalls a Serge who was very pessimistic, always talking about Schopenhauer... Yet he's truly at a decisive turning point which will come to a head during the last four months of the year, while he lives with his parents and resumes his job as guitarist-pianist at Milord.

> MICHÈLE ARNAUD: *"The first time I saw him I found him strange, both shy and impudent, an introvert and a show-off. It was months before he decided to talk to me, and that was just to say: I'm getting a divorce. I asked him why and he said that it was because his wife no longer measured up to his esthetic ideal."*

A witness who wishes to remain anonymous in this matter tells the following story: "I remember Serge introducing me to Elisabeth, a very pretty, bourgeois Russian. I almost ended up slapping him in the face over a nasty remark that he insisted was innocent. Like an ass, he told her, "If you'd stayed thin I'd never have dumped you." I was furious, and told him he had no right say such crap! Anyway, she just laughed. It was obviously hurtful to her but she didn't want to let anything show..."

The divorce decree is granted by the civil tribunal of the Seine, October 9, 1957, ten years to the day after they first consummated their relationship. Elisabeth Ginsburg becomes Elisabeth Levitsky once again before remarrying in 1960. Later, Lise will become a militant member of the CFDT

(Confédération française démocratique du travail)[3] and head of the Centre INFFO.[4] The Lucien that she had met in 1947 at the Académie Montmatre has blossomed before her eyes. They lived together through passion, bohemianism, poverty, and shared a love for painting and music. In ten years, from the age of 19 to 29, Serge would abandon his ideals: his dream of becoming a true painter with his own salon is compromised in favor of this minor art his father so despised. As a songwriter (from 1954 to 1957, Serge entertained no ideas about singing his owns songs), he could only succeed in getting his work performed by fat transvestites or maybe some scumbag burlesque star. And yet the idea that something big was just around the corner must have been a constant in his mind. How else can one explain the following "agreement" that Elisabeth describes below?

> ELISABETH: *"Our contract, as we called it, was all about silence and anonymity - a little game we played together for some 30 years."*

It might be amusing to push our analysis a bit further. So, Serge now finally decides to devote himself to songwriting. Faithful to the pride instilled in him by Joseph and Olia, it now becomes a question of forcing himself to be the best (which was his credo as a painter: genius or nothing... and of course he quit...). That's how it is with the Ginsburgs and we've seen it in the preceding chapters: that special pride, instilled as much by the mother as by the father, which is translated first and foremost as an acute sense of one's intelligence and uniqueness (a family of artists, cultivated, private, and withdrawn). They are convinced that they belong to an elite group, and it has nothing to do with bloodline or money. With their gifted, critical minds made even more powerful by their sense of humor - especially in the case of Serge - they love to poke fun at others, including those within their own family ranks (remember Lucien's aunt, the Polish Jew with a thick accent that the kids made fun of and who was also a source of shame?...) It's like they are saying, "Don't get us mixed up with those people!" The things that remind them of their origins (poor, immigrant, Jewish, Russian) are a source of crushing humiliation. In addition to their anguish and hardship, they suffer cruelly because of the anti-Semitic laws enforced during the war, and they respond

---

[3] French Democratic Federation of Labor. (T.N.)

[4] The International Development Research Centre. (T.N.)

to this indignation with a sort of carelessness that could have cost them their lives (the star pinned on instead of sewn in, the girls going out to the movies after the curfew time imposed on Jews).

Serge would always tell us from the start: "Don't confuse me with other singers!" One can understand neither the man nor his work without grasping this notion: the Gainsbourg clan is terribly proud. Although self-deprecation is a hallmark of Jewish humor, it is something that the family simply does not engage in. When he starts to poke fun at himself later, even in song, talking about his huge ears and how ugly he is, it is more like an act of self-flagellation. The truth is that he had suffered too much to be able to laugh about it.

The Gainsbourgs are also respectful of rules. They obey the law and are people of elevated moral fiber. Now, when transposed into the world of art, how does this play? Here's a lad who had so much respect for painting that he was afraid to question the rules. This art with a capital "A" leaves him intimidated and apoplectic. But since, on the other hand, he has no respect for popular music, he is ready to push all the boundaries, like Boris Vian before him, who undoubtedly paved the way. But Serge will put more time, energy and professionalism into it, combining the careless insolence and cutting edge humor that were both constants in Vian's work. Yet unlike Vian, he wasn't simply telling himself "Hey, I'll have a blast writing cheesy little pop songs and make a killing at the same time, just to show them it's all a joke." On the contrary: for all his talent with melody – and all that classical baggage that would later serve him so well – it still took years for him to write decent text (unlike Vian, the prolific journalist, who could spit out copy on demand). He even used four different lyricists between 1954 and 1957. Giving birth to his lyrics would be a painful process throughout his career, and Serge would often stay up all night long, waiting until the last moment to finish. In short, it wasn't simply seeing Vian onstage that triggered it all. It was for four years, night after night, accompanying singer after singer at Milord, four years of playing guitar behind Michèle Arnaud, four years of analysis, of dissecting his repertory (Mouloudji, Ferré, Brassens, etc.). Plus four years playing all night at Flavio's or Toquet! He finds the time to discover that it's actually possible to say something intelligent in a few rhyming couplets. All of these things will have time to ripen and magnificently appear in the months that will follow.

Lise makes her exit, and perhaps Serge even tells Michèle Arnaud the truth about the torch he's carrying for her. But her private life, as we've seen, is complicated. She is wildly pursued by Patrick Lehideux, a wealthy industrialist and son of a former cabinet member from the Pétain government. The two are eventually wed in 1964.

GAINSBOURG: *"I wrote for her because I was very much in love with her. This young woman fascinated me. There wasn't an ounce of vulgarity in her... Thinking about her makes me want to quote Balzac: "In love, there's always one who suffers and one who is bored..." It was one of my biggest breaks. She was smart enough to see a new kind of style in my work."*

FRANCIS CLAUDE: *"One night at Milord, Michèle, Serge and I are talking about painting. After a couple moments, he starts getting fidgety and ends up telling us how he's a painter and that we should come see his work. Michèle is both curious and quite excited, so the next day we head over to Serge's place. His paintings, as far as I can remember, were quite tender and not at all subversive. It felt like the work of Corot... Suddenly, Michèle notices a piece of music on the piano. It's called "Defense d'afficher" – words and music by Serge Gainsbourg. She says to him, "So you've hidden it!" He once again starts to squirm like a worm and then goes to fetch "Le poinçonneur de Lilas," "La jambe de bois"... five songs in all and each one a masterpiece."*

JACQUES LASRY: *"A few weeks before I quit Milord to work at Stuctures sonores, Serge came by with a bunch of scores and manuscripts. Michèle Arnaud had asked me to stay a few minutes because she wanted to know what Gainsbourg had written. She was wondering if she could perform some of his tunes. So he gives me the music and I see the painstakingly prepared scores, which was strange for someone who said he was so uninterested in popular song. He asked me to play them. He had never hinted that he wrote songs. He even seemed to be ashamed of it! A little while later he called me and said that Francis Claude wanted him to sing "Le poinçonneur de Lilas" on the radio. He brought me the music and I ended up being the first person to arrange that song."* [5]

---

[5] When know that Serge performed at least twice on the radio towards the end of 1957. He did "Le poinçonneur de Lilas" on Paris-Inter (later France-Inter, now defunct). On another occasion he sang and was interviewed by Cora Vaucaire.

Francis is enthusiastic, but Michèle... well, she only takes one of his songs. "Mes petites odalisques," "Le poinçonneur de Lilas," and "La jambe de bois" are too masculine for her. "La cigale et la fourmi" might do, but the piece is not as strong as the others. Finally, she sets her sights on "Ronsard 58," with lyrics by Serge Barthélémy. It's a monument to misogyny, not far from – in its theme and its cruelty – Raymond Queneau's "Si tu t'imagines," which launched the career of Gréco a decade earlier:

You may my dear have everything on your side
You may have lovers and have great success
Spend your summers lounging at the seaside
In nice bikinis that show off your breasts

You'll be draped in mink and drive fancy cars
Dandies and playboys will knock at your door
But as you smile and play your game like a star
Please don't forget that all you are is a whore

One can imagine how this tune might go over at Le Milord, especially with an audience full of older men with young chicks hanging on their arms... Maybe Michèle Arnaud initially only takes one song, but she asks her guitarist to get to work right away on some new tunes in the same vein. On December 20, 1957, Serge goes to SACEM to register "La recette de l'amour fou" and "Douze belles dans la peau," which she immediately appropriates:

When you've gone twelve rounds with the girls
With typists and royalty in pearls
This is what it comes of it don't you know
Laid out with a bullet
A belly full of lead
A man who's now lost his head

On January 5, 1958, Francis Claude invites Serge to perform on the radio show he does for Paris-Inter, presenting him as young talent that he has proudly discovered and "A full-fledged member of Le Milord Arsouille": "He was playing the piano a while ago, and later he might pick up a guitar. When he has time to himself he paints. He seems to have found a way of writing very unusual songs which he manages to champion with his own unique personality..." Then nervously, Serge belts out "Mes petites odalisques," which would be done one year later by new talent Hugues Aufray:

Gone are all the escapades
All that remain are tired charades
Gone are all the lovers, too
Searching slumber somewhere new
And from the bed, remember those
Unfaithful ones who brought you woes
Because they could no longer feign
Interest in your tired refrains

It's the same, all day long
My little sluts, this is your song
Turn and turn and turn once more
And dance this dance for evermore

A few weeks earlier, Serge, half-dead with stage fright, had been pushed onstage at Le Milord by Francis Claude.

JACQUES LASRY: *"I had stopped working for Michèle, and one day I see Serge on Avenue des Ternes. He was very excited and told me, "Last night I sang at Milord, Francis presented me... I sang 'Le poinçonneur de Lilas.' It was a smash!" I saw him onstage for the first time that night, and it was extraordinary. He trembled, very lightly, and looked like a man in the throes of some sort of prophetic communication, when in reality he was in communication with himself, not the public."*

In the February, 1958 edition of the monthly *Music-Hall*, there is an ad placed by Ducretet Thompson Records to announce the release of a new EP by Michèle Arnaud. The big number is Michèle's lovely cover of "Marjolaine," a popular tune by Francis Lemarque (really, at 40 years old, his first great personal success – he had lived over a dozen years in the shadow of Yves Montand, to whom he gave his best songs, including "A Paris" and "Quand un soldat.") On the same EP Michèle performs "Douze belles dans la peau" and "La recette de l'amour fou," which historically speaking are the first two of Serge's works to be committed to vinyl. Two months later, he finds another voice for his songs, the seductive Jean-Claude Pascal, who records the same two tunes for an EP on the label La Voix de son Maitre (at the time, the standout single is "Croquemitoufle," which is given to him by his friend, Gilbert Bécaud). But it's Michèle Arnaud, with her cold snobbishness, who gives us the superior version of "La recette de l'amour fou," a mini tragic-comedy in two acts and a denouement:

> *Do play the game of love's endeavor*
> *First say "always" then say "never"*
> *Do consummate*
> *'Fore it's too late*
> *But when you've settled the score*
> *If he starts to sleep and snore*
> *Just kick his ass right out the door*

It's common, in those days, for a song to be recorded by several artists. Between 1957 and 1958, there are 25 different versions of "Cigarettes, whiskey et pépées" (The Eddie Constantine version is the only memorable contribution), 26 takes on "Lavadières de Portugal," 32 covers of "Buenas Noches Mi Amor," and finally 91 versions of "Que Sera Sera." Wild inflation, it seems, leads to the rapid decline of this fad, leaving the music publishers all-powerful: in order to sell their songs, some writers have to go as far as paying the artists to sing them. The singer often demands 100,000 old francs (1,000 francs) to put a new song "on probation," as it were. Others, like Montand, simply refuse to take them. Also, the system allows for certain songs to prolong their success ad nauseum. It is not unusual for a hit to last six months, a year, or even a year and a half on the charts (for example "Cigarettes, whiskey, et pépées" by Eddie Constantine, released in spring of 1957, is still a big hit at the start of the 1958 school year some 15 months later).

At the very moment Gainsbourg starts to take off, French song is at its height: popular music is played all day on the three state outlets, including French TV and the outlying radio channels (Europe N. 1, Radio Luxembourg and Radio Monte Carlo). The French have come to see the powerful role of the television, the radio and the turntable in their everyday lives. The latter two especially are greatly profitable: the Philips factory in Louviers employs 500 workers in 1958, as does the Pathé Marconi factory in Chatou. In 1951, in France alone, they sold 5,450,000 78s, 90,000 33s, and 5,000 45s. In 1954, they had reached 5,500,000 78s, 2, 600,000 33s, and 80,000 45s. Finally, in 1957, they're selling 800,000 78s, 9,500,000 33s, and 10 million 45s!

While none of the records really allows us to determine who truly sold the most discs,[6] we can get an idea about a song's popularity through the "small format" sales (four page scores of words and music). And we also know that in the realm of "quality French song," the niche in which Serge hopes to establish himself with the public, an EP by Brassens ("La prière," "Chanson pour l'Auvergnat," etc) can easily sell 150,000 copies.

But the big fad had been launched a year earlier by Europe N°1 with the invasion of foreign songs, especially Italian songs, coming over the French air waves (even though the station managers organize, among other things, the *Coqs de la chanson* programs to offer French music as a show of good faith). Lucien Morisse, the station's boss, just loves the new scene: he drifts around from festival to festival, from San Remo and Naples, coming back with scads of new titles. The two who benefit the most from all his trips are Dalida and Morino Marini. Dalida, Morisse's lover, gives us "Bambino," "Buenas Noches Mi Amor," and "Tu n'as pas très bon charactère," all while making her debut at the Olympia. Marino sells over a million records in France, including "La Panse," "Bonjour à Paris," and "Oh La La."

The English-speaking world makes a big splash with *The Girl Can't Help It*, a film starring Jane Mansfield and 12 other musical acts that, according to the critics, "rang the bell that ushered in rock'n'roll." It's a time when a young Jean-Philippe Smet, the future Johnny Hallyday, sees Elvis Presley's *Loving You* time and time again. But certain journalists seem to think the calypso is dethroning rock and roll. Harry Belafonte is the new star, and "Day-O" is an enormous hit in France. It spawns over forty cover versions

1957 is a rather mediocre years for songs. Les grands prix de l'Académie Charles Gros[7] are awarded to a friend of Brassens, one René-Louis Lafforgue (for his 33 rpm of *Julie la rouse*), Lucette Raillat (for "La môme aux boutons"), and Simone Langlois (for her take on the songs of Jacques Brel). Raymond Devos, the year's other sensation, sells out the Alhambra, while Gilbert Bécaud packs them in at l'Olympia with Dalida as the opening act.

---

[6] This problem is a typically French phenomenon that the billboard charts and the local radio stations would not resolve until 1984, when Europe 1 and Canal+ helped impose measures to better represent real sales figures.

[7] The big musical awards that year, similar to the Grammys. (T.N.)

The next big hit on stage is the American Frankie Laine, nicknamed "Mr. Rhythm," who is but a cut-rate imitation of Elvis.

Near the end of 1957, it is also clear that Philips wants to launch a series called "The New Faces of Song," whose first eight EPs will be released simultaneously, with arrangements by Claude Bolling and Alain Goraguer. Signed by Jacques Canetti, who also runs Le Théâtre aux Trois Baudets, these newcomers, including Denise André, Claude Parent, Micheline Remette, and Ginette Roland all have one unfortunate thing in common: none of them make a breakthrough. And yet amidst these very circumstances, Serge will be offered a contract by the same company.

Beginning on February 28, 1958, Michèle Arnaud starts doing live shows at Bobino along with André Dassary (who had just taken the cure and had only recently been forgiven for having sung "Maréchal, nous voilà").[8] It is during this period that she starts doing "La recette de l'amour fou," and for the first time, we see Serge's name in the papers. Papa Ginsburg, aglow with pride as one might suspect, cuts out the notices and sends them via air mail to Serge's twin sister Liliane, who is living in Casablanca. The following is from Combat, March 8:

> Her naturally elegant voice fits marvelously with the carefully chosen repertory (...) I should also note the appearance of a unique talent, composer Serge Gainsbourg, whom we'll surely be discussing again.

Precisely: In May, when she returns to the Olympia (she had already sung there in 1957, on the same bill with French entertainer Henri Genès, and The Platters), Michèle performs eight songs, four of which are written by Gainsbourg. Meanwhile, she starts to make forays into television, producing the show Chez vous ce soir, which is hosted by Jean-Claude Pascal and premieres on March 29, 1958. Among the guests is one Serge Gainsbourg, and it's his first time on TV. As the Milord has shown us, his stage fright is terrible and still as bad as ever. The young entertainer Bernard Haller remembers these first difficult steps...

---

[8] Often sung in place of La Marseillaise, it was a key piece of propaganda for Pétain and the collaborationist Vichy government, and thus often the subject of ridicule and parody. (T.N.)

BERNARD HALLER: *"Gainsbourg did two songs, including "Le poinçon-neur." Not a big triumph. People were stunned by his physical appearance... I'm wondering if that second song was "La jambe de bois," which we never heard again and was a real riot!"*

A funny story really, this "Jambe de bois" business. The tune was also a big favorite of Boris Vian. So, as the story goes, a wooden leg, feeling useless and on the brink of taking its own life, stumbles onto a battlefield. The French are fighting the Cossacks. The peg leg doesn't want to end up on the stump of a Russian peasant, and thus asks the cannonball if it could do him a favor and change its trajectory a bit:

> *Take dead aim at that French officer*
> *And should you blow off his leg*
> *Heed my words and trust me true*
> *I'll be the man's new peg*
> *...if gangrene hasn't yet dug his grave...*

But alas, the soldier sees it coming, tries to duck, and gets his head blown off... Serge records this song for Philips on February 17, 1958, during a rehearsal session at Studio Blanqui. The recording is simply piano and voice. He also cuts four other tunes: "Le poinçonneur de Lilas," "Ronsard 58," "La recette de l'amour fou," and "Douzes belles dans la peau."

As noted earlier, Jacques Canetti is the artistic director at Philips, and without a doubt the most important man in French show business during the '50s. A person, perhaps, of questionable moral fiber, he's nevertheless top-dog at a major record company, the boss at Théâtre aux Trois Baudets (which is the main venue for the biggest stars in music), and the most important concert promoter for the major names in French music (Devos, Brel, Brassens, Béart, etc.). The in-house producers include both Denis Bourgeois and Boris Vian. Vian produces, among other artists, Magali Noël, Henry Cording, Kenny Clarke, and Alain Goraguer. He also does a compiled series of discs called "Jazz pour tous" (Jazz for everybody). At Fontana, he supervises the Miles Davis sessions for the soundtrack to *Ascenseur pour l'échafaud*. Last but not least, he is responsible for the very first Screamin' Jay Hawkins recordings released in France (an EP that is part of their rock and roll collection called A cracher des flames).[9] He also releases the first 25 cm single of "I Put a Spell on You."[10]

DENIS BOURGEOIS: *"When I went to see Serge at Milord, I immediately asked him to do a demo tape. When Canetti heard the tunes, it was like he had been struck by lightning, and signing Serge would take but a matter of days, even though Serge was being courted by another record company. My first instinct was to reunite Serge and Alain Goraguer."*

JACQUES LASRY: *"I knew that Ducretet Records, at the behest of Michèle, had already approached him. Philips was also interested in him, and Serge was drawing huge crowds at Le Milord. Although I was no longer there and thus not a first-hand witness, Serge still kept me apprised – almost daily – about all the goings-on. I was myself an artist represented by Ducretet and was not very happy with the outfit. I advised Serge to consider going to Philips because they were technologically well-equipped and had what it took to make Serge a true artist."*

JACQUES CANETTI: *"I offered him a contract almost instantly; in fact, at that time, I could do more or less what I wanted at Philips. I'd told myself that Gainsbourg was someone who could have a career of his own as a recording artist and not just as a songwriter, which would obviously prove to be true. Serge signed on right away. He was very docile, and his father and I grew quite close, for he appreciated the patience I showed his son."*

On May 3, six months before the release of his first 25cm album, Serge receives his first real review in the papers. It's comprised of two columns and written by Henry Magnan for *Combat*:

SERGE GAINSBOURG AT LE MILORD L'ARSOUILLE

People are talking about him and will keep talking about him. His name is Serge Gainsbourg, and he truly detests the kinds of songs that have nothing to say [...] What's more, he's right to believe, as an authentic poet, in the intrinsic value of words. Here's to you, Mr. Gainsbourg!

---

[9] This literally means "spitting fire." (T.N.)

[10] Screamin' Jay Hawkins died in February, 2000. Serge had always been a fan, and even did a screwball duet version of "Constipation blues" for the TV program Les enfants du rock in the 1980s.

Serge, who now sings four songs during the course of his show (five if an encore is called for) is soon to receive a visit: on the advice of Francis Claude, Yves Montand decides to come to a show, accompanied by Simone Signoret.

GAINSBOURG: *"I was quite moved. After seeing me at Milord, Yves called me over to his place and asked me straight out: "So what is it that you want, my boy? You want to be a singer, a songwriter, a performer?"... and me, like a cretin, I simply say: "I want it all." I didn't want to come off like an ass, but I did. I felt like I was now screwed. He wanted to work with me, but nothing ever came of it. In retrospect, I was lucky: had I given all my songs to Montand, a masterful stylist, he would have kept me waiting in the wings, and I would have become just a shadow, like Francis Lemarque, who met with that very fate while working with Montand."*

Serge and Yves run into each other a few months later on Rue Albert Hirsch, an area familiar to Serge from his childhood in Champsfleur, and Serge claims to have arrogantly spat out at Montand: "I feel nothing when you sing my songs!" This is Serge we're talking about - the guy who has been waiting for three years to get one of his pieces sung by a famous artist - and he tosses this magnificent stroke of luck right onto the trash heap.

Serge still can't manage, before taking the stage, to rid himself of the fear that is sometimes so intense it leaves him nauseous. It's a fear made all the more worse now that Francis Claude, working in another club, is not always around to introduce Serge in person. On these occasions, they use a recording of Francis' supple voice, which resonates through the silence: "You heard him playing piano just a while ago. His name is Serge Gainsbourg, and it's not a paycheck that they give him, but rather a pill!" Once he's behind the mic, the atmosphere becomes... well, not cold, but rather Siberian. This truth is relayed to us through the man who, upon the advice of Denis Bourgeois, will become Serge's arranger.

ALAIN GORAGUER: *"I'd already seen this type of reaction when I watched Boris Vian onstage. It was like a mixture of hatred and fascination. You could almost read it in the thoughts of the audience, a reaction waiting to burst forth but somehow it never did: "You ugly dope... You sing like an idiot." Neither Vian nor Gainsbourg exuded anything vaguely pleasant or likeable. They were mortified onstage and it was evident. Even if they had turned their backs to the spectators while performing, it would have made no difference."*

Gainsbourg lands at Philips at about the same time Brel is just gaining notoriety. Another Philips artist, Brel had just done his third LP for the company and scored his first big hit with "Quand on n'a que l'amour" (which won the Prix de l'Académie Charles-Cros). Gréco – yes, Gréco once again - was the first to sing Brel in 1954 ("Le diable (ça va).") Brel had been very gracious in writing for her two tailor-made songs: "Je suis bien" and "On n'oublie rien." In 1958, the hits that people are humming in the streets include "Hello, Le soleil brille...," from the film *Bridge Over the River Kwai*, Charles Aznavour's "Aye mourir pour toi" and "Diana," by Paul Anka. At the same time, people like Boris Vian and Georges Brassens, or Henri Salvador and Gut Béart debate each other on a monthly basis in the pages of *Music-Hall*, or sometimes in front of André Halimi's microphones, discussing the question of the "conspiracy of mediocrity" plaguing the world of song. Later, in *Music-Hall* once again, Halimi poses another question: "Is popular song a minor art form?"

Serge, slowly but surely, is building a repertoire. On April 16, 1958, he registers "Le Charleston des déménageurs de piano." On May 2, we get "La femme des uns sous le corps des autres" and "La purée," a kind of short, chatty play including a spoken monologue of mutual insults on the part of a drunken bum and a sly old fat cat: a song that would also never be released:

> *He's a wastrel and a phony*
> *Skeletal and bony*
> *Opening doors of fancy cars*
> *To pay for drinks in a dimly lit bars*
> *With a wit that's more than lucid*
> *What in fact some would call acid*
> *He's lost it all save for that bit of pride*
> *That keeps him from going to beg inside*

Is this song made to order for Philippe Clay? Very probably. The information about Clay then trickling down to the press suggests that he has the intention of recording at least two of Gainsbourg's numbers. Serge is tickled pink, of course, especially after the fiasco with Montand. Some six feet and three inches tall, Clay has for years been one of the most popular of all

French music-hall artists ("Le noyé assassiné," "Monsieur James," etc). He is, at the same time, an actor, acrobat, and dancer, and when it comes to breathing life into the songs of others, he is without peer as a performer. In 1958, we once again find him at the top of his game, thanks to song ("La gambille"), film (he is seen in Jean Renoir's *French Cancan*, portraying in superb fashion the character Valentin le Désossé, and then again in Jean Delannoy's *Nôtre-Dame de Paris*). He also graces the stage with a winning performance at the Olympia, and puts out, once again during the same year of 1958, an EP whose title track, as a strange coincidence might have it, is called "Les stances Ronsard."

The two share a singular physical resemblance which is often noted by the journalists of the day. That doesn't stop them, however, from having a serious falling out. If one believes the first version, Clay promised Serge that he would do an album comprised entirely of Gainsbourg pieces. The other version describes Clay as quite vexed to have learned Serge had recorded these songs himself – for the same company – while the songs had been promised to Clay, and this led to Clay having to cancel his own sessions.

> GAINSBOURG: *"Artists can really disappoint you. Take Philippe Clay, for example. I've heard him sing my songs some twenty times, but always at his home, never onstage. I was more or less forced to sing my own material because I was writing lyrics that nobody else wanted."*

> PHILIPPE CLAY: *"In the beginning, it was he who talked to me about "Le poinçonneur," but I never sang it. The song was for me and I should have performed it. Damn, have I done some stupid crap in my life!"*

They finally do end up burying the hatchet a few years later. Clay would start to experience a serious slump starting in 1962. That year, Serge offers him "Chanson pour tézigue." Then in 1964, they appear on television together for a duet of both "Accordéon" and "L'assassinat de Franz Léhar." Serge uses this occasion to lash out with a cruel remark in response to one of the journalists for *La Tribune de Genève*: "It's funny, working for other people. I used to really appreciate Philippe Clay and follow what he did. But he never took any of my songs. Now that I don't care so much about him, he wants them."

May 13, 1958. The French in Algeria take the central government by storm, creating the Comité de salut public (Committee for Public Safety) around General Massu while the National Assembly is reduced to a mad free-for-all. Gainsbourg is once more invited - this time by Roger Bouillot - to speak on the radio for the show *La Soirée du club d'essai* on Paris-Inter. There is a live recording made of the show, which takes place in the hall of the Alliance Française. That evening, Serge - who can't find a pianist and ends up using his father as his accompanist - sings "Le Poinçonneur" and the anti-militarist "Jambe de bois (Friedland)," a bit provocative considering the context.[11]

Serge, along with Denis Bourgeois, is in the process of meticulously preparing his first real recording session (the one in February was a simple formality before the signing of the contract), planned for June 10. The two of them are wondering about just whom they might get to look at "Le Poinçonneur": they're sure that the song can be a big hit, but if it's sung by a newcomer with a less than appealing physique... well, that's difficult. Montand is a has-been. Clay and Serge are on bad terms. They think of Les Frères Jacques, but are then approached by a newcomer named Hugues Aufray about whom they know nothing except that he is said to have published two EP's under the name of Bob Aubert et son Typic Brésilien, and that he's the brother of Pascale Audret, a young and promising actress who debuted in *L'Eau Vive*. He also had a bit of success running a club called "La Polka de Mandibules." In May, 1958, he participates in Numéros 1 de demain, organized by Europe N° I and the monthly *Music-Hall*. And from there, thanks to "Le poinçonneur de Lilas," he's able to sign a contract with Barclay.

> HUGUES AUFRAY: *"One night at Le Milord l'Arsouille, I catch Gainsbourg doing "Mes petites odalisques" and "Le poinçonneur." I'm immediately pulled into the performance and can see that this guy has real talent. So I go back to Le Milord - once, twice, three times, even - without ever trying to chat with him backstage. I was so timid. On the other hand, I was able to listen to and learn these beautiful songs by heart. I would mark down the lyrics on a piece of paper because at that time, of course, there were*

[11] For those less familiar with French history, this event surrounding General Massu primarily highlights the actions of the conservative and more politically and militarily reactionary wing of the French populace and government.

[139]

no portable recording devices… This was kind of my method. I'd done the
same for the Brazilian songs in my repertory: my friends would sing the
tunes and I would note things down. This is the basis of folklore and the
oral tradition. So I learned these songs and integrated them into my tour-
ing show. Being such beautiful pieces, they met with a lot of success. Denis
Bourgeois, Gainsbourg's artistic director, seemed to be worried, telling
himself: "Listen, you need to be careful. This guy is ripping off our whole
thing!" But as far as I felt, there was no dishonesty in what I was doing. I
hadn't committed any theft! I went to the offices of Denis Bourgeois and
explained myself, saying that I wasn't out to take advantage of anybody.
Gainsbourg, who was present, seemed rather flattered."

Jacques Lasry, the ex-pianist for Michèle Arnaud, recounts a somewhat
different version of the story: "One day Hugues Aufray calls me and says:
"I've just discovered the songs of Gainsbourg, and they're what I need." So I
set up a meeting with the wife of Francis Claude, who had a restaurant where
people drank by the bucketful, and on that day I encountered a Gainsbourg
who was overflowing with self-confidence. After an intense discussion, he
flat-out refused to give his songs to Hugues. He was almost aggressive about
it. He offered no explanation, just a radical refusal. He had quite elevated
critical sensibilities."

Despite this, Aufray's version of "Le poinçonneur" comes out in March,
1959, six months after Les Frères Jacques had their own success with the
song, as we will see later on. So the first to come is the last served. We can
understand why Aufray, for a long while, held a grudge with Serge, who nevertheless offered him exclusive rights to record "Mes petites odalisques."

Bourgeois' strategy is clear: in order to launch the career of his prodigy,
as both a songwriter and a performer, they need a prestigious name to back
Serge while he takes his first steps as an artist. Les Frères Jacques, nicknamed "the most complete athletes of song," famous for over a decade now,
with their tights, their moustaches, and their nutty hats ("La queue du chat"
dates from 1948, "Le complexe de la truite" from 1954) seem to be an excellent choice.

PAUL TOURENNE: *"We were looking for lyrics, and our manager, Canetti,*
told us about this amazing guy he'd just met, Serge Gainsbourg. We met

up with him in Francois' apartment, and he played us three or four songs, including "Le poinçonneur de Lilas." He was terribly shy and had to work like a slave just to get his songs performed by other artists. Really, it wasn't easy for him... I remember all four of us gathered around the piano, trying to understand what he was saying. We didn't dare tell him: "Sing more loudly... We can't hear a thing!" We had him do each song three times and we finally decided on 'Le poinçonneur." We recorded it in 1958, from June 23 to June 24, and then performed it onstage at La Comédie des Champs-Elysées two months later. The audience really took to the song, which was one of the only tunes we did without any theatrical staging. We did nothing; it was simply evocative. The four of us were onstage with our backs turned to each other. In this way, the song had great power because nobody was distracted by choreography. It's not a funny song, but rather seriously dramatic... Now as a group, we weren't a huge source of revenue when it came to selling records, even though we could always pack the concert halls. But "Le poinçonneur" did so well that it became our biggest seller in years. We had sold plenty of Prévert for decades, but this Gainsbourg piece was our hit and it belonged to us... That's why we were so proud of it."

Starting on October 23, 1958, on the stage of La Comédie des Champs-Elysées, Les Frères Jacques perform "Le poinçonneur" as the "First Gainsbourg Concerto." Their version, orchestrated by Pierre Philippe, is all over the airwaves during the summer. The Gainsbourg version comes out in September, at the same time as his 25 cm *Du chant à la une!*. The legend behind the song tells that Serge would often run into the same employee of the RATP in a metro station. One day, he asks him what his dream is. The ticket puncher responds with this superb answer: "To see the sky..."

> I've got a crummy little job
> A working stiff like any other slob
> There's no sunshine in my life, no
> It's utter strife, so
> To ease the drag of this routine
> I've Reader's Digest magazine
> And in the pages I peruse
> They say life in Miami's one long cruise
> But I've no time for useless scheming
> Or endless dreaming

They say you've got to work to eat
So I punch holes in little sheets

So on June 10, 1958, Serge, along with Alain Goraguer and his group, enters Blanqui Studios, owned by Philips. They record three songs that day: "La
jambe de bois (Friedland)," "Douze belles dans la peau," and "Le Charleston
des déménageurs du piano." The choice of Alain Goraguer was clear: He was
the ideal man, someone who needed Serge in order to expose his own singular talent. Goraguer, arranger and accompanist for Boris Vian, had done
the orchestration for Magali Noël's version of "Fais-moi mal, Johnny." He
also wrote songs for Salvador (who hired him for his concerts at Bobino). In
1956, he released an EP with his trio (Paul Rovere on bass, Christian Garros
on drums, who also played on the first Gainsbourg recordings) entitled
Go, Go, Goraguer!, which included the tunes "What Is This Thing Called
Love?" by Cole Porter, "Prelude to a Kiss" by Duke Ellington, as well as two
original compositions.

ALAIN GORAGUER: *"I was summoned over to Philips and there waiting
for me in the office was Gainsbourg, the same lad I'd seen a few months
earlier at the terrace of Le Toquet, looking perfectly like the background
pianist he was. Our first contact was simply amazing, and three days later
we were inseparable. We started the recordings, and even if Serge was
completely delighted I could still sense a sort of despair behind his belated
success. He wanted to make a big splash, and right away. What's more,
the deck was stacked against him. First of all there was his physical appearance, which he couldn't come to grips with and which he did his best
to exaggerate: each time he had a new suit, he'd do his best to demolish it
within twenty-four hours. It was his part of this whole "anti-whatever"
business."*

Born in 1931 in Rosny-sous-Bois to a Corsican mother and Breton father,
Goraguer had grown up in Nice and learned to play the violin (up to the point
where he detested the instrument), and then the piano. Upon the advice of
Jack Diéval, a famous jazzman, he decides to give up everything for music
and moves to Paris. Crazy for jazz, he adores Art Tatum, Erroll Garner, Bud
Powell and Thelonius Monk. When he sees the great bands of Dizzy Gillespie
and the Modern Jazz Quartet Paris, his head just explodes. As an arranger,

he's easily on a par with the big names of the time, such as Michel Legrand or André Popp.

Neither Serge nor Alain are satisfied with the first recording of "La jambe de bois (Freidland)," a song that won't be featured on the first album but is later re-recorded during a new session on January 12, 1959. On June 13, Serge registers "L'alcool" with SACEM, and then "Du jazz dans le ravin" and "Ce mortel ennui" are registered July 1. In the meantime, on June 17, and then later in early July at Studio Blanqui, he lays down the four other tracks that are featured on the first 25 cm album, which includes "La recette de l'amour fou," "Le poinçonneur de Lilas," "L'alcool," "Ronsard 58," "La femme des uns sous le corps des autres," "Du jazz dans le ravin," and "Ce mortel ennui."

Right away, because of his style, Gainsbourg sets himself apart from everything else out there, from all of the other singers that people are talking about. There is no common ground between him and Brassens, Brel, Clay, or Lemarque. There's a virtual abyss separating Serge from the Rive Gauche. On that side of the Seine, people are poetic and engaged, and they practice a witty and subtle form of irony. With Gainsbourg, the words, which meld with the music, are not simply grafted onto a score because they conveniently match the rhythm or harmonic structure. And they are ultra-pessimistic. With Gainsbourg, it's about sarcasm, not irony. Technically, since his very first songs, Serge refuses to follow the classic tricks of the trade: practicing scales, forcing himself to develop dramatic effects, etc. And he "sings in style of the time, very French, like he has a mouthful of marbles," as Eddy Mitchell so beautifully puts it. He avoids rolling his R's like Barbara or Brassens...For "Le poinçonneur," Goraguer imagines a lofty introduction embellished with a flute and pianistic glissandos, giving the music a joyous and lively character, all the while providing a story of a man trapped working underground. For "Ce mortel ennui," they concoct a very Monkish intro, and come very close to creating a masterpiece:

This black apathy
That grips me
When I am with you
This black apathy
That keeps me here
And follows me all the day through [...]

Of course there's really nothing left to say
On this pillowcase
But we're also at a loss of words
Standing face to face

GAINSBOURG: *"If don't listen much to my old songs, it's out of fear – the fear of running into a rather large contingent of female faces that have passed through my life. If I listen to "Ce mortel ennui," I instantly see the cute little looker that I thought about while writing the tune. And she wasn't any dope, either: when the song came out she simply said to herself, "That's about me," and then went her merry way..."*

Gainsbourg is definitely an odd-ball. He's pushing thirty and he sings for crowds of the same age, an intellectually blasé public, which is to say not a lot of people. Rather than being seduced by his songs, the listeners feel attacked. When the album comes out, journalists are quick to connect the cynicism of Serge to the film *Les tricheurs*, by Marcel Carné, where the characters forbid themselves, out of sheer pride, to fall in love.

For Serge, at the wheel of his Jaguar (a fanciful image, for Serge never learned to drive), it is always about seducing women with aggression from behind his shroud of black pessimism.

You or me, who's driving this trip?
Of course it's me, so button your lip
In the glove box you'll find some treasures select
American whiskey and good cigarettes
So listen intently, my little doll
To this tune that's playing, my favorite of all
Crank up the volume to maximum pitch
And don't be afraid, I won't drive into a ditch

Of course, the Jag does wind up in a ditch:

And while the two squirmed in agony
The radio kept blasting the melody

Life is rotten and Gainsbourg has every intention of illustrating this truth while Alain Goraguer and Michel Hausser perform their magic, the first on piano and the second on vibraphone. After the poinçonneur finishes his job, he or maybe his double, looks for oblivion in "L'alcool":

My delusions spill out on the street
Hopes are crushed under my feet

After slaving the whole day away
The only thing on display
Are the hideous flowers in my room

The best of all is that Gainsbourg's vaunted misogyny in no way scares off his first and foremost female interpreter, Michèle Arnaud, who does a version of "La femme des uns sous le corps des autres" on an EP that she also releases in the fall of 1958, just before opening at the Olympia for the likes of Georges Brassens. Bruno Coquatrix, the manager of the venue, asks her – as legend has it – to refrain from certain passages in "Les jeunes femmes et les vieux monsieurs" and especially "La femme des uns sous le corps des autres." She refuses. A bit snooty, maybe, but still a risky move made in the spirit of freedom of expression.

The woman of some
'Neath the body of others
Releases sighs
Of voluptuousness

At first we're polite
Then everything goes
We toss back a drink
And then toss off our clothes

When asked about this song, the author would speak about a "satire aimed at libertinage," all the while denying being jaded himself.

GAINSBOURG: *"Jaded? Certainly not. Only insofar as what I'd practiced, what I'd tried, what had left me desperate. I'm not a libertine. I might have dabbled with it and done a lot of stupid shit, but it just left me in despair. In reality, I have kept my ideals as far as love is concerned. I'm intact, or at least I think so. If I had really been a libertine, I wouldn't have been in such despair after every act of love."*

Since the month of February, when the first disc containing Serge's songs was released, Michèle Arnaud had betrayed Serge on several fronts: She released two other EPs, the most notable takes including Paul Anka's "Diana" as well as "Croquemitoufle," written by Gilbert Bécaud. But this doesn't stop her from asking Serge to give personal guitar lessons to her son Dominique, the future Dominique Walter, at the time just fifteen years old (we'll cross his path again, during his singer phase).

Only July 16, Serge has his second television appearance. He is invited by the beautiful Jacqueline Joubert, mother of the young Antoine de Caunes, for a program entitled *Avec le sourire*, during which he performs "Douze belles dans la peau," just after a short interview in which he's paralyzed by stage fright:

JACQUELINE JOUBERT: *So, Serge Gainsbourg, I'd like to know just why you are so harsh with other contemporary artists.*

SERGE GAINSBOURG: *It's... Let's just say it's an attitude...*

JJ: *Ah! An attitude. No, you're not the type of lad to affect an attitude. You're much brighter than that.*

SG: *Let's... just assume that it's...*

JJ: *You know, you could speak more loudly.*

SG: *...it's easier to attack than just grin and bear it [...]*

JJ: *In any case, you have some songs that are quite elegant in their attacks, I must say. In fact, they're so aggressive that I wonder, are big stars interested in doing them? [...] You're a little bit... I going to invoke a strong word, so don't be shocked... You're sort of the Daumier of song, aren't you?*

SG: *Those are strong words.*

JJ: *They're quite strong, but your works, in any case, are little masterpieces. I'm sure you're quite proud of having written "Douze belles dans la peau?"*

SG: *(icy smile)*

JJ: *It's funny, isn't it?*

The album cover is brick-red, a background for a mysterious collection of bizarre news stories ("The Haget murderer has no scar, but rather one eyebrow higher than the other!"). It's called *La chant à la une!*... This first 25cm LP from Serge, released in September, features a portrait covering three-quarters of the album: his stare is fixed on you coldly, with that contemptuous grimace of his. On the back cover is a piece by Marcel Aymé, the author of *Passe-muraille*, *La Jument verte*, and *Contes du chat perché*.

DENIS BOURGEOIS: *"I liked the idea of Marcel doing this because he's one of the idols of our generation. He was, at once, the most modern and straightforward of authors. His work was complex and cynical. When I went to see him out in his country home, carrying along a portable record player, I was a nervous wreck. On the telephone, his wife had told me that he didn't like much, certainly not the songs he heard on the radio. So he listened to the record right in front of me, expressionless, opening his mouth only to say "Come back tomorrow." Then, he gave me this text."*:

Serge Gainsbourg is a twenty-five year old pianist who's also become a composer of words and music. He sings of alcohol, women, adultery, fast cars, poverty, depressing jobs. His songs, inspired by the hardships of his youth, have a trace of melancholy, bitterness, and an ever-present hardness. The songs are sung over music that is a bit Spartan, in which, as the style of the times dictates, rhythm often trumps melody. I'm hoping that good fortune smiles on Gainsbourg, for he deserves it, and it might even brighten up some of his tunes.

Marcel Aymé

On the promo version of his first 25 cm, given only to the press, there is a double sleeve (wrapped in a band announcing "After Brassens, Brel, Béart: the new big thing!" showing that Philips was setting the bar high for its new artist). We learn that "he writes and sings his own blackly comic songs" and that "he likes shish-kabobs, Edgar Allan Poe, and speed." What's more, there's this hilarious interview:

—If you hadn't been you, who would you have liked to have been?
—*The Marquis de Sade (immediate response). Robinson Crusoe (After thinking about it).*
—What's your favorite line from Baudelaire?
—*Strangeness is one of the integral facets of beauty.*
—What would you take to a desert island?

—*Seven books: Une vielle maîtresse by Barbet d'Aureville, the poetry of Cattalus, Cervante's Don Quixote, Adolphe by Benjamin Constant, Poe's Fantastic Tales, and the fairy tales of Grimm and Perrault.*
    —*Five albums: Schoënberg, Bartók, Johnnie Ray, Stan Kenton, Ray Coniff.*
    —*Five women: Mélisande, Ophelia, Peau d'âne, a manicurist, Vivian Leigh.*
    —*And some blue jeans.*

Serge had sung every evening at Le Milord, along with the other regulars like Jacques Dufilho, Darrigade, Fouziquet, Francis Claude, and Michèle Arnaud. After the summer closure, the cabaret reopens its doors on October 2 with the same line-up, which continues without interruption and which also includes newcomer Jean Ferrat, who plays from November 19 to December 16 and then is replaced by Christian Nohel.

Among Serge's first enthusiastic fans is the much missed Lucien Rioux of *France-Observateur*. He would, ten years later, be the first to publish a book on Gainsbourg in the "Poètes d'aujourd'hui" series by Seghers.

> LUCIEN RIOUX: *"Onstage at Le Milord, he was quite uncomfortable... in real agony... And it showed. The public's first reaction was one of scorn and rejection, mostly because of his appearance. Then, he adopted the attitude of the provocateur: instead of him feeling uneasy, he'd tried to get the audience unnerved."*

> SACHA DISTEL: *"I immediately identified the very modern harmonic sensibilities he showed as a piano player. Jazz musicians – and I'm one – hear very unusual things that others might not perceive. And then there was that incredible mug of his, that Semitic caricature of a face that revealed a man with nightmarish complexes."*

> JEAN-CLAUDE BRIALY: *"Thanks to Michèle Arnaud, I'd known him a long time before I started working with him, back from his days when he was just a pianist at Le Milord l'Arsouille. Right off, I was seduced by his intelligence, his caustic humor, and that charm that made him seem like some sort of Renaissance prince. He reminded me of one of the Medicis, with those big eyes and that hook-nose and the rather elegant and arrogant way he had of looking down his nose at people, even though he himself was a penniless nobody."*

Rare press clippings from the day confirm this impression. From *Les Beaux-Arts Bruxelles*, we read the following: "We know his songs. He sings them himself with that reedy voice of his, without any gesturing. He gives the impression of being both melancholic and indifferent, with those dreamy eyes and ears like a flying elephant." From Paris, in *L'Officiel des spectacles*: "Gainsbourg writes exquisite songs and sings them quite badly, just as tradition would have it. He's scrawny and feeble and always seems to be a breath away from fainting or simply vanishing." In *Arts*, from a story called "Gainsbourg: Even Uglier than Clay," we find this especially harsh description: "Ears shoot out perpendicular to the head, enormous eyelids, pitiful arms. Still, as with Philippe Clay, such a horrific appearance only does more to bring out the sensitive soul inside." Nevertheless, the author of the piece believes that Serge will one day be as famous as his song "Le poinçonneur de Lilas": "In the coming months, he will be recorded, photographed, even have his name in lights. So when does he play the Olympia?"

Magazines are also publishing reviews of the album *Du chant à la une!*... In *Ciné-Revue* (January 16, 1959), we read: "It's been a long time since I've heard a singer who can do so much with the natural simplicity of modern verbiage. He responds to the blows that life deals us with his heart and his blood." From *Regards* (February, 1959): "His icy humor, his blasé lucidity, and even the little accents of bitter sadism bring to mind a certain biting journalism. It goes without saying that this is a pretty sickly atmosphere he conjures up. But Gainsbourg is no dupe: he's looking for the exit sign that will lead him away from the disenchanted cynicism of *Les Trichuers*." On November 22, 1958, Claude Sarraute, in Le Monde, recounts: "His performances are very Dean-Sagan, very à la mode and cleverly rendered. Tranquil, yet with an assured confidence, the disenchanted voice of this child of his generation, this former back-up pianist, sings of the intoxication of the senses, alcohol, and the velocity of life – impressions that seem almost painful for him to recall as he is planted there behind the microphone. His neurosis and his timid aggression denote a sensibility, an anxiety pregnant with even more possibilities yet to be exploited. What a fantastic surprise."

---

[12] "Machin" can be translated several ways – a thing, a thingamajig, etc... (T.N.)

Journalist Eve Dessarre, in *France-Observateur*, breaks a story towards the end of 1958 that is way ahead of anything her colleagues are doing: "Serge Gainsbourg, or the delirium of solitude." Here are a few chosen excerpts:

> *Yesterday, hardly anybody paid attention to him. At Le Milord l'Arsouille, the club run by Francis Claude, he was the house pianist [...] Today, he sings his own songs, and listening to them is enough to send a shiver up your spine because these "machins"[12] (Gainsbourg's own term), of which he speaks express a cold violence, frenzied but perfectly logical and calculated. He's a pale lad with ears that stick out and a nose that devours his face, with a red mouth twisted into a frown. It's like sitting in front of a Pierrot Lunaire who's mined the depths of despair to such a precise point that one can but laugh in unison at both him and the rest of the crowd.*

"La Jambe de bois (Friedland)" had already been blacklisted by the RTF.[13] Are they afraid that former soldiers and disabled warriors will be offended? Do they see the song as too anti-militaristic, considering that de Gaulle, now back in power, is trying to control the events in Algeria?

Gainsbourg takes great pleasure in responding:

> *"I'm very happy that these types of things bother them. When I'm singing at Le Milord or Les Trois Baudets, I'm simply gloating. People may give me snide looks [...] but why shouldn't a song illustrate something horrible? The surrealists afforded themselves this luxury in literature. Did Goya try to hide he horror in his paintings? (He lights a cigarette, tempting to calm his fidgety hands) This is also the state of modern life, and it doesn't mean you have to take everything so seriously. I'm a painter. I'm thirty years old. I felt terrible about myself and so many others like me who've wasted their time trying to do other things. It makes me sick to see all these people frittering away their time on jobs that they have absolutely no interest in doing. I'm trying to knock some sense into all these people and all the absurd jobs they've created. Just like the metro clerk in my song, spending day after day punching holes and more holes and more little tiny holes..."*

Gainsbourg detests sentimental songs, as we'll see later: "Before, I just hated pop songs, pure and simple. I never listened to the radio." Then come these pointed remarks from a journalist about his misogyny and his love life:

[13] Radiodiffusion-Télévision Française – A major French media outlet. (T.N.)

[14] A satirical and political French newspaper. (T.N.)

Suddenly the face relaxes and the voice becomes normal, almost that of a thirty-year old adolescent: "After a while, women just became an encumbrance. In all my solitude, I just don't know what to do with them. I've always been a loner, even when I was a kid."

In retrospect, Gainsbourg would say: "My first record came out too soon. It was dark. Too dark. And nobody wanted to have that record around the house." Still, he was able to count on the support of an influential supporter. Two weeks earlier, Boris Vian had begun his collaboration with *Le Canard enchaîné*[14] with a defense of George Brassens entitled "Hey music fans, get ready to be lambasted!" (and in fact, he dug into them for not appreciating the last LP by Tonton Georges, which included "Le phonographe du phonographe," "La femme de Hector," etc.). On November 12, he offends them again, delivering this dithyrambic article on the album *Du Chant à la une*:

DU CHANT A LA UNE: SERGE GAINSBOURG

Come along, all you readers or listeners, those of you ready to rail against all those phony songs and fake artists. Empty your pockets and run to the record shops, and demand that the owner give you a copy of the new Philips B 76447 B... This isn't any payola: I don't work for Philips any longer, and even if I did I'd be telling you the same thing.

It's the first 33 rpm from a witty individual named Gainsbourg, Serge, born in Paris on April 2, 1928. As for me, I'm hoping it won't be his last. As for you, well, you're the ones who can make sure it's not his last. An album is costly to make, and it's also costly to launch a new artist, especially when the owners of the record shops, drowning in a sea of mediocre product and paralyzed by rising sales tax, no longer have the time to listen to what the record companies send them.

So what will you hear on this disc?

First of all – honoring those who are often forgotten – you'll hear Gainsbourg's back-up players, thick as thieves and swinging together under the direction of Alain Goraguer, who provides the orchestration for the nine cuts on the album. Technically speaking, each one easily ranks a 17 to

---

[15] "This black apathy that grips me... whenever we're together..." (T.N.)

19 on a scale of 20, in spite of a piano sometimes poorly tuned. But that's not the fault of Goraguer: in a recording session, a piano should be tuned to a vibraphone.

You'll hear, tucked away in the middle of one side of the album, a song sure to disturb you: "Ce mortel ennui qui me vient... quand je suis près de toi..."[15]

You'll hear three absolute technical triumphs (phrasing, style, cadence, etc.): "Le poinçonneur des Lilas," somber, feverish, and lovely, has also been done by Les Frères Jacques, who are quite admirable. But listen to the real author do it. It's the prototype of powerful popular song that's missing among artists like Yves Montand. "Douze belles dans la peau" is also of superb quality. Michèle Arnaud sings it rather well, I believe. Jean-Claude Pascal also gives it a go: an homage to his good taste. "La femme des uns sous le corps des autres," with its South American rhythms, is also both a bitter and exuberant success.

By the way, if some numbskull wants to accuse Gainsbourg of pessimism, I'll permit myself to ask this same halfwit if he really loves pleonasm that much, and if, by chance, he really listened to the tune...

You'll hear "Ronasrd 58," not as imaginative, but still a worthwhile jazz number that's not some dated piece like the ones we currently hear in France that try to evoke the spirit of jazz from 1935 (which would be just fine if it were 1935).

You'll hear "La recette de l'amour fou" and you'll remember, since I'm going to tell you, that Gainsbourg regrets but one thing, which is not having been able to know the director of the Ecole universelle of surrealism, André Breton.

You'll also find "L'alcool," "Du jazz dans le ravin," and "Le Charleston des déménageurs de piano." This last tune is a great illustration of just what the piano can do, and it's simply delicious for those who play or those who simply like to listen. Still, from time to time, we should consider those who actually do the work of moving...

And after having heard all that, the phonies among you will tell me that Gainsbourg has a weak singing voice. And while it might be a bit muted or too nasal, remember that he's not singing opera. You want opera? Go buy some Xavier Depraz. Gainsbourg might remind you, now and then, of Phillipe Clay. Yes, because their voices have a similar timbre. And so what? Gainsbourg also has that tense and biting quality you find with Clay.

You'll also probably tell me that this young lad is a bit skeptical, that it is wrong to see everything in such dark terms, that there's nothing "constructive" in his work... (sure... fine... if that's what you say).

To which I would respond that a skeptic who writes words and music like this, well, you had better give him a second listen before just grouping him in with the other blasé artists of the nouvelle vague... It's still much more interesting than some idiotic enthusiast eager to attack whatever displeases him...

And after all, this is 1958. We're capable of coming up with something better than images of baroque pavilions with bluish-green cats staring down at us from the rooftops.

Still, there's something missing on this album. One song, perhaps Gainsbourg's best: a little love ditty about a cannonball and a wooden peg-leg searching for a home.

It's a piece called "Friedland."

Gainsbourg's already recorded it.

But alas, it's not part of this album. You'll have to go to Milord l'Arsouille to hear Gainsbourg sing it.

They must have taken it off the disc in order not to displease the good king Charles XI.

Nevertheless, if I am not mistaken, might not Freidland become the Usurper?

Boris Vian

GAINSBOURG: "When the article appeared, my first reaction was to take an eraser and see if could wipe out my name... I did this because I just couldn't believe my eyes. I was a bit of an idiot!"

SYLVIE RIVET: *"One day Boris said to me: "I'd have given ten years of my life to have been able to write 'La jambe de bois!'" This surrealist tune was by no means popular and everyone seemed indifferent towards it, except for Boris. Serge almost fainted when I repeated this to him!"*

It's high time that we introduce this new and essential character in the life of Serge, who is at a major turning point in 1958-59: Sylvie Rivet, his publicist "de luxe."

"De luxe" because we're talking not only about a very beautiful woman, but also because she represents a mélange of all the characteristics Serge admires most: class, humor, elegance, and charm. Printed on the calling card of this former flight attendant are the words "Director of public relations for the Philips recording company".

SYLVIE RIVET: *"Serge was kind, and very amicable about everything. He earned almost nothing at Milord l'Arsouille, maybe three or four thousand old francs that they would fork out at the end of each night. After that, he'd invite somebody over to drink and he was broke again. He'd borrow some money from me for a cab and return it the next day. Then, it would start all over again.... He had only one suit, a Prince of Whales, and at the end of the evening he would put in under his mattress as a way of ironing it out! I remember one day when we were leaving my place together. It was right after he'd released "Le poinçonneur de Lilas," and people were hanging out their windows. Someone had obviously recognized him and said "Hey, come look! That's Gainsbourg coming by!" So I said to him, "You see. People do recognize you!" And he responded: "Yeah, because of my big ears"..."*

The job of a publicist, although maybe less specialized than today (there is only a single TV channel, a few local stations, Paris-Inter and a few other state run radio sites), is still no less arduous when it comes to launching a new artist. In the dailies, the space reserved for pop music is extremely limited. Compared to the number of magazines that are devoted to the cinema (we are in truly in a golden age, with journals like *Ciné-Revue*, *Ciné-Monde*, etc.), television publicity is really in its infancy (*La semaine radiophonique* was in charge of producing a meager number of programs). Music covered by the press is non-existent, with the exception of *Discographie Française* (essentially a professional journal) and *Music-Hall*, a monthly which is more or less infiltrated by the big record labels with articles often written by the publicists themselves. In an issue dated October, 1958 (it actually appears in September) a page of advertising, which also includes some publicity for Ricet Barrier, presents Gainsbourg as a "poet of both the bizarre and of black humor." The next month, Serge finds himself on the back cover (traditionally paid for by Philips – a form of publicity that is barely disguised if at all), again alongside Ricet Barrier.

During the months of autumn, "Hello, Le soleil brille…" is still among the best selling tunes, as is "Si tu vas à Rio" by Dario Moreno, as well as "Mon manège à moi" by Edith Piaf. People are also dancing to the Champs version of "Tequila." For the reopening of Les Trois Baudets, Jacques Canetti has some amusing marketing ideas that are well ahead of their time. First of all, with the exception of Raymond Devos, who has head billing, he presents a number of new talents, including Gainsbourg, Simone Langlois, the humorist René Cousinier, Ricet Barrier, and Béart, the "vedette Américaine."[16] The year is 1959, and the event is billed as Opus 109, whose underlying meaning implies "this year's new blood."

> JACQUES CANETTI: *"I said to Serge, "You should stop by Trois Baudets. You're just the kind of artist I'm looking for." It was quite funny, especially because he was completely unknown. Shortly thereafter, Serge agreed to come and play. Michèle Arnaud was none too happy to see Gainsbourg traipsing around my club, but he was no longer anybody's protégé. He did as he pleased."*

Father Canetti's second bit of pseudo-marketing involves asking Boris Vian to write some introductory texts which could be read onstage by ten "speakerines"[17] hired expressly for the occasion. For Serge's introduction, Vian composes the following:

> *Take a thirty-year-old lad with a gift for painting, music, and song – let's just say gifted for life in general. Put him in a room with a piano and a pen and let him ruminate, let the fires burn, let him make his little hole, a hole that will become huge in the world of music.[18] Serge Gainsbourg!*

---

[16] A French term that refers to the person who performs after the main act. (T.N.)

[17] The term "speakerines" might be brought a bit more up-to-date. Canetti, who borrowed the term referring to those pretty young women who introduce television programs, had hired ten young ladies, for the most part models or debutant actresses, who had exotic names like Carole Grove, Juliette Vilno, Chan Tung, Vinka Parese, etc.

[18] Again, this is Vian showing off his genius for wordplay. The little hole refers to "les petits trous," a key phrase from one of Gainsbourg's most recognizable masterpieces: Le poinçonneur de Lilas.

The audience at Milord is rather bourgeois and snobbish, while that at Les Trois Baudets is much more working-class. The space, which can accommodate up to 350 spectators, is rather cold when Serge appears to do a few numbers, especially "Le poinçonneur" and "La recette de l'amour fou." Around November 24, or 26, they start to do live recordings at the theatre destined for distribution among a secret and privileged few. On December 15, Guy Dornand recounts the concert in *Libération*, and citing the author of *Journal d'une femme de chambre*, he spends some time talking about Gainsbourg:

> *This Mirabeau of song, who's coming off as the rival of Léo Ferré, will he continue on his path or prefer to be first and foremost the poet of "Poinçonneur des Lilas" and "Ronsard 58?" This is surely a man of artistic temperament and a gifted composer. But is he right, with that pale face of his and that flat voice, to try to also be a performer?*

Always chasing after work, his schedule doesn't leave him a moment of respite: after finishing his songs at Trois Baudets, he heads back down to Palais-Royal, seeing as he does a double at Milord. This is the dominant rhythm from the months of November to December of 1958, punctuated by a few meetings with the press. On November 25, Serge is invited to be on Radio Luxembourg for the show *Super Boum*. Directed by Gilbert Carpentier and hosted by Maurice Biraud, the show will also feature Jeanne Moreau. His songs are played infrequently on the radio, where the censorship is still ferocious: at the RTF, they slap an infamous stamp across anything that might incite a loosening of moral standards, and all this at the time of Ferré's "Temps du plastique," Brassens' "Pornographe," and our very own hero's "Ronsard 58." On television, he appears on the New Year's Eve variety show hosted by Roger Pierre and Jean-Marc Thibault, which also features Danielle Darrieux, Gilbert Bécaud, Raymond Devos, Guy Béart, and the couple that everyone's talking about: a young up-and-comer named Sacha Distel and star of stars Brigitte Bardot, who dance a pas de deux... In the middle of this *Who's Who* of music and screen, Serge sings "La recette de l'amour fou." Keeping a careful eye on all this bustle, one might believe that his career is well on track, and like Sputnik, recently propelled into orbit, he will soon find his audience. But that's nothing of the sort. 1959 will be a year full of hope, but also one full of disenchantment.

six

An Anthracitic Mood

The year of 1959 starts like all the others finish: Serge is gallop-
ing down Boulevard Clichy towards Rue Beaujolais. At Les Trois
Baudets, where he does both matinées and evenings, the poster is changed:
gone is Devos – now they are clapping not only for Gainsbourg, but Béart,
Barrier, and Les Cinq Pères. From February 17 to19, Serge gets a little taste
of the long days on the road that are waiting for him beginning in March,
where he'll perform in Geneva with Raymond Devos, Béart, Barrier, Simone
Langlois, Lafleur and Bernard Haller. Among the spectators, we find one
Pierre Koralnik, whom Serge will work with several years down the road on
the musical *Anna*. He sums up the situation rather well...

> PIERRE KORALNIK: *"I saw this man with a crew-cut in a tight-fitting blue
> suit, really ugly, a sort of early version of E.T, and he hadn't impressed me.
> It was more intelligent, more subtle than the whole Rive Gauche thing, but
> it was still that."*

At Milord, Claude Sylvain, wife of owner Francis Claude, rejoins the company. Such is the case until the March 3, when the show continues without

her. Meanwhile, the recording session for "La jambe de bois (Friedland)," on January 12 with Goraguer and his orchestra, don't render the piece any more commercial. Finally, on February 21, during a broadcast of *Chez vous ce soir*, Serge does "L'alcool," one of the coldest and most maudlin of his first songs.

Among his playmates at Les Trois Baudets, we find Ricet Barrier and Les Cinq Pères. The first is already a big star who has all of France in stitches with "La servante du château" and "La java des Gaulois." The second group, which includes Philippe Doyen and Fernand Moulin, is composed of veterans, whose debut at Les Trois Baudets goes back to 1948, when they still called themselves Les Compagnons de la Musique, and before Francis Blanche renamed them Les Cinq Pères.

> RICET BARRIER: *"Our careers were all launched by Canetti: One might say that I was in the pink with "Servante du château," while Serge, with his "Poinçonneur," remained grey in a black and white world. We would often have rather tumultuous discussions after the shows. Gainsbourg would go on about how ugly he found himself. He hated his big ears. He told me he wanted to have an operation, and I said: "You're a fool! Keep your big ears – they're the biggest in all of show biz.""*

> JACQUES CANETTI: *"It's true that the crowd really didn't take to him. Serge had the same attitude as Boris Vian. The inability to be seductive onstage is just a sign that one is not ready, that one does not yet possess that essential sympathy one needs to draw in the audience. At least Gainsbourg was aware of this. He had no illusions. It was the same way in the studio. He would continually laugh at himself, and over time, the recordings got better and better. He was a perfectionist. On the other hand, while onstage, he took this 'I don't give a damn attitude' to new heights. A lot of artists of Serge's caliber take themselves too seriously. This wasn't the case at all with Gainsbourg."*

In *Bonjour Philippine*, from the February-March, 1959 issue, Boris Vian adds another layer to the to the story of Ricet Barrier and Gainsbourg:

> *Born on April 2, 1928, as public rumor would have it, since which time Gainsbourg has already produced a substantial quantity of work, this new artist has shined brilliantly among the newly discovered talents promoted by Philips in 1958. Truthfully speaking, and not wanting to savagely trample all over the merits of Philips (my feet aren't big enough for that), it's*

a charming blonde lady by the name of Michèle Arnaud who gave Serge, her accompanist for four years, his chance to start performing on stage. Thanks to his employer, Canetti, and Canetti's partner, Denis Bourgeois, Gainsbourg was able to produce his first album, but not without the help of pianist-arranger Alain Goraguer. [...]

On your feet, Serge Gainsbourg. You are accused of writing ferocious and scathing songs, of interpreting life in the darkest of terms, etc.

Serge Gainsbourg has no need to respond. Better that he continue to write songs. During that time, I will answer for him. In any case, the accusations are absurd. Do we congratulate a blind man for being blind? No, we feel sorry for him. So are we going to reproach Gainsbourg for opening his eyes? That would be just as ridiculous! Now I can already envision a type of fat-headed listener with a big belly full of optimism protesting that all is well, and that this youth of today is full of hatred for all that is beautiful. Ha Ha! I say directly to this listener [...] your big, fat belly blocks your view - either that or it's your preconceived ideas and your lazy conformity. Let's look at an example: you criticize Serge for this song entitled: "La femme des un sous le corps des autres." Might I permit myself to pose a question: did Gainsbourg invent adultery? Did the word not exist before him? (quite a while before, I dare say).

—Well, nobody's forcing him to choose that subject matter, responds the die-hard romantic, with that schmaltzy look in his eyes.

—So! I say to him (and now it's I who am the clever one), Could it be that you're touched, dear sir?

And so he stammers to his feet and leaves. I recognize the person that's with him. It's my wife! What a hideous character!

Oh, please, Gainsbourg! Give me "la recette de l'Amour fou!..."

Boris Vian

GAINSBOURG: *"So Boris invites me to his place in Cité Véron, behind le Moulin Rouge, and he tells me, opening a book of lyrics by Cole Porter: "You have the same prosody, the same structural technique and flair for alliteration." I walk away with a new swagger..."*

SYLVIE RIVET: *"Serge idolized Boris Vian. I took him over to Boris' place and left them together. Boris was all alone with his cream-colored piano. Ursula wasn't there. On the door, Boris had tacked up a paper on which he'd written: 'It is only the college of Pataphysicians that is not trying to save the world,' which delighted Gainsbourg. He was very timid, and truly admired Vian. He would later dedicate his first film to him. I don't know what they talked about. They met only that one time. When he left his "master's" house, I didn't ask him a thing. I left him alone with his thoughts, his secrets. Until the day he died, Serge always talked about Vian with a twinkle in his eye."* [1]

After a two-year romance with Darryl F. Zanuck, who had tried to launch a cinematic career for her, Juliette Gréco decides it is time to get ready burst back upon the scene, once again, as a stage performer. Not only a major songstress but one the France's prime muses, Gréco always has a coterie of big names worshipping at her altar, including those from the world of literature (Françoise Sagan, Pierre Mac Orlan, Marguerite Duras, Sartre, and Queneau) as well as the finest names in song (Ferré, Brel, Brassens, Béart). For her comeback, she obviously needs a crack writer, and heads straight to Le Milord and immediately becomes a fan of Gainsbourg, whom she, as does the press, nicknames 'the bat."

GAINSBOURG: *"When we met, I was simply terrified. I was intimidated by this beautiful woman. And I adored her arrogance..."*

PHILIPPE DOYEN: *"The Gainsbourg that I knew at that time was very discrete! The night before his rendezvous with Gréco, he asked us: "Do you think it would be appropriate if I brought her a rose?" We told him "yes," and he did so. It was quite moving, the fact that he actually asked us this question..."*

JULIETTE GRÉCO: *"I'll always remember the day he came to my house with his songs. He was a clueless, frightened, panicked mess. I had some beautiful whiskey glasses, in cut crystal. I served him a drink, but his hands were so shaky and sweaty that he dropped the glass, which shattered at his feet."*

---

[1] To be clear, one must remember that Serge didn't like Vian as a writer: he found his work unreadable. What he appreciated in Vian was his "character above all" (from 20 Ans, compiled by Philippe Adler, June, 1968).

In spring of 1956, Juliette devotes an entire EP to Françoise Sagan, and then another to Guy Béart two years later. In February, 1959, when she releases the EP *Juliette Gréco chante Serge Gainsbourg*, a magnificent and prestigious step for Serge. She is accompanied by André Popp and his orchestra.

RICET BARRIER: *"During that period, people liked to sketch images of a woman seen from behind with her long hair, and on each side of these flowing locks they would trace two half-circles sticking out: a caricature of Gréco kissing Gainsbourg!..."*

JULIETTE GRÉCO: *"The design was in perfectly good taste. What was horrible was the utter meanness of people: this attitude that the public had in regard to Gainsbourg, which is to say: "My God, is he ever ugly! How can this be!" But he had his revenge, and well deserved it was. Nevertheless, this lack of love was in a way responsible for his passing. I found him beautiful. What I found pleasing in his songs was Serge himself. He was a passionate and seductive man, one of great tenderness. I loved "Il était une oie," a sort of cruel but very accurate portrait of certain type of girl. Just because he speaks the truth doesn't make him a misogynist. There wasn't a hint of baseness in Serge, but a grand lucidity. He gave me one of his paintings, the only one that he hadn't destroyed, tossed away, or burned – one of the most beautiful things I have ever seen and which I treasure to this very day."*

Among the other songs on the EP *Juliette Gréco chante Serge Gainsgourg,* there's a version of "La jambe be bois (Friedland)," as well as "Les amours perdues," one of the first songs he wrote in autumn, 1954. Finally, Gréco interprets "L'amour à la papa," a scathing text in which Serge condemns the idiots who lack any "technique":

> *This romance is a fake*
> *The kind of love you make*
> *It's tired and it's flat*
> *You'd best know that*
> *There's better things to do than that*

Evidently, rumors are starting to fly in the realm of the music hall world. And while Gréco today speaks of the perfectly respectful relationship she had with Gainsbourg, they are nonetheless seen walking arm in arm into the most fashionable of establishments.

JULIETTE GRÉCO: *"I would go out with Serge and people looked at me like I was exhibiting some sort of Neanderthal. There was a photo taken at Club Saint-Germain that was distributed worldwide. I was wearing a Chanel suit and Serge had his eyes turned to the side, rather strangely. People looked at us and said: "What's gotten into Gréco? How could she go out with this monster?" It was ridiculous! As for me, I took great pleasure in speaking with him, in listening to him. He was someone whom I adored infinitely."*

Michele Arnaud must undoubtedly be quite bitter seeing her protégé fall into the hands of her rival, Juliette Gréco. But she's not obsessed about it. On her new EP, which also is released at the beginning of the year, she does her own version of "Il était une oie," as well as "Ronsard 58," which she'd been doing for a year onstage at Le Milord.

Jacques Canetti, who as impresario handles the artists for Radio-Programme, launches his show *Opus 109* on the road in France, with a small change in the billing. Such it is that in March, Jacques Brel (accompanied on piano by Gérard Jouannest), Ricet Barrier, Serge Gainsbourg, Les Cinq Pères, and Simone Langlois take to the provinces to assault the public, bolstered by Bernard Haller (doing a mime number), Lafleur (poet, singer, cellist, an all-around crackpot who appears in a kilt), and Preston (an illusionist-humorist).

DENIS BOURGEOIS: *"Radio-Programme monopolized the forty most famous French artists and Canetti scheduled his protégés to play Les Trois Baudets or to tour in the provinces. That's how Serge found himself playing halls much too big, in front of a public that was unaware of him - and believe me, he was drenched in sweat. He wasn't exactly booed off the stage, but often the silence was even worse than that..."*

GAINSBOURG: *"Canetti was a real slave driver. I toured with Brel in the provinces, and we'd show up in these old auditoriums with broken-down pianos. Of course, there was no public address system, so we had to manage with that. From time to time, between gigs, Brel would take me for a spin in his convertible Pontiac, pushing it up to 150 or so. We'd make a game of not crashing ourselves to bits... Interesting, hey? In each town, Brel already had scads of admirers – I don't like the word fan – and he would flagrantly bring down the house. When we'd come out of our hotels, crowds - some men, but especially women - would harangue him for autographs. I'd simply wait in the wings until it was all over. But one day, amongst the throngs, I saw a girl some thirteen or fourteen years-old with a sublime look about her. So she comes up to me, quite intimidated, and says "I came to see you, Mr. Gainsbourg." That really threw me."*

ANDRÉ HALIMI: *"Artistically speaking, I could see that Canetti had real flair. But he was really tough. Rumor had it that he'd ripped off quite a few people. Someone told me about how Brassens had gone to see Canetti in his office and had grabbed him by his tie, full of rage, because the financial figures after one of his tours were completely out of line. Still, Canetti was a man who worked relentlessly and really believed in what he was doing."*

JULIETTE GRÉCO: *"He was intelligent, clever, a great businessman, but I had some very violent discussions with him. One day, while on tour, I arrived a bit late because I'd had some car trouble, and I saw the owner of the place come up to me, drunk with rage, and say, "Where do you get off!..." I told him that I was sorry, and he shoots back: "With what I'm paying you!" And being intrigued, I ask: "What do you mean?" So he tells me some enormous sum I'm supposed to be getting, which left me quite perturbed. It was always like that, for everybody. Patachou actually struck Canetti. I did so myself. It was never a question of money, but simply a matter of dignity."*

JACQUES CANETTI: *"I worked from the principle that what started out as something painful would eventually result in joy. But with Gainsbourg, that joy was never realized – there was always a heaviness weighing things down. Fortunately, he had friends who toured with him, a rich variety of performers on the same bill. But Gainsbourg was essentially a Parisian. He loved Paris and wished to remain there. If there was a reason that I put so much importance on touring, well, it was sort of a mad and gentle insistence - the only way to get my artists known in the provinces."*

The order of appearance for the artists in the *Opus 109* tour never varies: after Bernard Haller, Ricet Barrier lightens up the atmosphere, an atmosphere that tightens up once again upon the arrival of Gainsbourg, who usually does three or four songs, including "La femme des uns" and "Le poinçonneur." Then comes Lafleur, Simone de Langlois, Les Cinq Pères, and finally Preston, right before the star of the show, Brel. The day after one of the opening nights in Brittany, there's a bit about Serge in *Ouest-France*: "He seems to be oblivious onstage, to the point where one wonders if he is even there." On the other hand, Brel triumphs, singing "Au printemps," "Quand on n'a que l'amour," "L'air de la bêtise," "La bourrée du célibataire," and "Les Flamandes." Later in the same article, we read: "With huge ovations and endless encores, Jacques Brel obtained the success he was due for his formidable talent." Serge is depressed. To his confidant and lover, Sylvie Rivet, he sings his blues:

Quimper, March 5, 1959

This is a nightmarish town. So much rain falls that there is no use in crying to add to the flow. There isn't even a shadow of a real flower in this land, only the hideous flowers on the wallpaper in the rooms.

There's enough melancholy here to last me to till the end of my days.

On March 14, 1959, there's an event that consecrates a particularly remarkable arrival in the tiny world of quality songwriting: Serge takes Le Grand Prix du Disque from the Académie Charles-Cros for his first album, which is awarded to him by Juliette Gréco during a ceremony at the Palais d'Orsay during the International Festival de la Haute Fidélité et de la Stéréophonie. In retrospect, concerning the first twelve months of his career, he would later say: "It all happened too quickly. I was awarded the grand prix for my first disc. Theatrically speaking, I really didn't have a career." Yet on Tuesday, the March 17, at the behest of Juliette Gréco, he appears onstage at the Olympia as a part of the Europe n°1 *Musicorama* show. According to *La Discographie française* (April 1, 1959), Gréco sings four of the songs that he'd just written for her, and then "Leaves the spotlight to her new favorite songwriter." The next day, Serge, quickly returns to join Canetti's tour, finding all his buddies, including Fernand and Les Cinq Pères.

FERNAND MOULIN : *"When Gainsbourg received the Grand Prix du Disque, I don't remember exactly where we were playing, but it must have been a hellhole because there wasn't a thing there, not even the tiniest little café with a bit of charm. Right away, after the show, Gainsbourg tells us: "Get together at the restaurant at the train station!" So when the gang arrived, he had a surprise prepared: he had placed a bottle of cognac on each table to celebrate his win. The next day, I was sick as a dog. My mates had to hold me up onstage so that I could keep my balance."*

BERNARD HALLER: *"We scoured the whole of France, from Brittany to Normandy. Brel was the star of the show but not yet a big name. We would look for little hotels that were only two and a half francs per night. Even though we were broke, Serge would always go to the big hotels. He didn't give a damn. He was sure that he was well on his way and he'd blow big wads of dough on his hotel rooms. Every night I'd watch as he'd peep through his windows. I'd say, "What are you doing?" And he'd reply: "I'm counting them. A soon as I get to 150, I put on my make-up!" He was classy onstage, well shaven, a suit and black tie. He already had the idea of his signature look. Onstage, the rest of us were all lit up with every projector in the house. But when the stage manager introduced Serge, he'd say: "And now, winner of the Grand Prix de l'Académie Charles-Cros, Serge Gainsbourg!" And wham!... There he was with a single spotlight highlighting his face. Pale as he was with those ears of his sticking out, he was like Dracula under the lights, monstrous! The crowd would shriek, but that didn't disconcert him in the least. He started his set and would finish with "Le poinçonneur." He had already become a provocateur, and knew that he had that demented face, which he made brilliant use of, accenting all of his faults."*

GÉRARD JOUANNEST: *"It was me who accompanied him on tour. I also played behind Simone Langlois, Les Cinq Pères, and others. Canetti paid me nothing for that. A lot has been said about Brel's stage fright, but Serge's was even worse. I remember it being almost necessary to actually push him onto the stage. If not, he didn't even want to go out. Me, I was already there playing, and it made me nauseous to watch his arrival. He was so panicked... He had an unreal stance before the mic. His knees and his hand would shake, and if he could have I'm sure he'd have hidden himself somewhere. I'd tell him: "Just calm down. You can't pull people into your performance like that." But it was no use. Brel thought that Serge had the possibility of being a real success if he could just be a bit more sure of himself. He stopped singing in public not long after because of this panic. At the time, it was certainly not a matter of alcohol. He was quite well-behaved, like a child at first communion! I also remember travelling together. Brel would drive, I would ride shotgun, and behind us were Gainsbourg and Ricet. That tour was a fiasco. The halls were often only half full, sometimes almost empty, and Brel would say: "O.K. guys. We're not working tonight. I'll pay you." When there was absolutely nobody, it wasn't Canetti who paid, but Brel."*

Even with the weight of the Charles-Cros prize behind him, the sales of Serge's *La chant à la une!*... remain quite modest. Each night, the nightmare begins anew when he walks onstage. At the end of March, after a concert in Toulouse, Brel quits the tour, which continues on with Béart as the headliner. Before leaving, Brel gives Serge a gold Dupont lighter a few days before his birthday. Serge tells Sylvie Rivet about the last little spin the two of them take together:

Toulouse, March 24, 1959

It's now six in the morning and I've just gotten home. We were out pub crawling with Brel! I'm happy. I'm going to sleep and rest all day in this room [...] Brel has gone off now, taking with him his friendships, his litanies, and his guitars, all in good will. I'm going to find myself alone, but what a boisterous and charming fellow...

A few days earlier, Gainsbourg, Brel, Jouannest, Barrier and a few others had dined together after a show at a restaurant in Poitiers... There's a group of girls at the table next to them. Serge spots the prettiest and points her out to his comrades, but he's too shy to get up and do anything about it despite his friends' encouragement. The group decides to then leave and hit a club for last drink. Once there, he finds the girl and her friends. Joking around, Brel gets them to laugh, saying: "Let me do my impression of Gainsbourg onstage for you!" With his feet pointed inward, his knees bent, and holding a mic in his trembling hands, he fools around for a moment doing "Le poinçonneur." Everybody breaks up laughing, including Serge, who finally asks the girl to dance. Then when she gets up, everyone notices that she has a club foot. All of the sudden, Brel's joke has turned sour. Serge, embarrassed but always the gentleman, later offers to accompany her back to her room. At the hotel, the whole gang, in stitches, is waiting at the elevator for Serge. Each of them takes a turn cruelly imitating the girl limping around and making fun of his conquest of the poor, wounded woman. Unfortunately, it's the hotel porter who appears and ... he's limping. Second gaffe... The next day, the gang gets ready to leave town and Gainsbourg suggests that they stop and say goodbye to the pretty girl, who works nearby. He gives the address to Brel, who drives. When they arrive, they discover she that is a salesperson in a shoe store!

> GAINSBOURG: *"I never really got Brel's prosody, but the astounding thing about him was that he lived entirely for his craft. When he wasn't singing, he'd hit the depths of depression. In his dressing room, just minutes before going onstage, he be playing his guitar and composing new songs."*

The group of *Opus 109* is back on the road again, towards Italy, with, as always, Ricet Barrier, Simone Langlois, Lafleur, and Gut Béart. Simone Langlois had made her debut in 1949, at the age of 13, onstage at Les Trois Baudets. A famous interpreter of Brel, whose pieces she had sung when he was still a nobody, Langlois' repertory in 1959 includes some lovely versions of "Au printemps" and "Je ne sais pas." Two years later, of course, she will create her feminine interpretation of "Ne me quitte pas."

Lafleur had known Gainsbourg for a long time. He'd met him at Milord when he was accompanying Michèle Arnaud. Lafleur himself would make the rounds of the cabarets, as many as five a night, with his kilt and cello. This prize winner of the former conservatory Concerts Pasdeloup had a little hit at the end of the 1950s with a number entitled "Les ratés de la bagatelle." Canetti, always up to his old tricks, had also hired him for the tour because he owned car, specifically a Peugeot 403 – an automobile that was truly in-dispensable when it came to saving money...

> RENÉ LAFLEUR: *"At the beginning, I'd bring along Simone Langlois, and in there other car there were Béart, Ricet Barrier, and Gainsbourg. After a few days, they joined me in my 403 and we drove through the whole of Italy together. They were quite happy, he and Simone, because I drove them around everywhere."*

For Serge, just as for Béart and the others, the tour ends up being a total flop. The Italian public, used to great big voices, is unforgiving. In Rome, the press announces: "Una serata di music–hall con i *Tre asinelli* di Canetti," but the venues are almost empty, with the exception of Piccolo Teatro in Milan, which is packed full. Fortunately, there are the joys of tourism...

> SIMONE LANGLOIS: *"Serge was extremely elegant, and always wore a tie. I was the only girl in the group and I thought he was cute. But then*

when he started to chase after me, well, he smoked so much that at the moment we kissed, I told him: "No! I don't want to!" During that tour in Italy we blew all our money, and when we went back we owed Canetti, our tour manager, 600,000 francs! With Serge, I visited ancient Rome and Le Palais Médicis in Florence, and he would explain the history of the paintings. We enjoyed several truly extraordinary weeks. I remember that gallery in Milan where he'd had fun letting me run ahead of him. I was very blond and very young, and all the Italian men chased after me, so Serge would arrive with a ferocious look on his face like he was going to give them a good ass-kicking. I'd cry out: "It's my brother, it's my brother!" And all the Italians would beat a hasty retreat!"

RENÉ LAFLEUR: "We'd walk around in Siena in the middle of the night, with all the shutters closed. It was like something out of the middle-ages. In Rome, I took them to the Coliseum. Serge was eager to get to the top, but once there he was struck with vertigo. He couldn't move, and I had to carry him down on my back!"

After a final gala at Turin, the chattel of *Opus 109* does a few more shows in the provinces before heading back to Paris, most notably in Toulon, the night before Easter, when the crowd is very sparse. Serge, with that awkwardness of his that creates an uneasiness with the public, and "his long, limp hands and eyes perpetually lowered," appears very strange to the journalist Line Brun from *La République – Toulon*: "Certain songs of his didn't go over with the audience in the way they do over the airwaves," she adds, rather snidely, before recounting how he would cut short his number when some money was tossed onstage...

RICET BARRIER: "After that concert we went bar hopping and got hammered with some chicks. They were hostesses, but they were also married to the servers in the club! Serge had spent about two hours trying to hit on one of them and he became enraged. I saw him screaming from the sidewalk: "In a couple of years those girls will be trying to rip off my underwear!""

RENÉE LAFLEUR: "Serge had hang-ups about his looks. He was very uncomfortable... His hands would tremble and he'd turn red as a tomato when a pretty girl would pass by. In fact, at that time, it was the women who'd hurl themselves at him. They were very tender with him, wanted to *protect him. He and Sylvie were very discrete. No one could have guessed what was up between them. He was never the one who took the initiative to start things or to break up..."*

It's now the spring of 1959, and everyone's listening to Peggy Lee's "Fever" (in French, "39 de fièvre" was sung by Catarina Valente among others), "Dansons mon amour (Hava Nagila)" by Dalida, and "Fais ta prière (Tom Dooley)" by Les Compagnons de la Chanson. Facing the tide of real rockers, who detest the bourgeoisie and only listen only to Gene Vincent, they offer up the "Rock bien lavé" or "whitewashed rock n' roll" (as the publicity from New York dubs it) of Ricky Nelson. In Paris, people dance the sega, and in New York, the cha-cha. Everybody's crazy about Brenda Lee. The rumor is that she is a dwarf some thirty-five years old, while in truth she's only fourteen. In the monthly *Music-Hall*, Jacques Canetti, who's already moving on to newer pastures, presents his latest discoveries, his "four-leaf clover" as he call it: Pia Colombo, Roger Riffard, Pierre Brunet, and Anne Sylvestre.

As for Serge, he's dealing with other worries: namely getting ready to enter the studio again in Blanqui to record his second album. Among the eight titles that he lays down in six days, before picking up again between May 12 and June 4, we find two cuts already covered earlier by other artists: "Jeunes femmes et vieux messieurs" (Michèle Arnaud), and "L'amour à la papa" (Juliette Gréco). With just a bass, wood blocks, and his glacial voice, Serge really captures the minimalism of "Fever":

> *Juke-box*
> *Juke-box*
> *I snap my fingers at the juke-box*
> *When over your body they don't linger*
> *I don't know what to do with my ten fingers*
> *No, I don't know what to do with my ten fingers*
> *So I snap, snap, snap them standing*
> *At the juke-box*

In above-cited "Le clauqer de doigts," we find united for the first time the ingredients that Serge would master so perfectly in "Ford Mustang" or "Qui es 'in' qui est 'out' ": a sort of exploding "franglais," decomposed into purely rhythmic onomatopoeia. In the daily publication *Combat*, he confides:

I knew about this juke-box, between Blanche and Pigalle – a pretty shabby thing, really – that really left me feeling depressed by the brutal nature it shared with all coin-operated machines and electric games, usually surrounded by a groups of young punks. It was right when I would come out of Les Trois Baudets, before going to Milord l'Arsouille. The young people you'd find there were like the ones you'd see everywhere else, not so many French, but a lot of Americans, English, Italians.

Really, Serge is a big fan of pinball, some say out of shyness, seeing how it lets him turn his back to the other clients... Furthermore, certain Rive Gauche literary foibles pop up in "La nuit d'octobre," a poem by Musset that's set to a proto-samba backing. This is of great displeasure to the old grumps in the crowd who prefer their Musset to be more maudlin.

> It's your smile and your verse
> Your look that devours
> Which has taught me to curse
> Until happiness flowers

LOUIS LAIBE: *"When he pulled that stunt I said to him: "You bastard! Instead of using one of our old songs that we wrote together at Madame Arthur's, you go and dig up some old Musset that's in public domain so you don't have to pay for the rights. Then you stick your own music over it. What's more, you stole the idea from me!" Actually, when I was accompanied on piano, first by father Ginsburg and later by Serge, I would often read Musset's poem to my clients at the end of the night... I'd ask them to play me one of Chopin's mazurkas because I knew Musset had been George Sand's lover, and that Georges Sand left him for Chopin..."*

Goraguer has a blast using swaying rhythm and clever arrangements for the brass, like on "Mambo miam miam," inspired by a rhythm made popular by Pupi Campa and Perez Prado, and later popularized by Dario Moreno ("Oh qué! Mambo") and in the movies by Bernard Borderie's likeable idiocy *Ces dames préfèrent le mambo*, starring Eddie Constantine.

> Pirate or madman
> They all run for high land
> And those who aren't shrewd
> Will die wanting for food
> Soldier or poet
> Sadness, you'll know it
> The misery and strife
> Of a poor gutless life

For "L'anthracite," as Eric Godart points out, "the flavor of the text plays perfect counterpoint to the kitschy side of the music, a sort of nod to those Hollywood productions with young, beautiful slaves from the Orient dancing lasciviously for some despot." A despot who's mulling over some very somber thoughts:

If it's laughter I incite
It's that my humor's anthracite
My turns of phrase provoke your ire
But your disdain just fans my fire
But beware, my little doll
Of this black humor after all
I'll unveil the beast within
The cry of evil and of sin

As far as misogyny is concerned, Serge needs lessons from no one, and this time he pushes the envelope even further. Listen to "Indifférente" over the music of Goraguer:

In your eyes I can see mine
You're lucky
They lend you a brilliance so refined
What does time matter
What does the wind scatter
Better your disappearance
Than your incoherence

On the cover of the second album, released in July of 1959, we see Serge ready for everything, carrying in his hands a bouquet of roses and a pistol (the cover also includes these liner notes: "Those who like my songs get flowers, others get a taste of my gunpowder"). No more songs about little mundane jobs, no more poinçonneur, no piano mover, no trivial stories, no more "jazz dans le ravin," and no more dreamy illusions: it's now a matter of impossible love, jealousy, sex in dark corners, and break-ups, like the one in "Adieu, creature!":

Farewell, dear creature
I'm heading off to nature
And don't feel sad and lost
Some night our paths again will cross

Interviewed by Paris-Inter, Gainsbourg is, already, getting quite snooty about the success of "Le poinçonneur": "Really, what bothers me the most is that among my songs, it's the one I consider the simplest, and it only succeeded as sort of an obsessive fad." They announce the release of his recordings in stereo, and you'd better believe it's a big deal because he mentions it in his correspondence: "Listening to myself in stereo is very amusing, even impressive. It brings my songs together, especially when one considers my lack of vocal prowess." Now there's an artist who doesn't know how to sell himself, you must be thinking, and at Philips, the poor Denis Bourgeois has trouble defending his protégé, who's lagging far behind Brel, Béart or Brassens when it comes the company's priorities. His style is too aggressive, introverted, jazzy, and without concession. Nobody understands just quite how to take him.

> CLAUDE DEJACQUES: *"At that time, we were a terrific flop on the radio. Programmers would simply say no to us. I found his songwriting amazing: he could swing better than anybody. I think that his Slavic origins play a role in all that. Through jazz, and his father, who also was a pianist, he inherited a sense of cadence and tempo that was completely unique. For the musicians in the studio it was a blast."*

> ALAIN GORAGUER: *"During that period, there was a totally artistic ambiance in the studio. We came in order to make a great record, even if the conditions were sometimes deplorable. For example, in the studios at Philips on Boulevard Blanqui, we had only a three track and couldn't record on the weekends. It was more or less a theatre, a huge room used by le Syndicat du livre[2] for its meetings. But the vibe was so artistic. We never talked about sales. At least not out of shame. That would come later."*

Goraguer, the jazzman, often resorts to fits of screaming. Serge has the tendency to blather on about his passion for painting, to which Goraguer responds: "Well if you really want to paint then do it!" Then come the reviews of the second album, which, as we will see, are totally negative. Furthermore, Boris Vian, with whom Serge could have possibly collaborated in the future (there is some vague talk of the two of them writing some songs for Salvador) is no longer there to defend him: he dies a brutal death at the Cinéma Le Marbeuf on June 23, 1959, during the beginning of a private screening of *J'irai cracher sur vos tombes*, a film based on his novel written twelve years earlier under the pseudonym of Vernon Sullivan: "His head dropped back, and as his heart failed his huge carcass slid down in the chair." Alas, the stunned Collège du Pataphysique loses its most ruthless soldier, much to the chagrin of Raymond Queneau.

> JEAN-PIERRE LELOIR: *"For my generation, it wasn't God the Father, but rather God the Son. For one thing, he was a master critic when it came to jazz. He wrote articles for Jazz Hot and was the artistic director for Philips. I met him when I was a young photographer. He really intimidated me and I didn't dare speak because after all, this was Boris Vian, a living legend, someone always talked about in the press, and who, in his own way, had really pissed off the bourgeoisie. He had such a presence! I ran into him a while before his death, in the do-it-yourself department of a BHV. He stood there admiring the floating devices of a toilet flusher, which was no longer made of welded brass but rather polystyrene. He showed it to me and said, "It's not bad, really."*

Let's move on to the reviews of the second album, and remember that they are published just months after Serge wins the Grand Prix de l'Académie Charles-Cros. It is almost as if the expectations resulting from this distinction arouse suspicion, notably in the pages of *Marie-Claire*: "His desire to write intelligent songs makes him run the risk of becoming quite boring. That would be a pity. He would never realize the splendid career that we expect from him." This is the same *Marie-Claire* that would make up for this in October, 1959: "They say he's diabolical, but he's really intelligent and lucid. They portray him as disturbing, when rather he is disturbed. People believe that he's cynical when in fact he's timid. He makes his way alone down the arduous path that the songwriter treks. But advance he does."

In *La Dépêche du Midi*, from October 6, we read: "The latest of Serge Gainsbourg's songs have lost their originality and much of their power. They are, like the songs of so many others, weak and banal." The undated and anonymous piece continues: "He portrays himself as a disturbing character (which he certainly is not, but he nevertheless plays the role), a morbid intellectual nourished on Sade, Poe and Baudelaire. His thoughts, he claims in his songs, are as black as anthracite, and his heart a den of vipers. [...] But so much systematic darkness grows tiresome after a while! Musically

---

[2] Union for the workers and printers in the press. (T.N.)

and sentimentally, this parade of bitterness, from "Jeunes femmes et vieux messieurs" to "Adieu créature!," just ends up being monotonous. As for poor Musset, his "Nuit d'Octobre" gains nothing from being drenched in a bath of mediocre mambo!"

On July 9, 1959, in *France-Soir*, France Roche announces that François Truffaut (who breaks through that year with the film *Les 400 Coups*) asks Gainsbourg to write the music for his next film, *Jules et Jim*, but history has deprived us of the details of this meeting. Just a day earlier, Serge had been invited by Juliette Gréco to the RTF radio broadcast Soyez les bienvenus, from which the following dialogue is culled:

> *Juliette Gréco: Are you aggressive?*
> *Serge Gainsbourg: Yes, a bit.*
> *J.G.: Why?*
> *S.G: For me, it's a front.*
> *J.G.: What is the thing you hate most in the world?*
> *S.G.: Stupidity.*
> *J.G.: And what gives you the most pleasure?*
> *S.G.: Painting.*
> *J.G.: Is that your true love?*
> *S.G.: Yes. The one and only.*
> *J.G.: How do you see yourself?*
> *S.G.: At the moment, I'm no big deal. Just hopeful.*

A young hopeful who sings "Le claquer de doigts" on July 10 for *Discorama*, hosted by Denise Glaser on France's only television station. A few weeks later, Serge hits the road once more for the final Canetti/Opus 109 tour. It's the year when François Deguelt sings "Je te tendrai les bras" and Sacha Distel croons "Oh quelle nuit."

From September 4 to 10, Serge finds himself headlining at Les Trois Baudets in a program that brings him back together with Ricet Barrier, Les Cinq Pères, Roger Comte, Lafleur, Marie-France, and Juliette Gréco. Then he heads to the studios of La Victoire in Nice, where they are finishing the filming of *Voulez-vous danser avec moi?* It's his first appearance in a film. This one is directed by Michel Boisrond. The first assistant is Jacques Poitrenaud, and the star is Brigitte Bardot.

JACQUES POITRENAUD: *"In the script, there's a character who's a bit*

troubled, seedy and bizarre... I ran across the cover of "Le poinçonneur"
and went looking for the composer. I don't remember if Boisrond had him
do a screen test. He basically just played himself in the film. Same attitude,
same manner of speaking – a lanky, gangly vague sort which was just what
we were looking for."

So the first meeting between Gainsbourg and Bardot takes place eight years before "Bonnie and Clyde," but during the filming, they only pass each other in the hall since they don't have a single moment onscreen together. One might also ask oneself where Serge, with no training as an actor, ever finds the nerve to go before the camera. Perhaps he is thinking of his father, who was an extra in a 1936 movie...

As for Bardot, ever since *Et Dieu Créa... la femme* in 1956 (directed by Vadim, her ex-lover), she has been constantly making new films and her fame is at its zenith. In 1957, we see her with Gabin in *En cas de Malheur*, and in *Babette s'en va-t-en un guerre* (by Christian-Jaque), huge successes at the box office. All in all, she has twenty-four films to her credit: the latest, *Une Parisienne*, is a big hit, but the same can not be said about *Voulez-vous danser avec moi?*, a crime farce that is quite silly but very endearing in which B.B. dances non-stop: rumbas in the arms of Dario Moreno, slow and sexy numbers with Henri Vidal, and even some rock tunes with Philippe Nicaud.

According to Boisrond, Serge is supposed to stack up reels of film while Bardot passes by him. Overcome with fear or simply smitten with Bardot, he systematically flubs ten or twelve takes and the scene has to be scrapped.

GAINSBOURG: *"In that first film, I played the role of a small-time hustler who blackmailed people with compromising photos. Brigitte was charming, but approaching her was out of the question. She was surrounded like a diva by the director, the make-up artist, her secretary, her hair stylist or the first assistant. Our initial contact was amicable, but there was no spark. Young as she was, I found her too girlish, too cute. Later, she became sublime."*

While filming *Voulez-vous danser avec moi?*, Bardot is pregnant and has an argument with Jacques Charrier, who advises her not to do *La Vérité*. Without warning, she attempts suicide by swallowing a bottle of Phenobarbital and the filming is interrupted for several days. Then, more tragedies start to crop up: Sylvia Lopez dies of leukemia just days before the end of the film. All the scenes that Brigitte did with her have to be re-filmed in a mad rush with Dawn Addams, all in wide shots because Bardot's belly is staring to show. Then, on December 9, 1959, some eight days before the film's release, Henri Vidal, Michèle Morgan's husband, dies of a heart attack at the age of forty.

Following the film, press clippings inform us that Serge wants to write songs for Dalida and Dario Moreno, both hugely popular variety stars. This just goes to show that the idea of "changing his tune," as he would say later in respect to Petula Clark and France Gall, is already starting to germinate... At the same time, we learn that he's working on the music for *L'Eau à la bouche*. It's the time when Gilbert Bécaud is singing "La marche de Babette" (from the film *Babette s'en va-t-en guerre*). People are dancing to "La Bamba" with Los Machucambos, while Piaf has a big hit with "Milord" and Brel with "La valse à mille temps."

Still traumatized by a recent failure during a tour in Marseille, Serge sings "La recette de l'amour fou" on TV for the program *Rose cache-cache*. At the same time, he faces a new challenge when he appears for the first time in a grand Parisian music-hall, opening for Colette Renard at the Théâtre de L'Etoile, a hall that seats some 1,500 people and where Yves Montand had just completed a triumphant six-month run – at the time a record setting run in terms of duration. Bruno Coquatrix in is charge of the programming, and his Olympia is packed every night thanks to Josephine Baker. Anyway, from October 14 to November 2, the posters announce that in the hall on Avenue Wagram, one can catch, in addition to Colette Renard (the singer of "Irma la douce," who appears in her signature high heels and whose version of "Taxi Girl" makes a big splash), Gainsbourg ("the new revelation in *chanson*" who is also presented in the program as "a great composer and star of the future"), and for "the first time in a music-hall setting," François Deguelt. There are two shows a night and even three on Sunday, all of which are a great success. Serge, who performs between an acrobat and a group of puppeteers, decides to do five of his most aggressive numbers, only one of which is off his second album: "Ronsard 58," "La Recette de l'amour fou," "L'amour à la papa," "Le poinçonneur de Lilas," and "La femme des uns sous le corps des autres." Obviously, he is not looking to please the crowd. He might have chosen "Le claquer des doigts" or "Mambo Miam Miam" – songs that were much "easier." This does not escape Claude Sarraute, who publishes laudatory reviews in *Le Monde* on October 21: "What disconcerts us about him is the absolute frankness of his tone, his obvious concern of not falling into the trap of things already done or seen, to give us a piercing look at this world that surrounds us, unafraid of what others may think. From this comes his frequent entanglement with censure and his concern for a melody destined to smooth out certain allusions to an eroticism all too precise. [...] He is a curious character. The surprised public at l'Etoile reserves for him a welcome that is more reticent. And, even while he has received the Grand Prix du Disque, he'll have to wait a bit to see his style, although perfectly in step with the times, adopted by the public." In *Paris-Jour*: "With infinite talent, he mows down sentimental illusion and vitriolizes romance." In the review dashed off by Paul Carrère in *Le Figaro* concerning Gainsbourg's program, we find these keen commentaries: "without a doubt, he is the most original of the new wave, with that silhouette of his and those awkward gestures... his spider-like clumsiness... his dry and dark humor..."

His willingness to play anywhere and everywhere continues. Each evening, after playing the Théâtre de L'Etoile, he does a second gig at Milord. Then, in December, he runs back and forth from Rue de Beaujolais to Rue Vavin because he happens to be appearing at the College Inn. It's here where he creates onstage "L'eau à la bouche" before recording it, as always, with his good buddy Goraguer, with whom he also records simultaneously the different themes for his first two forays into film music. The first is for *L'Eau à la bouche*, by Jacques Doniol-Valcroze, a misunderstood stalwart of the new wave and film critic for *France-Observateur*. The second is for *Les Loups dans la bergerie*, by Hervé Bromberger, featuring Jean-Poron and debutant Françoise Dorléac.

Thus, 1959 comes to an end. A year that includes some three-hundred concerts, the Grand Prix de l'Académie Charles-Cros, a second album clearly less original than the first, the filming of a cute little third-rate movie, some savage humiliation, and as always the financial misery that he just can't shake. In the following months, Serge will finally get a taste - fleeting as it may be - of the delights of success. But the troublesome years are far from over: they will follow him into the decade of the sixties, which is just beginning.

Be Pretty And Keep Quiet

Full of discreet eroticism and irresistible melody, the super-45 of "L'eau à la bouche" is released in January, 1960, at the same time as the film by Doniol-Valcroze:

I will take you nimbly, there's no need to tremble
Why be so afraid, I'll be so soft and gentle
Please don't become so shy and flowery
When passion starts to devour me

Finally some relief for our composer! It's his first real success, selling some 100,000 copies – quite a nice score considering that the sales amount to roughly fifty times more than his four earlier EPs. In a nightclub, Serge runs into the stunning Pier Angeli, the Hollywood starlet and ex-girlfriend of James Dean. She scribbles on a piece of paper: "I just adore 'L'eau à la bouche'... In fact it makes my passion devour me..." Already quite the fetishist, Serge will carefully preserve this cherished relic...

On December 16, 1959, in addition to "L'eau à la bouche," Serge registers two new titles with SACEM: "Les nanas au paradise" and "Le cirque," two songs that are at the time recorded by Catherine Sauvage but not released until 1996, as part of the anthology Gainsbourg chanté par.

At the College Inn in Montparnasse, Gainsbourg is the sole headliner, and he appears nightly from the beginning of January to the end of April. It's an ancient cabaret that existed as far back as the thirties, and each evening Serge "...douses his audience in a cold bath of unusual and disconcerting poetry..." observes one anonymous reviewer. In February, Serge asks his father to replace his regular pianist, who has fallen ill, and in May, he is joined onstage by the club's artistic director, the one nicknamed "la dame blanche de Saint-Germain-des-Prés" – namely Cora Vaucaire, who does a show dedicated to the roaring twenties. It's here at the College Inn where Serge catches up with his old pal Jacob Pakciarz, who had assiduously studied Gainsbourg onstage and now offers us this passionate analysis.

> JACOB PAKCIARZ: *"Serge would start to sing, and there were moments that I thought he had been stricken with aphasia. I was worried about him because I was very fond of him...While he sang, he seemed to go blank, forget the words – things that happen to all artists – but with him it was a bit much. I wondered if he'd be able to continue. Now this silence is an essential part of Serge's nature. I can recall Lucien, the kid I'd known when he was just twenty years old, at the Académie Montmartre. You'd be lucky to get three words out of him in the course of a day. The way he'd whisper - at minimum volume and at the very boundary of the unspoken. His entire psychopathological nature is there in a nutshell – this desire to express oneself while holding back, just letting slip a scrap here or there, as if the words had to be coaxed out. It was a style in complete opposition to louder, gutsier voices that are so popular."*

Gainsbourg is more or less obliged to make himself part of the cabaret circuit because after the Liberation, it is, for a short time, the required route to take for anyone interested in carving out a niche in the world of "serious chanson" (the "yé-yé" crowd, following hot on the heels of Johnny Hallyday – who would release his first EP in March of 1960 – would change all that).

A disillusioned Serge would later offer this commentary about the places he spent so much time in: "The cabaret, it isn't real. A snobbish crowd applauds when you do something difficult but they never buy the records. The music hall public applauds the simplest of things and does buy the records."

It's 1960. Dalida has a big hit with "Ne joue pas" and "J'ai rêvé" (Bobby Darin's "Dream Lover"), Neil Sedaka croons "Oh! Carol," and Brassens gives us "Le mécreant." It's at this time that Gainsbourg is dumped by Sylvie Rivet. A dispute erupts on the steps of l'Eglise Saint-Germain-des-Prés and Serge, having really pushed her to the limit, gets a good slap on the face from Sylvie, who had up to this point put up with more than her fair share of his fooling around.

> SYLVIE RIVET: *"With Serge, it was really difficult to be jealous... You can't, he's just too funny, too honest, too sincere... I found it amazing! He would tell me that he wouldn't be back late and then he'd stroll in at 6 in the morning saying: "I'm an ass. Some chick picked me up, I know I'm disgusting..." Here he was all vexed and I just thought it was a riot. We would always address each other as "vous" when we were out in public. That added a little spice when we allowed ourselves to say "tu." He was so handsome in that photo with the bouquet of roses - that's the Gainsbourg I knew."*

On May 12, 1960, still working with Alain Goraguer and his orchestra, Serge records four cuts for a super-45 entitled *Romantique 60*, which is released the following month. On this occasion, the words are written for a melody composed six months earlier for the soundtrack of the film *Les Loups dans la bergerie*:

> *Come close to me my sweet*
> *And don't tremble in the least*
> *I'll be sweet and quite discreet*
> *I am not the*
> *The big bad beast waiting to feast*
> *Ou, ou, ou, ou*
> *Cha cha cha du loup*

As with *L'eau à la bouche*, he creates a seducer wanting to reassure his conquest of his lascivious intentions. Yet as far as skirt chasing goes, he can still be darkly humorous, as in "Sois belle et tais toi":

> *The woodpigeon coos*
> *The sparrow he peeps*
> *The chicken he squawks*
> *The magpie does screech*
> *The camel be bleats*
> *The owl does his hoot*
> *The panther he roars*
> *And the crane simply soars*
> *And you, you, you...*
> *Be pretty and keep quiet*

One thinks of "Boum" by Charles Trenet, done in the style of time. On the B-side, there are two pseudo-rock pieces peppered with a bit of Rumba, which is all the rage at that time – pieces both funny and a bit hammy.

We start to see Serge regularly on television. On June 6, he does "La nuit d'octobre" (the piece omitted from his second album) in *Chansons dans un fauteuil*. Three weeks later, on *Discorama*, he sings "Sois belle et tais-toi." After five months non-stop at the College Inn, he takes a few days of vacation in Toquet, where "secluded in a little hotel, he writes a nouvelle-vague musical comedy called *Poppie*, before leaving for Spain to play a role in the new version of *Fabiola*," as we learn from a press clipping. The first version had reunited Michèle Morgan and Henri Vidal, and was directed by Alessandro Blasetti in 1949.

When this masterpiece is released in April, 1964, it is more or less thrashed by the critics. Yet Serge escapes with some generous reviews: "Thanks to his physique, Gainsbourg brings out the required characteristics of an odious assassin." The comic number by Dario Moreno is also highlighted...

GAINSBOURG: *"It was an Italian production, but we filmed it in Spain. Dario played Emperor Maximum and I was his right-hand man, of course. Man, did we have a blast! He would keep pulling these sumptuous jewels from his pockets, diamonds and rubies. He'd drop all his dough on this stuff and he was simply rolling in it. The crew returned from Spain and Dario had these wonderful American convertibles in an almost nauseating lilac color. He asked me to join him and I accepted. At the time, there were these little Teppaz units that you could slip 45's into. He had one in the car. On the highway, he'd drive like a nut and when he'd get pulled over by the cops he'd say: "Yeah, I'm Dario Mareno. Do you want an autograph?" His trick was to pass through the village no faster than 30 kmp and put his 45 on the player at full blast! On the road, we'd stop for a break at a town like Chalon-sur-Saône, I don't know, some dreary place. Me, I adored the big palaces even though I couldn't afford them, and I'd say: "Great idea, this is the only place that will suit Dario." But not at all. He'd stop at the hotel by the train station, a lousy little dive, tacky, green windows, peeling paint, empty dining room. A nightmare! When we'd go down to eat he'd just have a bowl of soup, and then ask: "Don't you have discounts for artists?" Super.*

I guess that's how you become a billionaire..."

In 1960, it's clear that Johnny Hallyday is on the brink of becoming an immense star as his "Souvenirs souvenirs" plays non-stop on the program Salut les copains. This is also the time of Aznavour's "Tu t'laisses aller," Brenda Lee's "I'm Sorry," and Elvis Presley's "It's Now or Never."

In his rare interviews with the press, Gainsbourg continues to speak non-stop about stopping his musical career as soon as he has the means to buy a studio and all the necessary materials for painting, which he still dreams about. In the meantime, he offers Michèle Arnaud a sumptuous gift: it is in fact for her that he composes "La Chanson de Prévert," which she performs on December 17, 1960, on the television show *Dix minutes avec Michèle Arnaud*. Her version, recorded before those of Isabelle Aubert, Gloria Lasso, and Serge, is issued as a record in the spring of 1961.

As far back as the 1950s, Cora Vaucaire, Yves Montand, and Juliette Gréco had all sung "Les feuilles mortes," which later became an international standard in English under the title of "Autumn Leaves." Tipping his hat to this classic in the style of the Rive Gauche, Gainsbourg composes "La Chanson de Prévert." His intention is probably to make a big splash, but he feels very shy about approaching the poet (Prévert) for his authorization.

> GAINSBOURG: *"Jacques Prévert had me over at his place at 6 bis, Cité Véron. He was already hitting the champagne at 10:00 in the morning. He told me, "That sounds just fine, my boy!" and I timidly handed over the document, which he signed for me."*

"La Chanson de Prévert" is without a doubt one of the most popular tunes in Serge's songbook, and there have been countless interpretations, including that by songstress Claire d'Asta, which was still a regular on the play lists in autumn of 1981, a good twenty years after it was recorded. There's also the version by Jane Birkin, which she performed onstage at the Casino de Paris in May, 1991, and it's probably the best of them all, including the original, which is as conventional as it is minimalist:

> *Oh, I'd like so much that you know this is true*
> *This song was written just for you*
> *It was your favorite*
> *This I know*
> *Kosma and Prévert*

Made you glow
And every time
These autumn leaves
Make me think of you and I
Day after day
These autumn leaves
Fade but never seem to die

In the pages of the November 15 edition of *Cinémonde*, which at the time has a circulation of 500,000, there's an astonishing discussion between Gainsbourg, actress Micheline Presle, director Norcert Caronnaux, singer Jacqueline Boyer (daughter of Jacques Pills and Lucienne Boyer) and Léo Ferré. The host is Pierre Guénin, who has published, among other things, this text in a book called *Le Jeu de la vérité*:

Pierre Guénin: Do you consider songwriting to be an art?

Serge Gainsbourg: Can you be attached to commercial interests and at the same time produce art?

P.G.: Do you find it normal that a song, most often quite silly, earns so much money for its writer?

S.G.: It's no less normal than making a killing as a sausage maker. It's a great con game, perfectly organized. Songs simply enter into the homes of people without knocking. You put your face on the TV, whether it pleases them or not.

Later, we learn from Serge that, "For the moment, I'm living with my mom and things aren't going that well financially." Then there's the following cynical exchange:

P.G.: What is the first quality that you look for in a woman?

S.G.: Assiduousness (laughter).

P.G.: And the fault that you're least likely to forgive?

S.G.: Frigidity.

Then there's this exchange between Ferré and Gainsbourg which is worth its weight in copyright:

P.G.: So Gainsbourg, do you write songs for the love of art or for money?

S.G.: My situation is rather delicate. I was a painter for fifteen years and now I earn a living writing songs. The problem is that the better things get, the stronger my desire to write "unsingable" songs.

Léo Ferré: In principle, when you write something, it's with your heart, not for money. You're wrong to think of songwriting as a minor art, unless, obviously, you're just thinking about the contingencies imposed upon you by some owner of a record company. There's art, and then there's shit...

S.G .: If my publisher and my record company...

L.F.: Don't talk to me about them – they're businessmen.

S.G.: But in the end, if they shut me up?

L.F: I understand your circumstances. It's a difficult situation. But what you want to sing and write, you simply have to do it, my friend.

S.G.: At home?

L.F.: No. In the streets. You have to get a permit from the cops.

S.G.: Well, as for me, I'd be perfectly willing to cut off my ear for painting, like Van Gogh did. But not for music.

Off air, the debate transforms into veritable verbal pugilism and Gainsbourg ends up calling Ferré "old-fashioned."

PIERRE GUÉNIN: *"Serge was really troubled with money problems. He'd earned peanuts with "Le poinçonneur." He was happy to engage in this interview because at the time he wasn't widely seen. Ferré had come off as rather pretentious, speaking of some of his songs as masterpieces, and Gainsbourg did not at all share his opinion. They parted angrily. What's even more amusing is that Gainsbourg pulled the same stunt with Guy Béart in the 80s, again addressing the theme of song as a minor art."*

In terms of his discography, 1960 proves to be a low point in his career as a writer. He publishes only six titles under his name (one of which was a lovely success, it is true), puts out no new album, and finds no one to interpret any of his songs, the attempts with Catherine Sauvage yielding nothing for the moment. Meanwhile, it is not impossible that he once again meets with Yves Montand, to whom he had promised exclusive rights to "La chanson de Prévert." On April 21, 1961, an indiscretion in Paris-Jour informs us that upon his return from Tokyo, Montand is very unhappy to learn that Michèle Arnaud and Serge had recorded the song some two months earlier. Two meetings with Montand and two blunders? The possibility is amusing.

But in order to understand the milieu in which his career is developing, it is essential that we know what is happening in the minds of the big shots at Philips, these "businessmen" so despised by Ferré (who is currently signed with Eddie Barclay, a well-known patron of the arts). The big bosses at Philips now include Louis Hazan and Georges Meyerstein. In their minds, the time of Jacques Canetti is finished. Hazan, the voice of the Algerian broadcast for The Voice of America during the war, starts in the business early on and has a father who owns a number of music stores in Morocco. Upon returning to the company on January 1, 1956, Hazan is made director of exports. He is the one who hires Boris Vian as music director for the Fontana label. For Philips, Hazan discovers Nougaro and brings to France singer Nana Mouskouri, whose success is immediate. In 1961, he steals Johnny Hallyday, who had been wasting away at Vogue where nobody could see his gigantic potential. Barclay signs Chaussettes Noires, with Eddie Mitchell, who release their first EP in 1961. Johnny finally fires Canetti in a fit of rage, and Hazan, already having captured Barbara and Claude François, is now in contact with Serge. A lasting relationship will soon blossom between the two men. It is nicely summarized in this brief dialogue confided to us by the ex-boss at Philips:

Gainsbourg: I don't think that you like me.

Louis Hazan: Like is too pretty a word. Why do you say that?

S.G.: Because I don't sell records, and because I cause you to spend money.

L.H.: I really don't give a damn. I'm quite happy to have you.

It's true that Serge is not a big expenditure for Philips, which doesn't waste a penny promoting him. The cost of producing his records is always kept to a minimun. His third 25 cm, *L'Etonnant Serge Gainsbourg* - the title itself a poem - is finished in Blanqui in seven days, between February 8 and March 16, 1961. Alain Goraguer and his orchestra are still in the mix, but they

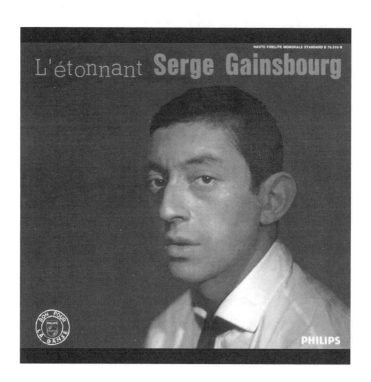

also add an artistic director named Jacques Plait, who up until that point had been busy with launching the early career of Richard Anthony at Pathé-Marconi.

On January 5, 1961, Serge registers four new songs at SACEM, one of which, "Faut avoir vécu sa vie," will be covered by Brigitte Bardot two years later under the title "Je me donne à qui me plaît." The final two, "Viva Villa" and "En relisant ta letter," are part of his third 25 cm album, published in the spring of 1961 (the cover is adorned with the words "Great for dancing," Jacques Plait's idea, no doubt), which also includes "La chanson de Prévert," "Le sonnet d'Arvers," "Le rock de Nerval," "Chanson de Maglia," "Personne," "Les oubliettes," "Les femmes c'est du chinois," and " Les amours perdues," one of his first songs registered with SACEM in the summer of 1954.

"En relisant ta lettre" is covered by Jean-Claude Pascal a few weeks before it is done by Serge. A real classic, it starts with this little criticism, in a neutral voice, at once cynical and disdainful:

> *While rereading your letter, I see that the spelling and you,*
> *That makes two*

The rest of the piece is a pitiless and cruel recounting of all the grammatical and spelling errors committed by the lovelorn female who authored the missive.

> JANE BIRKIN: *"When I met Serge in 1968 on the set of the film Slogan, I wanted to know more about him, and so I went to a bookstore and bought a compilation of his lyrics. Using a dictionary, I tried to grasp the beauty and complexity of his songs. One that I truly adored was "En relisant ta letter," and I had to put a lot of work into understanding all the humor because he writes at so many levels at once. All of the sudden I realized the enormous talent of this man for manipulating language, this guy who I thought I was just working with as an actor..."*

On the same EP, this masterful charmer of women, Jean-Claude Pascal, also covers "Les oubliettes," which is influenced by the realism of the songs from the 1930s that little Lucien had been exposed to:

> *If one must go on*
> *Regretting until dawn*
> *Better to move on*
> *My little turtle doves*

Come my little cuties
Oblivion is beauty
When you're there with me
The bread and wine flow free

L'Etonnant Serge Gainsbourg shows us the artist at his most unconventional: proof of this had been given to us with "Le poinçonneur" in 1958, when he succeeded in a genre that seemed to be already out-dated but which he transcended with unheard of talent. All this is contrary to what Brel would tell him later: it's Serge who is mistaken and Brel who is cheating (the unbearable pathos of "Ne me quitte pas," an enormous success in 1960). Brel overdoes it, sweating and sobbing, while Gainsbourg, acutely aware of himself and aware of his literary heritage, pays homage to Prévert and does not shy away from putting to music the lyrics of three great poets: Victor Hugo ("La chanson de Maglia"), Félix Arvers ("Le sonnet d'Arvers," which he undoubtedly penned while at lycée), and Gérard de Nerval ("Le rock de Nerval").

GAINSBOURG: *"The problem with this record was really quite simple: I had no lyrics for my music. Hugo's poem was a piece of crap, as was my music, and together they formed something ultra-crappy. Why did I choose only the romantic poets? Because I am, essentially, a romantic. This is why I had arrived at the following conclusion: "Take women for what they're not and leave them for what they are." I don't want them to love me, but I want them all the same."*

"Le rock de Nerval," with its grooving little sax, is about the only song that has held up well. It's a combination of an incredibly sentimental text whose music is set to the rhythm of a mid-tempo pop-rock piece, creating an effect which is at once amusing and poetic:

Come my sweet Spanish beauty
Night is jealous and moody
Its gloom reaches the skies
But even night's veil
Fails to make my star pale
It's the star from your eyes

The following "genre" piece, "Viva Villa," with its distracting Mexican flutes, makes it difficult for us to understand today why Serge would record something like this, unless it's simply a twisted reference to Castro's putsch two years earlier in Cuba:

> *Rifles and handguns for the raid*
> *And in each pocket a switchblade*
> *Heading to Guadalajara*
>
> *It's for a famous carnival*
> *This grand and mighty arsenal*
> *All in the name of Pancho Villa*

The flip-side of the cover for this third album contains this amusing text:

My sweetheart,

Here are a few songs that are only partly mine, and I ask that you listen to them carefully. Listen to one today and maybe another tomorrow, at your convenience. The next day I give you permission to dance to them. You recognize, I hope, I am now a bit less cruel with my remarks than I was yesterday, and if any bitterness remains I will cite, as a sort of excuse, this madrigal by Jean de Lingendes:

> *It all lies with God, above in the skies*
> *Their beauty is his fault*
> *Neither mine nor my eyes*

Affectionately Yours,
Serge Gainsbourg

It's true that's he's a bit less cynical, more lighthearted, when remarking that "Les femmes, c'est du chinois":

> *Like another when she comes to bed*
> *Sensation makes her want it more*
> *She laughs a little hollow laugh*
> *And counts the spiders on the floor*

It's no surprise that some of his songs are quite a hit with international lovers of lounge music, those who will rediscover the easy-listen sounds of Les Baxter and Martin Denny in the late 1990s. For fans with exotic tastes, "Personne" is a real joy:

> *No I should have never deigned to let my hand touch*
> *Your lovely person*
> *I should have controlled myself, I know that much*

About my person

Clearly, there is very little to remember from this album whose release is publicized by Serge's version of "La chanson de Prévert." The general impression is that he is drifting. The threat from the yé-yé crowd was becoming clearer while Serge was still trying to be a "good singer" in the fifties sense of the word. Twenty-five years later, he would confide to Noël Simsolo that he couldn't stand his voice in the beginning: "I was overly concerned. I projected too much, was too resonant. It lacked distanciation." Furthermore, in contrast to Brel or Brassens, already household names, Gainsbourg is still building name for himself. In marketing terms, one would say that he hasn't "found his demographic," assuming he has one. But in fact he does: at this stage, there are one or two thousand fans buying his 25cm recordings. One might easily guess what kind of people they are: people in the music business, students, dandies seduced by his attitude. But to sell more records, he needs to become more visible. With the lack of promotional support from Philips, he needs to be seen as an opening act for big-time stars, or on tour, or even better in grand Parisian music-halls. But nothing doing. The mess with Canetti after the hellish 1959 tours leaves him without a manager. Charley Marouani - Brel's impresario, who had run across Serge in 1958 when one of his protégés, Hugues Aufray had sung "Le poinçonneur" for him - is helping him out at the time purely as a friend, finding him some good galas to perform at, or even eight to ten day runs in Parisian cabarets.

The criticism of the new album is quite honestly no better than that of his second, some eighteen months earlier. In *Le Canard enchaîné* from April 20, 1961, we read: "In particular, we can chide Gainsbourg for having engaged a bit too much in his modernizations of the classics: Nerval, Hugo, and the overestimated Arvers. It's a lot to put onto a single record, even if the adaptations of the band are skillful. But honestly, we prefer the real Gainsbourg, who gave us "Amours perdues," "La chanson de Prévert," "Viva Villa," or "Oubliettes." In *Ciné Revue* on May 5, they are gentler: "His aggression always pays off because the surprises he gives us never fail to have a real effect. He gains your trust without you knowing it [...] The term *astonishing* is a perfect description of his originality. Serge Gainsbourg was, in our estimation, the newest talent in song – his ideas, his vision, and his perceptions were completely opposed to the whole "prêt à chanter" thing [...] He super-imposed over this gushing tenderness a glacial mask of fake realities. In a certain respect, he's almost the prude of French chanson."

After a period of depression, Serge finally accepts that Sylvie Rivet has left him for Brel. He continues to see her, but strictly for business matters as she is a press agent.

ALAIN GORAGUER: *"I too had to mother him. We'd stay up until 4 or 5 in the morning, just talking, and I'd try to cheer him up. He'd tell me: "I'm fucked. Three albums, and they don't sell or ever get played on the radio." His despair was real, and I felt for him."*

The first of his three films comes out in the Parisian theatres on April 1, 1961, but he only sees them a few years later with his newest romantic conquest...

GAINSBOURG: *"One day, I went to see La Révolte des esclaves at Barbès, with Jane. The guys in the theatre hated me! When I died on-screen, they applauded like madmen, yelling: "Yeah, that's it! Shitbag! Die, bastard!" All in Arabic, of course. I told Jane: "Let's beat it. If they see me at the exit they'll skin me alive!""*

When his new album comes out on April 5, Serge lines up a junket of promotional interviews. On April 12, he's on the television at Studio 4, and then rehearses on the April 21 at Buttes-Chaumont for the program *Superboum*, which is filmed five days later. On April 15, he does "Les oubliettes" on the show *Toute la chanson* (André Salvet's program, which is hosted by Jacqueline Joubert. The same show includes Bécaud, Brel, Les Compagnons, Colette Renard, Anouk Aimée and Michèle Arnaud).On the April 28, he's invited by Daniel Filipacchi and Frank Ténot on Europe N° 1, not for *Salut les copains*, but for a show later in the evening - *Pour ceux qui aiment le jazz*.

At night, he's gigging again at Le Milord with Francis Claude, Jacques Dufhilo, and Claude Sylvain. The monthly publication *Music-Hall*, in April of 1961, gives us all the details.

Tall and thin, with a diabolical look... Come to Milord l'Arsouille after midnight and you will be irresistibly fascinated. In the shadowy darkness and cigarette smoke, he speaks to you of despair and sings of things dread-ful, such as "La femme des uns sous le corps des autres" or "Jeunes femmes et vieux messieurs" or even "L'amour à la papa." He plays with his grave voice and dark humor. At night, he'll haunt and mesmerize you. Playing a Roman centurion in the film Fabiola, he kills the martyr Saint Sebastian by his own hand before being devoured by his own hounds...

Lights! In broad daylight, Serge Gainsbourg is not at all a creep with the ladies. He's romantic and gentle, and he wouldn't harm a fly. He loves Belafonte and Presley, drinks whiskey, and does figurative painting.

—Have you worked on your voice, Serge Gainsbourg?
—I don't have a voice...

The television promos continue through the month of May. He sings three songs ("La chanson de Maglia," "Personne," and "L'eau à la bouche"), accompanied by a band composed of a guitarist, bassist, drummer, and vibraphonist. There's also a big horn section for the set of *Discoparade* in Annecy on May 21. On June 14, he's invited to appear on a televised news journal to talk about his activities as a composer of film scores and as an actor. On June 26, he even travels to the Yugoslavian embassy – at that time still a country in the communist block – to obtain a visa, for he will be working there simultaneously on two films starting in the fall. He jumps at the chance, especially since the royalties paid by SACEM for the July quarter are becoming skimpier: his pay is a mere 6, 242 francs! Also, singers are not really pounding on his door for new songs. Only the faithful Michèle Arnaud, who we see constantly on television during the 1960-61 season, asks him for a new piece for her return to the Olympia, which begins on September 6. Serge suggests "Les goémons," part of an EP she does which also includes a successful version of Leny Escudéro's "Pour une amourette."

> *In brown and in red*
> *Sprouting from the sea's bed*
> *Seaweed and kelp*
> *My love is the same*
> *It's all that remains*
> *Seaweed and kelp*

Serge, acting in two films at the same time, figures in some really dopey scenes. As they're being filmed simultaneously, He loses track of where he is day by day - *Hercule se déchaîne* or *Samson contre Hercule?* Hercules is played by Brad Harris, a musclehead who does bench presses between scenes and whose thighs are so overdeveloped that he has to walk bow-legged. Invariably, Serge gets knocked off before the end of each film. In the first, he's decimated by arrows, and in the other – according to his memory – Hercules tosses a trunk at him, shouting: "Here's your booty!" before he falls into a ditch to be eaten by crocodiles (fake crocodiles, of course).

In short, he always plays a traitor who meets his end after getting involved in sticky situations with some cruel emperor or a princess whose throne he has his eye on. Most of the time, his lines are limited to phrases like "Kill him!" or "Get him!"...

Meanwhile, the eminent film critic and sometimes director François Chalais is after Gainsbourg to write music for his new film. On October 11, Chalais writes him with a few supplementary details: The filming of his short piece (50 minutes), called *Le chien*, with Alain Delon and Elke Sommer, will begin November 1. He tells Serge that he'll need a song called "Elke's Blues" for the bothersome Sommer, a German starlet who made her debut a year earlier in the English films *Don't Bother to Knock* and *The Victors*. Serge, already titillated, asks for a photograph of the young beauty (21 years old): "When reading the script I was able to come up with several ideas." Finally, on October 30, Chalais picks up his pen again to express his regret that Serge has not yet returned to Paris ("I want you to be a part of this adventure. I admire your talent, and I consider it as indispensable to my work as the faces of my two actors.") But it would simply never happen. Serge suffers a real bout of depression in Yugoslavia after a visit from Jacques Plaît, who talks to him about Johnny Hallyday, recently signed to Philips. At eighteen, he is the idol of every teenager and has already sold over a million records. In London, he records the material for two EPs that will contain, among other tunes, "Viens danser le twist" ("Let's Twist Again" by Chubby Checker), "Il faut saisir la chance," written by Georges Garvarentz, and "Douce violence," with lyrics by Charles Aznavour. Since springtime, Les Chats Sauvages and Les Chaussettes Noires have sold hundreds of thousands of records... So, why hasn't our accursed singer-songwriter sparked interest among this new generation?

> GAINSBOURG: *"My artistic director joined me in Belgrade. He gave me a bunch of records by Johnny Hallyday. "That's what you need to be doing!" he tells me. I was devastated. I hadn't written a note or line of lyrics in six months. Plus, I got kicked out of Yugoslavia for lighting a cigarette with a 100 dinar note. 100 dinars. That's 15 old francs! They thought in a was a 10,000 dinar bill because they'd seen me counting some a while earlier. "What provocation!" they railed, and then they tossed me out of the country!"*

Interesting fact: In 1961, Serge is already burning bank notes, some twenty-three years before the scandal on *7 sur 7*... Upon his return to Paris, he starts working the cabaret circuit again. On November 19, the press rails against the blousons noirs (the rock and rollers) who devastate Le Palais des Sports during the first rock festival in France, which includes Les Chaussettes, Les Chats, and also Vince Taylor et ses Playboys. 3,500 spectators, massive damage, undoubtedly, but the success of the event is obvious. On the other hand, the *franglais* singers like Gainsbourg (excellent reputation, modest sales) are in danger of being crushed by the yé-yés. On television, we see Serge perform on a couple of evenings before the New Year, including a date on *Vœux à tous vents* on December 31. At the beginning of January, 1962, Serge must have been wishing for a year less somber than the preceding one. In all reality, it couldn't be much worse. But this black will move towards gray, and we'll see things slowly start to get better, even if our hero is far from being out of danger. In the next twelve months, Serge will compose "Accordéon," "La javanaise," and other tunes for his album *N° 4*, his best effort since *Du chant à la une*...

eight

Let's take a walk inside of me

A s the year 1962 starts to unfold, French teenagers live and breathe the twist, which is all the rage at the moment. Johnny Hallyday finishes a triumphant stint at l'Olympia and his "Retiens la nuit" tops all the charts, along with, among others, Edith Piaf's "Non je ne regrette rien," Ray Charles' "Hit The Road Jack," and Jacques Brel's "Les bourgeois."

A few months earlier, Serge had seen a stage piece that simply blew him away: *The Connection*, written by Jack Gelber and performed by The Living Theatre. It features alto saxophonist Jackie McLean, a master of hard bop and someone whose praises Gainsbourg would continue to sing for the rest of his life, especially whenever the subject of jazz was broached. "Magnificent!" Serge would say. "I've never seen anything so beautiful," he later repeated in the magazine *Rock and Folk*, where he extolled the virtues this show - one of the harshest and darkest pieces ever staged on the subject of drugs. The Living Theatre, founded by Julian Beck and Judith Malina, two former students of Erwin Piscator, was for a long time (well after the sixties) one of the greatest experimental stage troupes to engage not only in theatrical works of narrative rupture (Brecht, Genet, Piandello, Strindberg), but also happenings and performance art. *The Connection* created deflagration wherever it was presented. Taking its title from the street slang for "dealer," Gelber's play started its run in July, 1959 in New York and is an illustration of what critics call metatheatre, or "a play within a play." The goal of the piece is to persuade the audience that they are in the presence of real junkies who are waiting for their connections to show up with their dope. To heighten the confusion among audience members, a supposed movie producer walks through the actual theatre with his team, pretending to make a film about drug addiction. Part of his entourage are four jazz musicians who engage in largely improvised jam sessions (among the players is, of course, Jackie McLean, with, as the French press reports, "his wild notes, his screams, his insane sonority." McLean would later include two of the play's pieces in his own repertory, one which he called "What's New," deemed by critic Jean Delmas to be a "sadistic masterpiece," as well as "Condition Blues," recorded the same year for the Blue Note label). In the auditorium, seated amongst the spectators, the film's writer protests whenever changes are made to his original script... The atmosphere created by The Living Theatre heightens the confusion even more when during the intermission, the actors go around trying to actually score dope from the audience members... It was even said that the dramatic collective overdose at the end of the play provoked actual fainting in the crowd and that the spectators, completely dumbstruck, often demanded their money back. After New York, the show goes to London and Paris before finally being turned into a film. A few months after seeing the play, Serge composes "Black Trombone," and in 1964, he writes a number on the same theme (jazz, drugs) called "Coco and C°," which comes out on the album Gainsbourg Percussions...

But back to our story. The year of 1962 doesn't really take off at full throttle. On February 2, Serge performs in Brussels, opening for Les Cousins (the Belgian group that wrote "Kiliwatch," a campfire song dressed up as rock and roll which was later covered by Johnny Hallyday). Then, with the help of Charley Marouani, Serge signs a contract with an Algerian TV station. He arrives in Algiers on February 5, just in time to perform at Le Bal de l'Ecole Normale that's taking place at the Hôtel Saint-Georges. The place is a real powder keg, and other artists simply refuse to play there at that time, what with the OAS[1] dynamiting anything that moves in a last ditch attempt regain

[1] The OAS was a radical, far-right group of armed French nationalist reactionaries willing take any measure to halt the realization of a politically autonomous Algeria.

control of the country. Serge must really need to sell some records and collect that 3,000 franc fee, so much so that he actually returns there some two months later!

Upon his return to Paris, other than for two television spots, Serge concentrates on preparing his latest 25 cm album, the fourth, judiciously titled *N° 4*. Meanwhile, Catherine Sauvage includes four of his songs on her new EP, just as Gréco had done three years earlier.

> CATHERINE SAUVAGE: *"One day on the radio, I hear these lyrics: 'In your eyes I see these eyes of mine/You're lucky/It lends you an intelligence quite fine.'" I remember saying to Canetti, "So you've got a guy like this in your stables and it never crossed your mind to introduce us?" Then I heard 'La recette de l'amour fou' and immediately added it to my repertory."*

During an aborted attempt two years earlier, Catherine Sauvage had recorded but not released "Le cirque" and "Les nanas au paradis." This time, she takes on "Les goémons," as well as two new songs, "Baudelaire" and "Black Trombone." Serge takes the Baudelaire poem, "La serpent qui danse" from *Fleurs du mal*, and sets it to a samba rhythm:

> Tes yeux, où rien ne se révèle
> De doux ni d'amer,
> Sont deux bijoux froids où se mêle
> L'or avec le fer.
>
> À te voir marcher en cadence,
> Belle d'abandon,
> On dirait un serpent qui danse
> Au bout d'un bâton[2]

Astonishing coincidence: this very text had already been interpreted by the same Catherine Sauvage a year earlier, set to music by Ferré and performed by the Jacques Loussier Orchestra! Unsatisfied with the result, might she have asked Serge to write new music for this poem? The second version, in all its methadone-inspired languor, is a testament to Serge's passion for jazz – at the time, he confides to the monthly *Diapason* that he listens to Gil Evans, Gerry Mulligan, and the Jazz Messengers:

[2] Seeing that there are numerous English translations of Les fleurs du mal, I will avoid committing literary heresy here and leave the text in the original French. (T.N.)

Black trombone
Monotone
The trombone
It is lovely
Swirling tone
Gramophone
And it moans
My ennui

The song he had offered to Juliette Gréco a few weeks earlier, surely at the origin of this cynical declaration, is in fact much more accessible and commercial. Juliette, who was surely moved upon hearing "La chanson de Prévert," soon has the same author's splendid "Accordéon" land in her lap.

JULIETTE GRÉCO: *"I still sing it onstage, some forty years later. Whether you like it or not, it's classic image of France for the foreigner, like Léo Ferré's "Paris canaille."*

God knows life is no treat
For musicians in the street
His only loved one
Is his accordion
It's what helps him get by
Like his bottle of rye
Neither mother nor son
Can be his accordion
Give it up, give it up, don't be so shy
Toss some change to the accordion guy

Meanwhile, Serge is broke once again and living with his parents. Then, between March 15 and April 22, 1962, seven days are dedicated to the recording and mixing of the album *N° 4* , again at Blanqui, and again with Goraguer and his orchestra of musicians who haven't had this much work – if not as much fun - since the twist was all the rage.

ALAIN GORAGUER: *"The yé-yés frightened everyone because they caused all the big recording companies to restructure. Every Thursday, you'd see 80, 100, 120 young boys and girls, fourteen to eighteen years old, lined up in front of the studios. They'd come to audition. They were treated like cattle. If they were chosen and their first disc was a hit, they lived like stars – fancy flats, limousines, the works. If the second record was a flop, they were back in their provincial hometowns. As for the human element, horrible things took place. What really worried those of us who were in the business was that the studios were grinding away, bragging about recording an unbelievable number of sessions. The studios were simply overburdened, obsessed with the idea of scoring a "coup."*

On this last 25 cm, which marks a turning point in his work and a place where he rediscovers the inspiration and diversity of his first forays in 1958, Serge offers us his own versions of "Black Trombone," "Baudelaire," and "Les goémons" (whose arrangement is ruined by a saxophone, imposed, much to the dismay of Serge, by artistic director Jacques Plait). Playing counterpoint to the penetrating mood and melancholic atmosphere he adopts for the latter tune, "Intoxicated Man" lets us appreciate a casual vibe and a subtle bass line uncannily reminiscent of Bois Vian's "Je Bois"...

> *Nightly*
> *I drink like a fish and*
> *I see*
> *Pink elephants that vanish*
> *Spiders crawling down the front*
> *Of my tuxedo*
> *Bats all flying 'round the ceiling*
> *Of my living-*
> *Room*

This newfound modernity is translated through the brilliant use of the rhythms of blues and jazz, an echo from the days of "Claquer de doigts," this time perfectly mastered, notably in "Requiem pour un twister," with its swinging electric organ:

> *Tell me have you ever heard of Charlie?*
> *If not I'd really be blown away*
> *There's never been a bar he didn't fancy*
> *What a fiend!*

A single, menacing voice responds, in a murmur: *Requiem pour un twist-eur.* It's not the voice of an opportunist using the word "twist" because it's hip. On the contrary, with this song, as with "Quand tu t'y mets," Serge is refining his style, and beginning to have fun with words, to master them even more. Hinted at a year earlier in "En relisant ta letter," he adopts a style that is half-spoken, half-sung, a forerunner of his future *talk-overs*:

You can be a real bitch
When you want
You don't do it much
But when you taunt
You have no idea...

In addition to "Baudelaire," Gainsbourg chooses samba rhythms for two other songs, "Ce grand méchant vous" and "Les cigarillos." The lyrics of the former are written by his old pal Francis Claude form Le Milord:

While the "you" is far away
For if it's near, I would fear
It would devour us both, my dear

Again, with great misanthropy and misogyny, Serge rejoices in simple contestation in "Les cigarillios":

These little cigarillos are so great at driving everyone away
I appreciate this herb
Kind and versatile
These cigarillos aren't like me, bogged down in such timidity
And a cruel acidity
Hides behind their style

For this album, Serge would also really love to set to music the poem at the end of Vladimir Nabokov's *Lolita*, which had been the talk of France ever since its publication in 1959. But while Stanley Kubrick obtains the rights to the film adaption, Serge is not authorized to use the text.

To announce the release of album *N° 4*, Serge returns to the stage of the cabaret La Tête de l'Art (formerly Chez Gilles), under the direction of Jean Méjean, from March 28 until the end of April, 1962. The ambiance is all whiskey and red velvet, and even Francis Claude or Jean-Claude Pascal would stop by to tell a few funny stories at the end of the show.

A pale face rendered almost pallid under the harsh glow of the spotlight; ears the color of those smitten by a frigid winter day; an ironic stare poorly concealed by heavy eyelids; a pursed little smile; hands twisted and clenched, hardly visible amongst the shadows; such is the astonishing Serge Gainsbourg as he takes the stage at "La Tête de l'Art."

Curious, sardonic, and diabolical, his songs are not passionate, but rather intelligent and cold. No flowers, no melodrama. He's a misogynist, and doesn't believe in the love of a woman; he sings of his numerous disappointments with neither revolt nor anger. And this cynicism – not that of a wounded Don Juan, but of a disillusioned man with neither the charm nor money for seduction – has left its mark. Cynicism, then. Yet if we scratch the surface, we often find tenderness in Gainsbourg's work. A tenderness that is discreet, hidden. And while he would never want to come off as tender, he wants to trouble us. Then again, he is more troubled than troublesome. He's tormented: a modern romantic with a passion for jazz and black humor who will one day end up singing of mad love. Gainsbourg's day will come, and I feel it is near.

Never stingy when it comes to a cheap play on words, *Le Canard enchaîné* had announced since February: "Quand il est en scène, le public boit du petit laid."[3] On April 28, in *Le Monde*, Claude Sarraute describes the show in detail. In addition to an illusionist, the crowd at La Tête de l'Art also enjoys the songs of Belgian singer Paul Louka and "the pitiful face of one Serge Gainsbourg and his stifled voice, working through refrains particularly apropos for the sensibility of a certain milieu, that of a certain Sagan or Vadim. Cigarettes, whiskey, and fast cars. He sings 'Jeunes femmes et vieux messieurs,' 'Le poinçonneur de Lilas,' and 'Personne.' " At the end of the show, the crowd welcomes Laura Betti, a superb Italian who will later become Pasolini's muse and star in several of his films. Some of the less serious papers report rumors of an engagement between Serge and Laura.

> LAURA BETTI: *"Engaged is a loaded word. Let's just say we saw a lot of each other. I liked him, but I would never have made love to him because he just made me laugh so much. I'd make fun of his whole poor, haggard soul routine. I didn't believe in his despair, and I could see there was sunshine inside somewhere. Had he really been sinister I might have given in, but his sense of irony was so strong, and when he did that melancholy routine I thought he was being really over the top..."*

When Serge meets Laura, she is also touring the cabaret circuit from l'Athénée to La Tête de l'Art, and she is pursued assiduously by another knight-errant who is at that time was a young actor. This is well before he would become one of the most popular producer-directors in France.

---

[3] If the end of the phrase read "boit du petit lait," we could translate it as "When he takes the stage, the crowd laps it up." But the word "lait" (milk) is transposed into "laid" (ugly), which turns the idiom into jab at Serge's less than handsome mug. (T.N.)

CLAUDE BERRI: *"She was pretty... I fell in love with her. Young love. Laura talked a lot about Serge, and according to what she told me she had really fallen for him. So this is my first memory of Serge, united by the fiancé we both shared."*

Michel Valette, at the time the boss at La Colombe (where Serge refuses to sing, unlike Béart or Pierre Perret, because there is no mic) and someone we will encounter later on as the future manager of Milord l'Arsouille, runs into Serge one night as the singer proclaims at a bar: "Even with my mug I'll make it. My goal is to make a lot of money and have the most beautiful women." This takes place at Port du Salut, where he happens to have a gig the coming May. Then at the end of April, he returns to Algeria, undoubtedly for an engagement at the Hotel Saint-Georges, where he stays for a few days.

Serge is becoming a regular on France's one and only television station: between March and July, he appears no less than seven times, including March 17 on *Histoire de sourire* and June 4 on *Toute la chanson*. It's all for the promotion of the new album which, judging from the newspaper clippings, is received with a sort of general indifference. *Combat* waits until August 9 to publish a review.

As for who is topping the charts or who is the latest darling on French television's *Salut les copains*, there are a few names at the head of the class, including Richard Anthony ("J'entends siffler le train"), Maurice Chevalier et les Chaussettes Noires ("Le twist du canotier"), and Isabelle Aubret ("Deux enfants au soleil"). It's a revolution in show business and Serge is overcome with discouragement. He's been slogging away for four years and still can't see a light at the end of the tunnel. Interviewed on Paris Inter in the month of June, the central question for Serge is, "Are you maybe going to stop writing songs?"

GAINSBOURG: *"There's no maybe about it. It's for sure. I could easily leave the world of music because in painting, which I practiced for fifteen years, there is no need for contracts and there are no concessions to make. Even though it may not seem like it, I know deep down that I make enormous concessions."*

On June 13, 1962, Georges Meyerstein and his wife throw a party at their home to welcome back to France pianist Errol Garner, whose work has been released on the Philips label ever since the brilliant *Concerts By The Sea* in 1956. Photographer Jean-Pierre Leloir immortalizes this fashionable shindig, which includes Garner, Canetti, Hallyday, Gréco, Salvador, Gainsbourg, and entertainers Fernand Raynaud and Roger Compte, as well as tour promoter Henri Colgran, or "the slave trader" as Leloir calls him, who "imports the great black American jazzmen to France."

It's while he's seriously considering abandoning his career as a songster (which is no pose... he's had little satisfaction since "Le poinçonneur") that he pens what some consider to be the most beautiful song in his repertory. In a letter to his daughter Liliane, who's living in Casablanca, Joseph Ginsburg soberly describes the tune as a "pretty waltz" ...

> J'avoue j'en ai bavé pas vous
> Mon amour
> Avant d'avoir eu vent de vous
> Mon amour
> Ne vous déplaise
> En dansant la javanaise
> Nous nous aimions
> Le temps d'une chanson[4]

And thus we have "La javanaise," which he first offers exclusively to Gréco. It is both a masterpiece and the ultimate reference of rupture generally identified by "Poupée de son, poupée de cire," giving rise to the exasperating cliché of "the great poet who sold out."

JULIETTE GRÉCO: *"La javanaise" is first and foremost a game – not a play on words but a game of playing with words, a game that instills in these words an even stronger value and nuance. 'J'avoue j'en ai bavé...' superb!... Regardless of the title he gave it the tune has nothing to do with the javanaise as it was spoken in the past. It is much more powerful and musical."*

Gréco performs "La javanaise" on a 25cm album but does not release it as a single until the beginning of 1963. It all starts with dinner at her home,

---

[4] Javanaise is a form of French argot, or slang, in which the phonemes "va" and "av" are inserted repetitively in between the syllables of normal words, forming a simple sort of pig latin with the "v" sound. I have chosen to leave the lyrics in French so that the reader might get a glimpse at the beauty and complexity of the feat undertaken by Gainsbourg, which really does transcend the simplicity of basic javanaise. A literal translation is given here, for it would be impossible to recreate "La javanaise" in English with the same rhyming meter and alliteration: It's I who suffered dear, not you/My love/Before I set my eyes on you/My love/Be not dismayed/While dancing this javanaise/Our love goes on/As long as this songs plays on. (T.N.)

Rue de Verneuil, a charming little street parallel to Rue de l'Université in the 6th arrondissement that is packed with antique dealers and where Serge will come to live several years later. They spend the evening listening to classical music and drinking fine wines. Then, at a certain moment, just before dawn, Juliette gets up and starts dancing in front of him. The next day she receives a superb bouquet of dangling orchids accompanied by a few words from Gainsbourg, who tells her he's just written a song inspired by that evening...

JULIETTE GRÉCO: *"He came to my home and played it on the piano. I just swooned... It was magnificent. Who wouldn't have been overwhelmed by that? There was so much of me in it, of the both of us. But that's my business. It's a secret!"*

> *À votre avis qu'avons-nous vu*
> *De l'amour ?*
> *De vous à moi vous m'avez eu*
> *Mon amour*

Two events separated by two months: Norma Jean Baker, aka Marilyn Monroe, kills herself on August, 5, 1962. On October 5, the Beatles release their first 45, *Love Me Do*. Six months later, when *Please Please Me* is released, Beatlemania starts to take off. Marie-Gisèle Landes, a reporter from *La Tribune de Genève*, is taken out for a night on the town by Serge (five different clubs until 6 in the morning, as she tells us in the September 17 edition), and he complains again about having "so far made too many concessions. My real songs, the only ones that interest me in fact, don't sell well or simply aren't played on the radio. You mustn't scare the kids! So, what do you want... Plus, I don't want to use conventional language. I want to remake vocabulary." During this time we read in *France-Soir* that "the ex-number 1 of the variety show, Gloria Lasso, wants to sing serious music or else retire." At ABC, in her long red gown encrusted with diamonds, she performs "Maintenant" by Bécaud and "La chanson de Prévert" by Gainsbourg...

Album *N°4* is dead on arrival. Very disappointing sales. When he is asked later why he started writing for the yé-yé crowd in 1963, he often responds: "So I don't die of hunger." In the fall of 1962 he must have been very frightened, wanting desperately to cut loose with something that would jumpstart his career. It's fascinating to imagine that at that time he might have thrown in the towel. There would remain only fifty or so of his songs, including "Le

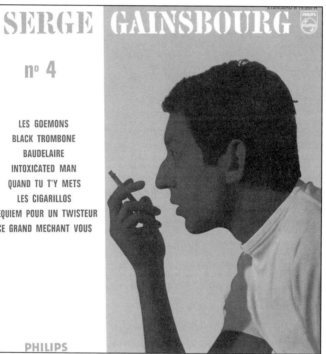

poinçonneur de Lilas," "La recette de l'amour fou," and "La javanaise," that would cement, some twenty or thirty years later – after the inevitable rediscovery – his status as the accursed, cult songwriter.

But he stands fast, and we see him singing on television ("Accordéon" on October 1, and then "Le Charleston des déménageurs de piano" on October 11 for Francis Claude's new show *Un pied dans le plat*). Still in October, there's a party at the Théâtre Fontaine for Raymond Devos's 40th birthday. All the big music-hall stars are there: we see Bouvril on the cornet, Nougaro on percussion, Gut Béart strumming an acoustic guitar and Serge playing an electric! Among the crowd are Jacques Tati, Juliette Gréco, and even Edith Piaf and her man Théo Sarapo.

> GAINSBOURG: *"So it appears that Piaf asks: "Who's that kid on the guitar? Gainsbourg? They say he's nasty but he looks really nice! Bring him over!" I hold her hand, already crippled with arthritis, and she invites me to her home on Boulevard Lannes, an apartment completely empty. She loathed furniture. She asks me to write songs for her... Shortly after that she was dead. What's insane about this is that Jane lived at the same address, in the same building. We could have run into each other! At that time, upper class Brits would send their children to Paris, to the home of wealthy women, so that they might learn about culture, needlepoint, and how to speak French. We finally met each other a few years later..."*

In November come the first signs that Serge's shaky situation is improving. France's biggest film star, Brigitte Bardot, is going to start singing and she asks him to write a song for her first EP, and then another for her first album, both of which are scheduled for simultaneous release in January, 1963.

> CLAUDE DEJACQUES: *"They met at Claude Bolling's. Serge came with me and he presented three lines of "L'appareil à sous." He would always give just a couplet or a sampling of the piece, and that way they couldn't reject it because it simply wasn't finished. But he had already showed them quite a bit with those three lines... It was because he was terrified of having a song rejected, and at the same time it was very clever on his part. Serge worked hard at being a success! Bardot always had a good feel for people who would make her look good. What's more, she really had a good time with Serge that day..."*

"La Madrague," the second hit from B.B.'s first EP, is written by the team of Jean-Max Rivière and Gérard Bourgeois, who over the years will pen a number of lightweight, sugary tunes for her, carefully exploiting the image of her as a sensual and liberated girl. Gainsbourg's "L'appareil à sous" is the first big smash and is clearly very ambitious despite its innocent pop surface – a little one and a half minute marvel:

> You're nothing but an arcade machine
> Boy
> Like a pinball you're a little
> Toy
> But that's a game
> I
> Just don't play

And the background singers doo-wop like mad...

At one point – it is even announced in the press – they are talking about Bardot doing "La javanaise." Then, the girl who in 1963 would make both *Le Mépris* and *Une ravissante idiote*, turns around and records "Je me donne à qui me plaît," a song perfectly befitting the image of the female Don Juan:

> I give myself to whom I please
> And
> Never twice with any ease
> And
> You've never suffered, never known
> Dear
> Don't be the first to toss that stone
> Dear

At years end, the girls are topping the sales charts: Sylvie Vartan with "Tous mes copains" (one of the only songs from the *Salut les copains* generation which addresses the war in Algeria), Francoise Hardy with "Tous les garcons et les filles," and Astrud Gilberto with "Desafinado." At the same time, the dazzling rise of Claude Nougaro destabilizes Gainsbourg. Nougaro's second 25 cm album, arranged by Michel Legrand, gives him the hit of the summer ("Une petite fille," music by Jacques Datin), as well as two other hits at the end of the year. As Louis Nucera puts it: "Claude, who was my friend, always greatly admired Gainsbourg. On the other hand, Gainsbourg was jealous of Nougaro's success, seeing as he, Gainsbourg, was still struggling. It's only human."

It's now time to discuss the letters of Joseph Ginsburg, who'll be along for the ride until April of 1971. These letters are sent by Joseph to Casablanca, to his daughter Liliane, Serge's twin sister. It would require several pages to evoke his epistolary talent, as Joseph would himself require six, eight, or ten for the job, and do so with strict and lovely penmanship. What interests us most is his "chronicles of Lucien." In each letter, roughly one every two weeks, he never forgets to report on the main events in his boy's career, and he never calls him anything other than Lucien.

Joseph speaks of those close to him with unbridled tenderness, in particular his grandchildren and his wife, Olia, for whom a great passion is still visible between the lines, especially when he talks about health problems or some of the nasty things she says to him, all the time showering her with attention... We also must note how cultured he is: in a single letter, he happens to quote François Mauriac, Ionesco, Verlaine, Chekhov, Léon-Paul Fargue, Oscar Wilde, and Francis Carco!

ALAIN GORAGUER: *"Serge had invited me to have dinner with his parents two or three times. They were absolutely delicious people. His father has a strong Russian accent and his mother was constantly taking the piss out of us. We drank vodka, we ate borscht, we lit candles, and the distance between France and Russia disappeared. His father would sit at the piano every now and then, and he was a very good musician. He was one of the last of a race of pianists that has since disappeared, pianists of extraordinary eclecticism. He was at ease in any style, a trait that we see in Serge. One could feel that his parents admired him, and that at the same time they were worried; after all, he had a late and difficult start."*

JOSEPH GINSBURG: *"Singing Serge Gainsbourg has become a mark of quality and youthfulness among artists. Petula Clark (the female Johnny Hallyday, she sells a lot of records) recorded one of Lucien's songs, "Vilaine fille, mauvais garçon." Brigitte Bardot took his song "L'appareil à sous," and Philippe Clay did "Chanson pour tézigue." And Lucien has a meeting on Monday (tomorrow) with Edith Piaf. Edith Piaf is asking him for a song! She's really great!"*

Petula Clark, born in 1932, had been a star in England since the age of sixteen. At the age of 25, she leaves for France and records her first French songs beginning in 1958. Shortly thereafter, Boris Vian writes for her "Java pour Petula." Her rather ironic image is co-opted by the intelligentsia and she seduces the masses with a string of hits. Starting in 1960, she has the good fortune of hitting it big on both sides on the channel: in France with "Prends mon cœur," "Marin," "Roméo," "A London," etc., and in Great Britain with "Sailor" (the #1 seller in Great Britain in 1961) and "Romeo."

> PETULA CLARK: *"I fell madly in love with a Frenchman who worked for me at Vogue. The only thing that mattered was being with him as much as possible in France. I sang whatever they asked me to because my French career was only of secondary importance. It wasn't my career. It just brought me love and adventure. And I was especially happy to be seen in a new light, not just as a child star of the British cinema of the forties."*

The Frenchman in question is one Claude Wolff, who had married Petula in 1961. He is always on the hunt for new writers and Serge is recommended to him by Denis Bourgeois, who will from this point on be handling his work. After Wolff sees him at l'Echelle de Jaocb and finds him "interesting," he brings Serge to the couple's apartment in Neuilly, on Rue Bois-de-Boulogne.

> PETULA CLARK: *"The first time I met Serge I was very shy. I had heard him on the radio before and thought that he had a fascinating voice and a unique way of combining words. I would sing his songs out loud in the house, not always understanding the lyrics. When I saw him I was instantly swayed by his charm. I always found him physically attractive, even before he became popular. He came to see me and brought the song "Vilaine fille, mauvais garcon." I was quite excited. He sat down and played the piano, and I heard that voice that I adored... After that, he brought other songs to me and I loved them right away. They were commercial, but not too obvious. There was something unpredictable about his music."*

> CLAUDE WOLFF: *"You've got to understand that songwriters at that time were a bit like pushy street vendors. Having your stuff sung by Petula was important because it would bring you huge royalties. Simply put, she sold tons of records... I remember a visit from Jacques Plante, who had offered me five songs, none of which I liked. He was a bit irritated, then*

he brought out "Chariot," claiming that nobody liked it. I took it and it became a huge hit for Petula... When we first met, Serge still didn't have much of a reputation for being commercial. Radio stations found his songs too offbeat. Seeing as he didn't speak much, we offered him a drink – the least we could do. He went to the piano and sang "Vilaine fille," and in his uneasiness he knocked the glass over on the piano. All of the sudden he was shattered. He thought it was over, that we would show him the door... Now, it's true that it's no good to spill stuff into your piano, but we took the song all the same."

The children of modernity are folly bound
But their slot machines will work to cover up the sound
Of all those nagging voices and incessant ploys
Naughty girl, bad little boy....

"L'eau à la bouche," "Le poinçonneur," "La chanson de Prévert," and "La javanaise": four classics and yet no substantial sales. Gainsbourg is still looking to hit pay dirt, and thanks to his letters to Joseph, we have a pretty good idea of what daily life is like for him. We learn from them that at the years end Serge does several charity balls in Lausanne (with Robert Lamoreux), then in Geneva and in Brussels (where he evidently hosts a charity event), and at the behest of Louis Hazan, the big boss at Philips, he spits out a tune for the young Nana Mouskouri, a jazzy improvisation called "Les yeux pour pleurer" from a source of unexpected inspiration: beneath the surface of a consistently black sea, the word "happiness" breaks through...

When your heart starts to cry
When you think that you'll die
Yes there's yet another love
One other marvelous love
Beneath your very eyes
Another love lies
And this is the love of your life

Since filming *Voulez-vous dansez avec moi?*, Serge has stayed in steady contact with Jacques Poitrenaud, Boisrond's ex-first assistant, who has been directing scenes from the film *Les Parisiennes*. Together, they come up with an idea for a short subject and begin to write it. It will tell the story of the birth of a song, with Françoise Hardy in the lead role (at eighteen, she has just sold four million copies of "Tous les garçons et les filles" all over Europe).

But the project is scuttled when Poitrenaud gets the green light for his first feature, *Strip-Tease*, with Krista Nico in the lead role. Serge is content to accept a rare role as a non-speaking extra.

Krista Nico is better known by her last name only, the future Nico of the legendary Velvet Underground. Born in Germany, she is still, at the time, unsure about whether to pursue a career in cinema (discovered by Fellini, she appears in *La Dolce Vita*), modeling (she poses for *Vogue*) or music. Shortly after *Strip-Tease,* she flies to New York and seduces Bob Dylan, with whom she will have a tumultuous love affair. In 1964 Dylan writes "I'll Keep It With Mine" for her, and then she heads for London to hang out with Mick Jagger, Brian Jones, and the rest of the Rolling Stones. They introduce her to Andrew Loog Oldham, who has her make a 45 for his label, Immediate. She finally returns to Miami and is adopted by the seedy crowd at Andy Warhol's Factory, where she joins Lou Reed and John Cale's Velvet Underground, earning herself a choice place in the pantheon cult rock icons. What's funny is that before meeting Dylan, the Stones, or Warhol, she first records in the studio with Gainsbourg. He had written the theme music for *Strip-Tease* and wanted to try something with her. He really didn't dig to her voice and her German accent, which he found too heavy. He gave up and called on his friend Gréco to sing the lyrics:

> *This is where they do the strip-tease*
> *For drunken fools dance flawless fairies*
> *Come see the skin this little doll*
> *Has draped in clothing scant and small*
> *Although I stand completely bare here*
> *An ingénue at heart remains dear*
> *And I will stay so every night*
> *In simple garments of delight*

From January 2 to January 5, Serge finds himself in a London recording studio for the first time. It's also the first time for his friend, Goraguer. Philips had convinced him to go there and find a more pop sound (in the Cliff Richards-Helen Shapiro sense of the word – the Beatles wouldn't release their second album until January 11) and there he falls under the sway of one "Lord Rockingham," i.e. Harry Robinson and his session players. It's obviously a last-ditch effort by artistic director Jacques Plait, who is just about to join Claude Carré in launching the career of Shelia. And seeing as how Serge

steers himself back towards the universe of jazz in the coming months, we can easily surmise that the experience must have been furiously disappointing for him. Two years will roll by - marked by the irruption of the Fab Four, the Stones, the Kinks – before he returns. He cuts six tracks in London: his own versions of "Vilaine fille, mavais garcon," "L'appareil à sous," and "La javanaise," as well as a lilting little number that is completely unexpected, an exercise in style for a poor lad who claims he has not a friend in the world, "Un violon, un jambon":

> *Put your fiddle and your banjo outside your front door*
> *Your pals will return and quench your sorrow*
> *To hell with your troubles, think on them no more*
> *Until tomorrow*

There's been no sign of Serge in Parisian cabarets for some time. He's had his belly full of concerts, an attitude nourished most probably by his future wife, whom we will encounter in a few pages. Jealous as she is, she must hate the idea of him hanging out with all those female barflies until all hours of the morning in shadowy, smoke-filled nightclubs.

The life of our hero has frankly not improved much. Here are a few figures (in old francs),[5] carefully gathered together by Joseph, still worried about his son's future:

—advance royalties "Accodréon"/J. Gréco: 50,000.

—advance royalties "Vilaine fille, mauvais garcon" / P. Clark: 50,000.

—actor's wages for radio play (Brecht) on France-Inter: 100,000.[6]

—net pay for charity ball in February at Cannes: 145,000.

—Salary for two months of filming in Hong Kong for Poitrenaud's new film: 800,000.

One can easily understand why Serge accepts a role in the new film L'Inconnue de Hong Kong, a real dog. At least it gives him the chance to see another country. A few weeks before flying to the English colony, he has longtime supporter René Quinson of Combat listen to "Vilaine fille." In an interview published on February 15, he explains:

---

[5] The new franc was introduced in 1960, and was worth 100 old francs. Thus if you do the math, 50,000 olds francs equals 500 new francs, which is about 100 U.S. dollars. (T.N.)

[6] Serge played in Brecht's The Exception and the Rule in 1963.

GAINSBOURG: *"So I think, "here's something commercial, but not in-famous." Obviously, I like to write things that are more aggressive and darkly ironic. But I also dig rock and the twist. It's how you steer the masses towards real jazz. [...] I only write on demand, never from inspiration. Brigitte Bardot wanted some songs, and I wrote her a few. But what I gave her was pure Gainsbourg, not a bunch of tunes that reflected her personality. What's more, she liked it."*

In February, 1963, Serge registers a song with SACEM that remains unreleased. We know not whom it was written for (certainly not for himself – he had just released a new album and he isn't the sort of guy who starts to immediately write material for the next one). Originally entitled "L'homme et l'oiseau," he changes his mind at the last moment and decides on "Le lit-cage":

Trapped here in my bed-cage
There lies a child none too sage
For whom burned a tender flame
Like the birds on tropic isles
Whose insouciance beguiles
This babe I wanted so to tame
But the task proved an ordeal
I could not bring the child to heel
It was useless I confide
I should have I snapped the wings
Of that hummingbird who sings
Or drained the life from his poor hide

At around the same time, Jean-Louis Barrault - Babtiste in *Les enfants du paradis* and since then director of the Théâtre de l'Odéon – hears Serge say on television that he wants to write a musical comedy. Barrault offers him his theatre and says Serge will have carte blanche. But our hero already has too much on his plate: in March, with Alain Goraguer helming the orchestra and handling the arrangements, he puts the final touches on four pieces of incidental music for *Strip-Tease*, which comes out in May. Then he records five pieces for the film Comment trouvez-vous ma sœur?, once again at Europa-Sonor studios, but this time with Michel Colombier replacing Goraguer. This contains the song of the eponymous title, a smart and pleasingly cretinous rocker:

All the girls are mine to take
Still
There are some I'd like to shake
Yes sir
But dig this
What'cha think about my sis'?

Serge also composes the first part of another song, "Avec moi," for this film by Michel Boisrond, but what is really interesting are the lyrics and music he writes for an operatic scene entitled *Les Hussards*, which requires 23 musicians, 12 chorus singers, a tenor, a baritone, and a soprano from the Opéra-Comique. An opera by Gainsbourg, even if it is only some 3 minutes 20 seconds long, deserves our attention!

A sort of temporary malaise starts to brew between Serge and Goraguer. It's simple: Serge is encroaching on Goraguer's territory.

ALAIN GORAGUER: *"I was the one doing all the work, but it was Gainsbourg's name on the credits. Film music is the job of an arranger. I just need eight bars of a melody and the rest is all ambiance – "happy," "sad," "car chase," etc. On 'L'Eau à la bouche,' he'd asked to take sole credit, and to be amicable about it I let him because I could sense his fear, his anguish about not being a success. He was terrified that he was too old, even before the yé-yés. So long story short, he got sole credit. But then he pulls the same crap on 'Les Loups dans le bergerie' and 'Strip-Tease.' That's when I lost it. It wasn't in any way a question of money. As far as that went, things were fair."*

The filming of *L'Inconnue de Hong Kong* unfolds over the course of April, 1963. Serge plays the role of a bandleader at a big hotel, a hardcore boozer who's titillated by the arrival of two music-hall artists, played by Dalida (the naïve songstress) and Beryll (the idiot songstress). At the start of the film, before it degenerates into a banal police investigation, Serge gives a great performance in the sequence where he hits on the two singers as the three of them go pub crawling one night. As he tells one gossip hound, "For the first time, I play a decent guy who doesn't die in the end, which is a big departure from my earlier films."

JACQUES POITRENAUD: *"The star of the film was Dalida, who was cer-*

tainly more of a singer than an actress. And even though Serge would sometimes scoff at the whole corny, romantic schoolgirl quality of her songs, I think he respected her professionalism."

Danyel Gérard does the soundtrack for the film and Michel Colombier handles the arrangements, but it's Francis Lopez, the composer of *La belle de Cadix*, who pens the tune "Rue de mon Paris," which Serge and Dalida turn into an incredible duo:

> On my Parisian streets
> Life is one big treat
> Even when they're pelted with sleet
> Avenues are named with such poetry sweet
> Poems we learn by heart, and beat by beat

GAINSBOURG: "'Inconnu:' like the title, the film remained unknown. I gave French lessons to Dalida because she had an accent that could stifle a chainsaw. One good memory: getting plastered on a French navy ship that was docked out there. I sat jiggling the ice cubes in my whiskey and asked, "Who sank the Titanic? Iceberg – once again, a Jew!"

JACQUES POITRENAUD: "One thing that he doesn't mention is that we were really living it up. We filmed by day, and partied by night. Everything was fascinating: the atmosphere of the city, the sampans, the port, the bars with those little fourteen year-old Asian girls... One night with Serge I saw my first porno film. Some street urchin led us through a bunch of sleazy neighborhoods in a rickshaw. He took us to a place where the storefronts were all smashed open, iron shutters torn down, and he tells us, "There it is. Go on up..." Needless to say, we were scared shitless, the both of us. We ended up getting taken to a room by three guys with big bulging eyes, and they set up a makeshift screen, just a sheet pinned to the wall. It was a girl getting humped by a dog..."

GAINSBOURG: "It was the most shocking film I ever saw – that pretty little girl getting her hole crammed by that mutt's cock, getting scratched up by his paws, reticent, but finally coming, in all that grim black and white..."

Among the cast of *Inconnu* is one Philippe Nicaud, a young man Serge had met on the set of *Voulez-Vous Dansez avec moi?*, in which Nicaud played the role of a transvestite.

PHILIPPE NICAUD: *"Dalida never went out with us. She'd spend the evening in her room on the telephone, running down info about her record sales! I remember driving around with the chief of police of Hong Kong, who'd taken us under his wing. One night, he very courteously delivered us to an opium den, where Serge puked his guts out. We quickly ran him back to the hotel where the chief looked after him and administered something to clean out his stomach."*

Upon his return Serge treats himself to fifteen days of vacation in Athens, where he hooks up with Béatrice, his future wife, just before having "almost perished," as Joseph puts it ,"When his plane from Hong Kong got swept up in a typhoon, the people on board all thought they were done for." In the offices of Philips, Serge runs across a singer who's rounding out the month working as a press agent. At the end of the fifties she cut a 45 under the name of Françoise Marin. Under the name of Sophie Makhno, she is known as both a concert promoter and lyricist for Charles Dumont, Jean-Claude Pascal, and Barbara, for whom she also works as a secretary. We'll catch up with her later when she is handling the Gainsbourg/Barbara tour in 1965, but for now she gives us this magnificent anecdote, almost too good to be true:

SOPHIE MAKHNO: *"So Gainsbourg's future wife flew from Paris to Tokyo just to slap Dalida in the face. That's what Gainsbourg told me. He'd done a film with her, and afterwards, those Ici-Paris types of rags invented a story of some romantic tryst between the two. When Béatrice learned about it, she took a plane to Tokyo, went to Dalida's hotel, walked up to her room, slapped her, and immediately went back to Paris."*

Contrary to what he says in the Combat interview before leaving for Hong-Kong, a piece in which he seems rather proud of the concessions he had made to the variety-show circuit, Serge suddenly appears more intransigent in *Le Figaro*, on March 9, 1963: "I realized that I was selling out, filling my gas tank with maple syrup. Now, it's the avant-garde or nothing." That remains to be seen...

nine

To The Beat Of The Yé-Yés

The avant-garde or nothing? It's true that the variety show is triumphing as never before. On the monthly program *Salut les copains*, Johnny, who's singing "Elle est terrible," finally finds a rival in Claude François and his "Belles, belles, belles." Eddie Mitchell does "Be-Bop à Lulu '63" and Sheila squeals "L'école est finie." As for Bardot, she prances around the charts of provincial radio with "L'appareil à sous," a premonitory title for its composer, who will soon say goodbye to his sorry financial state.

Once back in Paris, Serge digs right into his work, and as an appetizer gives us *"Sérénade* pour Jeanne Moreau," improvised around the titles of her most famous films. It debuts on the program *Sérénade* on Radio-Luxembourg, in June, 1963:

> *Forget the hours, forget the days*
> *But please do not ignore*
> *These words, I know you feel the praise*
> *Of all the fans that you adore*
> *Watch the pendulum, watch it sway*
> *And if the hours grow dim*
> *Forget Moderato Cantabilé*
> *Forget Jules and forget Jim*

On June 16, Serge has a long interview with Denise Glaser when he's featured on an episode of *Discorama*. He sings "La javanaise," "Les cigarillos," and "Un violon, un jambon," answering honestly and amicably the questions of the host, already famous for her softball interviews:

DENISE GLASER: *Serge Gainsbourg, you were once asked by somebody if you were a snob and you responded that you were the worst of snobs. What exactly do you mean?*

GAINSBOURG: *I mean that I hate vulgarity. I live in the 16th. I get manicures.*

Titillated by the subject of the yé-yés and the shake up they're causing, Serge gets straight to the point. The excessive timidity of his previous television appearances is now replaced by self-assurance and a healthy and provocative cockiness.

S.G.: *The new wave, well, I'd say that's me. New wave signifies the avant-garde in song. I don't worry about how Tintin or Babar are selling. I'm not going to add a "y" to the end of my first name. And I think that milky white teeth fall out quickly, while wisdom teeth come in only with pain. Maybe it's o.k. for the tennyboppers, because there's a ton of money in it, and if it permits them to buy boatloads of lollipops or even lollipop factories... That's o.k.... that doesn't bother me. But I do something altogether different, That stuff (the yé-yés), that's American pop. American songs with subtitles.*

D.G.: *Well, what is it that you do, or rather how do you see yourself now? What do you write about?*

S.G.: *Me, I represent French song. French chanson is not dead. It has to evolve and not hitch itself to America's wagon. And talk about modern subject matter. We need to sing about concrete, tractors, telephones, elevators... Not just tell stories about being eighteen and sad, about breaking up... I stole my friend's gal, now he's not my pal... That just doesn't fly, I mean, there's more to life than that. Modern life means inventing a whole new language, both musically and linguistically. There's an entire world to create, it just remains to be done. French song remains to be created.*

D.G.: *What do you want to say with song?*

S.G.: *Well you have to please the women first, because it's the women who root and the men follow suit.*

As *L'Inconnue de Hong Kong* hits Parisian theatres, Serge vacations from July to September in Toquet (he feels "sentimentally attached"), to write new songs. His friend Flavio lends him the piano at Club de la Forêt, which he uses to write songs commissioned by Jeanne Moreau, Juliette Gréco, and Zizi Jeanmaire, as well as those that will be featured on his new album, *Gainsbourg, Confidentiel*. Flavio's daughter gives us the rest:

DANI DELMOTTE: "*Sometimes his wife would kick him out of the room when he came back too late. He had rented the Villa Surlinks, completely isolated, at the other end of town. He'd go back on foot, three kilometers, and make the same trek back when his wife sent him packing. We lived upstairs, and he would wake us up, my father and I, and he'd come into the club and sleep in a booth. It happened at least ten times in the summer of '63. She was super jealous, and she gave him a lot of shit. It was unbelievable.*"

We have no idea at all whether this turbulent summer offers any inspiration for the songs he writes for Jeanne Moreau. On October 5, Serge participates in *Teuf-Teuf*, a program produced by Maritie and Gilbert Carpentier. The purpose: a tribute to the automobile. Serge, who doesn't even have a license, imagines an impromptu encounter with some young chick while driving a convertible. He calls his partner Gillian Hills and the song is entitled "Une petite tasse d''anxiété":

> (He) *Please climb inside*
> *Let me give this schoolgirl a ride*
> *And you'll have a taste of exquisite stress*
> *Before I get you back for your test*

He offers to drive her through the 'woods," but the girl turns the tables on him and asks that he please wait until she finishes her classes...

> (He) - *Now, now, you digress*
> *You think I'll wait on bended knees?*
> (She) - *You too should taste this exquisite stress*
> *And only then will I give you the keys*

For his new album, Serge keeps his word and decides to place himself at the front of avant-garde French chanson. He'll need two skilled accomplices to do so. Now several months earlier, in a club, he had heard the great black be-bop pianist Bud Powell, who was completely loaded but as nice as ever. Accompanying him were Belgian guitarist, René Thomas, and French bassist, Michel Gaudry. And could they swing! Daniel Filipacchi and Frank Ténot's show, *Pour ceux qui aiment le jazz*, broadcast on Europe n°1, often features a guitarist of Hungarian-gypsy origin, Elek Bacsik. He is known particularly for his version of "Take Five," the signature piece by Paul Desmond and Dave Brubeck. It finally clicked in Gainsbourg's head: if he's going jazz, he'll go all the way.

Before going into the studio to cut *Gainsbourg Confidentiel*, the trio warms up with a series of four concerts – every Tuesday during October, 1963 – at the Théâtre des Capucines, 39 Boulevard des Capucines, across from the Olympia. It is the first time that Serge finds himself headlining at a real music-hall, and the man responsible for it all is one Gilbert Sommier. Sommier, a law student, seems to be taking on the mission abandoned by Jacques Canetti, who, victim of a severe bout of depression, temporarily removes himself from the business. Heading up a little stable that includes Pia Colombo, Anne Sylvestre, Joël Holmes, and Ricet Barrier, Sommier wants to save "good" French song, the sort that which just can't find a home among the yé-yés. Johnny Hallyday's show at the Olympia a year earlier was essentially like a bomb going off: "It was sad seeing the Olympia transformed into the temple of twist. Wouldn't it be better to have a complete show by Gloria Lasso than to be subjected to this teenybopper frenzy..." writes Michel Pérez in *Combat* on June 26, 1963. It is as if the music-hall directors and the big bosses at the record companies are deciding to sacrifice not only a whole generation of artists, but also the (limited) public following they have.

> GILBERT SOMMIER: *"I was broke, and so to advertise my concerts at La Huchette I had to resort to hiring a street vendor from Boulevard Saint-Michel. I had only 80 seats to fill, and there was a sort of snobbism attached to the event. People like Christiane Rochefort started giving it great publicity and so it didn't take to much effort to sell out. I knew a lot of really talented songwriters and singers who no longer had a venue, and so I offered them a stage, a place to sing. There were plenty of unknowns and I was their conduit to the press. Pretty soon we had a regular crowd of reviewers, like Paul Carrière from Le Figaro, Claude Saurrate from Le*

Monde, and Lucien Rioux from l'Observateur."

Georges Brassens, quite in-the-know despite his reputation as a hermit, has sources who report him at his place on l'Impasse Florimont. René-Louis Lafforgue talks to him about La Huchette, and Brassens decides to grace the club with a visit without so much as an invitation from Sommier. Thanks to Brassens, and with a bit of help from Philips, Sommier soon finds himself at the Théâtre des Capucines with 400 rather than 80 seats. He's swimming in good will: Michel Siros, a high-fidelity nut, offers to handle the sound in exchange for the rights to record the featured artists. As for publicity, in addition to using the street vendor, he slips flyers under the windshields of parked cars. When the budget permits (for instance a show by Barbara), he takes out billboards. And so it is that Gainsbourg, who had never been to a single show at La Huchette, gets the honor of opening the new season of Mardis de la Chanson at Théâtre des Capucines on October 8, 1963.

Gainsbourg's memory has faded in respect to this evening. He forgets that all of Paris came out to see him, including Françoise Sagan, Joseph Kessel, Louise de Vilmorin, Guy Béart, Juliette Gréco, Philippe Clay, Félix Marten, Vercors, and Yves Montand. Serge even manages to coax Brassens out of his lair, not to mention his sister Jacqueline and his parents, Joseph and Olia.

If he was flipping out before he took the stage it was because he couldn't remember the lyrics. "Yeah, I was scared! Nauseous, even..." he tells Guy Vidal of the weekly publication *Pilote* in 1964. "I got plastered on bourbon... Now I just don't give a shit, which, as an on-stage attitude, is better than the aggression I showed at the beginning of my career. I used to frighten people; now they laugh their asses off."

"At the Mardis de la Chanson," remembers Gilbert Sommier, "Serge was accompanied by his wife, who always wore a leopard skin coat. He seemed to be really afraid of her. She was really acerbic." This observation is seconded by one of Serge's old friends from the Académie Monmartre, Simone Véliot, who has since become a painter.

SIMONE VÉLIOT: *"I saw his name on a poster and went to see him. Listening to his lyrics, you could tell things were starting to explode. He was going to be big. He would dress impeccably when onstage, but you could tell he was a bit uptight. Backstage, after the show, he gave me a warm welcome. I suggested that we get together some time, and he said, "I'd love to." He took out a notebook and jotted down my number. It was then that the tigress appeared, a raging fury who said: "Get over here, Serge!" He seemed to tremble before her, almost submissively. Timidly, he said: "Listen, call me." I never saw him again."*

At the Théâtre des Capucines, as one columnist puts it, "The room is composed of young, sweater-clad, intellectuals. Men wearing ties have already loosened the first button on their shirts, and their female companions, showing plenty of leg, are generally dressed in black with their hair either bobbed or in Morticia-like coifs." There is already the "cinéma d'art et d'essai," and now they are applying those same terms to the world of song.[1] They are talking about the "chanson d'essai," and how the Tuesday concerts serve as a "forum for independent song." Paul Carrière of *Le Figaro* takes notes at the first concert. He observes that Serge's performance creates a "very unique atmosphere," especially in that there is no piano and he is accompanied only by Gaudry's bass and Bacsik's guitar. Later on, Carrière shares his candid reactions with the reader: "what rhythm and originality," "striking figure, strange voice," "crippling, nasty irony," "still avant-garde – the most sure and most solid" and finally "always the most refined"... Serge does ten songs: "La femme des uns sous le corps des autres," "Intoxicated Man," "La recette de l'amour fou," "Ce mortel ennui," "La javanaise," "Maxim's," "Negative Blues," "L'amour à la papa," "Dieu que les hommes sont méchantes," and "Personne." There are three new tunes among the ten, two of which will appear on *Gainsbourg Confidentiel*, his first 30 cm album. We also get "Dieu que les homes sont méchantes," one of the pre-*Love On The Beat* era songs dealing with homosexuality, in a somewhat mocking and desperate manner:

> *Life is cruel*
> *Happiness scant*
> *I've left all my gowns*
> *Back at my aunt's*
> *A stint in the service*
> *Captain, what prater*
> *I've been discharged*

[1] A French term referring essentially to the independent, experimental, or art film. (T.N.)

I'm mad as a hatter

A few years later, he will give us the song's sister piece and write "Les femmes ça fait pédés" for Régine, queen of the night... There's also "Maxim's," which is soon covered by Serge Reggiani, in which we hear the dreams of a street sweeper, perhaps those of Serge before having met the very chic and very jealous woman he's now stuck with:

> *Ah, to kiss the hand of a worldly dame*
> *To shred my lips on her lustrous diamonds*
> *And then in the Jaguar*
> *Burn her leopard-skin coat*
> *With an English cigarette*

He gets good reviews in the press, beginning with Michel Pérez's in *Combat* on October 18:

> *The evening ends with Serge Gainsbourg's return to Paris. Here is a tower of song that in no way betrays even a hint of opportunism or demagoguery. Boldly flaunting equal measures of detachment, hep-cat irony, and insolence, he does nothing to gain the favor of those who wish to be flattered or rub shoulders with celebrities. There's no formal greeting of the crowd, just a little smile and a sly wink of the eye meant only for the players that accompany him. There's little room here for the sentimentally inclined.*
>
> *It goes without saying that Gainsbourg has something that many of his cohorts envy: elegance and lucidity. He understands his weaknesses and does not look to hide them. On the contrary, by forging a personality that is itself based in his limitations as a singer, he gains all the more our esteem. There's no point in being redundant about the quality of his songs. Their success is already well merited.*

Still, we can't forget that phrase: "his limitations as a singer!" On October 18, Paul Carrière of *Le Figaro* speaks of "his nonchalance, his sharp gaze and somber voice, which immediately create an atmosphere [..] Buttressed supplely behind his mic, yet still one with the group of musicians - including the fabulous guitarist Elek Bacsik - he "uproots" his audience, tugs at them with his beat. He never overdoes it. In the feverish rhythm of his unique brand of jazz, his irony remains glacial, all the while passing from intellectual refinement to full-tilt belly laughs. In the magazine *Arts*, which dons the subheading "The weekly of French intelligence" (Good God!), they speak of his "misogynistic ferocity," and say that he "distills a sprawling irony of acidic mannishness (sic). He's not bitter, which would be useless and petty, but virulent, morbid, and acerbic: he'll kiss you and kill you all at once. He's efficient in every way, not a single superfluous word, and he touches your heart as well as your head. His figure, which we see only as a permanent profile, is a testament to the Gainsbourg persona – poet of a masculine perfidy that seduces women, even those whom it irritates."

Claude Sarraute of *Le Monde* (Oct. 16) seems to have an unpleasant evening, at least until Serge shows up: "Finally someone worthy of being called an artist, in command of all of his talents and at the top of his game [...] His repertory is conjugated not in the past, but the present, even the future." Finally, the indefatigable Lucien Rioux of *France-Observateur* attacks the cheerful conformity of the "copains" crowd and predicts that "Once that insipid bubble-gum crap fades away, the public will come to love his adult lyrics."

Adult lyrics could have easily been the subtitle for *Gainsbourg Confidentiel*, which is recorded in three days, from November 12 to 14 of 1963 at Studio DMS with Elek Bacsik (electric guitar) and Michel Gaudy (acoustic bass). With Jacques Plait now gone, Claude Dejacques takes over as artistic director.

> CLAUDE DEJACQUES: *"He opted for this pure, trio style when he realized that tunes like "La chanson de Prévert" had been over-produced, rendered too didactic. I'm really proud of the terrific mix we got on this album, which was nevertheless recorded in a shithole of a studio on Rue Sussier-Leroy, an absolutely foul little garage, basically, where we managed to create miracles. All the material had been written and Serge came in ready and raring, so we finished the disc in record time."*

Everything ready and written?... Not so sure about that... Serge is always in the habit of working at the last minute, and in a letter from Joseph we learn that the he finishes the last two of the album's twelve songs the night before he enters the studio.

Some thirty years after its release, one is still stunned at how modern sounding this stripped down this little album actually is. Much of it is due to Elek Bacsik's guitar. Several months later, Serge would say about Elek: "With him I felt the groove of jazz rather than the force of rock, which I always found a little phony."

Elek actually writes the music for one the album's loveliest tunes, "La saison de pluies":

> *This is the rainy season*
> *It's the end of love*
> *From this veranda, I see him weep*
> *That child I so adored*

ALAIN BASHUNG: *"When I arrived in Paris from my native Alsace, the first artists I met were painters in Montmartre. They listened to Miles Davis, John Coltrane, and Gainsbourg's 'Confidentiel.' There was this exceptional guitarist named Bacsik. When I hear him it's like listening to J.J. Cale because of the way he plays, with a minimum of notes, but at just the right time!"*

MICHEL GAUDRY: *"Elek was both a guitarist and a classically trained violinist. A few years after this recording, he left for the U.S., where he died toward the end of the seventies. As for Gainsbourg, well, he put all his heart and soul into the album. He'd play the music on the piano and then let us do our thing. The record was put together in the studio. It opens with "Chez les yé-yé," which is both a driving piece and at the same time the articulation of frustration..."*

> *Not the yé-yés who pound the beat*
> *Nor the charms that you wear so sweet*
> *The "Doo-Run, Run" you listen to*
> *Or the club where you boogaloo*
> *Not all the bulls in the corrida*
> *Can keep me from my Lolita*
> *Chez les yé-yé*

The Lolita in question, whom we associate with Nabokov, of course, or even Kubrick (the film, with Sue Lyon in the title role, is released in France in 1963), manages to drive him nuts in this extraordinarily sophisticated and jazzy experiment ("Talkie-Walkie"):

> *I held a walkie-talkie in the palm of my hand*
> *Made in Japan*
> *Now all that remains is but a tiny grain of sand*

One grain, that's all
I gave the exact same model to the girl of my heart
We called one another night and day
Whether she was home or at the museum of fine art
I possessed her in each and every way

One fine day she forgets that the walkie-talkie has been left on next to
her bed, and he hears her moaning and sighing with another. He is then pre-
maturely transformed into "l'homme à tête de chou."[2] Gainsbourg continues
to mine the depths of the whole "franglais" and "modern gizmo" terrain,
giving us "La fille au rasoir," whose inspiration comes from a memory of
cinematic origin:

Razor, electronique
As it dances 'cross Clara's skin
The noise, metallique
I'm going to burst forth from within
No it wasn't so droll
Trying to maintain control

It's true, women are always driving him mad, especially when he has to
chase after them through the Russian mountains of the "Scenic Railway":

Yes
I'll show you the best
The old scenic railway
But those old feelings there
Are thinner than air

[...]

Yes
I have to confess
I'm bitter, but please stay
These machines are made
For those who want to get laid

Gainsbourg Confidentiel is released in January, 1964, and on top of the
charts are Aznavour, with "La Mamma," the Beatles, with "She Loves You,"
and Johnny Hallyday with "Excuse-moi partenaire." Not much space here

---

[2] "L'homme à tête de chou," or "cabbage-head man," will later become the title of Serge's 1976 concept
album. (T.N.)

for a strange question like this ("Sait-on jamais où va une femme quand elle vous quitte?"):

We never know where women go after they leave us
Whether this is true
Is something that you
Never knew
We never know where women go after they leave us
But me I really do
When all is said and through
Landru...

The film *Landru*,[3] by Claude Chabrol, came out in 1962, with Charles Denner in the lead role. During his trial, while speaking about one of his victims, Landru states simply: "She just left one morning. She left, your honor. What goes on in the head of a young woman? Go figure..." Yet later on, in "Negative Blues," Serge wonders again: *Where's my girlfriend?*

I see my cherry pie at last
Posing for my Rolleflex
A little doll in black spandex
And she really wears it well

"Le temps de yoyos" seems to be a good indication of his inner state, although as we will soon see, he is on the brink of drifting into this new yé-yé tide:

Silence I must
This sad despair
This malady
I cannot bear
The yo-yos time has
Faded fast away
Let's pass the torch now
To the new yé-yé

Just a few months into his second marriage, Serge takes stock of the situation on "Amour sans amour":

How many flowers I have plucked dry
They blossom open but to die
So many tears and garments have been shed

---

[3] The film depicts the life of an infamous serial killer, Henri-Désiré Landru. (T.N.)

Here at the footstep of my bed
A comedy unfolds, hear the chorus sing
For these forgotten, fragile beings

Finally, the centerpiece of this pivotal album is not really a play on words, but on letters themselves:

L, A, E, T, I
Five little letters
L, A, E, T, I
Make up Laetitia
Pounding out letters here on this page
Laetitia, your name I do spell
I am consumed with grief and rage
Typing your name I'm trapped in hell[4]

Serge hits the road as soon as the album is finished, zigzagging from Strasbourg (a TV concert) to Hilversum (Dutch TV), and then passing through Caen, Marseille, and finally the casino at Knokke-le-Zoute, Belgium, for a disastrous Flemish radio recital on November 29. Johan Anthierens, host of the weekly broadcast *De charme van het chanson*, remembers that the concert was organized for the benefit of Davidsfonds, the Dutch Catholic cultural organization. The reactionary audience turns so cold that it becomes uncomfortable for everyone, including Serge, who pushes his indifference to the point of finishing the concert with a barely audible voice, hands in his pockets. After the concert, the organization's president explodes in an embarrassing sermon, apologizing for having invited such an artist... A new nightmare awaits him in Paris, and is described in detail by the late Claude Dejacques in his book *Piégée, la chanson...?*:

The boss at Milord l'Arsouille had convinced Serge to write the songs for his new album right there at the club [...] so that it would be a big deal when the record came out. Francis Claude, who really admired Serge, had put everything together, but Philips didn't believe it should be responsible for the publicity [...] The only journalist to help get the word out was Lucien Rioux. So on opening night, Bacsik, Gaudry, Serge, his wife, and me, we all

---

[4] In the first two lines of "Laetitia" (it sounds the same whether spelled out either phonetically or as alphabetical letters), Serge sings the first three letters of a girl's name, the preposition "dans" (in), the phoneme "la," and then proceeds to spell ou the last five letters. In doing so he's actually singing something like the following: "There's an L, A, and an E in Lae-ti-tia." It's virtually untranslatable, and much prettier and more sophisticated in French. (T.N.)

get together in the basement backstage. There would be three musicians onstage, matched by just three audience members when the show began. And the three who dropped in were looking for a traditional chansonnier. It was just dead in there – like they were staring at three hit men. He turns coldly towards his musicians to avoid the dumbfounded faces before him. Afterwards, backstage, he sits like a zombie smoking cigarette after cigarette.

The day after this colossal failure, Serge is beside himself: "It was crushing," said Dejacques in private, "For him it meant that *Gainsbourg Confidentiel* was done for. In an instant, he decided to permanently retire this style of music."

The television show *Cœur de Paris* is broadcast on December 12, 1963. Created by Roland Petit and Zizi Jeanmaire, it includes Zizi doing a lovely "Javanaise" in a little square on Rue Saint-Vincent in Monmartre. For the grand finale, she's dressed, according to the papers, in a "lavish, diamond-studded gown and feathered headdress", and she performs the song "Zizi," specially written by Serge for her and her alone:

> *This life*
> *Zizi*
> *Is but*
> *A dream*
> *This life*
> *Tells you*
> *Not one*
> *Damn thing*

Serge, who's sick in bed with a splitting earache and getting two shots of penicillin a day, watches the premier of the *Sacha Show* on December 30. Sacha Distel, whom we've encountered before, was both Bardot's boyfriend and one of France's most popular stars in 1959-60. But his loveable novelty songs, like "Les scoubidous" and "Mon beau chapeau," can't stand up to the shock of the whole yé-yé thing. Still, thanks to the immediate and lasting success of the *Sacha Show*, Distel is able to launch a new career for himself. Until this time, he had never liked TV, but now he jumps at the chance to help create his own show along with producers Maritie and Gilbert Carpentier. They are American-style shows, the Dean Martin/Perry Como sort of thing with songs, often duets or trio performances, choreography and sketch comedy.

SACHA DISTEL: *"The three musketeers at the heart of the show were Petula Clark, Jean-Pierre Cassel, and Jeanne Yanne. And me, of course, I was d'Artagnan. Maritie Carpentier had suggested using Serge as house composer, and so he started to write tunes for us on a regular basis, all still unreleased, beginning with "Distell et Cassel," which was written for the first show broadcast on December 30, 1963. It was really just a paycheck to him. He was usually late, impossible to find..."*

This ends our interlude. Serge gets married for the second time, to a grand beauty, Françoise Antoinette Pancrazzi, known as Béatrice (like Serge, she hates her real first name). The wedding, on the afternoon of January 7, 1964, is a small affair in the 8th arrondissement. Béatrice, born in Algeria in 1931, is the daughter of Robert Pancrazzi, an industrialist. She had been divorced from Georges Galitzine, hence the nickname "princess Galitzine." The witnesses are Claude Dejacques (for Serge) and Yvonne Barrois (for Béatrice). Coming out of city hall they stop to pose for photographers and reporters.

Serge, as we have seen, had always been intoxicated with beautiful, bourgeois women. He had always admired them during his childhood, when he visited those elegant seaside resorts. They enchanted him, especially those in Toquet, where he was the pianist in the hotel bar. He had been fascinated by the snobbishness and class of Michèle Arnaud, his first interpreter. He was proud of having won the heart of Sylvie Rivet, his very elegant press agent. Now with Béatrice, he is set: she comes from the haute-bourgeoisie and her family has made a fortune in real estate. The polar opposite of his first wife, Elisabeth, with whom he had lived like a bohemian, Béatrice proposes that they live a cushy existence in an apartment behind La Madeleine, at 12 Rue Tronchet, in the 8th arrondissement. Even if that means putting up with her rather extreme personality: she will have tried to kill herself four times before Serge leaves her, and never as a joke. Each attempt will require urgent medical intervention.

They had known each other for just a short while, and Béatrice was surely pregnant when they got married. Natacha, their daughter, would be born in August, 1964, just seven months later. Olia and Joseph are apprehensive. What's more, they are not invited to the wedding. They only attend the reception at the restaurant, along with the couple, Jacqueline, and the witnesses. On the way to the reception, an inopportune phone call that Serge had received earlier sparks an argument which reaches its climax right when they pass the apartment on Rue Tronchet.

> GAINSBOURG: *"At the beginning, we lived together and everything was hunky-dory. Then it all turned sour. My job required me to take meetings with people, and even a rendezvous with an innocent young girl, like France Gall, was just unacceptable. It started on our wedding day. Coming back from city hall I get a phone call from a young girl, some crazy fan. It was completely innocent! Well she just blew up, and me, I felt like I was in a prison. "That's it," I thought. "I'm screwed." I knew immediately it would all turn into a nightmare... Anyway, it was a good idea to have the reception at a Russian restaurant, seeing as how the atmosphere afterwards was like a Siberian winter."*

In retrospect, it's easy to understand what has happened: Serge has thrown himself into the belly of the beast. Seduced by his love for this woman, a woman who just doesn't fit into his universe, he quickly comes to understand that this fatal attraction has landed him in the claws of a tigress.

> JULIETTE GRÉCO: *"One day, she interrupted us while we were working together. She was stunning and all, but you could see the rage in her eyes. I had to watch while Gainsbourg was in the grips of this absolutely murderous panther, and ready to move heaven and earth for her. What a spectacle! Still, I understand how someone could be jealous with such a man..."*

> SOPHIE MAKHNO: *"A few months earlier, Georges Meyerstein had asked me to look after Gainsbourg. He said, "I set up a meeting for the two of you. I'm sending my chauffeur and he'll take you to Serge's place on Rue Bugeaud." I wondered why Rue Bugeaud and not Rue Tronchet, where he lived. He told me: "He'd rather see you at his father's place." When I got there, Serge was pacing around the piano in a state of incertitude. He explained, "My wife just won't let another woman come to our home. Things usually go wrong and it turns into a big scene."*

Serge and Béatrice head to Morocco for their honeymoon. When Serge gets back, he starts promotion on the *Confidentiel* album, and although he has great hopes for the record, it will not sell more than 1,500 copies. *Télé-Revue*, nevertheless, heaps upon him this laudatory praise:

It remains still all too "confidential" that Serge Gainsbourg possesses a talent which merits much greater esteem. Still, it's true that in the world of song, being on top is usually a testament to one's utter mediocrity, to being an artist of complete insignificance, completely clueless [...] (But) Serge Gainsbourg's universe is an El Dorado where children, like brilliant insects, give birth to words that sprout wings. He is an alchemist creating lexical combinations that are much more clever than one would guess at first glance [...] He is without a doubt the most original singer-songwriter of his generation. His work is already testament to that, and in the future it will be much more.

On February 2, Serge sings "Chez les yé-yé," "Le rasoir électrique," and "No No Thanks No" on *Discorama*, and Jackie Lawrence, new girl on the block and host for the moment, does "La saison de pluies." On February 15, he stars on Daniel Lab's show *Trois annés trios success*, where he sings "L'eau à la bouche" and "Chez les yé-yé," while Philippe Clay performs "La recette de l'amour fou" and Gréco gives us "La javanaise." Finally, on February 20, he and Philippe Clay do a cheeky version of "Accordéon" on *Demandez le programme*.

Also earlier that month, he had invited Philippe Koechlin, editor-in-chief of *Jazz Hot* and future founder of *Rock and Folk*, to dine at his parents' house, snubbing, as it were, other magazines, especially *France-Observateur* and in particular the smaller *Musica*. It turns out to be a terrific interview and is published in April. Some highlights:

PHILIPPE KOECHLIN: *What kind of personality do you think you've forged through your songs?*

SERGE GAINSBOURG: *Certainly not any kind of pop-culture hero. My talents were honed among snobs, dilettantes. I don't make music for the throngs and masses of the city streets. [...]*

P.K.: *Aren't you tired of making music for such a limited audience?*

S.G.: *I don't even think about it. Just because I don't have a big following doesn't mean that I'm speaking only to the elite. I don't know who likes my songs. What is certain is that I have gained notoriety as a composer.*

P.K.: *Are there any French singers that you like?*

S.G.: *No, they all whine. They lack virility. They want to show all the little teenybopper girls that they understand. Those chicks hear me and they head for the hills. No, I don't like pop music.*

P.K.: *So what would you like to do?*

S.G.: *I believe that songwriting will lead to writing musical-comedy. I admit that my dreams are a bit unrealistic at the moment, but I don't see myself onstage at fifty years old. Singing, for the time being, is like painting was for me: a means of living a fringe existence.*

My dreams are a bit unrealistic! Living a fringe existence! This flabbergasting sincerity stands as a perfect statement of his feelings towards the singer-songwriter profession, and it is at this precise moment in his career that he composes "N'écoute pas les idoles" for his new client, France Gall, who without knowing it will save his life.

LES GRANDS AUTEURS & COMPOSITEURS INTERPRETES

SERGE GAINSBOURG

"gainsbourg percussions"

joenna
là-bas c'est naturel
pauvre Lola
quand mon 6,35 me fait les yeux doux

machins choses
les sambassadeurs
New York – U.S.A.
couleur café

marabout
ces petits riens
tatoué Jérémis
coco and c°

PHILIPS

ten

Don't Listen To Pop Stars

our months earlier, on October 9, 1963, France Gall (her real name
was Isabelle) had her sixteenth birthday, and as a special surprise,
she got to hear herself on the radio for the first time when Daniel Filipacchi
of Europe n°1 played "Ne sois pas si bête." The record company gives the
song the hard sell towards the end of November and soon France Gall is all
the rage: with 200,000 copies sold she is now a real threat to Sylvie Vartan
and Sheila.

It is Denis Bourgeois who pushes for the meeting with France, who had
been pulled into the profession by her father, composer of Aznavour's "La
Mamma," (a big hit in 1963). Bourgeois, responsible for signing Gainsbourg
to Philips in 1958, had since left to form another company, Bagatelles.

DENIS BOURGEOIS: *"I had the happy task of asking Serge to write for
France Gall. He had in fact remained, as it were, in his own territory,
writing for mostly cabaret artists like Gréco, Michèle Arnaud, or Isabelle
Aubret. He never wrote for the young, for this massive new wave. But once
he started, he dove right in, and he wrote classics!"*

FRANCE GALL: *"I'd meet writers in my producer's office. It was me, my
dad, and a piano. The guy would do his song and then take off. I hardly paid
attention. I remember Gainsbourg as being a timid guy with a very soft*

voice. I always loved his tunes. Afterwards, we'd talk about the right key
and then we wouldn't see each other until we met in the studio. Usually,
Alain Goraguer did the orchestrations for all four tunes in the morning,
then I'd sing in the afternoon and we'd mix at night and the record would
be finished."

Charles Aznavour is one of the first to put himself at the disposal of the new generation. He writes "Retiens la nuit" and "Saisir sa chance" for Johnny Hallyday. In fact, right when Serge finishes "N'écoute pas les idols," Sylvie Vartan is topping the charts with Aznavour's "La plus belle pour aller danser." Serge would later admit, "When the French rock groups came along, I wasn't too sharp about it. France Gall saved my life, because I was really lost."

France will sell more than 300,000 copies of "N'écoute pas les idoles," the title cut from her second EP, released in March, 1964:

> These little ditties that you hum
> How could it be
> That you want me to like them
> It just cannot be
> You would like it if I fell
> Head over heels
> And then just forget it all
> How would that feel
> Forget those pop singers please
> Listen please do
> For I'm as mad as can be
> Crazy for you

France sings it for the first time in public on a Jean-Pierre Cassel TV show, which we'll come back to later. Before that, we must discuss a new nightmare festering among our young married man. Serge is doing a show in Brussels with Elek Bacsik, with Romain Bouteille as the opening act. There are five shows scheduled from February 12 to February 16 at the former parochial hall, now transformed into a theatre under the direction of Jo Dekmine which specializes in the avant-garde. But one show is cancelled due to a lack of ticket sales. A night before the opening, there is a cocktail party in Serge's honor at the Martini Center, a hot-spot for hipsters in 1960s-era Brussels. The press is there.

ROMAIN BOUTEILLE: *"He was interesting because through him we understood that one could be considered "Rive Droite" and at the same time have literary aspirations. The crowd at 140 was a bit cold, and we were watching Gainsbourg and saying to ourselves "Impossible. He couldn't have said that... done that!..." There was a sense of disdain about him. Between songs, he'd take long pauses onstage on walk over to a cardboard mannequin who was holding the set list in its hand. He'd look at the title of the next song and then sit back down. There was also a model of a circular staircase. Just two elements of décor – a stroke of genius."*

The review in the Belgian dailies aren't terrible: One title in *Le Soir* reads "Serge Gainsbourg, or the danger of wanting to shock at any price," and describes the crowd, though composed of ardent supporters, as "a bit taken aback by this strange bird." It goes on to say that "Gainsbourg the performer cannot compare to Gainsbourg the songwriter [...] he doesn't possess the stature of a star." *La Lanterne* gives us another perspective: "Serge Gainsbourg: a monotonous delivery and lack of inspiration." The journalist is disappointed with his "morose" music. He questions Serge's misogyny, which to him "seems to be simply the result of facile intellectual speculation and an easy source of inspiration."

Nevertheless, it's Belgium that leaves us with the best televised record from that period. In early March, a team led by director Léo Quoilin more or less invades Olia and Joseph's Avenue Bugeaud apartment, still intermittently inhabited by their son. The show, *Venez donc chez moi*, will feature seven songs, including "Scenic Railway," "Elaeudanla Teiteia," "La javanaise," (with Jean-Pierre Cassel and Valerie Lagrange in bit parts) and "La fille au rasoir" (which once again show off Valerie's legs). Elek Bacsik and Michel Gaudry are also seen during a short instrumental.

A year earlier, Serge had done the music for Michel Boisrond's *Comment trouvez-vous ma sœur?*, which is released on March 4, 1964. Then on March 12, Carpentier productions scores a big hit with the new show *Top à Jean Cassel*. Along with France Gall, who does "N'écoute pas les idoles," Gainsbourg is also along for the ride, and he performs "Chez les yé-yé," as well as four other tunes composed just for the program: "Clicuediclac," "Viva la Pizza," "Oh la la la la," and "Al Cassel's Air."

The film of this show and all the film for the *Sacha Shows* was unfortunately destroyed or erased. Thus we'll never know what the silly tune "Oh la la la la" was like, but the beginning was interesting ("For little girls and little boys / My pockets hold some noisy toys"). Finally, Serge appears in an interview for the magazine *Music Hall*, soon to be defunct in the face of the colossal success of *Salut les copains*. His musings about the nature of song are still quite profound:

At its heart, song must be popular. It shouldn't be too much work. It's really difficult to express feelings in a natural and authentic way, so I simply do what interests me: I write about sophisticated women and dress them up in my words. I don't think I have ever written about a women who could be mistaken as something as provincial as a secretary from the suburbs. My songs unfold in a universe of luxury and neurosis. It's the polar opposite of the music of Damia or Berthe Sylva, of that world of the miserable street urchin.

The same year, in *L'Union de Reims*, he answers the question "Where is chanson headed?":

I'm no prophet... Maybe rock will lead to something... I'm still waiting for their more intelligent acolytes, and they haven't arrived. All this high fidelity, all this sound, it's exasperating... In the end, it's the same goddamned question we ask about all modern art... What's the future of painting? Of music?...

As for his personal life, well, the prison cell is growing smaller. On April 2, for his 36th birthday, Béatrice gives him a Steinway baby grand.

GAINSBOURG: *"I told her: "We get married on one condition – I keep working at my parents' house. That's where I work best, at my father's piano. You, you stay in the apartment." Then comes the Steinway. The message was clear..."*

Next, Serge will hunt down Bacsik and Gaudry and do the music for the film *Les plus belles escroqueries du monde*. Gaudry's big, fat bass lines lay the foundation for the cutting lyrics of this still unreleased tune:

Patience is bitter
Why wait in disgust
While Jaguars and furs
Are trampled to dust

She makes it well known
She wants rocks on her rings
And won't wait for someone
To buy her these things

The one who supports them
Is vile we are told
He counts all his strumpets
In silver and gold
You say he's a scoundrel
At fault, is this true?
Or is it the girls
He delivers to you?

Serge sets his mind to the task of his next album. He has a new idea in mind, another exercise in minimalism based simply on Afro-Cuban rhythms and background singers. It will be a few months, however, before he starts recording *Gainsbourg Percussions*. In May, we see him again on TV, and for the first he's time on a show with a teenage audience, *Seize millions de jeunes*, where he sings "Chez les yé-yé." A month later he's on Demandez le programme, doing duets with Philippe Clay. He performs "Accordéon" and "L'assassinat de Franz Léhar."

An unexpectedly calm summer - devoted mainly to anxiously awaiting the birth of Natacha – draws to a close when France Gall asks Serge for new material. Since we last spoke of her, she has released a rather weak EP, fea-turing Alain Goraguer and Robert Gall's "Jazz à gogo" and Jacques Datin and Maurice Vidalin's "Mes premières vraies vacances." Thanks to Serge's "Laisse tomber les filles," the title cut of the super-45 released in September 1964, she's off and running with her second beauty:

Stop your running 'round
Yes, stop your running 'round
Or one day I'll run around on you
[...]
When all is said and done it's true
You're the reason that we're through
You're the reason that we're through

Gainsbourg's lyrics are obviously unlike anything else in the bubble-gum world of the yé-yés - a world not completely bereft of charm, but still a bit insipid. His work either comes off as deliberately negative, or else it demands a more in-depth reading. What he sees in France Gall is a sad nostalgia: an awkward young girl who doesn't always like what people make her do. The songs he writes lend her a strength and clearness of purpose, as if she's refusing to take part in the insane "farce" that is love, the fairytale love of "nevers" and "forevers." Then again, this time we're not listening to some guy in his thirties belt it out, but rather a teenager... In a 1964 interview, Georges Bratschi of *La Tribune de Genève* questions Serge about the songs he writes for France Gall:

> SERGE GAINSBOURG: *I would say that they're exercises in style. Obviously, I'd like to do something more difficult. After all, that yé-yé stuff is all Tino Rossi and electric guitars. Still, if Brassens could write for Hallyday, he would do it. I don't know why Hallyday doesn't like me. Really, I could write some stuff that is much less stupid than the crap he sings. That would be easy. Anyway, as a composer, I truly must one day write a classic, something like Trenet's "La mer" [...]*

> G. BRATSCHI: *You write for others only out of necessity?*

> S.G: *In my profession, there's no such thing as "kind of successful." You make it big or die trying. Anyway, I love elegance. For me, living big is a way of destroying the notion of money. I feel I've managed to do that.*

Serge sends a new tune to Claude Wolff, who is asking for a piece for Petula Clark. It's the amusing "O o Sheriff," one of two featured songs on a super-45 that is released October 15, just before she finishes out the year with "Downtown," the huge, worldwide smash.

> *Oh, Sheriff, Oh, Sheriff, Oh, Oh*
> *If you really want to get a kiss from me*
> *Wo, Wo Wo Wo, Sheriff, Oh, Oh*
> *Take that chewing gum and toss it in the street*

CLAUDE WOLFF: *"Gainsbourg was less prolific; he didn't just churn stuff out. Still, I never turned him down. When I'd ask him for a song, he'd bring me one with a clear idea in mind, tailor-made for the artist in question. He knew the needs of the singer. He'd write really theatrical songs for Petula that were much different from the rest of his body of work."*

On August 8, Béatrice gives birth to their first child, little Natacha, also known as Laurence, or Totote. Serge is on cloud nine.

JOSEPH GINSBURG: *"We couldn't stop laughing about this very unusual mom and pop couple. Lucien is already dreaming about getting a pony for Totote. Well, later on, at least. Anyway, they adore their little girl. Lucien caresses her non-stop, a real doting dad!"*

Before getting into the production of his second 30cm album, *Gainsbourg Percussions*, which is slotted for release in mid-October, Serge decides to brush up on his knowledge. He doesn't want to do some pseudo-exotic kitsch for tourists, but rather the real deal. Now in 1964, no one is talking about *world music*. Sure, Brazil is doing a good job of exporting the samba and bossa nova, as evidenced by the success of Astrud Gilberto and Stan Getz, but there are few African artists making records, and even fewer of those are heard in France. Miriam Makeba, the South-African singer, is one exception. At the start of 1964, she releases two Dynagroove recordings: *Chants d'Afrique n°1* and *Chants d'Afrique n°2*. Through his friend Guy Béart, Serge is also discovers Babatunde Olatunji's *Drums of Passion*.

GUY BÉART: *"I would often go to the States, and when I was in New York, Harry Belafonte gave me this wonderful record, a disc by a Nigerian named Olatunji. It was all percussion with just a single melody line on top. I told Claude Dejacques: "That's where the world is headed, towards percussion." I had to have Serge listen to the record, and the result, for better or for worse, was that he moved from a small combo to a huge outfit for the recording of his new album."*

Of course we know that Béart was really angry with Serge for the stunt he pulled on the stage of the TV show *Apostrophes* in 1986. We also know that they never really liked each other, even when they were touring together for Canetti in 1959. Béart was always very jealous of Serge. Sure they had both written for Gréco, but nobody was coming to Béart and asking him to write for Bardot and France Gall. And we must admit the following: Serge did borrow liberally from Olatunji's "Akiwoko," a key cut on the virtuoso drummer's *Drums of Passion*, when he recorded "New York USA":

I saw New York
New York, U.S.A.
I saw New York
New York, U.S.A.
Never have I seen anything

> Anything, not anything, so high
> God! How big it is, New York
> New York U.S.A.

But it continues: Serge also transforms Olatunji's "Jin-Go-Lo-Ba" into "Marabout," while he uses "Kiyakiya" as the model for "Joanna." That makes three sources in all that are never credited to Olatunji.

GAINSBOURG: *"I remember thinking about it like this: "Abstract art caused an explosion in painting. In music, when form explodes, all that remains is percussion. Harmony disappears." Also, I was always listening to this album of ethnic music, and rather cynically I stole a few ideas from it... Ha, ha, ha... "New York U.S.A." is based on a Watusi war chant, while "Là-bas c'est naturel" plays counterpoint to a theme by Miriam Makeba."*

> Down there it's natural
> Down there in Ken-
> Ya
> For all the natives there
> It's just fine

GUY BÉART: *"Yeah, Gainsbourg took the arrangement note-for-note from Olatunji, but I didn't say anything. In that business, people depend on influences, and what's more he was a friend. It was only after the scene on 'Apostrophes' that I called SACEM and learned that "New York U.S.A." had been credited solely to him: words and music by Serge Gainsbourg, arrangement by Alain Goraguer. Still, I kept quiet. What good would it do? I was sick, and so I just forgot about it. A year later Claude Dejacques calls me and says: "Remember that recording by Olatunji? Well a lawsuit has been brought in the U.S.!" One of Serge's records had been released there and Olatunji took notice."*

CLAUDE DEJACQUES: *"So here's the story. Yeah, I gave Serge Gainsbourg a copy of Olatunji's LP a few months before we recorded the 'Percussions' album together with Alain Goraguer. Béart had turned me on to the record. I'd had Claude Nougaro listen to the whole thing before he did "L'amour sorcier." So where does plagiarism begin? Nobody denies that literature is born of literature [...] It's the same exact thing with music [...] quotes in classical music ... are so common that you could write a reference work on it that would blow your mind [...] But folk, or ethnic music is what is ripped off the most [...] It is both the root of success for much modern music and the means through which our ancestral melodies are passed on."*

This is a sensible way of ending the debate. Now back to the moment when Serge enters the studio in October 1964, with his favorite arranger.

ALAIN GORAGUER: *"I'd hooked up again with Serge for the France Gall tunes, and then we did this album. I've got great memories of it. We had a real blast, especially when teaching our French back-up singers how to sing in the upper register like young African girls. Other than a couple of pieces which feature a sax and guitar, there's nothing but percussion..."*

While the previous album was drenched in the vibe of nostalgic jazz, *Gainsbourg Percussions* is a riotous explosion in which the exoticism created by the back-up singers combines with various sound effects to create a showcase for texts that are one after the other both trivial and astounding. We start with the laid-back groove of fat Joanna:

> *Joanna's fat as hell*
> *She almost weighs two tons*
> *The biggest hippo in*
> *All of New Orleans*
> *Even so...*
> *Joanna*
> *Joanna*
> *Joanna*
> *You dance like the wind*
> *You're light as air*

Twelve cuts, seven days in the studio, a budget of 15,000 francs (his highest to date), and a cover which almost seems to declare that Gainsbourg is next in the line of "great composers and interpretive artists." On the back, Claude Dejacques describes the origin of this new work.

At first, he's just tapping his fingers on the edge of a wooden empire table. Images and ideas take shape. No longer can Serge ignore the beat of the drums, a cluster of beats which reveal the natural rhythms of life.

Two months later, both Alain Goraguer and I find ourselves in the same state of mind: it's time to get a move on. The result is a studio that starts to groove to the beat of five percussionists and twelve back-up singers. A few tunes with a sort of jazzy vibe are easily blended into a palette that is purely African.

Above it all lie the lyrics, chiseled into the sound: the mark of Gainsbourg.

Among the musicians are Michel Gaudry on bass and his pal André Arpino on drums. Along with René Urtreger, they perform regularly as a trio in Nancy Holloway's club.

During the recording session, Serge is reminded of the Living Theatre, of those pseudo-stoned junkies waiting for their connection with Jackie McLean playing in the background. On "Coco And Co," which could have easily been a part of the album *Confidentiel*, Serge adopts the personality of a correspondent. Seated in a jazz club, he describes the musicians in a muted voice, informing us as to what each player is jacked up on:

> *Listen*
> *As he swings his axe*
> *This cat*
> *Plays one crazy sax*
> *And he's*
> *Doped up to the max*
> *Coco and Co*

This late-night vibe that ushers in a foggy state of mind is echoed in the song "Machins choses," with its electric organ and ultra-cool sax:

> *You're a machine*
> *You, my thing*
> *We sit and chat*
> *No big thing*
> *Simple as that*
> *Nothing at all...*

Evoking the style of Jackie McLean, the saxophone on "Quand mon 6,35 me fait les yeux doux" plunges us into oppressive, hard bop while the lyrics chill us to the bone:

> *The thought just grabs me, but*
> *Where does it come from?*
> *It's vertigo*
> *And I'd like so*
> *To scream and fire*
> *Bang! Bang!*

A few years later, Serge discusses the idea of suicidal dizziness with Michel Lancelot on the radio show *Radio Psychose*, broadcast by Europe n°1:

"I get vertigo - I mean physically, I get dizzy spells. For me it's something fascinating. I'm fascinated by that ability to pass through the looking glass, as it were." Still, he's having fun on this new disc. We can almost see him smile on a number of cuts, for example on "Pauvre Lola," where France Gall supplies the laughter:

> *You should just let go*
> *But take it slow*
> *My poor Lola*

In an interview from that time, Gainsbourg explains how this album is not only a departure from everything he'd ever done, but also a break from tradition.

> GAINSBOURG: *"First of all, chanson is old hat, outdated. There is no modern chanson for our time. Look at painting, look at literature... Chanson hasn't moved an inch! These guys are still strumming their guitars and singing tunes like in the days of Bruant. I've tried – casually and without taking myself too seriously – to do something where the words and the music meld into one. To make this record, I sampled African rhythms and used them abundantly. It's not a surrender to contemporary tastes. This music has a form that it corresponds to, a rhythm that characterizes it..."*

It's when he's playing around and cheerfully detached that he becomes the most incisive, like when he describes the misadventures of "Tatoué Jérémie," or when he cuts loose with "Petits riens" in that nonchalant tone of his:

> *It's better to ponder nothing*
> *Than to think of you*
> *It does me no good*
> *No good, for we're through*
> *But it's as if from nothing*
> *All again is new*
> *These little nothings*
> *That all come from you*

Finally, there's the album's classic gem, "Couleur café," which is released at the same time as a single:

> *The effect is oh so fine*
> *Utterly sublime*
> *Watch while you unwind*

Just let go and don't stop shaking
Let the coffee do its thing
Make me step and swing
Make me dance and sing
All night long till dawn starts breaking

Evidently a hit, yet it's nowhere to be found in the charts. It takes backseat to tunes by other artists like Petula Clark ("Downtown"), Johnny Hallyday ("Le pénitencier), and the Rolling Stones ("It's all over now").

It's at this very moment in England when Jane Birkin, daughter of naval officer David Birkin and actress Judy Campbell, is literally swept away by composer John Barry just weeks before her eighteenth birthday. Jane grew up with brother Andrew and sister Linda in an environment both strict and aristocratic, and she had just returned from five years in a boarding school on the Isle of Wight ("The origin of all my hang-ups" she tells us). She also spent a few months in Paris, trying, without much success, to learn French... John Barry, some thirteen years her elder and divorced, is at the time preparing for his musical comedy *Passion Flower Hotel*, to be staged at the Prince of Wales Theatre. It's a somewhat naughty little piece that requires six young men and ladies. He met Jane – made famous by the David Bailey photos - at the trendy Ad Lib Club in London, a spot frequented by the Beatles, Stones, Roman Polanski and Sharon Tate. John suggests that Jane come in for an audition. She can neither sing nor dance, but it's precisely her shortcomings that charm the play's producers... The John Barry Orchestra had just released its tenth hit, the theme from the James Bond film "From Russia With Love."

> JANE BIRKIN: *"John was a brilliant man, absolutely brilliant. One day, when I was only seventeen, he came and made a proposition to my father. He wanted to elope with me... My father, wanting nothing but my happiness, acquiesced, and I climbed in to his Jaguar E-type. I told John that we could not make love until he asked me to marry him. I don't know why, but I thought it was an absolute must. If not, people would think I was some fast and frivolous chick. At the time, I thought it was a life that I was cut out for, taking care of the house and cooking his steak for dinner. I would be his ideal woman."*

Back in Paris, Serge is starting to promote his new album. In his book *Piégée, la chanson...?* Claude Dejacques tells us: "When *Gainsbourg Percussions* came out, I was convinced we were on the right track. I was working all the angles, talking to everyone in the nightclubs and in the media. Still, we had no luck, and no sales. The solution? Find some other performers to help us spread the word. I'd seen Canetti use this to his advantage for Brel, Brassens, and Béart." But the reviews in *Le Monde* are not so hot:

> *Gainsbourg has a pretty small following: very Rive Gauche, but very faithful. My guess is that they will be disappointed with his latest disc, 'Gainsbourg Percussions.' If you want sophistication, there's nothing better [...] But the mish-mash of sound effects and echoes of Africa, or New Orleans for that matter, come across as unnecessary embellishment. Does this recording really point the way to a rebirth of chanson?*

'Salut les copains' continues to snub the "old" Gainsbourg, but *Music-Hall* publishes a long interview with him in the January, 1965 issue. Here's a tasty morsel. Listen to a journalist who loves to listen to himself:

> —*Your music has made us accustomed to rather sardonic wordplay. In fact, words almost lose all importance. It's like we find ourselves trapped in an auditory triangle that evokes an almost physical reaction. On the one hand, there is absolutely no syncopation in your voice. The voice is like an instrument, like a tenor sax. There's this zigzagging agility: words transformed into muffled sonority. On another level, we have the female background singers, an almost lemony-yellow timbre, an octave above what we are used to hearing. Then the most striking element, usually reserved for voices speaking words, is here taken over by the instruments, all percussive... It's the rhythm that speaks...*

> —*Right, says Gainsbourg. Agreeing to who knows what.*

A new boss takes over at Le Milord: at the helm is now Michel Valette, an actor, singer, and ex-artistic director of the cabaret la Colombe, where he had presided over the debuts of Gut Béart and Pierre Perret. Opening night features Romain Bouteille, Maurice Fanon, Daniel Prévost, and headliner Catherine Sauvage. On November 4, it's Gainsbourg's turn. Given what they're paying him, there is no way that he can bring a bunch of pseudo-African backup singers or the group of drummers he just used on his record.

He just makes do by adding two more songs to an already established repertory ("Machins choses" and "Ces petits riens") and then he immediately hires Elek Bacsik.

"He's the king of soft-spoken, acerbic insolence," says *Elle*. Then there is the following caveat in *Paris-Presse*: "When Gainsbourg hits the stage, it is obvious that one is witnessing something unique and unexpected. As a performer, he does nothing to please his audience. In fact, he has nothing but disdain for the crowd." In *Le Monde*, on November 18, Claude Saurraute says: "More aphonic and unnatural than ever, his reflections on love are strewn like pearls before swine." In *Arts*: "Each of his songs is like an experiment in the vivisection of the soul, and quite a successful one at that." Finally, we have Jean Paget's lyrical passage in *Combat*:

Gainsbourg, the poet of *franglais,* just hammers away. His long, mocking face leans into the microphone, unveiling secrets passed by word of mouth. Fascinating. Like a caustic daydreamer. Heavy eyelids and acerbic smile. A contemptuous courtesy. Then all of the sudden, as if to beg our pardon, his manner is transformed - with the cool indifference of the ultimate hipster – into something almost charming and tender.

Le Journal de Genève, in its November 22 issue, expresses astonishment: "One hand moves forward, fumbling for invisible objects, while the other uses the cord of the microphone to trace peculiar shapes [...]; with supreme elegance and dazzling ease that moves back and forth from total restrain to refined spontaneity, he is at once distant and unguarded." *La Tribune de Genève* also reviews his performance at the club. In the article "Serge Gainsbourg, or the ghost of Landru," the criticism is more severe: "Each time, we have to ask ourselves just what's up with this guy. He seems to be asking himself the same question. Moments after walking onstage, he wants to flee. And he doesn't perform for long, either." Still, the same paper prints a lengthy interview with Serge at the beginning of November, where he starts by explaining that he hadn't performed in public for some eight months:

> —*Sure, it's a mistake not to prepare. But as for making everything slick, what stars call "polished" - that bores me. When I sing, it's like spitting in people's faces [...] and worrying about applause is something I find antiquated... I can't abandon all modesty. Someone like Brel can bring down the house at the end of a song, you know, hitting the big note at the end,*

but I find that too manipulative.

—Is it better on TV?

—Yeah, TV is more my thing. My face, on a TV screen, it works for people. Onstage, I'm just too awkward with myself.

Again in the *Tribune de Genève* article, Serge declares that the idea of making money has lost all significance to him, even though his income from the songs for Petula Clark and France Gall certainly gives him some breathing room. As for those singers who are fifty years behind the times, he continues to elaborate, using Anne Sylvestre as an example: "She sings about mountain springs and shepherd girls over melodies that date from the middle-ages. In the age of concrete that's an insult to one's intelligence. Pretty maybe, but..."

GAINSBOURG: *"Rive-Gauche style chanson is over. I know because I watched it die when I closed the last of those kinds of clubs [...] I was a pianist, then a headliner, and then they closed... And those that are still around are old hat. What's more, it's a sorry sight to see someone who supposedly has something to say if he's accompanied by crappy music. He strums his guitar, maybe three chords... And still, people listen... What can you do? They've never been exposed to anything better."*

The Geneva concerts lead us back to Sophie Makhno, who is busy preparing the double bill of Barbara / Gainsbourg at the Théâtre de l'Est in Paris.

SOPHIE MAKHNO: *"In the middle of the night, I get a call from the infuriated theatre director who tells me: "You've got to do something about your artist." What happened is that Gainsbourg had sung about ten songs, as usual, and simply refused to do any more. No encore. So at the bar next door, his wife overhears a conversation between two concertgoers who are complaining about Serge's attitude. Unable to handle any criticism about her husband, she goes berserk and physically accosts them."*

The TEP concerts take place from December 22 to 27. In *L'Humanité*, Serge reveals that he has opted for "a relaxed attitude and a hand-held mic, not because it's trendy but rather because it puts him at ease." Marie-France Brière, who was great at getting Serge booked on TV when she worked at Europe n°1, is also part of the promotion team for the concert. Finally, Serge recruits the René Urtreger trio to accompany him. Urtreger, a Bud Powell fanatic, is one of the best bop pianists in Paris. In 1957, he played with Miles Davis, Pierre Michelot, Barney Wilen, and Kenny Clarke on the *Ascenseur pour l'échafaud* soundtrack.

RENÉ URTREGER: *"Before writing the arrangement for the trio, we got together to rehearse for the concerts at Théâtre de l'Est. I went to his place, near la Madeleine, and he said something I'll always remember. My foundation is jazz, and when I had to accompany a variety singer I'd force myself not to get too complicated, just keep it simple. Serge told me "No! Let's get twisted." He didn't want any simple chord changes. He wanted me to be myself. So at TEP, he used my trio as backup. Albi Culaz was on bass and André Arpino on drums. The space was enormous and Serge was more used to small clubs, so we really boozed it up in order to able to face the crowd. Gainsbourg was particularly ill at ease. The audience was composed mainly of clueless old bats from Ménilmontant who knew nothing but "Le poinçonneur," maybe. All the other songs went right over their heads. One night things went so bad that he called my wife in the middle of the night to cry on her shoulder. He wanted to chuck it all in."*

SOPHIE MAKHNO: *"The audience at Théâtre de l'Est was in agony during the show, and Serge was frozen with stage fright. You could see his legs shaking in his trousers, and his back was almost completely turned to the crowd. From time to time he'd look out into the hall but mostly he kept his eyes on René Urtreger. Some liked this demeanor of his, but others started to boo, and the two opposing factions almost came to blows."*

BARBARA: *"What was nice was that we met each other during one of those big parties at TEP, on the day after some reporter had commented on how ugly the both of us were. I thought he was really handsome. We were similar in that we had the same hang-ups, we were both skinny, we both loved black... I asked him to go on tour with me, and he very politely accepted. I never thought of him as my opening act: we shared the billing... His stage fright and his shyness could make him nauseous before taking the stage."*

Serge is in fact scheduled to do a series of ten concerts with the Great Lady in Black, planned by Sopie Makhno to take place in various college towns. After a few shows he drops out...

Gainsbourg: "The people accepted me only reticently and I could tell they thought I was dreadful. I could see from their faces that they didn't un-

derstand a thing. I told myself: "They just seem to be so exhausted, there's really no sense in me staying"... I blamed it all on their utter laziness."

One fateful night of this aborted tour is, however, worth mentioning...

BARBARA: *"The crowd wasn't booing, but rather heckling him. You could feel some uneasiness, a strange reaction in the hall. After a moment, I was so angry that I had to do something, and I found myself going onstage to tell the audience that I just didn't understand. That night, we talked about it. He told me he wanted to leave the tour. I was quite sad because it was really discouraging. His desire to perform live had never been greater. Had he continued, he'd have conquered his stage fright and then some!"*

A few weeks before that, on January 3, 1965, we had seen him on *Discorama*, this time the guest of the incredible Denise Glaser, where he sang three songs from his new album. During the breaks he responded to some interesting queries:

DENISE GLASER: *One day we talked about the whole yé-yé and rock thing. Now, I really have to remain impartial, being that for the moment at least, I am the arbiter. But you told me one day: "Let 'em go buy a boatload of lollipops for all I care".... What do you think now? Now that they're older?*
S.G.: *Well, now I've changed my tune.*D.G.: *Changed your tune?*
S.G.: *Yeah, because the tune I'm singing now makes the same sound as a cash register. I think it's better to produce unpretentious rock than to do bad chanson that's full of literary pretense. That's just tiresome.*

Seeing that song titles serve as the inspiration for his future songs, Serge is getting accustomed to scribbling down his impossible language in little notebooks. One of them, dating from autumn, 1964, contains more or less everything of substance that he would come to realize in the following months, even years. Jotted down inside are the following titles: "Bébésong," "Les animals," "Pauvre Lola," "Ford Mustang," "Docteur Jekyll et Mister Hyde," "Lolita Go Home," "Olive Popeye et Mimosa," "Le groupe anglaise," "Le bluff," "Le fin du fin," etc. As for "Ford Mustang," we see the following reminder on the margin of the page: "All in English sung by background singers." Right next to it we find "Poupée de cire poupée de son," accompanied by the remark: "Eurovision."

eleven

Who's "In" Who's "Out"

Things are turning sour for Serge and Béatrice. The birth of Natacha, as we have seen, is doing nothing to quell his wife's jealousy, and life is not always a bowl of cherries up on the sixth floor of 12, Rue Tronchet.

Gainsbourg: "It's an important detail because it's the root of two great stories. Here's the first: there was this little balcony that looked over a street where all the whores worked, Rue Vignon. I heard shouting, and down on the street I saw a bunch of girls laying into some American dude. So I said to myself: "Shit, I'm gonna put an end to this!" I took a bucket of water and aimed for the girls, but before the cascade hit they'd taken a step back and the Yank had moved forward. He got the whole thing square in his face. So I guess you could say while looking to fuck, he actually got fucked... The second tale involves Béatrice... She'd given me a gold watch from Tiffany's. One night I came home late, maybe a little hammered, and she says: "Give me your watch." I knew just what she would do, and I was right: Bam! Right out the window. I remember counting the seconds before it crashed to the ground. The next day she gave me another one, again from Tiffany's, but this time in platinum..."

As for his music, in January, 1965 the magazine *Diapason* explores the "Gainsbourg paradox":

He is both the exacting composer behind the *Percussions* album, and at the same time the writer of "O o sheriff" and "N'écoute pas les idoles," both mainstream pop hits. There seem to be two sides to his persona, something like Dr. Jekyll and Mister Hyde. Who will kill whom?

On television, Serge blurts out, "I want to be a star in '65!" And how will he accomplish this? "I'm going to do rock n' roll. Real rock n' roll. I'll write a dozen tunes this year. I've been waiting six years. That's long enough!"

By this time, the Beatles have released "Eight Days a Week," the Kinks have put out "All Day and All of the Night," and the Stones have scored with "Time Is On My Side." The English wave has turned into a tsunami, and this will be followed in 1965 by Bob Dylan and a surge of soul music: Wilson Picket, James Brown, the Temptations, etc. Even before the change that will be brought about by the establishment of Eurovision, people are beginning to whisper that Gainsbourg is "selling out" now that he is actually earning a living. His own records may not be selling but he's writing hits for other stars. The reality is that we are moving towards a crucial point in his career: from 1965-1969, Serge will live through some of the more turbulent periods of his life – divorce, two love affairs, movies, television shows, several huge hits, and over a hundred songs sung by fifteen different performers, including "Qui est 'in' qui est 'out'," "Harley Davidson," "Sous le soleil exactement," and "Je t'aime moi non plus." It all starts with the epic "Poupée de cire poupée de son":

> I'm a dolly made out of wax
> A toy that sings you a song
> I'll bear my heart as I croon for you
> Oh won't you please come sing along

Written at the behest of Gilbert and Maritie Carpentier, "Poupée de cire" – the song that will represent Luxembourg in the Grand Concours Eurovision de la Chanson – is performed by France Gall on March 29 in Naples and broadcast live to 150 million television viewers. Serge books a first-class sleeping berth and makes the train trip with Louis Hazan and Louis Nucera, future author and ex-cub reporter from Nice's *Patriote* who's currently the press agent for Philips. Goraguer is leading the band and Pierre Tcherina is the television commentator. After all the other European artists perform, our little representative from Luxembourg comes away with 32 points, which is 6 more than English contestant Kathy Kirby.

FRANCE GALL: *"I didn't see much of Serge during the competition. The musicians had been humming the song since our first rehearsal and they didn't like the military cadence of the tune. Others said it was schmaltzy. Serge got pissed off and just left..."*

The musicians weren't the only ones who couldn't stomach the song. In fact, the French-speaking countries gave it fewer votes than the rest of Europe.

FRANCE GALL: *"I don't remember much about the competition except for the singing and being really thirsty. I went to the cafeteria with a friend and had a big glass of milk afterwards, and we must have chatted for a long time because the results had already been announced. When we came back, we had to walk through this long hallway and we saw a horde of photographers swoop down on us. Then I was pushed back onstage and I sang again... I was really unaware of what was happening to me."*

After an almost inaudible "Thank you," the song's composer is also swarmed, and finds himself trapped by a throng of both new admirers and old stalwarts.

> My songs form a mirror for you
> Look at me and you'll find
> I can be everywhere, this is true
> My voice explodes inside your mind

LOUIS NUCERA: *"I remember that at the time, France Gall was with Claude François and he was quite cruel to her. When she won, she called him on the phone and he really put her down. He was quite rude to her, and she fell in my arms and started sobbing."*

It is worse than that: instead of congratulating her, Clo-Clo, her then secret fiancé, shouts into the receiver, "You sang off-key. You're worthless!"... "She came out of the phone booth crying," remembers Serge some twenty years later. "It was really nasty. This business can be really squalid... just disgusting... I would call it utter abjection, but it's worse than that..."

JOSEPH GINSBURG: *"It really caused as big stir. They were already selling 20,000 copies a day (Lucien told me on the phone). Congratulations poured in by telegram. Tomorrow, Philips is throwing a cocktail party for 200 people. This little "side-trip" is going to make him a pretty penny... His mind is just running wild. We were squirming in anticipation on Saturday evening while we watched the TV [...] At the end, we all needed a handful of aspirin. Nobody could sleep until 4 in the morning!"*

Along with success come dopey interviews – in the provinces they are asking France, for example, if Serge is "her type":

Well, no, not really. I like guys with blonde hair and blue eyes. What I do like about Serge is that he's really weird [...] God, I would never marry him, but I hope he can write for me for as long as possible.

Serge would respond rather cruelly to this some twenty-five years later during an interview in the magazine *Les Inrockuptibles*:

France was just too harebrained to be a Lolita. A Lolita at least knows how to turn you on. She couldn't turn on anybody... Ha, ha, ha... My tank was full, but she couldn't even get the motor running..

FRANCE GALL: *"Serge wrote songs that corresponded to the image he had of me. I was a sad and lonely person back then, and I hated to talk. I made my first record when I was just fifteen and a half. At twenty I was still a total baby. I liked Gainsbourg's words and his style, which was more modern, and I found much more pleasure in singing his songs compared to the others. At the time of "Poupée de cire," I was very afraid of boys, and this song painted a good picture of me..."*

All I do is sit and sing
While boys just walk on by
Passion for me is a foreign thing
Why dream of love when I'm so shy

The victory at Eurovision means first of all that the song is covered all over Europe in a variety of languages, including German ("Das war eine scone Party") and Italian ("Io si, tu no"). The papers tell us that Serge is now a hot item. Henri Salvador, Sacha Distel, Eddy Mitchell, and Jeanne Moreau all ask for songs, but Sacha is the only performer who actually gets one in the months following France's hit. The best interview from this period is found in the Belgian weekly *Télé-Moustique*. Serge begins by saying that had he written for Yves Montand, he would have hit the big time much sooner:

Early on, I refused to make any concessions. I tried making imagistic concessions and I tried to stamp out my cynicism and misogyny, but I just couldn't make it work. It was too brutal! [...] Sure, I had some success on the Right Bank, but that's a very limited audience. The public, meaning the throngs of people who buy records, are the type who trash the Olympia at an Animals concert or invade Orly to see the Beatles. It's an audience that I have yet to seduce [...] When I was a teenager, an astrologist told me that I would have success abroad, and just so. I don't have a single French fan in Naples, yet it's the foreigners who voted for me! [...] So what does it mean to succeed? Money? I make enough, enough to live without worrying about it. Still, it seems that to really succeed means realizing the dreams of one's youth. As far as that is concerned, I haven't succeeded. In fact I've failed, because I wanted to become a painter and I never did.

Twelve days after Eurovision, on April 1, 1965, René Urtreger accompanies Serge for his very last concert in Nice, where he plays the Hall des Expositions for la Nuit du Droit. "I never expected that one day I'd be popular," he confides to Léo Chirchietti from *Provençal*. "I consider myself to be more of a cerebral singer, a guy who doesn't put too much bullshit into his songs. It's kind of funny, winning this prize." The next day, which is his birthday, he decides to spend his time "in complete intimacy with the mysterious young brunette who is accompanying him," reports *Provençal* before Serge returns to Paris.

> RENÉ URTREGER: *"I played with him in Nice. He came down to Negresco with his wife. Me, I was staying in a cheaper hotel because it was customary at that time for the band to be in a different hotel than the star. So I was all alone. It was ridiculous. A half hour after we arrive, he calls my hotel and tells me: "Come on over. I'll get you a room here." Probably because he knew I had a bottle of whiskey with me. Booze was another of our common interests back then. Anyway, his wife looked really pissed off. I could see that they were utterly bored with one another. He was on the road to stardom, and she was just trapped there, like a creature from another planet."*

This 1965 tour permits Serge to close the book on eight years of disasters, eight years of failures, eight years of cut-rat dances, smoky clubs, and hostile, snobbish crowds. Eight years of stage fright and crippling shyness, awk-

wardness, and nasty comments in the papers, such as t
pointing to "his limited skill as a singer"... Eight years of
establish anything but the smallest following.

Serge had no idea that Eurovision would put him bac
Dejacques soon introduces him to Valérie Lagrange, a you
ered at the age of seventeen in Claude Autant-Lara's 195   ... La Jument
verte. She is also on the very first cover of *Lui* in November 1963, photographed by her husband, Serge Beauvarlet. Her first EP is released in 1964,
with four tunes arranged by Maurice Vanger. On her second super-45, from
April, 1965, she is accompanied by the exotic South American combo Los
Incas. In contains Gainsbourg's "La guérilla":

> *Is this love we have, or just guerilla war*
> *Our life without tequila is just a bore*
> *Our life without tequila is just a bore*
> *Is this love we have, or just guerilla war*

VALÉRIE LAGRANGE: *"Back then, I was on this Latino trip, singing with
Los Incas and all. Serge adapted himself to this. I remember going out
together one night, and Serge was both a playboy and very timid at the
same time. I'm sure he wanted to take things further, but I was very much
in love with Jean-Pierre Kalfon, whom I had just met. I can see us going
from bar to bar, both very self-conscious, hardly speaking to each other...
It was a dreadfully boring evening, to tell the truth..."*

Valerie has quite a bit of success even though the show-biz people in
France prefer less independent and much more malleable personalities, such
as Sheila, Sylvie, and Gall. Serge will soon be doing business with Michèle
Torr, certainly one of those more marketable personalities. Fresh from her
native Vaucluse, she had broken in a year earlier with "C'est dur d'avoir
seize ans" and "Dans mes bras." Unconcerned with her image as a provincial
vamp, Serge writes for her "Non à tous les garcons":

> *If you're going to be a pain*
> *It just may be that*
> *You end up with nothing*
> *That is just a fact*
> *If you play coy*
> *Always coy*
> *Coy with all the boys*

Thanks to the royalties from "Poupée de cire," Serge is finally able to express his enormous generosity. First of all, he decides it's time for Joseph, now almost seventy, to retire. Olia has reservations about this. She had always worried about their financial situation and must have surely seen times when Joseph didn't have a penny to his name. Still, Serge succeeds in setting them up with a nice little nest egg. He also starts scouring antique shops and buys an astrakhan and an 18th century dentist's chair... Then, there are his sister's kids, Yves and Isabelle, the nephews that he so adores...

ISABELLE LE GRIX: *"In 1966, he took us both to a restaurant and then over to Le Train Bleu, a toy store, where he told us: "Go ahead. Take anything you want." You can imagine my brother, eleven, and me, just six... we went wild..."*

Serge, nicknamed by singer Robert Rocca "a character in Serge of an author's royalties," starts to hit the clubs, such as New Jimmy's, which is owned by his friend Régine. He and Régine have more than a thing or two in common: born just a couple of months apart, they had lived through the same trials during the war, both having to run and hide. Régine is also drawn to chanson, even the "grand chanson" of the masses, which is something of a contradiction to her "Queen of the Night" persona. After doing a 45 written for her by Aznavour, Serge spoils her with "Les p'tits papiers":

Just let them speak
These little scraps
Old tissues
Lying in your lap
A memory
Printed on map
To ease your pain

RÉGINE: *"I'd known him from Le Milord. I was the barmaid next door, at the Whiskey à Gogo. Before opening up, I'd go next door to see him, and I thought his songs were incredible. He got married and we didn't see each other for a few years, and then I ran into him at some industry party and I later called him to ask that he write me a song. He came with his wife, who was insanely jealous – she wouldn't let him out of her sight. I just stayed in my robe, my hair all messed up, and she must have told herself that I was nothing to fret over. And she was right: there was never anything between*

Serge and me... The next time he came alone and left at a sensible hour. The third time I said, "Let's go have a drink and a bite to eat." It was seven o'clock, and we ate with some friends. After that, we hit the club and he never went home afterwards. At eight in the morning, we were pounding Calvados, and Serge was getting more and more wasted. By nine, it was out of the question for him to go home to his wife. He said, "If I go home it'll be a nightmare. I'm sure she's looking for me everywhere!" So he went and holed up in a hotel. It was just before they separated."

> *Here, I'll loan you Charlie*
> *But he's mine you see*
> *Take good care for he*
> *Belongs just to me*
> *Don't forget, chérie*
> *Tonight do as you please*
> *But tomorrow bring him back to me*

RÉGINE: *"In fact, he brought me a song called "Il s'appelle reviens" (But he's mine you see), which I found amusing but a little too short. I asked him: "Can't you make it longer?" He says no. Then he adds: "I thought about something else, and I don't know if it's any good. Just a little number without a real beginning or end. I just wrote it that way." So he takes a piece of paper timidly from out of his pocket, sits down at the piano, and mumbles: "Be honest. I say it's garbage." In fact he was quite blasé about it. So he starts to play "Les p'tits papiers" and I was just floored. It was and still is a masterpiece!"*

Years later, Serge will write the following line about this interpreter of his who came along quite by chance:

Regine's is a private club and she calls all the shots. Not just anybody can walk in. One night I was on the list, and there was booze, but no music. So I made sure a few of my best tunes stuck in her mind.

It is interesting to note that in Greco's version of "Accordéon," Régine's "Les p'tits papiers," and Zizi Jeanmaire's "Bloody Jack," there is a constant thread of popular and farcical chanson that has nothing to do with the avant-garde period of *Gainsbourg Confidentiel* nor with the yé-yé pop of "Poupée de cire." To understand why Serge was drawn to this genre, we have to go back to his youth and the influence of Charles Trenet and Fréhel... He sees in Régine a vaguely cynical businesswoman and imagines her giving advice to fledgling streetwalkers. Thus, a song like "Si tu attends qu'les diamants te sautent au cou" becomes linked to themes he explored at the beginning of his career, in early songs like "Jeunes femmes et vieux messieurs" and "Ronsard 58":

What a lump of useless flesh is man
All you serve to do is fan his flame
In the end it's only you to blame
When it's said and done you've lost the game

If he is all you're holding in your hand
Hurry while you are still young and fine
In the eyes of all those aging swine
Youth is worth more than the rarest wine

From June 22 to June 24, Serge meets up again Brigitte Bardot in the studio at Blanqui. His ever-faithful comrades are along for the ride: Claude Dejacques as artistic director and Goraguer as arranger and bandleader. Two of the four titles cut are penned by Gainsbourg. Released in July, "Bubble Gum" becomes one of the summer's biggest hits:

Always love the same old guy?
Stuff like that is flat and dry
Love like that is just no fun
Old and tasteless bubble-gum

Over the corny, old saloon piano from the wild west, we hear B.B., who will soon star alongside Jeanne Moreau in *Viva Maria*. She also sings the song "Omnibus." Starting from the assumption that men are like trains – some are sleepers, some express, some Pullmans, or even cattle cars - Gainsbourg writes for her:

Local trains are just the tops
I love all those impromptu stops
In little towns with tiny shops
Where it's so easy to get lost

France Gall's seventh super-45 is also released that summer. "Attends ou va-t'en," with its breathtaking melody, is one of Serge's greatest hits from the yé-yé period:

Stay or don't stay
Just make up you mind

Stay or don't stay
I'll be fine
Stay or don't stay
But don't torture me
Stay or please let me be free

Let's tally the score. In the last fifteen months, Serge has written eight hits: "N'écoute pas les idoles," "Laisse tomber les filles," "O o Sheriff," "Poupée de cire poupée de son," "Les p'tits papiers," "La guérilla," "Bubble Gum," and "Attends ou va-t'en." Not even counting "Poupée de cire," these titles most likely represent between 1 and 1.5 million copies sold. *Gainsbourg Percussions*, on the other hand, sells maybe 3,000 to 4,000 copies (there are no reliable figures for record sales from that period). And that isn't all. To Petula Clark, he gives the song "Les Incorruptibles," inspired by the American TV show *The Untouchables*, with Robert Stack. It takes place in Chicago at the height of prohibition, and there are plenty of mafiosos... When he writes for Petula, it's like he is already imagining her in a Carpentier TV show, with costumes, décor, and choreography. As for the words, they are simple as can be:

All of this booze
Clandestine
Just gasoline
That rests in
Rusty stills
It's destined
To knock us flat on our ass while digestin'

PETULA CLARK: *"I loved performing "Les Incorruptibles" on stage. I always had the feeling that Serge wanted to come off as a slacker when he was really completely professional. It was as if everything was a joke to him, but at the same time he was very effective. It was both irritating and fascinating."*

From 1965-66, Petula's massive sales made her one of he biggest stars in Europe, second only to the Beatles. And although she does more than 300 songs in French, many remember her for one specific tune, "La gadoue," released at the start of 1966. It is Gainsbourg's tenth straight hit:

Both in the fall and in the spring
Galoshes are vital thing

For cloudy days and what they bring
Muddy things, muddy things, muddy things

During the months of July and August of 1965, Serge mopes around Toquet with his wife and little Totote. He has twelve tunes to compose for his next Philips album, but at summer's end he hasn't a single note. Also, things are getting even worse between him and Béatrice. He had already given her a hint about how bad it was when he disappeared for three days, but she didn't get the message. She starts to panic about Serge recording with Bardot. Gréco calls and she makes a scene. If Michèle Arnaud or some big female TV producer has a meeting with Serge, she assumes they've had an affair and slams the door in her face. And when she flips out, well, that's the worst. Dishes broken, antiques destroyed. Her last resort is always emotional blackmail.

In the coming months, we see Serge sing on TV, most notably re-doing "L'eau à la bouche" on *A chacun son la* in June, and "Couleur café" on *Parlez-nous d'amour* in July. In September comes an unexpected surprise – in this period of censorship he actually sings "Quand mon 6.35 me fait les yeux doux" on *Fric frac en chansons*. But the big news is his return to acting. He has not done a thing since *L'Inconnue de Hong Kong* in 1963, but then Claude Lourais calls on him for an episode of the popular program *Cinq dernières minutes*. The episode, called *Des fleurs pour l'inspecteur*, is shown at the beginning of the season. Serge plays the role of a bum suspected of murder, but for once, he's not guilty...

One might wonder why Serge hadn't done a film in over two years. The answer is simple: his jealous wife. Promiscuous little actresses are strictly off-limits. Serge is now thirty-seven and suffocating. Still, he manages to sell his wife on him doing a film in Switzerland that starts shooting in November. Jean-Louis Roy is directing this spoof, a mix of both spy movie and the fantastic that is entitled *L'Inconnu de Shandigor*. For some unknown reason, it will not be released until 1968. Anyway, Serge manages to calm his spouse by promising to take her along for the shooting.

Ever since Eurovision, Gainsbourg has become a hot commodity. He is forced to decline a countless number of requests, and not just from the lesser talents. In September, 1965, Johnny Hallyday, fresh from military service, asks him for two songs. Serge is no longer snubbed. Eddy Mitchell will follow suit a month later. Then for Sacha Distel, whom he had helped out even back when he was on the skids, Serge fires off "Mamadou" – much less innocent that it appears – which is found on the B-side of the super-45 that Sacha releases at the end of summer:

Mamadou Mamadou said to me
Whitey, you'd better not mess with me
So I told him "Mamadou, put back your knife"
And strummed my guitar for my pretty blonde wife

A sort of flip-side to "La nostalgie camarade," which he will record sixteen years later, "Mamadou" is an implicit reference to the fall of African colonialism.

SACHA DISTEL: *"If you listen to it carefully, you could interpret it as a totally racist song. Maybe that's why it wasn't so successful. It's funny, sure, but still it's about some colonialist reclining in his chaise lounge, talking to his slave, Mamadou, who ends ups sticking a knife in his master's belly..."*

Just a few months after the success of "Poupée de cire," France Gall's stardom starts to fade. "Attends ou va-t'en" isn't the hit they had hoped for, and her new EP, featuring "Le temps de la rentrée" and "L'Amérique" is even worse (unfortunately Sheila releases the inane but popular "Folklorique américain" at the same time). Next to these mediocre titles is another Gainsbourg tune that's not much better, "Nous ne sommes pas des anges":

All the lads these days look just like girls
With all that flowing hair
And all of us girls
Make the boys all stare
At the pants that we wear

The whole thing is shouted rather than sung by the hyperkinetic France Gall... One has to laugh when considering that the unisex anthem precedes by three months the tune "Elucubrations d'Antoine" (My mom told me, Tony, you'd better cut your hair...), a massive hit at the beginning of 1966 that leads directly to Johnny Hallyday's "Cheveux longs, idées courtes" (Big hair, small mind).

Meanwhile, Serge and Béatrice have settled back in at Rue Tronchet. The Beatles are doing "Yesterday," the Stones hit it big with "Satisfaction," and Johnny Hallyday releases "Quand reviens la nuit." As for Serge, he starts filming a little French TV bio called *Gainsbourg tel quel* for the program *Central variétés*. Claude Dejacques, still determined to sell Serge as an artist and not just a singer-songwriter, is behind the idea. The show, fifteen minutes long, is directed by Claude Dagues.

CLAUDE DEJACQUES: *"The now notorious filming of "La javanaise" is what finally caused the break between him and his wife. My idea for the scene was that Serge would be writing the piece and at home and then we would move throughout Paris as the song took shape. So we started filming on Rue Tronchet. Well, a technician had somehow tracked mud from his galoshes all over some spotless wall-to-wall carpeting... His wife was absolutely furious. I know that they had it out after we left."*

Béatrice is none too happy with the idea of a invasion into her home. She also isn't that impressed with the worth of the whole project and seems really pissed off by the presence of the film crew. During this final confrontation, she throws a jar of jam at Serge's head. He avoids it and it smashes into a wall. He just stares at the exploding mural, at the strawberries that drip down like bloody treacle.

CLAUDE DEJACQUES: *"Then she took the diamond and ruby bracelet he had given her and tossed it out the window, telling him to go fetch it. But he didn't..."*

GAINSBOURG: *"It was a big scene, and I remember leaving with nothing but my I.D. and my military record. In the beginning, I stayed in big hotels and passed my time – not romantically, mind you – with Valérie Lagrange and Mireille Darc... I was completely unaware that my ex-wife had police connections, and because I had to register at hotels, she knew exactly where I was. Luckily she never turned up. When Koralnik contacted me to do the musical Anna, I holed up at his place, which permitted me to get off the grid altogether..."*

The divorce will be announced in fall of 1966. As for the little telefilm, it is broadcast on October 12, 1965. Some extracts:

Claude Dejacques: What does it mean for you, the success of "Poupée de cire poupée de son?"

Serge Gainsbourg: Forty-five million.

C.D. Nothing else?

S.G.: Nothing. A certain satisfaction, I guess. Yeah, it's funny. I was known as this loner intellectual hipster, misunderstood by my peers. And then...[...] I just can't imagine myself onstage. The way I am, it just won't work. It's like a hazing. And that's a drag for someone who wants to be creative. To feel marginalized, you know? I can be funny when I want to. I know something about making people laugh. But I would prefer to be less of a clown, to be able to be myself. And that's what's sad.

But really, when has he ever "been himself?" When he was painting? When he was the hardcore misogynist of his youth? Does the mask of success suit him any better than that of the fringe cult songwriter? So is this just some new pose, or does he really feel bullied? It's a interesting problem for a psychoanalyst, the whole dual personality thing with Serge (Dr. Jekyll/ Mr. Hyde, Gainsbourg/Gainsbarre). Any way, being such an idealist, he's not going to be satisfied with this first taste of financial success.

Then Serge, the man who has sworn to never perform again except on television, brings up his concerts: "When people used to come and watch me sing, they said I had no stage presence. Now I'm seen as a cynic and they say I'm pretentious. Make up your minds!"

Let's end this by recalling a couple of things he said to Denise Glaser just two year earlier:

French chanson is not dead, it has to evolve and ... talk about modern subject matter. [...] Modern life means inventing a whole new language. [...] There's an entire world to create, it just remains to be done. French song remains to be created.

In this 1965 television portrait, Serge seems considerably more mundane, proving that he has reached the end of his ruminations about French chanson and the avant-garde:

Theoretically, in order to be truly modern, a twentieth century artist in the same vein as painters and poets and contemporary composers, one has to make atonal music in free verse. Now how are you going to sell that in the sticks?

A few months later he explains it in more detail to the ever-faithful Lucien Rioux from *France-Observateur*:

I want to be misunderstood as a painter, but that's the not the case when it comes to music. It's pretentious to say that one is writing for a minority. Right away we associate the minority with the elite. Me, I want to write for the majority.[2]

After lending his singing voice to the TV cartoon *Dim Dam Dom*, Serge works again with France Gall, whose producers are looking for a new hit after the fiasco of her last super-45. When Serge gives them "Baby Pop," he hands them all the necessary ingredients: rhythm, melody, a catchy hook... And still, they can't make it work. When it is released in January, 1966, it just doesn't perform like "N'écoute pas les idoles" or "Laisse tomber les filles."

> Sing and dance now, Baby Pop
> There's no tomorrow, Baby Pop
> Tomorrow, little Baby Pop
> Doesn't mean a thing

In "Baby Pop" Gainsbourg is without a doubt painting his most exaggerated portrait of the contradiction between the new generation that identifies with sweet little pop tarts like France Gall and the more sordid and dramatic reality beneath it all. The facts are hard to swallow:

> Finding love for you is a dream
> But you don't understand at all
> Yay, Yay, Yay!
> One day he'll dump you baby
> You're headed for a fall
> You'll end up just tying the knot
> With some poor slob that you don't love
> Yay, yay, yay!
> On your wedding night dear
> Pray to god above

Just the type of song we think we know by heart, up until the moment we stop to think about the words...

FRANCE GALL: *"Baby Pop" is for all girls. We were all that girl! And I really loved those lines "Sing and dance now, Baby Pop/ There's no tomorrow, Baby Pop/Tomorrow, little Baby Pop/Time for you to die." The*

---

[2] Serge, in the grips of some strange schizophrenia, seems to be telling us, some eight years after giving up painting, that he suffers from both an inferiority complex (in respect to painting) and a superiority complex (his ability to write a song in record time, a song that will earn him a lot of money, which is also at the root of his guilt). More than just dime store psychology, this is something to ponder.

only thing that bothered me was that high pitched voice of mine and that mix, which is kind of shrill. For TV spots and promos, they dressed me in wigs and black and white make up. I thought it looked ridiculous. It ruined everything."

Serge has since left the family domicile. After living in hotels for a few weeks, he is approached by Michèle Arnaud, who offers him a place at her daughter Florence's little apartment on boulevard Murat, where Swiss director Pierre Koralnik is also staying. Koralnik is known for the famous variety program *Douche ecossaise*, which debuted just months ago. At the time, Koralnik is on the cutting edge of avant-garde television, as is another protégé of Michèle Arnaud, Jean-Christophe Averty.

PIERRE KORALNIK: *"When I wanted to do the musical 'Anna,' Michèle suggested Gainsbourg. We became fast friends and soon he came to live with me. He stayed for two or three months, which was good all ways around: his wife couldn't find him and he got a lot of work done."*

It's the end of 1965 and teenagers are still determining who is atop the charts. Sonny and Cher are a big deal, and everybody is copying Ronny Bird's Kings Road look. Johnny Hallyday is still on top ("Le diable me pardonne") and the Beatles are ever-present ("Michelle"). Still, what everyone is talking about is president Charles de Gaulle's enormous drop in the popular opinion polls. Even worse, he has to face a run-off in the presidential elections of December 5. He nevertheless ends up crushing his opponent François Mitterrand just two weeks later.

Serge is notoriously oblivious to political issues and happily performs at the televised electoral soirées of both parties. Between the two events, he heads back to London after a two year absence to record his new EP, "Qui est in qui est out," at Fontana studios. Four cuts, four classics. While his last London experience, the recording of "La javanaise," was cut short, this time Serge finds a perfect match in producer/arranger Arthur Greenslade. His band of crack studio players lay down a driving tempo, with all that mod organ and screaming guitar that Serge wants... In a word, it's "very pop":

> Up to nine, you're IN it's OK
> Afterwards you're knocked OUT, it's KO
> It's the same
> As boxing, see

Fashion and movies and even TV

This is when we run into "Docteur Jekyll et Monsieur Hyde," whose words evoke as rather strange vibe in light of his recent sentimental tribulations:

> *Doctor Jekyll had such trouble and strife*
> *A bunch of lousy bitches messing up his life*
> *Mister Hyde deep inside*
> *Would soon come out and skin their hides*
> *-'Hello Doctor Jekyll'*
> *-Doctor Jekyll's long gone...*

That's right. Doctor Jekyll is long gone because one day he discovers that what they like in him is in fact Mr. Hyde. So which one is asking innocent Marilu these questions?:

> *Have you embraced it yet Marilu?*
> *Tasted it just once yet Marilu?*
> *Will I be first to get Marilu?*
> *Answer me Marilu*

The inspiration for the song is Italian starlet Marilu Tolo, who according to the press has "the same measurements as Sophia Loren." She starred in Edward Dmytryk's Bluebeard, alongside Richard Burton, Raquel Welch, and Nathalie Delon. Did she and Gainsbourg ever met? Should we lend any credibility to what the press reported at the time – that Marilu's agent forbade Serge from calling the song "Marilu Tolo?"

Serge's new super-45 is released in January, 1966, at the very moment when Petula Clark's "La gadoue" and France Gall's "Baby Pop" start to make their assaults on the provincial radio stations (and our little English girl is by far outselling France). But the real news is that Serge is for the first time going to find himself at the same place on the charts, starting in March with "Docteur Jekyll," and then with "Qui est 'in'."

Gainsbourg had finally completed his metamorphosis. Not only is he ahead of the trends, but he's creating them and pushing them forward. He's making "pop music," a term that "the kids are nuts for" as Joseph sardonically reminds us in one of his letters to Liliane. In it, he quotes Claude Dejacques' liner notes for this pivotal album:

Serge got off the plane in London carrying a little attaché case with a few ideas [...] He just needed one night of clubbing in Soho and all the rhythms of pop music pulled these four melodies right out of him.

In the first few months of 1966, the tiny world of French chanson and rock will experience a furious wave of change and innovation: In "Elucubrations," Antoine sings about birth control pills for sale at Monoprix; behind his rather goofy image, Nino Ferrer turns out to be a real R&B singer; and finally, the irreproachably cool Jacques Dutronc also makes it big in the springtime of the very same year. Dutronc's first two EP's contain no less than half a dozen classics (including "Et moi et moi et moi" and "Mini mini mini") co-written by lyricist by Jacques Lanzman, the writer and editor-in-chief of Lui. While waiting for Dutronc to become the girl-trap/boy-toy that he will eventually become, we should address the matter of the fantastic little gadget that Serge gives to his girlfriend:

> When she pulls
> SHOO BA DOO BA LOO BA
> On his cord
> SHOO BA DOO BA LOO BA
> He squeaks and says
> SHOO BA DOO BA LOO BA
> You drive me nuts

In the meantime, the boss at Philips, Louis Hazan, comes up with a crackerjack idea: after squatting with Koralnik, Serge moves into a room at la Cité internationale des Arts on December 18, 1965. For a monthly pittance (270 francs at the time), this famous institution founded by André Malraux would house artists of any nationality who had received a grant. The building is located on the Right Bank, and Serge, being on the highest floor, has a magnificent view of L'île Saint-Louis, Notre-Dame, the Pantheon... The director of the establishment is one Simone Bruno.

SIMONE BRUNO: *"I saw him in my office and I remember that he refused to sit down. He was kind of hunched over, uneasy – a strange mix of shyness and arrogance because, in all honesty, he thought he was quite a big deal. He wasn't the only musician of his ilk that was there: there were two or three other chanson artists along with the sixty classical musicians that we had. We had a music hall, and I asked him - as I did all musicians - to give a concert. He told me that he would look stupid, like an idiot, things like that. I think he just didn't want to do it. He had a little studio, with a small room and a kitchen and a bathroom. It was on the fifth floor, over-looking the Seine."*

GAINSBOURG: *"It was pretty Spartan - a little studio some 23 square me-ters, a crappy little tub, a bed, a kitchenette, and once the upright piano came in there was no room to move around. I bought a daguerreotype of Chopin that I placed on the piano. It felt like he was watching me laughing in my face...I stayed at la Cité des Arts for two years and I was very happy. There was a floor for engravers, one for architects, floors for painters and musicians. The hallways seeme d to go on forever. I would listen as great concert musicians practiced their scales, and I felt embarrassed to be writ-ing my shitty little songs. That's why I started to say that I practiced a minor art made for adolescents."*

SIMONE BRUNO: *"It's true that he was pretty uncomfortable because we housed mostly conservatory students at the doctoral level. The residents talked about him as if he were a neighbor, at times a strange one with nu-merous fiancées and unannounced visits. Some thought of him as a wild child. It's true that he wasn't very talkative and always seemed distracted. Whenever we ran into him he seemed to be out of it."*

In order to pick up girls, Serge uses a foolproof formula: he makes them laugh, treats them like princesses, and behaves with rare gallantry. His con-quests speak of a man who acts "like someone from the 19th century"...

GAINSBOURG: *"I was a mad playboy at that time. I had girls lined up 'round the block, I dare say. They may not have been sleeping on my door-step, but there was a line. Sometimes, I would grow tired of it all and make up my mind not to see anyone. I would go and buy a bunch of canned food and cook it up myself, then I'd sit at my little table and say, "Finally! No more broads!" Two days later I'd be back in the saddle."*

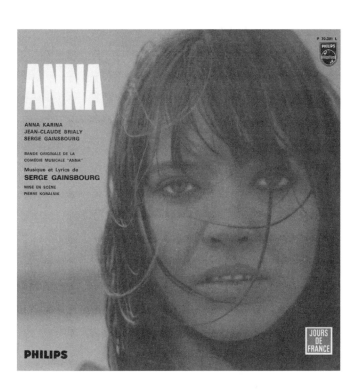

twelve

Lollipop Annie

On January 10, 1966, Serge takes time out between television appearances to attend a special event given for him at Radio Luxembourg. A number of his most famous interpreters are on hand, including Sacha Distel, Valérie Lagrange, Michèle Torr, France Gall, and Régine. Juliette Gréco appears via special link-up. The next day, Régine and host Hubert from Europe n°1 throw a big party at the Bus Palladium to honor "P'tits papiers." Then on March 5, Dominique Walter, Michèle Arnaud's son, competes at Eurovision de la chanson. He represents France with the song "Chez nous," written by Jacques Plante and Claude Carrère, which earns him just a single vote, giving him 16th place among 16 competitors. What should have been an illustrious beginning becomes a nightmare for the young man, who will soon be singing Gainsbourg...

> JOSEPH GINSBURG: *"And listen to this. I almost forgot: he was at the telephone, right in front of us when he jotted down something about a meeting with Salvador Dali. And just guess what it was – he was to compose music for a new dance that Dali wanted to introduce, something he brought back from who knows what exotic country."*

These plans are never realized, but that doesn't stop Serge from buying one of Dali's sketches, *La chase aux papillons...* Next, on March 13 - as is always the case when he releases a new album - Serge meets with Denise Glaser for the show *Discorama*, where he sings "Docteur Jekyll" and "Marilu." Once more, the interview is illuminating, intimate, and revealing.

> DENISE GLASER: *It's funny... Serge Gainsbourg, every time you come on Discorama, which is just about once a year, I feel like you're seeing the doctor for a check-up. I feel like I should be taking your pulse. Tell us how you are and what you're up to today.*

> S.G.: *Are you saying that I'm ill and incurable?*

> D.G: *Incurable, certainly, but I don't believe you're sick.*

> S.G.: *Incurable in what way?*

> D.G.: *Incurable insofar as you're Gainsbourg, and always tangled up in contradictions.*

> S.G.: *Not contradictions. Evolutions, not contradictions.*

> D.G.: *Well, now you yourself are singing a bit like the Beatles. What's happened?*

> S.G.: *It's just that there's this global trend that started in Liverpool and one can't ignore it. It's that simple. I can't just sit and turn to stone. I write difficult songs and they call me an intellectual. I write simple ones and they say I'm selling out... They don't cut me any damn slack, you know... They're just looking for anything to pick at [...]*

> *Denise then brings up the subject of Serge "changing his tune," which they had discussed at their prior meeting:*

> D.G.: *So why have you changed your tune?*

> S.G.: *My tune?*

> D.G.: *Your tune.*

> S.G.: *Because I can do much better this way, much better. I'm at the age where one has to succeed or pack it in. I made a very simple, mathematical calculation. I did 12 songs for a prestigious LP with a pretty cover. 12 pre-*

cious little elaborate pieces. Out of those 12, two got radio play and the rest were completely ignored. Then I wrote 12 songs for 12 different performers and each was a hit.

When Denise Glaser asks him if he wouldn't like to explore something other than songwriting, Serge brings up the possibility of writing a book, which would be about women, but he assures us that he is "not yet ready for that" and that music "has never been anything really important," except in the eyes of his public. The host is titillated by the subject matter of this forthcoming book...

S.G.: *Personal experience, personal disappointment, and then my personal ideal. Very complicated.*

D.G.: *If you're talking to me about your personal ideal, that means that you're not as misogynistic as you were a few years back?*

S.G.: *I was never a misogynist. I was reserved, that's all. And not very nice. What do you expect from me with this mug of mine, that I be some nice guy [...] I'm nice in my private life, but not out in public.*

D.G.: *Well, do you know that face of yours has garnered you many admirers?*

S.G.: *Yeah, I know. But women like that aren't stupid.*

D.G.: *What do you mean, not stupid?*

S.G.: *They know very well that it's me there behind the songs. My music is my job, it's my uniform, but once in my street clothes I'm myself, which is something altogether different. It's something that's a little easier to be. And why say, "You should be like this, you should smile, you shouldn't be brutish, you should be sweet?" What's this idea that it has to be either sunny or cloudy? Christ, maybe it's raining! In films, there are some great guys, guys like Jack Palance, who are always really brutish. People love those guys. At the music-hall that just doesn't fly. They say: "He's a goddamn sinister bastard, that one, a brute, nasty fellow..." But why? Why can't we see these things in a different light? [...]*

D.G.: *Well, I don't know if that guy is nasty or brutish, but I did see you a minute ago when you went to put on your tie. You moved across the studio with a little dance in your step, like a man happy to be alive.*

S.G.: *Maybe... I'm not so sure about that.*

After bringing up what Serge had said previously about young singers ("If they want to buy lollipop factories"), she reminds him that he's now writing for these same young artists:

S.G.: *They've grown up, and so have I.*

D.G.: *Now it's you making lollipops for them. You've even become a lollipop factory.*

S.G.: *Yeah, but I make ginger-flavored lollipops!*

Precisely! He must be really taken with the whole lollipop theme considering the song he writes for his youngest performer, France Gall:

> *Lollipop Annie loves lollies*
> *Licorice lollies are best*
> *When Annie sucks that tasty*
> *Lolly*
> *Her kisses drive the*
> *Men to folly*
> *Sugary droplets she swallows*
> *Tasty licorice delights*
> *Sweet little pearls so*
> *Very nice*
> *Take her to paradise*

The song "Les sucettes" is featured on France's tenth EP, released in May, 1966. Of all the hits Serge has written, it's this one that will cause the biggest stir. Is it a salacious hymn to innocence, or just the opposite? People often forget that Serge is terrified of any potential scandal, and these same people tend to make too much of France Gall's naïveté. The story, as rumor has it, has never been verified. Supposedly, when France Gall is made aware of the meaning behind the double entendre in "Sucettes," she is so shocked that she locks herself up and refuses to come out for three weeks.

DENIS BOURGEOIS: *"France always paid close attention to the music and lyrics. She would have never sung anything vulgar, ridiculous, or old-fashioned. She already had an innate sense of what was necessary in a song, without being calculating. In fact, her very first record, 'Sacré*

Charlemagne,' had caused a bit of a stir. When it came out, her yé-yé pals made fun of her and said that her music was for little kids. That hit her a lot harder than whole "Les sucettes" thing. She even wanted to pull the record!"

FRANCE GALL: *"Serge missed the mark with "Les sucettes" – the song was simply not a good picture of me. I was very modest and sang with an innocence that I was proud of. I was quite hurt to find out that he had mockingly turned that situation to his advantage. I had no normal relationships with boys, and when you sing, you know, it can be scary. I thought I was singing a story along the lines of Sophie, Comtesse de Ségur. When I understood the deeper meaning I was so ashamed, and afraid of being scorned."*

Towards the end of the eighties, Serge fiendishly relishes the opportunity to quote France when a reporter asks him, "Why do you no longer sing 'Les sucettes?'"

GAINSBOURG: *"France put it admirably: "I'm too old for that stuff..."*

> *Annie only needs*
> *Ten cents*
> *For those lollipops*
> *Immense*
> *Candy that shines like her own two eyes*
> *Bright as the sunniest skies*

After all is said and done, the song has no problem with censorship, unlike Michel Polnareff's "L'amour avec toi," which is much more explicit and almost completely blackballed. What's even funnier is that on the show *Au risque de vous plaire*, France performs "Les sucettes" amidst a sea of dancers decked out as lollipops and models walking around eating long candy suckers. The message is quite clear...

On March 21, Serge appears at a big gala for the Union des artists. Those in attendance include Jean-Paul Belmondo, Barbara, and Leslie Caron. Serge performs a parody of "Le poinçonneur de Lilas," singing from the bottom of a grave that he's digging himself. Then on April 12, 1966, at 4:08 in the afternoon, there is that historic event for the children of the yé-yé generation: Jean-Marie Périer takes the "photo of the century" for the magazine *Salut les copains*. There are 47 stars in the shot, the oldest of whom is Gainsbourg, nestled right in there along with Johnny Hallyday, France Gall, Nino Ferrer, Françoise Hardy, etc. After the shoot, all the beautiful people celebrate the anniversary of Johnny and Sylvie and dig into a big wedding cake. Thanks to France, and thanks to his "glissement" into the world of pop, Serge is now accepted by the new generation.

> MICHEL DRUCKER: *"Everyone knows that Périer photo, and what strikes me about it is that Serge is the only one of his generation. There's no Béart, no Brel, no Brassens. And what's more, his look would become all the rage. With that snarling mug of his he was helping to put the nail in the coffin of the whole dandy thing..."*

The photo, published in poster format in issue 47 of *Salut les copains,* will end up covering the bedroom walls of thousands of teenagers. In this same collector's issue, the article "Who is Serge Gainsbourg? An eccentric loner" informs us that he is five feet ten inches tall and weighs 139 ponds. We learn that he practices no religion and that his politics are "individualistic and non-aggressive." His hobby is "women," his favorite dishes are "pigeon, quail, bunting, thrush, and in general all types of small birds." His favorite painter is Paul Klee, his favorite musicians are James Brown and Igor Stravinski, and he reads Nabokov... We also read that he has a collection of very old, finely-crafted walking sticks and some sort of gadget whose "magnificent light is ideal for intimate evenings": essentially one of those lava lamps that is all the rage with hippies on the West Coast. In a more serious vein, Serge declares:

> *The Rive Gauche style, or intellectual chanson, is for half-wits. This ir-relevant and demagogic intellectualism is by far the most mediocre thing on the market. [...] The age of science that we live in leaves me completely indifferent, as do politics or social issues.*

Finally, concerning his piano playing neighbors at la Cité des Arts:

> *"There are just as many cut-rate players in the classical world as there are in the pop world... So why should I feel intimidated!"*

It's still springtime, 1966 when Serge writes a little novelty number for Régine. The style is somewhere between Guy Marchand and Henri Salvador, and starts with a metaphysical query posed by opera singer Régine Crespin, who was a background singer that day: "Pajamas you say / In yellow, in red, or in gray?" And Régine responds:

Me I'd simply never wear
No I would never even dare
Be caught in anything like a
Pair of pajamas

This timeless masterpiece is released in the month of May, and Régine invites virtually anyone who's anyone in Parisian nightlife. All guests are instructed to come only in pajamas or nighties...

In the meantime, divorce proceedings are scheduled at the county courts of the Seine for October 20,,1966, and in order to speed things up, Serge decides to accept all the blame and concede to all of his wife's demands. Among said demands is that all visits with his child take place in the mother's presence.

On May 9, 1966, Serge sings "Docteur Jekyll et Monsieur Hyde" and composes three sketch-songs for a new episode of the *Sacha Show*. Three weeks later, Michèle Arnaud proposes yet another program called *Cravate noire / Black Tie*. The guests include Sylvie Vartan, the Moody Blues, Nino Ferrer, Valérie Lagrange, Marianne Faithfull, and the producer's son, Dominique Walter. Michèle, who had never stopped singing, asks for two new songs from the man she helped to discover nearly 10 years ago and to whom she had just rewarded by commissioning for him the musical *Anna*. Obviously inspired by the title of Michèle's new show, Serge writes her the piece "Les papillons noirs," which they perform as a duo. It's a misunderstood little gem that the group Bijou, in a show of good taste, will save from total obscurity in 1978:

Sorrows fade in this drunken night
With all our heart we'd like to find
Chased from the corners of our mind
Those black butterflies
Those black butterflies

Historically speaking, Mireille Darc is the second actress to get a song from Gainsbourg after Bardot. For her second EP (she had already done a super-45 a year earlier), he writes her an insignificant waltz, "La cavaleuse." Then comes a ghost from the past, Jacques Canetti, who has been busy with the immense repertory left behind by Boris Vian. In 1966, he persuades Serge Reggiani (from Casque d'or, etc.) to try singing, starting with an album devoted solely to Vian (the consecration of which will take place one year later with "Les loups"). At the behest of the "slave driver" of the Trois Baudets tours, Serge composes the music for Vian's vexing and humorous poem "Quand j'aurai du vent dans mon crâne":

> When the wind whistles through my head
> When my bones lie bleached and I am dead
> Perhaps you'll say I'm mocking you
> But nothing could be farther from the truth
> For I'll no longer possess this physique
> Physique zique zique
> Long since eaten by rats

A *People Magazine* interlude: it's towards the end of May, 1966, at the Bonne Fontaine restaurant in Saint-Tropez, when Brigitte Bardot meets German multimillionaire, international playboy, and ex-bobsled champion Gunther Sachs. Among his numerous conquests is Soraya, ex-empress of Iran, just to mention one... It's love at first sight on both sides. Bardot is hypnotized, and the first volume of her autobiography tells of "his salt and pepper temples, his superbly and somewhat rebelliously long hair, his cocky, suntanned face, his immense build and that indefinable accent..." Gunther knows just what to do to seduce a woman, even one as blasé and donjuanesque as Bardot: a romantic evening serenaded by a gypsy ensemble until the break of day; a shower of roses falling from a helicopter onto the shores of La Madrague; a ride in his speedboat, which he pilots wearing a tuxedo and an immense black and red cape on a night illuminated by the full moon... After a few weeks of this whirlwind courtship, the hipster Hun reaches his goal: he marries Brigitte in Las Vegas on July 13, 1966. She thinks she is living a fairytale, but the enchantment will soon fade. The man she thinks is prince charming is revealed to be an inveterate philanderer.

A literary interlude: at least twice during the course of interviews in 1966, Gainsbourg mentions the work of poet Georges Fourest as among his favorite bedtime reading. Fourest is so rare and obscure that he merits a bit of examination. Fourest (1867-1945) is a 19th century decadent poet and a forerunner of Surrealism. He is educated as a jurist but his true vocation is living off landed property, and he dedicates his life to the joys of laziness. Ever the amateur - he even defines himself as such –Fourest's guiding principle is: "Never take anything seriously, not yourself, not others, nor anything in this world or the next." He publishes his first collection of poems, *La Négresse blonde*, in 1909, which is followed by *Contes pour les satyres* (1923) and *Géranium ovipare* (1937). Why is Serge so drawn to this unknown poet? Obviously for his meticulous rhymes, his complicated verse riddled with all sorts of oddities, his irreverent humor, his burlesque erudition:

> *This man-eating ingénue*
> *Lies naked here in front of you*
> *Upon the skins of kangaroos*
> *From the isle Tamamourou*
> *Where tightrope-walking potoroos*
> *And platypus with duck-shaped bills*
> *Phascolomes set for the kill*
> *Prepare to mate as she sits still*

Now onto the production of the musical *Anna*, previously relegated to oblivion before being brought back to French TV in 1990. As for the soundtrack, it sees only a limited release in January, 1967 and is now a collector's item for Gainsbourg fanatics. It is re-released in 1989 on the compilation *De Gainsbourg à Gainsbarre*. It's rarity is one of the major reasons for the mythic reputation of this astonishing work, which when one re-evaluates historically represents an extremely popish moment of grace, if you will – something completely atypical in the history of de Gaulle-era France.

GAINSBOURG: *"It was French rock before French rock existed, really. I think the soundtrack has aged poorly, but the visuals still hold up. I always thought Koralnik was going to have an amazing career. He's a great director..."*

PIERRE KORALNIK: *"'Anna' is the story of a guy – Jean-Claude Brialy – who works for an advertising firm. He accidentally stumbles across a photo of a girl – Anna Karina – and from that moment has but one goal: to find her. He looks all over Paris, and the point of the story is that all along it had been his assistant. He didn't recognize her because she was hiding behind a pair of glasses... It was really original. Serge conceived of the music as a writer does a script. It was very rock n' roll. You could see the modernism in Gainsbourg's work, and the lyrics were magnificent."*

GAINSBOURG: *"'Anna' happened at the time of television's first color broadcasts. It was shown on the second channel in January '67. I was captivated by Anna Karina's beauty."*

PIERRE KORALNIK: *"She was magnificent, at the height of her beauty and talent. Plus, she liked to sing. She had a great voice, but nobody had ever dreamt of using it..."*

Anna Karina, 26 years old in 1966, is divorced from Jean-Luc Godard, with whom she makes *Vivre sa vie* (1962), *Alphaville* (1964), and *Pierrot le fou* (1965). She also works with Jacques Rivette (the scandalous *La Religieuse*) and Visconti (*L'Etranger*)...

ANNA KARINA: *"During our first meeting, I found Serge to be very shy, very sensitive. I never understood how one could find him ugly. He had such beautiful gestures, and was very distinguished, princely, I would say... Anna was very important for me. I had always wanted to sing and he had written great lyrics for me. I loved it when Serge would show me his songs. It made me think of my adolescence, when I was 14. My father would take me in his arms and he'd play with me and sing..."*

The director of photography, Willy Kurant, is Belgian. His name can be found on the credits to many of Serge's films, including *Je t'aime moi non plus, Equateur,* and *Charlotte Forever...*

WILLY KURANT: *"That's where I met him, or rather as Serge would say, that's where he spotted me. Koralnik was 20 years ahead of the times. The lighting he wanted is very trendy today, but at the time no one understood it. When the president of the technicians union wrote the director of the TV station, he said about 'Anna': "the work of Mr. Willy Kurant merits a prison sentence." That gives you an idea of the atmosphere back then ..."*

PIERRE KORALNIK: *"Serge had already been attracted to the idea of writing a musical with, among others, Jean-Louis Barrault. It was a passionate experience and the creative atmosphere was ideal. We would argue sometimes because he was writing for a lot of other people, and I thought he was casting his pearls before swine. I understood his talent and knew that he was capable of producing rare and precious things, things that I loved."*

JEAN-PIERRE SPIERO: *"Serge was supposed to deliver the lyrics and just 15 days before filming started we had only half the songs. It was a disas-*

*ter because we had to have everything storyboarded, every set ready. I
remember Serge writing day and night and giving singing lessons to Anna
Karina. It was insane. He wasn't hyper, but nervous, and at certain times
he'd hit a creative block and just keep chain smoking. Then at four in the
morning he'd telephone Pierre to say that he finished such and such sequence. It was created under considerable pressure."*

GAINSBOURG: *"It was at that time I set my record for successive nights
of intentional insomnia – eight nights. At night I'd compose music that
would be recorded the next day. In the mornings I had studio sessions and
in the afternoon I was playing a convict in the Loursais film, Vidocq. When
it was over I slept for 48 hours straight..."*

During a somewhat depressing instrumental, we see the soggy shores
of the beach and seagulls spiraling into infinity... It's the intro to "Sous le
soleil exactement":

> *Lying beneath tropical skies*
> *Capricorn... Cancer... Which is it?*
> *I've long since forgotten it seems*
> *Right 'neath the sun I surely am*
> *Not in the shade nor somewhere else*
> *Under the sun, just right below*
> *I surely am, under the sun*

One of the prettiest sequences is filmed in a chateau at Rochefort-en-
Yvelines with England's Marianne Faithfull, at the time Mick Jagger's fiancé.
The front man for the Rolling Stones, currently atop the charts with "Paint
it Black," is along with his newest conquest during the filming. "Marianne
Faithfull was my idea," Koralnik tells us. "In the script, there was this
strange girl, beautiful but quite wild, who was supposed to play counterpoint
to the sophistication of Anna Karina." For contractual reasons, her song -
"Hier ou demain" – isn't included on the soundtrack but rather is issued
as a separate 45:

> *Yesterday's a dried up sea*
> *I never loved you, dear*
> *Tomorrow you may think of me*
> *But I'll be nowhere near*
> *Yesterday or tomorrow*
> *I'd have said "yes" to you*

Yesterday or tomorrow
But today we're through

Another high point in this musical, which draws its inspiration from the author's literary tastes, is the song "C'est la cristallisation comme dit Stendhal"... Brialy runs across the photo of Anna and it's love at first sight. He murmurs to himself: "Not bad, not bad at all..." The jaded seducer, the one who was destined for "casual relationships," is now hooked:

I'm the type who has to play the field
My independence, it's the rule
I'm the type that
Just can't settle down

Getting Brialy ready to sing is no piece of cake. The brilliant, young actor, 33 years old, had broken through seven years back in Claude Chabrol's *Le Beau Serge*. He releases a 45 in 1964 that contains the song "Horizontalement," which is given to him by Jean Ferrat. When Koralnik has him listen to Gainsbourg, he is completely floored.

JEAN-CLAUDE BRIALY: *"Serge said, "I'm going to teach you how to sing. Me!" And he did just that, with a great deal of patience and kindness. I dubbed my voice over his as to not screw up the rock tunes because they were very difficult. I really had to work..."*

The results are a bit rough, especially on "Boomerang" (where Serge's voice is sometimes dubbed in for Brialy's, who must have been off-beat) and also on the rock number "J'étais fait pour les sympathies." Much more successful is another dialogue – "Rien, rien, j'disais ça comme ça" – between the cynical Serge and the indifferent Karina.

JEAN-CLAUDE BRIALY: *"He was charmed by Anna, whose style of singing was a breathy and erotic foreshadowing of what we would come to find on later Jane Birkin albums. I think that Serge was in love with her, and anyway, he was unable to work with people without being in love with them. He even told me he was in love with me! He came to see me on set with a little bouquet of flowers, and he was very affectionate, tender."*

Finally, we have a sort of rough draft that hints at what would be coming with B.B., namely Anna Karina as "Roller Girl," the Lolita of the comic strips:

The girl whose face they paste
On Harley Davidsons
On BM double-U's
Yeah I'm the Roller-Girl
Roll Roll Roll
Roller Girl

Serge recruits Michel Colombier as musical director/arranger for the *Anna* sessions. On the advice of Alain Goraguer, he had hired and gotten to know the young arranger during the sessions for the soundtrack to *Comment trouvez-vous ma sœur?* His star is now rising considerably and he has his finger on the pulse of the sixties, writing all the little "jingles" for *Salut les copains*, as well as the credit sequence for *Dim Dam Dom*. Serge will later use him for his film music, for the "Bonnie and Clyde" arrangement, and on the first version of "Je t'aime moi non plus."

MICHEL COLOMBIER: *"Serge had what I didn't, and vice-versa. Working on 'Anna' was definitely the most fun we had together. I found it interesting how we worked together with no concern for ego – we were simply participating in a collaborative work. For example, I would choose the color palate for the orchestrations, but he would never just give me a melody and then simply take off for a stroll. He was at every session and would always tell me if something displeased him. It might be a note in a chord or even the precise voicing of the note. I was really passionate about it all. Besides being fascinated with his lyrics, I also loved his utterly unique melodic sensibility, which was rooted to a great degree in his Russo-Jewish background. Blacks and Jews have that in common, I think – they're the only people who really know the blues..."*

Meanwhile, in August,1966, Gainsbourg the actor finds himself embroiled in another mess: he's stuck for six weeks shooting another load of rubbish in Colombia, Jacques Besnard's *Estouffade à la Caraïbe*, with lead actress Jean Seberg, unforgettable next to Belmondo in *A bout de souffle*. It's a detective film that's all action, set in an exotic locale with a brutal dictator and an oppressed populace to make it all the more believable.

As usual, Serge accepts a minor role just as a means of enjoying a vacation. On his flight from Paris to Cartagena, he meets up with one of the other actors, Paul Crauchet. Crauchet remembers the wooden bungalows in which they are housed, right in the heart of the jungle. There is just a tiny partition separating his room from Serge's, and the two of them stay up talking trash all night long. Crauchet also remembers the bordellos in Cartagena.

PAUL CRAUCHET: *"They'd put us up in a fine hotel, but Serge wanted to go out and hear some Afro-Cuban music. He was crazy for that stuff. Well, the two of us wound up in the city's bordellos, and over there, a bordello is nothing but a hovel. It's just some open-air joint, but with a modicum of discretion. There is no exposed flesh and you can hear some great musicians. Serge took some notes and actually pointed things out to me, made me appreciate the music. At two in the morning I was beat and had to split, but he stayed there and transcribed his notes into music."*

GAINSBOURG: *"In the bordellos, you would walk onto a patio where the girls were sequestered behind doors with iron bars. They would have them step out and you could choose... Women as beautiful as the Algerian girls painted by Delacroix... I choose one, but I tell her pimp I don't want to fuck her at the brothel and I take her somewhere else. No, that's not right: first I fucked her in the whorehouse and then I took her away. I remember her bed was covered with stuffed animals and there were postcards pinned all over her walls. What's more, she let me do whatever I wanted, which is rare with prostitutes... So afterwards, I take her to the hotel where we get it on again. The next few days after that she accompanied me to the set. At that time there was always a row of chairs that had the names of the directors or actors printed on them. I sat her down in the one marked Gainsbourg and the whole crew was shocked, especially Seberg..."*

He also amuses himself with professionals in Paris...

GAINSBOURG: *"I head to Rue Godot-de-Mauroy and spot a couple of girls in a car. I tell them: "I want both of you. We'll do it in stereo!" When we're in the car, one disrobes, but not the other. She was a bit burnt out. I'm really nervous, I start yelling, and finally I just end up paying them. I take off, and in the staircase, I can hear the little sluts shouting at me: "Faggot! Faggot!" The quarrel spills over into the street and I start to kick the shit out of their car. I feel like slapping the one who's a real cunt, but they manage to push my arm back when they roll up the window...Luckily, they were stuck between two other cars. If not, they'd have mowed me down! I hear the police sirens, so I decide to duck into a side street. Later, when I became Gainsbarre, I had top-shelf call-girls, from a catalogue, in really plush brothels frequented by ministers and aristocrats, the types who say, "I want that one..." and five minutes later they've shot their wad."*

It's also the city of Cartagena which unmasks Gainsbourg the pyromaniac. In a restaurant decorated with dried-up old plants, Serge lights a cigarette and distractedly tosses the match over his shoulder. 15 seconds later the place is in flames and things are sheer panic. Outside, Serge beholds the blaze with fascination, asking himself: "Did I do that?"

GAINSBOURG: *"No one hurt, fortunately, but nothing of the place remains. I tell myself I'd better beat it, then I go back to my whore and wait for things to calm down. Also, it was the last day of filming and everybody was to return the next day. That morning, I'm back at the hotel and I run straight into some Colombian cops who stop me with their sidearms drawn. Then this lawyer shows up, straight out of an Orson Welles film, this huge guy in a white linen suit who's trying to catch his breath."*

PAUL CRAUCHET: *"I remember that night. I was dining with my friends and sitting a few tables away from Serge. But I left at about 10:30 and the fire broke out around 11:00. The next day we had to take the plane back to France, to film exteriors in Nice that we couldn't do in Colombia. When we were leaving, I found out Serge was in the can."*

JOSEPH GINSBURG: *"The production company ended up paying for it and Lucien was released. 13 hours of interrogation and no smoking, which was for him a real ordeal, but he had to hold it together because he told the police he didn't smoke. And just before leaving, when he took a cigarette that they offered him, one of them said: "So you do smoke, huh?" He answered: "I said that I didn't smoke, but I didn't say that I wasn't a smoker!"*

In fall of 1966, the sounds on the charts are changing. France is now all about soul music and Californian pop, while a new monthly publication, *Rock & Folk*, is just hitting the stands. James Brown scores with "It's a Man's World," the Beach Boys with "Good Vibrations," and the Troggs do "With a Girl Like You." The Stones give us "Mother's Little Helper" and the Beatles release "Yellow Submarine," while Dylan puts out "I Want You." French stars, like Johnny Hallyday, Jacques Dutronc, and Michel Polnareff are also making waves.

Upon returning to Paris, Gainsbourg (as unbelievable as it sounds) goes back to Béatrice, even though their divorce is finalized. His little girl has just had her second birthday and he misses her terribly. This reconciliation – conditions state that they must live apart – lasts less than a year, from November, 1966 to October, 1967. He'll need Bardot to come into his life before he can finally exorcise the woman at the root of such profound pain. In fact, he would never be able to recall it without great reticence.

Then he goes back to work. They offer him a fortune to compose a little commercial jingle for Dalida, for some brand of wine. "20 million for 20 minutes," he would confide to his friend, journalist René Quinson.[1] Dalida, who's in a slump (she hasn't had a hit for over a year and won't have another until next fall, with "La Banda"), inspires nothing in him. After her commercial, he craps out an abysmal little ditty for her called "Je préfère naturellement," which is part of a super-45 that she releases at the end of the year. At the same time, he composes and sings the title sequence for the TV show *Vidocq*, starring Bernard Noël, which starts broadcasting on January 7, 1967 on channel 1.[2] It's impossible not to hear the parallel with Bob Dylan's "talking blues," which was itself inspired by Leadbelly and other blues pioneers:

> *Ah, ah, ah, if you know not what torture prison brings*
> *Ah, ah, ah, you know nothing of the freedom that I sing*
> *I'm a fugitive, I understand these things*

A year later, in issue 14 of *Rock & Folk*, Philippe Constantin will goad him on about his cynicism while recalling one of his appearances on *Discorama*:

PHILIPPE CONSTANTIN: *(When Denise) Glaser asked you about plagiarizing Dylan on the Vidocq recording, you calmly responded: "I didn't think anyone would notice."*

SERGE GAINSBOURG: *Yeah, that's true. But really all I took was the rhythmic groove. I don't know if you can really accuse me of stealing the harmonic progression of a blues, and melodically it's mine.*

P.C.: *I guess I just bring it all up because in the eyes of the French public you're considered our number one cynic.*

---

[1] Old francs, of course.
[2] The song is called "Chanson du forçat." (T.N.)

S.G.: *Well it's strange that in such volatile times I'm accused of being a cynic. [...] People accuse me of cynicism without understanding my romantic nature... Or my nature as a man... of 40 years... I'll show them, all those two-faced swine, and nice little boys and girls in this business... What a bunch of phony assholes! I'm the one you should be putting a halo on...*

There are also business meetings. Upon the advice of Charley Marouani, Serge meets with Eddie Barclay, who had long since wanted the writer of "La javanaise" to be one of his artists. He sees him again in the end of 1966 when his contract with Philips expires, at the end of eight good years of loyal service.

EDDIE BARCLAY: *"I'd always said I'd wanted to work with him and he was impressed that I'd signed Brel to a lifelong contract, which is something rare in this business. I offered him a better contract than he had at Philips, and I offered my studios, which were at that time the best in Europe, if not the world. Duke Ellington and Miles Davis had just cut records there... He also knew that I could guarantee excellent promotion, like I did for Brel or Ferré, who both sold more records than him. A lot more! With a personality as strong as Serge's, we could expect him to sell a lot of albums. Finally, Philips got wind of our negotiations and the bidding war began."*

Serge is in a quandary. Sure, he had only sold 15-20,000 records under his name compared to Johnny Hallyday's 800,000. Like his father, who is also always respectful towards people of importance, Serge wants neither to annoy nor to appear ungrateful towards the bosses at Philips, Louis Hazan and Georges Meyerstein. They had always supported him. On the other hand, they had gotten the most out of their risky investment, be it through the sales of France Gall records or those of other Philips artists between 1964-65.

Still, his royalties are the same as when he signed with Canetti in 1958: a meager 5%, which is raised to 7% after he is approached by Barclay. Hazan also proposes a 100,000 franc signing bonus. Barclay offers more, of course, but Serge remains with Philips.

This ends a turbulent year. On December 23, Serge appears on a Christmas show, *Noël à Vaugirard*, billed as a "beatnik nativity show" and broadcast as part of Dim Dam Dom. "I don't remember. Did I play Joseph or the jackass?" he jokes some 20 years later. In this humorous sketch, filmed in slaughterhouses, he does in fact play Joseph, standing next to Chantal Goya as Mary and surrounded by guest stars Jacques Dutronc, Régine, Guy Marchand, etc. On December 31, 1966, for a televised New Year's Eve show, he sings "Docteur Jekyll et Monsieur Hyde."

One day Doctor Jekyll he could see
It was Mister Hyde they wanted and not he
Mister Hyde vile and base
Soon would take poor Jekyll's place

Like a resume of his life...

He wants to become a painter, but instead becomes a popular singer-songwriter who's invited onto TV shows. He is romantic and reserved, but his love life is a disaster. People love his incisive and original songs, and then he has to change his style to earn a living. He is both timid and hostile, and now does rock songs and poses with other stars from Salut des copains. He is neurotic about his ugliness, and then finds fame and hits 40, which both turn out to be upturns for him. Lucien Rioux, one of his most faithful aficionados, remembers that in the time of "smiley faces" (we can all remember those little yellow circles with the happy smiles), the public - other than the few thousand who will always wait with baited breath for his next disc - is not yet ready to accept Serge. So who will win out: Doctor Lucien or Mister Serge?

thirteen

Zip! Shebam! Pow! Blop! Wizz!

It's 1967, and the Beatles release their most famous album, *Sgt. Pepper's Lonely Hearts Club Band.* Gilbert Bécaud, Donovan, and the Rolling Stones are also all over the charts. As for Gainsbourg, although he hasn't given a concert in a year and a half, he enters French living rooms by means of television every two weeks. In fact he does 27 television shows in 1967 alone! One of the most successful is *Dents de lait dents de loup,* directed by Pierre Koralnik.

JEAN-PIERRE SPIERO: *"It was completely wild. We had a couple of surreal hosts: the M.C. Rosko, who came from English pirate radio via Radio Luxembourg, as well as Annick Beauchamps from France-Inter. We placed the singers and dancers right in the middle of the crowd, and I created a décor built around giant photos that I hung everywhere. It's where we got to see the famous duo with France Gall and Serge doing "Les sucettes." She sure understood the words that time!"*

The show, with its totally grooving pop vibe, is supposed to be the first of a series, but such a stink is raised about it that the producers' ambitions are cut short. Looking back at it now, the show, largely inspired by the British program *Ready, Steady, Go!,* stands as one of the best pieces of television from the second half of the sixties. All the big stars of the day are there: Claude François, the Walker Brothers, Eddy Mitchell, Sylie Vartan, Marianne Faithfull, and Serge, doing "Marilu." The opening sequence is sung by France Gall and Gainsbourg himself, inspired by the driving organ behind the tune "96 Tears," a minor hit by the American group ? and The Mysterians:

> SERGE: *You're just a baby*
> *A little baby wolf*
> *Your teeth are pretty*
> *But you're no big bad wolf*

> FRANCE: *Yes I'm a baby*
> *A little baby wolf*
> *Yes I have baby teeth*
> *But there a carnivore's*

Among the show's dancers and extras is one Marie France, the legendary Parisian transvestite and future star of Alcazar, where she is renowned for doing a spot-on Marilyn Monroe.

> MARIE FRANCE: *"I had an orange mini-skirt and long hair. I could tell he was checking me out when I was dancing. At lunchtime, he invited me to a bistro, and later that afternoon he came over, claiming that we had been invited out by some of the technicians from the SFP. We ended up in some room drinking whiskey. He took me to dinner and told me, "Let's go have a drink, wherever you'd like." We took a taxi to l'Entresol, in the Marais. Then we went to his room at la Cité des Arts [...] He played the piano. He was real charming, and in no time I wound up in his arms. In the morning we had breakfast in the brasserie at Pont Louis-Philippe. Then we went back up to listen to the Anna Karina album he'd just received."*

The above-mentioned album is most certainly the soundtrack to *Anna*, which he had just finished mixing a few weeks earlier at studio Hoche with Michel Colombier. He's condemned by some critics for the words to "GI Joe," one of the film's craziest songs:

> *GI Joe*
> *You're going to die under American flags*
> *GI Joe*
> *Bombs will shred you up into American rags*

One should remember that this is the middle of the Vietnam War. Interviewed by René Quinson, Serge responds: "I wanted to do something paradoxical. People saw political statements in that, statements far from what I had in mind."

Anna is scheduled to be shown on January 13, two days after *Dents de lait dents de loup*, and in color, for those lucky few possessing newly adapted televisions. In spite of the good promotion, the reviews are mixed. Certain newspaper headlines poke fun at the show, for example "Gainsbourg wants to write intelligent lyrics on top of a jerk-style dance beat." Gainsbourg responds: "The music in *Anna* has a new sound. Some people will look at it and say: 'That's yé-yé.' But what does that mean, yé-yé? Nothing! It's time to assimilate new sounds into the music, without any preconceived or pejorative notions." In *La Dépêche du Midi*, he says: "Our composers are usually influenced by American musicals. But if you go to Broadway, you'll see that they haven't evolved. They continue to write music in the style of the thirties with lyrics for 50 year-olds. I am totally immersed in Anglo-Saxon music. I have tried to mix that English sound with rock and rhythm & blues, and at the same time add a few passages that might be deemed lyrical. In any case, I don't have the kind of musical experience necessary to write a true modern opera."

Three days after its televised broadcast, *Anna* is given a special screening at the Translux cinema, but no one is interested in distributing this unclassifiable product. Serge still thinks it will have a great run in theatres, especially because of the lighting, the direction, the exploding colors – all those things that risk alienating the television spectator. In no way discouraged, Gainsbourg and Koralnik briefly entertain the possibility of collaborating with writer Joseph Kessel on a French adaption of the famous *Fiddler on the Roof*. Serge would later tell Philippe Constantin, "With Anna, I simply proved that I still had it together." In other words, he's not totally a victim of his concessions.

Serge writes another tune for Eurovsion, which takes place in Vienna in April, 1967. The singer this time is the 17 year-old Minouche Barelli, and her performance fails miserably. At about the same time, Serge declares that he's writing 12 songs for Anna Karina, 12 for Jeanne Moreau, and another dozen for actress Elsa Martinelli, whom he had just met on a television set:

"That one's exactly my style. She's really modern, really jazz." None of these projects will see the light of day, and there's a reason why as far as one of the performers is concerned. "I was good friends with Anna Karina," Claude Dejacques tells us. "Serge tried to bed her and she gave him the blow off. That's why there wasn't any album." Finally, Serge settles on composing the music for *Au risque de te déplaire*, a 45 by Marie-Blanche Vergne, with lyrics by husband Jean-Cristophe Averty. He also writes "Néfertiti," which is part of France Gall's new EP (the one that contains "La Petite," the inane duo with Maurice Biraud):

> *Nefertiti*
> *Don't worry so*
> *Those strands of cloth*
> *As you should know*
> *Will preserve your scent so fine*
> *Until 1999*

Serge writes "Les petits boudins" for Dominique Walter, and it appears on the EP that also contains his version of "Penny Lane" and Polnareff's "Je n'ai pas osé." Thanks to this new tune, which is especially cynical and in direct contrast to Walter's pretty mug, the "mama's boy"- as some others in the profession cruelly refer to him – carves out his meager 15 minutes of fame amidst an already overcrowded sea of seductive heartthrobs. When the song, sung by the young Robert Farel, makes a comeback in 1987, it crawls its way up into the top 50...

> *When I've got the time*
> *I need to unwind*
> *With a little cooze*
> *She's with me all night*
> *Not for her to choose*
> *Come my little cooze*
>
> *This life suits me fine*
> *What is there to lose*
> *With a little cooze*
> *It's a simple thing*
> *Never have the blues*
> *With my little cooze*

In a typical display of showbiz compromise, Serge writes for Claude François, who is also offered the male lead in *Anna*, a role which later goes to Eddy Mitchell. He offers him "Hip Hip Hip Hurrah," which Clo-Clo (Claude Français) sings on an EP released in June, 1967:

> `Politics
> Is my biz
> The trade of women scorned
> I love them and leave them
> Be forewarned
> There's one love in my heart
> But if one day we had to part
> I would say
> Hip Hip Hip Hurray
> Hip Hip Hip Hurray

GAINSBOURG: *"Those words in his mouth, it was a nightmare. But the lyrics weren't bad. I almost used it on my next 45, instead of "Chatterton," but lucky for me, Clo-Clo put it on the B-side of "Mais quand le matin," a huge hit. I'd hitched myself up to a speeding locomotive. Another jackpot!"*

CLAUDE DEJACQUES: *"At that time, he still so resented the humiliation of his earlier failures that he was flattered to have his stuff sung by any asshole. Years later, at his place on Rue de Verneuil, he had displayed all the album covers of his interpreters, even the shittiest! For him it was a trophy case..."*

At this time, he also gives two tunes to his old pal Régine. Just before summer there is "Loulou," with its lovely melody and simple lyrics:

> It's all
> Permitted
> Loulou
> The silks and furs you
> Wear over nylons and old cheap shoes
> Use it
> Your beauty
> Loulou
> We're crazy for you
> For you Loulou

Then comes "Ouvre la bouche, Ferme les yeux," released at year's end:

> To put up with their lies and hear their cries

Just being wise
Is not enough
A cast iron gut is just the thing you need
When your heart bleeds
You must stay tough
Open up, swallow down
Close your eyes, you'll lose your frown

On April 1, Serge makes another television appearance, this time in Abel Gance's series *Présence du passée*, which recounts the events of the summer of 1792. Serge accepts a non-speaking role as the Marquis de Sade. Meanwhile, Jane Birkin's first daughter, Kate Barry, is born in London on April 8, and Serge will soon be raising her as if she were his own. At the same time, John Barry walks away with two Oscars (best music and best song for *Born Free*). One of the English headlines reads: "John Barry: Two Oscars and a Baby Girl!" At his side is Jane, who is at the heart of the scandal caused by Antonioni's *Blow-up* (which hits French screens in May), especially with regards to the scene where she dyes her hair blonde for the little nude wrestling match with her girlfriend, Gillian Hills, and David Hemmings, a big-name photographer who's trying to solve a possible murder in swinging London. Jane, much too busy to play mama, is unconcerned about the wave of disgust unleashed in the conservative press. In fact, it's the first English film to show the pubic region, and the press dubs her Jane "Pubic Hair" or Jane "Blow-up." Now, some time has already passed since Newsweek referred to "John Barry, with his E-type Jaguar and E-type wife"... There's no longer anyone who will touch Jane, and her career is stopped short. When she does the film Wonderwall, she's nothing but an extra. Things turns sour with John Barry, and within months, she asks for a divorce.

In February, Serge is interviewed by René Quinson for *La Dépêche du midi*. He talks about his interpreters, especially Brigitte Bardot, with whom he will experience an extraordinary adventure in the future:

I'd have liked to have written songs for Marilyn Monroe, and I believed it was possible to replace her with Brigitte Bardot. This was my biggest disappointment. The recording was first-rate. Bardot shimmied around voluptuously when she sang, caressing her thighs and overflowing with sensuality. But the image didn't translate onto the disc. B.B. would only be good for the scopitone.[1]

In the same interview, he explains why he thinks he's more advanced than other singer-songwriters:

The French ignore it all - the rhythm, the music, and the words. Our singer-songwriters, the "Rive Gauche" sort, still write in alexandrine, that silly, old, obsolete one-step stuff that they compose on the guitar. The rhythm lacks all originality. The day one of them decides to compose something more complex and play around with the phrases and syllables, my livelihood will be threatened.

On April 16, Serge appears once more with Denise Glaser on Discorama. He sings no new songs – he's expecting to be in London in June to record his next EP – but rather simply answers the always clever questions posed by his hostess, who asks him how a songwriter so famous for being ahead of his time can compose so many commercial songs:

SERGE: *What do you mean by that - that it's a paradox? I adapt. I have more avant-garde goals for myself. Simply put, I can do what I want. A song for Gréco, one for France Gall, and then one for me. Three styles.*

DENISE GLASER: *Then you're like certain master forgers.*

S.G.: *If that's how you want to put it, why not?*

D.G.: *But ones who also have a certain amount of talent themselves. Generally, we can't say that about most master forgers. [...] They copy quite well, but don't do anything original.*

S.G: *And so why do I muck about in that mire? [...]*

D.G.: *Does it bother you?*

S.G.: *It's like finding a bone in my fish. Let's start again. [...]*

D.G.: *I said you were like certain master forgers who can imitate any style. And I said you are like those rare forgers who have an original talent themselves. That's to say that you have a personality that no one else could copy.*

---

[1]The scopitone was the forerunner of the music video, essentially a jukebox that played strips of 16mm film along with the music. (T.N.)

S.G.: *That's what I've heard. But I suppose I wanted to hear it again.*

D.G.: *Why? Is it really so amusing?*

S.G.: *Yeah, it's hilarious. Really, I have never aspired to be myself.*

As far as film is concerned, Serge is taking it easy until shooting starts again in summer and then fall. *Estouffade à la Caraïbe* comes out on March 22, and is more or less ignored. This is followed in May by *Toutes folles de lui*, a rather tawdry story of how a dry-cleaning establishment is transformed into a whorehouse, music coutesy of Serge. But as far as disasters go, the most interesting one is ecological: the Liberian oil tanker *Torrey Canyon*, loaded with 120,000 tons of crude, runs ashore and starts leaking just southeast of England, at Cornouailles, on March 18, 1967. The oil slick spreads down to Brittany and Cotentin, covering over 150 kilometers by April 15. The *Torrey Canyon*, built in 1959 and enlarged and modernized in 1965, is the largest oil tanker on Earth, some 300 meters long.

On May 31, after once again singing "Docteur Jekyll et Monsieur Hyde" on the Sacha Show, Serge and Claude Dejacques jump a ferry and return to London to cut his new super-45. Of course, we should in no way be expecting Serge to turn into an ecological activist. All he has to say about "Torrey Canyon" is the following:

> Constructed
> In Japan, now I'm rusted
> The truth is I'm entrusted
> To Americans
> A factor
> Of naval subcontractors
> My home was in the Wild West
> In Los Angeles

The press is talking more and more about what hot property comic books are becoming. *Spirou* and *Barbarella* are quite popular, but especially so is Astérix, whose misadventures are published weekly in *Pilote*. Serge uses an English choir to record the first version of "Comic Strip," which he will present on the television show *Tilt*, with Mireille Darc as his partner:

> Come my doll inside my comic strip
> Come fill my bubbles, come and take a trip
> Go clip! Crap! Go bang! Go vlop and go

Zip! Shebam! Pow! Blop! Wizz!

Mixing is done at the Philips studios in Soho, and it is handled by Giorgio Gomelsky (who produces, among others, The Yardbirds with Jeff Beck). The band is led by David Whitaker, who at the time is also working with the Rolling Stones, Marianne Faithfull, Claude François, and Sylvie Vartan. The first meeting takes place in Paris, in the offices at Bagatelle publishing, and then Whitaker goes to London to prepare the arrangements according to the composer's specifications.

> DAVID WHITAKER: *"He was real professional and we worked very hard. There wasn't much screwing around. He was quite strict with me, even though I happened to be older than him. He gave of lot of instructions to the musicians and often had spontaneous ideas and would want to change the groove or something else. And he would take meetings during the session... I found that really irritating..."*

With his organ and his horn section grooving like the best Nino Ferrer, he cuts "Chatterton," a tune that is for a long time a forgotten piece of his repertory inasmuch it is ignored in every compilation until the complete version of *De Gainsbourg à Gainsbarre* in 1989. Serge is remembering the terrible fate of an obscure English poet from the 18th century who winds up destitute and poisons himself. Based upon the play by Alfred de Vigny, which is based upon the life of Thomas Chatterton, here is "Chatterton":

> *Chatterton, killed himself*
> *Hannibal, killed himself*
> *Demosthenes, killed himself*
> *Nietzsche, crazy as hell*
> *As for me....*
> *As for me...*
> *It's not going very well*

Shortly after the release of the EP *Mr. Gainsbourg* at the end of June, we read in the magazine *Top* that Serge is "The king of pop music [...] The insane onomatopoeia of 'Comic Strip.' The black humor and puns of 'Chatterton'... 'Hold-Up,' which is like the incidental music in a thriller... A delicious and irresistible cocktail.":

> *I came to steal your heart my dear*
> *It soon will all be clear*

A billion kisses dear
And my lips they hide
Teeth so sharp inside
Which will pierce your hide

France is just barely recovering from the shock brought on by the Six-Day War between Israel and Egypt. Panicked crowds swamp stores and buy emergency supplies, sure that things will evolve into a third world war. But instead of following suit, Serge uses the time to indulge in an extemporaneous exercise in style, which his father explains in a coded language that leaves us grinning – after all, he is writing to his daughter Liliane in Casablanca.

JOSEPH GINSBURG: *"The prefecture of Britain has asked that Lucien compose a glorious hymn dedicated to the region and its brave sailors. He's been busy at work, and the task should be completed in 24 hours... [The next day:] The recording, which includes Michel Colombier on electric organ, is headed for Rennes where it will be translated into old Breton and sung by a Breton."*

This is the story behind the only military march Serge will ever compose, written at the behest of Israel's cultural attaché in Paris. "Le sable et le soldat" would be broadcast over the airwaves and sung everywhere from Gaza to Tel-Aviv:

Yes I'll defend the sands of Israel
I'll defend the soil and the children of this land
When Goliath comes from the pyramids afar
He'll turn tail and run at the sight of David's star

GAINSBOURG: *"I was asked to sign petitions for Israel and I did. They asked for a song and I wrote one. The tape was sent with the last plane before hostilities ended and they used it over there to lift the morale of the troops. I'm Ashkenazy – I have nothing in common with Sephardic Jews..."* [2]

A few weeks later, the new France Gall EP comes out, but things don't go so well for her. The bubbling little adolescent has become a young woman whom the public will soon grow tired of. "Bébé requin," which imitates the

---

[2] As usual, Serge plays down the question of his background, but this is still an act of engagement, and it is very revealing. To our knowledge, he is the only French Jew to have accepted a commission like this under such dramatic circumstances.

style of Gainsbourg but is actually by Joe Dassin, Frank Thomas, and Jean-Michel Rivat, is one of her last hits before a long dry spell that will last from 1968-1974. The other, "Teenie Weenie Boppie," is classic Gainsbourg:

Teenie Weenie Boppie
She took some LSD
One tab, now what remains
Is one real messed up brain

Look at all these pretty colored flowers
Coming from the Thames as it does flow
They're the remnants of our Mr. Jagger
Drowned there in his smart and stylish clothes

France Gall: "It was when all those groups were talking about acid. I thought it was a prophetic song and all, evoking the image of a drowned Rolling Stone not long before Brian Jones was found dead in a swimming pool."

On July 30, a portrait of Serge is presented on a television series called *Les Quatre Vérités*, itself part of the parent program *Central Variétés*, filmed back in April... This is the reason why Serge performs only "La javanaise" and "Docteur Jekyll" – both lip-synched, which is from now on the rule – and not a thing from the new EP. It's then that he meets André Flédérick, a director with whom he will do an impressive number of shows over the following years. After displaying his photo of Chopin, who looks down in judgment on him from atop the piano ("He looks just about as happy as me"), Serge gets to the meat of things in *Quatre Vérités*:

REPORTER: *Why did you come to live at La Cité des Arts?*

SERGE: *Because I have serious personal problems. Heartbreak. I didn't want to live anywhere too private, like a Parisian apartment. So I found La Cité... I disappeared into the community.... I'm a bit brutish, you know, so the transition wasn't easy.*

He takes us there and provides commentary:

Here's the musicians' floor, so you'll hear Chopin, Stravinsky, Bartok in the hallways... It also reminds me of my childhood because my father used to wake me up with Chopin. He'd do his scales and play those Chopin etudes that I recognize each day here. It's like having a 25 or 30-year flash-back now.

There's a certain gap between me and the others because I make a lot of money doing things that aren't so serious, while they struggle to do quite serious things. It makes me feel like a bit of an exile, which isn't really true. I'm the one who has adopted an aggressive attitude because I feel guilty. They claim I'm stuck-up, but it's not true. I'm just uncomfortable in my own skin.

I can't explain my lifestyle. I smoke a lot, which leaves me feeling really spaced out. People say I'm a doper, which is absolutely false... I know that it's trendy [...] People do that to get spaced out, but I'm that way naturally. I'm always a bit absent minded, but dreaming is my only form of drug use.

The painter Noël Pasquier is in the studio just above Serge's, on the sixth floor. Sometimes he comes down to watch Serge's little Japanese TV or listen to recordings of James Brown, Ornette Coleman, or Stravinsky. Pasquier remembers Serge spending a lot of time in the hallway at La Cité, where there is a phone booth.

NOËL PASQUIER: *"He was always in a suit, always the dandy. I can see him in that cramped phone booth, copying down numbers. He was hidden away most of the time. I never remember him giving a concert during his entire stay here. He would let down his guard when we were among friends. I'd say he was more pessimistic that anguished. He'd always say, "It's not important" – that was his favorite expression. His success with women was surely a kind of revenge, and he was a fine connoisseur who went through quite a number. His painting, at least what I saw of it, didn't seem highly personal. I could see that he hadn't found his style. He loved painting, but it was a harsh mistress to him. He really wasn't a failed painter, he just threw in the towel. At La Cité, where people entertained a lot, he hung around almost nobody but painters. That was his masochistic side..."*

From July to August of 1967, Serge has his last vacation together with Béatrice and Natacha, alias Totote, at Belle-Ile-en-Mer. In September, Serge starts acting in a new film, *Ce sacré grand-père*, near Aix-en-Provence. His old pal Poitrenaud is directing and Michel Simon has the lead role.

During the filming, Serge is visited by both his parents and Béatrice. He returns to Paris just when they release *Si j'étais un espion*, the new Bertrand Blier film for which he do the soundtrack. This is when his ex-wife tells him that she's having a second child: Vania, alias Paul, is born in the spring of 1968. Meanwhile, Gabin asks Serge to appear in La Pacha, which begins shooting in November. It's a good little detective story by Georges Launter in which cadavers abound and where Michel Audriard, at the top of his game, gets to speak two of his most famous lines of dialogue: "When they start sending idiots into space, you'll be the next astronaut," and, "You don't pack a sausage when you're going to Frankfurt."... Before filming, Serge, along with Michel Colombier, must first record the music for the soundtrack at Studio de la Gaîté. The session also includes the two sides of his new 45, with the first version of "Requiem pour un con":

> *Listen to the organs*
> *Blasting just for you*
> *It's frightening just what they can do*
> *Really hope you like it*
> *Me I think it's slick*
> *It's a requiem for a dick*

GEORGES LAUNTER: *"It was amazing that he agreed to do the music and actually act in the film. Even more amazing is that Alain Poiré of Gaumont, who has a very bourgeois background, agreed to use "Requiem pour un con" on the credit sequence. He was even enthusiastic about it, which was really unusual because it was way out there for that company!"*

At the same time, he does the original soundtrack for Jacques Rouffio's *L'Horizon*, a film based on a novel by Georges Conchon which is released in Paris on November 29. On the 45 that is issued simultaneously, we hear the instrumental called "Elisa," the name of the character played by Macha Méril. It turned out so well that Serge didn't want to waste any time putting lyrics to it, first for himself, then for his friend Zizi Jeanmaire.

MICHEL COLOMBIER: *""Elisa" is an excellent example of how we work together. We were very demanding with one another, and at each session we felt like we had to just blow away the other. Serge would bring in eight measures, and I would find it just great, but he'd say, "I don't know what to do next." So I'd try to come up with something and then I'd contribute the next eight. After that, we worked on the idea of using four percussionists and four pianos: an upright, a baby grand, a honky-tonk piano, and one that was out-of-tune."*

In the fall of 1967, the charts are full of "peace and love." Scott McKenzie sings "San Francisco." The Beatles do "All You Need Is Love," and Procol Harum puts out "Whiter Shade of Pale." Michel Fugain scores with "Je n'aurai pas le temps" and then on October 5, Jimi Hendrix releases *Are You Experienced?* Finally, in the October issue of *Rock & Folk*, an anonymous but clairvoyant piece denounces all this "lazy hippie" stuff, and asks:

When will a colossal article be written about the greatest of the French pop singers, the most anarchic and subversive of musicians (true despite of and because of his money and success), this genius of well-tempered cynicism who calls himself Serge Gainsbourg? Something that also gives us a close-up of his "nuclear option" France Gall, who has had the courage to lend herself to the audacities and obsessions of her perverse Pygmalion...

The writer's wish will soon be granted: two editions later, *Rock & Folk* dedicates three pages to Serge, who confides to reporter Philippe Constantin how much he is impressed by Roger Coggio's staging of Gogol's *Diary of a Madman*, which he sees at the Théâtre Edouard VII.

ROGER COGGIO: *"Serge came backstage and there were 20 or 30 people who were praising me with the types of platitudes that actors often hear when they leave the stage every night. At the perimeter of the bustling crowd there was this guy standing completely motionless, just silently staring at me. I didn't recognize him, and I was at first struck by his attitude, not because he was famous. I went into my dressing room to take off my make-up and change my clothes, and when I came back out he was still there, all pallid. He was stammering when he approached me and there was an uncomfortable moment. I'm also very shy... Then he started to talk to me, and not about my acting but rather the text of play. I could see he was very impressed by the piece, that it had really gotten to him. One of the first things he said to me was "I'm Russian, my name is Ginsburg." Then he spoke of the genius of Gogol, whom he had read and knew like the back of his hand... He talked to me about the manuscript of Dead Souls, which Gogol was unhappy with and which he ended up burning... Only a Russophile could know about such obscure details! I felt that when he*

spoke about Gogol it was sort of an act of transference for him. Gogol was
never heralded in his time. The star in 1830 was Pushkin, definitely not
Gogol, who was looked upon as a failed madman - a view that Pushkin
shared. What had captivated Serge in the play was not the madness, but
the solitude of the character I played. He pointed out bits of dialogue and
phrases, talked to me about the "cancer of solitude," and how that man,
who was like every other, goes about forging a life because of the fact that
he is humiliated and offended - of how forging one's own character is the
only way to overcome the suffering, that one must become king, number
one, the who is bowed down to. I went to my car, and just before leaving
he said something astonishing about the end of the play, where the char-
acter calls out for his mother and winds up in the fetal position: "When a
character gets back to his origins is when he becomes almost normal." And
that's true. For five minutes, the character speaks to his mother and says:
"Take pity on your sick child, etc..." Later, I was often reminded of this
when I would hear Gainsbourg in interviews, talking about his parents
with infinite tenderness."

Not wanting to go into any hardcore psychoanalysis, we still must admit
that this testimony is very informative. Plunging into *Diary of a Madman*, we
learn of a diabolically nasty little bureaucrat driven to madness over a love
affair turned sour. We follow him as he comes to believe he is the King of
Spain, scampering around and treating the doctors and nurses as courtesans
as servants... "You think I'm a mythomaniac, presumptuous even?" Serge
says in 1967, "No, I am aware of and able to criticize myself. These last few
years I've written very few good songs. I'm successful, but not as an actor,
singer, or writer. I am only successful as a character. Anyone who sees me
once never forgets me. It's funny. I'm so ugly. And my praise is owed to this
hideous mug I so detest."

I am only successful as a character... A character that he controls and
for whom he writes the dialogue, naturally, but who is not really him! This
stunning lucidity will twenty years later lead him to say the following on
Radio-France:

I wear a mask as a defense mechanism. I believe that I've put on a mask
and that I've been wearing it for 20 years. I can't take it off – it's stuck to
my skin. On the outside, there's the masquerade of life, and then behind

that is the ghost, me.

On Saturday, October 1, Serge finds himself part of a regular column in *France Soir* called "It could only happen to him." Apparently, he'd been at some outrageous, Dadaist happening that started early in the evening between Pont Louis-Philippe and Pont Marie. Later, sitting at the terrace of a small café, a truck driver calls out to him...

GAINSBOURG: *""Mr. Gainsbourg," he says to me, "If you want to see something funny then come with me. I'm going to drive my truck into the Seine!" I half-heartedly try to dissuade him but to no avail. A cop passes by, but I say nothing. I want to see those 10 tons plop into the water. And was it ever a sight. After that I took the guy to the bistro to buy him a drink and wait for the cops."*

Serge owes an album to Philips, which since *Gainsbourg Percussions* has only released two of his EPs and some film music. All the singers are after Serge to write for them and his love life is once again a wreck. Sophie Makhno, who had organized the Gainsbourg/Barbara tour, serves as our witness:

SOPHIE MAKHNO: *"It was during Nana Mouskouri's premier at Olympia, on October 26, 1967. Serge Lama was the opening act. The Gainsbourgs had been invited by Louis Hazan and his wife, who adored Serge. They were all seated up front, and Béatrice starts to confide in Hazan, telling him: "Serge is crazy. Look, he bit me!" She starts to pull back her dress. Hazan tries to calm her down before she makes a scene right there during the show. Then she suddenly starts crying during Nana's performance. Again, Hazan tries to calm her down. Gainsbourg had split, and he never came back home. He left without a penny in his pocket and went to the Hôtel Georges-V. He later told me: "I just had the most woeful night of my life. I had a notebook filled with the names of different girls. Each time I called, I got the blow off. I just sat there all alone in my gloom."*

This time there's no going back – the rupture is permanent. He goes to great pains, as always, to point out how he remains classy and takes the high road:

GAINSBOURG: *"I was very noble about it all. I purchased an apartment for my daughter on Rue Arbalète, in the Latin Quarter, which her mother also had access to. I also bought Béatrice a very chic car, a 404 coupe..."*

La Cité now makes it clear that it's time Serge find other accommodations. Most artists are allowed to stay only a year and he has been there since December 1965. He works out a loan with his record company, which is approved by Hazan, and asks his father to start looking around. Work is simply nonstop. He hunkers down for a few days to compose tunes for the television program *Show Bardot*, scheduled to air on January 1, 1968.

Brigitte is still married to Gunther Sachs, but he's getting on her nerves. He dreams of making a movie with her and recruits Gérard Brach to write the script. But Bardot hates the project. To avoid doing it, she signs on for *Shalako*, which is supposed to start shooting in Andalusia come January, with Sean Connery. In May, 1967, Gunther forces her to present his film Batouk at Cannes. It is a documentary he had produced about the animals of Kenya. Rumors of divorce are rampant... On July 13, their first wedding anniversary ends in a huge fight. During the summer, Brigitte shoots a short piece with Alain Delon, part of the film *Histoires extraordinaires*, based on the book by Edgar Allan Poe and directed by Louis Malle, and it is then that she cheats on her husband with one of the assistants, a story she tells in her autobiography.

Another one of her lovers from this time, who wishes to remain anonymous, recounts the following: "Gunther Sachs was a despicable character, a total bore, with no moral standards or any warmth - a reactionary teuton, odiously arrogant and nasty, who would indulge himself by screaming at gas station attendants or waiters when he wasn't served promptly enough. Take away his money and he was nothing. For him, marrying Bardot was a question of social status. He really put one over on her."

Now it's impossible to understand what will follow – namely the mad passion that will unite Bardot and Gainsbourg for no more than a few weeks but which will have serious repercussions for the both of them – without taking into consideration the reckless Don Juanism of this woman, who at the age of 33 is at the height of her beauty. Our anonymous contributor continues: "She dealt with her conquests like a praying mantis: Serge, like me and like all the others, was zombified by Bardot. That woman had a supreme talent for grinding men into rubble. Serge was a totally atypical lover for her. He had the authenticity of a real artist, he hated money, and he led his life with a sort of heedless existentialist ethic. He was the exact opposite of the clean-cut types she had been with. I am convinced that Serge fascinated her much more than her other lovers. He brought her into a world of intelligence and talent, which no one had ever exposed her to before. Little did it matter that he had a face like a gargoyle from Nôtre-Dame. What's more, he brought a whole new world to her, served up on a silver platter, which is just what she needed at the time. Thanks to Serge she was hip again."

It all begins on October 6, 1967, with an innocent little breakfast to discuss the Sacha Show and the special broadcast of January 1. She tells Serge about certain scenes already filmed back at the end of summer – "La Madrague" at her place in Saint-Tropez, and then "Le soleil" on the beach at Pampelonne. The scene with flamenco guitarist Manitas de Plata is finished by director François Reichenbach on the night of Bardot's birthday, during a party on September 28. Gunther is absent and makes due with sending a telegram... Then in London, she films *Le diable est anglais*, a stupid little piece by Bourgeois and Rivière in which she wears a charming little uniform that brings to mind those worn by the Beatles on the cover of *Sgt. Pepper's*. In the television studios in Boulogne, the remaining sequences are given to another director, Eddy Matalon. Things go poorly and the star is perturbed. She is annoyed by the incompetence of the people around her and complains about having to fend for herself, without costume or makeup people:

> I was just about to chuck it all in when I got a call from Serge Gainsbourg. He said very little and spoke very softly. He wanted to meet with me alone and have me listen to two songs he had written for me. Did I have a piano? Yes.
>
> He came to my place at Paul-Doumer.
>
> I felt just as intimidated as he did.[3]

Serge plays "Harley Davidson" for her on the piano. Brigitte has no particular interest in motorcycles and expresses doubt. Serge responds with a "bitter and sad smile" that this doesn't mean she can't do it in her own style.

> I didn't dare sing in front of him. There was something in the way he looked at me that made me freeze up. A sort of timid insolence, like he was waiting, with a hint of superior humility. He was full of strange contradic-

---

[3] All of Bardot's remembrances are culled from her autobiography. Initiales B.B., Editions Grasset, 1996.

tions, a scornful glare in an otherwise sad face, a cold humor betrayed by
a warmth in his eyes.

Shy, she tries to sing, but without much conviction. So Serge then asks if
she has any champagne. They pop open a bottle of Moët et Chandon just to
break the ice. Rehearsals start the next day and continue until they record
"Harley Davidson" and "Contact" in October, 1967, at studio Hoche with
Michel Colombier at the helm and an assistant engineer named William
Flageollet. The result is a 45 that is released on December 10. The night of the
recording, Brigitte, as she recounts in her autobiography, invites Gloria, her
"Chilean Amazon," who is accompanied by husband Gérard Klein. After the
session, the four go out to eat together, and Brigitte furtively grasps Serge's
hand under the table.

I had a visceral need to be loved, desired, to belong body and soul to a man
I loved, admired and respected.

The moment my hand touched his was a shock for the both of us, an inter-
minable and endless melding, an uncontrollable and uninterrupted elec-
trocution, a desire to crumble and melt, a magical and rare alchemy [...]
His eyes met mine and his gaze never left me. We were all alone in the
world! Alone in the world! Alone in the world!

Gloria and her husband discreetly retire and leave the new lovers alone.

From that very minute, which lasted centuries and still lasts today, I never
left Serge, and he never left me.

This little champagne-fueled diner in a Montmartre restaurant marks
the beginning of a torrid love affair that is chronicled in astonishing and meticulous fashion by Joseph as he writes his letters to Liliane. On October 30,
he gets it straight from his son's lips that Brigitte is in love with him.

JOSEPH GINSBURG: *"Serge worked his charm while they were rehearsing*
a song for Show Bardot. It's no secret in the showbiz world. Thus are the
ravages (or blessings, depending on one's point of view) of Slavic charm.
He told us: "I've lost all my hang-ups about being ugly. Women look at me
differently.""

WILLIAM FLAGEOLLET: *"Bardot was the ultimate star. When she en-*
tered a room everybody was under her spell. Even though she wasn't a

real singer, we recorded quickly, and she had no problem getting it right, which was not the case with Dalida or Mireille Mathieu, whose sessions were endless. I remember that for us, the technicians, when we worked with Bardot, well, it was a bath every day, our Sunday best, and our finest suits and ties. If the session started at eight, we didn't come five minutes early, like usual, but rather a half-hour early. That first night we looked around at each other and broke out in laughter."

EDDY MATALON: *"We had imagined a song set in a stylized garage, with a big Harley. It all seems so tame today! I am surprised at how legendary it became. My only explanation is this: from 1967-68, the whole poster thing really took off, and the image showing Bardot straddling her bike was one of the first to be reproduced like that..."*

The chains, the red and white oil drums, and a superb chrome machine... And Bardot, black leather miniskirt, shiny, high-heeled boots that climb up to her thighs, the dark eyes, that blonde mane of hair: one can't help but visualize this amazing and fantastical image when you hear her sing...:

I don't need a thing at all
When my Harley calls
Nothing means a thing at all
When my Harley calls
Hot leather on my jeans
I feel the vibration of my machine
Gun the motor one more time
The pleasure's so divine

GAINSBOURG: *"I worked according to the desiderata of the directors and Brigitte, For example, when I learned we could shoot at an exposition of kinetic art and that Brigitte would be dressed by Paco Rabanne, I wrote "Contact," a futurist piece..."*

Help me out of my flight suit, if you please
It's covered all over with space debris
Contact!
Contact!

On November 1, 1967, Serge sings "Comic Strip" with Brigitte on the *Sacha Show*. He is also an extra in the background while Distel and Bardot –

who were lovers in 1958, don't forget – wearing flowery shirts and necklaces, perform "La bise aix hippies," an amusingly silly little sketch.

SACHA DISTEL: *"I spoke with Serge, so I knew that Bardot was the dream of a lifetime for him. During the taping of that episode of the 'Sacha Show,' I could see onstage that there was clearly something between them."*

Serge and B.B. go out all the time. One night he takes her to Raspoutine, on Rue Bassano. Emotion is running high: the gypsy band plays romantic serenades and accompanies the couple all the way to his green convertible, an English Morgan, which "smelled of leather and rosewood [...] my toy, my passion, my whim," as Bardot reports. They drive to her place at 71, Avenue Paul-Doumer:

I was really dolled-up for him.

We didn't try to hide it. On the contrary, we flaunted our passion. Régine knew about it. We spent a few nights dancing at her cabaret, holding each other close. [...] We left there, inebriated by our own selves, by champagne, Russian music – we were lost in the same vertigo, drunk on the same harmonies, the same love – we were mad for one another.

RÉGINE: *"They came to eat at my place several times because they needed to avoid being seen in public. I remember having a real good time and Brigitte seemed very relaxed, laughing all the while. She was really in full bloom, and I think she really admired him, and he was quite flattered because he considered himself so ugly. He was astonished that this woman who epitomized beauty was so enamored of him. I had always told him he was beautiful because of his talent, and that women who put importance on looks were idiots..."*

JOSEPH GINSBURG: *"Lucien exulted... "The most beautiful woman in the world wants me at her sides!" And right he was! But then he continued: "But beware the wrath of Gunther Sachs," and "I don't want to walk into a trap." Subtext: "If I fall in love, I'm screwed..." That's just how he was. I was dumbfounded."*

Serge is burning the candle at both ends: he films during the day and composes at night. After *La Pacha*, he appears in *Vivre la nuit* with Marcel Camus, the director of *Black Orpheus*. He plays a small-time reporter with a big heart who looks on helplessly as his friends (Jacques Perrin and Catherine Jourdan) tear each other apart...

It's at this moment that Brigitte is invited by Gunther Sachs to come and celebrate her 33rd birthday at his place on Avenue Foch. "I spoke to Serge, who advised me to go," says Bardot. "After all, I was his wife. But I didn't go. I was really the illicit wife of Serge, and I adore the illicit." She neverthe-less sees Gunther out of a sense of "obligation" and a terrible fight breaks out. He reproaches her violently for her tryst with "that horrible fellow, that clownish Quasimodo" with whom she flaunts herself just to "make him look ridiculous." She comes back at him and says that she's "the most cheated on woman in the world" and that she has every right to take revenge:

Serge was the worried sort, always fretting about losing me. Each time I came back to him he thought it was a miracle. It seemed impossible, in his eyes, that I'd chosen him, and our reunions were as passionate as those that take place after an interminable separation, even if I was gone only for a few hours. He bought me a wedding ring at Cartier which he slipped onto the ring finger of my left hand after I had taken off the red, white, and blue rings Gunther had given me.

I have a very personal divorce ritual.

Serge is totally overwhelmed on the work front. Two studios are reserved for him at Barclay, on Avenue Hoche. In one he records with Bardot; in the other, he works with Mireille Mathieu on the song "Desesperado" – a piece still unreleased, at least by her. It winds up in the hands of Dario Moreno a few months later:

The stars are like explosions in the sky
That just before he dies
A desperado casts
Up to the heavens vast

One might wonder what drives Gainsbourg to accept or reject writing for certain artists. All his choices seem to be made according to esthetic concerns, dominated by willful misappropriation and by an apparently tor-turous refusal to compromise. Among those whose requests he refuses in-clude Johnny Hallyday and Sheila, as well as Stone, Jeanne Moreau, and Sylvie Vartan. But that doesn't stop him from writing for Dalida or Mireille Mathieu. In *Les Lettres françaises* (1969), he attempts to explain it:

I know the limits of my modesty. When Piaf was selling 500,000 records and I was flat broke, I refused to write for her. I refused Montand because I didn't agree with him ideologically. I refused Hallyday, and others who sell tons of records. Compromise is O.K., but my condition is that it be a bit tongue in cheek. I don't want to just fall into the mainstream.

In all truth, with the exception of certain cases where he isn't in the position to refuse (pressure from his recording company, a service owed a publisher, etc.), it's impossible not to notice a certain spite that seems to whisper: "If they're stupid enough to ask me for songs, then they're going to get what they pay for." The exception seems to be Dominique Walter, whom he sees again in 1967. For one thing, Serge is fascinated by this lad with a destiny completely the opposite of his (born in opulence, handsome mug, never experienced misery or emotional problems, neither with women nor with his career as a singer, which he practices as a dilettante). There's also a moral debt with respect to his mother, Michèle Arnaud, his first interpreter, who is more powerful than ever at television stations (she's very close to the Prime Minister, Georges Pompidou) and has always been faithful to a fault. Yet we can't help detect a sort of perversity on the part of Serge. The songs he gives to Walter are unusually aggressive, which is the exact opposite of Dominique's image of a charming songster. After "Les petits boudins," he has Walter sing "Johnsyne and Kossigone," a spoonerism on the names of the heads of states of the U.S. and Russia, Johnson and Kosygin.

> *Johnsynne and Kossigone*
> *Two cuties both well-known*
> *But not a thing to say*
> *A bachelor I will stay*
> *Kossigone I don't care*
> *And Johnson's just hot air*

The producers of *Manon 70*, a film starring Catherine Deneuve and Sami Frey, had commissioned music from Serge, but he's simply beat and wants to be left alone. All this work is coming at a bad time...

MICHEL COLOMBIER: *"It was at the apex of his romance with Bardot. We were supposed to meet at my place at nine o'clock Monday morning. We had very little time to write the different themes. I wait, but he doesn't show. He ends up calling me at noon to tell me: "Listen, I'm going to be a little late..." He's still not there at five, so I call and tell him I'm going to proceed without him seeing as how we had to be in the studio in just three days. I think he finally showed up the night before the recording session. He told me that he couldn't pull himself away from Brigitte and gave me this great line: "Every time I put my shirt back on she rips it right off.""*

Serge really loves "Manon," and goes so far as to include it in his concert at the Zenith in 1988. Jane will also do a lovely version at the Casino de Paris in May, 1991:

> *Manon, Manon*
> *I'm sure you don't have a clue Manon*
> *How much I despise*
> *All that you are*

One evening, Serge and Brigitte head out to the King Club, where they are spotted by Jacques Chancel, at that time the gossip columnist for *Paris-Jour*, who's dining with Françoise Sagan. The next day he writes that Serge and Bardot "spend all their evenings together." On Wednesday, November 22, Serge calls him to complain. Chancel discourteously and hastily tries to explain his intentions:

SERGE: *You've embarked on a campaign that's a real pain for me. Now I'm going to have all the weekly rags hounding me...*

CHANCEL: *You should be flattered....*

SERGE: *Don't you understand that I'm the anonymous type? I live on the fringe, and now all of the sudden I'm portrayed as some kind of playboy. I'm no Casanova [...] I've found this great love, which is nobody's business, but it's not like I'm her future husband. B.B. is happy. B.B. is working. B.B. is having a grand time. We're happy together and there's no law against friendly relationships.*

Back to the *Bardot Show*: amidst a décor of floating balloons painted with psychedelic letters representing phylacteries, Tito Topin directs B.B. as she rips through a backdrop and insolently moves forward, covered from head to toe in a white one-piece jump suit, a little comic-strip style superhero cape hanging from her shoulders, and - one more spicy detail – a black wig making her look like the photographic negative of Barbarella. It's "Comic Strip" of course. The producers find out that the Americans are buying the program and they record two versions, so we have Bardot going "zip-shebam-blop-whiz" in both French and English...:

It's Serge's talent that made the show a success.

He's was in charge of all the visuals. Among other things, he chose my wardrobe, the things that suited me best, or sometimes he'd just have me half-naked. He directed me and advised me. At the recording session for the song, "Oh! Qu'il est Vilain," which out of jealousy was written by Jean-Max Rivière against the wishes of Serge, he still handled the difficulty of the situation and adeptly directed the recording session, even though the song was a flop.

For the final apotheosis, after the sketch created around the song "Bubble Gum," we have the superb imagery of "Bonnie And Clyde." The fugitive gangster couple, brought to life on film by Warren Beatty and Faye Dunaway, will become popular in France only a couple of months later. On November 10, 1967, Serge, in the style of Jack Warner, had screened the film and took the time to pay close attention to Dunaway's monologue:

> *You've heard the story of Jesse James*
> *And how he lived and died*
> *If you're still in need*
> *Of something to read*
> *Here's the story of Bonnie and Clyde*

GAINSBOURG: *"I have dinner with Bardot and I intentionally get plastered. She calls the next day and asks why I did that. I'm all silent, as if to imply: "I was overwhelmed by your beauty." So she tells me: "Write me the most beautiful love song you can imagine."*

That night he writes "Bonnie And Clyde" and "Je t'aime moi non plus"..."

> *The story goes Clyde had a doll so pretty*
> *A lovely little thing whose name was Bonnie*
> *The two of them create the gang of Barrow*
> *Their names - Bonnie Parker and Clyde Barrow*

Imagine an abandoned warehouse, Bardot in a long skirt whose slits give way to garters, short wig, beret covering her ear, eyes as dark as ever, finger on the trigger of her machine gun. And Gainsbourg, alias "Ladykiller" – her name for him – shirtsleeves rolled up, tie a mess, ready to draw his Colt from the holster:

> SERGE: *One of them is going to find us sometime*
> *To hell with it for Bonnie's love is all mine*
> BARDOT: *What do I care if those bastards snuff me*
> *I would die for Clyde and in a heartbeat*

Serge and B.B. are also being hunted. The paparazzi are hounding them. They're camped out in front of her place on Avenue Paul-Doumer and also in front of La Cité des Arts, as the establishment's director tells us:

SIMONE BRUNO: *"It caused a lot of gossip because it was really out of the ordinary as far our daily routine at La Cité was concerned. One day I ran into Brigitte Bardot in the hall. She had come with an exquisite dog, and in fact I had noticed nothing but the dog and my secretaries broke out laughing when I told them we were being visited by an Afghan with beautiful long hair. They asked me: "Didn't you notice who was holding the leash?" I hadn't looked at the owner! That being said, we had a night watchman who was feeding details about Serge's visitors to 'France-Dimanche.' The poor guy got the boot – he had violated the discretion of the establishment."*

In Catherine Rihoit's biography of Bardot, published in the eighties, Serge recalls their paranoia.

Serge: "People had a kind of hatred for her. I saw her accosted in the streets: "You're disgusting!" What did that poor girl ever do? She never hurt anybody. She lived her life, she chose her men... When we would walk around together on the streets, she had a sort of sixth sense – she could sniff out photographers. She could smell them, literally. She'd say: "I know there's one around." I never saw anything, but she was always right, like an animal that could smell its hunter..."

In the meantime, the producers of *Shalako* send Brigitte the script for the film, which starts shooting in the coming weeks. Madame Olga, her agent, doesn't look kindly upon her relationship with Gainsbourg and struggles to make Brigitte face the facts and accept her duties. Isn't she the one who wanted to shoot this western in order to distance herself from the cinematic ambitions of hubby Gunther? But she doesn't read the script and she pokes fun at the American producers rounded up by "Mama Olga" who try and convince her of how lucky she is to be able to work with Sean Connery and a director as famous as Edward Dmytryk.

As the days pass, Brigitte comes to the brutal realization that her marriage to Gunther Sachs, with whom she is temporarily out of touch, is nothing but a "sham," a "show-business spectacle":

Serge spent the nights composing marvels on my old Pleyel Piano. One morning, he played me his gift of love: "Je t'aime moi non plus."[4]

CLAUDE DEJACQUES: *"The recording of "Je t'aime moi non plus" took place at Barclay studios. The arrangement was by Michel Colombier, and the only people there were Denis Bourgeois, the sound engineer, Serge, Brigitte, and me. It took two hours tops. There was an extraordinary atmosphere of love that permeated the studio. They were truly in love – it wasn't just some stupid flirtation, but real love."*

> Brigitte: I love you, I love you
> Oh God I love you
> Serge: Not me
> Brigitte: Oh my love
> Serge: Like a wave not yet breaking
> I come, I come and I glide
> Thrusting inside

WILLIAM FLAGEOLLET: *"On the first session the voices didn't record well. We had changed reels, the musicians were playing their asses off, everything was in place but nothing was happening. There was no emotion – neither from Serge nor from Brigitte. So the next day we took up where we'd left off and the recording got underway with, let's say... emphatic body language. In short, Bardot had loosened Serge up. The two of them were standing very close together and not a single movement was censored by modesty... a very hot session. They were very cuddly and we just dimmed the lights..."*

When we recorded "Je t'aime moi non plus" it was late at night, at the Barclay studios. We each had a mic. We were maybe three feet away, holding hands. I was a little ashamed about imitating the lovemaking between Serge and me, sighing with desire like I was coming, all in front of the engineers. But after all, I was simply interpreting a situation, as if it were a film I was shooting. Then Serge comforted me with a wink, a smile, a kiss.

---

[4] When he wrote the words, Serge wasn't thinking of Dali's quote, but he loved the following quip: "Picasso is Spanish, me too. Picasso is a genius, me too. Picasso is a communist, not me." He even claimed to have been inspired by it.

It was great, beautiful, pure. It was us.

In his book *Piégée, la chanson...?*, Claude Dejacques lets his lyricism run free and describes this historic session:

It's about 10 o'clock and I'm waiting to put down the vocal tracks. No reporters or photographers. They bolt out of a black taxi, crazy in love, just like in the song, and make their way down the hallway to the studio. Things are going swimmingly and as soon as they hear the playback music that they're to sing over they plunge into the heart of the fantasy that is devouring them, clothed only in the music and lyrics, drunk with each other and so honest that the take becomes much more than a simple duo by singers in front of a microphone: they are leaving their mark for eternity. First thing the next day I'm in the mixing booth. This time, I can see that Brigitte is really holding her own and I know that this is going to be something big. We make promotional copies (which were later saved), but towards 10 o'clock we get hit with a cease and desist order. Brigitte's lawyer had blocked the release.

This probably doesn't all happen as quickly as Dejacques recounts. At least a weekend goes by between the recording session and this drama, enough time for *France-Dimanche* to publish a petty little piece by François Marin that appears on December 12, and which describes the song as "4 minutes and 35 seconds of amorous panting" before going on to tell how the session had been recorded behind closed doors:

Even Gunther Sachs, Brigitte's husband, was not permitted to enter the studio. I called him to get his side. His maid told me: "Mr. Sachs has left on a trip. I don't know where he is or when he will return."

Gunther is, in fact, in Switzerland. Once advised, he hops on the first plane to take charge of the matter.

CLAUDE DEJACQUES: *"Gunther just blew his top. He demanded that she choose between him and Serge. It's at that moment she decided to send the telegram blocking the release of "Je t'aime moi non plus."*

The indiscretion immediately causes Bardot to panic, as she points out in *Initiales B.B.*:

Madame Olga had warned me that if the record came out, Gunther would leave me and the result would be an international scandal which would forever tarnish my image. This whole thing had left Olga beside herself,

*and she scolded me vehemently for my bad behavior, my lack of discre-
tion and morality, my dissolute and undisciplined life! In short, she gave
me a working over that no amount of tears could abate! I had gotten what
I deserved!*

Olga demands that she write to Philips immediately and make them halt
the release of the record:

Gainsbourg, apprised of the situation which was now assuming unheard
of proportions, accepted at the last minute, and with his usual elegance, to
remove "Je t'aime moi non plus" from the album, which was scheduled for
release in just a few days.

That morning, he receives a letter that he would later display among
other souvenirs at Rue de Verneuil. It is perched atop a lectern: on letterhead
that reads Brigitte Sachs Bardot, we can make out the words of the manuscript – "Serge, I implore you to halt the release of 'Je t'aime'..."

"Her husband forgot about the relationship, but he couldn't accept that
song," surmises William Flageollet, the engineer who reminds us that the
record is actually played one time during an afternoon news broadcast on
Europe n°1: "The reporters ignored the interdiction, saying *It's just this
once that you'll hear this censured piece!*" Who gave it to them? Gainsbourg?
Dejacques?

> CLAUDE DEJACQUES: *"The masters had to be seized. I had arranged
> to put them to the side, but the officials who grabbed them only took
> one copy!"*

As all this unfolds, hot on the heels of the *France-Dimanche* story, the
scandal rags realize that they have hit pay dirt with this story, and Bardot
will suffer the consequence for a good 15 years. *Paris-Presse l'Intransigeant*
affirms: "Gainsbourg frightened about his duo with Bardot." The writing is a
classic example of the genre:

> *I have just listened to a most scandalous record. So scabrous that I must
> hesitate each time I put pen to paper in order not to make you red with
> shame when I convey what I have heard. [...]*
>
> *Believe me when I say that the lyrics to this song will in no way quiet the
> rumors we have been hearing about Serge and Brigitte. The song begins,
> quite innocently, with some very pretty organ music that is almost liturgical.*

Then, B.B. sings: "I love you, I love you my love"...

"Not me" answers the composer, straight-faced.

Nothing shocking so far. But wait for the rest [...] B.B. sings:

"You come and you glide, thrusting inside. Oh! My love, you're a wave."

Later, things become almost surreal in this paragraph printed in bold, capital letters:

FROM TIME TO TIME BRIGITTE LETS OUT LITTLE MOANS OF PLEASURE AND SIGHS OF COMFORT. FRANKLY, IT IS LIKE LISTENING TO TWO LOVERS IN THE THROWS OF COPULATION.

On December 20, the very same *Paris-Presse* publishes stolen photos of Bardot and Serge doing their Christmas shopping. In reality, they had been taken before the scandal broke. Bardot, "kidnapped" by Gunther, spends a week in Gstaad. He takes this opportunity to try and seduce her anew. He even suggests that she take an apartment right next to his at 32, Avenue Foch. But he is oblivious to the fact that Bardot and Serge still dream of living together. Upon her return, Serge has Brigitte visit the little house that his father has found on Rue de Verneuil, in Saint-Germain-des-Prés, swearing to her, as Bardot tells it, "that he will build his love the palace from *A Thousand and One Nights.*"

JOSEPH GINSBURG: *"Two weeks earlier I'd called and told him: "If you want to see this nice little house, you better go do it soon. – Give me the address!" The two of them went there and he told me that he liked the house and that he'd go back and see it during the day. When he went back the next day at 11:00, with Brigitte, there were interested parties on site, but as soon as the agent saw the two of them arrive he exclaimed: "It's sold! It's sold!" The second visit sealed the deal and Lucien concluded the business. The house - street-level and second story – is at 5 bis, Rue de Verneuil, the same street where Gréco lives."*

On December 24, Serge is interviewed by phone on France-Inter. The reporter mentions how single was shelved at the last minute and asks Serge for an explanation...:

S.G.: *There was a scandalous article printed in some rag and there is no reason to make a scandal out of this song because it's too beautiful. It's an erotic piece that would have been restricted to those under the age of 18. But the music is very pure... For the first time in my life I write a love song, and what happens? They take it the wrong way...Bardot interpreted the text wonderfully. I'm delighted to have worked with her. I had her sing in a real dramatic style and it's a good song.*

Reporter: *Are you having a nice Christmas?*

S.G.: *Yeah, alone...*

The January 1 television show is an "immense success" as Brigitte puts it:

I watched it at Avenue Foch, where Gunther had invited some friends over. Everyone raved – I was beautiful, I sang well, even Gunther was proud. It was only when Serge came onscreen that things turned sour. Everyone criticized him, said how ugly he was!

How horrible!

I had tears in my eyes! [...]

Where was he?

He must be sulking somewhere, depressed, in his little dorm room all alone with nothing but his piano for company.

The next day she has to take off to Almería to make *Shalako*. Gunther, feeling stung, decides to go with her. She no longer wants to do the film and calls her agent in a fit of tears to say that she doesn't want to leave. Madame Olga flies into a rage and tells her that she's reckless:

I saw Serge again at Paul-Doumer while I was packing. Madame Renée, my housekeeper, in strictest confidence, had orders not to open the door for anyone. Serge filled my suitcase with little words of love scribbled over sheets of music, every which way. [...]

At the last moment, I pierced the skin of my right index finger and wrote "I love you" with my blood.

He did the same and wrote "not me."

Then we melted into each others' tears, hands, mouths, breath.

When the door closes behind him, the separation is for good, but that's still ignored today. Brigitte offers this analysis in retrospect:

> *It's because this love was shattered that it was so intense. We had escaped the everyday, the grind, the scenes – all that destroys even the wildest passion over the course of time. With Serge I have nothing but sublime memories of beauty, love, humor, folly.*

Over the years Serge often amuses himself and pretends to be some sort of conspirator, playing dumfounded reporters the test pressing of "Je t'aime moi non plus" with Bardot, which remains unreleased until 1986. Of course, the pressing is all scratched up and worn out, but it still exudes the formidable sensuality that the public at large would discover when Bardot finally permitted it to be released, with the profits going to her foundation for the protection of animals.

> CLAUDE DEJACQUES: *"In spite of my immense affection for Brigitte, I was always convinced that she had really blown it by stopping the release of "Je t'aime moi non plus." Her versi on was twice as powerful as Jane's, and the record could have been the peak of her career. At the international level the success would have been enormous..."*

> JANE BIRKIN: *"When I met Serge it wasn't hard to see that Bardot had occupied an important place in his heart. With her voice and her beauty, she seemed to him to be the ideal woman. I met her later on and it is impossible not to be moved by her sensitivity and her total disregard for ambition. Bardot is someone that I personally adored, even though Serge was smitten with her... I would have found it abnormal if he were not!"*

In 1985, when the author of these lines was writing a first book on Serge, Bardot was asked to comment. But it was necessary to wait for the publication of her memoirs for her to finally speak on the subject of this amazing love affair. In 1985, she spoke but a few words:

Gainsbourg is both the best and the worst, the yin and the yang, the white and the black.

The boy who was probably the Russo Jewish little prince, dreaming while he read Andersen, Perrault, and Grimm, has become, in the face of the tragic reality of life, a Quasimodo, touching or repugnant depending on how the spirit moves him. Deep inside this fragile being, both timid and aggressive, there lies the soul of a frustrated poet of tenderness, truth, and integrity.

His talent, his music, his words, and his personality make him one of the greatest composers of our sad and afflicting times.

-Brigitte Bardot

fourteen

Jane B., English, Sex: Female

The *Bonnie and Clyde* album by Serge and Brigitte is released the day after the show's broadcast, on January 2, 1968. In addition to the key pieces performed on the television show ("Harley Davidson" and "Contact" are missing), Dejacques adds six more of Serge's own tunes, from "Baudelaire" to "Docteur Jekyll and Monsieur Hyde," which makes the album Serge's first anthology. Serge expounds upon the recordings in this brief text:

These 12 titles by Brigitte and me are really love songs – combative, passionate, physical, fictional love songs. It is of little importance whether they are amoral or immoral because they are absolutely sincere.

Contrary to the popular belief - which is diligently supported by Serge himself - the break-up does not happen when Brigitte goes off to shoot Shalako in Andalusia, but rather after Gunther Sachs drops Brigitte off in Almería, from where she has long telephone conversations with Serge, who is working with Michel Colombier. They are discussing whether or not Serge should come to Malaga for a brief, amorous tryst. It seems that Brigitte's mother is delighted with their relationship and tells anyone willing to listen that her daughter has found herself again after meeting Serge, as we learn from a letter that Joseph sends to Liliane. The first days of the shoot are a nightmare. Bardot is having a nervous breakdown, and there's no end in sight.

MICHEL COLOMBIER: *"I had the feeling – even though I really didn't know her – that Brigitte was a woman who really loved him. Serge was so different from all the other men in her life... I could see he was completely out of it, and he wanted to go and join her in Spain even though we had work here in Paris. One time he was so desperate that he suggested taking everyone - including me, my wife, and my kids – to go there so he could be near her. We had to work to dissuade him..."*

Jean-Louis Barrault meets with Serge once more to discuss the musical-comedy that they've been talking about since 1962. They come up with a title, *Kidnapping*, but the project is still in limbo. Joseph, however, is still very enthusiastic about the idea...

JOSEPH GINSBURG: *"The director at the l'Odéon had him visit the theatre along with Madeleine Renaud before declaring: "It's going to be for January, 1969. Get to work. You're a poet, and I trust you. You can help me with the direction if you want..." But upon hearing the news, Brigitte exclaimed: "Oh no! I come first!"*

Joseph's letters allow us to bear witness to every last detail concerning the end of this love affair. Serge has just been kicked out of La Cité and is now back in at Avenue Bugeaud, so Joseph is now privy to each morsel of information. Later on, in the same letter, Joseph tells Liliane that "Lucien won't be going to Andalusia: the minuses outweigh the pluses – a pack of reporters is following B.B. everywhere. It would be a glaring scandal." They call each other whenever it's possible, but Brigitte is afraid that her phone is tapped: "They call each other twice a day, so the ties between them are still strong," says Joseph. "He's walking on air because she is coming home for him – poor Lucien is really hooked." The lovers have actually found a solution: Bardot negotiates with her producers for a round-trip ticket to Paris and back, and Serge sends mom and dad to Fontainebleau while he awaits her at Avenue Bugeaud. In a letter dated January 6, Joseph explains the rest:

JOSEPH GINSBURG: *"It's been a while since we've come back from Fontainebleau, but only recently have Lucien's wounds begun to scar over. He says "It's no big deal, tell mom not to fret over me," and he had this*

air of detachment when he called Fontainebleau. But that's all rubbish [...]
The poor boy's lived through the martyrdom of transitory love, waiting in
vain... Alone, alone, alone! Not a single sympathetic shoulder to cry on [...].
He really suffered here in the apartment, just waiting for four days, never
going out. He saw her... at her designer's place..."

So what happened? To understand it, we must cull details from Brigitte's
memoirs. She talks about her time in Almería, where she distracts herself
after the long hours of filming by transforming her room into a nightclub,
spinning trendy records, and inviting all sorts of actors over to spend the
evening with her and her "amazons," which is what she calls the coterie of
friends and secretaries that never leave her side. One day she shows up late
at the set and Edward Dmytryk shoots a nasty look her way. There's a shot
planned with her and Stephen Boyd, the dashing Irish actor whose 15 minutes of fame had come in *The Fall of the Roman Empire*. Sensing Bardot's
distress, he decides to try his luck:

He took me tenderly in his arms and whispered sweet little things [...] He
was very comforting to me and I needed that terribly. I stayed by him
constantly and found in his presence a certain protection. I would hold his
hand and throw my arms around his neck [...] They took photos, of course,
which made page one in all the world's newspapers!

It was like I was cheating on Serge and Gunther at the same time, vicari-
ously.

If we are to believe Brigitte's story, Boyd was never her lover, but rather
her "tender and attentive friend." The photos cause swift reaction: Gunther
once again threatens divorce and Serge, through an intermediary who happens to be a photographer for France-Soir, sends her a "long, sad letter" explaining that he has just composed "Initiales B.B.," a "nostalgic hymn that
will forever glorify her image as an adored goddess."

As a funny coincidence would have it, there's another film being shot
in Almería, *The Magus* with Michael Caine. Andrew Birkin is the assistant
director, and to help comfort his little sister, who has just split with John
Barry, he invites Jane to spend a few days on the set. So off she goes with her
nine-month old baby and a wicker handbag. Bardot runs into her but has no

idea at all that this little English girl will soon be famous the world over for singing "Je t'aime moi non plus," which Brigitte had passed on...

As Serge puts it to his father on January 25, Gunther "has succeeded in re-establishing the relationship." The story has come to an end: "Things are back to normal," he adds, spitefully. Joseph, pragmatic as ever, thinks first and foremost of his son's career, concluding: "That relationship was always a dead end... In any case, she aimed the spotlight on him and there's no sign of it dimming. It was an adventure that was worth having, even considering the initial troubles..."

The day after the break-up, Serge is feeling terrible. He spends his nights with Claude Dejacques, hitting all the bars on l'île Saint-Louis. He can't stop repeating how he wants to throw himself in the Seine.

> CLAUDE DEJACQUES: *"I was at his sides the whole time during that week when Bardot dumped him. Serge wanted to blow his brains out. He was really in love with her, but his pride was also shattered. Going out with her was an enormous boost to his ego because it was like he was triumphing over his own ugliness, which early on had caused him great suffering."*

> GAINSBOURG: *"It's like when you break a string on a guitar, it's very dangerous. It scarred me. It was very fast and very short – no more than three months, and then over for good. She left her mark, no question. Nothing more to add."*

Early in February, 1968, Serge gets back to work. He's worried about his image and starts to be seen with pretty girls. The gossip hounds in the press imagine him in the midst of rebound, still faithful to the sublime star. We see Serge having breakfast with Anna Karina at Lipp, and their arrival causes more of a stir than that of Belmondo and Ursula Andress, at least according to Joseph, who is fretting over his son's welfare...

On February 8, Brigitte's secretary calls to inform Serge that the star is "bitter" about him no longer telephoning her in Spain. In the middle of the night, Serge acquiesces: "You haven't understood what's going on," Brigitte tells him. But he is profoundly hurt and remains irritable: "After those four terrible days I spent waiting for her, I am now healed [...] Anything she might say now goes in one ear and out the other," says Serge to his parents. He distracts himself by going out with a different girl every night, and like a teenager organizes his little black book according to blondes, brunettes, and redheads.

In February, 1968, we also Serge sing "Manon" on the television show *Tilt*. It's the a-side of his new 45, a little record that he sends Bardot (and from the lyrics it is easy to see that it is dedicated to her). At the same time, the March issue of the teenybopper monthly *Mademoiselle Age Tendre* publishes a long interview between Serge and Philippe Charles, along with a photo of Serge on a throne, with Mireille Darc and France Gall as two splendid hippies seated at his feet. In the article, he makes the following declaration: "I'd like to discover a 12 or 13 year old girl – no older – and find a style for her. If necessary, I'll have thousands of auditions. She'll have to be very beautiful, of course. I'd be a kind of Pygmalion to her, create a character in the world of song." And on Mireille Darc: "I imagine Mireille as an acidic mix of impertinence and sensuality, so I have to write words and music that bring this out." In fact, he offers her two new tunes in 1968: "Hélicoptère" and "Le drapeau noir":

> My bed is just a raft on the river fair
> And upon it, on it, float like air
> Float your little undies dear
> A little flag of black letting out its slack

A March 4, 1968 article written by Michel Derain for *Paris-Jour* is entitled: "Serge Gainsbourg is frightened: He's fallen in love!" We see him in the company of "Odile, a photographer," but he declares in the sensationalist piece: "I will never be gentle with women. I hate them. It always ends badly between us." The press is constantly harping about his past conquests and this has cemented his reputation as a seducer, now a central part of Serge's trademark persona and something that makes him the envy of most of the male population. *Marie-Claire* asks: "Why do pretty girls go for ugly men?" Gainsbourg proclaims: "They adore me. I don't even have to lift a finger and my phone never stops ringing. Every day there are more love letters in the mail..." Then again in March, he is interviewed for *Paris-Press*: "I like women as objects, beautiful women, like models. I guess that's the painter in me. I never tell them I love them. It's they who tell me, all the time [...] Equality for women doesn't exist. They're just like rabbits who've had roller skates strapped on their feet. They might be able to pirouette around on them, but they're still rabbits." Like gasoline on a fire, Serge's heartbreak drives his misogyny to new heights. Yet years later, he will be wise enough to see that the ordeal had actually been beneficial to him. When a reporter reminds him of how his look changed radically during that time, Serge responds:

> *There's been no plastic surgery, if that's what you mean. It's obvious that Bardot had a huge influence on my destiny. She gave me confidence when she told me that I'd be making films.*

And in fact, in the less than three years between "Poupée de cire" and the *Bardot Show*, everything changes for him. He goes from being an accursed poet known only by a select elite to being a popular composer. After the *Percussions* album tanked, apart from some film and television music he had released only two original super-45s. The ambitious musical *Anna* had never received its just acclaim, yet another disappointment for the Gainsbourg who might be "credible" in the eyes of intellectuals. Sure, the singers of his songs are scoring hit after hit – his hits – but the frustration of always remaining behind the scenes must be starting to seriously bother him. Then, when everything was starting to click with Bardot and the recording of "Je t'aime moi non plus," it all crumbled.

In a book he's preparing on Gainsbourg in the late sixties, Lucien Rioux talks about how Serge's cynical character is now producing songs that are "too harsh." One of these is "La plus belle femme au monde n'arrive pas à la cheville d'un cul-de-jatte." It's written, at the height of his depression, for Dominique Walter.

> The world's most beautiful doll
> Whether in love or not
> Shallow or on the ball
> Has only what she's got
> Whether she walks on all four legs
> Or hangs upside down
> She is useless as a cripple
> Another silly clown

Not necessary, really, to even point out that the song with its idiotic diction was a total flop. In early 1969, Walter will inherit two more songs for a 45 that is in every way destined for disaster. Side A, "La vie est une belle tartine," is a suicidal hymn explicitly about Bardot:

"Lusitania, Titanic"
The bodies washing up ashore
Although their destinies were tragic
Not one would have me come aboard

Yes, life is such a pretty story

I was sleeping near the tracks
Waiting there for my B.B.
But as I lay there on my back
The train derailed and came for me

The other cut Serge writes for him resonates like a confession - "Plus dur sera la chute" narrates the trials and tribulations of a rock star on stage:

The girls here in this theatre
Screams cracking VU meters
And way down deep inside of him
The violence is like lightning
The cries they become frightening
Reporters' ceaseless din
He dives into empty space
Filled with pride and sublime grace
He knows that he is born to win

On March 14, there's a novel distraction for our convalescent – the release of *Pacha*. As it's out of the question to drag Gabin around to radio stations to do promotion, the job falls to Georges Launter, the director, and also to the composer of the film's soundtrack, which contains the celebrated "Requiem pour un con," released simultaneously as a 45. On April 2, 1968, Gainsbourg celebrates his 40th birthday, which coincides with Tchou publications putting out a limited collection of his lyrics called *Chansons cruelles*. A week later he's back to serious business.

CLAUDE DEJACQUES: *"We left for London to record Initiales B.B., and of course Gainsbourg had prepared nothing but the title cut. But he worked according to an infallible method: he starts every song with the title because he understood long ago that the title should be the key phrase in the refrain and also the theme of the song. We took the train and then the ferry instead of the plane, so that he'd have time to write. We took off from Gare du Nord, where he put away a couple of bourbons, and during the trip he wrote the words to the three other songs and he was ready..."*

YVES LEFEBVRE: *"I had remained in contact with Serge since 'Ce sacré grand-père,' and I can say that I followed each step of the production of Initials 'B.B.,' from when the first words were committed to paper until the recording with Arthur Greenslade in London [...] I knew he was doing a song about Bardot, and he told me: "I think I'll use the theme from Dvorak's 'New World Symphony...'" His musical background permitted him to do things like that. I never sensed that he was burdened, but rather amused and astonished. He paid homage to B.B., all while winking at her from the corner of his eye."*

The words were inspired by Baudelaire's translation of Poe's *The Raven*. Serge starts by remembering a book Bardot had given him, and then he jumps right in:

> *Looking at the stars*
> *Feeling abandoned*
> *In an English bar*
> *In London, stranded*
> *Reading "L'amour monstre"*
> *By Louis Pauwels*
> *A vision in my drink*
> *My mind now travels*

Constructed like a mini-symphony, "Initiales B.B." is a sublime homage in which Serge's voice is detached, like a narrator's, at once sardonic and loving, over a background of trumpets, violins, a piano, and background singers.

> *Sporting leather boots*
> *This wondrous Alice*
> *Her beauty there contained*
> *Within this chalice*
> *She wears not a thing*
> *And smells so fair*
> *With essence de Guerlain*
> *Upon her hair*

For these new London sessions Serge hooks up once more with arranger Arthur Greenslade, already put to the test in 1965 for the "Docteur Jekyll et Monsieur Hyde" EP. Greenslade has been working with Phillips since the time of Johnny Hallyday's "La generation perdue." After collaborating with Serge, he produces three cuts on Françoise Hardy's album *Comment te dire adieu*.

ARTHUR GREENSLADE: *"Serge was very anxious, and this final song of his to Brigitte seemed very important to him. You could feel in the air how meticulous Serge was being."*

CLAUDE DEJACQUES: *"We were really uneasy because we knew we had really hit on something with "Je t'aime moi non plus." Serge mulled it all over and it all got condensed into "Initials B.B." When the tune was released in June, 1968, Brigitte called and asked me to bring her the record. She listens very attentively, quite moved, and tells me: "Phone Serge, would you?" I did so and passed her the phone, then I discreetly left. In fact I never saw Brigitte again..."*

As writer Georges Conchon points out, Serge loves the artifacts of this consumer society and the press from now on will continue to tease him about this. He even has a weakness for words with a "franglais" consonance: Kool cigarettes, Zippo lighters, Brownings, fluid makeup... He mixes it all together and jumps into his buddy Yves Levebvre's Mustang:

We French kiss in
My Ford Mustang
And bang!
Smash into rocks and trees
Mustang here
Mustang there
Parts all here and there

Like the heart of "Bloody Jack," a song he offers to Zizi Jeanmaire, Serge's heart is also cold. Still, he's lighthearted enough to cook up a little nursery rhyme, "Black & White," which brings the super-45 to a close...

Sipping her milk the young negresse did say
Oh how I wish that there just was some way
If I covered my face with this liquid today
I'd be white as the English wouldn't you say?

On April 13, 1968, Béatrice has Paul, Serge's first son. Also, Jacqueline Joubert does a television special devoted entirely to him as part of the *Entrez dans la confidence* series. Serge sings "Ces petits riens," "Comic Strip," and a duo with Anna Karina, "Ne dis rien," taken from the musical *Anna*. There is also a superb interview with the aforementioned Georges Conchon, from which this extract is pulled:

GEORGES CONCHON: *Does your life march in step with - pardon the phrase - your work?*

SERGE GAINSBOURG: *In every way, yes.*

G.C.: Your work is one with your life and your work is nothing but your life and your life is nothing but your work?

S.G.: Could there be anything more?

G.C.: Certainly.

S.G.: And what's that?

G.C.: You have no passions?

S.G.: Abstracts passions. I'd prefer to have animal passions.

G.C.: But, and I'm going to say something stupid here, is intellectual contact at all necessary for you?

S.G.: It's unbearable.

G.C. Unbearable... you mean in general?

S.G. Not only in general, but specifically speaking especially.

Two months earlier, Serge had met Pierre Grimbault, who had had him read the script for *Slogan*, which he wrote with an African-American named Marvin Van Peebles. He was immediately seduced and accepted star billing. Grimbault, a commercial specialist, now wants to get back to his first love, the cinema. Furthermore, in a letter from Joseph we read: "Lucien has found a friend, for once, and it appears that this friend is fellow playboy."

PIERRE GRIMBAULT: *"True, except for the fact that Serge was not a playboy but a polygamist, which is much more serious! At that time – it's rather odd - we looked like each other. I was looking for someone onto whom I could project the autobiographical story of the film. I had known Gainsbourg back when he was the pianist at Toquet, and later I had invited him onto my radio programs when I was a host at France Inter. The story of 'Slogan' is based on a romantic affair that I was just not able to get over. It was François Truffaut who told me: "The best way to get over it and forget the girl is to make a film. You'll be able to transpose everything onto the characters and it will no longer be your story."*

For the part of Evelyne, Grimbault first thinks of Marisa Berenson, one of the worlds most famous models at that time. She is not yet an actress (she would later work with Visconti and Kubrick) but her screen test shows her to be very convincing. Serge is delighted and already imagines inevitably seducing her during the filming, just as he had seduced that girl with whom he spent three days in Brussels at the end of April, like all those one-night stands he had had at the Hilton... After Bardot, Berenson would make a really nice little notch in his belt. But there's a small problem: Grimbault changes his mind and starts to visualize another Evelyne. Saying nothing to Serge, he takes off first for Rome, then Munich, and finally ends up auditioning actresses in London. It's there where he spots a girl wearing an ultra-miniskirt.

PIERRE GRIMBAULT: *"She has these crazy legs that are just unsightly, and I give her a hard time: "Do you really need to show me those things?" She responds: "Not if you'll pay for an operation." Very witty, right of the bat. So I ask if she can come to Paris for some screen tests. I write down her name: Jane Birkin..."*

JANE BIRKIN: *"The first time we met, I had trouble understanding Serge's name. I thought it was Serge Bourguignon. I only knew three words in French, among which were Beef Bourguignon – the source of my confusion, I suppose. Before doing a screen test with him in Paris I had learned a few lines of dialogue, but it was a disaster. This language was stranger than Chinese as far as I was concerned. I remember when Grimbault and I went over to pick him up at his parents place. He was surrounded by posters of Bardot, giving an interview and having the reporter listen to "Je t'aime moi non plus" at full volume, the version he had done with Brigitte. I said to myself: "Who is this poseur in the mauve shirt?" I was utterly captivated. He was grimacing: Pierre had just told him he had chosen me instead of Maria Berenson."*

GAINSBOURG: *"We go to the studio to shoot a couple of scenes and I ask her straight away: "How can you accept a part in France when you don't speak a word of French?" So she immediately starts whining. But when I saw the rushes I said to Grimbault, "This little English chick isn't half-bad..."* "

Afterwards, Serge was beside himself for having provoked such despair in her: "It was a scene from a tragedy," he would confide to Yves Salgues in *Jours de France* in 1969. "Jane bemoaned her fate. It was all a jumble for her – fiction and reality, life and the script. 'I have nothing left,' she said. 'I've lost everything. Even a wild beast wouldn't touch my flesh.' I could only conclude that this girl was fabulous."

PIERRE GRIMBAULT: *"I think that the truth of the matter is that this little English chick really pissed him off, and that it was a blow to his ego to have to shoot a film with an unknown. During the screen tests he behaved like a real bastard, feeding her what we call dead lines, a trick used by pros to trip up beginners. But she dug in her heels and fought like a soldier. So I go out at night, like usual, and find myself at Régine's. Revolution was erupting in the streets, so we had to enter discretely, through the back door... After a moment or two Régine comes over and warns me: "You have a red Porsche, right? Well the students are going to use it to reinforce their barricade!" I run out like a madman and scream: "I'll help you! I have the keys!" The crowd shouts: "Super!" I jumped behind the wheel hauled ass back to Boulevard Montparnasse at 100 miles per hour, in reverse, ruining my engine."*

JANE BIRKIN: *"Then I went back to England, waiting for the trouble to die down in Paris. Serge seemed to me to be someone completely arrogant and sure of himself. This thing with his superiority was very humiliating. Still, he was very interesting. I was simply of no interest to him..."*

Serge is much too individualistic to get involved in the events of May '68. Later he would say: "Revolution? It's what I call blue-collars, red with shame." In reality, he's afraid of a Bolshevik-style revolution and even fears that his house, on which work has just begun, might be confiscated.

Jane comes back to Paris to stay with Andrew at Hôtel Esmeralda, in a 17th century mansion with a view of Notre-Dame. She moves in with Kate and a nanny and gets up every morning at five o'clock to take French lessons and study her lines. Actual shooting starts at the beginning of June in the Parisian apartment of photographer Peter Knapp. Serge, ever the creep, doesn't lift a finger to help Jane. As for Grimbault, he sees his film turning into a disaster: if there is not at least some small hint of chemistry between

his main actors, who have supposedly had a torrid love affair stretching from Venice to Paris, then it just won't work. Jane's brother bears witness...

ANDREW BIRKIN: *"As chance would have it, I was working as an assistant to Kubrick at the same time. After '2001, A Space Odyssey, he had asked me to scout locations for a film on Napoleon, which was never made. I was staying in the same little hotel as Jane. The first night she tells me: "The guy is unbearable, totally egotistical. He treats me like shit." The second night: "Today was even worse. I'm really unhappy." The third night she's just plain furious, and says: "Something weird is going on..."*

"So on the fourth night I tell them that things just can't go on like this, that we have to talk and that I want to see them for dinner at Maxim's at 10. It was a Friday... I slyly forget to show up and just what was supposed to happen did happen: on Monday they were holding hands. If I hadn't set things up there would be no movie. I would have had to stop filming..."

JANE BIRKIN: *"My marriage was ruined, and that was the most important thing in my life. My career hadn't even started and I had no ambition in that regard. I dreamt only of some sort of sublime love... After dining at Maxim's, Serge takes me to New Jimmy's, at Régine's. Still trying to show off, he asks me to dance, but it has to be a slow number. So when the disc-jockey finally plays a slow tune he takes me out on the floor, and he steps all over my feet. I could see he didn't know how to dance and I was completely delighted. I fell in love with him because of his shyness, his awkwardness... We later finished up our night in Pigalle, at Madame Arthur's, with all the transvestites who came and sat on our laps like a bunch of noisy roosters. They all knew him because his father had worked there as a pianist. They would shout "Oh, hi Serge!" and shower him with kisses, the feathers from their hair sticking into my face the whole time... I asked why he hadn't even said "How do you do?" the first time we met, and he answered: "Because I didn't give a damn"... I understood that all these things I had seen as aggression were really just defense mechanisms of someone infinitely too sensitive, terribly romantic, with a tenderness and sentimentality that no one could imagine existed. One day he told me that he was a "phony villain," which is true..."*

GAINSBOURG: *"After our bar-hopping I took her to the Hilton, and they made a terrible faux pas: "The usual, Mr. Gainsbourg? Room 642?"*

Anyway, nothing happened. I was dead tired. So in they morning she takes off and leaves me with a 45 that I really liked at the time, "Yummy, Yummy, Yummy" by Ohio Express. Five days later, same thing happens: Hilton, dead tired, sleep. She must have asked herself: "What's with this Frenchy?" It was a perfect plan, this nothing business."

Serge is quite smitten, and ever the romantic. One night, he convinces Jane that his love for her has driven him to request that all the monuments of Paris be illuminated. Actually it is just eight o'clock and all the monuments light up as usual. Still, Birkin believes him because "he's just so cute"... Then, his latest conquest has to head back to London for a few days. He stays in her room that night, at l'Hôtel Esmeralda. He lights a candle and watches it burn all night. The next day he sends an overseas telegram:

> *I would like that this telegram*
> *Be the loveliest telegram*
> *Of all the telegrams*
> *That you will ever receive*
>
> *Upon opening this telegram*
> *Upon reading this telegram*
> *When finished with this telegram*
> *May you cry a tender tear*

A talisman, as it were, that Jane will return only 11 years later, when they break up. We'll later see how he got Catherine Deneuve to sing it and how he himself appropriated it for the album Mauvaises nouvelles des étoiles.

JUDY CAMPBELL BIRKIN: *"My daughter came home and declared: "I have to tell you something. You know that horrible Frenchman I told you about? Well I think I'm in love with him. I believe he loves me, too." Serge was just fascinated by her 'Englishness,' the fact that she'd go out to a nightclub in a pair of jeans with her wicker handbag. Jane was ravishing, funny, sexy – she was even the first flat-chested girl to grace an English magazine cover."*

Shooting on *Slogan* starts at again at a breakneck pace: they continue in Paris until the end of July and then must begin again in Venice in September. Meanwhile, Grimbault has recommended Jane to Jacques Deray. She'll play the second female lead in a movie he's filming in August in Saint-Tropez: *La*

Piscine with Maurice Ronet, Alain Delon, and Romy Schneider, reunited for the first time since their separation five years earlier.

In a letter dated from August, Joseph gives us the particulars of the situation. First, Serge is very much in love and has left to be with Jane in Saint-Tropez. Then they run into B.B., who "kisses them both as if nothing had happened..."

Jane's brother photographs them on the beaches of Escalet and La Moutte. Serge quickly takes him under his wing.

ANDREW BIRKIN: *"He became a great teacher - he had me read Huysmans' 'A rebours,' taught me about great wine... That's when I starting collecting old bottles. But it was his childish side that pleased me the most, and I like seeing that we had this trait in common, especially because he was someone who seemed to have succeeded in life. As for my dad, David Birkin, he was a free-thinker. He would have been delighted to see Jane marry a black man and have a coffee-colored baby... he was a lot like Serge in the sense that he liked to shock his entourage... He later laughed about them never having married..."*

JANE BIRKIN: *"Oh, and was he ever jealous of Delon! He thought he was too handsome! In Nice, Serge managed to rent a car four times bigger than Alain's but it was useless because the roads were too narrow. We had to change Kate's diapers in that big, flashy limousine, and then there was the nanny and the baby carriage. Serge just moaned: "My beautiful car has been turned into an Arabian caravan!"..."*

PIERRE GRIMBAULT: *"It wasn't only Delon who drove him nuts but also Ronet. They were the two icons of French seduction. I had a house nearby and we'd set up a meeting to discuss the next part of 'Slogan,' which was scheduled for September in Venice. He shows up stark raving mad and tells me: "If one of those scumbags even touches her, look at this..." He opens a little case and shows me a revolver. He was ready to plant a slug in their bellies!"*

Broke down and beaten, Alain Delon remains nevertheless a gallant gentleman till the end. He drives Jane to the train station where she says goodbye to Serge before he returns to Paris – against his will – for professional reasons. In fact, he has a meeting with Françoise Hardy, whom he dines with in a restaurant at Place Vendôme. He tells her that he is beside himself, convinced that "Rocco" will seduce Jane, and that she will leave him (if she hasn't already), recreating just several months later the misery he knew when Bardot left him to go and film in Almería. This is the second time that Serge and Françoise are working together. In April, he had written for her the magnificent lyrics to "L'anamour," the "story of your loveless love / that changes like the clouds above...":

> I love you but fear
> I've wandered astray
> Sowing poppy seeds
> On the dead and lifeless clay
> Of loveless love

FRANÇOISE HARDY: *"There's an interesting story behind "Comment te dire adieu." It was originally an instrumental called "It Hurts To Say Goodbye" that I had heard through a record producer. I liked it and was convinced that I could make it work. Serge accepted to do the lyrics even though the melody wasn't his. When it came time to record I was surprised at how hard he worked. He knows exactly what he wants. In fact, he's probably a bit lazy and really works best when he's under pressure..."*

> By no means would I
> Dare to expose
> What is in my eyes
> I'll keep them closed
> Better off to cry
> Than let you know
> It hurts to say goodbye

Released in November, 1968, "Comment te dire adieu" was an enormous hit by early 1969, the last big one in the first part of her career (along with "Etonnez-moi, Benoit," with words by Patrick Modiano). Shortly thereafter, Françoise Hardy says her farewell to live performing after a gala event in London. She can no longer tolerate being separated from the one she loves.

In September, shooting resumes on *Slogan* back in Venice. In the film, Serge plays a commercial director who is receiving an award in Venice. There he meets Evelyne (Jane), with whom he falls madly in love. Back in Paris, his wife (Andréa Parisy), who is taking care of her own baby and pregnant with another, sees that this is something serious, unlike his other one-night stands, which she tolerates. Finally, after series of psychological and emotional upheavals, Evelyne dumps him for some dandy, athletic Guido (who is incidentally an Italian speedboat champion, an important detail), and he is lost in a broken-hearted abyss. All in all, a great film with quick and stylish editing, sometimes a bit gimmicky but always effective. Jane is superb and Serge is funny and cynical. It's easy to understand why they are nicknamed "couple of the year" some six months later upon the film's release.

> PIERRE GRIMBAULT: *"So I hook up once more with the dear couple who are making my life torture. It's Venice, they're holding hands all the time – all very lovely. So we get back to shooting and I see that it's no longer my story but rather Serge's and Jane's, which is just what Truffaut had predicted. So the first thing that happens is during the Television Commercial Festival. I had rehearsed things with two actors and we were supposed to shoot over on the corner of the stage, without disturbing the actual event. The organizer knew me because I had been nominated several times in Venice... Well, just 15 minutes before it starts he comes and tells me: "Pierre, you have to be ready. It's you. You're getting the grand prize this year." Like every year, I had things that were nominated, but I hadn't expected this. I informed Serge: "This will be super! Go up there in my place and I'll keep shooting!" He was petrified, all green. I had to push him. So we see him walk on stage and receive the grand prize from the mayor of Venice amidst an explosion of photographers' flash bulbs! Instead of having to fake it, the first scene of my movie is the real deal..."*

During the filming, reality merges with fiction when Jane runs into a boy she had known quite well in London, but with whom she claims "nothing happened." She kisses him probably a bit too enthusiastically and Serge digs in for their first quarrel.

> PIERRE GRIMBAULT: *"At a certain moment towards the end of the film, there is an insane speedboat trip down the canals of Venice at 70 mph. Of course it's totally against the law. Playing up the documentary film angle, I manage to convince the guy who's piloting the craft, and I position assistants along the route so that we don't crash into any gondolas. Then we start filming. An hour later we hopped a plane: they were looking to throw us in jail..."*

Back in Paris, Serge and Jane move in to L'Hôtel on Rue des Beaux-Arts because work is still being done at Rue de Verneuil. One evening, at the jazz club in the hotel's basement, Serge runs into pianist René Urtreger, with whom he had played his last concerts in 1965.

GAINSBOURG: *"It was a nice little neighborhood hotel at that time, the place where Oscar Wilde had died. You know what his last words were? He'd come to Paris to drop out. He was a pariah in England because of his homosexuality. So he's dead broke and he knows he's dying. He calls the doctor and informs the man that he is penniless... The doc says, "That's just great. Now who's going pay me?" And Wilde responds: "I see that I am going to die as I have lived: beyond my means..."*

JANE BIRKIN: *"At the time I met Serge, I knew nothing about love. After John Barry left, I got my act together and got down to business. I immediately told Serge that I wanted to work, that I would no longer lie around the house waiting for my man. I wanted to work at all costs. Even though I had devoted myself to my husband, I ended up losing him. I said to Serge: "I never want to experience that again."*

Meanwhile, renovations are continuing at Rue de Verneuil, closely supervised by Serge's father each time Serge is away from Paris. He wants to make his house into a jewel and he contacts Andrée Higgins, a famous antiquarian and designer in Saint-Germain-des-Prés.

ANDRÉE HIGGINS: *"We met on the day after he broke up with Brigitte. He had some really dark ideas and asked me to make the house all in black... He wanted to live in a Bardot universe. He had these sublime, life-size photos framed, all done by Sam Levin, and in the hallway leading to his room he had the idea of placing a series of smaller, black and white photos, lit up from unusual angles. When Jane got there the Bardot photos were replaced by portraits of Marilyn Monroe. He even wanted the curtains and lampshades to be black. I remember his father calling and saying: "Serge is completely mad. Change the color!" He acquiesced when it came to the curtains, but even the toilets had to be done in black... One day he comes over with a chandelier some six feet high and says: "We have to put this in the bathroom." I tell him he won't be able to get to the bathtub and he says: "Who cares, I never bathe anyway..."*

In September and October, 1968, Serge makes some television appearances and performs a few songs. He is approached to do the French adaption of *Hair*, which never comes to pass, and then he and Jane go to Zizi Jeanmaire's opening night at l'Olympia. Serge gives her not only "Bloody Jack," but also "L'oiseau de paradis" for the occasion:

> *Just like a bird of paradise*
> *That shines as bright as stars at night*
> *Our love is shaped from fragile clay*
> *And from our hands a life is born*
> *That precious jewels will soon adorn*

After the show, Zizi throws a little shindig at Maxim's for 50 of her close friends...

GAINSBOURG: *"Salvador Dali shows up and gives Jane and me both a kiss. It's mind-blowing because he is calling me "Maître" ... "Maître, they tell me that you own 'La Chasse aux papillons...' Could I borrow it for a book that I'm preparing?..." I tell him, of course, "Yes, whenever you like..."*

On October 30, live on Europe n°1, Serge takes part in a fascinating radio broadcast: he is psychoanalyzed by Michel Lancelot. With respect to his incommunicability and solitude, there is the following exchange:

DOCTOR: *Don't you have any deep regrets about your attitude, the fact that you can't manage to share yourself with others?*

GAINSBOURG: *Absolutely not. I'm like a sponge that never gives up its water. I can loan myself to others, but I never give. And I'm not talking about love, but about my relationships with men. I have no regrets. I'm like I was as a child, I haven't changed. I'm true to myself, unsociable, reserved. I'm not going to change my behavior just because I happen to practice this craft.*

On November 18, 1968, *France-Dimanche* gives us the following headline: SURPISE MARRIAGE FOR SERGE GAINSBOURG. For him, we read, "Jane Birkin has left her rich husband." It's the first of endless rumors... In the meantime, they have better things to do. Serge and Jane have two sessions in London, the first in November and the second in December, 1968, where they record songs for the January, 1969 album at Chappell Studios, with Arthur

Greenslade manning the helm. The jewel of the this new opus is Jane's version of "Je t'aime moi non plus."

JANE BIRKIN: *"Early on, Serge had asked me to sing it with him but I refused. Bardot's version was just too good. Then my pride was hurt watching the parade of actresses like Mireille Darc who were just begging to do the song with him. Furthermore, I was jealous: the idea of him cooped up in that little studio with that stunning girl, well, I said to myself: "Yikes! Anything but that!"*

As an appetizer, they release in December a 45 of his own version of *L'anamour* with a b-side (under Serge's name only) that includes "69 année érotique," a demonic little cut that could not be any more amorous:

> *Gainsbourg and his Gainsborough*
> *Took off on a ship*
> *Watching from their state room*
> *Their never-ending trip*
> *They're in love and like this song*
> *The trip will last the whole year long*
> *Taking every comer on*
> *Until the New Year dawns*

It's played in clubs, as is "Je t'aime moi non plus," but it never makes the charts, which at that time are dominated by the Beatles, Johnny Hallyday, and Joe Cocker. Still, "Je t'aime moi non plus," sung an octave higher than Bardot's version, is both a masterpiece and a future worldwide hit.

JANE BIRKIN: *"The recording was done at a Piccadilly studio, just Serge and I both intertwined... We did two takes, no more. I remember how later, like the conductor of an orchestra, he directed my amorous sighing. When it became a hit, people imagined all sorts of crazy things. They thought we'd placed a tape recorder under our bed. Serge said if that were the case the recording would have been a lot longer than four minutes!..."*

> *Jane: I love you I love you*
> *Oh God I love you*
> *Serge: Well not me*
> *Jane: Oh my love*
> *Serge: Carnal love, it's a dead end*
> *I come, I come and I go*
> *Thrusting so slow*

I come and I go
Thrusting so slow
Trying to control...
Jane: No, just let go

JANE BIRKIN: *"When we got back from London and played the track for the head of Philips, he told us: "O.K. I'm ready to go to jail, but for an album, not for a 45." So we headed straight back to London on the ferry... "*

That's when Serge, caught off-guard and feeling pressure from Georges Myerstein, decides to include "Manon" as well as his own takes on "Sous le soleil exactement" and "Sucettes" (recorded two years earlier by Anna Karina and France Gall respectively). He also writes some words, which are dedicated to Jane, for the song "Elisa," previously an instrumental composed for the soundtrack to *L'Horizon*:

Elisa, Elisa
Jump onto my shoulders please
Elisa, Elisa
Try to pick off all the fleas
Run you fingers fine and fair
Make sure there is nothing there
In the jungle
Of my hair, Elisa

He composes four other songs for Jane, including "Orang-outang," which is inspired by Jane's stuffed animal monkey (that is in fact named "Monkey"), and which she has been carting around since she was a baby. Two years later it will grace the cover of *Melody Nelson*:

I love my little stuffed orangutan
Orangutan, orangutan
He sleeps beside me here on the divan
Orangutan, orangutan
Eyes all open wide
No more teeth inside
But I must confide
I love his mangy hide

Wanting to do more than simply pilfer a bit of a Chopin prelude, Serge decides on "Jane B." to use a poem from Nabokov's *Lolita*, something that he had always wanted to set to music (Wanted, wanted: Dolores Haze./Hair:

brown Lips: scarlet/Age: five thousand three hundred days/Profession: none, or "starlet.") Jane's voice is like the quivering of a tightrope walker, and she already possesses an extraordinarily moving fragility. Serge had told her: "You sing like a choirboy..."

> *Description*
> *Eyes: blue*
> *Hair: Blond, pale*
> *Jane B.*
> *English*
> *Sex: female*
> *Age: Twenty maybe twenty-one*

At the end of September, Serge sees Béatrice again. She's planning a Christmas dinner for Natacha (fours years old) and Paul (six months). In January, while Jane does her first cover – or "covering" as Gainsbourg calls it – for *Jours de France*, the film *La Piscine* hits the screens and "Je t'aime moi non plus" is in the record stores, under Jane's name. The scandal can now begin, much to the chagrin of Brigitte, who in her autobiography concludes the story of the affair with these words:

> *I thought I'd die when one month later I heard the recording of that song with Serge and Jane. But that's how things are! I'm not angry with either one of them. Really, I felt bad about my own cowardice, my uncertainty, the way I believed that I deserved it all, the harm that I unconsciously created and which found its way back to me like a dagger in my heart.*

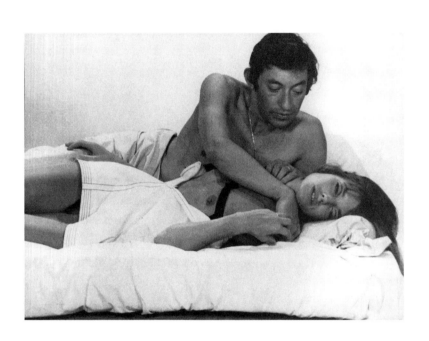

fifteen

Erotic '69

On January 29, 1969, we find Jane in the arms of a crooning Serge while he sings "Elisa" on the program *Quatre Temps*. Then, before she sings "Jane B.," she is interviewed by Gainsbourg himself:

–So your name's not Elisa?

–It's Jane

–Jane what?

–Jane Birkin.

–And you're a film actress, right?

–Yes.

–And you've been in...

–'Blow-up.'

–With David Hemmings, a handsome lad... then?

–With you!

–[He breaks up] Yes, in 'Slogan...' and then...

–'La Piscine,' with Alain Delon.

–Handsome lad.

–You bet!

–And now you want to sing. Who gave you that idea!

–You!

MICHEL DRUCKER: *"I've seen it in people who become successful and I saw the same change in Serge: that awareness of the profession and the public. One becomes polished, relaxed. Success had finally reassured him – he'd lost all his hang-ups."*

Jean Hugues, the house photographer for Philips, is given the task of shooting the cover of "Je t'aime moi non plus."

JEAN HUGUES: *"It was really early on a winter morning, in front of the bronze statues at the Alexandre-III bridge. It was cold and overcast. The shoot lasted 10 minutes, then Jane and Serge took me to the hotel at Rue des Beaux-Arts. Serge drops a record onto a portable Teppaz and says: "Jean, I'm going to play something for you. It's going to be scandalous but the clubs will eat it up." It was "Je t'aime moi non plus." I understood then and there why we had just taken that photo."*

The 45 is released in January and in no time the press dubs them "the scandalous couple"... They are baptized "the moaning duo" by *L'Express*, and their "pornographic" song, as one songwriter calls it, is almost never played on the radio, except late in the evening on France-Inter, especially on José Artur's *Pop Club*, for which Serge and Jane also do the intro music:

> Serge: Forget the past, forget the future
> Here's the 'Pop Club,' here's
> Jane: José Artur
> Serge: For all the ones whose hearts demur
> Here's the man
> Jane: José Artur
> Serge: Slip into your finest furs
> Here comes the 'Pop Club' of
> Jane: José Artur

Just as Gainsbourg had predicted, "Je t'aime moi non plus" gets off to a roaring start in the clubs before hitting the international market.

Isabelle Adjani: "I was at school and I got hold of a copy in spite of the warning label: "Forbidden for minors"... I would hide and listen to it and my mom blew her top when she found out. It was a riot. There was something transgressive about it but there was also this sweetness, which seduced me and plenty of other teenagers, I suppose..."

Despite numerous television appearances, performing the song on air is out of the question. Anyway, Serge's mother is sick and depressed, and he is worried. Her arthritis is causing her more and more suffering and she is so down that she is starting to have some morbid thoughts. Ever the attentive son, he prepares her meals and chips in when Jacqueline takes a few days off for vacation. As for Jane, she is welcomed wholeheartedly by the press. Two months after *Jours de France* she does the cover of *Mademoiselle Age Tendre* and explains "Why I love Serge Gainsbourg." Then Serge, interviewed in *Noir et Blanc*, answers a reporter who asks if Jane is his type of woman:

I don't have a specific type. I'm eclectic and I've known many different kinds of women. Jane is more like a pictorial ideal. When I was a painter, I only depicted women that were a bit androgynous, diminutive, flat-chested. All my paintings look like Jane. I painted her before I knew her.

Just when the sales of "Je t'aime moi non plus" are going through the roof, Serge and Jane leave for Nepal to shoot the film *Les Chemins de Katmandou*, directed by André Cayette. Cayette's dud gives us Jane transformed into a wastrel lunatic and Serge in the role of a pathetic bastard.

GAINSBOURG: *"Cayette tells me: "We're going to slap a moustache on you because your face is too recognizable." I say: "But hey, didn't you already use Aznavour in 'Le Passage de Rhin' and 'Brel for Les Risques du métier?'" But still, he had to put me in a moustache. So those imbeciles stuck some unmovable piece of crap on me and I walked around for the whole film with an upper lip stiffer than an Englishman's. But Cayette isn't the type who's prone to changing his mind. He told me: "As far as I'm concerned, once the script is finished, so is the film." So we're in India and Nepal but he won't take his nose out of that script. I pointed something out to him: "Look at those two fantastic kids. Let's do a shot with them," and he says: "No, the shot is what's on paper." He had taken off to scout a location earlier and he had wanted to do a lateral tracking shot, some 50 meters of flowering trees in a superb setting in northern India. But when we got there, everything had been killed by the blazing sun. So what does Cayette do? His script reads "flowering trees," so instead of coming up with another shot he sends five techs out there to stick paper flowers onto the trees..."*

JANE BIRKIN: *"Everyone was talking about Indian philosophy, but when we got over there it was a different story. I saw deformed hands, children sleeping on railroad tracks in Calcutta [...] It was impossible to enjoy the beauty of things. They would distribute our food and we'd consume it inside an air-conditioned car. Once I saw a woman starring at me and salivating. So you roll down the window and give away everything, not out of generosity, but because you're so terribly uneasy that you feel guilty about eating."*

The only upside is seeing Nepal in such exceptional conditions. They take advantage of this, testing out the regional specialties and smoking some hash. "I don't know what happened," says Serge, "but after a few hits we chickened out and a doctor had to inject us with a camphor solution. My heart was ready to explode. My pulse was nearly 200." A photographer from *Jours de France* witnesses the whole thing: "He felt ill and was really quite frightened. At that point there was no more of his usual cynicism. He lost his head and showed his fear because he knew this was a serious health issue!"

Once back from Nepal they are finally able to move in at 5 bis, Rue de Verneuil. As Jane puts it, the house resembles its owner: to the very end, he would reign like a despotic maniac over this imaginary museum, this mishmash of precious objects gathered together over the course of years which are meticulously repositioned should they be misplaced by even the slightest millimeter. By opting for black, he not only abolishes color but sublimates it. His living room is a rigorously ordered display case that plays counterpoint to his disorderly interior.

MICHEL PICCOLI: *"Serge and I lived on the same street. One day I'm taking a taxi past his place and the driver says: "You know that Gainsbourg? He's a dope fiend!" I answered: "Not really, sir, it's much worse than that!" But he just didn't get it."*

A Swiss reporter gets the privilege of publishing the first piece on what she calls "the lair of the beast"...:

All black. Black from top to bottom. Walls and ceilings. Checkerboard black and white tiles. Even at daytime it's all black: a Moroccan partition, a black wooden grill with openwork design, is placed in front of the window in lieu of a curtain – a black filter for the white light. The few pieces of furniture are all black. Some strange objects: an enormous taran-

tula in a glass globe, a lifelike crab placed on the floor that seems to have surged forth from God knows what hole, a life-size écorché. Brrr. Amidst this diabolical décor stands the beast. All dressed in black with big, pointy ears. Deformed nose and protruding eyeballs. His skin is pale, his mouth immense, his smile satanic.

The sales of "Je t'aime moi non plus" are already approaching 200,000 in France when, in the middle of June, Serge makes an appearance in the Gérard Pirès film, *Erotissimo*. During this period of equanimity, Serge continues to promote the song "Elisa" on any TV show that will have him. On July 26, *Slogan* has its gala premiere at the Cinéma Colisée on the Champs-Elysées, where Jane appears next to Serge in a transparent mini-dress. *France-Dimanche*, never missing a beat, declares: "SERGE GAINSGOURG IS NOT ASHAMED TO SHOW OFF HIS WOMAN NUDE..." Behind all the sensationalist press, another phenomenon is growing and will last over the coming years: Serge and Jane are becoming a highly charged media symbol of a certain moral liberation in France that had been hindered by de Gaullian morality, as the following television director points out:

ANDRÉ FLÉDÉRICK: *"Everyone remembers those photos of Jane in that transparent mini-dress, through which you could see her breasts and panties... For my generation they were a couple that did something positive. They took risks and they helped expand our ideas about freedom. Through them, the behavior of younger people became more accepted. Don't forget that at that time people didn't dare kiss in the streets, or at least almost never! We saw extraordinary love and a rapport of absolute freedom. Jane, with her straight-talk, was the antithesis of the female object. Thanks to Serge, she had learned to exist. Before, she had been just an English shop-girl - pretty but without substance. With Serge she completely bloomed."*

Undoubtedly aided by the blistering success of "Je t'aime moi non plus," *the* slow dance of 1969 in all the hip nightclubs, *Slogan* makes a big splash, and the reviews, with a couple exceptions, are almost globally positive. One detraction comes from *Journal du dimanche*, which refers to it as "sentimental marmalade." In *L'Express*, André Bercoff assures us of some good moments: "The way in which they wholeheartedly devour each other with their eyes and tear each other to pieces without respite is a pleasure to watch. The film is bittersweet, the love-child of pop-art and the pill." Michel Duran, on the other hand, seems repulsed by Serge's appearance: "Gainsbourg makes me nauseous. I suffered through an hour and a half of this film, wrecking my eyes by trying to watch it without looking at Gainsbourg. Impossible. He's always there. For you women who love him, you're in for a treat. Pierre Grimbault shies away from nothing, showing him in bed, in the tub, making love. As I am not a lover of horror films, these were some of the most painful moments for me." Soon all of France is postered over with the four-color prints of the sensational couple. The success of *Slogan* lasts into November, 1969, at which time Serge and Jane receive French cinema's Triomphe award, precursor to the Césars.

> ISABELLE ADJANI: *"One Thursday afternoon when I didn't have school, I went to see 'Slogan' and 'Les Chemins de Katmandou' at a local theatre. I found Serge really handsome, he had a romantic presence... It was like looking into a mirror – observing him gave me the feeling that it was possible to look at myself freely and find myself beautiful. When I saw him on TV I felt he was constantly re-inventing himself. He'd hold himself like an adolescent. His stare, his look, it was aggressive, that way he never smiled. People in my generation tried to imitate that nonconformity."*

Grimbault of course asked Serge to do the soundtrack for *Slogan*, so Serge gives him an orchestrated duet over a moving melody, contrasting the high-pitched voice of Jane against his own murmured growl, which since "Manon" seems to have settled into the delights of the half-sung/half-spoken thing that will soon become his stock in trade. The superb arrangements are by Jean-Claude Vannier, whom he used on the soundtrack to Paris n'exitse pas and who will soon become a key figure:

> JANE: *You're vile, you're vicious, you're vain*
> *You're vapid, you're venal, a real pain*
> SERGE: *Evelyne you are unfair*
> *Evelyne you are so shrill*
> *Evelyne are you aware*
> *You love me ever still*

> GAINSBOURG: *"Pierre Grimbault asked me to do some romantic "American style" music for 'Slogan.' I told him: "Just let me be and let me do what I want, or else go get fucked." He really wanted me to add some romantic touch to his film, but music can't add anything to a film! If the*

film isn't romantic you can't make it so by adorning it with little melodic ditties. What's more, I'm not a romantic character. I'm a spineless bastard. So I didn't do the music he wanted because you just shouldn't cheat with music. First of all, film music should serve as counterpoint, and secondly, it should never be pleonastic."

The success of "Je t'aime moi non plus" has for some time now been reaching across the borders, well beyond Switzerland and Belgium. Just like Max Romeo's "Wet Dream," the song is immediately censored in Great Britain.

JANE BIRKIN: *"When I played the record for my mother, I just skipped to the next song when the sighing started. Unfortunately, my brother played it again and she quickly realized that her daughter, still tainted from the Blow-up affair, was going to become even more scandalous. 30 years later and the English still think of me as "Je t'aime" Birkin. No use trying to tell them that I made 60 films and recorded a dozen albums. It follows me around like a criminal conviction."*

In August, 1969, Serge spends a few days in England, where Jane is filming *Delitto A Oxford*, a small Italian film. While at the Oxford Bear hotel, with neither radio nor television – "freed from all parasitic information" as he would later say – Serge lays the foundations for *l'Histoire de Melody Nelson*, the story of a young girl on a bicycle who is run over by the composer's Rolls Royce. The first of his "concept albums," it will be a painful 18 months before being fully realized. Meanwhile, "Je t'aime moi non plus," put out by Philips' English branch, Fontana, climbs all the way to number two on the charts in Great Britain in September, just behind Creedence Clearwater Revival's "Bad Moon Rising."

Then out of the blue, Fontana senselessly and abruptly halts production of the record. In spite of this, "Je t'aime moi non plus" continues its march, this time on the Major Minor label. It's number three at the start of October and actually climbs to first on the British charts – for one week only – before dropping back off. All this while a phony group dubbed Sounds Nice cuts an instrumental version dubbed "Love At First Sight" after the BBC and Radio One ban the sung version of the song.

To understand what's happening with "Je t'aime moi non plus," we have to remember what's happening in the rest of Europe during this time of Pope

Paul VI. On August 25, Italian Radio (RAI) censors "Je t'aime moi non plus," considered an obscene and intolerable record that must at all costs be kept away from minors. That same day, *Osservatore Romano*, the mouthpiece of the Vatican, enthusiastically approves, going so far as to cite the most scandalous parts of the record as a means of shocking its readership:

When such subjects become themes for music, it is simply obscenity at 33 rpms. The popularity of this song confirms the level of stupidity to which we have driven the modern man of mass culture.

Worse yet, there is a "seizure undertaken by order of the district attorney of Milan for violation of article 528 of the penal code concerning obscene publications and performances." It takes place at the Milan factory where the record is being made, right at the moment when it is number two on the Italian charts. This order, which extends to "wherever the record is found," affects all of Italy, where it will soon be sold under the table for 50,000 lira or distributed with an innocent looking Maria Callas cover. As for the distributor, he will receive two months suspended sentence and a 352 franc fine.

Thanks to the great push provided by the press, sales of the single take off in all directions. After Italy, however, the record is banned in Spain, where it is classified as "pornographic" by the country's Minister of Information. The same happens in Portugal and Brazil (thank you Catholics!), and even stranger, in Sweden, where the Lutheran empire follows suit on September 10.

But that's not all. In France, Philips finds itself forced to sell off its reserves - which thanks to the Vatican is a done deal by October 1 - and replace the offensive cut on the album with "La chanson de Slogan." The masters of "Je t'aime moi non plus" are officially returned to Serge, who's ready to sell them to the first comer, in this case Lucien Morisse, the head of both Europe 1 and Disc'AZ, whom he had worked with on the Dominique Walter recordings.

By September 8, thanks to the nightclubs, Serge had sold 780,000 copies of the 45. By October 15, 1969, thanks to the Vatican, that number passes the million and a half mark, including 250,000 in Great Britain, 200,000 in Germany, and 280,000 in France. Before the year's end, the number will double (in France alone, AZ sells 300,000) and in the following months Serge earns over an estimated two million francs and Jane over a million.

GAINSBOURG: *"Lord Snowdon, who did the covers for my reggae albums, told me this extraordinary story. He was accompanying Princess Margaret to some far-off South Sea Island and they're greeted by this darkie band that only knows two songs: "God Save The Queen" and "Je t'aime moi non plus." People kept standing up, sitting down, standing up, sitting down..."*

For the Michel Audiard film *Une veuve en or*, which comes out on October 22, 1969, Serge writes a great little tune which is performed by Michèle Mercier: "La fille qui fait tchic-ti-tchic" comes out as a 45 on Disc'AZ:[1]

> *My silver gown is like*
> *A current when it spikes*
> *200 volts that climb*
> *Their way along my spine*
> *It runs from head to toe*
> *And I can feel it flow*
> *Steering the men I know*
> *To Sodom off they go*

Serge and Jane are newly glorified on the September, 1969 cover of *Rock & Folk*, which had published the transcription of Serge's appearance on Radio Psychose a year earlier:

> *I feel like I'm torn between good and evil. I feel like I have a pure soul, but there's also something impure about me. By impure I mean my sexual hang-ups. I'm, let's say, a fetishist and a sadist. My sadism is abstract, a mental thing. As for my fetishism, for me it's a question of dissociating myself from the animal condition. It's about being sophisticated in one's physical relations. This is a purely esthetic problem – I've been a painter for too long, so I see first and foremost with my eyes. Being a painter, I was around a lot of models, nude women. For me, a naked woman means absolutely nothing. A naked woman on the beach, it's animalistic, and the animal state is anguishing to me, something I want to escape. Thus I need to embellish.*

In fact, there are numerous reporters clamoring around the composer of "Je t'aime moi non plus" and waiting for him to say something provoca-

---

[1] The title is obviously a reference to Irving Berlin's "Cheek to Cheek."

tive, yet Serge is squarely opposed to the sexual liberation that both he and Jane have come to represent. He admits that he is nostalgic for old Victorian morality. He wants to restore the intensity of the touch and taste of sin, obviously...:

> *"Je t'aime moi non plus" expresses the superiority of eroticism vis-à-vis sentimentality [...] there are millions of songs about romantic, sentimental love: the first encounters, the discovery, the jealousy, illusions and disillusions, the rendezvous, the betrayal, the remorse, the hatred, etc. So why not devote oneself to a song about love that is much more contemporary: physical love? "Je t'aime" is not an obscene song. It seems perfectly sensible to me, it fills a void.*

Coming back to the song some 12 years later, he finally explains the hidden meaning, which many have suspected for quite some time:

> *The explanation is that the girl says "I love you" while they're making love, and the man, with his ridiculous machismo, doesn't believe it. He thinks she says it in a moment of bliss, while coming. There have been times when I have believed it. In a way, I'm afraid of letting myself be had. But that's really something esthetic, a search for something absolute.*

When *Lui,* "the modern men's magazine," publishes its first photos of Jane (with Serge in charge of the shoot), we see a mysterious little chain with a key hanging on it. Serge wore an identical one for many a year. What it opens we dare not ask... They are magnificent shots, and there's text from the master:

> *Antibardot, antifonda, a touch Antinous, Antina, my Jane, my little androgyne, they will love you, them neither, and they'll pin your photo up next to Mick Jagger, next to Marilyn, Jean Harlow, Bertha von Paraboum, all those little soldiers in their gray barracks on a little winter morning. You will destroy their health...*

On October 15, 1969, Serge and Jane hit the U.S. for the shooting of Cannabis, a sex-charged detective thriller restricted to those over 18. It doesn't open until August, 1970. Still, he does get to meet up again with Koralnik, his old Swiss pal who directed Anna. Today, *Cannabis* is of no interest to anybody but the fans of the numerous scenes of torrid tenderness acted out by the couple... Serge plays a killer who receives his orders from the New York mafia. His mission is to take control of the drug traffic. Jane plays the role of daddy's little girl, and Serge obviously falls for her, ready to give up everything, including his partner and blood brother. It all ends in a tawdry and tragic bloodbath. The only pleasant surprise is the cinematography of Willy Durant, who was director of photography on the set of Anna.

The year comes to an end with Serge being invited to perform on several television shows. He does "69 année érotic" on La Nuit de Paris. He also does television performances of "L'anamour" and "Elisa." The orchestra and choir of the ORTF even offer to do a "clean" version of "69 année érotic" under the title "70 année fantastique." Nice way to close out the sixties. Joseph Ginsburg, proud as ever, sums up the decade thusly:

Serge wanted to be a painter, which is why he did music and finally ended up (successfully) in the cinema, where he's like a fish in water. Highly unusual. We haven't yet gotten our heads around it – it's a long way from the studios of Montmartre to the soundstages of Boulogne...

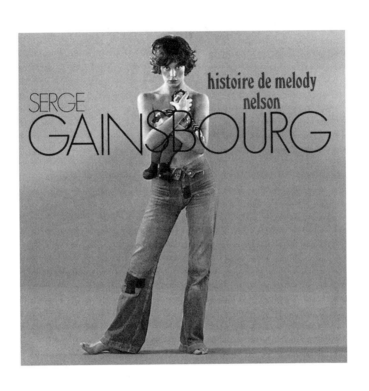

sixteen

Ah! Melody

1970 is, for all intents and purposes, a transitional year. After the recent media blitz, Serge makes himself scarce. He only appears twice on television, and he only does one radio show of any note when he appears on Philippe Bouvard's Radio-Luxembourg to perform a live version of "La Javanaise," with France Gall singing backup. This is followed by a duet of "Les sucettes." France is now living with Julien Clerc and temporarily out of show business. We will soon see her attempt a comeback with a little help from Gainsbourg.

Serge's breakneck work pace now slows considerably. He wants to spend as much time as he can with his fiancée, so he tries to get parts in the same films as her or simply accompany her when she's shooting, as he had done a few months earlier in Oxford and as he will do again when she acts in *Trop petit mon ami* and *Sex Power*. He's also devoting a lot of time to the joys of family life: raising little Kate as if she were his own, spending Christmas with Jane's parents, and of course taking care of Joseph and Olia.

In January, 1970, Serge meets up again with Jean-Claude Vannier to do the soundtrack for Pierre Granier-Deferre's film *La Horse*, which is hitting the screens the next month. It's time we deal with Vannier, the composer, arranger, and bandleader with whom Serge will do three film scores. He will also be Serge's partner in crime for the astonishing *Melody Nelson* album and will continue to work with Gainsbourg up until the time of Jane Birkin's *Di Doo Dah*. Born in 1943, Vannier is used to composing "at the table" and without a piano, which impresses Serge. In 1968, he does a number of arrangements for Johnny Hallyday and then accompanies him as bandleader in spring of 1969 for Hallyday's famous *Show de l'an 2000* at the Palais des Sports. In May, he accompanies Michel Polnareff on TV, and then he does the arrangements for Barbara's album *Madame*, which is released in February, 1970.

> JEAN-CLAUDE VANNIER: *"People have always told me that they can recognize my arrangements right away. I don't waste time trying to figure out if that's a compliment or not. Maybe I have what's called a style, maybe they are obsessions. I can't really say. It's true that I hate useless harmonies and rhythms that serve no purpose, so I try to hone things down. I have never had (we've heard this recently) three guitars playing the same part along with a piano and a bass line – which is already a rhythm section – and then two drummers and percussionists on top of that. I reduce it all to a simple expression: piano, bass, and drums. What's more, the pianist can't use two hands, and the guitarist must make do with no more than two notes at a time. The drumming is completely minimalist because I've always hated cymbals... On a lot of records I've made, you only hear the toms, the snare drum, and the bass drum - nothing else. Sometimes you even find really rhythmic songs where I use absolutely no drums. I have other idiosyncrasies, of course. I adore it when things go haywire, which means out of key, so I use notes that are off-key all the time: I love discordant instruments, the kinds of things you don't hear everywhere."*

In March, 1970, Serge flies to the U.S. with Jane for the launching of "Je t'aime moi non plus." But the scandal hardly attracts the attention of radio programmers and the cut only reaches 58 on the charts. Then from April 21 to 23, they lay down the rhythm tracks for *Melody Nelson* in London. Another session takes place in early May at Studio Dames in Paris with engineer Rémy Aucharles. Then nothing happens until winter of 1971.

> RÉMY AUCHARLES: *"The sessions started at five and we stopped at nine to eat dinner at restaurant across the street. Then we went back and worked all night. The reason the album was done in two parts is because Serge re-*

ally lost inspiration towards the second half of the record. It was a creative block."

Looking at the official records of the session, the documents where the titles of the recordings are written down, this is hardly surprising. One can find songs that are started but never finished, such as "Es-tu Melody," "Le papa de Melody," "Melody et les astronauts," and two versions of "Melody lit Babar," the only piece whose lyrics are actually finished but somehow does not make the album.

So what's happening? Why this lack of inspiration as these sessions drawn out over 10 months? The answer lies in the ambitiousness of the project. Evidently, Gainsbourg wants to make a statement. He wants to re-establish that aura of the authentic, avant-garde poet and composer who has been damaged, if not destroyed by his commercial successes, from "Poupée de cire" to "Je t'aime moi non plus." Maybe he also wants to surpass Léo Ferré, the first to take a real step forward with the 1970 double album *Amour anarchie*. On both "La the nana" and "Le chien," Ferré, with the help of backing band Zoo, creates a stunning marriage of rock music and more literary chanson, taking his initial attempts of 1968 ("C'est extra") even further. But probably the real reason is that Serge wants to impress Jane, who had been married before to composer John Barry, let's not forget. In 1978, Serge will actually confide to interviewer René Quinson that he "could no longer remain simply a composer of little ditties." That's why he writes *Melody Nelson*, which he defines as "a truly symphonic musical..."

JEAN-CLAUDE VANNIER: *"I must say that I was extremely flattered when he had his record company contact me. I told myself: "Finally an interesting adventure." He had me come to London and I remember getting sick in the plane. I was a wreck when I arrived, and he looked at me and said: "What happened to you?" That was our first meeting... Then we worked on the music for 'Paris n'existe pas' and we started to hit it off, we found common interests. We both like similar turn of the century songs and American standards, like Cole Porter... We have similar artistic loves, and in a variety of fields he turned me on to the new ones... He used "vous" with me at first: "Shut up, I could be your father." Then, very gently he would tell me: "You see, you're Cole and I'm Porter."*

Serge and Jane head to Morocco for a few days and visit Serge's sister, Liliane, in Casablanca. There, with the love of his life, far from Paris, he holes up in a little hotel in Marrakesh to write the words for *Melody Nelson*. Serge tells a reporter: "The result was a real disaster. Jane went sunbathing and me, I was happy as a clam, but unable to put two words together. We went back to Paris, and there everything kicked into gear." One amusing anecdote from the trip is when Serge is invited to Rabat by the sister of Hassan II, whom he had met at Hôtel de Crillon.

GAINSBOURG: "*It was hell. Reception after reception, a fantasia, a circus. One day they take us into a room, Jane and me, and there's a piano. The king's piano. Totally out of tune. And so they ask us to sing "Je t'aime moi non plus." Jane tells me, "I don't want to sing." Of course. Out of the question. I explain that I have forgotten the words but then some lady in the audience takes out that book published by Seghers.[1] We had to sing. Plus, as is always the case in these conditions, I screw up at the piano. The worst is that at the moment the groans start, everyone chimes in with their own "ahs" and "ohs." A nightmare. I swear, never again. Invitations come at too high a price.*"*

Just before he and Jane leave for Yugoslavia, Serge, along with Jean-Claude Vannier, composes the soundtrack to *Cannabis*. The theme song stands out:

Death comes, in the countenance of an infant dear
Holds a gaze crystal clear
Draped in finery her elegance nocturnal
Our kinship eternal

By name she beckons me
And now I've lost my head you see
Is this hell or bliss
Or the subtle touch of cannabis?

Arriving in Yugoslavia in June, Serge and Jane do two films: first, eight weeks on Abraham Polonsky's *Romance of a Horse Thief*, then three or four

---

[1] The book, by Lucien Rioux, was published in 1969, and half it is comprised of the lyrics of Serge's biggest tunes.

more weeks to do a local film, Milutin Kosovac's *19 Djevojaka I Mornar.* Polonsky, exiled since the McCarthy era, meets Jane in Paris and immediately falls in love with Serge's mug, offering him the role of Sigmund, her phony, city slicker fiancé. Polonsky had suffered through quite a long spell of not being able to make films, so when Serge expresses his desire to direct, he says: "Make your film as soon as possible. Don't put it off!"

JANE BIRKIN: *"The filming was really fun. I was the only goy in a film made by Jews about the history of Jews... I met up with Yul Brynner again, an old friend from my days in London... One day, Serge organized a costume party around a circus theme and everyone came. Polonsky, a very dignified, elder man, came as the tin man from 'Wizard of Oz.' Yul Brynner dressed up as a clown, Serge as a female clown, and Eli Wallach as a gangster. We partied all night."*

Andrew, Jane's brother, comes to spend a few days with them...

Andrew Birkin: *"One evening, just for fun, I decided to listen to a record by John Barry, my sister's former husband. Serge noticed this. He gave me a strange look and then disappeared. He spent half the night brooding on a hilltop! He was sick with jealousy. I couldn't believe my eyes..."*

Marilu Tolo, the starlet who inspired Serge's song "Marilu," also has a little role in the film. She provides a few sparks herself...

JANE BIRKIN: *"We were all staying in the same house, which had been transformed into a hotel. There were frogs jumping right out of the Danube... One day a circus came to town. There was girl who did a number with a pistol and she was giving Serge the eye. He sent her a note, and man was I beside myself! I was jealous all night. She was built like Jane Russell, really powerful, and with a revolver [...] When he played the piano with Marilu Tolo I was so jealous that I left for Dubrovnik, where I caught a plane to England in order the see my gynecologist so I could get pregnant right away [...] I was really distraught. I was so afraid that this girl would become something explosively dangerous."*

And this is why Charlotte is conceived... During this scene that Jane refers to, Serge sings a song that will appear neither on *Melody Nelson* nor on any subsequent album. To this day, it remains unreleased. This magnificent piece is "La noyée":

You have gone astray my darling
Swept away by memory's tide
From the river's shore I'm calling
Please come back here to my side
But you drift into the distance
Down the frantic path I stride
Trying to with such persistence
Close the gap of our divide

GAINSBOURG: *"For the Polonsky film in Yugoslavia, I had written an incredibly beautiful waltz, and while I was convinced of this I nevertheless said to myself: "This isn't something for me, but who could sing it?" And then one day it came to me: Yves Montand. I call him up. He sets a meeting for the next day. At 10 in the morning I'm at his door and he sees me in, very elegant, while Simone suggests we get the ball rolling with straight whiskey. I want to show him I know how to drink, so I jump right in. I play my waltz and Montand says: "It's beautiful!" Before I leave, he shakes my hand and tells me: "Write a b-side, we'll make a record." After that whiskey on an empty stomach, my trip back was hallucinating. I puked pure alcohol into the gutter! After that, there was no more news, even though I'd written a number, "Satchmo," for the other side. I later heard through the grapevine that he no longer wanted to record it."*

You are but a poor dead collie
Floating sadly down the stream
But I am your slave my darling
I dive in and chase my dream

Let's recap... Early in his career, Serge sees Montand, but his awkwardness torpedoes any possibility of a future collaboration. In 1961, he promises Montand (the first to perform "Feuilles mortes") the exclusive rights to "La chanson de Prévert," which he then gives to Isabelle Aubret. There is another meeting in 1963, just before Serge leaves for Hong Kong, but nothing concrete comes of it. Finally, there's this business with "La noyée," which Montand rejects because he fears it will be misunderstood by malicious journalists...

Next, Serge and Jane are hired by some Yugoslavian producers to star in Le Traître?, in which they play resistance fighters hunted by the Wehrmacht. Upon his return to Paris, Serge uses the 50,000 francs he earns on this weird little schlock film and pays cash for a 1928 Rolls Royce. He has neither a chauffeur nor a license, and the car almost never leaves the garage until he sells it 10 years later. He does keep the hood ornament, the famous "Spirit of Ecstasy" that we encounter again in "Melody," the opening cut of Melody Nelson. Serge is now back to work on the album after his four months in the Balkans. An incomplete manuscript with the working title of "Sonnet au bouchon du radiateur de la Rolls" gives us a glimpse into the creation of this piece, one of the most sophisticated in this major work:

> For you I've braved hairpin turns and figure eights
> I've run down mangy dogs and sent crowds screaming
> Like a stunt pilot whose motor is dying
> He sees the horde below him run for the gates
>
> Oh Rolls you've bogged me down with endless traveling
> You've cost me just how many pounds of sterling?
> Upon the hood you spread your wings to the skies
> And like a Goddess sing "God Save the King"

Finally, in a letter from Joseph to his daughter Liliane dated January 11, 1971, we learn that "Yesterday Lucien started recording Melody Nelson, and the session will last all week. He's happy with his lyrics." He is, in fact, in the studio until January 14, and then he spends three days mixing in early February. The album ends up having seven cuts, including two longer than seven minutes. Over a rocking rhythm track of drums/bass/guitar there is an orchestra some 50 strong and in certain places a back-up choir of 70 singers.

JANE BIRKIN: *"Jean-Claude Vannier played a big role in 'Melody Nelson.' The Vannier years are marked by a certain "color," the color of his orchestrations. He's very modest and very sensitive, and he suffered when the media gave all its attention to Serge, which was completely unjust and yet inevitable."*

The story starts off with an innocent quatrain that sets the scene, provides the ambiance, and introduces our hero:

> The pylons graze the chassis of my Rolls Royce
> Which in spite of me has wandered free
> My Rolls seems called here by some sort of strange voice
> A dangerous, desolate place to be

He then dedicates these lines to the silver Venus hood ornament, whose weightless wings soar past the outposts:

> *Haughty and scornful, while the radio blares out*
> *Covering the silence of the motor*
> *Perspective's lost, she leads my mind astray*
> *Ignoring all the sidewalks that I rout*

Lost in his dreaming, the narrator and his Rolls run down a red-headed girl. The story continues with the "Ballade de Melody Nelson":

> *A little animal*
> *This Melody Nelson*
> *An adorable tomboy*
> *A delicious little child*

RÉMY AUCHARLES: *"Even tough he was sometimes fatigued, Serge was doing really well at that time. Jane was always with him and took care of his every need. What hit me was how distressed she would get if Serge wasn't doing well. It was catastrophic for her. She was maternal with him, and they were so tender with each other in the recording booth."*

The cover of the album, which is released during the second half of March, 1971, leaves no doubt about the identity of Melody Nelson. Even under the china doll make-up, rosy red cheeks, and curly red wig we can see that Jane=Melody and Melody=Jane. The photograph by Tony Franck really makes her seem like the fourteen and a half year old girl the song describes, even though we know that she's hiding her pregnancy behind her favorite toy, Monkey. Still, the "Waltz de Melody" is ephemeral, and the drama inevitable:

> *The sunshine is scarce*
> *No happi-*
> *Ness just strife*
> *And love's lost*
> *As we wan-*
> *Der through life*

JANE BIRKIN: *"We hear unusual instruments on that album, ones that we're not at all used to hearing, which gives it something mysterious, mystical, oriental, something pure and perverted at the same time."*

JOSEPH GINSBURG: *"Lucien called us up and said, "Grab a taxi and come*

over to our place at six!" He had us listen to the 'Melody Nelson' tapes. It
was monumental, an avant-garde work!"

> Ah! Melody
> You would have made me do
> Such foolish things
> Hey hey hey ho
> It's dada daddy-o

> Oh! Melody
> Love's a thing that's never come your way
> As you've told me
> But is there any truth to what you say?

Histoire de Melody Nelson is deemed by the press a major album, and dubbed "the first true symphonic poem of the pop age," with more superlatives to follow. When interviewed by reporters, Serge draws a comparison with Arthur Hiller's hit tear-jerker, starring Ryan O'Neal and Ali McGraw: "*Love Story* is a gumdrop. *Melody Nelson* is a Red Hot." Serge gives Gérard Jourd'hui, from the "superweekly" *Pop Music*, the following explanation:

On the level of phrasing, the question of whether or not to sing in French is still being debated. In jazz, it's an unsolvable dilemma. As for rock and roll, the groove sometimes permits it – it has those unique tonic accents – but I've been careful to simply speak instead of sing. As for the theme, it's perhaps taken from my life: the story of a 40 year old man with a pretty young girl. As for death, it's been eliminated so that love remains eternal.

RÉMY AUCHARLES: *"He was a real perfectionist when it came to the sound. He had very precise ideas concerning the arrangements, the chord voicings, the piano, and the vocals. He intervened a lot in the actual mixing, which was unusual for him because he always knew how a song would come out in the end. He knew the result in advance."*

GAINSBOURG: *"I don't do the orchestration, but I always work closely with the arranger: I hear the trumpets, I hear the violins, the woodwinds, the tubas – I hear it all... and I never want a tuba replaced by a cello. I am very precise about what I want. So yeah, I don't write out arrangements, but I don't feel guilty about it. Mussorgsky didn't do his own orchestration either."*

But the story doesn't end here. The driver of the Rolls, in love with Melody, takes her to "L'hôtel particulier" at "fifty-six, seven, eight ... whatever, on Rue X":

> *If it's free, room forty-four and I'll pay extra*
> *It's the room round here they call the Cleopatra*
> *`Rising from the big black ornate bedposts*
> *Are four tribesmen with torches all aglow*

But little Melody longs for the skies of Sunderland and steals away on a 707 that never reaches its destination. In a distraught murmur, a voice floats over a repetitive bass line. It's our delirious narrator:

> *I know of sorcerers who can pull planes from the skies*
> *In the jungles of New Guinea*
> *They look to the clouds and lust for all the pennies*
> *That the wreckage will bring them when everyone dies*

Like the island's primitive natives, the narrator, obsessed with Melody, also implores the deities:

> *And the hope remains alive in me*
> *That a plane crash may reunite*
> *Me with my long lost minor Melody.*

The inside cover of *Melody Nelson* gives us a peek at Gainsbourg's new look: long hair and a five o'clock shadow, which in 1971 is something new.

JANE BIRKIN: *"I think I had had an influence. I bought him his first pair of Repettos from a discount bin and I begged him to grow out his hair and beard. I like guys with sloppy beards because they have that needy look, and I think it gave his face a pretty, sculpted quality. He had too smooth a look when he was clean shaven, like Oscar Wilde. I didn't like it so much. I like a sort of haggard look. I can't stand it when people spend too much time on their appearance. Plus, for him it was like he'd finally gotten over his adolescence because he hadn't had a single hair on his face before he was 25 or 30. That was part of his eastern heritage, and the fact that he wasn't so hairy was something I found exquisitely refined. He was really bothered about it in the army and had a huge hang-up about not having to shave, kind of like me having no breasts when I was at boarding school, with all the girls laughing at me."*

In mid-March, there's the promotional push by Philips, and the company really believes in the record. The walls around Paris are covered with posters and the sidewalks are studded with stickers reading simply "Melody Nelson."

> FRANÇOISE HARDY: *"It's one of my favorite albums. Musically, it's completely new, extremely original, and pure in an inimitable way. I know from having spoken with plenty of musicians that this record influenced a lot of people."*

> ISABELLE ADJANI: *"I adored it. It was musical literature. I felt like I had slipped into some book I loved, a world both ideal and ominous, everywhere signs of both joy and death. I remember that my love for the dark side came from him and that horrified my parents. For them, darkness is synonymous with mourning, but Serge had transformed this concept..."*

So at that time, exactly how innovative is *Melody Nelson*? First, it's a concept album (a term popularized in England) which means that it's an LP whose separate songs are related by a narrative thread or common theme. Next, the songs are like nothing else we've seen: the usual structure of couplet/couplet/refrain/couplet/refrain is replaced by an extremely refined poetry set amidst pop music that is beautifully married to classical instrumentation. Ferré, as we have seen, pointed the way, but Gérard Manset's album, *La Mort d'Orion*, also played a role. It got a lot of play on Michel Lancelot's radio show Campus, where it created a craze upon its release in 1970. Gainsbourg may not have been the first, but he will remain the most significant influence and he will continue to explore the concept album in his next two works, *Rock Around The Bunker* and *You're Under Arrest*.

On April 13, 1971, Joseph sends Liliane his final missive. He's spending Easter vacation with Olia in Houlgate. He apparently receive two birthday telegrams, one from Serge and the other from Jane and Kate. Sitting on a bench at the little villa which he is renting for a few weeks, he lays the plans for a July trip to Saint-Nectaire. "I still need to shake myself out the doldrums. Lately, it hasn't been going so well in Paris. I'm tired," Joseph writes to his daughter, signing "The duo of Papa (darkly ironic baritone) and Mama (affectionate mezzo-soprano)." On April 22, at seven o'clock, he dies violently from a stomach hemorrhage at the age of 75.

GAINSBOURG: *"I passed through a terrible phase when my father died. Jacqueline phoned me and I could tell from her voice that it was something serious. I let out a cri de 'cœur:' "has something happened to mother?" It was really hard for her. She and Liliane were father's little darlings. He was playing cards and he just bled out... My sister and I cried all the way to Houlgate. When I walked up to his body I had a rather childish reaction: I thought he was angry, I was afraid he'd yell at me, I was ready to say: "Dad, I'll never do it again!" I found a charming little cemetery that looked over the sea... Later, Mama complained about not being able to go and meditate at his grave. It was too far for her. So I pulled some strings and found him a place in Montparnasse, just 20 meters away from Baudelaire. A few years later, Jean-Paul Sartre became his neighbor. Then Mama joined him, and one day I'll take my place there...*

... Later I had this mind-blowing dream. I know that my father was in a film around 1936. I've never seen the film, and what's more, he's just an extra in it. But in my dream I said to myself, "I'm going to go to the movies and see my dad..." I'm sitting in a big theatre, and there, up on the screen in black and white and bigger than life, is my father. I shout out, "Papa, it's me!" and at that instant he steps out of the screen, in color... And in the dream I was 50 while he was only 30... Being an atheist, perhaps because of my sins, I drew no conclusion from it...

... With my father, I guess it was like losing a friend. We were both shy lads. Still, he was there at all the important crossroads in my life: Les Beaux-Arts, Le Toquet, Le Milord l'Arsouille, Rue de Verneuil... He would cut out all the articles about me. When I was attacked in the press, he would respond to the reporters. I'd say: "No, dad, don't do that. Papers come and go but I'll always be here..." One day he complained: "What good is all your fame if we never see you anymore?..." I will never forget him!"

After Joseph's death, Serge spends a few days with Jane's parents at the Isle of Wight. Jane, Andrew, and Kate are all in tow. Then he gets back to promoting *Melody Nelson*. On May 23, 1971, we see him again on *Discorama* with the irreplaceable Denise Glaser.

SERGE GAINSBOURG: *I decided that the French were more or less allergic to modern jazz, which at the time I really liked. So I dropped jazz and went into pop. Now pop music, that doesn't mean cheesy trash, I never did that.*

You know what that means in French, right, the verb do?

DENISE GLASER: *The most glaring proof of that is certainly those songs of yours that have become international hits. Let's not exaggerate, but there's one song that really caused a stir [...] I'd really like to talk about "Je t'aime moi non plus."*

S.G.: *The French version was number one, which had never happened before. I thought I'd sell maybe 25,000 copies and I ended up selling 3.8 or 4 million. I hit pay dirt with that one. I'm going to be accused of being cynical again, but this job is about getting paid. But that's not cynical at all. It's the truth. The song made me a fortune. It wasn't calculated. I did the song because I found it beautiful and more erotic than anything.*

D.G.: *I'd like it if you spoke a bit about Jane. We see a lot of beautiful women here at 'Discorama.' This girl, she's like flower. There's nobody that looks like her.*

S.G.: *Well I hope she's a plastic flower because real ones, they wither. No, I really shouldn't say that. That's boorish. She is beautiful. She could have been my daughter, some 20 years younger. Yeah, I've been lucky. I think it's because of her that we had such success with "Je t'aime moi non plus." It's not me. I could feel it, and I put her name in big letters and mine really small... and her photo. It's a song that wasn't written for her, but rather for Bardot [...] I had sworn to myself that I would never again record it. I had Jane listen to it and at first she was shocked by the idea. Then I sat at the piano. We kept it in the same key – C major, like the original. She sang it practically a whole octave higher, which gave it a truly unique, juvenile feeling and made it such a hit. I'm not sure if the original would have been so successful internationally. I'd like to make that clear.*

D.G.: *You just said that Jane was shocked in the beginning by the subject matter and by the song itself. I'd like to know why.*

JANE BIRKIN: *I think it was the panting. I didn't understand the words because...*

S.G.: *She had just arrived from England and didn't speak French.*

J.B.: *[...] I blushed like mad when I heard it and I didn't want to listen to it again. After that it was a question of singing it, and I'd always loved the tune, the melody. It was very, very pretty. So I did it. I understand the people who were shocked by it, but I also think that it was pure. Serge is funny. He makes me laugh. After that, everyone said: "What are you doing with that cynical monster who hates women and everything." I didn't see it like that at all. That's how he seduced me, by being so funny like that [...]*

S.G.: *I'm not, like everybody claims, a cynic. I'm a romantic. Always have been. As a young boy I was shy and romantic. I only become cynical upon making contact with my fellow man. People hassled me because I was ugly and because I was upfront about things. They say I'm ugly, and that's fine. I am and I don't give a damn. It's worked for me. I once wrote: "When people say I'm ugly, I laugh very quietly so that I don't wake you." I was thinking about Jane when I said that. I've had some beautiful women in my days and right now I'm with the most beautiful. So if people are bothered by my ugliness, it's no big deal...*

J.B.: *I'm fine with the fact that others find him cynical. That way, his private side is all for me. I've got this dog that bites everybody but me. That's very nice. I don't like dogs that lick just anybody's hand. I like it when others say: "Your dog is a nightmare!" Because later he'll come to me all gentle. That's something very special.*

S.G.: *I once said on the back of an album cover, "Women should be taken for what they're not and left for what they are." That doesn't apply to her.*

J.B.: *Anyway, that's not true. Sometimes you say things that are pretty but completely false.*

S.G.: *No, that was for the others in my past, but not her. With her, I take her as she is and I will not leave her. Maybe I'd leave her if she pretended to be something she's not... No. I'd never leave her.*

On July 22, 1971, in a small private clinic in London, little Charlotte makes her way into the world.

JANE BIRKIN: *"While I was giving birth, Serge and my brother were getting plastered on banana liqueur across from the clinic. Every 15 minutes they'd come to the door and listen through a stethoscope. She was very pretty when she was born and Serge just completely lost it. After four or*

[381]

five days there was a huge drama. Yul Brynner, her godfather, showed up, but it was bad timing. The doctors had asked me to sign papers permitting them to change the baby's blood because she was jaundiced and her bili-rubin had risen to alarming levels. The clinic wasn't equipped for this, so they took Charlotte away to Middlesex Hospital. I was sick myself, with a virus I'd gotten in Yugoslavia. Serge really wanted to see her, but the baby was checked in under my name and they wouldn't let him in no matter how he begged. What's worse is that the next day, coincidentally, the papers wrote about a madman who was attacking babies in the hospital! Sounds like a joke but it's true. Haggard and desperate, there he was at two in the morning wanting at any cost to see his little girl! They finally let him in and he felt reassured."

GAINSBOURG: *"After that, I went back to Jane's little apartment over near Chelsea. It was the middle of the night, not a single bus or taxi in sight. I left on foot and it started to rain. I must have walked about two hours, traversing the whole of London. It was the most joyful stroll of my life. That night, I held happiness in my very hands."*

Meanwhile, the press has a field day when Serge and Jane themselves announce: "We're getting married in the spring of 1972, six months after the birth of our baby."

JANE BIRKIN: *"We weren't trying to be provocative. Both of us believed it. It was all planned out. He wanted to get married at the Gare de Lyon. He said he'd decorate the banquet hall there with white balloons. We'd have a masked ball and we'd hop on a train going who knows where. He'd even arranged it all with a decorator and Georges Cravenne, who organized all the big Parisian parties. Then I hesitated at the last minute. I felt the party and the marriage had gotten out of hand, that it had all become one enormous publicity stunt. I asked him to give me a small wedding with only close friends, but Serge said, "Come on... At least one reporter from 'France-Soir!'"*

Serge trades the little key hanging around his neck for a Star of David from Cartier's. He then hooks up with Gréco once more for several tunes, including "Un peu moins que toute à l'heure":

Less than I did just a while
Still I love you
It dies a bit with every smile
Still I love you

His female interpreters, other than Jane of course, are becoming rarer. Still, Serge remains faithful to Régine, and writes for her "Laiss's-en un peu pour les autres" and "Mallo Mallory," a melodramatic tale that starts with a rape:

Mallory had barely just turned 16 years old
When one day there came a gangster nasty and bold
He took her on a cold floor that was covered in grease
She bit her hand until the nightmare came to a cease
And that bastard left her there
In her eyes a half-dead stare
Although mom had said quite clear
Watch your back my Mallory dear

In the different television shows that Serge participates in towards the end of 1971 - as prestigious as they may be - we see nothing approaching the quality of the work he released some six months earlier.[2] Fortunately, director Jean-Christophe Averty proposes a filmed adaption of *l'Histoire de Melody Nelson.* The shooting, postponed due to the birth of Charlotte, takes place in November, 1971. The special is broadcast on Wednesday, December 22 at 9:30 in the evening.

JEAN-CHRISTOPHE AVERTY: *"I had permission from the Belgian painter, Paul Delvaux, to use his paintings as backdrops for certain scenes in Melody Nelson. This collage of Delvaux's work, the sets that I designed, and some other visual trickery worked in perfect harmony with Serge's songs. Serge just laughed about it all, especially seeing me running around like a nut and popping out of the control booth 200 times a day to come and yell at the technicians. It was a madhouse. All the superimpositions and visual effects – he'd never seen anything like that."*

---

[2] The sales of Melody Nelson are disappointing - an estimated 20-30,000 copies.

[3] Marché International du Disque et de l'Edition Musicale, the world's largest music industry trade fair.

In December, 1971, at Francois Patrice's Club Saint-Hilare in Paris, then at MIDEM,[3] and later in January at the Whisky à Gogo in Cannes, Serge attempts to introduce a "vertical suite," as he puts it, based on "Je t'aime moi non plus" as well as another almost liturgical melody called "La décadanse." His intentions are explained in a press release:

A slightly erotic dance that is at the same time less vulgar than the paso doble, where the man looks like a barnyard rooster. "La décadanse" is for intimate couples, couples now together, or ones that desire to be. When one dances a slow dance, whether or not the person is conscious of it, there is an ulterior motive. One wants to get his or her partner in bed.

> JANE BIRKIN: *"It was a great idea and a very original dance. I think people just didn't have the guts. Really, it's embarrassing for the girl because she has nowhere to look.[4] For the guy, it's fine. It was very exhibitionist. When Serge told me about it I said to myself: "How is it that no one has ever thought of this before?" I think the song is a religious hymn."*

> SERGE: *Turn away!*
> JANE: *No...*
> SERGE: *As I say*
> JANE: *Not like that!*
> SERGE: *And dance*
> *The deca-dance*
> *Yeah that's the way*
> *Move and sway*
> *Slowly*
> *Come my way*
> *[...]*
> SERGE: *God!*
> *Forgive our transgressions*
> *The deca-dance*
> *Has control*
> *And now our souls*
> *Simply wander astray*

---

[4] Her back is to her partner.

At MIDEM, "La décadanse" causes a minor scandal. The press speaks of "distressing and spectacularly bad taste." Anyway, the whole premeditated "coup" essentially fails. Beginning in 1972, there are certain members of the press that are starting to grow weary of the sensational media couple of 1969-70, regardless of the fact the *France-Soir* announces that the wedding is set (this time suggesting some 900 guests at Maxim, all dressed up in Empire fashion, with Gainsbourg himself supposedly coming as Napoleon at the Pont d'Arcole). *Melody Nelson* has certainly found critical praise, but not success. Is the triumphant hero behind "Je t'aime moi non plus" - after having "cashed in," as he confided to Denise Glaser – once again becoming the fringe poet, the respected composer who can't sell records, just like 10 years ago? That's it exactly. He has just released the first of four essential recordings (Melody will be followed by Vu de l'extérieur, Rock Around The Bunker, and L'homme à tête de chou) in which sales will be inversely proportional to artistic merit. Art with a capital "A" - that doesn't bother him. But poor sales? A return to square one? Not really. However, in the coming months we will see the realization of one of his worst fears: becoming "Mr. Birkin."

O Di Doo Di Doo Dahe

On February 14, 1972, Serge invites Jane's parents to Zizi Jeanmaire's opening night at the Casino de Paris. It is understood that after the show, the next stop is Deauville, where they arrive at two in the morning. Serge, apparently, has no desire to go to bed and so he drags Jane's mother to the casino.

> JUDY CAMPBELL-BIRKIN: *"He bought me 500 francs worth of chips and said he wanted to see me play. So I started to win, time and time again. The chips just piled up, and I very proudly told him that I was going to cash in and go back to the hotel. "No! You can't just stop like that! When you're winning you've got to keep playing! - And if I start to lose, then I can quit? – No! If that happens you keep going till you've lost it all!" That is, of course, exactly what happened."*

Distraught by the lousy sales of his previous two records, Serge accepts a deal to write the jingle for a commercial featuring a new men's fragrance by Caron. As for the films, things have cooled down a bit. Jane will from now on follow her own career path, not wanting to expose herself to the insinuations of scumbag journalists who are constantly pointing out that one never sees her onscreen without also getting Gainsbourg acting in some supporting role or maybe even writing the score. In fact, at the end of 1971, Serge accompanies her to Rome to shoot a dog of a film that rivals even the inanity the toga movies he did in the early sixties. This time it is a vampire movie: *Les Diablesses*, by Anthony M. Dawson (alias Antonio Margheriti). Serge plays a police inspector and is forced to wear a Sherlock Holmes hat because the action supposedly takes place in a haunted house in Scotland.

> JANE BIRKIN: *"I was almost certain the film would never come out. No such luck. In January, 1974, I'm walking by the Georges V one day and see that 'Les Diablesses' is playing. They'd changed the title to suggest that it was some lesbian story. There was a photo of me and another girl, and they added Serge's name so that it would be risqué. It was hilarious [...] I got completely disguised when we went to see it, afraid that someone would recognize me amidst the bustling crowd. It was a needless precaution. There wasn't a soul and so I dropped the disguise. We laughed so much during the film that people shushed us!... We even got yelled at!"*

In Richard Balducci's *Trop jolies pour être honnêtes*, which they film in the spring of 1972, Serge plays an Italian gangster and once again composes the score. The film is Jane's first comedy and her way of signaling the end of a certain era. Bernadette Lafont is among the co-stars:

> BERNADETTE LAFONT: *"It's the story of four girls who do a hold-up, with Serge as the head of the rival gang. We filmed in Tarragone, near Barcelona. I remember that one evening, after drinking a lot of green Chartreuse, Jane and I dared one another to go and take a midnight dip. Serge in no way wanted to join in. I can still see him grumbling on the beach, his dog doing the same at his side, more and more afraid with each second that Jane would drown the further we got from shore."*

He was right to have worried, especially if we are to believe the story of that insane night in Paris which took place just before that. Jane narrates:

> JANE BIRKIN: *"We were at Castel's and I'm pretty sure I was plastered. It didn't take much. Then again I was no saint, either... Serge did something that evening that I found to be the most vicious thing in the world: he turned my wicker basket over and emptied it out in front of everyone. Goaded on by the crowd, I noticed a pie just within reach... He was right in front of me and it took just seconds to grab the pie and toss it in his face... I immediately realized that it was something you just never do. Never in all your life should you do something as vile as hit someone with a cream*

pie in public... And Serge was great about it. He got up and walked to the door with pie falling from his face at every step, left Castel's, and walked straight towards Rue de Verneuil. Having no idea how I'd get out of this one, I got up, rather stupid looking and not at all dignified like him... There was almost no more pie left on his face when he arrived at the corner of Rue de Verneuil. Suddenly I had an idea: I would run past him and throw myself into the Seine... Neither of us was thinking very clearly... And it worked, because he saw me dash by him and he came running after me. He followed me, because after all, he is very kind, and he wanted to know what was going to happen. I crossed Quai Voltaire and sped down the stairs, taking four steps with each stride. Soon I saw Serge standing on the same steps, trying to get a glimpse of me, and three seconds later I found myself in the Seine. I was really screwed because I didn't know how to swim and plus there's a nasty current... I was fished out by Serge and some firemen. He forgave me for everything, which was just like him, and we walked home arm in arm. My Yves Saint Laurent blouse had shrunk five inches... When I think back on it, the whole thing seems so charming. I can't get over the naïveté ... I think that memories like this belong to a world without cruelty..."

Now we come back to France Gall, the singer who had "saved his life." It's like she has just stumbled out of the desert. The innocent little pop-tart of the mid-sixties doesn't know how to re-invent herself. Sylvie Vartan is doing American-style variety shows and Sheila is performing pop tunes, catering to the lowest common denominator. But France had simply retired from the business to give herself to Julien Leclerc and their perfect love. In 1972, however, she wants to make a comeback. Bertrand de Labbey, Julien's manager and record producer (also Gainsbourg's future agent), takes charge of finding her some songs.

BERTRAND DE LABBEY: *"I called Gainsbourg and he was exquisitely courteous. I thought he'd tell me to take a hike because France hadn't sold any records in such a long time. He wrote two pieces for her: "Frankenstein" and "Les petits ballons." I supervised the production in the studio. Serge was in charge of the session, and infinitely respectful of everyone. It was marvelous working with him. We were naturally disappointed that it wasn't more successful."*

It seems, though, that Serge is really straying off track, giving France these novelty tunes fit only for a television show. Who can expect a comeback with some trivial song like "Frankenstein," no matter how amusing and clever it may seem:

> It took a guy with brains like ol' Einstein
> To slap one in a guy like Frankenstein
> And make from all the dead men on the block
> A corpse that walks

FRANCE GALL: *"I came back to see him then because nothing at the time was working, and he, along with Jean-Claude Vannier, agreed to write two songs for me. The words were perfect, but not what I was expecting. I wasn't happy about recording them. That's when I understood that he'd said to me everything he had to say. Really he never knew me. He was only interested in what he could project onto me."*

"Les petits ballons," which rides atop music by Jean-Claude Vannier, clearly illustrates what France is talking about: Serge continues to confuse her with a doll, this time one made neither of wax nor sound, but rather latex:

> With your mouth you blow me up and
> When I reached desired size
> Mouth to mouth and hand to hand
> We are free to improvise
> There's nothing that can move me, no
> I'll never feel a thing
> Only if you touch my balloons
> Does my heart begin to sing

The other little doll that Serge dotes after is Charlotte. Behind "shocking" photographic evidence, *Paris-Match* reports with its typically impeccable taste: "The champions of anti-conformity - the outlaw couple - have been transformed into a picture of domestic bliss by Baby Gainsbourg."

In the fall of 1972, Serge and Vannier together compose the score to Claude Berri's *Sex-Shop*, which comes out on October 25.

CLAUDE BERRI: "It was a comedy about the new relaxed morality, swinging, and pornography, so the climate of the film perfectly reflected the real universe. I played a bookseller facing bankruptcy who transforms his store into a sex-shop. I asked Serge if we could use "La décadanse" and I asked him to do original music."

Speak whore, open up and tell me
What it was like with you and he
And was it better than with me
Just how much and in just what way
You vicious cunt, what did he say?
And did he take you all the way?

In the meantime Jane starts filming Roger Vadim's *Don Juan 73* with Brigitte Bardot. In one scene we see the two beauties naked together on a bed. The script called for them to sing a song, and Brigitte teasingly suggests "Je t'aime moi non plus."

Serge starts writing the words and music for Jane's first album, but we also see him a lot on TV. On November 4, 1972, he performs "La noyée," the most beautiful of his unreleased songs. On November 11, he's back on *Top à...* for a show dedicated to his pal Régine. He returns on November 29 for a show with Petula Clark, where he does "Les anthropophages" with Petula, Dalida, and Claude François. The last weeks of this quasi-sabbatical are dedicated to Jane's first album with Vannier. In January, 1973, we get the 45 "Di Doo Dah":

Di doo di doo dah
Oh di doo di do dah
Melancholy, disenchantment reign
Di doo di doo di doo dah
Oh di doo di doo dah
This messed-up boy is giving me a pain

JANE BIRKIN: *"These songs come across immediately as portraits, mini-interviews. I was lucky in that I inspired in him these little films. I only wanted to sing sad songs, but he wanted songs that were also funny and rhythmic."*

"Encore Lui" works as a master shot of a wild run through the streets of Paris in which a host of religious references appear in a none too haphazard fashion:

I go down to la Chapelle
And that man he follows me
I head for Rue Evangile
Turn around and there is he
Rue de Rose, Rue de Fillettes

Turn around
He's there you bet

For "Puisque je te le dis" Jane sits at the bar, playing the role of a chick who's had her fill of some sentimental fool:

Since I'm telling you now
Oh, I love you so
Since I'm telling you how
You're ever so droll
We've been talking now for
Two hours at least

There's a conclusion in the form of a confession, over a pretty Vannier melody, in which Jane affirms that one can take her or leave her just as she is, because after all, "C'est la vie qui veut ça"...:

I would like to tell you that I'm faithful
But for starters I think that would be unwise
For don't you see that's it's not true and that you'll never
Ever know what to expect from me

During the sessions for *Di Doo Dah*, Gainsbourg and Vannier will part ways after three years of very fruitful collaboration.

GAINSBOURG: *"He's a truly great musician, but one day we had a big fight. We were both completely plastered and he said to me: "Listen, it's simple – you've made me play second fiddle." And I said: "So beat it, then!" He could have been one of the greatest orchestrators, but he's so intelligent and hyper-sensitive that he told himself: "If I do that I'll get nowhere." So he decided to perform onstage."*

In fact, Vannier later releases several albums on Filipacchi and RCA, writes the soundtrack for Martin Veyron's 1985 film *L'Amour propre*, gives concerts at Dejazet, releases some all too rare albums (*Pleurez pas les filles*), and even publishes a collection of stories, *Le club des inconsolables*. In 1996, five years after Serge's death, he works again with Birkin on the album *Versions Jane*, later touring with her.

JANE BIRKIN: *"Afterwards, Serge always paid close attention to what Vannier was doing. He really liked the kid. He went to see him in concert, and he even sang with him I think. Vannier is very endearing. He never changes: he's an adolescent who loses his temper with grown-ups, which is what happened with Serge. It was a real father/son relationship, with the same break-ups, the same difficulties, the same attachments. Serge never had another relationship like the one with Vannier. They were on the same wavelength, and there's never been anything like it since. He really respected Vannier, and was very proud to see him evolve as a composer and performer. I believe he felt like he had launched his career."*

The absence of Vannier's skills as an arranger will be all too evident on the next two albums, when the responsibility falls to Philips' Alain Hortu and keyboardist Alan Hawkshaw and his group of London session men, whom Serge had discovered during the *Di Doo Dah* sessions. Born in 1937, Hawkshaw gets his start in a beat group, The Checkmates, in the early 1960s before becoming a session player for a number of British pop stars, including Tom Jones, Dusty Springfield, Engelbert Humperdink, and Shirley Bassey. He also does television music and makes easy-listening albums. Over the years, he works with Cliff Richards and Olivia Newton John, and he is involved with the albums *Rock Around The Bunker, L'homme à tête de chou*, and all of Jane's albums up to and including *Amour des feintes.*

From March 26 to March 28, 1972, Serge records the instrumentals for what will become Vu de l'extérieur. Like with *Melody Nelson*, the notes from the session tell quite a story. We find several scuttled tunes ("Tout mou tut doux," "Les papiers qui collent aux bonbons") and others that will evolve over the course of the sessions ("Dans les nuages et la musique" becomes "Pamela Popo" for example).

Next, six arduous weeks are dedicated to writing the lyrics. He maintains radio silence at Rue de Verneuil and his name appears but once in the press, on April 18, 1973, when Serge July tells the newspaper *Libération* that he needs another 230,000 francs to start his new publication. He then thanks the generous donors, who include Jean-Pierre Chevènement, Alain Geismar, Jean-Paul Sartre, Maurice Clavel, Jeanne Moreau, and Serge...

On May 5, Serge plays the joker at the annual gala for the Union des Artistes, dressing up as a convict and imitating a tightrope walker. It's later broadcast on television. From May 7 to May 11, then again on May 14, he lays down the vocals to *Vu de l'extérieur*. Then on the May 15, he has a heart attack.

JANE BIRKIN: *"I came back after a long day of filming and found two women in my living room who should not have been there. They asked me to sit, and my world just crumbled to nothing. We'd had such crazy times together that I'd forgotten he was a flesh and blood person, with a heart and veins. The night before we'd quarreled because he'd kept me up. I was nasty that night. Serge's villain thing might be a pose, but so is my nice girl persona... So I went to see him at the American Hospital and I found little Lucien Ginsburg there. Little devil was putting everybody on, pulling out the connection to the "beep beep" sound on the heart monitor to make all the nurses come running. When they showed up he would make faces at them. I later found out that when he left the house at Rue de Verneuil, he refused the blanket that the ambulance drivers wanted to put on him. He didn't like the color, so he took his cashmere blanket instead. Plus, he insisted on walking to the ambulance because he didn't want to be seen in a stretcher. He even took the time to pack a briefcase full of Gitanes because he knew there would be restrictions at the hospital. It really didn't scare him as much as it should have."*

"I was quite frightened," Serge tells the magazine *Les Inrockuptibles* in 1990. "I had a paralyzed arm, high blood pressure. I started to cry. I was alone. Jane was shooting a film. For 15 minutes, I thought it was curtains." He does find the strength to call Odile Hazan, the wife of his boss at Philips, whom he is very close to. She manages to save his life by sending help immediately.

JACQUELINE GINSBURG: *"After a few days in the hospital, he started insisting that Jane bring him Old Spice spray-on deodorant. Everybody wondered, "Where has this newfound obsession with cleanliness come from?" In reality, he was smoking and just using the deodorant to mask the smell. The only time he didn't smoke was in intensive care because he thought the oxygen would explode."*

JANE BIRKIN: *"Three days later, he was so sad. Nobody knew he'd called a reporter from 'France-Soir' and given him an exclusive interview from his hospital bed. He wanted people to know that he'd almost died. He made me go out and buy all the papers to make sure that no world event pushed him back to page three. Then he framed the cover. It wasn't anything freakish or unwholesome. For him it was proof he was loved."*

Serge gets pretty serious for six or eight months after the incident, going without almost any alcohol or tobacco. The hospital had diagnosed him – already – with the beginnings of cirrhosis.

DR. MARCANTONI: *"I started caring for him in 1975. Before me there was another cardiologist who died. His first incident was actually a small infarction on the posterior wall of his heart, which is to say it was minor. Sure, I felt guilty about not being able to persuade him to take more precaution, especially to smoke less. I really don't think he smokes for pleasure. Rather it's gestural, part of his look. In a sense, his alcoholism protected him from his heart attack. In France, we have a lower rate of cardiovascular disease, and the only reason seems to be alcohol..."*

JANE BIRKIN: *"Then I took him to Normandy to recuperate. I was near Lisieux, where I own a little presbytery. After a few days, I think I see some tobacco on his teeth and I scream: "You're smoking!" He says: "No! Not at all! It's just pepper from the Bloody Mary I made myself." I didn't notice anything until we got back to Rue de Verneuil. As usual, he took his dog Nana for an evening walk, but this time I was suspicious. I watched him until he turned the corner, and when he got back I asked him to kiss me. He tasted like tobacco. I slapped him hard. I was crying, and I ran upstairs to call my father. I told him: "Serge has been secretly smoking for six months!" and he answered: "That was a mistake. Now Serge will smoke in front of you and the dog will just piss on the balcony, which is bad all around. You should have pretended to ignore it."*

It's November, and Serge happens to appear in a TV movie, *Le Lever de rideau*. Also, for a month now, "Je suis venu te dire que je m'en vais" has been playing on the radio, and people are discovering the album *Vu de l'extérieur*, with its superb cover by photographer Jean d'Hugues, in which Gainsbourg's head is surrounded by big shots of chimpanzees, orangutans, marmosets, and other baboons.

JEAN D'HUGUES: *"Everyone thought that "Je suis venu te dire que je m'en vais" was Serge saying he was leaving Jane, which was not at all the intention. In his mind, it meant "I'm going to die and I have to prepare you for that." When he played it for me, we were in the living room at Rue de Verneuil. When Jane came home, he stopped the recording. "She can't stand this song," he said. Then he took his cigarette and his glass of whis-*

key and shoved them into my hands, saying: "If she asks, it's you who are smoking and drinking!" The cover was his idea. He wanted it to look like old family photos, stuck together haphazardly, only he wanted a family of monkeys that were all better looking than him. He insisted that I find a proboscis monkey. I used archival photographs and also added a few of my own, including a negative that we used on the back where he's walking out of a street urinal."

For the 45 of "Je suis venu te dire que je m'en vais," Serge offers us a rereading of Verlaine's "Chanson d'automne." The poem had already been set to music in the 1941 song "Verlaine," by his idol Charles Trenet – a detail that Serge cannot ignore. Gainsbourg deconstructs it, rearranges it, and makes, with the same pieces, a different puzzle, creating the classic that we know. It is magnificently reinterpreted by Jane onstage at the Casino de Paris:

> *As soon as it happens, you're breathless and you're pale*
> *This farewell it is true*
> *I regret telling you*
>   *Telling you that it's all through*
> *I loved you, but what can I do*

The final sessions for *Vu de l'extérieur*, which include the mixing, take place on September 17, 19, and 25 at Studio des Dames.

> *Your outsides, yeah baby they're stunning*
> *So on the inside, I know that baby you're cunning*
> *It's not nice, but rather nasty my belle*
> *So don't be surprised when I tell you to go straight to hell*
> *Go get screwed, go screw somebody fast*
> *All those old men, find 'em and then*
> *Go round shaking your ass*

Serge is happy at home, and even if he's still flipping out about his accident, his touch is light and humorous. He turns out songs with the sole aim of making us smile, such as "Panpan cucul":

> *When I drive some chick*
> *All over town I'm really thinking*
> *That it's just like giving her*
> *A little spanking*

"Take women for what they're not and leave them for what they are." The aphorism has become his leitmotif, and the characters we encounter are like something from the comics: the Incan princess in "Titicaca"; the black stripper in "Pamela Popo"; "L'hippodame," soft as a marshmallow, accompanied by her gigolo. In "Sensuelle et sans suite," he plays with onomatopoeia like he did in "Comic Strip":

A one night stand with you madame
It goes wham, it goes bam
Wham I take you girl, and then bam
I'm on the lam
These little dolls all fall for my scam
I lay it on, wham and then bam
Wham they're in my bed, then it's bam
Bye-bye, ma'am

At Rue de Verneuil, Michel Lancelot films an episode of his excellent series *A bout pourtant*, which is dedicated to Serge. He looks furiously punk: messy hair, crumpled shirt, three-day growth of stubble. In the December 19 broadcast we hear Serge declare:

When it all turns sour you have to sing about love, splendid love. When it goes well you sing about breaking up and other horrors. She's the woman I was waiting for. I didn't know it at the start – there was a mutation that took place. I believe she is the last, and if she leaves me... I love this girl, I can tell you that. I have never said that about anyone. [...]

I'm handsome, I'm superb, I've got money, I'm a success, I'm famous...

No, I'm getting carried away.

As a little kid I was super cute, then these ears and this nose started to grow. Now it's not as bad with long hair, but then it was trendy to have short hair and... the ears really stuck out more. Then I worked on my look, it got a little better... I think that men improve with age. Women fall apart and men get better. It's not fair, but that's how it is.

"Par hazard et pas rasé" hints at the theme of "Flash Forward" (from the 1976 album *L'Homme à tête de chou*) and harkens back to "Talkie-Walkie" (from 1964's *Gainsbourg Confidentiel*). The narrator makes a surprise visit to his fiancée, who is cheating on him:

Haphazard, haggard am I
I knock at her door
And who do I see

[398]

From out of the blue
A skydiver
The kind of guy
Who steals girls' hearts

The prettiest song on the album, "La poupée qui fait," is obviously dedicated to Charlotte:

A little doll who makes peepee-caca
Just a little doll who says papa
You've got to grab her by the sleeve
You shouldn't be unwise
Or she'll fall down and tears will fill her eyes

Vu de l'extérieur is rather well received by the press. In January, 1974, the weekly Pilote writes: "Serge Gainsbourg offers us an album that he wrote while staring at Petit Baudet's line of pink underwear for little girls. Even if it evokes curdled milk at times, or a certain mustiness, it's still enjoyable - amidst all those sheep bleating *je t'haiime* - to find someone who thumbs his nose at everything (at himself, at us) with such talent." In volume 86 of *Rock & Folk*, he's given a two-page piece called "The Adolescent Man." But despite Serge's numerous television appearances, "Je suis venu te dire que je m'en vais" doesn't make the slightest dent in the charts. The end of '73 and beginning of '74 are dominated by tunes like Johnny Hallyday's "Noël interdit," the Rolling Stones' "Angie," Pink Floyd's "Money," and Michel Fugain's "La fête."

Six months after his heart attack, Serge gives the magazine *Spectacle* an interview in the form of a confession, which is broadcast on television November 3, 1973:

I had some friends. Now I'll have fewer. I'm becoming a little more difficult. I was already a misogynist, and now I'm a misanthrope. You see, there's not much that remains, but I still have the essentials, like my children, my wife, and my work. That continues. With a more lucid mind and hands that no longer tremble - or at least very rarely. Alcohol had a very harmful effect on me. I was so completely saturated that I'd go all night long without any inspiration. I was moving really fast and I saw all sorts of landscapes pass me by, but I'd hit a wall. Now I know I have a minor heart condition, and I hope it won't get too serious. I hope I'll survive.

Jacques Dutronc is one of those few close friends. They had known and admired each other for years yet never worked together. Finally, and for the first time, Gainsbourg writes him some lyrics. Naturally, he is invited to be on *Top à... Jacques Dutronc* on March 2, 1974, where the two of them, along with Jane, perform "Les roses fanées" as a trio.

Serge writes "L'amour en privée" for Françoise Hardy. The music is by Jean-Claude Vannier, who meets up with Serge again for just this project. The song is for the François Leterrier film *Projection privée*, which is released in October, 1973 and wins Jane, the lead actress, laudatory praise from the critics, who are in love with her grace and beaming presence. As her biographer Gérard Lenne points out, even though the film is a commercial failure, it permits Jane to be taken as a serious actress after a series of third-rate films. In fact, she works constantly and her popularity steadily rises. After *Le Mouton enragé* with Jean-Louis Trintignant (1974), there will be a series of burlesque comedies: *Comment réussir quand on est con et pleurnichard, La moutrade qui monte au nez, La Course à l'échalote*. Success, yes, but the sort that risks to stereotype her as the sexy English girl with a funny accent. At that same time, trouble starts brewing between Serge and Jane.

> "Relations between a man and a woman in this business can be very trying. It's better if they're both at the same level. Just when Jane reached the heights of stardom, I started to crack. It was very difficult, almost like I was "Mr. Birkin." I never liked that. Everything seemed to be taking off for her, and while I was doing truly great stuff, there were still no gold or platinum albums. It was a distortion, and one that left me feeling ill at ease. I wanted to experience with her all the stress of fame. I was suffering at that time, and then presto-chango, I did "La Marseillaise" and the concerts at the Palace... "

Five years have gone by since "Je t'aime moi non plus" and its four million copies. The sales of *Vu de l'extérieur* top out at 20,000. Jane's album is a failure. It's funny how the sales of the couple's records are inversely proportional to their visibility! All this happens at a time when French song is in the midst of a metamorphosis. Slowly but surely, the new generation is gaining a foothold. It is foreshadowed by Julien Clerc and Veronique Sanson (and before them, Michel Polnareff, who was ruined and relegated to fiscal exile in 1974). Yves Simon picks up the baton starting in 1972 with "Au pays de merveille de Juillet," followed by Maxine Le Forestier's "San Francisco" in 1973. Soon we'll see Michel Jonasz, Gérard Manset, Jacques Higelin, and Alain Souchon. Some of them even grew up listening to Gainsbourg, but their public doesn't know this. In fact, there's a certain parallel between the years of 1971-1977 and 1958-1964, relatively speaking. Gainsbourg was an outsider from the Rive Gauche, an unconventional figure in the world of "nouvelle chanson." To the yé-yé, he was an old man. To the mainstream public he was a relic that was respected but not understood.

At the same time, there is an unconscious "chipping away" that takes place which paves the way for his success with reggae in 1979. Gainsbourg may not be selling to the masses, but he's always on the radio and on television. Each time, he's there to say something nobody else dares say, to adopt a position no one else would champion. He smokes, he's unshaven, he curses, he's cynical, he lip-synchs, and each time, his songs – without fail – contain something that will shock daddy or grandma. The little brats from eight to 12 who see Gainsbourg in the seventies may not be old enough to buy records, yet for some of them, it's something electric. They see something in this 45 year old punk. Once he finds the right musical vehicle, things will take off. And that, as we will see, is exactly what happens.

But in 1974, Serge makes a blunder. A few days after the death of the president Georges Pompidou, Valéry Giscard d'Estaing announces his candidacy for head of state. Like other artists (among them Johnny Hallyday, Charles Aznavour, Gilbert Bécaud, and Mireille Mathieu) Gainsbourg signs a petition of support for Giscard, which is expansively covered in the press and for which he is roundly snubbed by left-wing intellectuals through weeklies such as *Le Nouvel Observateur*. "If I supported Giscard," he tells Noël Simsolo one year later in an interview for *Absolu*, "the reasons were understandable. I have no fondness for Mitterrand. In the past, he was involved in some all too questionable business [...] I had long since identified Giscard d'Estaing as an upright and rather brilliant man. That's all... I should add that I was being willingly provocative in my choice, something that I haven't done in quite a while." Later on, he will justify his decision by calling it "Dadist," finally admitting: "Hey, I screwed up. I thought Giscard was a good minister of finance and a very good lieutenant-colonel. He turned out to be a shoddy general."

To comprehend this gaffe, one must understand the context. In 1974, the Union of the Socialist Left, led by François Mitterrand and Georges Marchais, invokes the ire of people like Gainsbourg who have a visceral hatred for communism, which in Serge's case is motivated by the Soviet Union's flagrant anti-Semitism. What's more, the presence of a number of pro-Palestinians in the French left is something that does not fit with his convictions, which are instinctive and familial rather than well thought out. Now chided, Serge would be careful to never again fall into that trap. Only in 1990 does he lend his name to another petition, and this time for a good cause: an appeal to the mayors of France to stand against Jean-Marie Le Pen's National Front...

On March 4, 1974, the eve of the presidential elections in France, there's another Top à... , this time dedicated to Gainsbourg, finally. Jane performs "Bébé gai," her new 45, and the Carpentiers give Serge carte blanche. He chooses the décor and runs the whole show, along with director André Flédérick. The guests include his dog Nana, Jacques Dutronc, Françoise Hardy, and Guy Bedos. Jane and Françoise perform "Les petits papiers" together. As a trio, Jane, Serge, and Dutronc do the "Les lolos de Lola," a comical and unreleased number:

> *Jane: Soldiers love me so*
> *Watch their passion grow*
> *For me*
> *Listen as I walk*
> *To all their sleazy talk*
> *They say*
> *Jacques: Oh what great*
> *Titties*
> *Serge: Lola's are such*
> *Pretties*

MARITIE CARPENTIER: *"There's really no rational criteria when it comes to Gainsbourg, so we were never worried when he screwed up his lip-syncs. What would be a disaster for someone else is normal for him. We offered him 'Top à...' knowing full well we wouldn't draw a large audience. What's more, the provincial press really made a fuss..."*

The reviews are in fact very negative. Pierre Jean writes in L'Union de l'Aisne:

On Saturday night, the Gainsbourg couple gave us the "Tops" in bad taste. They spent no less than an hour and a half assassinating us with dull-

ness in a program straight from the dumpsters of Paris's nouveau chic. It was pretentious, crass, and above all, incomprehensible. Why invite Serge Gainsbourg? He's talentless, filthy, and unshaven.

Obviously, Gainsbourg shuns the usually glitzy décor of *Top à...* in favor of a sort of warehouse, or suburban London parking structure, with red benches and other vague accessories strewn amidst the asphalt and metal girders. It does not please *Nice-Matin's* Monique Fort:

> *Nobody with any sense likes Gainsbourg. He's depraved, contemptuous, and sings like a dope fiend. On Saturday night, he invited us to a parking structure in some place as grimy and nondescript as he himself, all while gargling songs that nobody understands – at least nobody outside a very specific circle and certainly not the 8:30 crowd. It's nice to know that Annie Cordy will be on next week.*

It's a universe that perhaps does not appeal to the mainstream but which does catch the eye of producer Jacques-Eric Strauss, whom Serge meets two weeks later at the Cannes Film Festival. "I saw your show. I could tell that some of the ideas came from you. Day comes you want to make a film, come and see me." Gainsbourg really doesn't believe him at first. He takes it for the usual sort of festival bla-bla-bla. Still, the idea of directing is something he's been thinking of for the last 10 years. During the filming of *La moutarde me monte au nez*, while Jane is doing her "hurly-burly British" thing (*dixit* Serge), he starts writing the script for *Je t'aime moi non plus*.

Meanwhile, Just Jaeckin's *Emmanuelle*, starring Sylvia Kristel, has been doing monster business ever since its release in June, 1974. Serge had refused to do the music for this now legendary film, and the task was given instead to a rookie named Pierre Bachelet. It's a gaffe that will cost him untold riches, as he liked to say, seeing as how the film will run for another 10 years at the Cinéma des Champs-Elysées. He had predicted a mere 10,000 seats at Midi-Minuit! Indirectly, however, Serge profits from this iconic piece of yuppie erotica...

> GAINSBOURG: *"I'd acted in a short film that played for two years because it happened to be the lead-in to Emmanuelle. It was called 'Derrière Violette,' and I played the killer, of course. I was the "Eraser" - I snuffed out old fogies with a syringe..."*

Serge makes up for his blunder in 1977, doing the music for the third installment of the franchise, *Goodbye Emmanuelle*. But his lack of style – or maybe it's his lack of an arranger, seeing that neither Goraguer, Colombier, or Vannier are anywhere in sight – makes him miss out on another opportunity at the start of 1974...

> BERTRAND BLIER: *"I'd asked him to do the music for my second film, 'Si j'étais un espion,' in 1967. I met him at La Cité internationale des Arts, and he and Michel Colombier had worked out this great theme for me, really James Bond-ish. Then we lost touch until 'Les Valseuses,' for which I wanted him to do the soundtrack. I set up a screening of the working cut but he didn't like it. He later came to regret it. Maybe the film was too "in-your-face" for him. He likes to shock, but it has to be done with style – that was the dandy in him. Me, on the other hand, my provocation is crude and dirty. Or maybe he just felt a sort of jealousy or competition between the two of us. I didn't hold it against him though: 10 years later I used him for 'Tenu de soirée...'"*

After a couple of television appearances, Serge gets down to the business of writing his new album, which he will record from November 26 to December 2, 1974 at Phonogram Studios in London. The band consists of Alan Hawkshaw on keyboards, Alan Parker on guitar, Dougie Wright on drums (more than ever the minimalist beat man) Brian Odgers on bass, and for the first time since "Initiales B.B.," three female background singers.

> BRIAN ODGERS: *"While others would ask us to play the same piece 20 or 30 times, Serge got right down to business. He accepted most of our arrangements the first time he heard them. For 'Rock Around The Bunker,' we were hired for four days, and we worked from 10 in the morning till 10 at night. Later he added vocals and did the mixing. The last day, seeing as how we finished ahead of schedule, Serge found excuses to keep us around and improve certain numbers, but it was really so that we could earn a bit more money, which was very good of him."*

Is it possible to go too far? Upon the release of *Rock Around The Bunker* in 1975, we see fans, devoted ones, plunged into consternation, completely floored by this devastating album. Gainsbourg had not only struck a sensitive nerve, he had pounded upon it in a way that made the hypocrites flinch with indignant modesty. That being said, there were precedents. Others had used Nazi imagery with the obvious desire to provoke, namely Liliana Cavani in *The Night Porter,* the controversial film starring Charlotte Rampling and Dirk Bogarde. *The Rocky Horror Picture Show* is all the rage on London stages, with men traipsing around in corsets and garters, wearing swastika armbands. But Gainsbourg thrusts his knife into the wound with particular relish and devastating humor. Only he, the son of a Russian-Jewish immigrant who had worn the yellow star during the war and escaped the crackdowns, could be permitted this:

> *Slip into your nylons laddies*
> *Pull those garters over your knees*
> *Strap your fishnets to your panties*
> *Come on boys lets make it spicy*
> *Let's all dance the*
> *Nazi Rock Nazi*
> *Nazi Nazi Rock Nazi*

Did Serge chicken out at the last minute? "Nazi Rock" would have been a much better title for the album than *Rock Around The Bunker...* It's the Night of the Long Knives revisited: over a rock'n'roll soundtrack, he cuts into flesh, narrating the story of Otto, the "Tata teutonne":

> *All full of vermin and fleas*
> *Using his titties to tease*
> *Twisting them just as he please*
> *Firing his guns with such ease*
> *Tatatatata tata*
> *Ratatatata[1]*

It would be a mistake not to recognize in this album a longstanding and legitimate rancor. The targets of this chiding are not the bastards of 1939, but rather those of 1975, with Gainsbourg-Adolf asking who spilled the beans:

> *The voiceover I hear*
> *Is saying Adolf dear*
> *A catastrophe is near*
> *I just yawn and sigh*
> *I know it's a lie*

---

[1] "Tata" is French slang for queen, or fag.

JACKY JACKUBOWICZ: *"Before I was a TV personality, I was a press agent with Phonogram. I worked there from 1973 to 1980, and I took care of the "difficult" artists like Gainsbourg and Bashung – difficult in the sense that radio programmers were frankly offended at the suggestion that they play a record by Segre. When I went to see Monique Le Marcis at RTL, I got turned down flat. The only support I found was from the director of France Inter, where programs were broadcast at night in outlying regions. 'For Vu de l'éxterieur,' it was difficult; for 'Rock Around The Bunker,' it was almost impossible."*

In the bunker, Adolf goes mad because Eva keeps listening to her favorite American tune, "Smoke Gets In Your Eyes." Eva Braun actually did love the original 1934 recording by the Paul Whiteman Orchestra:

> *Eva loves "Smoke Gets In Your Eyes"*
> *Oh how'd I'd like it if some other guy*
> *Was fucking Mrs. "Smoke Gets In Your Eyes"*
> *In my eagle's nest*
> *Where we both rest*
> *Laughing slyly*
> *She spreads her knees*
> *And lets me see*
> *Her bearded lady*
> *But I am spent*
> *My nerves are rent*
> *Can't do it baby*
> *Not when I hear "Smoke Gets In Your Eyes"*

GAINSBOURG: *"The album was obviously an exorcism for me. I remember those girls, the English background singers, wishing me "good luck" when we left the studio. They'd figured it would be a tough sell. They thought I'd laid an egg, but for me it was a golden egg."*

On the album's title song, things go south. Hitler gets pounded in his bunker, and it's a bitter pill to swallow:

> *Bombs drop*
> *It's shock*
> *Walls rock*
> *Can't talk*
> *Sublime*
> *Metal*

It falls
The world
Is mauled
Death's mine
Rock around the bunker!
Rock around rock around!

Later on, obviously, there will be plenty of douchebags – Klaus Barbie and the like – who beat it for tropic shores and live the good life:

SS in Uruguay
The rabble here does as I say
Never getting in my way
Heil! They obey...

Sure, there are the "dopes who keep wishin' for some extradition," but Gainsbourg isn't crying out for vengeance. He'll leave the dirty work to someone else. Still... when interviewed in *Absolu* about *Rock Around The Bunker*, a reporter gets him to talk about the rise in terrorism (Palestinian, Red Brigade, the Baader group in Germany), and elicits this surprising response:

I prefer to play the destroyer. It's more fun. I'd liked to have been a terrorist. [...] If I became a terrorist today, I'd go to South America and blow away all the old Nazis. I'd also stop off in Spain. There's a former commissioner of Jewish affairs over there, a French aristocrat who's a doddering old fool. He asked if he could come back after Pompidou died. He's just an old fossil, but a bullet in the belly would serve him just right. That's a euphemism! What would I do if I saw him back in France? In a word, I'd buy a pistol and knock him off. In 1940, I was 11 years old and it's my only regret. I'm no coward in these situations. If the Nazis regained power, I'd warn them that I was an elite machine gunner in 1948. I still know the basics.

Serge is referring to the vile Darquier de Pellepoix, commissioner of Jewish affairs under the Vichy government, who hid out in Spain after the war. He was neither pursued nor convicted, and ended up dying there in 1978...

With this album, Gainsbourg truly wants to provoke, to toss insults around over a rock 'n' roll canvas. In the April, 1975 issue of *20 Ans*, he is interviewed by Alain Wais:

ALAIN WAIS: *It's not every day you hear things like Rock Around The*

Bunker in France.

SERGE GAINSBOURG: *How should I have put it? "Dansons autour de la casemate"? That sure wouldn't have gotten people grooving... [...]*

A.W.: *So it's to please the younger crowd?*

S.G.: *Groucho Marx said something very interesting about this topic. He'd just become a grandfather and they asked him how he felt. He said: "I'll never get used to being married to a grandmother." The public and women, they're the same thing: I'm ready to abandon that part of my public who've grown old and now spit on me.*

For the 1974 Christmas issue of *Lui*, Serge poses Jane for a series of photos that are now famous (one becomes the cover of her next album, *Lolita Go Home*), in which she is naked except for nylons, a pair of high heels, and handcuffs. The only décor is an iron bed. Then on December 27, the program *L'Enchaînement* is recorded, but because of a strike it is never broadcast. It does, however, contain the unreleased song "Telle est la télé," recorded especially for the occasion:

> They keep playing those old flops
> Before the war these bombs were dropped
> Hardly hits when they were wrapped
> Really they were crap
> Then they try to sell me books
> Useless ads with useless hooks
> And God knows if I pass the time just daydreaming
> Such is T.V, TV, TV is the thing

A rather insane anecdote from January, 1975: Serge contributes to the lifestyle magazine *Au fils des jours* for an issue dedicated to the evils of tobacco. Television studios - as can be expected given the nature of his latest album – have pretty much slammed the door in his face. There are a couple of exceptions, including an appearance on the March 8 broadcast of *Z'heureux rois Z'Henri*. On April 12, for the show *Un jour futur* featuring

Jacques Dutronc, he performs "Nazi Rock" and "Rock Around The Bunker." At the end of May, he's part of *Bouvard en liberté*, but there's no way he can do anything from the scandalous album. Instead, he does "Je suis venu te dire que je m'en vais" as well as "Comic Strip" in a duet with Jane. The only way that Philippe Bouvard can imagine to be provocative is to ask Serge to shave on live TV : "I know," he slyly says, "that when you make a public appearance you don't shave for three days before hand." Serge responds "Exactly!" and proceeds to cut himself while shaving, bleeding profusely. "Oh no!" moans Jane. "Come here my darling..."

It's all rather pitiful. In Giscard's France, where the hits are Serge Lama's "Je suis malade" and Michele Sardou's "Une fille aux yeux clairs," Gainsbourg is more and more the destroyer. And things aren't finished. In his new film, *Je t'aime moi non plus*, which monopolizes all of the last six months of 1975, he'll stir up even more shit. Jane doesn't hesitate for a second, and out of her love for Serge and for the story she inspires in him, she risks her career and jumps right on board for this sordid and sublime adventure.

eighteen

There Are Days I'd Give God Knows What To Be Able To Shit My Whole Being Away

It will be several months before filming starts on *Je t'aime moi non plus* in September, 1975, near Uzès in le Gard. During the first days of January, Gainsbourg starts recording a tune with the singer Dani. It's written especially for the Eurovision competition. Dani had already been selected to represent France in 1974's Eurovision with "La vie à vignt-cing ans," but when president Pompidou died, France decided not to participate because the competition was unfortunately on the same day as the funeral. Using a theme from "Boomerang," which is featured on the *Anna* soundtrack, Serge composes "Comme un boomerang":

> I can feel as booms and bangs
> Rip to shreds this tender heart
> Love is like a boomerang
> Coming back to where it starts
> I can feel the tears and pangs
> What I gave you has been torn apart

DANI: *"I'd run into him everywhere: Régine's, Castel's, where I worked at Alcazar's. He was a fixture of Parisian nightlife. The organizer in charge of Eurovision in France had a jury made up of people in the profession. When we presented "Comme un boomerang," they didn't want it, claiming that it was too provocative. But Serge refused to change a thing."*

[412]

Serge also takes the time to write lyrics for four new songs on Dutronc's February album, including "L'ile enchanteresse":

A thick lipped goddess did I find there
With kinky hair and kisses so fair
Standing on a little stool
My little whorish lovestruck fool
Shook her grass skirt while I drooled

Serge is probably thinking of Dutronc's "La compapade" when he goes to the studio in early July to record "L'ami Caouette," his first "summer hit" (he'll have two more with "My Lady Héroïne" and "Sea Sex And Sun").

When Dinah's tight
She'll dance all night
Dinah might[1]

Two pieces of news: first, Serge finds Philippe Lerichomme, a producer who finally is up to snuff; second, he gets a talented arranger in the person of Jean-Pierre Sabar, former accomplice of Hugues Aufray, Françoise Hardy, and Claude François. He'd used him as a pianist on *Melody Nelson* and on the song "Sex-Shop," and he runs into him again while working on the Dutronc album. Sabar is also hired as an orchestrator on Jane's second album, *Lolita Go Home*, and also for Serge's new 45. For "L'ami Caouette," Serge wants a West Indian rhythm. Sabar gets down to business and recruits Jean Schultheis for backing vocals.

SABAR: *"After Gainsbourg had his fight with Vannier, he proposed that I take over. I called Jean-Claude right away to tell him, and he said: "Go ahead. Don't worry about me. Anyway, sooner or later he'll dump you like he did me. He's done it with all his arrangers." And in fact he did end up dumping me, but our collaboration lasted through the Je vous aime soundtrack in 1980..."*

GAINSBOURG: *"The real drag was that kids would see me on the street and shout, "Hey! L'ami Caouette!" There's also another terrible story connected to this song. I was in Avallon with Jane, dining at the Relais de la Poste, and I suggested to the maître d'hôtel that he change his clothes and come have a drink with us at the bistrot. It was all fine at the start. He's*

---

[1] This is nowhere near the original, which in French reads "L'ami Caouette/Me fait la tête/Qu'a Caouette." The entire song is simply a play on words with proper names and rhyming homonyms. (T.N.)

buying us rounds and finally offers us a nightcap at his place. It was foggy and he led us out to the country... We went up to his loft and everything changed. It was like Jekyll and Hyde. He tells me: "Now you sing L'ami Caouette," and suddenly there was nothing friendly about his demeanor. I tell him: "Absolutely not. I sing only for money, and never in private. Not even in my shower." So the insane nut pulls out a shotgun and says: "I want you to sing!" But I'm unfazed, and just say to Jane: "Come on. We're out of here." A nice, quiet weekend turns into a nightmare."

One small problem: Serge is so busy preparing *Je t'aime moi non plus* that he has no time to deal with the lyrics for Jane's album. In fact, he writes the lyrics for only one song, "La fille aux claquettes." The lyrics are handled by Philippe Labro, who had also worked with Johnny Hallyday.

JANE BIRKIN: *"All Serge had was a title, 'Lolita Go Home.' It was sheer panic. Then Labro showed up with the lyrics. Neither Serge nor I were sure he'd be on our wavelength, but the words were great. The songs had a certain seediness that you don't expect from his work, and he was able to paint a very pretty picture of me..."*

PHILIPPE LABRO: *"Serge gave me themes, words, or titles, like "Lolita Go Home" or "Bébé Song," then he'd let me loose. I brought him the lyrics and he read them, sitting there smoking on his sofa in his amazing living room at Rue de Verneuil. Then he went to the piano, and there I saw him compose the songs for the texts, inventing melodic lines and refrains as he went along! It lasted all afternoon and all evening. In one session, without leaving the room, he wrote six melodies for my six texts. I was staggered."*

The album is released on time, with an attractive and sexy gold cover and a photo of Jane taken from the *Lui* "handcuff" sessions. Filming also starts on *Je t'aime moi non plus.*

GAINSBOURG: *"Jane was searching for a new style at the time. She could see the day coming when she'd never get offered anything but screwball comedies featuring her gimmicky English persona. Her impresario told her not to do 'Je t'aime moi non plus.' He said: "It'll ruin your career." But I knew Jane had real dramatic talent."*

In March, 1975, Serge is interviewed for the monthly publication *Best*, where he holds forth on the cinema: "I've never been used correctly, and I won't do any more of that stuff. Anyway, cinema is dead in France. Nice little actors and directors who make comedies. Just as mediocre as the world of music. I could only employ foreigners in a film. The only director I would work with is Elia Kazan. They all made me portray characters that were nothing like me. Still, acting is something I know how to do. That's all I've ever done."

Six months later, Serge reveals the intentions behind his first film as director:

Subject of part I:

It is a hyper-realistic and tragicomic relationship in a universe that could be situated either in America, France, or Italy. A marginal love lived briefly by two exceptional beings.

A crappy, yellow Mack truck with a figure of a pin-up girl on the side. Two homosexuals on board: Hugues Quester in the role of Padovan, introverted and tortured, always fiddling around in his plastic bag, and Krass (talk about a name!), alias Joe Dallessandro – buff, macho, steely-eyed.

The road leads straight to a desolate landscape, a sort of emotional and geographical no-man's-land, the asshole of the world. Also holding court there is a flatulist, Boris, who gets wasted on champagne all day and leaves little Johnny in charge of his snack bar. They serve burgers, Coca-Cola, orange juice... Everything there is American, which serves to accentuate the rupture with reality and neutralize the trivial. Johnny – a boy's name for a tomboy – is played by Jane without makeup, her long hair rolled up and hid beneath a short wig. Johnny, all flat-chested and skinny, short-haired, adorable and fragile. She lives through each hellish day with her irascible boss, looking out at a horizon that is at once deserted and inaccessible - a desolate countryside that surrounds her. Deserted, that is, until one day a crappy, old yellow Mack truck shows up.

Subject of part II:

Krassky, known as Krass, gay and vaguely Polish, and Padovan, an effemi-nate homosexual of Italian origin, make a living by using their truck to haul garbage from a nearby municipal dump. Krass is violent and taciturn, Padovan rather venomous. Johnny, the little, androgynous English girl, apparently pure as the driven snow, is named for her flat chest and big ass.

Krass can stand neither Boris and nor his fetid blasts, and each time he hears another trumpet call from flatulist's rear end, he lets out a torrent of abuse: "Disgusting motherfucker... Shit!" He starts flirting with the girl, doing the hetero thing, and she can't resist. This drives Padovan mad. Gerard Depardieu shows up next, a clumsy hick riding plow horse, and then Michel Blanc, pale and long-haired.

JACQUES-ERIC STRAUSS: *"Esthetically speaking, the visuals came very naturally to Serge because of his education. When we built the American bar at the airfield in Uzès, it seemed impossible. As a producer, I was worried. He just said: "You'll see. It'll look just like an American Bar. I promise." And American it was. Everyone was amazed. Everything was perfect down to the last detail. He had visualized it all in his head..."*

JANE BIRKIN: *"The first day we had to do a very complicated master shot that lasted six minutes. Serge had explained what he wanted the night before, and the next morning it was raining. We all felt miserable, really bad for him. The next day it was finally nice again and we dug into our ambitious shot.... Everything went swimmingly, and then... he cut it during the editing!"*

Originally, Serge thinks of Dirk Bogarde for the role of Krass, but an older man would have made it a completely different story. It's Anne-Marie Berri, the film's co-producer and wife of Claude Berri, who suggests Joe Dallessandro. He acts mostly in the films of Paul Morrisey and Andy Warhol, and is one of the "Warhol superstars." At nineteen, he appears in *Lonesome Cowboys,* and he follows that up with *Flesh, Trash,* and *Heat* - in short, the New York underground with all its emphasis on improvisation at the edge of nothingness and fleeting moments of near genius. Stunningly beautiful, Joe and his hips are featured on the cover of the *Rolling Stones Sticky Fingers* (designed by Warhol). He's just shot *Flesh For Frankenstein* (1974) with Warhol and Morrisey and also appears in Louis Malle's *Black Moon.*

Subject of part III:

Rides in the truck, Saturday night dances, fights, absentminded day-dreams about the public dump – it all starts to color their emotions. But at the hotel, Krass shows that his love is platonic. That's when Johnny instinctively turns over onto her stomach. Thus starts the sodomite love of Johnny and Krass. His excitement is cerebral, physiological, asphyxiating, paroxysmal, and in a word – orgasmic. His cries cause the couple to be chased from their flophouse to a whorehouse, where their next-door neighbors, either prostitutes or some couple that's just hooked up, are constantly up in arms, believing that they are the targets of an assassination attempt. The couple finally ends up completing their tryst in the cab of the truck, next to the public dump.

Kate Barry, just seven years-old at the time, only joins her parents on the weekends. One day, Depardieu notices she's bored and takes her over to some unidentified spot and tells her: "Come on, let's misbehave!" For two hours they amuse themselves by smashing empty bottles against the side of a wall...

Every Saturday, in the annexed kraut hangar/snack bar, there's a sleazy dance featuring the livid flesh of striptease artists. The local rock group – played by Au Bonheur des Dames – pounds out a suffocating slow tune (a ballsy version of "Je t'aime moi non plus") while Johnny and Krass embrace and a fat woman strips.[2]

JANE BIRKIN: *"'In Je t'aime moi non plus,' the theme is the despair of having to love someone at any price. Otherwise, life is just not worth living. When Johnny tells Krass "I'm a boy!", it's one of the most beautiful ways of wanting to belong to someone, in any way... For obvious psychological reasons, nobody but Serge could have written this film or have dealt with it in this manner. His sickness is infinitely more interesting than other people's health..."*

A piece of dialogue:
JOHNNY: *But you do love me a little bit?*

---

[2] The striptease was uncomfortable for everyone, and the fat lady in question was crying, finding it very hard to take the humiliation. As Ramon Pipin of Au Bonheur des Dames puts it, "There was the face of this ravaged girl, full of tears, and Gainsbourg kept shouting behind her to keep going. It was real harsh."

KRASS: *It's not important whether I take you from the front or the back. It's the fact that we're comingling, having a synchronized epileptic fit. That's love, baby. Believe me, it's rare.*

During the filming, they try to get Dallessandro to speak French, but Gainsbourg brings a quick halt to that.

JOE DALLESSANDRO: *'I understand what you're saying very clearly,'* explained Serge, *"that's not the problem. But when you speak French your face contorts and you no longer look like yourself." I thought at the time that it was a very polite way of saying that he didn't like my French!"*

Finally, Joe Dallessandro's voice is dubbed by Francis Huster. Willy Kurant, "One of the greatest and most hated [men] in France," according to Serge, is the chief cameraman. He had met him on the set of *Anna* in 1967 and then again for *Cannabis* in 1970 – both Pierre Koralnik films.

WILLY KURANT: *"When I was hired for 'Je t'aime moi non plus,' my glory days were behind me. I'd started in Belgium, where I was born, but there I was considered a fool. So I came to France in 1962 and did a few shorts with Maurice Pialat, and then I worked in TV as a war correspondent [...] covering the Cuban revolution, Cyprus, Vietnam, etc. Agnès Varda offered me my first feature, 'Les Créatures,' in cinemascope and black and white. Then there was 'Anna,' Godard's 'Masculin-Féminin,' Skolimowski's 'Le Départ,' two films with Orson Welles [...]"*

As previously stated, the film has a completely hyperrealist esthetic, or in other words it features heavily saturated colors, and simple, clean shots that are amplified by wide-angle framing.

WILLY KURANT: *"In terms of sensibility, where to place the camera, I immediately saw that he was a meticulous man who knew exactly what he wanted. He had slyly observed others working, even when he was shooting something wretched. Plus, he was trained in painting and architecture. He knew how to compose an image. I saw him move a bottle of Coke one centimeter right in front of a dumbstruck Joe Dallessandro, who was so shocked to see someone directing that it must have been a huge change from the enlightened amateurism of Warhol. Gainsbourg is a fringe character and he made a film that might be qualified as underground deluxe..."*

A piece of dialogue:

JOHNNY: *Why do you always look so sad? Krass: There are days I'd give god knows what to be able to shit my whole being away.*

JACQUES-ERIC STRAUSS: *"During the filming, the relationship between Joe and Jane became a sort of game. Serge put Jane in situations that would have been unacceptable with any other director. To push her beyond the limits of exasperation, he'd play at forcing her to go farther than she wanted to go. And it's true that in the middle of it all, Dallessandro started falling for Jane, which Serge, even though he may have been aiming for that, did not like one bit. Anyway, it didn't blow up. In the end it all finished amicably around a nice bottle of booze."*

HUGUES QUESTER: *"There were some bothersome moments. Jane really got into her role, and her relationship with Joe really made Serge jealous... Jane was hot and bothered by Joe's good looks and Serge became jealous of his creation. To direct someone you love in that sort of situation is very dangerous, and at the same time an exceptional act of love. Once again, he'd really put himself out there..."*

"It was sometimes strange on the set," says Michael Ferguson, Joe Dallessandro's biographer. "This was because of the strained relationship between Serge and Jane, which was steeped in alcoholism at the time. And that made Joe think about his own relationship with alcohol, especially his father's alcoholism."

WILLY KURANT: *"This film was very important for Jane. She was directed by Gainsbourg the filmmaker and not Gainsbourg the man. She listened and did everything he said. Her part is tragic, pathetic, and she played it to the hilt."*

JANE BIRKIN: *"I couldn't screw this up because he had written the role for me, physically, and that's something very rare."*

Serge digs into the editing in November, 1975, along with Kenout Peltier, whose name he'd seen on the credits in Bertrand Blier's *Valseuses.* The only time he leaves the cutting room floor is for one or two television appearances – a means of assuring continuing sales for "L'ami Caouette." His look is still the same and he seems to be falling apart even more and more. His nonchalance is always apparent, especially in terms of his appearance, and he makes no attempt to hide his "dirtiness" for those viewers offended by his mere presence. In the monthly *20 Ans,* he answers the incessant criticism voiced in the letters received from indignant television viewers:

TV viewers want you show up at their homes in a tux while they sit in front of a plastic tablecloth in a pair of slippers. So I show up at their homes just as you see me. It's really extraordinary, a completely aberrant notion. TV barges in and attacks us at home. We need to be in black tie for that? The only guy I want to see in a tux is the one I'm ordering champagne from.

In a November 22 broadcast of *A bout portant,* which is dedicated to Jane, she confirms for Pierre Bouteiller that Serge never says he loves her. "I've tried," says Serge, "spitting out bad dialogue like *baby, I love you...* But that's not my role. That's the role of composition." The conclusion of the conversation is certainly booze-fueled, but frighteningly sincere:

JB: *His personality is very forceful, but he lets me grow. It's like a kid holding on to a balloon. I feel like if he cuts the string I'll float away. I like being a balloon, but I always want to feel that string, or else I'd just explode in the sky.*

S.G.: *I think that more and more she'll have an impact in the world of cinema and that I'll have more and more trouble. [...] In fact do you want me to be prophetic?*

P.B.: *Go ahead.*

S.G.: *If she has any misfortune, I lose her. And I hope she does.*

J.B.: *You want to lose me?*

S.G.: *No, I don't want to lose you. Things get reversed, and what do you become? A crazy bitch. You become a crazy bitch because you're jealous as a tigress, because until now it's you who have been stuck with me, old girl [...] But if my film is a success - and I think it will be - I'll become a director and I'll be auditioning stunning broads and you'll be there going: hello? hello?*

In January, 1976, just after Donna Summer's worldwide smash with the Giorgio Moroder produced "Love to Love You Baby" (the first extended remix), the news reports that Louis Hazan, CEO of Phonogram and friend of Gainsbourg, was kidnapped on December 31 in front of his house on Rue Jenner. He is the first French businessman to fall prey to this sort of terrorist operation. It is organized and undertaken by the small group Ordre nouveau, which is linked to Italian gangsters. For reasons of security, there's a three-day black out imposed on the press. The kidnappers ask for 15 million francs. On January 8, Hazan is freed and the money is recuperated when the kidnappers are arrested. Serge, very close to Hazan's wife, Odile, is quite shaken up by the event...

Serge suffers a terrible lack of inspiration while finishing the editing on *Je t'aime moi non plus*. He's composed a considerable number of soundtracks since he first did *L'eau à la bouche* in 1960, but he can't manage to write the music for his own film and almost ends up calling in another musician. At the last moment he finally comes up with the superb "Ballade de Johnny et Jane," an instrumental that he will soon write lyrics to for a future Birkin 45. Featuring Jean-Pierre Sabar as arranger, the soundtrack album, released in 1976, also contains three instrumental versions of "Je t'aime moi non plus," as well as some banjo variations inspired by the movie *Deliverance*.

Je t'aime moi non plus comes out in Paris on March 10, 1976. The next day, France-Soir publishes an ultra-provocative interview republished many times under an eponymous title. Some noteworthy quotes:

> *–Do you love yourself?*
> *–No. I don't like shoving into my mouth what's just come out of my nose.*
> *–Snob?*
> *–Snobbism is a champagne bubble teetering between a fart and a belch.*
> *–They say you're skeptical.*
> *–Man created the gods. The contrary remains to be proven.*
> *–You're speaking seriously?*
> *–No, that's a joke.*
> *–When are you going to be finished with cinema?*
> *–You putting me on? I just started.*

So will his support for Giscard two years earlier pay off for Serge? At least he and his producers wind up with Michel Guy, Minister of Cultural Affairs, who agrees not to give the film an X rating, which would have limited its distribution and branded it pornographic – exactly what the rating was created for a short while ago. The reviews are published without delay. "I am neither puritanical nor prudish," proclaims Louis Chauvet in *Le Figaro*, "but frankly I found Gainsbourg's film unbearable, shocking, and provocative in the most vile manner [...] Still, there is a sort of mystery in it: just how does an artist come to write such a script?" Jacqueline Michel of *Télé 7 jours* says of Jane: "After this seedy, androgynous number, I don't think she will be featured in anybody's fantasies." Gainsbourg is crucified by *La Croix:* "Seeing as how I only visit public dumps when I have rubbish to dispose of, I will abstain from all commentary."

Robert Chazal of *France-Soir* seems to be one of the only critics to have understood the movie:

In his first film as writer and director, Gainsbourg takes us into a universe where happiness is a word void of meaning and where the borders are melancholy, derision, tenderness without delusion, and despair. He has, unlike any other French filmmaker, imposed upon us a vision very close to that found in the very best American films that deal with misfits and losers, such as *The Postman Always Rings Twice* and *They Shoot Horses, Don't They?*

One might also cite François Truffaut, who gushes with praise about the film over the radio, or Pierre Tchernia, who calls to tell Gainsbourg how he and he wife were moved to tears, or the magazine *Positif*, which provides an intelligent comparison between Je t'aime moi non plus and the American regionalist painting of Edward Hopper and Andrew Wyeth. On April 5 in *France-Soir*, we learn that Madame Raymond, Serge's and Jane's "forty-something nurse," has had her hands full since the film came out: every morning she has to scrub down the walls outside the house at Rue de

Verneuil "since every night brings more filthy and threatening graffiti," such as "Keep this up and we'll have your head." Some of them simply "question the director's manliness." Each day, the mail brings him a bevy of insults. Finally, we learn that at the theatre in Montparnasse, each showing "brings hissing and applause that is louder than any political rally..." There's one more result of the malaise generated by *Je t'aime moi non plus*: in following years, everyone who participated in the film comes to be seen as a pariah.

> WILLY KURANT: *"That film was just assassinated, and so was I. For months I had no offers, and so I went back to the States, and under the name of Willy Kurtis I shot a series of B movies for Roger Corman's production group. Stuff like Michael Miller's 'The Incredible Melting Man...'"*

> HUGUES QUESTER: *"The film meant great promotion for me, but it was also a dead end. Everybody took me for the character I played in the film, and for two years I got offered nothing but similar roles. They kept waiting for me two take that plastic sack out of my pocket... I just went back to the theatre..."*

After *Je t'aime moi non plus*, Joe works again in France and then moves on to Italy to shoot an impressive array of second-rate junk. He takes advantage of his cult status to work on *Cotton Club* with Francis Ford Coppola and *Cry Baby* with John Waters, but the roles are always minor...

As for Jane, she is shunned by producers. Apart from a pretentious film by Bernard Queysanne and some Italian piece of schlock, it's a long purgatory - she does nothing until 1978's *Death on the Nile*.

> CLAUDE BERRI: *"I had suggested to Jacques-Eric Strauss that he co-produce the film with me, and I think that made Serge happy since the two of them knew each other so well... I loved the final result and we were all disappointed with the film's failure at the box office. It's no coincidence that the movie is dedicated to Boris Vian. I'd have liked to see Serge do a remake of 'J'irai cracher sur vos tombes.' I suggested it to him and I*

don't know why it never happened. He was thinking about making it a Jewish story, set in Berlin before the war. Anyway, he was really upset about never succeeding as a filmmaker. Success was very important to him and he'd been enamored of film since he was a kid."

JANE BIRKIN: *"One day my mom called from London to ask why the movie was only being shown in gay porno theatres in Soho. I didn't know what to say. In Paris it was being shown on the Champs-Elysées and Truffaut had spoken very well of it. I could have killed that moronic English reporter who wrote, "Has Mr. Gainsbourg forgotten how to use butter?" – a comparison between 'Je t'aime moi non plus' and Bertolucci's 'Last Tango in Paris.' I was really frustrated at the time."*

JUDY CAMPBELL-BIRKIN: *"That film shocked me. My husband and I went to see it in Paris, and he was speechless when it ended. I had to think about what I was going to say to Jane. I ended up telling her something stupid like "It's very interesting." And really, it is. Thinking back on it, after the initial shock, I compared the film to the story of 'The Little Mermaid,' who changes her appearance, despite the suffering it causes, to please the man she loves. As to the film's distribution in England, well, I was revolted by the horrible theatres it was reduced to playing in."*

On March 17, 1976, *Variety* gets it just right: "It's reminiscent of those old Yankee dramas, except for the gay thing. In those Yankee films, the men were macho, but not gay. Or else they didn't admit it." Later, Robert Murray, author of *Images in the Dark: An Encyclopedia of Gay and Lesbian Film and Video*, sums it up thusly: *Je t'aime moi non plus* was years, if not decades, ahead of its time. I don't understand why it's not considered a classic of the seventies."

Charlotte only sees the film much later, just months before Serge's death. She watches it at daybreak, after a night of sleeplessness, cracking up at the dance scene and the tracking shots in the truck. On Serge's answering machine she says, "This film is magic..."

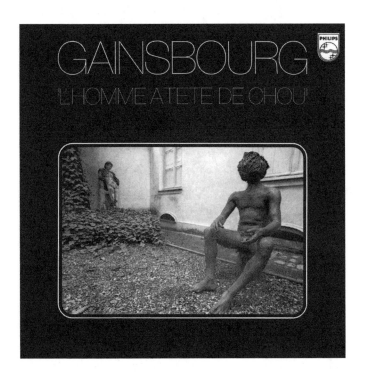

nineteen

I'm Cabbage-Head Man

The period just after *Je t'aime moi non plus* is painful for Serge. He doesn't feel well. Artistically speaking, he's both proud of himself (the praise from Truffaut) and cruelly disappointed (the poor box office). None of his latest records, nor any of Jane's for that matter, has met with the success he had hoped for. Thanks to his lifestyle, he's even hurting on the financial front, so when Jacques Séguéla suggests he direct some Woolite commercials Serge accepts right away. Three spots are recorded between 1976 and 1977, and they feature Brigitte Fossy, Jane Birkin, and Marlène Jobert. Séguéla also has him shoot the layout for a brand of disposable razors. The idea: "Cigarettes have killed my voice, alcohol has ruined my liver, women have stolen my heart, but nothing will touch my beard – except Bic." It is curtly rejected by the product's maker.

Some scenes pulled from domestic life at Rue de Verneuil, with the kid sisters whom Serge nicknames "Kékate" and "Charlotte ma crotte"... The oldest, Kate, is nine in 1976 and often the victim of dastardly remarks made by classmates. After Jane's nude photos in *Lui* and the release of *Je t'aime moi non plus*, Kate endures insults that all the little brats are most assuredly relaying straight from their parents' mouths: "Your dad's a dope fiend!" or "Your mother's a whore!" The simple fact that they are not married is enough to shock the children from so-called "good families." Sometimes,

Kate has to use her fists. With that tomboy look of hers, she earns the nickname "Madame Justice" out on the playground.

At home on Rue de Verneuil, the kids are very well behaved. They learn very quickly not to touch the objects in the living room and they spend most of their time in their room on the first floor. The écorchée at the entry to the hallway terrorizes the girls, but they have to pass by him to get to the toilet. Plus, some imbecilic nanny tells them that if they bathe at night, it will chase after them with glowing red eyes and steal them away. Alas, they start to pee out the window.

To make the kids laugh, Serge comes up with the most hideous faces. He comes up with ways to frighten them, dressing up like a ghost and holding a flashlight under his chin. On one occassion, he comes into their room dressed as a clown, and proceeds to console them with an accordion and a guitar. They are forced to stay at home when they catch lice, and to keep the neighborhood from learning about it he insists that Jane use a pharmacy far from home. Serge is also esthetically critical, especially with Kate, of course, as the oldest must set an example. One day she comes home wearing some toy rings she'd found as a prize in some Cracker Jack-like junk purchased at the baker's. He pulls them off her fingers and says: "No way you're wearing that. It's ugly!" He's very strict about courtesy and also monitors their table manners and their mode of dress. He really demands that everything be attractive, just like each object in his museum/house where all is pleasing to the eye. He takes his parenting role very seriously when it comes to Kate, whom he considers adopting. "There's no question that he was my dad," says Kate Barry. "He took responsibility for me when I was just one, and I don't think that blood relationships are very important. The people that matter are the ones that invest time with you. I know he's a part of me, right down to my behaviors."

ANDREW BIRKIN: *"It's impossible to describe the happiness, but there was this extraordinary side to life with Serge. He and Jane were happy, but not at all in the bourgeois sense of the word. Like a child, he loved to have fun. Once, for Christmas on the Isle of Wight, he said: "Let's have a magician over for Christmas eve!" Serge had read about some guy in a local paper and I went and found the poor slob. I think he was called Fred the Conjurer, and he arrived thinking he was performing at a children's surprise party. Not the case. It was just Serge, Jane, Linda, me, and my parents. We watched as the guy carted out all this stuff and did the stupidest tricks. We were rolling on the floor... Serge being Serge, he slipped the man a monstrous tip and applauded like a madman."*

In addition to the écorchée, Serge, a few years earlier, had acquired a sculpture by Claude Lalanne. It is called, simply, "L'homme à tête de chou," and represents a naked, seated man with a head replaced by the plump inflorescence of a cruciferous vegetable...

GAINSBOURG: *"I ran across 'L'homme à tête de chou' in the window of a contemporary art gallery. I came back by 15 times and finally walked in the door, paid cash, and had it delivered to my house. At first he ignored me, but then he loosened up and told me his story. A reporter for a scandal rag, he fell for a little shampoo girl who cheated on him with some rock and rollers. He bludgeons her to death with a fire extinguisher, drifts into madness, and loses his head, which turns into a cabbage..."*

CLAUDE LALANNE: *"Not more than five days after I finished the thing it started speaking. I was delighted that he was the one who bought it because I really admired him. Later he called and asked if he could use the statue on the cover of his next album. I said fine, and to thank me he invited me to the studio to listen to 'L'homme à tête de chou' before it was released."*

The recording of the new LP starts just five months after the release of *Je t'aime moi non plus*. The music is laid down over six days, from August 16 to August 21 in London. Mixing is finished on September 14 at the Studio des Dames. Sabar is not along for the ride, and the arrangements are handed over to the ever-faithful Alan Hawkshaw, while artistic direction is naturally handled by the henceforth indispensable Philippe Lerichomme. Without trying to avoid stress, an essential part of creation especially for him, Serge approaches the making of the new album in a radically different way.

PHILIPPE LERICHOMME: *"'L'homme à tête de chou' is a very personal concept album. It is without compromise, and contains astonishing exercises in style that are expertly sculpted. It's also the introduction to the talk-over, which is to say that rhythmic, spoken voice that he would regularly use in the future. He knew like no one else how to pace his words over each measure in a way that fascinated me. This time he got the lyrics really polished before setting them to music, which is not how he usually works."*

L'homme à tête de chou comes out in November, 1976 and is immediately hailed as a masterpiece, even by the punk generation, who in France, look upon Gainsbourg as a blood brother:

> *I'm cabbage-head man*
> *Half-vegetable half-bloke*
> *And for the love of Marilou*
> *I went down to pawnshop to*
> *Hock my Remington you see*
> *I knew not what to do*
> *Lost and penniless poor me*

The fatal meeting between the misfit journalist and the shampoo girl: we find ourselves amidst the sordid décor at "Chez Max coiffeur pour hommes" when the narrator happens to stumble in for a shave, and into that bitch...

> *Who quickly blinds me with her pagan beauty*
> *And with her soapy hands*
> *She bends down and what a sight*
> *Her tits a Turkish delight*
> *Rose flavored, bouncing off me, dynamite*

She cuts his hair and he pays through the nose. But there are some good times. For example:

> *When Marilou dances to reggae*
> *Unzip your fly as if to say*
> *I send you greetings and good day*
> *From my serpent down the way*

She drives him mad and he goes wild, becomes delirious, rambles, and wanders astray in his "Transit à Marilou":

> *I can feel the cabin vibrate*
> *I can feel my joystick rise*
> *From the control booth come sighs*
> *Cunnilingus-like voices state*
> *In syllables and cries*
> *We're reading you just great*

But the nymphomaniac nymphet starts to freely fuck around. The film stock in his head receives a "Flash Forward" in the form of a slap...:

She stood between two macaques
In a festival like Woodstock
Like a guitar ready to rock
From two jacks
One a bullet hole the other her asshole

Gainsbourg: "I did what they call a talk-over because there are words so sophisticated in the prosody that they cannot be put into a melody. You can't sing "One a bullet hole the other her asshole." It's not possible, you have to speak it. Very nice alexandrine also."

These aren't really songs and melodies in the classic sense, but rather atmospheres and ambiances. Atop the insistent rhythm of "Aéroplanes," Gainsbourg speaks of his opaque dementia:

My poor fool you dream and hover
Treat me like a penniless hick
A vile and miserable prick
What does it matter, when words like smoke simply vanish lover

As Serge put it, "A Lolita is like a flower that has just opened and has become conscious of both its perfume and its thorns." The man observing the masturbating girl now has homicidal tendencies, which leads to "Meurtre à l'extincteur":

Lying there on the tile
There's one last lifeless jolt
A final dying hiss
I grab the handle now
Marilou disappears in a cloudy mist

Marilou now rests under the foam, but the nightmare isn't over. The assassin finds himself in a "Lunatic Asylum." Just like Gregor in Kafka's *Metamorphosis*, who awakens one morning to find himself transformed into an insect, Gainsbourg's character has now become cabbage-head man:

The little Playboy bunny now munches on my head
Shoe Shine Boy
Oh Marilou, please don't stop
She used to roll me in her hands and round her bed
And suck me like a lemon drop

An artistic masterpiece but a commercial failure, the record sells just 20 to 25,000 copies. Peanuts. Still, certain pieces like "Marilou Reggae" are right in step with the times. In 1976, Bob Marley is already a huge star, not to mention Toots and the Maytals, U-Roy, Burning Spear, etc... Hawkshaw and his band may not groove like real Jamaicans, but the light bulb has already gone off in Serge's head. Two years later, Philippe Lerichomme won't have any trouble convincing him to go to the source and explore the music's roots in Kingston...

Jane, at 30 years of age, is at the summit of her career and the height of her beauty. This is when Serge, still finishing his album, writes a tune for her new 45. As already alluded to, he takes "La Ballade de Johnny Jane" from *Je t'aime moi non plus* and adds these superb and moving lyrics:

Hey Johnny Jane
With your big wide eyes and basket in your hand
Walking aimlessly around this no man's land
Hey Johnny Jane
You can feel those Spanish flies send you a kiss
From public dumps that form their Atlantis
Hey Johnny Jane
All those trash trucks pass by
And drop off waste that like dead children no one ever will miss

JULIEN CLERC: *"The first time I met Serge was backstage at the Olympia in February, 1969, when I opened for Bécaud. He came up and said: "I haven't heard anything as interesting as that in 10 years," which was a great compliment. I had always been fascinated by his gift for melody, but he really bowled me over with "La Ballade de Johnny Jane." There's a harmonic progression there, something I don't understand, that takes you to another world. It's dazzling. Every time I hear it I think: "That bastard! Shit, I wish I'd written that..." "*

In a November, 1976 interview for *Libération*, there's a long piece with the Gainsbourg devotee Gilles Millet, who had just had words with Delfiel de Ton over *Je t'aime moi non plus*. Gainsbourg speaks about the new album:

The music? Really, I never know what to do. I'm scatterbrained, I have no rules. It must be a symptom of my desires. I'm influenced by what's happening around me, but now that's starting to cause me problems because I'm to saturated with the rhythms of pop music. I'm not Brassens. He's a classical painter. He has no problem with form. Me, I question everything.

[433]

In March, 1977, *Le Matin* describes how Serge is now moving in all directions. He does a song for Nana Mouskouri, another for Françoise Hardy, and the soundtrack to *Goodbye Emmanuelle*. He also puts out a 45 for summer, "just to make a buck, for fun," and all while preparing Jane's new album, whose working title is still *Apocalypstick*.

For Nana Mouskouri, to whom he gave "Le yeux pour pleurer," he writes "La petite rose":

> *My poor little thing*
> *Never did you sing*
> *You were plucked all too soon*
> *Are you now something new*
> *Do angels sing for you*
> *Or rather have you met your doom*

For Hardy, he writes the somewhat flat "Enregistrement," where he seems to be trying to recapture what he did with "Comment te dire adieu":

> *If the past is just lost to you*
> *And future days are looking blue*
> *Yes if the present's changing too*
> *The tape recorder remains true*
> *To those words of love it plays the whole night through*

JEAN-PIERRE SABAR: *"All of Gainsbourg's arrangers were, to a certain degree, his slaves. Consenting slaves, because it was fun to work with him, they laughed a lot, spent all day cutting up around the piano while they should be working. Plus, he was also straight about the pay. At the beginning, he told me, "You'll get credit for the arrangement, but never the music." He didn't want to share the fame. But at SACEM, things were fifty-fifty. That's something they don't all do."*

Around May 20, Serge is in London again with Alan Hawkshaw and Philippe Lerichomme to try his hand at a summer hit, "My Lady Héroine." TV promos start in mid-June. The intro is catchy, and so is the melody, but the words are frankly third-rate...

> *Oh my Lady Héroine*
> *Just as pure as ol' Justine*
> *Pain in virtue is very nice*
> *Like the pleasure that's in your vice*

You might get a laugh if you flip the disc and find "Trois millions de Joconde," which happens to be one of Charlotte's favorites tunes:

> I made up three million Mona Lisa's
> An enormous mass
> And every morning I use her sweet smile
> To wipe my ass

It's now time to introduce Alain Chamfort. We'll quickly sum up his background to establish the context. He gets his start doing R&B in a Mod group around 1965-1966, which means 15 years or so of doing Otis Redding and Wilson Pickett covers. He puts out a 45 on Vogue at the same time that Dutronc releases "Et moi et moi et moi." Dutronc needs a keyboard player and Alain signs right up.

Chamfort later throws together a group of background singers and does sessions right and left, finally meeting up with Claude François, who hires him as a composer for the record company Flèche.

ALAIN CHAMFORT: *"In 1970, it was, "Hey, loser"... When I met Claude, it all turned around. I was a new man, the perfect picture of success, with an American car and chicks everywhere."*

Catapulted by the album *Podium*, Chamfort becomes one of pop's hot, young heartbeats. This is the time of "Bébé chanteur," and he's scoring two hits a years until 1975...

ALAIN CHAMFORT: *"I wanted to do something else but Claude stopped me. He wanted me to milk the formula for all it was worth. In 1976 my contract was up and I pulled out. I took a real beating. I'd signed with CBS and put out an album of disparate material. I wasn't very sure of myself. Then in 1977, I went to look up Gainsbourg, in spite of the fact that the people around me had advised against it, saying he was a has-been. People in my generation never called on him because he wasn't current. I felt right off that this was a good thing because it would permit him to get back in touch with the youth. Still, in the beginning he was hesitant, and it took a kick in the pants from Jane, who felt that I could do a good job with his lyrics. She convinced him..."*

> Out the edges of the town
> I saw you through my rearview mirror
> Like watching the credits roll on down

A film that you see but can't hear

Gainsbourg will write a total of nine tunes for Chamfort's *Rock'n'Rose* album, some of them quite pretty little numbers, like "Lucette and Lucie," the story of two identical twin girls:

> *Lucette, Lucie*
> *The two of you and in the middle me*
> *And we make love in stereo you see*

DOMINIQUE BLANC-FRANCARD: *"I was the sound engineer on the album. We worked at the little Studio Aquarium on Rue Lecourbe, and I can remember Alain's face when he heard the words for "Lucette et Lucie," which was a blow-by-blow recounting about Chamfort getting it on with two Swedish chicks... He quarreled with Serge about recording it. He was scared stiff and explained it was just impossible for his audience. Serge knew this very well and played around with the ambiguity. But at the same time he already adored Chamfort because he represented exactly what Serge would have liked to have been: a teenybopper heartthrob."*

ALAIN CHAMFORT: *"He worked real hard on the album but he didn't earn much from the sales. He was hoping to repeat the success he had with France Gall, but to no avail. He didn't want to do the lyrics for my next 45... When I started the album 'Poses,' in 1979, I went back to see him. He was the only one who could help me."*

We'll get back to the Chamfort story later, when he has his megahit with "Manureva." At the end of 1977, Serge has two other main projects: the *Apocalypstick* album for Jane, which has now become *Ex-fan des sixties*, and eight songs for Zizi Jeanmaire's new show which starts in December. The most ambitious of these projects is Jane's new album, which is released in February. The album's title cut even climbs to 26 on the charts before brutally disappearing in April:

> *Ex-fan of the sixties*
> *Where are those crazy days*
> *All your stars seemed to have passed away*
> *Gone now is Brian Jones*
> *Jim Morrison, Eddie Cochran, Buddy Holly*
> *Same for Jimi Hendrix*
> *Otis Redding, Janis Joplin, T-Rex*
> *Elvis*

JANE BIRKIN: *"I had a horrible time trying to sing "Ex-fan des sixties."* *It was a question of rhythm. Serge couldn't understand what the problem was. After 50 tries we just gave up. It was tragic. Finally, we started again six months later, and during that time, Elvis died, which made Serge change the lyrics. If not it would have ended with "poor Janis Joplin."*

> I make a mark as I pass through
> With all this makeup that I'm wearing for you
> Apocalypstick, Apocalypstick
> Regardless of anatomy
> My lips inflict décalcomanie

Five years after *Di Doo Dah* and two years after *Lolita Go Home*, *Ex-fan des sixties* is a total success, in an altogether different register than the forthcoming *Baby Alone In Babylone*. Inspired by his friend Dutronc is a song that Françoise Hardy refused to sing: "L'aquoiboniste":

> Mister Idontgiveadamn
> He is always such a ham
> Always I don't give a damn
> Give a damn
> Sir Idontgiveadamn
> Blows off each and every fool
> Looks ahead and says just who
> Gives a damn

In spring of 1978, while Jane is filming *Death on the Nile*, Serge, in tow as usual, writes the screenplay for a new film called *Black-out*.

MICHEL PICCOLI: *"A few years earlier, we dined together and I told him I was going to start shooting Grandeur Nature in Italy. It's about a man who shares his life with a blow-up doll that he treats like a real woman. He looked at me, livid, and said:*

"That's' dreadful. I just started writing the same story."

CLAUDE BERRI: *"I remember that weekend in Normandy, at Jane's, in the summer of 1978, with Jean-Pierre Rassam and Carole Bouquet. Serge read us some scenes, or rather poems – I always thought of his films as cinematic poems – from 'Black-out.' He began it like a kind of puzzle. He was always dreaming about cinema, even in the middle of songs."*

Serge had been obsessed with the film and its difficult subject matter for some four years. He imagines three characters, two men and a woman, stuck in a Hollywood villa during a blackout in Los Angeles - a long "No Exit" made all the more oppressive by the fact that the only source of light comes from the headlamps of a Cadillac... For the female roles, Serge thinks right away of Jane and Isabelle Adjani. He wants Robert Mitchum for the male lead and even has a meeting with him in a big Parisian hotel (he even saves a cigarette butt put out by the famous star of *Night of the Hunter*). He then considers Dirk Bogarde, David Bowie, and finally Alain Delon, whom Serge just loved in *Rocco et ses frères*.

Delon refuses to see him or even read the script. He simply arranges for himself a screening of *Je t'aime moi non plus* and then dictates this cutting letter to his secretary:

Dear Serge, I believe that we are evolving in two completely different universes and moving toward different horizons. But this is nothing new, and it's something I regret.

GAINSBOURG: *"Moral of the story: it was easier for me to meet Dirk Bogarde and Robert Mitchum than Alain Delon. Of course I have nothing more to say..."*

ISABELLE ADJANI: *"There were two female characters: one was almost his wife, and the other his mistress. On that fatal night we take part in a diabolical little three-way game, very clever and very deadly. I really liked the idea of the Cadillac - its headlights fading as the battery dies. The denouement was also terribly calculating. I'm sorry that the film never got made."*

GAINSBOURG: *"My producers didn't know what to make of it. It was almost Hitchcockian, like a horror film with a climax that never happens... Still, I've held on to one line, a sort of epigraph that must have given them cause to reflect: "The light of reason gives birth to monsters..."*

From May 22 to 24, there's another studio date at Phonogram in London, and once again Alan Hawkshaw accompanies him on his third and final summer hit. This time, the disco shtick succeeds beyond all expectations. "Sea Sex And Sun" is a huge smash in the nightclubs and on radio:

Sex Sea And Sun
It shines so very bright
You dear excite
Your fake tits are dynamite
Oh so tight

The song climbs the charts all summer long, finally peaking at number four thanks to, among other things, the numerous television appearances Serge makes during the month of June, each one harder than the next. The tune, spat out in just minutes, is by his own estimation moronic, but it succeeds where none of the sophisticated pieces from *L'Homme à a tête de chou* did. Plus, it gets a shot in the arm when Patrice Leconte uses it for the soundtrack to *Les Bronzés*, which makes a killing at the box-office.

Since the death of his father, Serge has been even more attentive to his mother. On Sundays, they usually dine at Avenue Bugeaud, where Jacqueline and her children are now permanently ensconced. Jane, Kate, and Charlotte all adore Olia, who can never stop nagging her son. She opines about everything. If he looked like a slob on TV the previous night, she'd say: "Why are you wearing that shirt with holes in it? It's frightful!" Serge explains for the hundredth time that it's part of his image. Then for the hundredth time she harps: "I don't know why you never had your ears fixed!" One day she mutters an insult in Russian, and Serge, not missing a beat, says: "What's that, crazy?" Surprised, she looks up and says: "Oh, so you understood that?" ...

NICOLE SCHLUSS: *"One day I saw this extraordinary scene. Serge showed up out of nowhere with Mastroianni, the two of them thoroughly plowed. He tells us: "I want to introduce Marcello to my mother!" Olia was on cloud nine. "Oh, I'm so pleased to meet you! I've seen all your films!" Mastroianni kneeled down for 15 minutes, kissing her all over her cheeks and hands: "So bella, your mamma!" She was floored. "Hear that," she said, "The most seductive man in Italian cinema finds me beautiful!" They then continued their escapade. Serge decided to lie down in the middle of the street to stop a taxi."*

MICHÈLE ZAOUI: *"Serge was the star, and we accepted that. We idolized him. He'd do some big hit and we'd ask to hear it again. He knew nothing of our lives, but that wasn't because he was egotistical. We knew he really loved us."*

KATE BARRY: *"For us, Olia was like a real granny. She would hide 50 franc notes under her pillow and tell us: "Come see what I have here!" She had a crazy sense of humor and could be very nasty, even more so with her children than with us. When she didn't want to listen to something she would pretend to be deaf. When she was bored with the conversation, she'd start to whistle..."*

What really bothers Charlotte is that she's asked to cover her ears whenever there's a dirty joke, which of course she gets anyway. Another rite is the after-dinner film on Sundays, accompanied by Serge's voice-over commentary, especially critical when it's some flop from than sixties that annoys him: "Cut this crappy scene! Your reaction shot is botched! What's with this shitty music!" But if it's a western by John Ford or a crime film with Bogart, he's fascinated and quiet as a mouse.

In the summer of 1978, Serge gets a visit from French rockers Bijou. The sensational power trio signed by Philips is comprised of Vincent Palmer (guitar, vocals), Philippe Dauga (bass, vocals), and Dynamite Yan (drums). In the shadows is also Jean-William Thoury, manager, lyricist, and eminence grise. "The boys," as Serge calls them, just after giving their second performance at Mont-de-Marsan's punk festival and already with one sharp and frenetic album to their credit (*Danse avec moi*), come to ask Serge's permission to cover "Les papillons noirs," which he'd done 12 years earlier as a duet with Michèle Arnaud. Even better, they suggest that he come and sing in the studio with Dauga on this piece that he can barely remember. Serge is flattered, and decides it would be fun to accept. What he doesn't know is that he has had one of the most important encounters of his life.

VINCENT PALMER: *"I think I qualify as a hardcore fan, and that goes back to the first time I heard "Quand mon 6.35 me fait les yeux doux" on a Denise Glaser show when I was a kid. I was impressed and I started buying his records."*

> *In the vague shadows of the dawn*
> *The troubled visage in a mirror*
> *As if by chance you see yourself*
> *Now the black is clear*

JEAN-WILLIAM THOURY: *"On the original, Serge's deep voice anchors that of Michèle Arnaud. We thought it would fun if he did the same for us.*

He came to Ferber studios. "Why did you go dig up that old stuff?" he says. "If you want, I can write you an original." So we all said "Absolutely!"

JACKY JACKUBOWICZ: *"Being the press agent for both Gainsbourg and Bijou, I played the intermediary. I guarantee you, when he came to the studio for "Papillons noirs" he was scared stiff. It was the first time he'd sung with a rock band. Afterwards, he did some television shows with them, and then there were the concerts."*

PHILLIPE DAUGA: *"We first met him during a radio show and he thought it was super that we were fans. At the café afterwards, he put us to the test. We brought up songs that even he had forgotten. He was stunned."*

JEAN-WILLIAM THOURY: *"I'd met Serge when I was a reporter for the rock magazine 'Extra.' He had an insane talent for charming people, seducing them. Everyone changes his attitude when faced with different interlocutors. From what I've read, Elvis Presley was a master at it. Gainsbourg was the same. With intellectuals, he was an intellectual, with artists, he was a painter, with militants, he was a rebel, and with junkies he came off as wasted himself. With us, he played up the rocker thing, showing us the inside of his custom-made Louis Vuitton cases, which were filled with cassettes of Eddie Cochran, Buddy Holly, etc. I really don't think it was Machiavellian, but rather an incredible desire to please, to seduce."*

"Papillons noirs" is done over by Palmer with an elegant take on the original riff. Gainsbourg wastes no time returning the favor, writing "Betty Jane Rose" for them, which comes out as a 45 in 1978:

> *Down in the parking lot she finds her key*
> *Opens the door of a car our minor she*
> *Betty Jane Rose strikes a major pose to tease*
>
> *Down in the parking lot she strolls around*
> *Strutting her stuff she sings her minor sounds*
> *Betty Jane Rose is the major tease in town*

VINCENT PALMER: *"My best memory from the "Betty Jane Rose" session is when Serge broke his foot but still decided he'd come to the studio in a cast. He tapped his cane to the rhythm and kept saying: "This is amazing!" He always laughed at my penchant for collecting things, but I'd started very young, when you could find old EPs for just a few francs.*

There's hardly anything crappy in his whole catalogue. He's one of those rare French artists who never made a fool of himself..."

PHILIPPE DAUGA: *"We got along perfectly. He joined right in with us and our insane shit... We were real pals. We'd hit all the bars and he'd drink us under the table. He'd call and say: "I'm bored. Nothing to do. Come pick me up in your (Citroën) DS." He was like a kid. He thought my DS was better than his Rolls! We got swept up in his frenzy and it became hellish. The next day he'd be fresh as a daisy. We'd need three days to recover!"*

During one of these blowouts, Serge signs one of Palmer's ties, which is covered with naked ladies: "Faites joujou avec bibi"...[1]

JEAN-WILLIAM THOURY: "We rehearsed several times with him in the cellar of Dynamite's house in Savigny. For the release of *OK Carole* in 1978, Phillips organized a promotional tour in Epernay, the Mecca of champagne, where Bijou did a concert. Serge came along, and the press and other guests were transported in a special train. He joined them for two songs at the end of the show. It was the first time he'd been onstage in 13 years."

That morning, Vincent Palmer and his friend go to pick up Serge at Rue de Verneuil. They are accompanied by a Gainsbourg fan from Brittany who at the time has no idea he'll wind up as his hero's publicist seven years later, first at the Lyon bureau of Phonogram, and later at the end of 1987 in Paris. This native of Nantes, one Jean-Yves Billet, is like Palmer an aficionado of Serge's heroic period, and is obsessed with rediscovering the Gainsbourg discography, using all his patience and dedication to establish a complete collection of his work.

PHILIPPE DAUGA: *"In Epernay, we played in a big town hall. Nothing had been confirmed. There was nothing but a rumor that he might appear onstage with us. The kids were asking, "Will he show or not?" It was strange seeing him backstage later on. He was petrified and he pounded down several drinks to get his courage up. He had to go onstage for two songs, "Les papillons noirs" and "Des vents des pets des poums." When he took the mic the kids went berserk, they couldn't believe it. For an hour*

---

[1] Difficult to translate. Serge is deconstructing the word "Bijou," of course, which in French means "Jewel." What it says, essentially, is "Make joujou with bibi." Alas, an obvious sexual pun and one that not only evokes his new partners in crime, but harkens back to an old lover. (T.N.)

after that, back in the dressing room, he was dazed. He kept repeating: "I can't believe it, I can't believe it..."

JEAN-YVES BILLET: *"After the concert, we head over to some dive for a dinner thrown by the promoter of the gala. Here I am for the first time face-to-face with my idol, the man who completely blew my mind with 'L'homme à tête de chou.' I felt really out of my element that night. At the next table, people were saying things like: "Yeah, but did you see that other guy, the ugly one!" Don't forget this is 1978, and Gainsbourg's not at all a big star. At a certain moment, one of the men gets up from where he's been eating with a few friends and some skanky broads, and he hands Serge a paper, asking for an inscription. Without hesitating, Serge writes "Champagne should be dry, but not a whore's thighs." I can't start to describe the look on that guy's face when Serge handed back the paper. Even so, one of his tarts got up and came over to shake her ass in front of Gainsbourg, who just looked up and said: "You know what you're in for tonight? Nothing!""*

Towards the end of 1978, Philips puts out a series of anthologies to celebrate Gainsbourg's 20 years in the business. He's seen a lot on popular TV shows, doing old titles like "L'eau à la bouche," "Le poinçonneur de Lilas," and "Couleur café." Reporters swarm Rue de Verneuil to sift through his memory. Interviewed by Bill Schmock for *Best*, Serge comes off as depressed and confirms that he has trouble relating to the young generation, all the while delighted at what's happening with Bijou and Starshooter, a punk band from Lyon that had just recorded a maniacal version of "Le poinçonneur de Lilas." These 20 years have, like "Sex Sea And Sun," eaten away at him. He has no idea about where to go musically on his next album, other than to ask the aforementioned groups to accompany him, all the while telling himself he doesn't have the vocal chops to do battle with "amplified guitars and drums." On the other hand, he's already got the photo for the cover, shot by Lord Snowdon in the deserts of Nubia. The concept is as follows:

It's about a man who's been technically dead from a heart attack for several minutes. He tells us what he saw in the afterlife: people who die young remain young when they're dead, and those that die old remain old shits for eternity. He's finally resuscitated, but there's a problem: he's 20 years-old, so he's going to blow his brains out. Not bad, eh? [...] Musically I don't have it, it's not there yet. There are so many diabolical instruments [...] they can do whatever you want [...] but I don't want to fall into that electric trap.

At the same time, in *Elle* magazine, Gainsbourg declares: "I have no desire to be psychoanalyzed. I'd never let another person mess around in the deepest recesses of my thoughts. I find it inconceivable. No artist needs this. Their work is already a means of projecting their hang-ups." He continues:

> S.G.: *For 30 years I've been taking barbiturates to sleep. Without them I dream, I obsess, I tell myself stories.*

> REPORTER: *These become films, songs?*

> S.G.: *Not at all. It's evasion, fantasy, pure imagination. I don't start thinking about songs until two weeks before the deadline.*

At the time of his 20th anniversary in show-business, Serge also pens a letter for *Le Monde de la musique*. It's on one of his favorite themes: major art and minor art, and the need to study:

After the initiation, it's up to each person to find his style and his voice and make sure there is a place for his genius. It was the same for Rimbaud, Alban Berg, and Le Courbusier. But in the minor arts, like mine, you simply have to take aim and not miss the target. We're the one-eyed kings in the land of the blind. Also, the elite marksmen are possessed of only visionary genius. They ignore the closer targets and other nuggets of gold in order to shoot for the stars. They follow the implacable laws of ballistics, aiming at the hearts of future generations. I've always allowed myself to believe that Marlon Brando used earplugs in order to block out the responses of other actors and thus, completely isolated and tetanized by his own auto-admiration, his acting gained even more dramatic intensity. Perhaps I should do the same. But how would I know I was still pleasing the teenagers?

twenty

Le Jour De Gloire Est Arrivée

Slowly but surely, things are falling into place. The *Vignt ans de car-rière* anthologies are reminding everyone of just how important Gainsbourg is in the history of French song, even if the recordings of the seventies never sell as well as they should. As he alluded to in the quote from *Monde de la musique*, "Sea Sex And Sun" was successful in seducing the "teenagers." Their older brothers and sisters, who read *Best* and *Rock & Folk*, are intrigued by this 50 year-old who screws around with Bijou. Certain punks even recognize in *L'homme à tête de chou* a work representative of the *no future* generation. Just one more big step and he'll finally reach the right-fully earned level of superstar that has eluded him all these years. And now he's but weeks away from that...

PHILIPPE LERICHOMME: *"Marilou Reggae" had pricked up my ears, but I will never forget the real moment of revelation. One Sunday night I was at Rose-Bonbon, downstairs from the Olympia, to see a group that never showed. I was watching all the punks dancing, and it must have been one or two in the morning. I was cynically listening to the club's playlist of disco, punk, and reggae, when it suddenly came to me: "You gotta go to Jamaica for real Reggae." A few hours later, I phoned Serge and told him: "I think we need to go to Jamaica and do a Reggae album!" He said: "Super, let's go!" I spent four months setting it all up, first by going to Lido*

Music to buy a dozen reggae albums so that we could pick out the best musicians, and then by using Chris Blackwell's team at Island to help me track them all down."

Lerichomme is in a good position to handle this since for the last 10 years he's been working at Phonogram, which distributes all the Island material put out by Chris Blackwell, the man who made reggae popular all over Great Britain and Europe. He'd put out Bob Marley's *Catch a Fire*, as well as albums by Burning Spear, Jimmy Cliff, and Lee "Scratch" Perry. Among the local musicians, there are some real heavyweights, notably the rhythm section formed by drummer Sly Dunbar, bassist Robbie Shakespeare, and percussionist Sticky Thompson. They're everywhere at once, forming the backbone of Peter Tosh's group and playing as well with Black Uhuru, Gregory Isaacs, Third World, U-Roy, Culture, etc.

On January 12, 1979, Gainsbourg and Lerichomme start recording the album *Aux armes et caetera* at Dynamic Studios in Kingston, Jamaica. Serge is the first white artist to use Sly and Robbie's band. Later, Bob Dylan, Ian Dury, and Joe Cocker will follow suit. Grace Jones records the album *Warm Leatherette* with them in 1980, and the classic *Nightclubbing* a year later. Along with the rhythm section is keyboardist Mikey "Mao" Chung and guitarist Radcliffe Bryan, both on leave from Peter Tosh's band, and also there's the I Threes, the backup singers for Bob Marley, comprised of wife Rita, Judy Mowatt, and Marcia Griffiths. In short, the best Jamaican musicians on the market.

Before leaving, the head of Phonogram asks Serge if everything is ready. As usual, he flat out lies. Still, he and Lerichomme decide on four cuts. First, of course, is Marilou Reggae from *L'homme à tête de chou*, done this time as "Marilou Reggae Dub." Compared to the original done with the white boys from England, it's night and day. Next is "La Marseillaise," already rebaptised "Aux armes et caetera," and "Vielle canaille," an old American hit done in French by Jacques Hélian in 1951.[1]

Finally, there's a new version of "La Javanaise," aptly titled "Javanaise Remake." The av/vé alliteration works marvelously well with the pulsating

---

[1] The American tune, "I'll Be Glad When You're Dead, You Rascal You." (T.N.)

reggae groove. Serge is so happy with it that he decides to add a last couplet of original Javanaise jive.

PHILIPPE LERICHOMME: *"During my life with Serge – and I say life because that's a better word for it – I always wanted to be his first audience, the first "kid," as he'd say, to hear what he was doing, and each time I was too wrapped up at the mixing booth. I had to take a step back, put myself in the shoes of the ordinary listener, and see how things were evolving without getting too technical. I would give him my advice and make strong arguments, all while giving him the final word in case of disagreement, which was rare. We left for Jamaica with quite a few melodic ideas [...] and titles, even more than were necessary, but we had no lyrics – the Japanese painter's syndrome. I had no idea of the impact that "La Marseillaise" would have, but Serge was completely aware. We were dead beat upon arrival in Kingston that evening, and the next day we learned that our sound engineer would be held up in New York for two days. No way to record! So we met the bassist, Robbie Shakespeare, who right away assumed I was the singer and Serge the producer, given the difference in our ages... Two days later we're in the studio with our celebrated sound engineer and our Jamaican musicians, who couldn't have cared less about the record. For them it was "Take the money and run!" Plus, it was nothing like our usual recording environment. Around the studio there were goats and the carcass of an old car. There was a certain uneasiness until Serge went to the piano and impressed them by playing a few harmonies. Out of the blue, he asked if they knew any French music. They broke out laughing and we were even more embarrassed... But then one of the musicians mentioned a French song called "Je t'aime." He meant "Je t'aime moi non plus" of course, and the others knew it as well, so Serge blurted out: "That's me!" It all changed then. They were completely under his spell."*

SLY DUNBAR: *"At first, we thought he wanted a real clean sound, but he told us: "No, play it like you feel it!" The result is that we did it in the studio without overdubs, almost live."*

ROBBIE SHAKESPEARE: *"It had to be raw, no embellishment to pretty it up. In France it went double platinum, right? We didn't get any royalties. All we got was a Polaroid!"*

GAINSBOURG: *"Philippe Lerichomme is a remarkably capable guy. I've never seen anyone like that in my turbulent career. He's more what I'd call a cineaste rather than an artistic director. He puts it all together, sound and image, after I give him the material of course. He's a very important fellow. I have to tell you, I hate show business and the people involved in it. Absolutely unbearable. Nasty. They are vicious and jealous. Me, I'm neither of those things, and Philippe has not one ounce of vulgarity."*

Aux armes et caetera becomes a huge jackpot upon its release in March, 1979. It goes gold, then platinum in record time, finally selling over a million copies. The kids that watched Gainsbourg on TV between 1970 and 1975 are now between 15 and 20. Serge, now nearly 51, gives them "Brigade de stups" and suddenly the age difference disappears. Who else would have dared?:

> The narcs have cornered me
> My back's against the wall
> They're looking for my stash
> They only found my balls

His talk-over explores the charms of "Lola Rastaquouère"[2] while Bob Marley's background singers innocently chant "Rasta!":

> Her sex a Cyclops I heard its call
> Like Ulysses I pierced her through and through
> I was bitter and brutal, true
> And I good god was blinded by it all

Gainsbourg, "the monster who charms" as they used to say, finally puts to rest his biggest hang-up in an elegy for his poor dog Nana, "Des laids des laids":

> Same music, same reggae for my bitch
> The mutt they found ugly as a witch
> Poor little pooch, I'm the one who drank
> But its you whose liver tanked
> Osmotic victim you have been
> All my words you drank them in

---

[2] Rastaquouère hints at "Rasta" or "Rastafarian" obviously, but is also a reference to Francis Picabia's 1920 publication, Jésus-Christ Rastaquouère (Collection Dada, Paris, 1920). In French, the words means "flashy foreigner" – someone smooth and yet shady.

The studio at Dynamic Sounds is a factory: two days to record the band, one for the back-up singers, the I Threes. All that's left is the vocals, but of course Serge has left that until the last minute.

PHILIPPE LERICHOMME: *"That night at the hotel I told Serge: "You sing tomorrow!" and he answered: "I know..." That meant he still hadn't written the songs. So I walked him back to his room, which was next to mine, and I saw something I will never forget. On his bed he'd strewn out sheets of white paper corresponding to each cut on the record, with a title atop every page. So, understanding the situation, I left him alone with those blank pages and went to my room, where I also hardly slept at all. The next morning I went to knock at his door. He hadn't moved an inch since the night before and the papers were on the same spot on the bed, only now they were covered in writing. He was exhausted, of course. I rearranged the tunes because they were going off in all directions, and then at eleven in the morning we went to the studio and he sang... until two in the morning! The album was finished! Over the next two days we did the mixing, and then we headed back to Paris. The musicians had hung around, aware that something important was happening, and I remember when the session was over, Serge came up to me and said: "What have we done?" and I answered "I don't know, but we've done it!" The only idea we had was to go home and see "what we had done" in a non-Jamaican context. He had literally spat out this record under total duress, without a break."*

When reporters and programmers receive *Aux armes et caetera*, it is accompanied by this text which expounds upon his premonition:

The punks came and really only Sid Vicious fascinated me because he was dangerously logical and suicidal. So I'd guessed right – the burnt out figurehead of a movement that would have captivated me if I hadn't been seduced some 30 years ago by Dada, Breton, and Sartre's 'Nausea.' So what else is there to slip on the turntable other than, and always, Screamin' Jay Hawkins, Robert Parker, Otis Redding, Jimi Hendrix, and that which has really moved me for the last few years: ska, blue-beat, rocksteady, reggae, reggae, reggae...

So I dreamt of Jamaica, of a music where one can simply say what one wants – instinctive, animal, pure and contentious, violent and caustic, so close to Africa, so far from the gray skies of London and the blue skies of

Nashville and Los Angeles.

Just before going to Jamaica, Serge had expounded again on the theme "Pop songs - a minor art." To his previous musings he adds the following: "One can't be a visionary in fields dominated by money. But I can be useful insofar as being subversive. Pop music is a great means of subversion because it's so ubiquitous."

> *The Klan the Klan dressed in hoods*
> *Relax baby be cool*
> *The blood it flows in these woods*
> *Relax baby be cool*

This subversion will become a media scandal and assume enormous dimensions in France during the following months, as well as two years later when Serge's purchase of a manuscript of "La Marseillaise" brings the affair to a conclusion in 1981.

So Serge dares to recite the national anthem over a reggae groove. And to give it a new name: "Aux armes et caetera." Practicing the technique of collage – one that he had employed in the late fifties when starting to doubt his talent as a painter – he pastes the patriotic hymn over an exotic tempo. The Surrealists would have appreciated this. "The Marseillaise" he claims in *Libération*, "is the bloodiest song in all of history. 'Aux armes et caetera' is kind of like Delacroix's painting where the lady with the flag, atop a mass of Rastafarian cadavers, is nothing less than a Jamaican woman, her breasts overflowing with sunlight and revolt while belting out the heroic refrain [...] over a piercing reggae beat!"

On May 6, 1979, "Aux armes et caetera" places Serge on the top of the French charts for the first time, displacing Supertramp, Elton John, and the Bee-Gees. Meanwhile, he kicks off another series of concerts with Bijou. Together they pound out not only "Betty Jane Rose" and "Relax Baby Be Cool," but also the reggae version of "La Marseillaise."

JEAN-WILLIAM THOURY: *"The onstage collaboration took place at Mogador, the Palais des Sports, and at Lyon, at the trades council, where the success was such that a second gala was organized the next day. Jean-Pierre Pommier, the producer, was astonished when Serge didn't ask for a fee, and so he gave him a pinball machine that he installed in the Rue de Verneuil house. Then Serge invited Bijou to play with him on TV, most notably on the Jacques Matin show. I think that marked a turning point for him, a step towards the new generation. Maybe it was also a good luck charm. His gratitude towards us was evident, as was ours toward him. The relations were always pleasant, but we really were from different worlds, and we ended up going our separate ways."*

GAINSBOURG: *"Those concerts set off something extremely important: the kids gave me an ovation. There's no doubt that it was Bijou that sparked my desire to return to the stage."*

JACKY JACKUBOWICZ: *"It was magic. He was never so well received and he wanted to tour with the group. June, 1979 was French Rock Mania. Six months later he was playing the palace with his rastas."*

On June 1, 1979, the "Marsellaise scandal" explodes when Michel Droit, a 56 year-old ex-Gaullist lackey, bonafide reactionary, and spiteful essayist, publishes this nauseating piece in *Figaro Magazine*:

GAINSBOURG'S MARSEILLAISE

By recording a parody of "La Marseillaise," Gainsbourg undoubtedly knew he'd be creating a scandal, but his undertaking is more than a simple insult to our national anthem.

The rhythm and melody are vaguely Caribbean. In the background, a chorus of nymphets emits some thoroughly unintelligible onomatopoeia. And with his face in the microphone, his dying, mumbling voice exhales words that escape like bubbles from dirty water - words taken from "La Marseillaise."

Such is the latest piece by Serge Gainsbourg, who thanks to, or perhaps in spite of his national anthem, has been able to climb right up the charts.

Until now, this spirited spouse of the gracious Jane Birkin, this singer and songwriter who, when looking into a mirror must dream of a time and a place and a young public for whom looks would not have been an issue, has delivered both the best and the worst. The best is his songwriting, pieces like "La javanaise" or "Le poinçonneur de Lilas." The worst are a certain number of elucubrations that apparently mine the erotic phantasms of his precocious senility, as if he were exposing himself and in doing so trans-

posing the vocabulary of European highschoolers for what we might call "monetary compensation."

Thus, Gainsbourg has often sought and frequently found scandal through different sorts of trendy provocation. But this piece reaches the heights of immodesty and exhibitionism - he should have chosen something else. This time he has decided to simply blaspheme that which, for 200 years, has been among the things we hold most sacred.

From Lily Pons to Line Renaud, how many great lyric artists have sung "La Marseillaise" when the occasion presented itself? Now, to see it vomited up thusly – I'm thinking of another word less polished but more colorful – vomited up in scattered fragments, well, we have never witnessed this.

And hearing him is one thing, but seeing him! And see him we did the other day on television. We saw Serge Gainsbourg! Before slobbering out "his" Marseillaise, he obviously polished up his stage presence, his body language, his attitude: sleep still in his eyes, a three-day beard, a worn-out but pricey shirt... In brief, calculatedly dilapidated and crustier than ever.

Forgive my bluntness and basic lack of the most elemental charity, but when I see Gainsbourg I can feel myself turning into an environmentalist. By that I mean I find myself in a state of constant defense against the ambient pollution that seems to flow, as from a drainage ditch, so freely from both his person and his work. Of course, "La Marseillaise" has been sung by ragged, unshaven, filthy men. But first off, it was the real Marseillaise they sung. Furthermore, the rags they wore were real rags. The dirt they were covered in was real dirt. Their unshaven beards were not some carefully crafted artifice. These were men that Malraux referred to as "epic tramps," men who sang "La Marseillaise" knowing that they may very well die in battle or before a firing squad.

Has Serge Gainsbourg never heard of these men? Is this why he cannot even bring himself to simply respect the song that enabled their sacrifice?

And finally, we have to address the most delicate and not unimportant aspect of this shoddy and odious debacle.

Many of us get alarmed, and with good cause, when anti-Semitism rears it *head in our modern world – an anti-Semitism that we thought was buried along with the six million martyrs sent to their deaths by the worst incarnation of this phenomenon.*

But we know as well that there are those who propagate anti-Semitism, and there are those who provoke it.

So I say, as I weigh these words, that Serge Gainsbourg – unconsciously, I must believe – has just placed himself in that second category.

There is clearly not a single man of good faith, not even a simpleton, who would dream of associating this scandalous parody of our national anthem with Gainsbourg's Judaism. But it's not exactly men of good faith who make up the hordes of anti-Semites. Is this really the time to give them some cheap opportunity to make light of all the Jews in France who suffered and who died with not only their faith, but also "La Marseillaise" in their hearts? For someone who dares to make it an object of derision so that he might make few bucks in publishing rights?

In addition to being a disgusting insult to our national anthem, this is a low blow to his co-religionists.[3] Was this the only way Serge Gainsbourg could find to resuscitate a career that has been bankrupt for so long now?

On June 16, *Le Figaro*, feeling that its editorialist may have gone a bit too far, decides to publish three letters in support of Michel Droit. The next day, Serge responds in *Le Matin Dimanche*:

THE STAR OF THE BRAVE

Perhaps Droit,[4] a journalist and man of letters - let's say four letters - member of a African group of professional francophone hunters (c.f. Bokassa I), high priest of the Order of State, decorated soldier, holder of the Croix de Guerre and Croix de la Legion d'Honneur, also known as the "Star of the Brave," perhaps he would like me to put back on my cross, the Star of David, which I was forced to display in June of 1942 in yellow

---

[3] A terrible choice of word, especially in this context. It recalls the anti-Semitic propaganda literature of WWII.

[4] It's useful here to remember that "droit" means "right." (T.N.)

and black, after having been relegated to a ghetto by the militia. Should I, thirty-seven years later, return there, pressured this time by a former neo-combatant, and should I, until the day I die - which shall not be long for him, I hope ("One less Jew in France" he'll be able to say) – should I be condemned to ceaselessly live and relive that flashback from an adolescence in occupied Paris, or even one from my not far-removed ancestry: the pogroms of Nicholas II which were narrated for me by my father?

Perhaps the wax in the ears, the cataracts - these remnants of post-Gaullism – perhaps we could operate and extract them from this extremist Droit so that he might in some measure be able to judge my Marseillaise, heroic in its pulsating rhythms and dynamic harmonies, and equally revolutionary in its initial sense and in its "rouget le lislienne" call to arms.[5]

It pains me even more to have to inform this poor man that I am still able, unlike he, to be everywhere at once, thanks to radio waves and cathode rays and records, and thus this personal version of the national anthem, which is wholly mine whether he believes it or not, will be played all over Europe, Africa, Japan, and the Americas, including Jamaica, where it was given birth.

I have nothing else to add, except perhaps for a few words taken from an editorial by Edouard Drumont and printed in his paper 'La Libre Parole.' It is inspired not by Beaumarchais but rather a 'France for Frenchmen,' dated Sunday, September 10, 1899, and it concerns one Captain Dreyfus: "Long live the army! Down with traitors! Down with the Jews!"

Lucien Ginsburg, a.k.a. Serge Gainsbourg

During this time, the controversy starts to build. It's discussed in *Le Monde*, and the weekly *Tribune Juive* publishes an interview with Gainsbourg on June 21, 1979: "What Michel Droit can't stand is that the television, during prime time, had me singing my Marseillaise in front of a blue, white, and red flag. A Jew on their tricolored flag and a reggae version of 'La Marseillaise' – it was too much for him."

---

[5] Claude Joseph Rouget de Lisle is the composer of "La Marseillaise." (T.N.) foreigner" – someone smooth and yet shady.

Droit continues to publish his missives, and Jane, outraged, goes so far as to write him. He responds in a rage-filled letter full of old and dated French in a ridiculous style. In December, 1979, six months after his first editorial, he spouts off again, more cantankerously than ever, in *Les Nouvelles littéraires* (meanwhile Serge's record has already gone platinum):

> *Even if "La Marseillaise" is our common treasure, that does not mean we can permit just anyone to handle it, or permit someone to make of it something that it is not. For example, to take a few phrases from here and there and transform them into a sort of hodgepodge placed over a foreign rhythm, spiced up by horny background singers muttering a parody of the refrain which amounts to nothing more than derision.*

> *But it goes even further than that. It should never be permitted of any of us to make a commercial work by exploiting "La Marseillaise," which is recognized as our national anthem. One should never be able to enrich oneself with either all or part of a song that makes one's spine tingle, that prepares us for battle and death. One might wish to ignore it, contest it, refuse it, but one must never profit from it, lest one become a simple whoremonger of the very glory it represents and the blood spilled by others.*

"Whoremonger," "hodgepodge," "foreign rhythms," (read enemy of France): it's all there, a sort of despicable perfection. The nicest thing about the whole incident is that the provocation, if there even is any, comes from a lad named Lucien Ginsburg, who as a citizen is above all suspicion. He honestly and scrupulously pays his taxes and never choses fiscal exile, unlike Gilbert Bécaud, Charles Aznavour, or Alain Delon. This little Jewish immigrant who so masterfully handles the French language with such grace and invention is far more French that Michel Droit could suspect, a citizen who has no need of military hymns to provoke feelings of patriotism and who has had a blast taking a good old tune and setting it to good, new rhythms.

There's a menacing preamble to the parachutist affair in Strasbourg, which is detailed further on. A dedication ceremony for his record at the International Trade Fair in Marseilles, where Serge is to be the guest star at the Jamaican stand on September 28, 1979, is canceled due to pressure from the National Parachutists Union (UNP), which states that it is ready to oppose the recording "by any means necessary." What's more, the Marseille division of the UNP announces its decision to block the sale of *Aux armes et caetera!* The mayor of the city, Gaston Defferre, strikes back, asking Serge to come and sing at the Rose Festival being held by the Socialist Party on October 21 and 22. Serge declines, and the official reason given is that he's shooting abroad. However, it's more likely that he does not want to be held hostage for the purpose of political maneuvering.

20 years after the fact, other than pointing to the controversy, how does one explain the success of *Aux armes et caetera?* First, there's the fact that the groundwork is already laid with *L'homme à tête de chou*, "Sea Sex And Sun," and the reissuing of the "classics." Then, by adopting reggae, Serge finds a musical language at the forefront of modernity, which perfectly suits his style, more spoken than sung. He also (perhaps on purpose?) largely simplifies his lyrics and makes them accessible to the entire public without minimalizing them to the extent he does on "Sea Sex And Sun." *Aux armes et caetera* gives us the perfect mix of subversion/challenge (the Marseillaise à la reggae, "Relax Baby Be Cool") self-deprecation ("Des laids des laids"), sex ("Lola Rastaquouère"), a wink at harmless drugs ("Brigade des stups"), and pure humor ("Pas long feu"). Although not a concept album, the LP is remarkably coherent, almost without weakness, and packed with hits and catchy melodies. In short, much to the displeasure of the fans of the *underground* Gainsbourg of the early seventies, it's completely out of the blue: on his trip to Kingston, he has himself a face-lift, a staggering makeover. And we should not forget that pirate radio, all over the place in 1979, plays a role as well. Many stations have their FM signals blocked and their facilities seized, but the number of young listeners keeps growing and Gainsbourg's Marseillaise is one of the most played tunes, along with "Des laids des laids," which is encroaching on the terrain of traditional radio like RMC and RTL.

It's a metamorphosis: Gainsbourg, a celebrity who had always been in the background, is now a superstar, a matinee idol, and this newfound popularity completely recharges his batteries. He's on cloud nine, just sniggering. The man who had such trouble "taking off his mask" as he used to tell interviewers in the sixties, finds himself 15 years later with a mask that is doubly schizophrenic, thanks to a triumph he never envisioned. Soon, the image will be muddled by Gainsbarre, the public beast and unforeseen gold mine in TV ratings, whose encroaching presence will add yet another layer to his strata of personalities, making the understanding of his work even more difficult.

In fall of 1979, there are rumors of Serge returning to the stage. The Palace, which over the last few months has become the nightspot in Paris, is mentioned. In the provinces and in Belgium, certain promoters are already at work. Earlier, he had written the words to "Chavirer la France" by Shake, a little variety singer whose lightweight songs earned him 15 minutes of fame in the mid-seventies. Next, it's Alain Chamfort's turn.

> ALAIN CHAMFORT: *"In 1979, I found myself with plenty of good music for an album and one tune that was a sure hit, providing that the words were good. That melody became "Manureva." At the beginning, Gainsbourg, whom I'd returned to after I was unable to find any other lyricist, wrote me this real piece of shit, "Adieu California," with a bunch of worthless lyrics, all the clichés imaginable from Sunset Boulevard to Malibu. Long story short, I still recorded the tune, and my record company, as usual, found it splendid. The bigwigs all decided to go forth with producing it, but I was convinced that if we kept those words we'd be sunk. I really panicked. I went to Serge and said: "Write me some new lyrics, and make it snappy." The next day he had to dine with Eugène Riguidel, who was participating in the La Transat.[6] Jane had christened his trimaran. It was during this period Alain Colas' boat, 'Manureva,' disappeared. Serge had this idea, like a light bulb going off. He called me, and I told him: "I have just what you need," all the while reminding myself that this was a delicate matter to tackle since it was based on a recent news story. But he'd written me this imposing text. I asked CBS to halt everything. The 45 for "Adieu California" was tossed to the trash heap, and we had a huge hit with "Manureva."*

---

[6] Transatlantic yacht race. (T.N.)

Manu Manureva where are you
Manureva lost amidst the blue
Like a ghostship that is heading for
Tropic isles that simply have no shore
Any more

Jane writes a cute little text for Alain, "Let Me Try It Again," and Serge does two other songs, the opportunistic "Démodé" and also "Bébé Polaroid":

Baby Polaroid
She comes into focus
Let's her image stroke us
Baby Polaroid
Flashes for the camera
Frozen in mascara
There in freeze frame she waits for me
Posing and smiling and so carefree

It's during this time that Jane meets Jacques Doillon and starts work on the film that will become *La Fille prodigue*. Jane, in fact, "becomes" the film. Doillon falls in love with her, but there is a small problem: she's been half of one of the most famous couples in France for more than 11 years now. She is of course not indifferent to Doillon's attentions. At the same time, she looks on powerlessly as Serge metamorphosizes. She can't stand going out every night, but Serge keeps asking her for more. That year, he sells more records for Philips than Johnny Hallyday. Like a kid, drunk on success and excited by the forthcoming NRF publication of his "parabolic tale" *Evguénie Sokolov*, Serge, now more than ever, wants to make himself seen out doing the town, to savor every moment of his success, to sign autographs for the hordes of little teenyboppers who just a year earlier would have considered him a has-been.

JANE BIRKIN: *"In my opinion, the change took place during the concerts at the Palace. Gainsbourg was taken over by Gainsbarre, the blowhard. Suddenly the majority had spoken. Before, he was a marginal character, difficult, not easy to like. That's true. But Gainsbarre really took over. It was fatal. It's normal that something should change as a result of all this. From that point on, Serge would belong to the public. I had to admit this, even if I still felt nostalgic at times."*

Philippe Lerichomme pulls off a master stroke 11 months after the Kingston recording. He convinces Sly and Robbie, as well as all the other musicians (save for Rita Marley and the other back-up singers, who are touring with Bob Marley in the States) to come and do the Palace concerts in Paris in December. They don't have much time - just a few days for rehearsal – which explains why they're only doing the cuts from *Aux armes et caetera* and three old tunes: "Harley Davidson," "Docteur Jekyll et Monsieur Hyde," and "Bonnie and Clyde." They plan to record the shows on December 26, 27, and 28 for a double-live album whose release is scheduled for January, 1980. It's not simply by chance that after 15 years, he choses the Palace for his comeback. He could have chosen the Oylmpia, but he would have been trapped by a "chanson" crowd demanding an "authentic" recital, which he has no intention of doing. The Palace is the hip, young, trendy, superficial Mecca of Parisian nightlife, full of people who read *Rock & Folk* and *Best*, and who are expecting something special (namely Gainsbourg up on stage, surrounded by Rastafarians singing "Aux armes et caetera"). Gainsbourg is hoping the crowd will be on its feet, as it should be for a reggae concert that prompts one to dance. It all comes together, and the Palace is reserved for December 22 through 31, 1979. There will be other dates in Lyon, Strasbourg, and Brussels.

All of Paris is there for opening night: Karl Lagerfeld, Rudolf Nureyev, Louis Aragon, Roland Barthes, Diane Dufresne, etc. Scheduled for 9:00, Serge actually takes the stage at 11:15, probably paralyzed by stage fright.

Francoise Hardy: "Serge is very keen on compliments. I had gone to seen him in his dressing room at the Palace, which was thoroughly embarrassing. When he saw me he asked : "Well? Well?" I spoke about his "class" and his "presence" and I could see he was quite touched. He answered: "Just what I wanted to hear."

Every night, Serge, imperial and radiant, has a parade of celebrities, nymphets, and parasites pass though his dressing room. Jane and the girls come to the first show, but then on December 24 they go to London for Christmas with the Birkin family. That night, on the way to midnight mass, they have a car accident. Jane, out of her head, spends the night at the hospital with Kate and Charlotte, 12 and 8 years-old, respectively. This shock, which comes on the heels of the death of her friend Ana, in no way improves her mental state. At a time when she needs her man to take care of her, Serge can think only of milking the present for all it's worth. Furthermore, a new scandal takes shape just days later.

On January 4, 1980, the eve of his double concert in Brussels, Serge is supposed to sing in Strasbourg. Motivated by the hateful tirades of Michel Droit, the parachutists succeed in discouraging the organizers of the Marseille concert, which is eventually canceled. In Lyon, on January 3, everything goes fine. The next day, things turn sour.

Since December 29, head of the UNAP (Retired Parachutists Association of Alsace), Colonel Jacques Romain-Defossé, has been asking the mayor of Strasbourg to stop the Marseillaise from being sung. In spite of some serious threats, including threats of violence, neither the police nor the mayor give into the pressure. During this period, Gainsbourg's supporters and detractors write letters to the readers of *Dernières Nouvelles d'Alsace*, some simply horrific: "Gainsbourg is really Ginsburg, in other words part of a cohort of people who, pushed out by Russian pogroms and Nazi ovens, have taken up residence – very comfortably, I might add – in our country. A soldier who walks in step with people named Krivine, Cohn-Bendit, Levy, and Glucksmann, merchants of revolution and brewers of philosophical soup. A new legion whose rule is simple: when you stand and face the French flag, spit."

On January 4, the concert is supposed to take place in Wacke Hall. The technicians have no problem setting up. At seven, the audience enters, among them 60 parachutists who also buy tickets. Their plan is to crowd the front rows and intervene when Gainsbourg breaks into the national anthem. While waiting, they distribute tricolor leaflets amidst a backwash of insults from the 3,000 wild youth - "France? You can have it, old man!" With their red berets cocked over their ears, they are described by Brigitte Kantor of

Le Matin as "...no longer young or dashing [...] quaint, if not pathetic." They organize an impromptu press conference: "We will show that there are still real Frenchmen," they proclaim. A former stormtrooper gets carried away while pointing to the crowd: "Look at them! They're just like their idols – slovenly, filthy, a bunch of fools!"

Backstage, Serge is bargaining with Sam, the big Jamaican road manager responsible for the whole crew. Each time he looks out at the crowd, Sam comes back even more terrorized. Serge wants to sing with his Rastafarians. The police wouldn't have permitted this were there a real danger. He's sure that the paratroopers will back off when confronted with 3,000 screaming fans. He thinks he's convinced Sam when he sends him to pick up the others at the hotel, but Sam doesn't return. While Wacke Hall is filling up, things are getting hot in the city. A bomb scare causes an evacuation at the Holiday Inn where the musicians are staying. The Rastafarians are now completely flipped out, and understandably: the background singers are carting off their young children, who've been taken hostage by a debacle that in no way concerns them. When Sam finds them hiding on the bus, they refuse to come out. Their only desire is to leave town as soon as possible.

Deserted by his band, Serge decides to go and confront the crowd with Phify, his sometimes bodyguard that he had just met at the Palace.

> PHIFY: *"Strasbourg was amazing. The Rastafarians had chickened out, and you really can't fault them for it. So Gainsbourg tells me: "I'm going get up and sing the real Marseillai se." I took the stage with him and held the mic. It was great, really moving. When the paratroopers heard the national anthem, they stood at attention like a bunch of morons. They weren't really dangerous, either. They were more ridiculous than anything. Luckily, there were police vans to help them make their getaway, but they still got spat on by the crowd. Serge went back to his dressing room in tears. He was enraged. But he proved that he had balls."*

When the hall empties, Colonel Jacques Romain-Desfossé, orchestrator of this pitiful operation, admits that Gainsbourg is "a very intelligent man, who understood that there are people who want to hear the real Marseillaise. He showed himself to be a marvelous tactician tonight."

Later that night, the cancellation of Serge's Strasbourg show is announced on Belgian television, paving the way for a huge success the next evening. Upon arriving in the Belgian capital the next morning, Serge is swarmed by reporters. The images of his performance the previous night are shown on TV We see him brimming with emotion, fist raised in the air, screaming: "I remain a rebel! I've restored the Marseillaise to its rightful place! I ask that you sing it with me!" The shots of those fatheaded paratroopers with their stupid berets pushes things into the realm of the absurd. The craziest thing is all those old cops and soldiers would later become Gainsbourg's die-hard drinking buddies.

Upon returning to Pairs, Gainsbourg is even more shaken by the affair, especially since the controversy has been kicked up a notch. In *Le Monde*, Patrick Boyer defends Gainsbourg and asks: "Will there never be an end to this stupidity over the French colors? With these hypocrites who splash blue, white, and red all over their curriculum, their intolerance, their racism, and their small-mindedness?" Gaston Wiessler, former Resistance commander, replies that he'd like "to make Mr. Gainsbourg and his entourage understand that earning money – because it goes to whomever has copyright – by screwing around with a hymn that is sacred for us former Resistance fighters, is a sacrilege that I compare to pillaging the bodies of the dead on the battlefield! A certain artists' union has judged it necessary to claim freedom of expression as a means of justifying this Marseillaise, and so if tomorrow I decide to sculpt something out of fecal matter, would the same union call this art as well?" Admiral Joybert, several lines later, praises the paratroopers in Strasbourg while the radio and television union condemns the attacks to which Serge is objected, calling them "an attempt to block artistic freedom of expression." A week after the event, on France-Inter, Jean-François Khan dedicates his show, *Avec tambours and trompettes*, to Serge. Incited listeners call in to beg for "respect for the values that remain," which the Marseillaise is the symbol of. Some are full of bile, saying: "Everything

Gainsbourg touches, he dirties. He doesn't sing, he vomits," and "It's because he's a Jew he wrote that, he's not French," or "He should go back to Israel and marry Barbara..."

In March, 1980, Michel Droit enters the Académie Française, succeeding Joseph Kessel. As tradition dictates, he must, during his speech under the dome, pay homage to the man who died and left him the seat. Serge breaks up and declares: "Kessel was a Jew... We're going to watch Michel Droit pay homage to a Jew [...] That's pretty funny... Otherwise, I couldn't give a damn."

Yeah, I'm Gainsbarre

Financially, things are, as Serge would put it, frankly ridiculous. Even more so now that Bertrand de Labbey, whom he had met during France Gall's aborted comeback, is handling his affairs. It all began a few months earlier, when Gainsbourg, still hoping to make Black-out, slammed the door behind him after leaving the offices at the Artmédia agency, where the directors had found the project too difficult and were in no hurry to support it. Labbey, who had meanwhile stopped producing records to work at Artmédia, where he already represents Catherine Deneuve, understands the situation and is distraught.

BERTRAND DE LABBEY: *"I ran after him on Avenue George-V, and I took him for a drink at Francis. I said I wanted to work with him and that I was ready to get him films. My enthusiasm touched him. I put forth one condition: I wanted him to sign a contract that would allow me to represent him in all areas. It's not the type of thing you ask for at this stage in a collaboration, but I really wanted work with him. We had a meeting at his place a few days later, lunch at Rue de Verneuil, to go over the contract. But the night before, I don't know how it happened, Serge, Catherine, and I found ourselves club-hopping until six in the morning. The meeting was just too important, so I went anyway, haggard and spent. We had breakfast and he proceeded to go over the contract line by line, like a businessman, which he*

*certainly was not, asking me in a very serious tone to make little changes.
I defended myself on every point, but it went on and on, and after three
hours I was exhausted. I said: "Listen, Serge, I'll sign whatever you want.
We're changing everything anyway." And he said to me: "My boy, I'll sign
your paper just like it is." He wanted to test me."*

With his new mandate that encompasses stage, screen, press, and recordings, Labbey is seen by Serge as some sort of magician. In little time,
Gainsbourg's income is doubled.

In spite of his newfound celebrity, Serge's life at Rue de Verneuil remains
normal. Parked in front of the home is Jane's new brand-new, gunmetal gray
Porsche, a recent gift from Serge. Jane is visiting Jacques Doillon regularly.
He likes to show her his other films: *La femme qui pleure, Les Doigts dans la
tête*. The filming of *La Fille Prodigue* will soon start in Trouville.

Although he'd sworn off acting, Serge had agreed earlier to appear in
Claude Berri's new film, for which he'll also do the soundtrack. The future
director of T*chao Pantin, Manon des sources*, and *Jean de Florette* – not to
mention future actor in Serge's *Stan The Flasher* – Berri had written *Je vous
aime* for Catherine Deneuve, finding inspiration in his own love life: a woman
closing in on her forties remembers the men in her life, both husbands and
lovers, first encounters and break-ups. The cast is all stars: Depardieu, the
stud, the beautiful animal; Souchon, the sentimental book proprietor; and
Gainsbourg, the aging bohemian.

CLAUDE BERRI: *"I wanted to do a portrait of a woman who lived her
life in stages. There is a lot of suffering in this film and it's very close to
my heart, despite the weakness in its construction. Catherine really dove
into 'Je vous aime,' especially because each character represented someone important in her life. Of course it's all transposed. I had witnessed
the affair with François Truffaut and was looking for something similar.
It wasn't about finding somebody to incarnate Truffaut, but about finding Catherine a partner who could make the relationship very personal,
heartbreaking, and aggressive. That's why I thought of Gainsbourg. He
alone would inspire me to write those scenes. I didn't try to make him play
a director, which would have been too difficult, so I kept him a singer."*

CATHERINE DENEUVE: *"During the filming. Serge was happy about being able to act, but also he seemed worried inside. There were a lot of exterior shots where we had to wait for a long time, so we did a lot of talking. He's the type who has a hard time going back home at night, and me too. I like discussions to last late into the night, and that's how we spent those long evenings together. Yes, Serge is very difficult, but he's also great company, really lively, very ingenious. He's not so blasé as people think."*

Meanwhile, Gainsbarre's mug is plastered all over Paris. One poster has him in an inexpensive suit, with the caption: "A Bayard changes a man – right, Mr. Gainsbourg?" It's not the only ad campaign to use his image, which in 1980 becomes iconic. Shortly thereafter, he shoots a spot for Christian Blachas' magazine *Sortir*, which is shown in French cinemas. In April, 1980, bookstores put out *Gainsbourg*, by Micheline de Pierrefeu and Jean-Claude Maillard, a biography brilliantly illustrated but not widely distributed by the failing publisher. Serge also goes to visit Yvelines, a primary school where he is invited to meet a 5th grade class. Finally, NRF comes out with his parabolic tale, *Evguénie Sokolov*. Claude Gallimard spent seven long years waiting for these 80 pages of powerful sensations. Sophisticated writing, precise style, rich vocabulary, and devastating humor make this strange literary creation one that merits a bit of attention:

> *From my life, a life now here trapped in this hospital bed with shit-flies hovering above, come images occasionally precise but more often blurred - "out of focus" as photographers say – some overexposed, others murky, and which if placed end to end would constitute a film both grotesque and atrocious, because its peculiar soundtrack, running parallel to the longitudinal perforations on the film, would contain nothing but blasts of intestinal gas.*

Sokolov, a poor lad suffering from "that iniquitous misfortune of constant wind-breaking," starts off in the first few pages with an itinerary not unlike that of Gainsbourov, except for the farts: chased out of school and propelled forward by his anti-establishment gas, he enters the School of Fine Arts, were he decides "with no real conviction to study architecture" before moving on to painting. His gaseous infirmity earns him nicknames in the army: Bombadier, Gunner, Gust O'Wind, Snowblower. All until he decides to return to painting and drawing with the quill...

A particularly violent explosion broke a pane of glass and made my hand tremble like that of an electro-epileptic child. I contemplated the broken glass at my feet and then lifted my eyes to my sketch, fascinated. My arm had operated like a seismograph. Upon reflection, the dazzling beauty of what I had drawn seemed to emanate from a dangerously exacerbated sensitivity brought on by some stimulating drug.

Responding to insidious inquiries from the magazine *Art Press*, Gainsbourg defends himself:

The only laughter that might escape upon reading my book would be nervous laughter, because the concept is thoroughly tragic. 'Evguénie Sokolov' is a wide-angle autobiography, meaning it contains distortions – atrocious distortions that may call to mind one Francis Bacon.

In fact, we know that Francis Bacon paints tortured and lacerated faces and bodies, silent screams, oral afflictions – a sort of sublime bedlam of very poetic monsters amidst a décor of raw meat, crucifixion, and sordid coitus:

Thus, I told myself in the dark of night while vainly searching for sleep, the premonitory stench of my bodily death would become a means of moving towards and transcending that which is the most pure, the most vivacious, and the most desperately ironic in the deepest recesses of my creative spirit, and after so many years dedicated to pictorial technique, so many days spent spreading my gas before the frames of the great masters, these broken lines, frail and tortured, had just freed me forever from my inhibitions.

Sokolov suddenly becomes a fashionable painter, adored by critics and groupies whose sighs of admiration are echoed by the artist's derriere. They salute his "hyper-abstraction," his "stylistic insistence," his "formal mysticism," his "rare eurhythmy." He comes up with a name – gassograms – for his pictures, which sell like hotcakes. This brutal notoriety is unfortunately accompanied by new anal pains. Evguénie, now tortured by his rear end, starts to slowly die. His ascension to glory is abruptly halted by a lack of gas, making all work difficult or vague. Worried, Sokolov dives into a host of medical treatises, such as *Intestinal meteorism in gastro-intestinal pathology* by Roux and Moutier. Again, here's Gainsbourg in *Art Press*:

This book took six years of work. I took quite serious notes, did research at the school of medicine, bought several scientific works. It's not just any old thing – it's highly structured and very precise.

Serge reads numerous descriptions of anal surgeries, and it's in the eight volumes of Bruno Péquignot's *Manual of medical pathology* that he finds most of the terms used by our lamentable protagonist in the course of his medical procedures. We then see Evguénie follow a strict diet in order to produce unheard of flatulence: gusts blown forth into infectious miasmas that curdle the atmosphere so much it becomes unbreatheable. To isolate himself from the world and also his own stench, he thinks of protecting himself with a gas mask.

Don your mask, Sokolov, so that your anaerobic fermentation might spread your fame from blasting tubas, so that your irrepressible wind might transform abscissae and ordinates into sublime anamorphosis.

In *Le Journal du dimanche*, literary chronicler Annette Colin-Simard doesn't hold back: "It's Gainsbourg's first, and let's hope, last novel. The subject matter is grotesque beyond imagination. His talent is non-existent. One only hopes its black cover is indicative of the destiny this rubbish deserves – a hastily dug grave in the backyard."

Others will find a synthesis of Serge's main literary influences in this little tableau so harshly rendered. Through Sokolov, we see the silhouette of Des Esseintes, the alter-ego of Huysmans in *A rebours*. The clinical horror of the descriptions evokes both Lautréamont's *Chants de Maldoror* and Defoe's *A Journal of the Plague Year*. The profound disgust for humanity brings to mind Rimbaud and Léon Bloy.

GAINSBOURG: *"Given that I am a man of the 19th century, so is the language. I remain a gentleman, and perhaps a bit of a punk. The idea is disgusting, but it allows me to deal with the nostalgia of never having made it as a painter. Evguénie is a man who consciously destroys himself because he wants glory, and glory destroys him. Thus in a way, it's autobiographical."*

In the months following the publication of the book, there's also the appearance of *Au pays des malices*, a collections of lyrics compiled by Franck

Lhomeau and Alain Coelho, which is followed by a number of aphorisms including: "Snobbism is a champagne bubble teetering between a fart and a belch."; "Cock is masculine, cunt is feminine. A question of genre."; and one of his favorites, "The one walking the dog wears the leash." Serge will often speak of another literary project over the coming years, a fictional journal that would be nothing but lies and fabrication. There's nothing to suggest he came up with anything more than the title.

At the same time, Jane dives into her part in the Jacques Doillon film. Serge, aware of the threat posed by Doillon, doesn't want her to do it. He's also jealous of Doillon as an artist. Hasn't Jacques given her a great dramatic part, comparable to that of Johnny Jane in *Je t'aime moi non plus*? And at just the moment when Serge discovers he won't be doing *Black-out*? Instead of rallying himself and following her to the set, as he had done before when a threat arose (with Alain Delon in *La Piscine*, for example), Serge loses himself in alcoholism. In the midst of a suicidal and self-destructive vertigo, as if he were facing the inevitable end of their love affair, he is playing with fire, literally driving his wife into the arms of his rival while doing all he can to disgust her.

> JUDY CAMPBELL-BIRKIN: *"Over the years, his alcoholism was bearable, even when he was very drunk and putting away entire bottles of cassis. Then, when the kids got older, it wasn't as funny. Jane really wanted to do 'La Fille prodigue', but Serge had warned her: "If you do it, I'm not coming home."*

When she comes home from school, Kate Barry, 13, never knows what to expect – the 50 year-old child who jokes around and plays games with her and Charlotte, or that "frightening person who was brutal and harsh with his words."

> RÉGINE: *"One day in Deauville, he calls to tell me 'The Blue Angel' is on TV and he wants us all to watch it together. In the afternoon, he takes off with my husband, and five hours later they're nowhere to be found. Jane and I start to worry. Turns out that he and my husband, who never drinks, were making the rounds of all the bistros. Finally they get back, and Serge declares he no longer wants to have dinner, so he heads off to the bar at Club 13, where he starts screwing around with all the assholes that are sending him drinks. I had to go and get him. I grabbed him by the collar*

and dragged him back. I said: "You made such a stink about 'The Blue Angel,' well now you're going to watch it with us!" Right in front of me, he starts to insult Jane, Charlotte, and Kate. Everyone was crying. I grabbed him and said: "This stops now, unless you want a sock in the face!" He sat down and started blubbering. He didn't even know where he was..."

On July 15, 1980, the day after Bastille Day, Gainsbourg sings "Aux armes et caetera" under the Arch of Triumph, lighting his smoke off the flame at the Tomb of the Unknown Soldier. At the same time, he's contacted by Gérard Blanc and the other surviving members of French pop outfit Martin Circus, who have dropped off the radar over the last few years, doing mostly variety TV. Serge writes them the mediocre lyrics to "USSR/USA":

> *USA*
> *Stop today*
> *Stop playing the fool*
> *USSR*
> *You guys too*
> *Just like the tsars*
> *All wanna be stars*

Just before his series of shows at the Palais des Congrès, Julien Leclerc finds himself short on lyrics for his new album, which must be released almost immediately. Through Bertrand de Labbey, he asks Serge for lyrics to two songs: "Mango" and "Belinda."

JULIEN CLERC: *"He came to the studio with Jane in the midst of their break-up. They were both suffering, but she already had that look, like she was somewhere else. She looked like those women who know that they're leaving. Serge had stood me up several times in the past, so this time I was forced to shut him up in the studio with his mini-cassette, just so that he'd write. I watched over him from behind the glass in the control booth to make sure I got my lyrics!"*

> *My little vine you're dancing in the breeze*
> *Me, the macaque, I chase you through the trees*
> *I want to bite into your mangos so fine*
> *That hang upon your vine*

In mid-September, 1980, during a very grim night, Jane leaves Serge and takes the girls with her. His excesses are driving her over the edge. Kate and Charlotte have for some time sensed, confusedly, that things aren't going well. Their mom, who in their eyes had always been "head of the family," no longer sees in this hyper-alcoholized Gainsbarre any trace of the Gainsbourg she once loved. This is the terrible duality that Serge would set irrevocably into memory a year later with "Ecce Homo." Everything happens very quickly, very brutally. Jane tells the kids to pack their bags. Distraught, she joins Serge in the kitchen to talk, swearing that she loves him passionately, that she wants to stay, that she doesn't think she can make it without him. She remembers him looking like a little kid who couldn't understand the seriousness of what he had done.

The first official story about the break-up appears in *Le Journal de dimanche* on October 9: "I miss my children's laughter so much it's killing me," declares Serge. On October 24, Jane and her kids are on the cover of *Paris-Match*. The headline: "Gainsbourg and Birkin: Split – In Love for Twelve Years – The Brutal End of a Love Affair". "I'm unhappy," she says, "very unhappy. I prefer not to talk about it." There's nothing more: the story explains that her lawyer, Gilles Dreyfus, has advised her to not say anything to the press.

> RÉGINE: *"Serge caused the rupture. He wanted it and he planned it. He could never forgive her for having considered a romance with someone else. When she left, he told me he'd never take her back."*

> GAINSBOURG: *"It's my fault that Jane left. I abused her too much. I'd come home thoroughly plastered, knock her around. When she'd yell at me I couldn't stand it – two seconds and wham... She put up with a lot from me, but it's since turned into an eternal affection..."*

> KATE BARRY: *"It's true that at the end, things were a mess. It was like the Elysée Matignon each night, with the same spectators, the same nightlife assholes. Jane couldn't take any more. She felt like she was suffocating, like a witness to self-destruction. He didn't understand that Mom had had it, that she couldn't breath. They were no longer a true couple – this was a monologue."*

The blow to Serge's morale is frightening. While wrapping up on *Je vous aime*, Catherine Deneuve calls Jane to convince her to come back. There is an attempt to reconcile for a few days at Rue de Verneuil, about which Serge says: "In a moment of pride, I refused. I had cried too much, for too long."

In the meantime, he had asked his friend Jacques Séguéla to loan Jane his home at Villa Montmorency, a sinister but luxurious private development in the 16th arrondissement.

Serge spends three days with Gérard Depardieu, working through his blues and listening to sad music while never uttering a word, all right in front of the wild-eyed, nine year-old Guillaume. Then he admits to *Le Quotidien de Paris*: "I thought I'd hit bottom, but it was a false bottom. I'm all alone in my millionaire's bachelor pad [...] I have a platinum record, but what I really need is a platinum girl. I had a golden girl, but she's dumped me."

On November 9, at midnight, he goes on the radio program *Vous avez du feu*, and makes a "staggering confession":

"I've just learned a serious lesson. [...] At 52 years-old I've just experienced my first failed relationship. And I know it is just as violent, even more so than if I were 20. I know there are those out there who take me for a cynic, but they should know that I have been crying tears of fire for months now, real tears [...] I've never been as unhappy as I am today."

Still, he does recognize that he's difficult to live with:

"You've got to take risks. Me, I race Formula-1, not go-carts. It's exhausting in the sense that I recognize I am a dipsomaniac chain smoker. I'm moody and anxious. [...] Now it's time to move on to other women, but not like a skirt-chaser. I'm not a playboy. Plus, I'm too sad. I can't do it now. I've never known how to pick up girls. I've always known by instinct if I had a chance. [...] I'm a romantic, which is why I'm hurt. I am in despair. It's very difficult. I'm a boy. A boy who's suffered greatly, but a boy nonetheless."

Jacques Doillon is afraid that Charlotte hates him. He tries to explain to her that he can't help himself, that he just loves her mother too much. Now nine years-old, when she sees her father after the separation, Charlotte tries to comfort him by talking trash about Doillon. Not out of meanness, but rather to establish a sort of complicity. Serge, for his part, is much too realistic about his wrongdoing and cannot come to blame Jane.

JANE BIRKIN: *"That's also something I admire in him. He was never aggressively bitter, never showed any spitefulness towards me, and many men would have given the fact that it was I who left [...] He forgave every-*

one who left him, both Brigitte and me. He was very faithful, and decided to create an image of us that no one could touch, a sort of perfection. It wasn't a question of betrayal. It was understood that he was unbearable and I was simply saving my own skin. There was no dishonor in that. He would argue with people who spoke ill of me. It's very rare, not having the desire to sully the image of the other person."

For Julien Clerc's birthday on October 4, 1980, Serge takes the stage at the Palais des Congrès. The third partner in crime is Gérard Depardieu, who's also just put out an album, lyrics courtesy of his wife Elisabeth. Serge and Julien do a duet on "Mangos," and then the trio does an impromptu version of "La Javanaise." On the same day, *France Soir* publishes a promotional photo of Catherine Deneuve with Gainsbourg. Like a little kid - and like a braggart - Serge cuts it out and runs around backstage showing it to everyone, letting people believe that something is going on with the two of them...

JULIEN CLERC: *"Like everyone, I had first sung "La javanaise" in the shower, but I also did it on TV with Miou-Miou. Anyway, after that memorable show, we went out and partied at a restaurant and then in a nightclub. That's when I discovered that Serge was capable of incredible physical courage, along with a kind of heedlessness. I saw him get into a little brush with Gérard. Serge was giving him a bunch of shit backstage, and when you think of how big Depardieu is, well that takes some nerve. Anyway, he was looking for trouble and he found it. It all came to a head early in the morning when Gérard grabbed him and slammed him down on the hood of a car, saying: "This stops now, or it ends badly!"*

For his nighttime debauchery, Serge finds an ideal drinking buddy in Daniel Duval. The actor and ex-husband of Anna Karina, whom Daniel had married in 1978, had just found big success on the other side of the camera. His film, *La Dérobade*, featuring Miou-Miou (who takes the César for best actress), was the tenth highest grossing movie of 1979.

DANIEL DUVAL: *"The first time I met Serge was at a nightclub, of course, at two in the morning. After a while, I wanted to leave, but he told me: "No, you're not abandoning me!" We stayed by each other's side for three days, and we became immediately very close because we had a lot to talk about. We were friends. We didn't talk about cinema, music, work... We had both just separated, Serge from Jane and myself from a woman whom*

Serge also knew and once loved, Anna Karina. We were heartbroken. I always wondered how he could party like that, until the early hours of morning, and then I realized he was vomiting, that fucker! He would excuse himself and then head to the toilets to barf, me four steps behind him. These dark nights were populated by a coterie of the most beautiful girls in Paris, but we would ignore them and just screw around together. It was a real love relationship, but not homosexual. He was insanely jealous, and if one of my friends approached me he acted like a rooster! Now and then, some doped-up chicks would come over and ask if he was holding - Serge, who never took drugs, never even smoked pot! This would really piss him off... When he found out that I was taking drugs, he shook me and said: "Motherfucking doper!" He wouldn't stand for it."

Serge gets together with old pal Jacques Dutronc on a regular basis. The latter is getting ready to release his first record in six years, graciously entitled *Geurre et pets*. Until now, these "summits" have yielded little fruit. We're well aware of their respective faults: both lazy, drunken schoolboys, they obviously know each other too well for there to be any surprises. Yet when it comes time for the album, the alchemy kicks in:

Hajji, chink, kike, paki
Wog, gringo, rasta, brownie
Polack, kraut, gook, hymie
This is a love song
What bullshit!

Gainsbourg writes only lyrics for this album. Dutronc covers two of his old tunes, "Le temps de l'amour" and "La vie dans ton retroviseur," beautiful melodies that he croons marvelously. Then Serge writes him a lovely little story ("Mes idées sales"):

I have made clean
My dirty thoughts
Both for real
And for a joke
My script now horizontal
Like your cries
And like my stroke

"L'éthylique" bears both their names, and we'd be wrong not to see it as a little love letter, man to man:

I don't have the words
Gainsbourg has gone astray
That's how it is
When he drinks
But oh my word
It's looking good today
Into a fizz
He sinks

Serge isn't the sort to be self-critical, but he loves bemoaning his fate, as Dutronc tells us in an interview with Jean-Marie Périer during a video recording of his concerts at the Casino...

JACQUES DUTRONC: *"He's one of those rare people in this business who only talked about himself, but at least he did it well. [...] You could break both legs, both arms, and fall out a six-story window, then call to say, "Sorry I couldn't make it." And he'd respond: "Yeah. I'm a mess, too. I've got a splinter." Gee, that's nice of you... Anyway, I believe he was a great artist. He was at least smart enough to never turn into his caricature. Sometimes it came close. It would have been easy... [...] And what no one understood is that is wasn't booze, or cigarettes, or his cock that killed him. Destruction is something different - that simple. Really, the only thing that made us laugh, and since he's dead I can talk about it – he's finally dead, resting in peace! - was when we thought about Yul Brynner. We'd say: "When people die, their hair and their fingernails continue to grow."*

On December 17, 1980, at the end of a year rich in both remorse and rebirth, *Je vous aime* hits the theatres. In a *France-Soir* interview, Serge declares: "In a way, Claude Berri drew from my own life. In the story, I make Catherine suffer. Myself, well I'm also very cruel." And the film really does contain some huge screaming matches between the two, to the point of it being uncomfortable. The viewer is left to suspect that this is just what happened a few months earlier between him and Jane:

CATHERINE DENEUVE: *I'm sick of knocking around all night. That's no life!*

SERGE: *Well I need to have some fun if I want to write songs. It's because I don't give a shit about life that people like what I do. Some people sing about hope and it's a depressing bore. I sing about despair and people laugh.*

[477]

Je vous aime does rather poorly – just 300,000 tickets sold in Paris. "Bardot was an Ingres, Jane a Gainsborough, and Catherine is a Van Dongen," says Serge, giddy over the media-perpetuated rumors that he maliciously nourishes.

CATHERINE DENEUVE: *"As an actor, he was great because under all that reserve, all of his hiding behind that mask of smoke, one could sense his fragility. Also, he must have worried about not being up to the task. In the film, when I meet him, I'm a reporter who's come to interview a successful singer, then we have an affair and I start to write lyrics for his songs. I remember one of his most beautiful lines. Instead of saying that he wants to be happy with me, he makes this supreme declaration of love: "You're the one I want to be bored with." It's an offer you just can't refuse!"*

CATHERINE: *When you say women are bitches, is that supposed to be a compliment?*

SERGE: *Absolutely.*

CATHERINE: *A compliment for dogs?*

SERGE: *No, for women!*

With a bit of help of from Jean-Pierre Sabar, his old arranger, Serge releases the film's soundtrack at the same time. It opens with "La fautive," his most misogynist piece in ages, which bounces over an R&B groove lifted from the Four Tops' "It's The Same Old Song":

The guilty one, it's you
If you're in a pile of shit then the blame's on you
The guilty one, it's you
You're gonna pay for all the grief that you put me through

We'll pass over the tiresome reggae version of "Je vous salue Marie" to look instead at a funny little tune sung by Serge when his character in the film goes to a kennel to shoot a piece for a TV show:

I like tail
Lovely hounds
From the pounds
Bitches all 'round
Heat abounds
I like tail

Catherine and Serge, as a duo, have a modest hit at the time with "Dieu fumeur de havanes," which later becomes one of his most widely played smashes:

> *Catherine: You're but a smoker of Gitanes*
> *Round your head a cloud of blue*
> *Now and then I get teary it's true*
> *God's my only master then there's you*
> *Serge: God is a smoker of Havanas*
> *Paradise a smoky cloud above*
> *These words did he speak to me my love*
> *Of things thereof*

On December 27, 1980, they do the tune on TV for Michel Drucker's show, *Stars*. During the lip-sync, Serge pretends to be sloshed and tries to feel up Catherine in an attempt to fuel the rumors.

CATHERINE DENEUVE: *"Serge is a tortured soul, but he is also able to get downright giddy over the tiniest details, and that's when he's amazing. When you get to know him, he can be irritating or provocative, and then he'll let loose with some mind-boggling phrase. He always ends up winning. He's betrayed by his profound kindness. He's certainly had his sorrows, and I think I did help him. But I'm no nursemaid. I was also troubled because I have a great affection for Jane and I found the whole thing very sad..."*

GAINSBOURG: *"Yeah, I was terrible. Catherine... She not only helped me get out of a bad place, but it was maybe also because of her that I didn't shoot myself."*

Excited at the idea of being Catherine's pop music Pygmalion, as he had been for Brigitte Bardot, Anna Karina, and Jane Birkin, he suggests they team up soon and do an album. Catherine accepts, and the date is set for February, 1981.

Another woman now comes into Gainsbourg's life. He meets the Paris-Planning model, Caroline (alias Bambou),[1] at the Elysée-Matignon. Bambou gives her account of the meeting in her 1996 book:

A trendy nightclub. It's the first time she's set foot there, her agency was throwing a party. She never goes to these dumb-ass parties. This is the

---

[1] Caroline von Paulus, distant niece of Field Marshal Friedrich Paulus, former Nazi general. (T.N.)

first! She's on the dance floor, moving to a disco beat, lights flashing all around. The boss at the club comes over and says the man across the way demands to see her at his table. She looks over at him, surprised. No way. Who does that old fuck take himself for?

She shrugs her shoulders and with a detached air replies:

–Don't know the guy. Tell him to go to hell. Who's he to give me orders?

She keeps dancing, like mad. She's unbridled. She loves the music. She doesn't want to think about anything, nothing...

Exhausted, she goes back to her table where her friend's waiting.

–It's been ages since I've danced like that. I'll have one more drink with you, another dance, and then we can split if you like.

She looks up. He's planted himself there with a bucket of champagne.

–Hi.

The old fuck has come to her table since she wouldn't come to his.

–Mind if I sit down, you little tart?

He sits down and looks at her, laughing. She smiles. This guy has style. Better yet, she likes him, and it looks like he likes her...

It's the beginning of a torrid and violent relationship, one of love and hate, insane screaming matches and immense tenderness. In the beginning, she slips little love letters under his door, things like "To my adorable papa, whom I'll love forever," sealed with a kiss. Charming. He's seduced. In December, 1980, he invites her to Los Angeles, where he is set to work with one of his pet interpreters.

ALAIN CHAMFORT: *"I was preparing for the album 'Amour année zéro' and I went back to see Serge. We had parted on good terms after "Manureva." Seeing as how he was always hounded to write for everybody in Paris, I suggested that he come to L.A. with me. At first it was just us two, and it was rather rude of me, I suppose, to tell him the night before we left that Lio was coming with me. Still, it was fine in the beginning. We looked for a house and partied for about 10 days, just cruising around in a Rolls on Sunset Boulevard. "Amour année zero," the title cut, was indica-*

tive of what we were both living through: the rebirth of love. Serge had left Jane and found Bambou. I'd left my wife and found Lio... Serge was lonely, so he had Bambou join him, and that's when things turned sour. We lived together in that house, and the girls, who couldn't stand each other, just lounged around the pool. The tension got so bad that it was unbearable, so much so that Lio became nasty with everyone."

LIO: *"I think on one hand, Serge was bored, but he also imagined that he was living in some heightened reality, as does everyone who's dazzled by the idea of discovering Hollywood, Sunset Boulevard, those big names one dreams about. As for Bambou, maybe she'd been dreaming about crazy recording sessions with the wildest musicians on the West Coast, parties till the break of dawn. Anyway, nothing was exciting enough for her."*

Chamfort is unhappy. He rejects Gainsbourg's lyrics and asks him to work a little harder.

LIO: *"Gainsbourg was really loafing, which was tough on Alain. He only ended up writing things like "Malaise en Malaisie" and "Bambou" because Alain was there and constantly pushing him."*

> *Bambou*
> *Your vacant eyes seem to invite me*
> *Bambou*
> *Into the tropics hot and sweaty*
> *Bambou*
> *The troubled waters of your blank stare*
> *Bambou*
> *Reflect a swamp and danger lurks there*

ALAIN CHAMFORT: *"Gainsbourg was fascinated by the fact that Bambou was a junkie. It was an unhealthy curiosity, because Bambou wasn't afraid to take things to the limit, to follow that same self-destructive logic they both shared. Serge would say nonchalantly: "Yeah, she's pushing the envelope. I found a bunch of syringes again in the bathroom!"*

In her book, Bambou narrates the events around a dinner at a Japanese restaurant, which ends very badly:

She doesn't like alcohol and so she doesn't drink much. He, however, is quite lit up. The mood is still festive. He talks about work, life, everything... He is by nature more than shy, a man-child who's been flayed alive. After a few more drinks, he takes us for a ride through the frenzied delirium of a total madman, all while anchoring himself to a paradoxical lucidity. Sometimes she can't make sense of it all. He's complicated, this guy! She listens, amused. He starts to stagger a bit as they leave the restaurant. Hot sake, although not super strong, goes right to the head... Does he drink to tame his shyness, or to deal with the trials of creativity? She does not know. He was like this when they met, and she accepts him as he is. But it's no picnic...

He's really tanked and starts to get belligerent, berating her constantly. His monologue is not wholly coherent, and the conversation disintegrates. She keeps her cool...

"Look at me! Aren't you happy?"

"Sure, but I don't like to see you so plastered."

"Just like you to say something like that! ... You piss me off! I'll get plowed when I please, and if you don't like it, then you can go back to where you came from!"

She remains silent.

"Don't pout, you fucking cunt. I get bitches by the truckload. You're not indispensible."

"Listen, you'd better stop. Keep it up and I won't love you anymore!"

He gets up with his fist raised, ready to strike.

"Say that again!"

She looks in his eyes and knows it would better to keep her mouth shut, but she can't stop herself from pushing his buttons:

"Keep it up and I won't love you anymore!"

Wham! He strikes and she hits the ground.

"What? I didn't have you come thousands of miles so that I could hear that! So you don't love me anymore!"

He's mad. He grabs her by the hair and drags her down the stairs. He flips out and starts beating the hell out of her with all his might. She tries her best to protect herself, rolling up in a ball and covering her head. She knows if she says anything he'll kill her, so she keeps quiet. She no longer feels the blows. The booze had made him insane. He no longer knows what he's doing, and the blows keep raining down.

Out of energy and out of breath, he finally stops. He sits down, haggard. He immediately comes over to her, conscious of what he's done, full of shame and regret.

GAINSBOURG: *"Three months in L.A. to make an album, that's nothing to me. Sunshine, swimming pool – that's nothing to moan about. I recorded 'Mauvaises nouvelles des étoiles' in six days in Nassau..."*

ALAIN CHAMFORT: *"Serge was just getting plastered and then he finally split without a word. And he took the lyrics to a song we were working on, "Souviens-toi de m'oublier," which was going to be a major cut on the album. Catherine Deneuve had just arrived in L.A. to promote Truffaut's 'Le Dernier Métro,' and Serge, who'd just filmed 'Je vous aime' with her, went to meet her. He wanted to write an album for her, and to convince her, he offered her this beautiful text. Obviously she accepted. Still, I found it rather crass."*

"Lio was jealous," said Serge. "She wanted the song herself, but that was out of the question," he tells us later in *La Palace Magazine*. The song that was originally written for an Alain Chamfort melody now becomes a duo for Serge and Catherine Deneuve:

> *Catherine: Please remember to forget*
> *Serge: I haven't yet*
> *Catherine: Please reflect like a mirror*
> *Serge: I'll try my dear*
> *Catherine: And do your best to forget*
> *Serge: I mustn't fret*
> *Catherine: Amnesia like a blessing*
> *Like black magic comes*

LIO: "The record company had invested hundreds of thousands of francs, we were in this luxurious mansion in Beverly Hills, and all because Gainsbourg was part of the deal. Thus his departure was quite a blow to Chamfort."

The day of Serge's hasty withdrawal, Chamfort meets up with him at the airport and digs into him. Then Chamfort gets a round-trip ticket to Paris and goes off to explain the situation to Alain Lévy, the head of CBS, who sets up a dinner with Gainsbourg. Serge promises to do the work and send on the missing lyrics.

When he gets back, Gainsbourg dives into the recording of the Catherine Deneuve album with his English musicians. There are 11 cuts, including a remake of "Ces petits riens," an insipid plagiarism of "Docteur Jekyll et Monsieur Hyde" called "Monna Vanna et Miss Duncan," a reworking of "Initiales B.B." which becomes "Digital Delay," and then "Marine Band Tremolo," a poke at the English national anthem just two years after "Aux armes et caetera." Serge is sorely lacking in inspiration. He thinks he can improvise, as usual, but he has no concept, no unifying idea. He makes do with sending subliminal messages to Jane, using Catherine, his messenger deluxe, to sing the words to his "Overseas Telegram," the one he sent her when they met in 1968 and which he took back after the break-up.

> CATHERINE DENEUVE: *"If the record was poorly prepared, it's as much Serge's fault as it is mine. I didn't have experience. I just told myself, "Well, I guess that's how this works." But as time moved on I understood that something wasn't right. I'm partly responsible too. One can't be 'only' the performer..."*

The only success on the tiresome record are the words to "Dépression au-dessus du jardin," a tune that Serge is so attached to he will perform his own version of it onstage at the Casino de Paris in 1985:

> *The garden is steeped in depression*
> *Chagrin dominates your expression*
> *You just let go of me*
> *As if it were a spree*
> *And summer just came to an end*
> *The flowers have all lost their scent*
> *Killed by that assassin*
> *Time, our dark friend*

The stunning melody is credited to Gainsbourg, who once again fails to cite the source, Chopin's 10th etude in F minor, probably taught to a young Serge by his father. Catherine's voice, in contrast, is not up to the task. Serge had dreamed of recreating with her the same miracles he pulled off with Bardot and Birkin, but really it's only the album's cover - Catherine, shot by Helmut Newton, decked out in black silk and reclining on a fur - which bears any merit...

On February 23, 1981, the newspaper *Libération*, crippled by serious financial problems, publishes – for the time being – it's last edition, and the headline reads: "Je t'aime... moi non plus." Serge frames it. In the pages of women's magazines, he declares that he's once again polygamous. There are photos of him with a certain Yaëlle, a university student, which come out just after the official arrival of Bambou. Then he's seen escorting Valentine, the daughter of Zizi Jeanmaire and Roland Petit. But his escapades don't last long, and he's photographed back in the arms of Bambou, dancing at a nightclub on the Champs-Elysées. Also, posters are up all over Paris for the release of *La Fille prodigue*, the film that had hastened Jane's departure. The critics are unanimous in their praise of her performance: "The polar opposite of her usual lightweight, comic roles, here she is powerfully moving..."

reappears the day before Mitterand is elected President of France, just in time for it to review the Catherine Deneuve album. Also inside is a cowardly bit of wordplay from her would-be Pygmalion: "Deneuve? Non, d'occase!"[2] Catherine immediately sends him a cutting telegram:

> *As far as I'm concerned, there's no amount of drunkenness that will ever justify your wordplay in 'Libération' STOP One must know how to control certain impulses STOP You'll never be able to drown all your regrets, and in spite of your success I know you are inconsolable for reasons that have ceased to be of interest to me STOP I was fond of you but further indulgence would simply be smug.*

Catherine

A crude and drunken Gainsbourg, who beats his women and vomits up all that alcohol that makes him so sick... There's nothing about his attitude in the last year and a half that is in the least bit likeable. But the public at large ignores the most unpleasant signs of his depression, and Serge's popular-

[2] A play on her name – "neuve," as in "Deneuve," means "new." Serge is essentially saying, "New? No, second hand!" (T.N.)

[485]

ity does not wane. A media icon, Serge's likeness even makes its way into Grevin's wax museum in Paris.

Family interlude – Serge produces a 45 for his nephew Alain Zaoui, newly christened Alain Ravaillac (he later settles on Zackman). His wife Nicole fills us in.

> NICOLE SCHLUSS: *"We'd come back from the States, where Alain had played with some of Zappa's musicians. He had Serge listen to some demos, and Serge was smitten with "Discométèque." He gets us a meeting the next day with Alain Levy, the head of CBS. The contract is signed, they go into the studio, and Serge lets Alain choose his musicians. Then it's time for the lyrics. Alain starts in: "A drink and a smoke, I dance till I drop/ The disco wop..." Serge interrupts: "What's that crap? No, nothing doing." Alain explains that he could have read him the lyrics earlier but that Serge didn't want to hear them. There's a big pow-wow in the studio, and just as a joke, Alain sings: "A joint on my lips, a cock like a rock/The disco wop." Serge says, "Super!" not noticing how the record company guy in the back is starting to squirm... Obviously there wasn't a lot of airplay, and later Serge was kind of pissed. He could get away with lyrics like that, which wasn't the case for his nephew..."*

After a relaxing summer, Serge tackles the recording of his new reggae album, *Mauvaises nouvelles des étoiles*, at the famous Island Studios in the Bahamas from September 21 to 27. His artistic director fears it will be a useless imitation, which is in fact what the media points out when the album is released in November. The argument is nonchalantly brushed of by Serge, who claims that it serves as the second part of a diptych.

> PHILIPPE LERICHOMME: *"As much as I'd believed in Aux armes et caetera, where the margin of error was maybe 100%, I was convinced that we shouldn't do another reggae album. That's where we disagreed. Serge persuaded me one day by trapping me in a room with the heads of Phonogram, who were asking for nothing more than that."*

In the studio, the atmosphere is not as cool as it was two years ago. This time, Sly Dunbar and Robbie Shakespeare walk around with copies of *Billboard* under their arms, checking out sales, monitoring the climb of Grace Jones' album, or negotiating a recording deal with singer Gwen Guthrie.

These guys are no longer *musicos*, but rather openly traded stocks whose hourly rates are continually on the rise. Bad vibes with the rastas...

BAMBOU: *"When they came to France for the Palace concerts, Serge bought them all gold chains, and they chose the thickest ones because they said people back home try to rip them off their necks and steal them. When we came to Nassau they didn't have a single tune ready and every two hours they'd ask for 10 bucks, claiming they hadn't eaten in 10 days!"*

Like before, Serge leaves for the Caribbean with nothing more than titles and secretly stays up burning the midnight lamp to finish the words. During this time, he's running on bull shots – a concoction of vodka, beef bouillon, and Tabasco which Bambou prepares and serves to him in the studio. After his version of "Overseas Telegram," the album gives way to "Ecce Homo." Behold the man:

> *Gainsbarre, yeah that's me*
> *You can find me where you please*
> *In nightclubs or on the streets*
> *In Yankee bars, life is sweet*

Extraordinary invention, this Gainsbarre stuff. It inevitably leads to the play on words "Gainsbourg se barre, Gainsbourg se bourre."[3] Serge is making it easy for the next 10 years of reporters and TV hosts: their subject matter is predetermined and their principal target will use and abuse the cliché to the point of schizophrenic overdose.

GAINSBOURG: *"It's arrogance, and at the same time I'm giving myself shit. It's definitely not narcissism... I don't see why the great masters can all do self-portraits but I can't."*

PHILIPPE LERICHOMME: *"That name, Gainsbarre, really translated the duality of Serge, who was always pushing the envelope and often going over the limit. There were times when Gainsbarre would get away from me and go too far, because the danger was in not having any more boundaries to cross, in going to the other side, the point of no return. I forced myself to*

---

[3] "Gainsbourg leaves, Gainsbarre boozes." (T.N.)

know these boundaries, to understand his way of playing with the limits, which was not easy."

Gainsbourg the blowhard can guess what the "boys" want from him. It's ironic to see him become the flag-bearer for all these kids when at 53, he could be their father or grandfather. His intentions become even more solemn in "Juif et Dieu":

> *And if God were a Jew, girl that would worry you*
> *Don't you know that the Nazarene*
> *Hasn't a drop of the Aryan*
> *If he's the son of God, if that's true*
> *Then*
> *A Jew is God*
> *God and Jew*

Later he quotes Einstein, the Jewish Karl Marx, and the trio of Semitic Bolsheviks comprised of Zinoviev, Kamenev, and Trotsky. His skirmish with Michel Droit still haunts him. He can't accept having been obliged to wear the yellow star once again. And he hasn't yet said his piece to the paratroopers who stopped him from playing in Strasbourg...:

> *What the hell got into you to bust up the shack*
> *Of this poor indigene, why'd you take that knife*
> *Open the belly, drain his life*
> *When from the bush he just got back*
> *It was nostalgia, my friend*

In "Negusa Negast," he looks condescendingly but lucidly at the beliefs of his Jamaican musicians:

> *Man created the Gods, not at all you say*
> *But religion makes you as foggy as ganja*
> *Pull on that joint Mr. Rasta*
> *Keep on believing one more day*

Following all this are 2 minutes 48 seconds of the gusts, farts, and blasts of "Evguénie Sokolov," just published six months earlier by NRF. "The rastas were shocked when he recorded the farts," remembers Bambou. "The guy at the mixing board didn't want to do it. Serge felt obliged to explain his book to them, but you could see they didn't like it. They thought Serge was insulting their music!"

"There's another person in France who has also written of his *Flowers of Evil*, and I don't mean Baudelaire," declares Patrice Blanc-Francard on France-Inter. Lionel Rotcage goes even further in *La monde de la musique*: "Somewhere between Bacon and Picabia during his monster phase"... *Libération* declares: "The biggest sham – and maybe the most celebrated one of his career. 100% reggae. 100 % pathetic. 100% moving. 100% provocative. 100% magisterial. Gainsbourg. More cynical than ever, more lyrical than ever, more urgent, and casual at the same time..." In another interview with Bayon, Gainsbourg stages his own death. He imagines his suicide, in 1989, from a bullet to the back of the neck, and he talks to the reporter from six feet under:

BAYON: *Now that you're dead, are you going to build yourself a tomb like all the great artists?*

GAINSBOURG: *Maybe a bit later, when I'm understood. Not right away. Anyway, it's utterly useless. Useless to live on through one's creation. To want to live on is monstrously arrogant. The only way is to procreate. Like dogs.*

JANE BIRKIN: *"Serge doesn't like the idea of death. He thinks, like a kid, that it won't happen to him. Like a little boy, he believes that in the end there'll just be a scolding: "I won't do it again," he'll say. He'll get another chance and then start his bullshit all over again, of course. Serge is a suicidal optimist. He's a big-time Russian gambler: why play it safe? Why behave myself?"*

GAINSBOURG: *"My heart problem is a hand grenade. The pin's been pulled but it hasn't exploded. Anyway, I am the master of my destiny, and not the other way around. I work like mad, it's true. Stress is a rhythm to me. The goal* isn't to upset myself, but to get amped up. It's not literal stress either, but intellectual. It's motivation for survival. Otherwise I'll just blow my brains out."

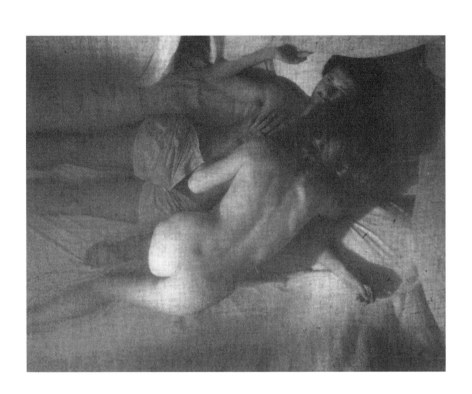

twenty-two

Escape Happiness
Before It Escapes You

In November, 1981, just when *Mauvaises nouvelles des étoiles* comes out, a charming little singer named Claire d'Asta is moving up the charts with her country-tinged version of "La chanson de Prévert." The song's composer is right behind her: in February, 1982, Gainsbourg is fifth on the charts with "Ecce Homo," right behind France Gall, Chagrin d'Amour, Jacques Higelin, and Nana Mouskouri...

Back when he was with Jane, Serge had published erotic photos. Some were quite hot, and even appeared in *Lui, Playboy,* and *Photo.* Now, Filipacchi Publishing is asking for a new set of negatives featuring Bambou for the November, 1981 edition. Eight days later he delivers the photos - with captions - of *Bambou et les poupées.* It's icy eroticism, dominated by electric blues and pale reds, a Surrealist orgy in which we can no longer distinguish between the human body and the amputated mannequins.

Serge explains the harsh and unsavory eroticism of *Bambou et les poupées* to Georges-Marc Benamou in *Elle* on February 15, 1982:

> For me, love is found in the alcoves, in the vagueness of transgression.
> Love should be something shabby and clandestine. Hidden from others.
> What's more, I'm not a liberated man, in any sense of the word. I believe
> that my upbringing, rife with restrictions, is interesting, for it allows me to

live the life of a secret pornographer. An upbringing without limits leads to impotence. It will lead every generation to impotence.

Priggish and timid beneath his façade of obscenity, Serge makes us his confessor in *Le Quotidien de Paris*:

Timidity? Its ultimate incarnation demands that one be timid with oneself, that one not dare even approach oneself. One can only 'moumoyer;' one can never be informal. As for the formality of vous, well that is the timidity of aristocracy. I don't say that lightly - if I walk in front of a mirror, I cover my genitalia... Really, timidity is an excess of narcissism. That being said, I don't indulge in narcissism, but something much more vicious: onanism by way of a middleman.

One of the captions:

Tuesday, 2:15 in the afternoon

The first symptoms of photophobia. Looking for chiaroscuro and back-lighting. Abusing Bambou like a legionnaire in Tonkin. She cries yellow and lies white. My little Chinese Princess coils herself up in the bed's spirals, her eye and crotch almond-tinted. 'Nice girl.' From my camera's viewfinder, I can see that this girl has a Rolls Royce of an ass. There's nothing missing but the lime green license plate of L.A. My camera slides under her chassis, and she, her crimson fingernail up her tailpipe. Freeze frame.

Are these images a hint at a return to painting? He's already been speaking of it for a few years now. He talks about a "Unique and definitive painting" which would reconcile him with those major arts, the memory of which haunts him still...

GAINSBOURG: *"In an antique shop, I found an 18th century easel staring right at me. I'm going to buy it. I'll transform Jane's old bedroom into a studio and in a few years I'll do some painting, for sure. When this whole circus is over. One day I'll relax. I'll go back to writing, as well. I like the silence of writing, the pen scratching across virgin paper."*

On November 29, 1981, sporting a black eye and a trashed eyebrow, Serge is invited onto Philippe Labro's one o'clock afternoon TV show. In a belated conclusion to the Strasbourg affair, there was supposedly a nightmarish run-in with three paratroopers who knocked him around while he was on a peaceful little stroll home "during milkman's hours." The truth is altogether different: the night before he had dined with Jacques Wolfsohn, accompanied by Bambou and Bertrand de Labbey. He was really lit up, almost to the point of delirium tremens.

> BERTRAND DE LABBEY: *"It's by far my worst memory. That night he got me very angry. Both Wolfsohn and me. Serge was playing with fire. He'd started by daring me to tell Bambou how pretty I found her. He was being foolish. He probably thought I was young and seductive, and he asked me to do that because he was afraid that otherwise I'd do it behind his back. After he'd gotten drunk he could barely recognize me. It was a real pain... Then, he started to knock himself around, bash his head into the walls. It was horrible. Wolfsohn and I stayed around because we were afraid he'd die in the middle of the night from all the blood he'd lost. In those moments, he was possessed of a desire for destruction, to hurt himself. Absolutely uncontrollable."*

Having regained a semblance of lucidity, Serge, live in front of hundreds of millions of TV viewers, turns things to his advantage (or so he believes) with this pathetic manipulation and plea for sympathy. Then another televised mini-scandal erupts on TF1 in December. While discussing the problems in Poland, Gainsbourg declares: "I have only five words to say: Those Soviets are some motherfuckers."

On December 13, he's at the heart of another controversy when he buys a manuscript of the Marseillaise, penned by Rouget de Lisle, during an auction in Versailles. It's not the original, which was lost in the upheaval of revolution, but one of two authentic copies signed by the author himself, dated 1833 and addressed to Composer Luigi Cherubini. Serge is ready to spend anything, and finally does obtain it for a little over 130,000 francs. After each refrain, it is even marked with the words "Aux armes et caetera" because the composer hadn't wanted to repeat the words every time! An old man in his seventies, on the verge of passing out right there, hisses at a reporter: "It's pitiful, scandalous. Tell him if I were 20 years younger I'd rip it right from his hands!" The following reaction is published as a letter to the editor in *Journal des orphelines de guerre*: "Could the Minister of the Army and the Minister of Culture not have sent buyers? Are we still Frenchmen, or are we men without countries who simply let such things happen?"

> GAINSBOURG: *"The return to Versailles was grandiose. I was accompa-*

nied by Phify, a Polish bodyguard and bouncer from the Palace. Then there
was Bambou, my chink girlfriend. Me, I'm a Russian Jew, and the car was
a Chevrolet, an American! And on the back seat there was an original
manuscript of the Marseillaise! Amazing!"

Thoroughly full of himself, he shows up next on January 3, 1982 on TF1's
Droit de réponse. This "jewel of Mitterand television," hosted live by Michel
Polac, aims at creating a space of total freedom, and no debate show has
ever rivaled it since. There are five million viewers for Polac's broadcast
on the death of *Charlie Hebdo,* a satirical weekly (later brought back) that
had its heyday during the days of Pompidou and Giscard. Seated with
Professor Charon, the legendary agitators from the paper - a touchstone for
an entire generation - proceed to behave like a bunch of old drunks even
more pitiful than those "stupid and malicious" fools singled out in their by-
gone slogan. Incidents start to take place backstage between Jean Bourdier,
a couple of right-wing journalists from *Minute,* the designer Siné, and Phify,
Gainsbourg's bodyguard, who interjects with his switchblade. High school
students are insulted by Charon when they admit they don't read *Charlie
Hebdo.* The program quickly turns into bedlam and the chaos is indescrib-
able, and then Gainsbarre, in the middle of the entire, catastrophic non-event,
decides to contribute to the madness by blowing farts from a penis-shaped
balloon before finally insulting the right-wing journalists. Speaking about
the Strasbourg concert two years earlier, he accuses them of being inform-
ers, and sloppily blurts out: "Those paratroopers, I put 'em in their place!"
Polac plays a tape to calm everyone down, but the show is turning into a
brawl. Chairs fly and there's a volley of cursing never before heard on television during prime time. The next day, Michel Polac feels obliged to apologize
on TF1.

Two days later, *Minute* strikes back and publishes Gainsbourg's address. On January 2, 1982, a tear-gas canister is tossed at his house on Rue
de Verneuil. The neighbors sound the alert while Serge, who's taking care
of Charlotte, sees smoke pass under the door. "I didn't know what was happening outside. It could have been anything," he tells the police that evening.

On February 15, 1982, Gainsbourg is featured in *Elle.* He photographs
Bambou, who is dressed by Azzedine Alaïa, and in the interview with
Georges-Marc Benamou, he speaks, very surprisingly, about the two chil-

dren from his second marriage, despite the fact that he wants his past life to "remain in a fog of anonymity": "I have a 16 year-old girl. I also have a son. Nobody knows that. He's 14, very handsome. He's mine, and I've recognized it." Later, he confirms what he'd said at the beginning of his love affair with Jane Birkin, namely that a woman should maintain a certain "aura of availability."

Life with Bambou is following its course, punctuated by horrific quarrels and tender reconciliations, the likes of which are recounted in her book *Il et Elle*. In March, 1982, Serge directs a short subject for Claude Villiers' Ciné-Parade. It is to be based on *Scarface*, one of his favorite films. While Chabrol proposes a reworking of a scene from *M. Le Maudit* with Maurice Risch, Gainsbourg rewrites the rules of the cinematic game set forth by Villiers and creates a scene that doesn't exist in the original film, one centered on the relationship between Tony Montana (Scarface) and his sister Cesca, played by Daniel Duval and Jane Birkin respectively. This subject is dealt with in the subtext of Howard Hawks' original and much more bluntly in the Brian de Palma film. For Serge and Jane, this is the first professional reunion, and the situation is delicate.

> JANE BIRKIN: *"I was a little intimidated. It's funny after a relationship has changed. I came to work as an actress, and I didn't sleep for three days - maybe just an hour or two out of exhaustion. I was really nervous. I knew I wasn't looking very good and I was exhausted even before the filming started. I was dreading the moment when I'd have to shoot with him, but he was an angel, all sweetness and kindness. I was very flattered."*

The nighttime escapades with Daniel Duval are all over the news. Here's just one story among a hundred:

> DANIEL DUVAL: *"One night when we were screwing around at l'Elysée-Matignon, surrounded by all the 'grande bourgeoisie' of France, we decided to leave for Pigalle, where we knew someone who owned a bar. We rented it out for the night. It was just us and two whores, so we shut the doors and until dawn's early light we amused ourselves by taking turns being the barman, the client, and the waiter. We spent the night in an imaginary world, and at the crack of dawn we drank champagne before going back home to sleep."*

In order to flee his melancholy and pay his taxes, Serge goes back to filming commercials. In 1980, he receives the Lion d'argent at Cannes for a little spot he does for Brandt dishwashers. In 1981, there is a commercial for Rouder Saint-Michel cookies, and year later there are spots for Lee Cooper Jeans, Renault, and instant soup. Between 1982 and 1984, he also does three commercials for Gini lemonade.

After a month at Mas de Chastelas in Saint Tropez spent recovering from all his debauchery, Serge receives a new gold record for his last album straight from the hands of Pierre Lescure, head of variety programming at Antenne 2. This is a preview to the May 23, 1982 broadcast of the special *Enquête sur une vie d'artiste*, an excellent portrait by Pierre Desfons, with Gérard Lanvin in the role of the detective who identifies all too well with his subject. The Quebecer Diane Dufresne sings the unreleased piece "Suicide," words by Gainsbourg and music by Claude Engel:

> *I can see myself atop a mound of C-4*
> *And like Larousse scatter to the wind*
> *Each and all of my severed limbs*
> *Like plastic surgery gone to war*

On July 13, 1982, Gainsbourg dines with Patrick Dewaere and offers him the lead role in *Equateur,* the film he's just finished writing, which is based on a Georges Simenon story called *Coup de lune* and set in Africa. Patrick promises to think it over. Coming home that night to Rue de Verneuil, Serge has the misfortune of discovering he's been burglarized. Luckily, the police had already nabbed the cat burglar, whose bag was full of Serge's collectables, as he was leaving Gainsbourg's domicile. The next day, Serge goes to confront the thief, André Philisot, who tells him how he scaled the façade and broke a pane of glass in the door. Serge, not at all bitter, offers to buy him a drink when he gets out of prison...

Two days later, after dining with Claude Lelouch, Patrick Dewaere kills himself: an overdose of despair.

BERTRAND BLIER: *"Patrick didn't want to do that film with Serge. He was afraid to go to Gabon with him because he knew it would be bedlam and they'd just end up getting thoroughly plastered together. The night before they dined together he told me: "Two of us will leave, but there won't be two returning." He was really afraid of Serge."*

Jane is busy living her life with Jacques Doillon, and when she gives birth to her third daughter in September, 1982, Serge actually offers to be the godfather. It's around this time that he crosses paths with Alain Bashung. Quick resume: Born in Alsace, he grows up playing parties, is nuts for country music, and tours American army bases. In 1977, there's an album called *Roman-photos*, which reveals the influence of Dylan, Lou Reed, and J.J. Cale. It's a bust. On a small budget from Phonogram two years later, he records *Roulette russe*, but the album doesn't take off until the release of a new 45, the sensational "Gaby Oh Gaby." Now, at 36, he's finally hit pay dirt. A million copies later, he records *Pizza* in London and he's off again, scoring with "Vertige de l'amour." The album sells over 400,000 copies and the single a million.

ALAIN BASHUNG: *"Two years of maximum pressure and touring, and in the end I wasn't happy with any of it, especially on stage. It was strange. I was in a difficult place. The kids only came to hear the hits – they knew the words to "Gaby" and "Vertige" better than I did. Whenever I sang a line differently I could see them grimace. They weren't into any of my other songs and the rock crowd wasn't coming to my shows. They figured, as usual, that hits=money=sell out=it's not rock. Some crap like that."*

A dispute with Boris Bergman forces him to look for another lyricist, one likely to follow him in his extreme quest, which from the record company's point of view is commercial suicide.

ALAIN BASHUNG: *"I'd followed Gainsbourg's entire career. First of all, there aren't many guys like him. Like Dutronc, he seems to not give a damn about the world, like he's screwing around. But those types are obviously the most sincere. They told me I was the first to imitate his look on TV because there is doubtless a resemblance in our style and I'm often unshaven. I'd wanted to do something with Serge for a long time and I knew what I wanted to say with this record."*

Success late in life is destroying Bashung's nerves. He feels ill, physically. He tells *Libération*: "I had to do *Play blessures*. I had no choice. I was inches from death. I mean clinically. That's where these minimalist melodies come from, the rigorous cacophony, the crisis. From music that's physical. It was everything but easy, really." Like this tune in the form of a confession, "C'est comment qu'on freine":

> All these Cossacks are aiming at me
> I'm in the gulag, long to be free
> I'm a screw up don't know how to say yes
> My head is just a muddled mess
> That's how you slow down
> I'd like to get off this ride
> That's how you slow down

ALAIN BASHUNG: *"Gainsbourg and I worked totally as a team. It's not his words pasted over my music. I had written down my ideas, some phrases, and he, knowing the power of words, brought order to my puzzle... I'd meet him around three in the afternoon at his place. After he finished not shaving, we'd dive right into vodka and Ricard. I mean, why add water when vodka is the same color?... He also had another great drink, the Tequila Rapido: 1/3 tequila, 2/3 champagne. You cover it with a napkin, slam it down so it fizzes, and then gulp it in one shot. It's like an explosion. We'd work till midnight and then go out to party, sometimes just right out on the sidewalk until dawn. It's interesting – why go to a club to drink when it's nicer outside?"*

> I dream about a show for carnivores
> Some underground carnage they'd adore
> Please keep that stethoscope away from me
> I'm dreaming that this remake sets me free
> I dream about a meeting face to face
> I dream...
> I dream of the worst

ALAIN BASHUNG: *"'Play blessures' is an album of extreme lucidity. It's like two alcoholics drying out. Reality is sordid enough, we didn't need to make it more sordid that it was..."*

> I dedicate this anguish to a vanished singer
> Dead from thirst in the Gaby desert
> Let's please have just a minute of silence
> Pretend I've not as yet arrived

ALAIN BASHUNG: *"We had some great times together. I saw him cry. This man who had done so many magnificent things was ready to do it all over, start from scratch again. He was thinking about his life. He was the loneliest guy on earth. We had a relationship that was very beautiful, like father and son. With me, he wanted to be at the top of his game... He had the nerve to do something immense. I think back to the table in his living room with all the precious objects... It had to do with some sort of telluric current and he found his energy within these coordinates. To be creatively insane, one needs an atmosphere of order. You can't run a 100 meter dash in a swamp. Gainsbourg had mixed together memories, culture, and sentimental trophies, and his whole apartment was mapped out, his mind was impeccably compartmentalized[...] He was a prince. He reinforced that idea that you have to really go for it, or else it's not worth it. He gave me the desire to do things with elegance, even if I wouldn't be understood by the whole world. He played with pop music and beautifully refined it. I have never seen a guy so strong and sensitive at once. He never lost his touch, regardless of the state he was in..."*

Pizza had sold 400,000 copies. *Play blessures* would peak at 60,000. A flop? No. A new direction, clearly. Since them, Bashung's itinerary has been impeccable.

On November 3, 1982, while Play blessures is hitting the record shops, France Culture dedicates a special day to Gainsbourg, highlighted by a remarkable interview with Noël Simsolo. A sample:

GAINSBOURG: *I'd say the same as Victor Hugo - "It is strictly forbidden to set my verse to music."*

NOËL SIMSOLO: *If you had to, absolutely?*

GAINSBOURG: *I dunno... The sound of a toilet flushing? What could one put? It's difficult. A little Rachmaninoff? No way! Mahler? No. Schoenberg? No. Berg? No. Debussy? Absolutely not. Scarlatti no, and not Bach either. Certainly not Chopin, that would be redundant... I know: a little Art Tatum!*

That same evening, by chance, he is on Antenne 2's *Cinéma Cinémas*, speaking about three of his favorite films: Jean Vigo's *L'Atalante*, Merian Cooper's *King Kong*, and Tay Garnett's *The Postman Always Rings Twice*. Some of the commentary:

Realism? Shit, there's enough of that off-screen. I want nothing to do with realism. Because I want to escape. I have no desire to sit down in some dark theatre to see, or re-see reality. I want a trip. I want to escape like when I was a child with Luc Bradefer or Pim Pam Poum.

The filming of *Equateur* starts at the beginning of December, 1982. In the press kit that will be distributed at Cannes in May, 1983, we can read the director's statement concerning his intention:

> *My idea is to make a sepia-colored sketch of the progressive deterioration of a profoundly idealistic and perfectly integrated human being whose constant lucidity and romantic weakness come to work against his humanist instincts, at the same time as he becomes exasperated with his controlling loves. Probably in the 1950s, colonialist subtext.*

Equateur is a commissioned job, but Serge, who dreams of returning to cinema after seeing many of his projects go belly up, really dedicates himself to the project and signs on to do the directing, the music, and the script. The team, including his faithful cinematographer Willy Kurant and cameraman Yann Lemasson, assembles in the jungle of Gabon. The actors include René Kolldehoff, Francis Huster, and a couple of big names like Jean Bouise as the public prosecutor and François Dyrek as the police chief. The female lead is Barbara Sukowa, one of Rainer Werner Fassbinder's favorite stars - a mixture of purity, power, and voluptuousness whom Serge discovers through Fassbinder's *Lola*.

The film's story is simple: in Libreville, during the 1950s, a young, well-adjusted man, Timar, shows up at a sleazy hotel run by a couple, Eugène and Adèle (Kolldehoff and Sukowa). Adèle and Timar become lovers. There's a double murder in the jungle, Eugène dies, and the couple breaks up.

GAINSBOURG: *"I liked this Simenon book, this tragic passion set in a racist milieu. I'd never have adapted a Maigret [book] – I don't like detective stories. In Equateur there was this parable that I related to: the impossibility of relations between two races, male and female. Sukowa was the only choice for Adèle. She's a powerful and instinctual woman, like Lana Turner in 'The Postman Always Rings Twice.'"*

BARBARA SUKOWA: *"I came to Paris to meet Serge. First we lunched together, then had tea, ate diner, and finally we closed out the night at a club. He took me to a Russian restaurant, Le Raspoutine, where his father had played, and when we left the musicians followed us out onto the streets. It was really funny. Other than "Je t'aime moi non plus," I knew none of his songs. He just showed me his first film as a director, which I really liked. I felt that with 'Equateur,' he wanted to do something even more stylized."*

WILLY KURANT: *"Serge and I had stayed in touch since 'Je t'aime moi non plus.' He kept me up to date on the hassles with 'Black-out' and I of course immediately accepted to work with him in Gabon on 'Equateur.' We had financial problems from the get-go. He really thought the money would be there, but after a short while the technicians started to worry."*

According to Gainsbourg, the film's producer had blown a large part of the budget playing baccarat, not to mention "the tidy sum handed over to president Bongo." At week's end, Gainsbourg starts paying the crew with his American Express card. Once in Libreville, Serge is supposed to meet the Gabonese president for a photo op. He shows up on time - in a suit and tie – at the palace gates. He passes by iron bars and armored doors, and then waits in a room until a subordinate comes to tell him the photo shoot is canceled. Bongo's (white) advisors had just informed him that a photo with Gainsbourg, a subversive from France who ridiculed the Marseillaise, could in turn be used by the press to ridicule the regime...

WILLY KURANT: *"The filming was extremely harsh because of the climate and an eye infection that everybody got, except for Gainsbourg, who nevertheless had his share of parasites – a tic that set up shop between his toes. For me it was total horror. I had tendonitis that wouldn't heal because of the humidity. In short, it was no picnic."*

BARBARA SUKOWA: *"We were all sick at one time or another, which meant that the shooting schedule would change depending on the day's sickness. I really enjoyed the filming, even if it wasn't easy. Francis Huster was frightened by the diseases, especially in the scene where he had to go into the river."*

WILLY KURANT: *"In spite of the problems, Serge kept everyone reassured morning till night. Francis talked about the shooting like it was hell in the heart of the jungle, but it wasn't so bad. Sure, it was a slow film, especially the dialogue, and the elliptical narrative was too much for some critics. It's true that there wasn't much in the book and that Francis complained too much."*

Interviewed after his return from Africa, Huster is hysterical. He tells of how his character is eviscerated by "Gainsbourg's scalpel-camera," and how some of the erotic scenes are "excessively shocking," and obtained only by "burning our brains; it's the fire in my head, and in Barbara's, that illuminates and sets ablaze our naked bodies."

As for Serge, he'll be asked why he'd gone so far for just a few scenes in Africa...

GAINSBOURG: *"It was already decided. There was no one who'd say I could have shot this in a studio. That's absurd. I'd never have gotten these performances from the actors. They were crushed by the heat, devastated by fever or fear, dulled by quinine. And just filming nature would have meant surrendering to exoticism. Simenon's book is claustrophobic: elephants and hippos are fine for epics, but I'm not making 'Tarzan', so I made do with a few shots of mangroves. I find the twisted roots of these trees extremely dramatic. I don't see how I could live there, although I did have friendly encounters with the natives, who carved me crutches out of bamboo. My roots are in the micro-climate of the smoke-filled shittiness of the 7th arrondissement."*

FRANCIS HUSTER: *"Gainsbourg is a poet with the camera and a remarkable director of actors. He was one himself and you can feel in his look that he admires his actors. He's very baroque, a hyper-realist of the soul... I'm really proud to have done the film, and consider it to be one of the best I've made, along with those of Zulawski... He and I were like Cocteau and Jean Marais..."*

Back in Paris, in January, 1983, Serge digs into the editing of 'Equateur,' which he knows will be shown out of competition at the upcoming Cannes Film Festival. In April, he accepts an interview with Fabienne Issartel, who's come to speak with him on the subject of women for 'F Magazine.' Serge asks her to be patient while he wraps up a press junket for 'Equateur.' She waits, has a scotch, and an hour later the interview finally begins. But Serge starts telling his prostitute stories. The reporter is disappointed, tells him so, a nd ridicules Jane Birkin before leaving. Serge becomes furious and rips her tape recorder away. They insult each other, fight a bit, and finally Serge kicks her out.

The night before *Equateur* is shown at Cannes, in May, 1983, Serge, while still limping and using a cane, is thinking about Patrick Dewaere, with whom he had dreamed about making the film. He tells this to a reporter whom he's dining with at the Majestic. When he walks into the restaurant, Dirk Bogarde gets up and kisses him, which makes him giddy as a kid: "Did you see that? He kissed me! He kissed me, yeah? That's something. He's a nice guy, hey? One of the world's greatest actors gets up to greet me. That's class. He knows how to live. A great man…" The film, which never comes out on video because of a screw-up between co-producers, is memorable for the line, "Africa, goddamn it, is the white man's graveyard," as well as for its interminable canoe shots that inspire this definitive critique in *Libération*: "You can really feel the heat!" At Cannes, the chaos created by Serge's presence causes a brawl even before the screening of the film.

> BARBARA SUKOWA: *"I discovered another side to Serge in Cannes. We were at the Palais des Festivals, and rather than return to the hotel by car, he convinced me to walk. He wanted the crowd to follow him. He relished in how well-known he was and he loved to prove it to me."*

In the projection hall, the film is booed and the reviews are unanimously negative, with the exception of Michel Perez's, and even he points out that Serge is giving himself over to "pathetic provocations that would serve to trouble no one but a moron[…] It's fine to reimagine Simenon's novel and take from it an almost unbearable image of colonial Africa, both lyrical and vengeful. Unfortunately, the Africa offered to us in *Equateur* is unique only for the timidity of its violence."

Equateur opens in Paris on August 24, 1983, to general indifference. Serge is sick of it all, so he moves on to something new. In the space of a few weeks, he writes 22 songs, 11 for Jane Birkin and 11 for Isabelle Adjani. A nice little two for one, with two gold records at the finish line. As is now his habit, he records demos by placing a cassette recorder atop his piano, which he uses as a Dictaphone to add commentaries, as one of the most celebrated engineers and producers in eighties French music points out.

> DOMINIQUE BLANC-FRANCARD: *"He'd say, for example, "That's the refrain, that's the stanza, then you just wing it!" Philippe Lerichomme would give it to the arranger, who'd embellish the melody and build around it.*

Serge would let the musicians fill in the rest. He wasn't interested in doing the arrangements himself."

While recording the backing tracks in London, Serge still doesn't know which tracks will go to Jane and which will go to Isabelle. After the tracks are finished, he'll give them to the performers and the voices will be recorded.

DOMINIQUE BLANC-FRANCARD: *"He was drinking a lot and would already be well into it when he showed up in the morning. At the time of those two albums, he was running mainly on cocktails. He'd bring a shaker in his briefcase and make bourbon-based concoctions, stuff that would kill a horse. He'd make up three shakers a day, a thimbleful of which would have been enough to wipe out the average human. He'd drink them down in big beer mugs. Then he'd move on to 102. He had drink in each hand – stereo, you understand – but that didn't stop him from working."*

Gainsbourg is terribly interventionist in the studio, but he and Lerichomme make an impeccable duo. Serge takes care of the singers, gives instructions, helps with phrasing, etc. Philippe is in the mixing booth, carefully supervising all the takes.

The two albums come out simultaneously in October, 1983, but even though the sound is similar, as Alan Hawkshaw remarks, their superb covers evoke different worlds: Adjani's is more lighthearted, mischievous, and spicy; Birkin's is more mature, sophisticated, and intoxicating.

ISABELLE ADJANI: *"We were both interested in the same subjects: heartbreak, separation, tragic fascination, the fatal love at first sight. This album was maybe a bit lighter. I think with me, he was taking a break..."*

> *I'm in some state that's out near Ohio*
> *And I am feeling so low*
> *I'm in some state that's out near Ohio*
> *Nevada's getting closer all the time*
> *I want to flee at all cost*
> *Cross the borders and just get lost*

ISABELLE ADJANI: *"I remember wanting everything to go to Jane because I really liked what he did with his language and hers: the most elegant franglais in the world, like the work of certain artists at the end of the 19th century who would take unsimilar things and make them into an original piece."*

Much more inspired than he was for the Catherine Deneuve album, Serge hands Adjani hits on a silver platter. The first 45, "Ohio," climbs to 25 on the charts in spring of 1984. "Pull marine" will do even better, hitting number one on November 4, 1984, one year after the album's release.

> The bottom of the pool shone through
> Through my sweater marine blue
> Torn up and far from new
> Repairs long overdue
> You had given it to me
> And now I'm all alone you see

In a moment of subtle nostalgia, Serge, whom Isabelle calls her feeling-director, writes her "Le mal intérieur." Isabelle murmurs, on the verge of tears:

> I feel you inside, so near
> Yet I know that you're far from here
> I can feel you everywhere
> But I know that your heart's not there

ISABELLE ADJANI: *"I could have sung it differently, but he made me understand that he didn't like real singers, the kinds with real pipes, a real voice. That's why he liked to work with actresses, because he could push them to do things they weren't used to. It gave his world a sort of magic... He'd direct me with hand gestures, a look, by lowering his eyes or giving me a little smile. He exuded seduction, and it had nothing to do with any phony shtick."*

DOMINIQUE BLANC-FRANCARD: *"Adjani is an astonishing and very colorful person. The two of them never stopped bickering, but Serge provided a great atmosphere. He had made the two albums with the same arranger, and he didn't want Isabelle to know they'd be doing Jane's album right after hers, or Jane to know that they'd just finished Isabelle's..."*

If Isabelle's album is seductive, then Jane's is intoxicating. It is, without a doubt, the best of their collaborations, finished three years after an affair that was never really over, but which rather followed other paths as a means of prolonging itself. During the making of this masterpiece, Jane sometimes catches Serge crying behind the glass...

JANE BIRKIN: *"Con c'est con ces consequences"... Singing that in front of* him, such emotion – *It was the most beautiful gift he could give me. He manages to find beauty in the abyss. It was almost spiritual. When I managed to sing it, I could see he was proud of me..."*

> More than moronic this mess
> Moronic that we split
> We have to face the evidence
> That tonight is it
> Your tale of tail this shaft I mine
> Already it is more
> Than moronic this mess

MICHEL PICCOLI: *"My favorite of his songs is "Les dessous chics." A most refined rendering of the love of eroticism."*

> Fine underwear
> Emotion's tender modesty
> All made up outrageously
> Blood red
> Fine underwear
> Creates a private world for you
> That's fragile as the morning dew

JANE BIRKIN: *"On this album, I sang his wounds, I become l'homme à tête de chou, I became Serge in drag."*

> Escape happiness before it escapes you
> Tell yourself there's an over the rainbow
> Higher than the sun that's up above
> Radiant
> Believe in god and in heaven
> Even when it all seems so grim
> Know our heart is forged in blood and fire

DOMINIQUE BLANC-FRANCARD: *"It was always the same routine with everybody. There were real tough moments. I saw Jane roll around on the ground and I didn't know what to do. Philippe would just ask me to proceed like usual. It was just their game. After a half an hour she'd dry her tears. It would all be over and she'd start recording. When one's not familiar with it, it can be quite scary."*

> Baby alone in Babylone
> Dead beneath the waves

[507]

Waves of light
Waves of dust
Waves ephemeral
Your dreams eternal
You will find her there

What more can one say about this album? It is pure emotion, stripped bare, raw. Two fragile beings paralyzed by a past that cannot be resuscitated and a complicit and delicate present where not the slightest faux pas is permitted... In 1984, Jane receives the Académie Charles-Cros award for *Baby Alone in Babylone*, the same prize Serge won 25 years earlier for his first 25cm album. Jane, away filming *La Pirate*, has Serge accept the award for her. He has tears in his eyes.

After the recording sessions for these two albums, Serge speaks about his future plans in *Paroles et musique*:

This time I'll need a double album. 30 minutes won't be enough. I've already done the reggae thing, and this time I think I'll either contact a famous English group – I won't say which – or move between simple guitar stuff and the London Philharmonic, depending on the tracks. It'll be a real test. I plan on really pushing things, screaming, crying... This album has to go beyond anything I've ever done before.

At the same time, Serge makes his entry into the Larousse encyclopedia, volume 5. The following is culled from his 24-line entry:

With a gift for sharp and subtle humor, he knew how to impose upon the public a casually disenchanted and sardonic personality that hides a lively sensitivity.

Well said, Larousse.

GAINSBOURG LOVE ON THE BEAT

A Whore Among Whores

When Charlotte spends a weekend at Rue de Verneuil, her dad shows her his old films, like *Hercule se déchâine*, just to get a few laughs out of her. He also does his big chef routine in the kitchen. He cooks her chickpeas from the delicatessen, adding his special herbs and spices. If he reheats some borscht, he never forgets the sugar. In the taboule from Hédiard, a drop of olive oil is always a must. Charlotte is in heaven when they go to a restaurant. Serge always goes to the most prestigious places, just so things are always a party, always a success. He doesn't want her to be disappointed. Also, Charlotte discovers something while her mom is filming *La Pirate*. A few months earlier, she had watched a shoot. Seated in the corner and hidden behind some furniture, she observed little Laure Marsac acting opposite Jane. Everyone says that since that moment she had dreamed of making films. In the summer of 1984, she's in her first film, Eli Chouraqui's *Paroles et musique*, and the critics all agree that she steals the show. Meanwhile, of her own volition, she enrolls in a Swiss boarding school, where she spends the school year in peace, far from the media and her parents. Only 12 years old and already she's already making her first adult decision.

In September, 1983, Serge is interviewed for the weekly Belgian publication *Télé-Moustique*:

S.G: *I'm broke, that's the scoop! Socialism has bankrupted me. I'm in the red.*

REPORTER: *How much?*

S.G.: *600, 000! It's like a spinal tap, this racket! Shit, I don't care. I live day-to-day, but on the other foot now.*

REPORTER: *The right?*

S.G. *No, the third one. The one with Cinderella's slipper on it. I'll get by. I'm one of the most highly paid commercial directors out there.*

REPORTER: *So there's no love loss between you and Mitterrand.*

S.G.: *What's important is 'ça s'arrose!' No, that's dreadful. Forget that.*[1]

Gainsbourg does in fact make a volley of new commercials for everything from Friskies cat food to Palmolive detergent. Then in the beginning of 1984, he's called to help rescue old pal Jacques Dutronc, who's recording the 45 that will end his engagement with Gaumont Records. Serge is supposed to create lyrics around the title "Merde en France." When the day arrives, he hits the studio armed with his famous briefcase and starts making cocktails. Dutronc, who had always considered Gainsbourg's alcoholism a joke compared to his own, soon realized that he will never have his lyrics in time and simply improvises a bunch of gibberish over the tune.

During this time, Gainsbourg develops a real friendship with Thomas, the son of Dutronc and Françoise Hardy.

THOMAS DUTRONC: *"I remember watching 'Jaws' with him and Charlotte, on his big screen. I was really afraid. I started crying, and with tears in my eyes I went back to take refuge in my mother's arms. The next time, we watched Stanley Kubrick's 'The Shining'... And the first time I drank was with Serge. We were in a Chinese restaurant and my dad had ordered champagne, so he let me have a taste. I liked it, so Serge kept slipping me more under the table. The more I drank, the more I liked it, and*

---

[1] "Ça s'arrose" actually means "Let's drink to that." But this is really a reference to Gilbert Bécuad's huge hit "L'important c'est la rose" – the Socialist party had made the rose its symbol of victory in 1981.

when we left the restaurant I was super happy. I told my mom: "Now I understand dad!"

Another time, Serge and Jacques stumble home at nine in the morning to find Françoise, who's been waiting up all night and is filled with rage and jealousy. She pulls his glasses off and crushes them under her feet. Dutronc heads to see his kid and says, "Now that's real clever! No more glasses. Your mom's hysterical. That's the thanks I get for putting up with Serge all night!"

This brings us to March 11, 1984, and the scandal on TF1: Serge, live on the TV show *7 sur 7*, burns a 500 franc note in front of reporters Erik Gilbert, Jean-Louis Burgat, and millions of outraged viewers.

> JEAN-LOUIS BURGAT: *How do economic and social problems affect the life of one of the best paid artists in France?*

> S.G.: *I'm in a hell of a fix. Let me tell you a little parable. In May, 1981, I was walking down Rue Saint-Denis and I spied this super hot little street walker. "Hey Gainsbarre, want a date? – You know my name, but what's yours? – My name is socialism!" Now she's superb, wild makeup and all. I say: "So how much do you want? – You can pay afterwards." So I go up and when she strips, I see it's a hideous transvestite. She turns to me and says: "Come on, take me by my communism!"*

> *Of course, it's a parable. That said, we're so far into the shit now that pretty soon we'll be drinking hot water instead of coffee. This tax thing is a racket, that's what it is. I'll show you... This isn't a parable, this is real... I take this 500 franc note... So I'm taxed at 74%, right? I'll tell you how much is left over (he lights his Zippo). What I'm doing is illegal, but I'm going to do it all the same. I don't give a damn if they toss me in the can (the bill starts to burn). I'll stop at 74%... Let's not be stupid, this isn't for the poor, it's for nuclear... And that's what remains (he puts out the flame) out of 500 francs... It's fucked!*

> J.L-B.: *What's fucked? You can't still work like before?*

> S.G.: *I'd like for all the poor to have Rolls Royces. And I sold mine! That's socialist labor for you.*

> ERIK GILBERT: *"Two days earlier, we had lunch and prepared the show with him, but he didn't let on about the stunt, which he had certainly*

planned. What struck us during the show was that little briefcase of his, which contained a huge stack of bills. He told us that he never left home without a considerable sum of money."

The station is bombarded by thousands of calls from viewers mad with rage, unable to accept that the station would let Serge burn the bill on live television.

ERIK GILBERT: *"He wanted to show what was left after he paid his taxes, and he did it without any bitterness, while wanting, at the same time, to shake you up, and the shock was immense. The switchboard exploded with extremely violent calls. I've only seen it twice on '7 sur 7:' once with Serge and also with Daniel Balavoine, when he said he didn't give a shit about old soldiers. It became a benchmark moment. As journalists we were surprised about how he acted. He had this sort of flat diction and we had to work to decode it. We didn't understand the significance of the gesture, but we knew right away that it was an extraordinary thing to burn a 500 franc note, insomuch as we were already in a crisis... Still, I was oblivious to the illegality of the act: the bills don't belong to us – they belong to the Bank of France. Gainsbourg could have been dragged into court for having done it, we too for having permitted it."*

The consequences of the act are, unfortunately, more negative than positive. The management of TF1 is overwhelmed by angry letters. Letters to newspapers are full of hostile rants. Serge is criticized for being a rich provocateur who laughs at the poor. His speech lacks clarity, so when he says "... it isn't for the poor, it's for the nuclear..." it is lost behind the big shot of the burning bill. You can't hear him (plus his speech is never that intelligible). There's no doubt he is playing the bad boy, excited by the idea of breaking a taboo (money is sacred). He even receives hate mail at home. His housekeeper, Fulbert, sorts through the letters. He comes across a devastating one from a little boy who had cried in front of his TV because the bicycle of his dreams costs 500 francs. Serge is touched, and sends the child the most beautiful of bikes...

JULIEN CLERC: *"The day after '7 sur 7.' I was dining with Serge, who was like a proud little boy. We had to stop by his place so he could show us the tape while he made commentaries, rewinding and replaying certain parts. After that, we hit the clubs. I can still see him dancing those beguines at*

Keur Samba. Then we hit La Calvados, one of his stomping grounds, to see his old friend Joe Turner, the blues pianist who died in 1990. They had a ritual: Serge would buy him I don't know how many cigars, line them up at the piano, and call out the titles of standards he wanted to hear. But every half-hour Turner took a break and was replaced by a Mexican group that would pound out cucarachas, and Serge, who always carried around wads of money, would stuff bills into their guitars, producing cries of "Viva la revolucion!" That night really wiped me out. When I took him back home – he was so wasted that I couldn't have just plunked him in a taxi – it must have been seven in the morning, and after a period of silence he turned to me and said this great phrase: "No, you're right. After a while you wear out your welcome..." Another time, for Renaud's anniversary, we got hammered on Tequila Rapidos and I just turned into a wallflower while he and Renaud burned up the dance floor at Les Bains Douches... Oh la la..."

BERTRAND DE LABBEY: *"Serge would drink to simply forget the flow of time, his worries, the tribulations of creation. At the same time, it was difficult for him in public because he always had to push the limits farther each time, or else he just wouldn't go out. When he was drinking, I couldn't take him for too long. He was extremely repetitive and could become belligerent. It was tiresome, for him and for everyone who loved him. There would always come a point in the evening when you had to leave, when you couldn't do anything else for him."*

In April, 1984, Serge and Philippe Lerichomme get together in New York with a new plan: Manhattan funk with a pinch of New Jersey rock. The one who sets the groundwork is a French expatriate with his finger on the pulse of Big Apple trends...

JEAN-PIERRE WEILLER: *"I'd told myself it would be a great town for Gainsbourg. I was in touch with Philippe, who himself was thinking of recording 'Love On The Beat' there. So I sent him some cassettes of some WBLS radio shows but they just didn't click. One day I brought over some albums, including the Herbie Hancock stuff with Bill Laswell, and another by Southside Johnny and The Asbury Jukes called 'Trash It Up,' which Serge completely loved. He told me: "That's what I'm looking for." On the cover were the words: "Produced by Nile Rodgers and Billy Rush"... "*

Nile Rodgers is the leader of the group Chic, the composer of "Freak Out" (1978) and "Good Times" (1979), two of the best funk-disco singles of the time. Jean-Pierre gets hold of him, but Rodgers declines. He's too busy. He's just done Bowie's mega-seller, *Let's Dance*, and is moving on to produce Madonna's *Like a Virgin*, whose sales will go through the roof in 1984. So now there's Billy Rush, the backbone of Southside Johnny, who is fairly famous on the East Coast thanks to his connections with Bruce Springsteen, his longtime pal from the days when they were both forging their careers and at the head of their own groups. In the Asbury Jukes, Billy Rush is both producer and chief songwriter.

BILLY RUSH: *"When Jean-Pierre talked to me about Serge, I didn't know anything about him, not even "Je t'aime moi non plus." We set up a meeting at my place in New Jersey, in my garage/studio, and I saw this real shy guy show up. He only spoke a few words of English. He had me listen to one of his little cassettes where he'd laid down some of the melodies for his songs. The vibe was kind of strange – I'd never have guessed he was such a big star in France... So I set out to work right in front of him. I chose a beat, slapped some bass over it, added some keyboards and guitars. We didn't even speak, and I felt uneasy, as if he were sizing me up..."*

JEAN-PIERRE WEILLER: *"That meeting fascinated me. Here's the two of them - Serge trying see what Billy can bring to the table, and Billy probably thinking Serge was from Mars. It was unbelievable, there in that garage with this total rocker and Gainsbourg the dandy, with all his finesse and classicism. It was a head-on crash of two cultures...»*

BILLY RUSH: *"At the end of the day I'd done two or three tracks and they took off with the tapes. As they walked away, I thought: "Who knows? It was fun, even if it doesn't pan out..." But they came back the next day and said: "It's great! Let's continue!"*

PHILIPPE LERICHOMME: *"Once again, it's a new musical world for Serge, and therefore a delicate time. One night, he called me from his room to say: "What the hell are we doing here? My music is Chopin. It's got nothing to do with this..." To which I responded: "That's exactly why we're here, to try something new..." "*

Serge starts to feel comfortable in Manhattan, and two months later they go into the studio. Billy recruits some big names, including synthesizer whiz Larry Fast, who also plays with Peter Gabriel, and two guys from Bowie's touring band, sax player Stan Harrison and backing singer George Simms. *Love On The Beat* is recorded in New Jersey and mixed in Manhattan at the legendary Power Station, all in 10 days...

> GEORGE SIMMS: *"So we show up at Billy's place in New Jersey and listen to the first two songs, and Steve and I look at each other dumbfounded, as if to say: "What the hell are we doing here?" I'd never heard of Gainsbourg before, and knew nothing of his reputation, his career, his fame, or his artistic genius. At one point we even thought he was just some rich guy whose favorite pastime was paying American musicians a bunch of dough to record songs that he'd play for his friends. It all happened real fast, I think he sang nine songs in just seven hours. I'll never forget how animated Serge was during the session, how he'd jump around and dance like a leprechaun when he wanted to describe something."*

Before leaving, Serge tells himself: "This time, I'm going to try to avoid stress, and not improvise everything the night before I go to the studio." He rents a suite at the Ritz in Paris. Three bars, three pianos, but nothing comes of it. There's just Serge, cornered:

> *From a piece by Francis Bacon*
> *I have stepped out*
> *To make love to another man*
> *Who tells me*
> *Kiss me Hardy*
> *Kiss me my love*

They're the last words of Admiral Nelson at the battle of Trafalgar in 1805: dying with a bullet in his chest, he calls to his faithful lieutenant and lover and murmurs into his ear, *"Kiss me, Hardy..."* Serge is seriously addressing homosexuality for the first time in song. Interviewed by Philippe Manœvre, he declares: "I wanted to go beyond sexual relations between man and woman to speak about relations between man and man, in all the tragedy that it implies. Just like that James Joyce line, "I'm the boy that can enjoy invisibility...":

A whore among whores
I dive into the mire
Where beasts they do roar
And angels do expire

BILLY RUSH: *"I was very quickly drawn in by Serge's aura. I saw him as a sort of bohemian artist, completely unique, especially for an Anglo-Saxon like me. He was unlike anybody! Musically, we hit it off right away. All the players I brought in would say the same. He inspired us, made us want to push ourselves for him. And man, he drank enough to kill a horse. He made me these crazy strong piña coladas. And he smoked! If I have lung cancer, it's his fault!"*

Once again, Gainsbarre pushes the envelope. But his obsessions resonate poignantly in "Sorry Angel," a 45 that will climb all the way to number two on the French charts in February, 1985:

It's I who caused your suicide
My love
I who sliced open your veins
I know
And now you live among the angels
Forever
Forever and ever

"Put your work twenty times upon the anvil," said Desnos. 8 minutes and 5 seconds of orgasmic cries, absolute climax – this is *Love On The Beat*:

Burning from every orifice
All three that god above bestowed
I decided with no remiss
To let myself completely go

Love On The Beat
Love On The Beat

Watch me as six million volts
Escape this sturdy staff of mine
Our limbs are now joined in revolt
A spasm synchronized divine

Love On The Beat
Love On The Beat[2]

BAMBOU: *"We were promoting "Love On The Beat" on Enfants du rock, and Serge asked me to dance behind him half-naked. I really didn't want to. We recorded one version with me in a T-shirt, and one topless, and of course the topless version was broadcast. I didn't want to show my breasts, but Serge told me: "You're disgusting. You're going to ruin the show. Don't you understand, if this record tanks it'll be your fault!" So when you're shouldering a burden like that, you go topless... There were two or three shows like that where it was basically blackmail."*

Why push things so far? Because Gainsbourg is trapped. Trapped by his trademark image, by a reputation he needs to defend, and by the success he has so loved since reaching the height of fame. But it's also because he knows full well that no one else would dare explore the kind of eroticism he deals with on this album. And then there's that cover... Gainsbourg, photographed by William Klein, is made up as a transvestite. We see only his face, his slicked back hair, a slender cigarette, fake fingernails, and some simple jewelry. A shocking image for a raw album. Provocation, with Gainsbarre in heat...

Finally, there's the superbly emotional duo with Charlotte and Serge, based once again on a theme by Chopin:

Charlotte: Inceste de citron
Lemon incest
I love you so I love more than all the rest
Papapapa
The love that we will never make
The frightening kind and the most rare
It's drunken pureness strips us bare
Serge: So exquisite
Lovely child my own
My flesh and my bone
Oh my baby my soul

---

[2] A double-entendre: "beat" is a homonym for the French word "bite," which is slang for penis. (T.N.)

Apart from the fact that she sings off-key – she herself admits it – Charlotte is quite happy to have recorded the song. She also has no problem with the video a couple of months later. If it's misunderstood, she's all the more delighted: "I like it when people are confused. It's better for my privacy." A good rule of thumb...

Superb décor, circular bed, Serge shirtless and in pajama bottoms, his daughter next to him wearing his top. These so-called heretical images manage to shock even the most hardened. With the video for "Lemon Incest," more than with any other song, he strikes a very raw nerve. He gets a kick out of it, and comes back to the same theme two years later with the film *Charlotte For Ever*. But it's a less happy experience...

Love On The Beat comes out in October, 1984, with the support of a huge promotional campaign - what we call in English *overkill*. Gainsbourg is everywhere, even in the voices of his *intreprètes*: Jane Birkin and Isabelle Adjani are both climbing up the charts with "Fuir le bonheur de peur qu'il ne se sauve" and "Pull marine" respectively. One inspired reporter tells him: "In Japan, they consider you a national living treasure." Spot on. More than ever, he's a man of his time.

BERTRAND DE LABBEY: *"He was trapped. The public was detestable, constantly waiting for him to swerve off course, as he always would. They paid more attention to the faux pas than to what he actually said or wrote. He was in a permanent state of derision and provocation, especially when faced with television hosts. When the other interlocutors were more cultivated journalists, he could develop much more passionate ideas. During the time of 'Love On The Beat,' I was at interviews where he'd make up homosexual adventures that he never had or which he would embellish to heighten the effect. He constructed a character for himself so that the reporter across from him would always leave with "good material," something meriting, for example, page one of 'Libération' the next day. Underneath it all, he was working really hard on those interviews. It was an example of his exquisite courtesy. If, for example, the reporter didn't make the cover, he was sorry – for both himself and the reporter."*

Interviewed about the theme of his current album, love between men, Serge says the following in *Libération* on September 19, 1984:

I was always unhappy with boys. First of all, I had a repulsion - a repulsion towards skin. And also I felt... I wouldn't say weakened, shit... and not guilty, either... Distant – that's it! I was very modest and it just didn't work. It's a life I just missed out on. In my youth, in the army, I could have... fucked or gotten fucked...Anyway I did fuck guys.

At 20 years-old, I cruised the streets a couple of times. If you combine shame and shyness, it's an erotic mixture... They're what I call "fortuitous encounters," when I didn't feel like a whore, or when I wanted a guy. It always went very badly. I picked up some real pretty boys, cute as hell, and had it off with them. Three times. And it just didn't work...

He does a couple of interviews for gay magazines, including one for *GI* which is overflowing with romanticism about a young boy who had made him "the most beautiful declaration of love. The most beautiful I have ever heard. Even the word sublime cannot describe it. He had understood everything about me." Serge made love to him: "It didn't go well. I told him: *This is a disaster*. Beat it! I kept one of his sketches that came from China. It's in a frame. He passed like a shadow evaporating under the harshness of the sun, the future, extravagant futures."

On March 15, 1985, Jacqueline, who's been taking care of Olia for the last 14 years, finds her seated unconscious in an armchair. Oddly enough, their mother, practically bedridden, had gotten up, made her bed, and stylishly dressed herself.

MICHEL PICCOLI: *"The night his mother died, we were together, with Serge and Jane. They called right when he was launching into a funny story. He answered, hung up, told us what happened, and then said: "Shit, I'm going finish my joke anyway." There was nothing egotistical about it. He just wanted to finish his bit. He was a sulking child facing a catastrophe that he wanted to deny for a few more moments."*

JACQUELINE GINSBURG: *"She was just sitting there in the dark. We called a doctor, but she'd had a thrombosis. She was brain-dead, but Jane and I thought we should still probably try to do something."*

Olia is taken to the hospital in Boulogne where she is pronounced dead at the age of 91.

GAINSBOURG: *"I think she was sick of it all because next to her bed we found a bottle of vodka I'd given her along with some sleeping pills. At the hospital, the doctor took me aside and said, "If we take off the mask, it's over. If not, she'll go on in a vegetative state." I told him to shut it all down.... The day of the burial, I'll always remember, we hadn't yet closed the coffin and I leaned over to kiss her, on the lips, and I started to stamp my feet with despair and with rage in the face of death... Then those guys took her down into the tomb and they stumbled, so I said: "Hey, watch out! Shit, don't disturb her!" After that, I never went back to Avenue Bugeaud. It would have been too painful. And I always wear this ring that belonged to her."*

LILIANE ZAOUI: *"This distance between us made things rather impersonal between me and my brother. He struck me as rather cold at times. He had this routine: he'd bring me inside to admire the fabulous interior. But the day Mother was buried, he totally broke down and asked me to come with him to Rue de Verneuil, where we listened to Ravel's 'Pavane pour une infante défunte,' one of the pieces she loved.... I was really moved... "*

Things are untenable between Serge and Bambou, and least for the moment. In June, 1985, he tells the magazine *VSD*: "There is no more Bambou. But I don't want to talk about it. I don't want to upset her." They had wanted to have a child together, but she lost it. Better that way, Serge tells himself, considering the age difference: "When the kid's 20, I'll be 80." To kill the time, he goes out with his friends, especially Buzy, a female singer who had a hit in the early eighties with "Dyslexique."

BUZY: *"I had the words for this song called "I Love You Lulu," and he was supposed to do the music for it. Bashung had tried, but I didn't like what he did. He's the one who told me to go to Gainsbourg, and I had no idea that his real first name was Lucien. We had a meeting at Rue de Verneuil, and when he read the lyrics he thought the song was for him! Anyway, I was behind schedule and he was dragging his heels, so I wrote the music myself and took advantage of the situation to write another song that this time really was for him. It was called "Gainsbarre." He was really moved. He came to the studio to do the cuts and he even took the cover photo for the album."*

There was one rather bizarre evening when Serge called her and said: "Get here immediately. There's dough to be made. We're going to do a commercial together!" Buzy arrives at his place around 1 A.M. and finds Serge telling his sex stories to about a dozen cops. For the record's photo shoot, he has her pose for five hours, topless, atop a 50 cm cube. She ends up losing it and starts screaming at him.

> BUZY: *"At the end of the shoot, I told him to switch roles and play the model. I used a whole role of film on just his face, and in spite of his fatigue and his haggard mug, I became aware of his charisma from all angles."*

Serge is invited by Patrice Sabatier to be on the live TV show *Jeu de la vérité*, and he's starting to flip out. The night before, he tells *Matin*:

> *What's left? Nothing at all. I lost all my chicks, and my mom. The loss of one's mother is the loss of one's youth.*

Even though the sales of *Love On The Beat* earn him a new platinum record, he's still afraid of the audience's questions, which he may not dodge. The only exceptions are the two jokers he can play. Those are the rules of the show. He's worried about blowback over burning the 500 francs, and he's right to worry. He wants to be clean, and so he stops drinking a week before the show.

> PATRICK SABATIER: *"I was there with him for 15 minutes before the show and I could tell he was really focused. He was smoking a lot, but I didn't see him drink. He knew very well that he'd soon be in front of 10 million viewers. Gainsbourg wasn't any nut who'd do just anything. He knew exactly where he was going to take things."*

That evening, he manages pull it all off marvelously. He prepares for battle first by choosing to perform Aznavour's "Parce que." He also memorizes a bunch of dirty jokes, carefully compiled in a little notebook by his nephew Yves. He really needs them because he is subjected to a flood of bullshit and predictable clichés. It is really low: he's dirty, he's a doper, he's cynical, he massacred the Marseillaise, he made fun of the poor by burning a 500 franc note, and worst of all, he didn't perform with Renaud and his friends on the record for Ethiopia. In an elegant and theatrical gesture of demagoguery, he makes out a check for 100,000 francs to Doctors Without Borders. For the majority of more or less hostile viewers, Serge now becomes a generous, respectable soul, and his trademark image, sullied by past excesses, is for the time being rehabilitated.

GAINSBOURG: *"Something really crazy happened after 'Jeu de la vérité.'
I'm out in the clubs and a pretty young girl comes over to my table and
starts showering me with compliments. She tells me her dad loved the
show, especially the story of the little immigrant that I told in the first
person: I go up to Mitterrand and ask: "How much will you give me to beat
it?" He answers: "10 francs." I go see Raymond Barre, same question, and
he offers me 50. Then Chirac offers 750,000. Finally I see Le Pen: "What
will you give me to leave? – Five minutes!" "My dad was doubled over in
laughter," says the girl, who keeps on flattering me. So I finally ask: "Who's
your father?" And it was Le Pen's daughter... We stayed out till dawn."*

In early July, 1985, Paris is awash in posters featuring the transvestite
image from *Love On The Beat,* hovering over a blue, white, and red background which reads: "Bastille Day, July 14: Mr. Gainsbourg respects tradition." At the same time, papers are full of inserts announcing his concert
dates, beginning with the Casino de Paris. On August 7, there's a long television interview with Jane Birkin, and then Serge flies to New York to rehearse
with Billy Rush and the ace players he's put together for the shows.

Back in France, Serge is awarded the Officer's Cross of the Order of Arts
and Letters. Coluche and Clint Eastwood, honored at the same time, are
given the lesser Knight's Cross. Serge, the son of Russian Jewish immigrants
who had worn the yellow star during the war, is extremely proud. Does it
bring to mind his parents, who arrived in Marseille with false documents in
1921? Most certainly... Serge loves awards, the tangible traces of his success:
gold and platinum records, trophies, badges given to him by his friends on
the local police force, and the rosette of the Legion of Honor, which is given
to him by a fan and which he wears in brazen illegality.

As Serge is getting ready for the concert at the Casino de Paris, the competition is stiff: also touring that fall are Jacques Higelin with Mory Kanté
and Youssou N'Dour, and Nougaro, who's playing the Olympia. Still, all the
shows are sold out up to October 20, and a fifth has to be added in extremis.
The kids are lined up on Rue de Clichy at nine in the morning to make sure
they get tickets.

The night of the premiere, there are plenty expecting Serge to take a fall.
And in fact, after the raising of the curtain, which opens like a pair of jeans
being unzipped, Gainsbarre, surrounded by stagehands and his American

musicians, teeters and slips on the fifth step and falls from atop the stair-case and breaks his face. The public cries out. Only it isn't Serge, but rather a stuntman. After a few nervous moments the real Gainsbourg enters to a standing ovation.

Of course, Serge is scared stiff. The stakes are huge, nothing like those concerts at the Palace in 1979 when the novelty of seeing him onstage was enough to make it an event. This time, he constructs a tower of song, cover-ing all periods of his career, from 1959 to 1985, from "L'eau à la bouche" to "No Comment," with stops along the way for highlights like "La javanaise" and "Ballade de Johnny Jane." This is when he first sees that sea of flames from all those lighters, which every night puts him on the verge of tears. Now and then, he busts out with a little dance step, undulating and jerk-ing his body around. Forget the fact that in Manhattan he'd said: "Come on! Have you ever seen Frank Sinatra dance around onstage? No, he just stands there behind the mic. I'll do the same, freeze frame." Finally, to surmount any memory lapses, he uses a teleprompter, a technique made popular by Johnny Hallyday.

BILLY RUSH: *"One day, two weeks before the premiere, we see this moving van pull up and they pull out velvet-covered panels, gold records, album covers, posters of Bardot, portraits of Jane and Bambou, and a whole mishmash of little knickknacks. Serge had decided to decorate his dressing room exactly like Rue de Verneuil... As for us, we were treated like kings – none of my tours in the U.S. compared to it. With him, it was first class, or nothing. He took us to the best restaurants, showered us with gifts..."*

MICHEL DRUCKER: *"Seeing him onstage at the Casino, I thought about his three-pronged revenge: the revenge on his humble Russian immigrant background, on his impossibly ugly face, and on all his years of hardship. He succeeded in pleasing the public at large and the intelligentsia. In our business, that is extremely difficult. One day, when discussing television, Adjani told me: "You know, the ratings never reflect esteem or respect ..." During those last years, Gainsbourg touched the deepest part of France, the France of Coluche, because he had that clownish quality that all the squares liked. But he never failed at seducing the more demanding crowd, the intellectual elite."*

While the reviews are overall good, the best analysis of the Casino show comes from Sacha Reins, ex-stalwart at *Rock & Folk* who now writes for *Le Point*. She talks about how the concert kicks off with "Love On The Beat":

> *For those not able to grasp the subtleness of this bilingual wordplay, Gainsbourg punctuates each "beat" with a vigorous 'bras d'honneur.'[3] He gives us just what we except of him: some peepee-caca version of provocation, which becomes more pathetic each year. [...] And the music? Rock, or so he thinks. Just like he thought all he needed were Peter Tosh's musicians to become Rastafarian, he's convinced himself that David Bowie's mercenaries would make him a rocker. A huge and tragic error, because from "Je suis venu te dire que je m'en vais" to "L'eau à la bouche" to "La Javanaise," everything is ground out to a rock 'n' roll beat. It's not the fault of his excellent musicians – they're doing what they're paid to do. All the spectator can do is try and remember these beautiful pieces as they were, before their creator subjected them to a disastrous facelift. It's strange that this great artist, who even today continues to write marvelous and earth-shaking songs (listen to Jane B.'s last album), could be so mistaken in thinking that what we want is this drunken and salacious caricature. It's even sadder when one considers that, as we saw on Sabatier's show, there is someone else altogether under this hideous mask: sensitive, modest, fragile, generous, touching. Two personalities reside in him: Doctor Gainsbourg and Mr. Gainsbarre. He thinks it's the latter we come to see. How wrong could he be?*

Among the crew, both at the Casino and on the road, is the astonishing mustachioed colossus named Robert Adamy, alias "Dada." In addition to his role as stage manager, he handles the star's private security, keeping insistent fans at bay and making sure reporters don't get too familiar. We'll see him later during the concerts at the Zénith and on the tour that follows.

> ROBERT "DADA" ADAMY: *"When we left the Casino to tour in the provinces, we started in Lille, a 14,000 seat venue compared to the Casino's 1,500! When he got onstage to rehearse, he said: "What's this, Dada?" He was really floored, and I assured him that the hall would be full of throngs of people waving their lighters... Anyway, I can assure you that as soon as*

---

3 The obscence gesture associated with raising one's forearm and fist, as if to say, "fuck you." (T.N.)

we started rehearsing for the Casino and the tour, he didn't touch a drop of hard liquor. He understood very well that he couldn't let himself drink, and thanks to that we had a magnificent tour - very clean, very civilized."

BILLY RUSH: *"During the tour, there were tons of young girls among the crowd, crammed into the front rows, and sometimes they'd faint. Evert time that security would break up the crowd, he would turn towards me and wink: "They're fainting over me," he thought. He was delighted. Then again, he could get depressed, start sulking around in hotel bars, and that would bother me. One day, in Toulouse, I told him: "Hey, it's nice. Let's take a walk! Just put on some sunglasses and the Simms brothers will come along. There's nothing to worry about!" So we go out and in five minutes there's a riot, a horde of kids on our heels..."*

On January 5, 1986, little Lulu is born. Bambou, the little junkie, has stopped messing around with needles under threats from Serge: "I told her, *If you don't stop, I'll break your neck!* I saved her life and gave her Lulu."

BAMBOU: *"Just before Lulu was born, Serge had to have surgery at the American Hospital in Neuilly, while I was still in the last months of my pregnancy. I asked for permission to stay with Serge at the hospital, to spend the holidays with him, and when I started to leave, the nurses held me back and said that I was ready to deliver. It was January 5, the day of the King Cake, and Serge joined me with the cake and some champagne. We placed a bodyguard at the door, but the paparazzi had dressed up in hospital whites to see if I'd given birth to a strung-out baby. Not at all! He was an eight-pound marvel! Serge wanted a girl, his own little China doll, and when Lulu was born he pouted for three days. Afterwards he apologized and told me that he was the king of all idiots, that he already had a little girl and that now he could play soccer with his son. When I saw Lulu, I told myself that I'd never again be alone. Serge came in right after delivery, cut the cord, and gave him a bath. He came back the next day with Dutronc and Jacques offered to be the godfather."*

On February 22, Charlotte Gainsbourg, fourteen and a half years-old, receives the César as best young female hopeful for her role in Claude Miller's *L'Effrontée.* Everyone can remember the little girl with tears in her eyes, blinded by photographers' flash bulbs and standing between her two proud parents, with Serge kissing her on the lips... The César is well merited for this role in her third film, where she acts alongside Jean-Claude Brialy and Bernadette Lafont. Meanwhile, the director of *Tenue de soirée* is waiting impatiently on Serge for the soundtrack he's promised.

BERTRAND BLIER: *"Unlike on 'Valseuses,' this time I got the ball rolling months ahead of time and made him read the script. He was clearly thrilled by the wild dialogue between Depardieu, Miou-Miou, and Michel Blanc. Of course, everything was done at the last minute. We'd bought a big chunk of studio time and it had to be recorded on Monday. So we got together Saturday and asked ourselves: "Well what are we going to do?" He'd come to the editing room to watch some of the dailies or get a vibe for atmosphere, but aside from that he'd done nothing. He started work late Saturday and into Sunday night, and he was half-dead when he had me listen to the 30 or 40 little bits of musical ideas he'd recorded on his tiny Dictaphone. It almost looked like he was just winging it, but later, in the studio, it turned out marvelously. We spent two insane days and nights on it. Sometimes, Bambou and my wife would take off to get food around three in the morning, and Lulu, a newborn just a few weeks old, would stay there on his father's lap while we mixed the soundtrack at volumes that would have burst the eardrums of any hardened commando. I didn't dare lift a finger, but I had to be ready to intervene. I watched aghast as the ash of Serge's Gitane hovered just centimeters over the baby's skull while one hand manipulated the controls and the other grasped a glass of Pernod..."*

JEAN-PIERRE SABAR: "That's the last time I worked with Gainsbourg. That's when I started to let myself be heard, to tell him he was just recycling tired old crap out of the bottom of the barrel, old stuff that he'd already used or ripped off from somewhere or other. And Blier just went on and on: "Oh, that's great!" I only just started work on the credit sequence when Bertrand had his sound engineer call and tell me: "Serge doesn't want you to come back in." I was pissed at him for dumping me, but I was consoled by the fact that this is what he did with all his arrangers..."

During his appearance at Printemps de Bourges, once again with his American musicians brought back to France expressly for the show, Gainsbourg is invited to be the guest of honor on Michel Drucker's *Champs-Elysées*, in front of a huge television audience. Everything proceeds normally until the arrival of Whitney Houston, the black American singer who's about as white and antiseptic as Michael Jackson. She does her number, joins the hosts, and overhears a tuxedoed Gainsbourg spout out: "I want to fuck her." Whitney is flabbergasted: "Whaaaaaaat?" The audience is in fits and Drucker is now just treading water. He cries out, "Mother, change the channel!" and then does his best to translate while picking up the pieces: "Oh, don't pay attention, it happens sometimes. He just said he wanted to give you some flowers..." Serge: "I did not, I said that I wanted to fuck her!" He's expressing out loud what three-quarters of the male viewers are thinking to themselves, while the American star, mad with rage, readies herself for the coming scandal.

MICHEL DRUCKER: "The worst was that none of this was supposed to happen in the show. I had asked Whitney over only because Serge, during her song, had said to me: "I want to meet that bombshell!" So when he came out with what is, for most Americans, the foulest of insults, for a second I almost forgot we were live. I wanted to get up and punch him, or at least make him leave the stage. But had I done that the show would have ended, and we had another 10 minutes. Serge still had to sing "Vielle Canaille" with Eddy Mitchell. And I suddenly saw in his little boy eyes that he had understood the scope of this farce, and that he had landed me in one of his shitstorms... At the end of the show, Whitney was insane with rage. Serge went to apologize, but she wouldn't even look at him. I remember being stuck in the office while the switchboard was besieged. At four in the morning, we went to her hotel. We had managed to find an enormous bouquet of flowers and we also left her a letter, but we never heard back... After that, Serge thought I was snubbing him when I didn't have him back, but I just wanted things to cool down a bit..."

There are lawsuits threatened. Both the French and Anglo papers report on the scandal while Whitney does her tour of the talk-shows and tells the whole sordid story – without, of course, ever uttering the notorious phrase.

Meanwhile, Serge wraps up production on his new film, *Charlotte For Ever*. For a few months now, he's been talking to reporters about the script, which he wrote for his daughter: "I found an actor who I think is going to have an amazing career, Christophe Lambert - a charming young man, super handsome, sublime eyes. It's the story of a failed writer who lives with his daughter. They share a bed but never touch each other. She cooks him vile grub, they fight..."

> BERTRAND BLIER: *"He wanted me to work with him on the script for ' Charlotte For Ever.' I'd asked him if he'd set anything down on paper, and he told me: "I have the whole story, a 10-page synopsis with everything!" So he gives me the 10 pages and there's nothing but a line or two on each page, essentially nothing, just the seed of an idea... He apparently wanted to film in just a couple of months, but I said I couldn't he lp him. A screenplay, for me anyway, is a real job..."*

> BERTRAND DE LABBEY: *"Blier, whom I'd asked to help with the script, called me and said he had no desire, that it would take at least a year of work. For me, it was a terrible dilemma: after Serge handed me his musical career, I was also obliged to help him get his films made, but each time I remained in the background because I knew the results wouldn't be up to his expectations. Serge loved success. He thought he was going to make millions with his films! I said: "Come on, Serge, with this kind of material it'll be very difficult..." And he'd just say: "You'll see, we'll get there..." "*

The co-producer of his first film gives us some valuable insight on this matter.

> JACQUES-ERIC STRAUSS: *"I didn't produce his other films because I didn't like the scripts. I'd tell him to rewrite them, but Serge had so many other talents, especially as a songwriter, that he just couldn't restrain himself. He was a little lazy, and a script is something that needs to be fully realized, or it just caves in... I was ready to support him, but not on just anything. I wasn't going to get involved in films I didn't believe in simply because he was Serge Gainsbourg."*

In June, 1986, Serge engages in a pathetic little stunt: he's invited by the French national tobacco company, Seita, to attend the launch of the new Gitanes Blondes. Completely wasted, he mumbles a bunch of aphorisms by Lichtenberg in front of gathering of worn out reporters. Then he goes out and paints the town red with his buddy's son, who's celebrating his 13th birthday...

> THOMAS DUTRONC: *"He always bought me great presents, like that beautiful pinball machine, a Spectrum... That night he took me to Maxim's with*

Charlotte. He'd rented a Rolls with a chauffeur just to blow us away. I remember him ordering an obscenely pricey bottle of wine, something like 7,000 francs, and after he tasted it he asked that we wait a bit to let it breathe. At the end of the meal, I noticed that he hadn't even touched it, which I found completely bizarre... Actually, he did it on purpose so that the guys in the kitchen could toast to his health! Then he took us to Raspoutine, where the boss fawned over him. He told the musicians it was my birthday and they came to play at our table, then he told them it was Charlotte's birthday and they came right back as we tossed vodka glasses behind us..."

In the June, 1986 issue of *Globe*, Frank Maubert, ex-art critic for *L'express*, interviews Serge about painting. Five years after these interviews, he'll publish the excellent little book, *Voyeur de première*.[4]

FRANK MAUBERT: *"For the Globe story, we met eight straight days in a row, two hours a day, sometimes at night. Twice he accepted my invitations to the Louvre. He hadn't set foot there in ages and he noticed that some of the paintings had been relocated. He didn't smoke in the Louvre at all. He had total respect for the paintings, and for him it was like a church. His commentaries were excellent. He was passionate, even exalted. He never said anything inappropriate. Then I went to see his paintings. I don't think Gainsbourg was really a painter, but rather he played at being a painter. His stuff was like the work of an art student. He lacked technique. He was looking for his voice, stumbling around. Painter? Architect? No. He only wanted to become an artist. He mythified painters. To him, painting was something noble. His famous "last painting" that reporters always mention, it was formulaic. He didn't try. He would have fallen short. Every time I'd show up at his house there were cops. For him it was some Dadist gesture – he thought he was Picabia."*

During the filming of the TV show *Les Dessous chics de Paris*, in July, 1986, for a program that is essentially devoted to Jane Birkin, Serge runs into Gilbert and Maritie Carpentier as well as their longtime director, André Flédérick.

ANDRÉ FLÉDÉRICK: *"Serge was really harsh and nasty with Jane. He was also a real boor towards Fanny Ardant, whom they had asked to recite*

---

[4] A biography of Gainsbourg. (T.N.)

"Dépression au-dessus du jardin." Serge wanted her to read it while eating a banana. I lost it and stormed off the set, saying: "There's one director too many here." It was like he couldn't stand himself. He was extremely uneasy in his own skin."

Producer Claudie Ossard, currently making a killing at the box-office with Jean-Jacques Beineix's *37°2 le matin*, lets herself be swayed by the meager treatment that Gainsbourg presents her. Christophe Lambert then pulls out, leaving Serge to play the role of Stan, the alcoholic forger in *Charlotte For Ever*.

As for the cast, Serge recruits Roland Dubillard and Roland Bertin, who play two lost wastrels, and also a few young girls, like Anne Le Guernec, Charlotte's friend. During the filming, which starts in August, 1986, it appears as if Serge has lost touch with the author within him and is simply adrift in autobiographical pity. During the filming, Charlotte and her father stay at a hotel, and he tells his set designers, Raoul Albert and Claude Plet, to remake the set like the interior of Rue de Verneuil. For authenticity, he even brings a few things over, like the hood ornament from the Rolls.

CLAUDE PLET: *"For one scene, he wanted to film from below when Charlotte dunked her head into the water. He had this special bathtub built, with a glass bottom, the cost of which made everyone grumble. But he just had to have that shot. He was even ready to pay for the tub out of his own pocket, just to get that image."*

Whatever one thinks of the film, Charlotte had never, up till then, been so beautifully filmed. Once again, Gainsbourg uses his favorite cinematographer.

WILLY KURANT: *"I enjoyed the filming, even though there were certain things I couldn't stand... Charlotte was sometimes uncomfortable, but she's a truly great actress. She acts like a pro with 25 years of experience behind her. Some people saw something sleazy in this film, or they refused to watch it because they feared it was some disgusting display of gratuitous incest. But the director is someone very chaste... He is always looking out for the moral well-being of his daughter. One day, in Charlotte's dressing room, he found a cigarette butt in an ashtray and started screaming, asking if she'd been secretly smoking behind his back, which wasn't the case."*

GAINSBOURG: *"During the filming, Charlotte just blew me away. What*

*stoicism... She completely trusted her father. Still, when I had her strip,
she came home crying and said: "Daddy's betrayed me!"*

For Charlotte, who doesn't like to discuss it, the filming turns out to be
sometimes difficult. The films she had done prior to that were based more
in reality. She feels disoriented, as if in another world. She must have a hard
time understanding a subject matter that is too mature for her. She's sometimes uncomfortable in front of her father, and Serge will come to fret over
having made her cry. He doesn't understand that she has her modesty. By
offering up an atrocious spectacle of his own decay – during the film we see
him vomit into the sink and piss blood – it's as if he wants to redefine the notion of the word "unwholesome," especially when he smashes his head into
the wall to chase away his nightmares... The script oscillates between utterly
botched and hastily slapped together, yet there are truly graceful scenes, especially when Serge and his daughter dance together, or when he declares,
as if it were a vow: "I must return to the silence, there is too much noise
around me..."

GAINSBOURG: *"There are autobiographical references in my film, for example, the story of my mother, who has an accident in a sports car and
dies. I'd given Jane a Porsche Targa just before she left me, and I could see
in her eyes when I gave it to her that she'd already been thinking about it.
At the time, I didn't know. And how can you film that? I came to the hotel
where she was staying while she filmed and I offered her the car. I could
see the guilt in her eyes, something fugitive. You can't film that. I could
see something fugitive and atrocious in her eyes, like she felt that the car
was an invitation to death. Her look seemed to say: "You're giving me this
Porsche for me to kill myself in." But it was all very innocent..."*

In front of Sophie Fontanelle and Marie-Elizabeth Rouchy of *Matin de
Paris*, Serge engages in some auto-flagellation and asks himself some tortu-
ous questions: "Why did I make Charlotte cry? Why did I cry? I don't know.
I can't write a comedy. There must be some sort of internal violence that
motivates me. A latent violence[...] This film shattered me. After the shooting, I couldn't bear to look at the rushes. Not because of me, but because
of Charlotte! How could I have written such a terrible role? I don't understand." A few weeks before the film's release, Serge puts together a screening
for a small group of people.

Charlotte leaves the room enraged.

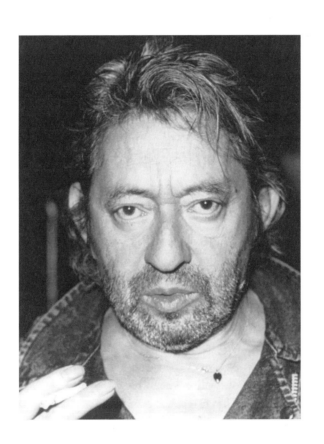

twenty-four

Hey *Man* *Amen*

From October to November, 1986, with the editing of *Charlotte For Ever* barely finished, Serge dives right into the recording of two new albums. Meanwhile, Brigitte Bardot's version of "Je t'aime moi non plus" comes out some 19 years after she stopped its initial release in 1967. The benefits will go to her foundation for the protection of animals. But she doesn't have much luck – without a promo campaign it is simply a non-event that attracts only a few die-hard fans.

In utter haste, Serge records the instrumentals and the backing vocals for Charlotte's one and only album at Billy Rush's place in New Jersey. It's a tender little thing full of restrained emotion from the performer's gracious voice. It comes out at the same time as the film, under the same title, *Charlotte For Ever*. There are only eight cuts, and the opening is a sort of polar opposite to "Lemon Incest":

> *Chorus: Charlotte*
> *Charlotte for ever*
> *Charlotte: My little dreaming dad*
> *Chorus: Charlotte*
> *Charlotte for ever*
> *Serge: Forever my heart's glad*

Three's a problem right off the bat: first, the lyrics are notoriously awful; second, Serge lifted the melody, note for note, from an andantino by Khatchatourian, and never credited him. A musicologist with *Le Monde* reveals it all, alerting the heirs of the Russian composer, who died in 1978. "O.K, I fucked up," Gainsbourg contritely admits to Bertrand de Labbey, "Charlotte was playing it on the piano, and I just lifted the melody." The upcoming trial will be won by the plaintiffs. Then Gainsbourg lifts another melody for "Zéro pointé vers l'infini," Charlotte's favorite song on the record, which comes from a popular Russian song. The title refers to the French title of the Koestler novel, Darkness at Noon:

From zero to infinity
Life's not reality
From zero to infinity
My fangs devour me
From zero to infinity
A drugged out reverie
Day and night I dream of thee
I thirst for Nelson, Melody

Serge then moves on to the new Jane Birkin album, *Lost Song*, recorded this time in London with Alan Hawkshaw and his band. The night before entering the studio to lay down the vocals, Serge had but one song, "On s'est fait pour entendre," which didn't even make the album. This record is anything *but* a follow-up *Baby Alone In Babylone*. It contains, for example, the song, "L'amour de moi," written in memory of Ava Monneret, Jane's deceased friend. Over a traditional French folk tune, Serge mixes modern expression with verses liberally inspired by Ronsard:

This love of mine inside is locked
Within a little garden fair
Where roses kiss the evening air
And lilies bloom near hollyhock

To life she simply said "no more"
And left to wander o'er the ground
Her body on some forgotten pathway found
Where she rests forever more

JANE BIRKIN: *"While recording this album, I knew that I was him, that I had become the hidden part of him, the part which I love best. The con-*

stant here is failed love, and it's sadder than 'Baby Alone In Babylone,' where there was still this battle with melancholy. This time there's not even any more violence... I think that with "Une chose entre autres," he wrote me one of my most beautiful songs, and one completely true to life."

> One thing among others
> That you do not know
> You had more than another
> My best my beau
> Is it your fault
> Don't feel remiss
> For perfect stories
> Do not exist

JANE BIRKIN: *""Lost Song" was my idea. I was coming back from Japan, where they'd asked me to do a commercial set to the music of Grieg's 'Peer Gynt.' I sang it with a symphony and I had him listen to it on cassette. During a press conference, the Japanese reporters had asked me if I felt more French or English, and I really couldn't say. I felt totally lost. I no longer knew where I was, what epoch I was living in – no longer young but not old, either. For the first time he was nice enough to listen to my suggestion. He said: "So it's a 'lost song' that you want?" and he wrote me this really pretty piece..."*

> Lost song
> In the jungle
> Of our now vanished love
> Disappeared in the clouds above

On December 10, 1986, *Charlotte For Ever* is released in Paris. "A script of substandard intelligence," writes Michel Braudeau in *Le Monde*, explaining how the author "tosses around a surfeit of curse words and low-brow poetry," all while lifting entire passages from Benjamin Constant's *Adolphe*. But he also reveals, with great finesse, how his slow-motion suicide, which started with his first heart attack, is one of the most constant themes in Gainsbourg's relationship with le public via the media: "It seems that people don't fire upon ambulances, or upon the mortally wounded. Ever since he started forecasting his inevitable death, he seems to have found the perfect scapegoat," concludes Braudeau.

One reporter, Alix de Saint-André, writes an article for *Le Figaro* entitled "Serge Gainsbourg: A tired salaciousness." She asks the question: "What's happened to his talent? Has it drowned in alcohol?" She also manages to record a few of the words spoken by the principal actress:

> *Charlotte, long and pale, with strands of hair escaping from her chignon, receives the reporters while nibbling at chocolate. Timid. Secretive. Uncomfortable.*

> *"For the first time, I'm really frightened. I don't know what the reaction will be. I haven't seen the film, but I'm afraid of what people will think. I don't want to talk about it. I don't want to hurt anyone."*

Especially not her father, who is already in a sorry state.

Eight days later, Serge puts his crudeness on display and salutes the reporter with a *bras d'honneur* at the end of a live TV show. The cinephile journal *Positif* is practically the only magazine to positively review the film, which is saluted in its February, 1987 issue for the "...enormous violence which elevates it without rendering it turgid and fussy, like the ramblings of Jodorowski and Arrabal." Our director/actor is congratulated on his performance: "A virtuoso display that hits on all cylinders: to hear him recite Benjamin Constant in that ultra-classic tone, with just a hint of irony, is magisterial." All this while Braudeau and the others see in it only so much filler...

In 1994, Jean-Luc Godard will give us this belated homage:

> *Serge Gainsbourg is the only one to understand, to be able to, to want to, to have to film the "for ever" that the cinematograph demands. Forever, therefore, must Charlotte be seen as standing alongside the most ardent work of Cassavetes, the most beautiful Vigo.*

On television, Gainsbourg is more and more unpredictable. It's sometimes funny, sometimes pathetic, sometimes revolting. One episode that is not well-known by the general public - Canal+ didn't have many subscribers back then - is when he came off as almost odious on March 4, 1986, while appearing with Catherine Ringer of Les Rita Mitsouko on a show hosted by Michel Desinot. Sure, we've seen him call singer Caroline Grimm a cunt; we've seen him say to Whitney Houston, "I want to fuck you." But this time his actions are truly unforgiveable. Catherine Ringer had done pornographic films when younger, and so Serge starts to degrade her, to call her disgusting

- an uncouthness that is truly out of place when one considers that it comes from the composer of "Je t'aime moi non plus," from the man who helped launch the sexual revolution in the seventies, the man who was unconditionally adored by Les Rita Mitsouko.

In the first few months of 1987, the person who certain polls have designated "the most loved man in France" starts to wear out his welcome. It's what they call in England "backlash." It's true that the media has given us an overdose of Serge. His dismayed fans can no longer look each other in the face. It's like watching the decline of a burned-out artist, half-senile, thoroughly intoxicated, unable to even hold his head up. His sob stories, his casualness, his exhibitionism – it all becomes irritating and unbearable.

Then the abscess explodes. In the January edition of *Globe*, entitled "Gloomy Gainsbourg/End of the Road," Serge Grünberg gives us a pitiless exposé of certain undeniable truths. The tone is almost spiteful, and it starts with the following words:

> *Gainsbourg, we love you, of course. You know it all too well. But you really broke into our piggy banks with that last incestuous flick. We feel like dried-up lemons. You're becoming vulgar, getting on our nerves. You might want to be Caligula, but you come off as Professor Charon. You are out! Your strip is no longer comic. It is decadanse!*

Grünberg asks if Gainsbourg's genius is all gone. He demands of the author of *Evguénie Sokolov*, after listening to his last few records, to prove that he is more than a has-been who now caters to the bourgeoisie:

Instead of allusion and understatement, it's all torpor and ranting. Elegance and metaphor have become a boring display of his "class." We would love to hear him think out loud, but for some time now, it's been impossible to say where the frenzy of the "wounded poet" stops and where the vile invective of the drunk begins[...] The auto-exploitation of his destructive alcoholism is starting to wear thin. The only people Gainsbourg titillates anymore are the housewives who read *Intimité*. It makes us think of the drunk at the corner store who makes everyone laugh, and is every day more smutty, facile, and unctuous.

Some reactions:

JANE BIRKIN: *"Serge is caught up in the gears. He likes us to talk about him. It's difficult for him to just fade away. I find it touching because it shows how unsure of himself he is... He lives vicariously, and he only feels alive when he's seen on TV or mentioned in the press. I despise the media like the plague: first they use Serge to sell their magazines or their shows, then they attack him for doing something stupid... He is capable of hurting people, but if he gets hurt it really floors him."*

GAINSBOURG: *"The author of the piece was a faithful fan, and to piss me off he just shat all over me. It was truly hurtful. I cried over it, which I am still able to do at this age. Why go and do Gainsbarre on TV when I can just be Gainsbourg? Is that it? It goes according to my mood, because I'm impulsive, not aggressive. If I overdo it, it's because I have no time to waste."*

BAMBOU: *"The public overdosed on Serge and he had a hard time recovering. He really suffered. When he is too fucked-up on TV and does stupid stuff, it really bothers me. It bothers him too when he watches it again, sober. But as he is very impressionable and because there's always someone who finds it funny, he keeps doing it. I've gone nuts telling him this and I'm sure he's sick of hearing it... But I love him, so I forgive it all. I don't believe another woman could put up with it. She'd be gone at the end of a couple months... You need a lot of patience to live with Serge... His private life is a non-stop public spectacle. He and Jane were the ideal media couple, but that's less true with me. It's not the same thing. I'm not a public person. Without him I wouldn't exist, and I know it."*

As for the commercials, things are slowing down. In 1987, he does only one for Pentex correcting fluid, and in 1988 he does his last for Tutti Free artificial sweetener, using once again Helen Nougerra, Lio's little sister.

DOMINIQUE BLANC-FRANCARD: *"He'd sometimes put me into the middle of incredible shitstorms in order to get those revolting commercials made. It was like highway robbery for him! For the Pentex commercial, we got to the studio at nine in the morning. I'd brought along two to three keyboards to do the music with, which was in fact a demo for a Jane Birkin song that didn't pan out. We recorded it in an hour. A girl came to do the voice-over, and that lasted five minutes. We'd finished by noon, and we just sat around talking rubbish till five. When the agency people came in and asked Gainsbourg if they could hear it, he exploded with rage and told them: "I said to wait outside! You'll come and listen when I tell you to."*

He made them wait around another hour... They came back to listen to it, and they said to him: "Not bad, but you don't think that the words are..." He told them it was fine the way it was, shoved the tape into their hands, and said goodbye! I've never seen anyone handle advertising people with such disdain."

In February, 1987, Serge returns from Morocco with Bambou and Lulu, just in time to participate on a live TV show. He meets up again with the singer Buzy, who wasn't as successful as she thought she'd be with "I Love you Lulu" and "Gainsbarre."

BUZY: *"We'd spent six months together just going nuts – it's was really crazy. At that time, Bambou was in London because of health issues, so her absence made that time possible. Then there was a publishing hassle because he realized his investment should have earned him dividends. At the beginning, things were simply spontaneous and friendly, and then he ended up asking me to sign a contract with his company, Melody Nelson, for the song "Gainsbarre." But I didn't want to. Anyway, he was totally upset about my album not being a big hit. I was really down, and then I released "Body Physical," which went through the roof. I remember seeing him on the set of the TV show 'Lahaye d'honneur.' He turned around and asked what I was doing there. I answered: "I have the same job as you, buddy! What's more, I have a big hit!" In the middle of all that I had a nervous breakdown. It's clear that when you live through something that strong with someone that powerful, creative, and he gives you credit as he did with me, that has an effect... The night of the last show on TV6, Serge came and clowned it up behind me. I was really afraid he'd make some obscene gestures, but nothing of the sort! And so I sang "Gainsbarre"... He was very sweet, but he couldn't stop himself from asking me at the end: "So, how much are you pulling down?" Since I knew his routine, I didn't get all bent out of shape. I replied: "With a song about you, I'm going to make a truckload."*

In March, 1987, officers accidently stumble across a trio of rich kids who get nabbed for clumsily stealing police uniforms in an attempt to kidnap Charlotte. When Serge learns about it he wants to ring their necks. He demands stiff punishment... In short, he's overcome with hatred and anguish. But the real news is the onstage debut of Jane Birkin. Her group is under the direction of Michel-Yves Kochman, and the drummer is future TV segment producer and author of children's books, Camille Safiris.

JANE BIRKIN: *"In a way, the 'Globe' article motivated me even more to sing at Bataclan. I was so exasperated. I wanted people to see the show and say: "Shit, he wrote some beautiful songs." It was my right to rebuttal."*

CAMILLE SAFARIS: *"I'll never forget the first time Serge showed up. We were rehearsing "Lost Song" with Jane while they were testing the smoke machines and projectors. Jane had walked out into the hall because she planned to go down into the audience while singing the song. We were enveloped in thick smoke and we lost sight of her for a minute. When the smoke cleared, there was Gainsbourg at a table with his pack of Gitanes. He appeared like a mirage, a supernatural image. Jane was just as surprised as us, and while still singing she went over to embrace him. It was really touching. After that, he would come to the concerts. He showed up several times, and even came onstage once during a song, tapping Jane's mic and asking the crowd: "Isn't it lovely, isn't she a cute little thing?" Despite the separation, you could sense great tenderness between them. I think he was still in love with her. Her singing his songs was proof of her love for him. She still loved him, but in a different way. They were separated, but all of her wounds had not yet healed."*

During rehearsals, Serge suggests that Jane move more, that she be more sexy, just like she had at the beginning of their relationship and on their first TV appearances. But he doesn't realize that she's changed. She's no longer the scandalous figure that shared his life, the sassy and petulant little English chick. In fact, she performs at Bataclan with sheer romanticism and the spectators are seduced by her delicate charm. At Printemps de Bourges, Gainsbourg films her for a television report by FR3. With a cameraman at his side, Gainsbourg plays the reporter. After three days, his all too visible presence ends up getting on people's nerves, and the crowd occasionally boos him. The finished product, released shortly thereafter, is a disappointing 52 minute documentary, in spite of the promising menu: Gainsbourg in the dressing room of the "Killer," Jerry Lee Lewis; Gainsbourg interviewing Ray Charles; Gainsbourg all hunched over greeting President Mitterrand... In short, a good idea gone bad.

Three new people now make their arrival. Each will play a more or less important role during the last few years his life. The first, Vanessa Paradis, is also the last of his Lolitas. The second is his confidant, secretary, and chief steward, Fulbert, who looks after everything at Rue de Verneuil. He is an exquisitely mannered young man who draws a pension from being disabled in a terrible accident from which he still bears a scar across his face. The third, Vittorio Perrotta, made his fortune in clothing. He quickly becomes a close friend, one whom Gainsbourg would present with La Légion d'honneur de l'amitié - a red ruby from Cartier's - in early 1991.

In the summer of 1987, Vanessa Paradis, the darling 14 year-old, hits it big with "Joe le taxi," a song by Franck Langolff and Etienne Roda-Gil.

Vanessa Paradis: "My father always resembled Gainsbourg in his philosophy and in his way of viewing things. He'd buy his albums as they came out. I remember dancing like mad to his reggae Marseillaise, which really made me shake my little ass... I think I must have fallen asleep to his music ever since I was a little girl. I flipped over Adjani's "Beau oui comme Bowie," and Jane's songs really gave me goose bumps..."

Every day, fans send Gainsbourg cassettes, poems, petitions, and love notes. Enemies send hate mail. He needs someone to sort through all that, handle the bills, greet guests, and turn away over-zealous fans.

Gainsbourg: "I did have a black servant once, but everything in my place is black, so I could only see him when he smiled... Ha, ha, ha... He fixed me African food... And then Fulbert showed up... I cannot and do not want to be alone..."

In August, 1987, Serge and Philippe Lerichomme take the Concorde to New York. The recording of his new album, *You're Under Arrest*, is taking place between August 17 and 30 at Dangerous Music – in other words Billy Rush's place. He'll come back to Paris to lay down the vocals with Dominique Blanc-Francard in September. The budget for the whole thing is 499,680 francs: 5,000 dollars for Billy and 3,000 for each musician - just 18,000 dollars in all - plus 176,320 francs for the studio and 114,360 francs for travel and lodging. A pittance compared to other big recording artists. The group from the Casino concerts is reunited, and only the background singers have changed:

One night while in the Bronx
I was ever oh so anx-
Ious to finally find Samantha
Between Thelonious Monk
A few punks and also Bron-
Ski Beat was playing on my Aiwa

You're Under Arrest, his last studio album, comes out in November, 1987. Serge, who thoroughly grasps how much he needs to redeem himself and put out a successful album that is not a simple remake of *Love On The Beat,* has worked very hard, especially on the general concept. Thus he takes his fans on a quest for a prepubescent avatar, neither Melody nor Marilou, but rather little Samantha, a 13 year-old black junkie. In "Five Easy Pisseuses" (a play on the title of the Jack Nicholson film *Five Easy Pieces,* directed by Bob Rafelson), he describes his character:

Out of my five little tarts I prefer number six
Yes for you Samantha all five are now my ex
Your little socks
Pump up my sex

She shoots up and nods off, but that doesn't stop her from taking her man's member all the way down to her tonsils ("Suck Baby Suck," one of the most appalling pieces of his career). But he gets sick of his heroine, and between the lines we can guess whom he's directing his reproaches at:

The bloody marks on your left arm Samantha
Yawn yawn Samantha
The tracks on your arms a
Line of powder cross your lips
Oh Samantha

Serge also remembers "Sombre dimanche," that suicidal ballad sung by Damia in 1936. However, he prefers the English title, "Gloomy Sunday" (sung by Billie Holliday in 1941):

I'll die on a Sunday my suffering true and tried
And you might well come back but I'll have long since left
While candles burn away like hope that never dies
And for you with such ease my eyes will open wide
And have no fear my love should I not hear your cries
My eyes will tell you that without you I'm bereft

[543]

Dominique Blanc-Francard: "We mixed 'You're Under Arrest' in a Pigalle studio, but as the mixing didn't interest him, he'd take off to go drinking in a prostitute bar. Each time he'd come back with two prostitutes and two cops. He wanted them to listen to the new songs "full blast!" Then he traded badges with the cops and they kept screwing around. When they were tired of all the nonsense and said they had to get back to work, he whined like a little boy."

Another salvaged memory is "Mon legionnaire," sung by Edith Piaf in 1937. But in contrast to his reggae Marseillaise, it's not done this time to piss off old soldiers. Still, one can imagine how the tune would have gone over on the preceding album, between the homosexual provocation of "Kiss Me Hardy" and "I'm The Boy":

> *My buried love my long lost love*
> *I can still see the stars above*
> *Desire for you eats me alive*
> *And now just tears and dreams survive*
> *For when you were still next to me*
> *I should have vowed my love to thee*

Dominique Blanc-Francard: "It was all classic talk-over, which didn't cause any problem on this album. The only hassle was "Mon legionnaire," because he actually wanted to sing it. We stumbled around for four hours in an impossible direction. It was absolutely ridiculous. He remained stubborn even though Philippe Lerichomme told him it wasn't working at all. He finally decided to speak it like the other tunes, and I think that in the end that version was a great success."

During the interviews for 'You're Under Arrest,' Serge drifts into deep depression and seems to hit bottom. He's trying like a madman to get work done, walking the razor's edge, but psychologically and physically he can't take it anymore...

Gainsbourg: "Really, I've had my fill of music. If I do a new album, it's to prove to myself that I'm the best, all the while vigilantly proclaiming that it is a minor art... Do I care about posterity? Like the man said, what's posterity ever done for me? Fuck posterity. I've always been a rookie. In grade school I got my ass kicked by the big kids because I was a rookie. Same goes for high school, in the academy, in the army where I suffered all

*that hazing. I was a rookie when I started painting and when I started the
piano. Then when I started this profession in 1958, I was a rookie again.
And I'm telling you, I'll be a rookie again when I kick the bucket. In the
middle of it all, I was also a rookie to a few chicks. I'm fragile because I'm
disillusioned. I have it all, so I have nothing. I had it all, and now I no longer have a thing. Happiness is a foreign concept which I can't conceive of
and thus don't look for. My plan is the same as any other guy's - to look for
truth through perversion. The only thing I'm looking for is the pureness of
my childhood. I have remained intact, INTACT, that's my force."*

The press is more or less positive about *You're Under Arrest.* Serge is on
the cover of *Paroles et musique* along with Charlotte, and there's a 15 -page
spread on him inside. Then, on December 12, there's a special broadcast of
Les Enfants du rock which is dedicated to Serge.

In the press, Gainsbourg speaks about his new plans to act in Jean-Pierre
Rawson's film based on the journal of Paul Léautaud. "It's no longer the literary critic we find here. Rather, through his love affairs with Marie Dormoy
and Anne Cayssac, a veritable erotomaniac is unveiled, and one that could
easily resemble Gainsbourg himself," reports *Le Quotidien de Paris.* "Anne
Cayssac, for example, in the offices of *Mecure de France*, paying homage to
the writer while on her knees, not even bothering to take her hat off."

JEAN-PIERRE RAWSON: *"He was going to play a rather big character in
Léautaud, but that turned out to be a bad idea because Gainsbourg himself
was a character, and not enough of an "actor" to disappear into the role.
He would have just done Gainsbourg. But really, it didn't happen because
he was in poor health. After eight days of filming, he couldn't even put one
foot in front of the other. He was already quite ill."*

The year ends on an interesting footnote: Bambou gets questioned by
the cops after coming out of a dealer's house in the 12th arrondissement.
France-Soir puts it on page three of the December 1 edition, and then the next
day comes the following story: "Gainsbourg-Bambou: Drugs." That same day,
Serge has over the narcotics officers who nabbed Bambou. She'll have to
go to detox in order to avoid jail time. Then there's the following story from
his valet:

FULBERT: *"When he got back from the States, where he was rehearsing
with his musicians for the Zénith, Serge was surprised to find a guy who'd*

broken into his house through the skylight and made himself at home. He'd taken a bath and slept in his bed. Without losing his cool, Serge grabbed the phone and called the police, right in front of this happily inoffensive fellow who had just escaped from a mental hospital..."

On March 22, 1988, Serge is back to the salt mines: seven nights at the Zénith and then off in every direction for 30 more shows, from Nantes to Metz, and from Caen to Nice. The décor is superb, post-atomic, "a night-blue or fire-red background with the metallic ruins of a warehouse sinking into the Hudson," as described by Claude Fléouter in Le Monde. His musicians are the same, led by Billy Rush on guitar. Technical support is once again provided by Robert Adamy, a.k.a. Dada, imposing as ever, who watches over Serge and makes sure he's not hassled by unwelcome visitors.

Billy Rush: "Physically, he had really deteriorated since the last tour. We could see that he was tired and depressed. He could feel himself getting old and he talked to me about it. He kept working, but not in any specific direction. He had nothing more to prove, so he was just looking to keep busy. He hated the thought of going on vacation."

Onstage, in front of tens of thousands of "little lads" and "tiny tarts"- a crowd much younger than that at the Casino de Paris three years ago – he's obviously ecstatic, anything but blasé, as his niece and nephew tell us...

Yves and Isabelle Le Grix: *"We had tears in our eyes each night, as if we were telling ourselves: enjoy it, because it could be the last time. Back in the dressing rooms, an impressive array of stars paraded by: Catherine Deneuve, Johnny Hallyday, Robert Charlesbois, Renaud, Jean-Paul Belmondo... Sometimes, old has-beens would drop in – we won't mention names – and this would bust him up. One night the group Cock Robin came by. He gave them a really warm welcome, and after they left, he asked: "Who are those guys?""*

The show includes excerpts from his two New York albums, old hits like "Qui est 'in' qui est 'out,'" "Manon," "Couleur café" and "Les dessous chics." There are also three new tunes: the pitiful "You You You But Not You," "Seigneur et saigneur," and the very moving "Hey Man Amen," in the style of the testaments:

When I'm dead and cold as sno
I'll leave behind for my little Luli
My nothings and my so and soe's
You'll have to think of what to doo
Little Lulu
You've lost poor me
But worry not I'm here in Paradee

On April 28, 1988, Serge dines with Bambou and his musicians at Laserre, in Paris, to celebrate his 60th birthday. The next day, he's at Printemps de Bourges, which earns him this new commentary from Yves Bigot in *Libération*:

> *The problem with Gainsbarre is maybe that he waited too long for success. All of the sudden he's a glutton: talks too much, makes too much of things, shows his satisfaction too readily – his relief – at finally being recognized.*

On tour, in the buses, in the hotels, the dressing rooms, Serge and Billy are constantly playing never-ending matches of their favorite game – chess. Every time Serge beats his musical director he is overcome with joy and relentlessly teases him about it onstage. But when he thinks he may lose, he just sweeps away all the chess pieces in a fit of anger.

> ROBERT "DADA" ADAMY: *"The good thing about Serge's fans is that they're rarely aggressive, which is unusual. Still, the girls were often hysterical. At that time, we used to have fun counting all the bras and panties thrown onstage, and the number was considerable! Serge was happy. He enjoyed his success in a very serene manner and he used to tell us that it took 40 years for him to reach this level of fame."*

> BERTRAND DE LABBEY: *"Serge knew very well that he was one of the most important creative minds of the 20th century. At the same time - I saw it during the tour after the Zénith concerts - he took a childlike pleasure in being reassured of it, up to the point where he'd kiss the window of his car as it passed by and say hello to people on the streets so that he'd be recognized, so they'd say: "Hey, it's Gainsbourg!" This permanent fear of being forgotten, of no longer existing, was as touching as it was surprising."*

Finally, there's a three-week tour of Japan.

> ROBERT "DADA" ADAMY: *"In general, the Japanese don't move around much during the show. They're rather timid, even about applauding, be-*

cause they're afraid to be a bother. So they wait until the end of the show.
For Serge, they stood up at the beginning of the first song, and the Japanese
promoter came over, very worried, wanting Serge to tell the audience to sit
back down. Serge said no way, and the fans crowed the stage and remained
on their feet. That's exceptional in Japan!"

During the summer of 1988, Serge reaches the very pits of depression.
He's hunched over and walking with a cane. Alcohol is making him fat,
and he's suffering countless delirium tremens. He should stop, slow down,
take sleep treatment. Bambou can only convince him to spend a few days in
Portugal in August. His health problems are getting serious: vision loss, cirrhosis, cardiac flare-ups, pain, and even problems with impotence.

At sixty years of age, Serge is terribly worn-put. He has but 30 months
to live.

twenty-five

I'll Die On A Sunday, My Suffering True And Tried

In the fall of 1988, Serge's health is at its worst, and the descent into hell inevitably follows. With the exception of *Mon Zénith à moi* on Canal+, his television appearances are disastrous. On *Nulle part ailleurs*, he introduces his video for "Mon legionnaire," directed by Luc Besson. There's Gainsbourg, donning a hat and flanked by a photogenic young boy while hysterical dancers gyrate in the background, like an episode of *Fame*.

To assuage his melancholy, he can always count on Jacques Wolfsohn or Jacques Dutronc, or even Dutronc's son, nearly 16 now, whom Serge loves so because, according to Bambou, he sees in the boy all of the purity that Jacques had lost.

THOMAS DUTRONC: *"One day after buying new speakers, we listened to Elvis Presley's "Love Me Tender" at full volume. He told me he'd always wanted to write a song so simple and so beautiful. Then we listened to "In The Ghetto" and he cried... I met up with him at Raphaël a bunch of times. I'd go see him in a bar, or at his place, sometimes with my school friends. One night he insisted on introducing me to his cop buddies and we ended up in a paddy wagon with Serge begging them to hit the siren. The cops said they couldn't because it was nighttime, but to make him happy they flipped on the flashing lights. Later, at the post office, he pointed to some*

cops and said: "Look, my toys." I remember him taking me to visit some
big precinct headquarters on Avenue de Maine, where they keep all the
psychos locked up in glass cages. We saw an exhibitionist there who looked
like he might have had Down syndrome, and he'd slid his underwear down
and was jerking off behind the glass."

One predictable catastrophe is Bambou's album, which was finished two
months earlier. Musically, *Made In China* is more of the same, seeing as how
we find Billy Rush, Gary Georgett, and Curtis King Jr. all there again. The
lyrics are the main weakness. The only thing that stands out on this anec-
dotal record, released in March, 1989, is the remake of "Nuits d Chine" and,
doubtlessly inspired by Julie London's "Cry Me A River," the rather pretty
"J'ai pleurer le Yang-Tsé."

DOMINIQUE BLANC-FRANCARD: *"Serge was bored. He'd finished his*
tour, he was depressed, and he wanted something to do. Alain Lévy, the
head of Polygram, didn't want to do an album with Anthony Delon, which
they'd talked about, and instead suggested Serge make a record with
Bambou. But Philippe Lerichomme, who rightly feared the worst, said that
as long as he didn't have any lyrics in front of him, there'd be no record.
Suddenly, Serge pulled a vicious stunt: he called Lévy directly to say that
Lerichomme was refusing to do the record. I was in Philippe's office that
day. Levy called right away to ask what the problem was, and we finally
ended up doing this record that we didn't want to do."

Gainsbourg tries to argue that "Nuits de Chine" had tanked because of
the bad luck involved in releasing it at the same time that Tiananmen Square
was unfolding in Beijing, and that anything with an Asian flavor was being
boycotted.

DOMINIQUE BLANC-FRANCARD: *"The start of the recording session was*
a nightmare. Bambou was adorable, but she'd never worn a headset in her
life, and she knew nothing about the notes or the rhythms. Serge started to
flip out because he realized he was running into a wall. The machine was
out of control. He called her terrible names, and she fell to the studio floor,
in tears. She was lost. She couldn't understand why it wasn't working.
Serge felt it was his fault and he became really aggressive."

Serge's alcoholism reaches epic proportions. From 1979 to 1989, it's just one long slide into 10 years of dipsomaniac hell. He once got so plastered that he fell into a coma, and the delirium tremens hurled him into a nightmarish universe. The pleasant pink elephants of popular mythology are now replaced by horrifying visions. He talks about one night when he believed he was being attacked with daggers that he tried to avoid with convulsive gestures.

So is Serge really suicidal? Does he think he is immortal? Alcohol surely becomes a prison that he can not escape. It's true that in France, a drunkard's paradise, alcoholism is rarely treated as what truly is: a physical and mental disease. Of course, when your name's Gainsbourg, you can't just go and join Alcoholics Anonymous. That's why some of his close friends suggest that he go abroad for treatment. However, the hardest part isn't the detox, but afterwards: in his profession, there's just too much temptation. His solitude also renders any attempt futile, tortured as he is by anguish and the tribulations of the creative process. As a means of rationalization, he'd often say that he'd made his best albums while drunk. "With no alcohol," he'd tell himself, "what would happen? I'd never get anything done!" Sometimes, on his own initiative, he goes to the hospital just for a break. After a couple of days, you could the see the relief in his face. He really wants to beat it, and he understands that he can't do it alone. That's the reason he starts psychoanalysis – Serge, who had always abhorred the idea of anyone scrutinizing his mental process. He also consults experts on alcoholism... three weeks before his death.

GAINSBOURG: *"Ever hear of Cocteau's "Despair Highball?" I never tried it - let's be serious - but here's the recipe. I quote: "Fill the shaker half-way with ice and eau de cologne, put in two drops of Ricqlès crème de menthe, a finger of shampoo, shake, and serve all frothy in a toothbrush holder."*

In January, 1989, he's hospitalized five times in a row. The doctors tell him if he keeps hitting the bottle he'll go blind. Finally, in April, they decide to operate. Just before going under the knife, Serge, well aware that he's risking his life, records a series of sketches with his puppet caricature. Written by Arnold Boiseau, they promote his new album recorded live at the Zénith. Before his surgery, he also does this little interview with himself on the TV program *Lunettes noirs pour les nuits blanches*, which is broadcast on April 8, 1989:

GAINSBARRE: *Tell me Gainsbourg - and this an insidious question - in Strasbourg, with the paratroopers, did you think you'd end up dead like John Lennon? Have you got balls?*

GAINSBOURG: *It's not a question of intrepidness, but rather courage. Intrepidness is for fools, that whole "Damn the torpedoes!" stuff... Courage is a question of vanquishing one's fear.*

GAINSBARRE: *You said something that's not all too dumb: "Man created Gods, and the contrary remains to be proven." Are you still an atheist, my boy?*

GAINSBOURG: *No, I'm really a polytheist. I talk about God in the plural, just in case there's one who might be offended.*

GAINSBARRE: *So tell me Gainsbourg, you think there's still time to join Rimbaud in Abyssinia?*

GAINSBOURG: *Yeah. To me, he and Picabia, they're the greatest. Because anyone who hasn't read 'Jésus-Christ Rastaquouère' is really the ultimate idiot. And there are a lot of idiots. It only sold 4,000 copies. There are tons of idiots, we're surrounded by them. And you're the biggest one of all, Gainsbarre. You can go fuck yourself!*

The operation takes place on April 11, 1989, and Serge spends six hours under the knife. He survives, which is both a miracle and another reprieve. After watching the new video by Bambou, he makes his comeback on May 10, appearing on Canal+ in tip-top shape. To say that he's giddy would be an understatement. Emotional, laughing out loud, perfect elocution, sharp-witted, he proceeds, with a gleam in his eye, to talk about his stay in the hospital, where he underwent the ablation of two thirds of his liver. Was it a tumor?

GAINSBOURG: *"Here's the truth about my operation, and the first one to say anything about cancer or cirrhosis will get a punch in face, because you don't operate on that stuff. They found some disease I'd picked up in Africa while filming 'Equateur.' That's all. Seems I was the bravest guy in the whole surgical ward... It's no fun, kids. My body did suffer, but I'm a stoic. When they woke me after the procedure, there were tubes every-*

*where, in my nose, up my ass, in my kidneys, my cock, and seeing all these
wires, while still coming out of anesthesia, I had this screwy reaction. I
asked: "Are we onstage? Sound check! How is it? Where are my players?"
I thought I was at the Zénith."*

Christian Gerin of *France-Soir* nevertheless publishes all the details in
his April 15 story. But Serge refuses to accept any of it, and instead disappears
into a realm of fanciful lies. Hospitalized by gastric surgeon Professor Fékété,
Serge is treated for diabetes, blindness, and respiratory problems all at the
same time. Remember, every day he smokes as many as 80 Gitanes, the most
toxic cigarette on the market. His alcoholism, says the reporter, had caused
a "cirrhosis of the liver that itself brought on the liver cancer. The partial
ablation of the liver was aimed at removing the tumor. We also know that
Serge Gainsbourg was worried about going blind. The diabetic retinopathy
was also a result of the poor digestive abilities of the liver, which caused his
blood sugar to soar. Finally, the doctors also feared pulmonary complications
after the surgery[...] the result of respiratory failure brought about because of
all of the tobacco residue in his bronchial and alveolar lung tissue."

> GAINSBOURG: *"To recuperate, I rented a suite at the Hôtel Raphaël, and
> the bartenders on every floor were under strict orders not to serve me al-
> cohol. So I was drinking a glass of water when I got this incredible call:
> "Hello, it's Marlene Dietrich." I said to myself that it must be some nut,
> but no, it was her: "Mr. Gainsbourg, I'm crossing my fingers for you, take
> care of your health..." She's a little hard of hearing, so I had to speak very
> loudly. The bar was full of Japs and Yanks, and I had to shout: "Can you
> please shut up, that's Marlene Dietrich on the phone." They must have
> thought I was a lunatic."*

At the Raphaël, he starts writing the script to *Stan The Flasher*, the film
he's been obsessed with for several months, written specifically for Claude
Berri. Stan is the name of Serge's character in *Charlotte For Ever*. Stan The
Flasher is also the nickname of Stan Harrison, his touring saxophonist. A
quick summary:

> *'Flasher' comes from 'flash,' American slang, and the literal translation
> would be "exhibitionist." It's a morbid sexual perversion that pushes cer-
> tain people to impulsively expose their genitalia by flashing open a rain-
> coat in front of little high school teenyboppers as an initiation into the*

masculine. Stan's a sort of punk rock William Shakespeare, to show or not to show, if you know what I mean, before the final destruction and the unhappy ending.

CLAUDE BERRI: *"I didn't really believe in the project. I thought he'd never be able to find the money. After reading a few pages, I asked myself: "What madman would produce this?" After he got out of the hospital, he called to tell me that filming would begin on June 20. I felt cornered, but I couldn't pull out. I did it out of admiration, out of friendship."*

The demented producer whose very existence Berri doubts is named François Ravard, ex-manager of the group Téléphone, who gets the project up and running in record time with a hand from Bertrand De Labbey and Canal+.

BABETH SI RAMDANE: *"I made an exception, and out of love for the character, I accepted to do the script and also the editing. So I timed what we had and added a few scenes, and still it was only 25 minutes. I told Serge we were flirting with disaster, but he wrote supplemental scenes during the shooting, at night, and we finally brought in Stan at 65 minutes... We never wanted to make a TV movie, but rather a full-length feature."*

The story is as follows: Stan is an English tutor who falls for one of his little students, Natacha, while his marriage is faltering and he can no longer perform for his wife. He's obsessed with flashing and decides he wants to show his cock off to innocent little girls. After he brushes up against his young student with the intention of feeling her up, he gets punched out by the girl's father and winds up in the can with la Corneille. After a final drink with his buddies, he shoots himself without ever having realized his fantasy.

BERTRAND DE LABBEY: *"I was proud of having convinced Claude Berri to do Serge's last film. At the last minute, he almost changed his mind. I said: "Be decent, do it for him." I had to tell him the truth, that Serge didn't have long to live, and then he accepted."*

CLAUDE BERRI: *"The first day of shooting I showed up moaning. The more I read the script, the more clear it became that Serge was the character. So when the crew was rigging the lights, I went over to him and said: "Serge, what am I doing here? This is your role..." Well, he went pale, held his hand over his heart, and I immediately stopped protesting. An hour*

*later, when we started shooting, he started miming the role for me. We did
one take, two takes, and then I told him: "Let me do it my way. Afterwards,
you can tell me if it's O.K., but you can't play it through me. It won't work."
I had no idea about how to approach my character, but in the first scene
we shot, I was supposed to read some tirade out of Hamlet, in English. I
speak very little English, so what else could I do but screw around? And
he was delighted! I understood that this is want he wanted – for me to
tragically fuck around. A sort of osmosis took place and within a month I
became Stan. In the last shot, at Montsouris Park, Serge would never have
asked me to take it that far, but I went further in my immodesty than the
role even demanded, completely nude, just as I was under the raincoat.
Going nude gave me the ability to shiver like needed to..."*

Dismayed by the bomb that was *Charlotte For Ever*, Serge limits himself
to a single retort – the one on his answering machine: "To be or not to be,
question-answer." Here and there in the film, we find scenes that contain
words from his songs, along with other famous puns, like "There is thunder
in the air, now there is horror in the age." He doesn't even know how to pad
the script any longer... Which doesn't stop the reviews from being globally
positive upon the film's release in March, 1990...

BERTRAND DE LABBEY: *"At the Raphaël, he was just living on hope, the
desire to make his film. For him it was a question of life or death. He still
must have realized that he wasn't a natural when it came to screenwriting.
He had trouble accepting criticism and contradiction because he wasn't
sure of himself. Fortunately, he was saved by his esthetic sensibilities. He
also knew how to surround himself with talented people who adored him
and would do anything for him. He turned out some really strange stuff
that's perhaps better than anyone imagines. I guess time will be the judge
of how his films fit into his entire body of work. But I admit that I love him
unconditionally for what he did to help my career. Honestly, I have terrible doubts about his films."*

From the bums on the street, to trash men, to mail carriers, taxi drivers,
and couriers from Phillips who literally do battle over who will deliver his
letters – all of them receive princely tips, and this sometimes attracts leeches,
including a likeable group of cyclists from Haie-du-Puits, which becomes
Team Gainsbourg when he gives 100,000 francs to their captain in June,

1989. A year later, when Pelletier, one of his cop buddies gets killed by a drug dealer, he sends a 150,000 franc check to his widow without the slightest ado.

In September, 1989, the definitive box set comes out. With nine CDs and 207 songs, it is a remarkable artifact whose hype includes full-page ads in several newspapers. They read: "GAINSBOURG'S IMMORTALITY DOES NOT WAIT FOR DEATH." It's a nice bit of provocation which almost turns terribly sour when just a few days later he has another cardiac episode and spends 48 hours under observation in the American Hospital.

GAINSBOURG: *"It was just a little scare, all due to stress. But next door was Bette Davis, writhing in agony. I was the first to know, at daybreak, that she'd bought the farm. I said to myself, "Whoa, smells like a graveyard in here. Time to beat it."*

In reality, ever since *Stan The Flasher*, Serge has been hitting the bottle, in pure defiance of his doctors' ultimatum. He knows that he should be playing it safe, but life is sometimes painful...

GAINSBOURG: *"The box set isn't really a compilation, but rather my sarcophagus! I don't have the time to listen to it and I don't like how my voice was in the old days. I prefer it today. Now it's like Joe Cocker's – ruined by tobacco, tar, hard liquor... The hardest thing, after this period of rampant and frenzied alcoholism, is to remain clear-headed, because without booze you notice all the assholes around you, you see reality for what it is. In alcoholism, everything is pleasant. Can you imagine going to a club without being shitfaced? It's unthinkable... Sure, I gave some pretty lame performances on television. But I have no regrets. That would be cowardly. I like scandals on live TV - it causes a big uproar and keeps me from getting bored. I realize that I'm a lot funnier when I'm sober. When I'm not, it's all memory lapses, all blablabla, muttering a bunch of unintelligible crap... That's no good, all that. But nothing will ever stop me from popping off with some obnoxious comment.... "*

The eighties comes to an end as both dictatorships and the Berlin Wall crumble in the east. One of the many of the already hundreds of pieces of graffiti at Rue de Verneuil reads: "Here cogitates a Slavic soul." Soon added to that is "Jimmy Somerville to Serge," right when the ex-singer for Bronski Beat hits pay dirt with his petulant disco version of "Comment te dire adieu."

Sheila, much to the amusement of Gainsbarre, says her farewell to song each evening at the Olympia by sobbing her way through "Je suis venu te dire que je m'en vais." Finally, 26 years after recording *Gainsbourg Confidential*, his ex-bassist runs into him during some posh get-together.

> MICHEL GAUDRY: *"I was playing New Year's Eve on December 31, 1989 at the Ritz, with a dance band, and the maitre d'hôtel came over and told me Serge had just come in with Bambou. He came up onstage 10 minutes later and ordered a Magnum of Ruinart for the musicians, then sat down and played "My Funny Valentine" and a few other pieces with us. He got up to leave, grabbed the champagne bucket, and passed the hat around for us musicians, but nobody kicked in a single franc! He started shouting obscenities at the crowd!"*

Serge manages to write lyrics for Joëlle Ursull's "White and Black Blues," which climbs to number two on the summer charts, and then he moves right into recording the new Jane Birkin album, *Amour des feintes*, in February. Its release is scheduled for September, 1990, while Vanessa Paradis' album, which he tackles at the same time, comes out in May, 1990. Serge writes six last songs for the ex of his life:

> *And even when*
> *All is veiled in the night*
> *I'll guide myself by the North Star's light*

> JANE BIRKIN: *"When it came time to record the album, Serge was in a frightening state of anxiety, from sleeplessness. Seeing him like that, I just asked myself: Why are we doing this? Why knock our heads against the wall? Why make him suffer so just to release such intimate material? I had the theatre, movies - I didn't need to do an album!"*

Not content with simply writing the words and music, Serge also designs the cover in India ink, a curious little sketch with ink stains in which Jane seems to have inherited Bambou's mouth...:

> *My neurotic poses*
> *Give way to roses*
> *Blooming from the asphalt*

> JANE BIRKIN: *"With 'Lost Song,' love still seemed possible. This time I'm seeing someone in the depths of solitude. It's a fatal and fatalistic record*

from someone who is dispassionately admitting that love affairs never end well. In each song, we see a gullible person who's found his way back to reality: it's all hopeless but he's blaming no one – it seems perfectly clear. When I finished this album I asked myself if it wasn't the end of something."

> These loves are fakes
> Pretence abounds
> Like some dead child
> Who walks the ground
> Gripped by strange fear
> At hearing sounds
> Of wind-swept cries
> All around

"Amours des feintes," the above variation on Ravel's *Pavane pour une infante défunte*, becomes the title of the album, the last of which he will record in the London suburbs.

On March 1, 1990, as he will on the eve of his death, Serge takes Bamboo to a restaurant to celebrate his birthday. At Maxim's, he gives her a Cartier watch that he bought that very day, along with another gift for Vanessa Paradis. In his little house on Rue de Verneuil, his fussiness reaches maniacal proportions. According to Jane, whom he privately confides in, it's a direct result of the solitude he's sunken into: "He's not very interested in other people, and he doesn't go to the theatre or the movies, he doesn't read. He's just withdrawn..." He refuses dinner invitations and makes little dishes that he eats in front of the television. In short, the most popular man in France spends his evenings alone. With no bitterness or spite, his home becomes his cage...

BERTRAND BLIER: *"You could feel a terrible sadness around him. Like with a lot of artists, it must have been his fate to suffer. Still, it was distressing. He had meticulously arranged his time and space, down to the last detail. Nothing could be moved... It was the outward expression of his mind. When something has gotten to this point, it's time to move on. But not him. He stayed... Visiting him was no breath of fresh air, I can tell you. It was a downer..."*

Now and then, Serge accompanies Charlotte to Jane's, under the pretext of needing to see her for a few minutes. In fact, he stays two or three hours as the two of them stroll down memory lane. Charlotte finds it touching, and the closeness between them still seems to be intact.

Instead of taking a break or dealing with depression, Serge digs into a new project: he writes the lyrics for 11 songs on the new album by 17 year-old Vanessa Paradis. At first, her manager, Didier Pain, and composer, Franck Langolff, had thought of using lyrics from Renaud, Buzy, and Souchon.

VANESSA PARADIS: *"We first ran into each other on a TV soundstage, a Patrick Sébastien show where they had 30 little kids dressed up like Gainsbourg and sing for him "On est venu te dire qu'on t'aime bien."* [1] *It was very touching. Serge was just blubbering and there was this incredible atmosphere on the set... Then one day I heard a radio interview with him, and the reporter asked why he didn't write for anybody besides Jane, Charlotte, and Bambou. He said there was only one little Lolita that interested him, and it was me. I couldn't believe my ears. I thought it was a joke. I ran to my telephone and told my producer to contact him. I was a little shy, but I wanted to ask him to write me a tune for one side of a 45."*

> *Tandem*
> *I can't stand 'M*
> *Sometimes it shines like a diadem*
> *Always the same when*
> *Tandem*
> *It's idem*

VANESSA PARADIS: *"Then there was that fateful day I went to see him at his house, and that was atrocious. Imagine two painfully shy people who don't speak for hours. Every time I moved around I was terrified of breaking something, it was horrific... We started listening to Franck's music and Serge got some paper so we could number the songs and mark down which ones we liked. After a while, he said, "So can I do one?" I couldn't believe my ears. He was asking my permission to write a song. I went nuts and screamed: YES YES YES! A bit later he came back at me and asked "How about five?" At the end of our meeting he'd decided to write all the lyrics."*

---

[1] A bit of wordplay with Gainsbourg's "Je suis venu te dire que je m'en vais." In this case, the kids are singing, "We came to tell you that we love you." (T.N.)

DIDIER PAIN: *"I had asked Renaud to do the lyrics for Vanessa. I wanted "Morgane et toi," "En cloque,"... And then here comes Gainsbourg. So I'm now in an embarrassing situation. I told Gainsbourg I'd given the job to Renaud. He called Renaud before I could get to him and said he wanted to do the entire record. He ended up crying and pleading: "I want to do it, I need it."*

Things start to fall apart while he's finishing Jane's album. Serge is more or less burnt out.

DIDIER PAIN: *"He's tired, sick, smoking like a chimney and hitting the bottle. My assistant and I pick him up everyday at the bar in Hôtel Raphaël. It's easy to see he's not going to do any writing. He says he doesn't understand the music, he doesn't get the stuff that Franck put on the tape, and he can't follow the melody. So we do it again and take off Langolff's voice, and me, I count out the feet for him on a piece of paper. Serge is lost, so we prepare him very straightforward stuff. I think it was due to his exhaustion because a musician doesn't need things broken down like that."*

The songs begin to appear. Every day, Didier Pain picks him up and takes him to the studio in his Porsche. Serge loves it – when traffic backs up, people notice him, and he rolls down the window to say hello and gab with everyone.

DIDIER PAIN: *"At the beginning, Serge came to the studio to "direct" Vanessa, which wasn't necessary because she's a real singer, unlike certain actresses who need that instruction. After a while it got on her nerves, and we managed to get around it by making their schedules conflict. When you look at the images of him and Vanessa in the studio, his gestures are all off-beat. Still, he managed to be very fussy about the diction, and Vanessa respected his wishes because she respected the lyrics."*

> *I love you now, please tell him*
> *Or just download me to his IBM*
> *I don't want to break his heart*
> *But I know very well you*
> *Have caused us to part*

GAINSBOURG: *"Dis-lui toi que je t'aime" (I love you now, please tell him), is the story of a girl who wants to let her ex down easily. It's terribly cynical. I really sweated blood because I wanted to be at the top of my game. There's not a weak moment on this album..."*

That's false: 50% of the lyrics are of not much interest at all. What's true is that he did suffer, particularly because Vanessa committed an act of lèse-Gainsbourg that exceeded even that which Alain Chamfort had earlier perpetrated: she refused the lyrics to at least five songs and asked him to start over.

VANESSA: *"Sometimes, in the studio, it was like being with a little boy who wanted to be coddled, and it was very touching. I know that a few months later he said that my people had driven him back to drink. Gainsbarre can say what he likes, I don't give a damn. What I remember is mothering him, putting all the bottles away and saying, "I don't want you to be sick. I'm asking you to do it for me. Maybe you think it's all a joke and we've only known each other for three weeks, but do it for those who love you." I was very upset and it drove me mad, but I was also grief-stricken to see him destroy himself and I told him I couldn't handle it. Then he'd give me a big smile and I'd melt..."*

In addition to "L'amour du soi," another success on the album is "Ophélie," directly inspired by Rimbaud's homonymous poem:

> *Oh how I'd like so*
> *Down a river to flow*
> *Like Ophelia*
> *To forget the days*
> *Get lost in the haze, no*
> *Memorabilia*
> *Let this taste of fire*
> *Sink into the mire, into the night*
> *A meandering dance*
> *Of a love that takes flight*

GAINSBOURG: *"I used to have three B's, and now I have four: Bambou, Birkin, Bardot, and Banessa Baradis! That last one, like Brigitte, has female enemies. They all tell themselves: "That girl might steal my guy." She radiates an aura of seduction that's very rare, a light that only stars give off... I've told her, and I'll say it again: Paradis, it's hell!"*

Gainsbourg is getting thin. He's wiped out. For the first time in his life, he decides to take a real vacation and spends the month of August with Marc and Françoise Meneau at l'Hôtel de l'Esperance in Saint-Père-sous-Vézelay. He needs a change of scenery.

FULBERT: *"At Vézelay, nobody bothered him, nobody asked him questions. He left in order to write a book... He was at home there, like it was his own country house, and he spent hours at the piano..."*

One day Kate Barry makes a surprise visit and finds him at the bar with a drink in his hand. He giggles and says: "You've caught me red-handed!" The promising designer has come to ask for some help with her new collection, and Serge, quite moved, accepts. After dinner, he offers her the room's large bed while he sleeps in the folding cot with his stuffed toy monkey. For years their relationship has been rather volatile, but at Vézelay there's reconciliation. "In a way, I was frightened," remembers Kate, "I had this sort of feeling." Looking back on it, she fells like she was saying goodbye to him.

In mid-October, 1990, there are two sessions that comprise the last of Serge's interviews for this biography. He's funny, moving, and accepts to open up even more, to dig into his memory and share new secrets. A few days earlier, on October 12, we see him on television accompanied by Jane. He's at the piano doing a song dedicated to his faithful musical director, Philippe Lerichomme. "Unknown Producer," also known as "L'homme dans l'ombre," will be the last song Gainsbourg ever writes:

> *A man in the background*
> *Aren't many to be found*
> *That really stick to it*
> *I trust in his vision*
> *His clear-headed wisdom*
> *His feeling and cool wit*

Philippe, his eyes full of tears, is utterly surprised and blown away. Later we find out that Serge had already planned everything for his next album, which he wanted to call *Moi m'aime Bwana* and record in New Orleans with the cream of the city's musicians... Meanwhile, Philippe and Dominique Blanc-Francard see to the dance remix of "Requiem pour un con." As fate would have it, "Requiem 91" is sent to radio stations on March 1, the eve of Serge's death...

Gainsbourg also makes his entry into *Le Petit Larousse*, right between the painter Gainsborough and Nietzsche's *Gai Savoir (The Gay Science)*:

GAINSBOURG (Lucien Ginsburg, known as Serge): French singer and songwriter (Paris, 1928). Behind his aloof and disenchanted façade lies a keen sensitivity (Je t'aime moi non plus).

Serge remarks to his friends: "Not bad, but there's a date missing..."
On October 26, 1990, he arrives in Montreal via Air Canada on a non-smoking flight. The next day he presents *Stan The Flasher* at the Festival of International Cinema in Abitibi-Témiscamingue in Rouyn-Noranda, a one-hour flight from Montreal. Serge exhausts himself giving 20 or so interviews after the screening, and tells of how he bought a Mercedes for his cinematographer because he was so happy with his work... On the subject of Vanessa Paradis, he's much less kind, and proceeds to trash her and her crew in the *Journal de Montréal*:

> *She's a pain in the ass! They got me drinking again... I had to go to detox because of them. Never have I had problems on a record like the ones I had with that bunch of assholes. They wanted to control everything. That's the last time...*

> DIDIER PAIN: *"A few days later, Vanessa and I were in Canada, to promote 'Variations sur le meme t'aime.' The reporters asked her to respond to Gainsbourg's attacks. We weren't even aware of his remarks, so they showed us some press clippings. Vanessa was in tears all day long. She called him and said: "It's not cool, what you said." He answered, "Don't be mad. I was drunk as a Pole."*

In early December, Serge returns to Vézelay and the Meneau's hotel. There he meets the writer Jules Roy and also the cellist Mstislav Rostropovitch, who's preparing for a series of concerts at the basilica that overlooks the little village. *In Rostropovitch, Gainsbourg, et Dieu*, Jules Roy recalls this extraordinary coincidence:

> *Gainsbourg is a poet. Depraved, if you will, although one might ask oneself what that matters[...] An ingrate, a hedonist, and a spiteful provocateur ever since fortune smiled upon him and even before, Gainsbourg is the accursed poet who's made the big-time, the scumbag who lays golden eggs, or if you will, gives us hell[...] Gainsbourg wants to escape from Paris, from women, from his own world. At the basilica, up on high, it was as if he were afraid of God, whom he saw as someone more powerful than himself, and whom he did not believe in, and who must be, if he existed, a bit of a sadist.*

[...] He only came to the basilica once and did not dare enter – in search of something, but what? He found this monument to faith imposing. When we told him it was built in honor of an ancient courtesan he was astonished. It dazzled him.

MARC MENEAU: *"He left on January 5, 1991 because the hotel was closing. I sometimes think that had the hotel remained open, he'd still be alive. When he arrived he was tired, but after a few days he perked up. His face came back to life. He needed a calm, simple, normal, and healthy life. Paris was his ruin."*

For the soundtrack to *Merci la vie*, the new Bertrand Blier film starring Charlotte Gainsbourg and Anouk Grimberg, the director has the mad idea of putting Bob Dylan's voice to Serge's music. It is seriously considered, and Phil Ramone, one of the biggest rock and roll producers in America, serves as the go-between.

BERTRAND BLIER: *"It was either Dylan or Lou Reed, but negotiations with American stars are a nightmare, and we stopped when we saw we wouldn't have the time. But I can tell you Serge was like a madman. Just before he left us, he went to see the film with his daughter. He left with without saying a word..."*

On those rare occasions when he has a visitor, Serge refuses to reveal anything about his next album. "I'm sick of it all. I'm just chasing my tail. I've done everything I can with rhymes," he tells Dominique Blanc-Francard, "I'm going to do it as prose."

CHARLOTTE GAINSBOURG: *"He'd had me listen to a lot of music and I remember trying to be as critical as possible. I jotted down the ones I preferred. I'd have liked to have recommended more, but I wanted to be tough at that time. Then he had me read his lyrics, and he'd written quite a few. I felt, especially about the music, that it was haunted by a sort of melancholy... His musical ideas were sad, very Russian, and he kept saying it wasn't what he wanted to do but that he felt pulled to this melancholy."*

In mid-January, 1990, Serge flies to Barbados with his daughter, recently dumped by her lover after a long and tumultuous affair. The man, much older, had plucked her up when she was barely out of adolescence...

When they arrive at the hotel, the receptionist thinks Charlotte is his wife, and Charlotte is quite flattered. In extremis, she spills her guts and bares her soul to her father, this girl who is so very private. It calms her down. Serge, bit by bit, starts to understand what a big role he has played in her emotional life. He was the first man in her life, and until then he hadn't realized how important he was to her. "But there are things which are beyond words, things we can't articulate with speech...," murmurs Charlotte. We have to make do with imagining these things: Serge and Charlotte in their hotel in the Antilles, playing chess, Charlotte photographing him, Serge sharing his daughter's grief... One morning, Serge faints. A doctor rushes over and finds a menacing cyst on his neck. He tells Charlotte: "Your father is very ill." After looking him over very briefly, the doctor is able to pinpoint the symptoms of a widespread cancer that is eating away at him.

On the eve of his death, Serge has a heart-shaped diamond sent over from Cartier's. He wants to give it to Jane. March 1 is Bambou's birthday, and she decides to invite Charlotte to join her and Serge.

> BAMBOU: *"He was very weak. We made plans to meet at the Bistrot de Paris. He said: "Charlotte's fine, but don't bring Lulu," and when we arrived at Rue de Verneuil he asked: "Why didn't you bring Lulu?" He was starting to lose it... During dinner, he didn't touch a thing. He asked if he could have some port and I said yes. He wanted another, and I told him that was a bad idea, so he backed off..."*

Charlotte and Bambou take him back to Rue de Verneuil. Before leaving, they both give him a tender embrace. Serge tells Bambou he'll call around two o'clock the next day and then asks if she can come by with Lulu. At 9:30, Bambou receives a phone call but there's no one on the other end. Does Serge need help?

> BAMBOU: *"On Saturday, March 2, I waited all day for his phone call. At four o'clock, I had this flash – I saw him dead. I asked Lulu to call, but there was no response. I thought maybe he was out, so I waited until 10 in the evening, then I just lost it and went over there. I didn't have any keys, so I had the firemen break in. They stayed in the room for 20 minutes, but since they hadn't called the paramedics I knew what had happened. The doctors had told Jacqueline that Serge had a widespread cancer, which was strange, because when I arrived, I saw a bottle of Lexomyl[2] at his feet... I tried to reach Charlotte but she wasn't at home. She was with*

---

[2] A Valium family tranquilizer. (T.N.)

friends and had learned about his death from the television. I'd told the
firemen to keep their mouths shut, but they didn't respect my wishes. Then
the cop detained me as a murder suspect... They wanted to take him to the
morgue, but I asked that they wait for the family to arrive. One of them
must have spilled the beans because the photographers descended on us
right away. When the doctor arrived, he declared Serge dead from a heart
attack."

Serge dies naked. He had fallen back while sitting on the edge of his bed. Perhaps he'd gone up to his room for a nap. According to official documents, he died around 3:30 in the afternoon. That day, he had forgotten to take his heart medication, just like Boris Vian some 40 years earlier. He hadn't suffered, otherwise his fists would have been clenched... At one in the morning, the news is made official.

A long vigil begins around Serge. We see Jane Birkin, Kate Barry, Charlotte, Bambou, his sisters Jacqueline and Liliane, his friend Vittorio, his nephews Yves, Alain, and Michèle, Fulbert, his majordomo, and Philippe Lerichomme, with whom Serge had a three o'clock appointment the coming Monday. Serge was to give him the cassettes with the ideas for his new album...

His fans, devastated, start assembling in front of the Rue de Verneuil home in the middle of the night, and soon the street is teaming with people. The cops, many of whom are his friends, soon have to block off the area and keep fans at a distance, letting in only those who wish to deposit a bouquet of flowers at the door. Friends come to pay their respects, including Catherine Deneuve and her daughter, Chiara Mastroianni. The remix of "Requiem pour un con" and "Je suis venu te dire que je m'en vais" play non-stop on the radio. Brigitte Bardot is one of the first to officially comment on the radio:

He was a very vulnerable person, truly shy, full of humor, and always
questioning himself about his work. He was not at all sure of himself, and
when you look at the marvels he was able to compose, the beauty of the
music performed by both Serge himself as well as others, it's difficult to
understand this lack of confidence. He's a man who lived an extraordi-

nary and marvelous life. His death touches us deeply because we are losing someone irreplaceable. But how wonderful it is that he existed, that we knew him...

Just hours later, *Le Journal du dimanche* published his obituary. That night on television, we see not only teenagers weeping, but also people of Serge's own generation. On April 2, he would have been 63. It's a state of shock. On Monday, *Libération* sells so many copies that people start fighting over them and selling them on the black market.

On the Monday night news, we get declarations from the likes of François Mitterrand ("Serge Gainsbourg elevated song to the level of an art that will serve as an emblem of the sensibility of an entire generation") and Jack Lang ("He sensually incarnated that ideal of the Rimbaldien *liberté libre*"). Michel Drucker will pull in huge ratings when more than nineteen million tune in for homages by Claude Berri, Brigitte Bardot, and Isabelle Adjani. In private, Charles Trenet utters this dreadful phrase to a friend: "Gainsbarre killed Gainsbourg as vengeance for having created him."

The following Tuesday and Wednesday, thousands of fans get together at Mont Valérien in Nanterre, where an amazing phenomenon - almost akin to a Buddhist offering - takes place. Instead of flowers, the "crazed fans" as he would call them, bring fruit, cigarettes, and bottles of Pastis. Those with empty hands take off rings and bracelets, or leave their Perfectos behind. The guest book is filled with messages of farewell, such as "Aux larmes, citoyens" and "Up in heaven, Coluche is making them laugh, and you'll make them dance and dream. Down here we'll be bored stiff."

At the Montparnasse cemetery, Serge joins Joseph and Olia, Charles Baudelaire and Joris-Karl Huysmans, Jean-Paul Sartre, Jean Seberg, Tristan Tzara, and his former painting instructor, André Lhote. The paparazzi use every trick in the book to get shots of all the stars. We see Alain Souchon, Alain Chamfort, the group Indochine, Renaud, Johnny Hallyday (the only one to make the sign of the cross), Isabelle Adjani, Patrice Chéreau, Françoise

Hardy, Michel Piccoli, Bertrand Blier, Julien Clerc, Michel Drucker, Anthony Delon, Richard Bohringer, Louis Chédid, Jack Lang, Mademoiselle Rocard, Serge July, the Simms brothers, Vittorio, Bambou, Lulu, Jane Birkin, and Catherine Deneuve, who reads as a eulogy the words to "Fuir le bonheur de peur qu'il ne se sauve." Devastated, Charlotte doesn't have the strength to read the words she had prepared earlier...

BAMBOU: *"I dreamt of Serge the day after his passing. In my dream, he told me: "I'm not dead." Lulu was sleeping at my side. I told Serge: "Stop screwing around with me. I'm the one who found you, I know you're dead..." Then he tried to take me by my shoulders and tell me he's not cold, and just then I felt Lulu next to me, all warm. I was afraid and I turned on the light! The second dream was a year and a half after the first. We were on a little boat with Charlotte, and Lulu was over on the shore. We were crying because we knew he was going to leave again. Serge was at the end of the boat, all dressed in white with a look on his face that I'd never seen before. He was calm, relaxed, serene, and I told myself things would be much better for him on the other side. He was just shining while we whimpered like a couple of idiots! In that dream, Serge told me he was afraid that Lulu would forget him, and I said there was no chance of that... Lulu thinks that his father is magical, that he's there watching us. Over the years, he'd ask me to set another place at the table for his father because "he might be hungry..."*

On May 13, 1991, when Jane is onstage at the Casino de Paris, she sings "Je suis venu te dire que je m'en vais" at the end of a sublime show. The emotion is overpowering.

GAINSBOURG: *"I'm going to try and hook up with Rimbaud, I want to find him... One day I will, somewhere in Abyssinia, where he trafficked in weapons and gold..."*

epilogue

On September 25, 1994, Jane Birkin gave a concert in London called *A Tribute to Gainsbourg*, the first show in her native England, with profits going to colon cancer research. For the event, kicked off with a few words from Dirk Bogarde, she gathered together a series of quotes paying homage to Serge. These included words from Isabelle Adjani, Jean-Paul Belmondo, Jack Lang, Claudia Cardinale, Vanessa Paradis, Jacques Chirac, Antoine de Caunes, as well as the following:

> *Gainsbourg is a rebel. His poetry is a weapon. His angry despair is aimed at every species of lie and hypocrisy. His work is part of the greatest lineage of French song.*
>
> –François Mitterrand

> *Once upon a time there was "Gainsbourg" - a mad prince in a world too narrow for him. He knew how to seduce us, to enchant us with the beauty of his soul and his heart. He hid his vulnerability behind an insolent aggression which, like his face and his physical body, reflected only the visible surface of this fiery and generous iceberg. He will always be Gainsbourg!*
>
> –Brigitte Bardot

Serge Gainsbourg searched in secret places, for key words and double meanings found in both the precious and the sordid, in music and adolescence – words to calm the great pain of Baudelaire and Huysmans.

–ALAIN SOUCHON

Serge Gainsbourg – an incandescent man of fragile despair.

–CATHERINE DENEUVE

In 1995, Serge is still one of the top 10 composers in SACEM when it comes to royalties generated from his work, and that year also, a recording of his songs is released, intelligently adapted and translated by Mick Harvey, former accomplice of Nick Cave, frontman of the Bad Seeds.[1] It's a limited release, but one which contributes to Gainsbourg's ever-growing status as a cult artist in the Anglo-Saxon world.

In the U.S., certain Gainsbourg pieces, especially cuts from his soundtracks, are now sought after by hipster aficionados of cocktail music and lounge core. Gainsbourg is mentioned as a favorite artist of the most interesting of the new generation of Anglo rockers, including Beck, David Holmes, Rufus Wainwright, members of Sonic Youth, Eric Erlandson of Hole and Courtney Taylor of the Dandy Warhols. Johnny Depp, spurred on by Vanessa Paradis, has become his most faithful ambassador in the American press. On the album *Music*, released in 2000, Madonna invited Charlotte to perform on a piece in homage to Serge.

In 1997, the remarkable anthologies Couleur Café, Du jazz dans le ravin, and Comic Strip, put together by Jean-Yves Billet, sold tens of thousands of copies in the U.S. and Great Britain, especially after Rolling Stone published its extrav-

---

[1] "The title of the disc is *The Intoxicated Man* on Mute Records (TN)

agantly positive reviews. Spin called Gainsbourg the "Jean Genet of cocktail hour," and *Pulse*, the Tower Records publication, dedicated a two-page spread to him by Joseph Lanza entitled "A Lush Memory." On July 19, 1999, *Newsweek* came out with its "Stars of the Century" issue, in which Gainsbourg took his place next to the Beatles, Bob Dylan, and Elvis Presley.

In 1985, I got interested in becoming his autobiographer because one day, haphazardly, I had written this phrase that always stuck with me: "Gainsbourg hides his immense poetic modesty under a mask of flabbergasting obscenity." I wanted to understand why I loved him so much, why his songs spoke to me like no others. Why, at a time when I listened to nothing but Anglo rock, was he the only French artist I held in esteem? And yet it's all right there in that phrase dictated by the unconscious. Gainsbourg and Gainsbarre. The poet and the provocateur. The timid exhibitionist. The scatological esthete. The prude and the pornographer. The dandy and the punk. The nobleman and the scoundrel. The crybaby and the braggart. The dreamer and the egotist. The genius and the forger. And at the heart of all this tumult, the wild child, Lucien Ginsburg.

The Gainsbourg myth starts here. *That's it, man.*

Paris, June 11, 2000

ALPHABETICAL LIST OF THE PERSONS INTERVIEWED:

The Ladies: Isabelle Adjani, Micéle Arnaud, Huguette Attelan, Isabelle Aubert, Bambou, Barbara, Brigitte Bardot, Minouche Barelli, Kate Barry, Laura Betti, Jane Birkin, Simone Bruno, Buzy, Judy Campbell-Birkin, Maritie Carpentier, Petula Clark, Coccinelle, Dani, Mireille Darc, Daniele Delmotte, Catherine Deneuve, Sophie Desmarets, Chantal Franckhauser-Suggs, Charlotte Gainsbourg, Jacqueline, Liliane and Olia Ginsberg, France Gall, Therése Gaugain, Juliette Gréco, Mme Pierre Guyot, Françoise Hardy, Yvette Hervé, Andrée Higgins, Myrtille Hugnet, Zizi Jeanmarie, Jacqueline Joubert, Anna Karina, Bernadette Lafont, Valérie Lagrange, Claude Lalanne, Simone Langlois, Isabelle Le Grix, Anne Le Guernec, Elisabeth Levitsky, Sophie Makhno Elsa Martinelli, Vanessa Paradis, Mme Léo Parus, Régine, Sylvie Rivet, France Roche, Gabrielle Sansonnet, Chaterine Sauvage, Babeth Si Ramdane, Nicole Schluss, Claudine Sonjour, Stone, Barbara Sukowa, Michéle Torr, Aude Turpault, Cora Vaucaire, Simone Véliot, Ursula Vian, Anne Zamberlan, Michéle Zaoui.

The Gentlemen: Pierre Achard, Robert 'Dada' Adamy, Jean-François Agaesse, Gert Alexander, Paul Alt, Georges Arditi, Pierre Arditi, André Arpino, Jean Astima, Rémi Aucharles, Hugues Aufray, Jean-Christophe Averty, Ricet Barrier, Serge (and Georgette) Barthélémy, Alain Bashung, Guy Béart, Robert Benayoun Claude Berri, Roland Bertin, Jacques Besnard, Gérald Biesel, Andrew Birkin, Gérard Blanc, Dominique Blanc-Francard, Bertrand Blier, Michel Boisrond, Roger Bouillot, Denis Bourgeois, Romain Bouteille, Jean-Claude Brialy, Jacques Canetti, Bernard Cassaigne, Jean-Pierre Cassel, Alain Chamfort, Henri Chapier, Eric Charddedn, Georges Chazelas, Jean Chazelas, Professeur Choron, Francis Claude, Phillippe Clay, Julien Clerc, Michel Clerc, Roger Coggio, Michel Colombier, Georges Conchon, René Cousinier, Paul Crauchet, Jean-loup Dabadie, Claude Dagues, Joe Dallessandro, Philippe Dauga, Gilles Davidas, Claude Dejacques, Jo Dekmine, Claude Delorme, Jean-Claude Desmarty, Jean d'Hugues, Sacha Distel, Philippe Doyen, Michel

Drucker, Jacques Dufilho, Jean Dumur, Jacques Dutronc, Thomas Dutronc, Daniel Duval, François Dyrek, paul Facchetti, Robert Faucher, Boris Fiakolvsky, William Flageollet, Flageollet, Flavio, André Flédérick, Jean-Claude Forest, Jean-Pierre Foucault, Daniel Foucret, Tony Franck, Fulbert, Lucien Fusade, Michel Gaudry, Erik Gilbert, Gogol, Alain Goraguer, Arthur Greenslade, Pierre Grimblat, Pierre Guénin, Roland Guinet, André Halimi, Bernard Haller, Alan Hawkshaw, Louis Hazan, Bernard Herman, Albert Hirsch, Francis Huster, J. Izuno, Jacky Jackubowicz, C. Jérome, Gérard Jouannest, Jean Conrad Kasso, William Klein, Pierre Koralnk, Willy Kurant, Bertrand de Labbey, Philippe Labro, René (and Renée Lafleur, Louis Laibe, Jacques Lasry, Georges Lautner, Jacques Lebihan, Yves Lefebvrre, Michel Legrand, Yves Le Grix, Patrick Lehideux, Jean-Pierre Leloir, Claude Lepage, Philippe Lerichomme, Jean-Luc Leridon, Gabriel Leylavergne, Pierre Louki, Géerard Louvin, Philippe Manoeuvre, Charley Marouani Dr. Marcantoni, Jean-Marie Masse, Eddy Matalon, Marcel Maton, Franck Maubert, Jean Méjean, Marc Meneau, Eddy Mitchell, Guy Moreau, Ferand Moulin, Billy Nencioli, Vacha Neubert, Philippe Nicaud, Louis Nucera, Lucien Oberdorf, Brian Odgers, Jacob Pakciarz, Didier Pain, Vincent Palmer, Yves Parachaud, Léo Parus, Noel Pasquier, Kenout Peltier, Vittorio Perrotta, Carolin Petit, Phify, Michel Piccolik Ramon Pipin, Claude Plet, Goerges Pludermacher, Jacques Ppoitrenaud, Huges Quester, François Ravard, Pierre and Emile Riou, Lucien Rioux, Ernest Rosner, Paul Rovére, Billy Rush, Jean-Pierre Sabar, Patrick Sabatier, Camille Safiris, Jules Schneider, M. Schwindling, George Simms, Nicolas Sirkis, Martial Solal, Jimmy Somerville, Gilbert Sommier, Jacques-Eric Strauss, Jean-William Tghoury, Pascal Tonazzi, Paul Tourenne, Jean-Claude Vannier, Dominique Walter, Jean-Pierre Weiller, Claude Wolff, Jacques Wolfsohn, Claude Zylberberg, and Léonard Zurlinden.

And especially to Serge...

Gilles Verlant is a journalist, editor, and a TV / radio personality in France for the past 30 years, specializing in rock music and the french chanson. From 1980 to 1990, Verlant interviewed Serge Gainsbourg and had full access to his archives. He has written the most complete biography on Gainsbourg, who revolutionized French pop music in the second half of the 20th Century. Twenty years after his death, Serge Gainsbourg remains the very essence of scandal, sexual intrigue, and music brilliance.

index of names

Adamy, Robert, 525, 546, 547

Adjani, Isabelle, 357, 361, 378, 438, 504-506, 519, 568, 572

Alexander, Gert, 61, 95, 97, 100

Anthony, Richard, 189, 205

Antoine, 89, 106, 146, 275, 572

Apffel, Jacques, 84

Aragon, Louis, 17, 90, 460

Ardant, Fanny, 530

Arnaud, Michèle, 109, 114-115, 118, 120, 122, 125, 127-130, 133, 140, 145, 148, 152, 155, 160, 168, 170, 184, 187, 193-194, 235, 240, 268, 273, 284, 320, 440

Arpino, André, 249, 255

Artur, José, 357

Arvers, Félix, 190

d'Asta, Claire, 184, 492

Attelan, Huguette, 94, 96

Aubret, Isabelle, 205, 240, 373

Aucharles, Rémy, 369, 375-376

Aufray, Hugues, 129, 139-140, 192, 413,

Averty, Jean-Christophe, 273, 383,

Aymé, Marcel, 147

Aznavour, Charles, 195, 241, 401, 456

Bacon, Francis, 469, 516

Bacsik, Elek 225, 228-229, 241-242, 253

Bambou (Caroline von Paulus), 1, 479, 481, 485, 487, 489, 492-496, 518, 521, 524, 526-527, 539-540, 545, 547-548, 550-551, 553, 558, 560, 562, 566-567, 569

Barbara, 143, 187, 220, 226, 254-256, 282, 313, 464, 501-502, 504

Barclay, Eddie, 139, 187, 294, 319, 324

Bardot, Brigitte, 100, 112, 156, 189, 209, 211, 217, 266, 285, 303, 323, 392, 479, 567-568, 572

Barelli, Minouche, 300

Barrault, Jean-Louis, 217, 287, 333

Barrier, Ricet, 155, 159, 162-164, 168-169, 175, 225

Barrois, Yvonne, 235

Barry, John, 251, 303, 334, 350, 370, 372

Barry, Kate, 303, 343, 347, 368, 378, 379, 417, 428, 429, 440, 461, 471, 472, 473, 563, 567

Bashung, Alain, 230, 498-499

Baudelaire, Charles, 67, 147, 174, 200, 202, 203, 339, 379, 489, 568

Bayon, 38, 489

Beach Boys 292

Béart, Guy 109, 156, 162, 186, 226, 246-247

Beatles, 207, 214, 231, 251, 259, 262, 267, 269, 273, 279, 292, 298, 311, 315, 352, 574

Beauvarlet, Serge, 263

Bécaud, Gilbert, 117, 130, 132, 145, 156, 177, 298, 401, 456

Beck, Julian, 198

Benamou, Georges-Marc, 492, 495

Berri, Anne-Marie, 416

Berri, Claude, 205, 391, 416, 424, 437, 467, 477, 554-555, 568

Bertin, Roland, 531

Besman, Michel, XI, 42

Besson, Luc, 552

Betti, Laura, 204

Bigot, Yves, 547

Bijou, 284, 440-443, 446, 451-452

Billet, Jean-Yves, 442-443

Birkin, Andrew, 64, 334, 345, 347, 372, 429

Birkin, David, 56, 251, 347

Birkin, Jane, 28, 184, 189, 251, 289, 329, 342-343, 345, 347, 350-353, 356, 359, 362, 372, 374-375, 377, 380-382, 384, 389, 392-393, 395-396, 414, 416-417, 420, 425, 428, 437, 452, 459, 474, 479, 489, 496, 503-504, 506-507, 519, 523, 530, 535-536, 538-541, 558, 567, 569, 572

Birkin, Linda, 251, 430

Blanc-Francard, Dominique, 436, 504-507, 539, 542, 544, 551, 563, 565

Blier, Bertrand, 310, 404, 497, 527, 529, 559, 565, 569

Boehli, André, 84

Boisrond, Michel, 175, 218

Bolling, Claude, 111, 133

Bourgeois, Denis, 134-136, 139-140, 147, 160, 163, 173, 212, 240, 281, 324

Bourgeois, Gérard, 210

Bouteille, Romain, 107, 241-242, 252

Bouvard, Philippe, 410

Bowie, David, 438

Brassens, Georges, 109, 113, 137, 145, 226

Braun, Eva, 407

Brel, Jacques, 109, 117, 132, 163, 165

Breton, André, 17, 152

Brialy, Jean-Claude, 148, 286, 289, 527

Brubeck, Dave, 225

Bruno, Simone, 275-276, 323

Brynner, Yul, 372, 382, 477

Burgat, Jean-Louis, 513

Buzy, 521-522, 540, 560

Cale, John, 214

Campbell-Birkin, Judy, 388, 425, 471

Canetti, Jacques, 110, 133-135, 155, 159, 163-164, 170, 187, 225, 284

Carco, Francis, 109, 211

Carpentier, Maritie and Gilbert 224, 234

Carrére, Claude, 278

Cassel, Jean-Pierre, 235, 241-242

de Caunes, Antoine, 146, 572

Cavani, Liliana, 405

Cayatte, André, 100

Chalais, François, 195

Chamfort, Alain, 435-436, 458, 480-481, 483, 562, 568

Chancel, Jacques, 321

Charles, Ray, 541

Chazal, Robert, 423

Chazelas, Jean, 55

Chopin, Frédéric, 19

Cinq Peres (Les), 158, 159, 164, 166, 175

Clark, Petula, 177, 211-212, 235, 245, 251, 254, 267, 392

Clarke, Kenny, 134, 255

Claude, Francis, 108-109, 113-116, 128-130, 136, 140, 148, 150, 158, 193, 203, 233

Clay, Philippe, 107, 110, 117, 137-138, 149, 211, 226, 237, 244

Clerc, Julien, 368, 400, 433, 472, 475, 513, 569

Cochran, Eddie, 436, 441

Coggio, Roger, 311

Colombier, Michel, 217, 219, 290, 299,

307, 310, 316, 320, 324, 332-333, 404

Coluche 523-524, 568

Conchon, Georges, 310, 340-341

Connery, Sean, 314, 323

Cortot, Alfred, 71, 80

Cousinier, René, 155

Crauchet, Paul, 290-292

Cucco, Flavio, 102, 120

Culaz, Albi, 255

Dagues, Claude, 270

Dali, Salvador, 79-80, 278, 351

Dalida, 123, 132, 170, 177, 181, 218-220, 293, 317, 319, 392

Dallessandro, Joe, 415-416, 418

Dani, 119-120, 224, 412

Darc, Mireille, 270, 284, 305, 336, 352

Dassin, Joe, 308

Dauga, Philippe, 440, 442

Dejacques, Claude, 173, 209, 229, 233, 235, 246-248, 252, 263, 266, 270, 301-302, 305, 324-326, 329, 335, 338, 340

Delmotte, Dani, 119, 224

Delon, Alain, 195, 314, 347, 356, 438, 456, 471

Delon, Anthony, 551, 569

Deneuve, Catherine, 320, 346, 466-468, 473, 475, 477-479, 483-485, 506, 546, 567, 569, 573

Depardieu, Gérard, 472-473

Desmond, Paul, 225

Dewaere, Patrick, 497, 504

Distel, Sacha, 148, 156, 175, 234-235, 261, 269, 278, 318

Doillon, Jacques, 459, 467, 471, 474, 498

Donovan, 298

Doyen, Philippe, 159, 161

Droit, Michel, 452, 454-456, 461, 464, 488

Drucker, Michel, 283, 357, 524, 528, 568-569

Dubas, Marie, 25

Dubillard, Roland, 531

Dufilho, Jacques, 09, 114-115, 148

Dufresne, Diane, 460, 497

Dumur, Jean, 37, 38

Dunaway, Faye, 322

Dunbar, Sly, 447-448, 486

Dutronc, Jacques, 275, 292, 295, 400, 402, 410, 476-477, 509, 550

Dutronc, Thomas, 511, 529, 550

Duval, Daniel, 475, 496

Dylan, Bob, 214, 259, 447

Yan, Dynamite, 440

Dyrek, François, 501

Evans , Gil, 200

Faithfull, Marianne, 284, 288, 299, 306

Faucher, Robert, 53

Ferré, Léo, 88, 103, 108-109, 115, 123, 156, 185-186, 370

Ferrer, Nino, 275, 283-284, 306

Fiakolvsky, Boris, 82

Filipacchi, Daniel, 193, 225, 240

Flageollet, William, 316, 324, 326

Flédérick, André, 308, 360, 402, 532

Foucret, Daniel, 43-45

François, Claude, 187, 222, 260, 299, 302, 306, 392, 413, 435

Fréhel, 26-27, 105, 265

Frères, Jacques, 107, 117, 139-141, 152

Fourest, Georges, 285

France, Marie, 299

Gabin, Jean, 25

Gainsbourg, Charlotte, 372, 381, 382, 383, 391, 399, 425, 428, 435, 439, 440, 461, 471, 472, 474, 495, 510, 511, 518, 519, 526, 530, 531, 532, 534, 535, 537, 540, 545,

554, 560, 565, 566, 567, 569, 573

Gall, France, 177, 236, 238, 240-242, 244-246, 248, 250, 254, 259-261, 269, 272, 278, 281-283, 294, 298-299, 304, 307-308, 311, 336, 353, 368, 390-391, 436, 492

Gaudry, Michel, 225, 230, 242, 249, 560

Gelber, Jack, 198

Getz, Stan, 246

Gilbert, Erik, 512-513

Gilberto, Astrud, 210, 246

Gillespie, Dizzy, 113, 142

Ginsburg, Jacqueline, XI, 22, 26, 30, 40, 53, 119, 395, 519

Ginsburg, Joseph, VIII, IX, XI, 17-18, 22, 104, 206, 211, 246, 260, 278, 292, 307, 316, 318, 327, 333, 366, 375

Ginsburg, Lucian (Lulu) 14, 20, 19, 21, 22, 24, 26. 32, 35, 36, 37, 38, 39, 43, 44, 45, 48, 49, 50, 53, 55, 57, 60, 61, 64, 66, 69, 70, 71, 72, 74, 75, 76, 77, 80, 81, 82, 83, 85, 86, 87, 88, 89, 90, 92, 93, 94, 95, 96, 97, 98, 99, 100, 101, 102, 103, 105, 112, 113, 115, 116, 117, 118, 119, 120, 122, 123, 124,12

Ginsburg, Natacha, 235, 244, 245, 258, 309, 354

Ginsburg, Olia, X, XI, 33, 39, 43, 57

Ginsburg, Paul, 354, 310, 340

Glaser, Denise, 175, 223, 256, 271, 279-280, 304, 379-380, 385, 440

Gogol, Nicolas, 311

Gomelsky, Giorgio, 306

Goraguer, Alain, 110-112, 119, 133-136, 142, 144, 151, 160, 173, 182, 187, 193, 201, 211, 217-218, 241, 244, 247-248, 290

Gréco, Juliette, 107, 110-111, 161-165, 170, 175, 184, 201, 206-207, 209, 224, 226, 236, 278

Greenslade, Arthur, 273, 339-340, 351

Grimbault, Pierre, 341-343, 347, 349, 361

Grix, Julien (pseud. Of S.G.), 103, 114, 118, 122, 368, 390

Guyot, Pierre, 47, 49, 57

Halimi, André, 108, 164

Haller, Bernard, 133-134, 158, 163-164, 166

Hallyday, Johnny, 132, 181, 184, 187, 195-196, 198-199, 211, 231, 241, 251, 268-269, 273, 283, 292, 319, 352, 369, 401, 414, 459, 524, 546, 568

Hardy, Françoise, 213, 283, 347-348, 378, 400, 402, 413, 434, 437, 511, 568

Harrison, Stan, 516, 554

Hawkshaw, Alan, 394, 404, 430, 434, 438, 505, 535

Hazan, Louis, 187, 213, 259, 275, 294, 313, 422

Hendrix, Jimi, 311, 436, 450

Hervé, Yvette, 48

Higgins, Andrée, 350

Hills, Gillian, 224, 303

Hirsch, Albert, 93-95, 97-98, 136

Holly, Buddy, 436, 441

Hugnet, Georges, 79, 81

Hugnet, Myrtille, 79-80

Hugues, Jean, 357

Huster, Francis, 418, 501-503

Huysmans, Joris-Karl, 347, 470, 568

I Threes, 447, 450

Indochine, 568

Jackubowicz, Jacky, 407, 441, 452

Jaeckin, Just, 403

Jagger, Mick, 214, 365

Jeanmaire, Zizi, 106, 224, 234, 310, 340, 485

Jones, Brian, 214, 308, 436

Joplin, Janis, 436-437

Jouannest, Gérard, 163, 166

Joubert, Jacqueline, 146, 193, 340

Karina, Anna, 286-289, 299-301, 335, 340, 353, 475-476, 479

Klein,William, 520,

Kolldehoff, Réne, 501

Koralnik, Pierre, 158, 273, 286-287, 298, 418

Kosma, Joseph, 77

Kristel, Sylvia, 403

Kurant, Willy, 287, 418, 420, 424, 501-502, 531

Labbey, Bertrand de, 390, 466, 472, 494, 514, 519, 529, 535, 547, 555-556

Labro, Philippe, 414

Lafleur, René, 168-169

Lagrange, Valérie, 263, 270, 278, 284

Laibe, Louis, 104-106, 171

Lalanne, Claude, 430

Lambert, Christophe, 528, 531

Lancelot, Michel, 249, 351, 398

Lang, Jack, 568-569, 572

Langlois, Simone, 132, 155, 158, 163, 166, 168

Langolff, Franck, 542, 560

Lanzman, Jacques, 275

Lasry, Jacques, 114-116, 120, 128, 130, 135, 140

Launter, Georges, 310, 338

Le Grix, Jacqueline, 103

Le Grix, Isabelle, 264, 546

Lefebvre, Yves, 339

Léger, Fernand, 69, 75, 81

Legrand, Michel, 143, 210

Lehideux, Patrick, 128

Leloir, Jean-Pierre, 174, 206

Lelouch, Claude, 497

Lerichomme, Philippe, 413, 430, 433-434, 446, 448-450, 460, 486-487, 504, 514-515, 542, 544, 551, 563, 567

Levitsky, Elisabeth, 78, 88-89, 125

Lévy, Alain, 484, 551

Lhote, André, 75, 81, 90, 568

Lio, 480-481, 483

Lyon, Sue, 230

McLean, Jackie, 198-199, 249

Makeba, Miriam, 246-247

Makhno, Sophie, 220, 236, 254-255, 313

Malina, Judith, 198

Manoeuvre, Philippe, 518

Marcantoni, Dr., 396

Marley, Bob, 433, 447, 460

Marouani, Charley, 192, 199, 294

Circus, Martin, 472

Matalon, Eddy, 315, 317

Maubert, Frank, 530

Méjean, Jean, 203

Meneau, Marc and Françoise, 562

Michelot, Georges Meyerstein, 187, 205, 236, 294

Pierre, 255

Mitchell, Eddy, 143, 261, 268, 299, 302, 528,

Mitterrand, François, 56, 116, 273, 402, 568, 572

Monroe, Marilyn, 101, 207, 299, 303, 350

Montand, Yves, 71, 77, 88, 103, 117, 130, 136, 152, 177, 184, 187, 226, 261, 373

Moreay, Guy, 53

Moreau, Jeanne, 156, 222, 224, 261, 266, 300, 319, 394

Moreno, Dario, 123, 155, 171, 176-177, 183, 319

Morrison, Jim, 436

Mouloudji, Marcel, 107

Mouskouri, Nana, 187, 213, 434, 492

Mulligan, Gerry, 200

Nabokov, Vladimir, 203

Nana (SG's pet dog), 396, 402, 434, 449

Nencioli, Billy, 113-114

Nerval, Gérard de, 190

Neubert, Vacha, 76-77

Nicaud, Philippe, 176, 219-220

Nico, Krista, 214

Nougaro, Claude, 210, 247

Nucera, Louis, 210, 259-260

Odgers, Brian, 404

Olatunji, Babatunde, 246

Oldham, Andrew Loog, 214

Pain, Didier, 560-561, 564

Pakciarz, Jacob, 69, 74, 81, 92, 181

Palmer, Vincent, 440-442

Pancrazzi, Béatrice, 235

Paradis, Vanessa, 542, 559-560, 564, 572-573,

Parker, Alan, 404

Parus, Léo, 15, 18, 47-48, 66

Pascal, Jean-Claude, 130, 133, 152, 189, 203, 220

Pasquier, Noël, 309

Van Peebles, Marvin, 341

Peltier, Kenout, 420

Perrotta, Vittorio, 544

Petit, Roland, 234, 485

Phify, 462, 495

Piaf, Edith, 25, 71, 155, 209, 211, 544

Picabia, Francis, 449

Piccoli, Michel, 359, 437, 507, 520, 569

Pipin, Ramon, 417

Plante, Jacques, 212, 278

Pludermacher, Georges, 93, 96, 98-99

Poe, Edgar Allan, 147, 314

Poitrenaud, Jacques, 175, 213, 218-219

Polnareff, Michel, 292, 369, 400

Polonsky, Abraham, 371

Porter, Cole, 16, 119, 142, 160, 370

Powell, Bud, 142, 225, 254

Prévert, Jacques, 184

Quester, Hugues, 415, 420, 424

Ravard, François, 555

Rawson, Jean-Pierre, 545

Reed, Lou, 214, 498, 565

Redding, Otis, 435-436, 450

Reggiani, Serge, 228, 284

Régine, 228, 264-265, 278, 283-284, 295, 302, 318, 343, 383, 392, 471, 473

Reichenbach, François, 315

Reinhardt, Django, 73

Renaud, 77, 104, 333, 453, 514, 522, 546, 560-561, 568

Rimbaud, Arthur, 67, 88, 90, 444, 470, 553, 562, 569

Ringer, Catherine, 537

Riou, Pierre, 47, 49

Rioux, Lucien, 148, 226, 229, 233, 271, 295, 337, 371

Rivet, Sylvie, 154, 161, 165, 167, 181-182, 193, 235

Stones, Rolling, 214, 251, 288, 298, 306, 416

Romain, Tony, 125

Rossi, Tino, 123, 245

Roy, Jules, 564

Rush, Billy, 514-515, 517, 523-524, 526, 546, 551

Sabar, Jean-Pierre, 413, 422, 434, 478, 527

Sabatier, Patrick, 522

Sachs, Gunther, 285, 314, 318-319, 324-325, 332

Safiris, Camille, 541

Salvador, Henri, 88, 137, 261, 283
Sansonnet, Gabrielle, 57, 66
Sarraute, Claude, 149, 178, 204, 229
Sartre, Jean-Paul, 79, 89, 379, 394, 570
Sauvage, Catherine, 103, 109, 180, 186, 200, 252
Schluss, Nicole, 439, 486
Schneider, Jules, 84
Seberg, Jean, 290, 568
Séguéla, Jacques, 428, 474
Shakespeare, Robbie, 447-448, 486
Shelia, 214
Si Ramdane, Babeth, 555
Simenon, Georges, 497
Simms, George, 516, 526, 569
Simsolo, Noël, 192, 401, 500
Sommier, Gilbert, 225-226
Sonjour, Claudine, 76,
Spiero, Jean-Pierre, 287, 298
Starshooter, 443
Strauss, Jacques-Eric, 403, 416, 420, 424, 529
Sukowa, Barbara, 501-502, 504
Sylva, Berthe, 243
Sylvain, Claude, 158, 193
Sylvestre, Anne, 170, 225, 254
Tati, Jacques, 209
Tatum, Art, 113, 142, 500
Torr, Michèle, 263, 278
Tourenne, Paul, 140,
Trenet, Charles, 28, 44, 71, 77, 183, 265, 397, 568
Truffaut, François, 175, 341, 423, 467
Turner, Joe, 516
Tzara, Tristan, 17, 568
Ursull, Joëlle, 558
Urtreger, René, 249, 254-255, 262, 350
Valette, Michel, 205, 252

Vannier, Jean-Claude, 361, 368-371, 374, 391, 400,
Vartan, Sylvie, 210, 240-241, 284, 306, 319, 390
Vaucaire, Cora, 77, 107-108, 116, 128, 181, 184
Véliot, Simone, 76-78, 226
Verlaine, Paul, 88, 211, 397
Vian, Boris, 3, 79, 103, 109-110, 117, 123, 127, 134, 136-137, 142, 151, 153, 155, 159-161, 173-174, 187, 212, 284, 424, 567
Vian, Ursula, 110
Wais, Alain, 408
Walter, Dominique, 145, 278, 284, 301, 320, 337, 363
Warhol, Andy, 416
Weiller, Jean-Pierre, 514-515
Whitaker, David, 306
Wilde, Oscar, 115, 211, 350, 377
Wilen, Barney, 255
Wolff, Claude, 212, 245
Wolfsohn, Jacques, 494, 550
Zaoui, Alain, 486
Zaoui, Liliane, 16, 23, 100, 521
Zaoui, Michéle, 439
Zurlinden, Léonard, 84
Zylberberg, Claude, 94

photo credits

Page 13
Serge Gainsbourg here as a child in 1934
Photo: © Hulton Archive/Getty Images

Page 91
Serge Gainsbourg late 1950's
©Photofest

Page 121
Du chant à la une!... 1958
Photo: © Michel Biguad, W. Carone

Page 157
N° 2, 1959
Photo: ©Jacques Aubert

Page 179
Film still from *Hercule se déchaîne*, 1962
Photo: ©Photofest

Page 188
L'Étonnant Serge Gainsbourg
Photo: ©Jacques Aubert

Page 197
Serge Gainsbourg late 1950s
Photo: ©Photofest

Page 208
N° 4, 1962
Photo: ©Jacques Aubert

Page 215
Film still from *L'inconnue de Hong Kong, 1963*
Photo: ©Photofest

Page 221
Serge Gainsbourg, early 1960's
Photo: ©Photofest

Page 239
Gainsbourg Percussions, 1964
Photo: ©Jacques Aubert

Page 257 & Cover image
Serge Gainsbourg, mid 1960's
Photo: ©Photofest

Page 277
Anna
Photo: ©D.R.

Page 297
Serge Gainsbourg – Brigitte Bardot
Bonnie & Clyde, 1968
Photo: ©Guidotti

Page 331
Initials B.B., 1968
Ill: ©A. Decamp

Page 344
Film Still from *Slogan*, 1969

photo credits *cont.*

Page 355
Serge Gainsbourg & Jane Birkin in
Slogan, 1969
Photo: ©Photofest

Page 367
histoire de melody nelson, 1971
Photo: ©Tony Frank

Page 406
Rock Around the Bunker, 1975
Ill: © Serge Gainsbourg

Page 411
Film still from *Je t'aime moi non plus*,
1976
Photo: ©Photofest

Page 419
Serge Gainsbourg & Jane Birkin on the
set of *Je t'aime moi non plus*,1976
Photo: ©Photofest

Page 427
L'Homme a tete de chou, 1976
Photo: ©Serge Gainsgourg. Scupture by
Claude Lalanne

Page 465
Evguénie Sokolov
Ill: ©Tom Recchion & TamTam Books

Page 491
Film Still from *Équateur*, 1983
Photo: ©Photofest

Page 509
Love on the Beat, 1984
Photo: ©William Klein

Page 533
Serge Gainsbourg, late 1980's
Photo: ©Photofest